PENGUIN BOOKS

WHEN ALL THE WORLD WAS YOUNG

Ferrol Sams is the author of seven works of fiction, including the novels *Run With the Horsemen*, *The Whisper of the River*, and *When All the World Was Young*, all available from Penguin. Also published by Penguin are *The Widow's Mite & Other Stories* and *Epiphany*. Ferrol Sams lives in Fayetteville, Georgia, where he practices medicine.

When All the World Was Young

FERROL SAMS

PENGUIN BOOKS

PENGUIN BOOKS
Published by the Penguin Group
Penguin Group (USA) Inc., 375 Hudson Street, New York, New York 10014, U.S.A.
Penguin Group (Canada), 90 Eglinton Avenue East, Suite 700, Toronto, Ontario,
Canada M4P 2Y3 (a division of Pearson Penguin Canada Inc.)
Penguin Books Ltd, 80 Strand, London WC2R 0RL, England
Penguin Ireland, 25 St Stephen's Green, Dublin 2, Ireland
(a division of Penguin Books Ltd)
Penguin Group (Australia), 250 Camberwell Road, Camberwell, Victoria 3124,
Australia (a division of Pearson Australia Group Pty Ltd)
Penguin Books India Pvt Ltd, 11 Community Centre, Panchsheel Park,
New Delhi – 110 017, India
Penguin Group (NZ), 67 Apollo Drive, Rosedale, North Shore 0632, New Zealand
(a division of Pearson New Zealand Ltd)
Penguin Books (South Africa) (Pty) Ltd, 24 Sturdee Avenue, Rosebank,
Johannesburg 2196, South Africa

Penguin Books Ltd, Registered Offices: 80 Strand, London WC2R 0RL, England

First published in the United States of America by Longstreet Press 1991
Published in Penguin Books 1992

22 24 26 28 30 29 27 25 23

All quotations of Edna St. Vincent Millay's poetry are from *Collected Poems
of Edna St. Vincent Millay,* Harper & Row. Reprinted by permission of
Elizabeth Barnett, literary executor.

LIBRARY OF CONGRESS CATALOGING IN PUBLICATION DATA
Sams, Ferrol, 1922–
When all the world was young / Ferrol Sams.
p. cm.
Completes the trilogy, the first two vols. being Run with the horsemen and
The whisper of the river.
ISBN 978-0-14-017227-0
1. World War, 1939–1945—Fiction.   I. Title.   II. Series.
PS3569.A46656W44 1922
813'.54—dc20 92–8856

Printed in the United States of America
Set in Baskerville

To
Helen

Lepanto

Gilbert Keith Chesterton

White founts falling in the Courts of the sun,
And the Soldan of Byzantium is smiling as they run;
There is laughter like the fountains in that face of all men feared,
It stirs the forest darkness, the darkness of his beard,
It curls the blood-red crescent, the crescent of his lips,
For the inmost sea of all the earth is shaken with his ships.
They have dared the white republics up the capes of Italy,
They have dashed the Adriatic round the Lion of the Sea,
And the Pope has cast his arms abroad for agony and loss,
And called the kings of Christendom for swords about the Cross.
The cold Queen of England is looking in the glass;
The shadow of the Valois is yawning at the Mass;
From evening-isles fantastical rings faint the Spanish gun,
And the Lord upon the Golden Horn is laughing in the sun.

Dim drums throbbing, in the hills half heard,
Where only on a nameless throne a crownless prince has stirred,
Where, risen from a doubtful seat and half attainted stall,
The last knight of Europe takes weapons from the wall,
The last and lingering troubadour to whom the bird has sung,
That once went singing southward when all the world was young.
In that enormous silence, tiny and unafraid,
Comes up along a winding road the noise of the Crusade.
Strong gongs groaning as the guns boom far,
Don John of Austria is going to the war,
Stiff flags straining in the night-blasts cold,
In the gloom black-purple, in the glint old-gold,
Torchlight crimson on the copper kettle-drums,
Then the tuckets, then the trumpets, then the cannon, and he
　comes.
Don John laughing in the brave beard curled,
Spurning of his stirrups like the thrones of all the world,
Holding his head up for a flag of all the free.
Love-light of Spain—hurrah!
Death-light of Africa!
Don John of Austria
Is riding to the sea.

Mahound is in his paradise above the evening star,
(Don John of Austria is going to the war.)
He moves a mighty turban on the timeless houri's knees,
His turban that is woven of the sunsets and the seas.
He shakes the peacock gardens as he rises from his ease,
And he strides among the tree-tops and is taller than the trees,
And his voice through all the garden is a thunder sent to bring
Black Azrael and Ariel and Ammon on the wing.
Giants and the Genii,
Multiplex of wing and eye,
Whose strong obedience broke the sky
When Solomon was king.

They rush in red and purple from the red clouds of the morn,
From temples where the yellow gods shut up their eyes in scorn;
They rise in green robes roaring from the green hells of the sea,
Where fallen skies and evil hues and eyeless creatures be.
On them the sea-valves cluster and the grey sea-forests curl,
Splashed with a splendid sickness, the sickness of the pearl;
They swell in sapphire smoke out of the blue cracks of the
    ground, —
They gather, and they wonder and give worship to Mahound.
And he saith, "Break up the mountains where the hermit-folk can
    hide,
And sift the red and silver sands lest bone of saint abide,
And chase the Giaours flying night and day, not giving rest,
For that which was our trouble comes again out of the west.

"We have set the seal of Solomon on all things under sun,
Of knowledge and of sorrow and endurance of things done,
But a noise is in the mountains, in the mountains, and I know
The voice that shook our palaces — four hundred years ago:
It is he that saith not 'Kismet'; it is he that knows not Fate;
It is Richard, it is Raymond, it is Godfrey at the gate!
It is he whose loss is laughter when he counts the wager worth,
Put down your feet upon him, that our peace be on the earth."
For he heard drums groaning and he heard guns jar,
(Don John of Austria is going to the war.)
Sudden and still — hurrah!
Bolt from Iberia!

Don John of Austria
Is gone by Alcalar.

St. Michael's on his Mountain in the sea-roads of the north,
(Don John of Austria is girt and going forth.)
Where the grey seas glitter and the sharp tides shift
And the sea-folk labour and the red sails lift.
He shakes his lance of iron and he claps his wings of stone;
The noise is gone through Normandy; the noise is gone alone;
The North is full of tangled things and texts and aching eyes,
And dead is all the innocence of anger and surprise,
And Christian killeth Christian in a narrow dusty room,
And Christian dreadeth Christ that hath a newer face of doom,
And Christian hateth Mary that God kissed in Galilee,
But Don John of Austria is riding to the sea.
Don John calling through the blast and the eclipse,
Crying with the trumpet, with the trumpet to his lips,
Trumpet that sayeth *ha!*
Domino Gloria!
Don John of Austria
Is shouting to the ships.

King Philip's in his closet with the Fleece about his neck,
(Don John of Austria is armed upon the deck.)
The walls are hung with velvet that is black and soft as sin,
And little dwarfs creep out of it and little dwarfs creep in.
He holds a crystal phial that has colours like the moon,
He touches, and it tingles, and he trembles very soon,
And his face is as a fungus of a leprous white and grey
Like plants in the high houses that are shuttered from the day,
And death is in the phial and the end of noble work,
But Don John of Austria has fired upon the Turk.
Don John's hunting, and his hounds have bayed—
Booms away past Italy the rumour of his raid.
Gun upon gun, ha! ha!
Gun upon gun, hurrah!
Don John of Austria
Has loosed the cannonade.

The Pope was in his chapel before day or battle broke,
(Don John of Austria is hidden in the smoke.)

The hidden room in man's house where God sits all the year,
The secret window whence the world looks small and very dear.
He sees as in a mirror on the monstrous twilight sea
The crescent of the cruel ships whose name is mystery;
They fling great shadows foe-wards, making Cross and Castle dark,
They veil the plumèd lions on the galleys of St. Mark;
And above the ships are palaces of brown, black-bearded chiefs,
And below the ships are prisons, where with multitudinous griefs,
Christian captives sick and sunless, all a labouring race repines
Like a race in sunken cities, like a nation in the mines.
They are lost like slaves that swat, and in the skies of morning hung
The stairways of the tallest gods when tyranny was young.

They are countless, voiceless, hopeless as those fallen or fleeing on
Before the high Kings' horses in the granite of Babylon.
And many a one grows witless in his quiet room in hell
Where a yellow face looks inward through the lattice of his cell,
And he finds his God forgotten, and he seeks no more a sign —
(But Don John of Austria has burst the battle-line!)
Don John pounding from the slaughter-painted poop,
Purpling all the ocean like a bloody pirate's sloop,
Scarlet running over on the silvers and the golds,
Breaking of the hatches up and bursting of the holds,
Thronging of the thousands up that labour under sea,
White for bliss and blind for sun and stunned for liberty.
Vivat Hispania!
Domino Gloria!
Don John of Austria
Has set his people free!

Cervantes on his galley sets the sword back in the sheath,
(Don John of Austria rides homeward with a wreath.)
And he sees across a weary land a straggling road in Spain,
Up which a lean and foolish knight for ever rides in vain,
And he smiles, but not as Sultans smile, and settles back the blade.
   . . .

(But Don John of Austria rides home from the Crusade.)

When
All the World
Was Young

> "... *The last and lingering troubadour to
> whom the bird has sung,
> That once went singing southward when all
> the world was young.*"

Remember who you are."

He had heard those words countless times and from no less an oracle than his grandmother. She used the phrase frequently, addressing him, his sisters, and even on momentous occasions his father. It was more than a shibboleth; it had become an incantation.

The words were her wisdom, the essence distilled from eighty years of joy, sorrow, confusion, serenity, and finally overweening assurance. Her wisdom was all she had to give. She gave it freely, but she never wasted it. The words were always appropriate, never adulterated with further specifics or moralizing. "Remember who you are."

She had thus admonished him this morning as she removed her snuff brush and wiped her mouth to accept his good-bye kiss. There was power in the phrase and there was power in the grandmother. She would protect her loved ones as best she could. For a Southerner of family, the words were enough; they covered everything.

He paused before the gates of Emory University. The tall straight oaks of Druid Hills towered with patterned bark on his left; to the right a portico of cream-colored columns thrust the tower and Moorish cupola of Glenn Memorial Methodist Church upward until it topped out above the trees. In the biggest city of the South, Emory was the supreme bastion of Methodism and also, with only slight incongruity, the ultimate sanctuary of intellectualism and graduate study in Georgia. His assault upon its portals was the most audacious moment of his life.

He looked down the curving, tree-sombre road to the stone-balustraded bridge spanning a dank and ivied ravine. He took a deep breath, squared his shoulders.

"Remember who you are," he said aloud and stepped forth.

As he crossed the bridge he spoke again. "I am Porter

1

Osborne." When he rounded the curve beyond the bridge, he caught the glimmer of white and pink marble from the buildings arranged like temples in majestic squat on the Quadrangle. "Junior," he added in prudent addendum. It was early June of 1942. Tomorrow classes began for freshmen in the School of Medicine.

Over his span of nineteen years, Porter had never entered any new environment without trepidation. Full of diffidence, imbued with dread of possible inadequacy, he could identify with the tuck-tailed dog sniffing with caution as it was led into a strange interior, spine bristling, eyes rolling, ready to yelp and bolt, or at the very least to piddle on the floor. A place by the fire was not to be taken on first introduction as a divine right. Thus he had felt in the first grade, when he left home for Bert Adams Boy Scout Camp at age twelve, on his entering day in high school, and certainly when he matriculated at college. He consequently assured himself that his present misgivings were the norm for him and that very soon he would acclimate: he would adjust to his new environment and it to him.

He thought of Old Man Kangaroo. "Make me different from all other animals; make me popular and wonderfully run after." He smiled and added, "By five this afternoon." He had done very well in grammar school; he had excelled in high school; he had finished college creditably and in addition partaken irrepressibly of high jinks that did not belong in academe. It would take some time, but he would do all right at Emory. "He was gray and he was woolly and his pride was inordinate."

It was a break with entrenched tradition that medical school was beginning in June rather than in September. Instead of a three-month hiatus between college graduation and the opening of med school classes, Porter had one hectic week crammed with so many chores of preparation that the days seemed compressed and choked. Roosevelt had barely lowered the summoning trumpet from his lips after the sickening, near-mortal wound of Pearl Harbor before the entire nation resembled a colony of ants, panicked but purposeful, frenzied in protective defiance, galvanically responsive to the sudden removal of the log or stone that had sheltered their culture, their existence. There was little time for shock; grief was futile, was rapidly transformed to rage. The United States was unified as never before in its history. People from diverse backgrounds and far-flung states came together with common purpose that was to prove irresistible. They went without the meat and rationed the gasoline. They planted Victory gardens to expand their larders and pared their budgets to buy more war bonds.

Young men swarmed the country in khaki, and hitchhikers in uniform were immediately and warmly accommodated by drivers who had previously looked the other way. Women were not drafted but thousands upon thousands of them volunteered, and Oveta Culp Hobby made khaki a color of fashion; one of the marching songs even opined that the Waacs and Waves were winning the war, and that on "twenty-one dollars a day once a month." The dun-hued garb of the infantry was the color of patriotism. It was accented by the white of the Navy boys, but khaki was the true color of war; it would lead to victory.

The eyes and forefinger of Uncle Sam, in heroic proportion, pointed from poster and billboard and proclaimed that he wanted You. The eyes followed the observer everywhere. So did the finger. That poster, combined with Kate Smith singing "God Bless America," Roosevelt's Brahmin resonance on the radio, and the sentimental promise that there would be bluebirds over the white cliffs of Dover, became as impelling as any altar call at a Baptist revival. Ants, in the thousands, responded by enlisting instead of waiting to be drafted, after which they marched while their fellows still scurried. "Just remember Pearl Harbor as we did the Alamo." The strains of "We're coming over" were heard again in the land.

Emory University, like other medical schools in the nation, answered the clarion call to war by speeding up its curriculum. The dons and deans proclaimed that they would sacrifice not one whit of the quality of education nor shirk on any ritual of training; they would simply accelerate their courses by abolishing summer vacations and by granting only long weekends between quarters. They would thus produce physicians in three years rather than four. Emory would prove its patriotism, would manifest its commitment, but would still uphold its reputation for excellence.

Porter Osborne, in his sector of the ant hill, raced as frantically as any of his fellows and arrived at Emory in its first accelerated class. He carried with him a not inconsiderable load that had nothing to do with remembering who he was. He had a firm grip on his burden and moved nimbly with it over the strange, newly erupted terrain; like a fully dedicated ant, he compulsively refused to lay it down. The burden was fear. It had several layers. He was acutely conscious that he was not garbed in khaki, and he feared the opinion that he might be a quasi-4F, a draft dodger. Obversely he had an even deeper fear of the foreign paths down which wearing the homogenizing khaki might lead

3

him, and he was shamed by the relief he felt at being free of it. That shame lay within him as mute and heavy as mud.

He had arrived at this point with a great deal of conflict but with very little controversy; he had discussed it with his father. Porter Osborne, Sr., an artist at conflict, was contemptuous of controversy. He had listened to his son with amazing manifestation of patience and even tolerance. Several times.

"What the hell you mean you're thinking about giving up your place in med school to enlist?"

"Well, Dad, it doesn't seem right. Here we are at war and everybody is being asked to sacrifice and support it; and all I'm faced with is doing exactly what I've wanted to do for as long as I can remember."

"You still want to be a doctor?"

"Oh, yes, sir!"

"Do you have any idea how badly an army needs doctors?"

"Well, no, sir. It just seems wrong for me to be going to med school when my friends are being drafted because they happened to major in journalism or business or education. I could always go back to med school when the war is over. Everybody else's life is being interrupted and it doesn't seem right for mine not to be."

"Who do you think knows more about running a war and the kind of manpower they need and when and where they need it — the President of the United States and all his generals or a farm boy halfway through his senior year in college?"

"Well, I'm sure they do, Dad, if you put it that way, but . . ."

"You're mighty right they do! And they think they need doctors and need them desperately. Do you know that they cut off the general draft at age thirty but keep on drafting doctors until they're forty-five? Did you know that?"

"No, sir."

"Did you know that they're out recruiting all the doctors they can get? They take an inexperienced one in with a rank no less than first lieutenant or captain and the older ones go in as majors or colonels, and that without one lick of previous military training. Did you know that?"

"No, sir."

"Well, they do. They need them like all get-out or they wouldn't be giving them all those special considerations. They have to have hospitals to treat sick boys and look after wounded boys. An army without doctors is no army at all."

"Yes, sir, I know that, but I can't get away from my feelings about . . ."

"Your feelings about what? You jump up and enlist now and you'll wind up in the infantry obeying orders from sergeants with half your intelligence. Then you'll really have some feelings. Son, the country needs your brain more than it does your body."

Porter winced but decided the intent was not to slur.

"Look, you were accepted at Emory well before those yellow bastards bombed Pearl Harbor. The Army knows where you are. They need you as a skilled physician, not as just another dog face. You're doing your part for the war as much as anybody else."

"But . . ."

"Look, I was a captain in 1918; I know what I'm talking about. As much as I hate noun verbs, what you've got to do is learn to compartmentalize. You go on back to college and keep those grades up and help us win this war in your way. OK?"

So. He arrived at Emory. He remembered who he was. He was prepared to compartmentalize. He was determined to excel and had *cum laude* on his diploma as confirmation of ability. His feelings about being a soldier, about dying, were buried deep. He strode with confidence. He looked even younger than his nineteen years, not quite a boy but not yet a man. He looked over his shoulder. Yellow Dog Dingo was nowhere in sight. He laughed at himself. "Hell, Porter," he said aloud, "you're not a kangaroo, you're just nuts. After all, Emory ain't Armageddon."

Forty-eight hours later he would have readjusted his thinking about that assertion, given the room in his consciousness for trivia or the time to contemplate it. A tidal wave of assignments for which even legend and rumor had produced inadequate anticipation washed over him, leaving him treading water frantically to keep his nose and mouth free. All other cares became relatively inconsequential in the unceasing struggle for academic survival; he was a *bona fide* freshman medical student.

Their work load was monumental. Just the exercise of reading the assigned material occupied the freshmen until midnight; learning it was another matter. They trimmed minutes from budgeted schedules wherever they could find them and became artists at the quick shower and the bolted meal.

The freshman year in any medical school requires serious adjustment and involves learning a prodigious amount of facts about

5

previously unexplored subjects. No other school anywhere, however, subjected its students to the same demands for memorizing five pounds of Morris's *Gross Anatomy*. No other school had an Anatomy professor with the ability to enslave, rule, and grind down a group of intelligent, for the most part personable, young American males, women medical students being still unthinkable. Emory was blessed, said some, cursed, said others, with such a professor.

He was muscular but also paunchy, so that he looked both solid and squat. His iron gray hair stood erect without part and was about an inch longer than the currently stylish crew cut. His eyebrows were untamed and wild; he had a gray mustache as rank and clipped as privet hedge. He wore spectacles with no-nonsense steel frames and a long white laboratory coat with permanent stains across the midriff. His teeth, however, were his most memorable feature. He had too many and they seemed too big. Porter at first meeting had decided that if the man had dentures they constituted a terrible professional mistake. On the street or on a crowded sidewalk he may have been a nondescript figure, but in the classroom and dissection laboratory of Emory University School of Medicine, he was an emperor, a rigid and absolute monarch, a Pharaoh who demanded more and more bricks but gave no straw to the children of Israel. His name was Horace Wingo, Ph.D., and his students called him "The Butch." Well out of earshot. The title was more than a nickname; it was the description of a condition and only the initiated could fully appreciate it.

The Butch did not bellow nor yell. On the contrary, his voice was soft, almost chalky, and he cleared his throat frequently, like someone not too long recovered from a spell of choking. He was said to have lost completely his sense of smell because of prolonged exposure to formaldehyde, and Porter wondered if it had also affected his voice.

"Look to the right of you," he said to the first meeting of the class, after he had ponderously called the roll and identified each responding student with a fixed and level gaze. "Now look to the left of you." When the boys had complied he silkily delivered his *coup de grace*. "One of you will not be here by Christmas."

There was total silence in the room. Porter darted a second furtive glance to either side of him. "Poor Rumble, poor Teate," he thought. "I wonder which one of them it will be." He observed that every face he could see was of a sudden either flushed or blanched and the necks of those in front of him had turned red. The Butch smiled blandly into the stillness, his lower lip a blood red crescent beneath the gleaming teeth, his upper lip obscured by the rank, grizzled mustache.

6

"Now, listen carefully to me. Your laboratory specimens in this course were once living, breathing human beings, that fact, of course, constituting their present value to you and, through you, to all of society. Remember this: If I catch one of you exhibiting the least disrespect to his laboratory specimen, the offender will automatically join the exodus from this group."

Porter's attention wandered, although he kept his gaze fastened raptly on the professor's face. "No wonder those Emory undergraduates are all so terrified of this old man. I thought they were kidding when they said he flunked at least a third of the class each year, but they're not. He really means it. He's going to do it." He swallowed. "Well, that's their problem; it's for sure and certain not going to be me. I've never flunked a course in my life and I'm not about to start now."

". . . This will be your Bible for the next year." Dr. Wingo had one hand on the tome by Morris. "That other school to the east of us uses Gray's *Anatomy*, and some of you who have to leave us may even finally find a haven there, but I chose this work because it is more detailed and a better authority. This," and he held aloft a second book, "is like unto it. This is Dorland's *Medical Dictionary*. You will be learning an entire new vocabulary over the next nine months; it will behoove you to pronounce it correctly." He cleared his throat. "Although actual points will not be subtracted from your grade for an error in pronunciation, I assure you that it will be taken into consideration in your overall assessment. Do not take for granted that you know how to pronounce a word just because you can spell it and have heard it previously. Look it up."

He turned and printed on the blackboard.

CADAVER

Then he drew a blunt, square-nailed forefinger down the page of his open roll book. The finger stopped, his eyes wandered over the room.

"Easley."

The tall, handsome boy two rows down from Porter corrected his slump into almost military erectness; his tight upper lip gave a slicing quality to his words.

"Yes, sir."

"You will be spending a large part of your waking hours with this object and it will even invade what dreams you may be privileged to have over the next few months. How do you pronounce it?"

"Ca-dă-ver, Dr. Wingo."

The teeth flashed. He thumbed the thin pages edged in red between the covers of the dictionary. The forefinger traveled downward and stopped.

"You are wrong, Easley. Dorland here says it is ca-$d\bar{a}$-ver. You will remember this."

His eyes went back to the roll book.

"Yarn."

There was the sound of shifted feet behind Porter.

"Yes, sir."

"You pronounce this one."

Dr. Wingo again printed on the board.

UMBILICUS

"I would say that's um-*bil*-i-cus, sir."

"Well, Yarn, so would a disgusting percentage of the rest of the class. Consult Dorland and you will find that it is um-bi-*li*-cus. A word to the wise, it is said, is sufficient. Keep Dorland at your elbow."

Porter's face felt hot, his buttocks were tight. He would have sworn that Easley and Yarn had both been right and was grateful that he had not been singled out. At the end of his row, a slick-haired boy named Conner was frantically taking notes.

"Why in the world," Porter thought, "is he bothering to do that? I'll not be able to forget those two words if I live to be a hundred."

Thus were the seeds of paranoia expertly sown. They fell on fertile ground and the birds of the air found them not; they sprouted and flourished and grew.

"You will all proceed immediately to the second floor, where you will be issued your dissecting kits and gowns. This should take no more than ten or fifteen minutes, after which you will assemble in the laboratory and be assigned your partners and your cadavers."

The medical school of Emory University in 1942 consisted of two buildings only. On the outside, they were identical save for the inscriptions carved deeply into the lintel over each entrance. One said Anatomy, the other Physiology. They were uncompromising rectangles of marble and they sat facing each other, unadorned by foundation planting or landscaping, bare of beauty, constructed unashamedly solely for function. The marble was of a dirty white streaked with gray and lacked the warming pink accents of the buildings on the Quadrangle. The warmth of red brick and living flesh awaited the medical student at Grady Hospital downtown in his third and fourth years, but the first two years were spent in these cold buildings on campus. There was an aura about them that seemed to breathe, "All hope abandon, ye who enter here."

The one architectural item of beauty in the Anatomy building was the stairway going to the second floor. It swept upward in gentle curve across the long front window, its marble risers and treads graduated in perfect proportion, its progress accented by a brass railing that glittered warmly in the stark hallway The stairway was inviting, full of promise, femininely graceful.

When the freshman medical students were dismissed by Dr. Wingo at his first meeting with them, following his instructions they proceeded upstairs. They found the steps of the flaring arch to second floor lined with young men, fine-looking young men, healthy, clean, well-dressed young men, some of them handsome, but all of them conspicuously solemn. They crowded in a row against the wall, leaving room for passage on the outside curve of the stairwell. The freshmen had to run that gauntlet to reach second floor.

"Who is that?" Porter asked Easley, who was directly behind him and was a sophisticated Emory graduate.

"Those are the sophomores; I recognize most of them. They just finished their first year one week ago. Those are the ones who survived."

"What are they doing here? What are they planning to do to us?"

"God only knows, and He hasn't spoken a word to me since He asked me to pronounce *cadaver*. Let's go."

As the freshmen bunched up like cows in a loading chute and, in single file, set foot on the stairs, there came a low hum, a moan, a lovely sound but eerie. Then the sophomores, their eyes uncrinkled by any semblance of smile, began singing, their only accompaniment the harmony of their own voices reverberating from the marble walls and floors. The tune was familiar but the timing was almost dirge-like. The words were unmistakably clear. The hair prickled all along Porter's neck.

CHORUS

The Eyes of Win - go are up - on you   All the live-long day.   The
Eyes of Win - go are up - on   you,   You can - not get a   way!
Do not think you can es - cape   him,   Rise   up   so ear - ly   in   the
morn.   The   Eyes   of   Win - go   are   up - on   you   Till
Ga - briel blows his   horn. ___   The Aaaaa-men. ___

Horn

Horn

10

Porter, overcome by awe, marvel, and fear, turned right at the head of the staircase instead of left into the proper line to procure equipment. He was in a short hallway at the end of which were double doors containing panels of ground glass that permitted the passage of light but not vision. With no thought except to distance himself from the singing sophomores, he grasped the knob and pulled, noting inconsequentially that the door was painted the ugliest, muddiest green he could imagine. He stepped into the room beyond and was transfixed, all his senses stimulated and assaulted simultaneously. He was in a cavern of concrete with high ceilings, bare windows along three sides transmitting unfiltered light devoid of either pity or mercy. The sudden sense of space made him dizzy. The room was furnished with starkly regimented rows of tables, their cast-iron frames bolted into the cement floor. The tops of the tables were slabs of marble, as cold and white as chipped ice. On each table, supine and rigid, sight-less, soundless, lay a human being, immobile, distant in death. They were uncaringly naked, impersonally male and female, some of them white but most of them black. Even from the doorway the skin looked thick and hard, as unyielding in vertical wrinkles along their thighs as that of a country-cured ham.

Porter heard his blood pulsing through his ears with swish and thud. He became conscious of the odor. He recognized formaldehyde. It stung and burned the nostrils and provided annealing tears; he had encountered it in college when dissecting animals, all the way from earthworms and frogs up to cats. He recognized an undertone of carbolic acid, recall carrying him back to childhood in the days before plumbing when slop jars were rinsed each morning; carbolic acid would kill any germ on the planet. It was a full and comforting smell, redolent of cleanliness. What he did not recognize was the sweet component that permeated the air of this room; it was revolting; sickening; it dominated. He thought that if a smell could be greasy, this one would. Of a sudden he realized this nauseating fragrance was the putrid dominance of human decay over the strength of formaldehyde and phenol. It assured the power of death in the face of any unnatural effort to stay its progress; it was almost rotten and it would have its way. He smelled it incongruously all the way down into his throat. He swallowed full and fast to keep from retching.

The white-coated figure of a laboratory assistant came into the room. "You're not supposed to be in here yet."

Porter bolted through the door without looking at him. "You're absolutely right," he said.

11

Hurrying down the hall toward his classmates clotted around the supply room, he muttered to himself, "Yet, hell! I'm not ever supposed to be in there. What in the world made me think I wanted to be a doctor? Dear God in Heaven, what have I done?"

He fantasized about marching down the stairs and out the front door. He could then walk with leisure to his home town through the singing June hours of this sunny afternoon and all through the night without a backward glance at the new world he had entered, and he would be done with it. Forever. Freedom. Instead, he made himself join the other students, put on his white gown with long sleeves, and spend the afternoon scrubbing a cadaver.

His partners were Townsend and Hutchins, a union appointed by no less a deity than the Butch himself and one not to be questioned. Townsend was an Atlanta native and graduate of Emory, a high school football player with eyelashes and full lips that made him almost pretty. Hutchins was from Milwaukee, had finished at Northwestern, and spoke in strident tones and accent that made him sound officiously authoritative. Porter exhibited meekness all afternoon in the presence of these sophisticates, did his part of the bathing, and completely repressed any sign of distaste for his task. "Daddy, if this isn't compartmentalizing," he thought, "then God didn't make little green apples and the sun won't come up tomorrow. You'd be proud of me; I can do it."

The freshmen moved by explicit direction in the Anatomy laboratory, following minute instructions about each procedure, supervised by a roving, carefully watching group of Wingo satraps. When he wished to gain attention for an announcement, the Butch rapped on one of the marble tables with the butt end of his metal probe. It made a ringing sound that reverberated commandingly through the room and produced silence and stillness in the students like that of children playing "Statue." It was a sound that appeared in the dreams of many of them for years to come. It came on that first afternoon after an hour.

"You have had enough time to clean your specimen. Now you will remove the integument in order to prepare for the dissection and demonstration of underlying structures. Nothing will be destroyed or removed with the exception of the fat. You will begin on the back until you get the feel of it." They labored.

Porter washed his hands six times before supper and still had to hold his breath to get food into his mouth.

He studied until midnight, soaped twice in the shower, resolutely put both hands beneath his pillow upon retiring, and prepared for sleep. He reviewed in his mind the origin, attachment, innervation, blood supply, function, and pronunciation of the platysma muscle. He also reviewed the train of emotional experiences that had sped through and over him in one afternoon. He wondered if anyone else had felt the same. He spoke in the darkness to his roommate in the lower bunk.

"Derrick."

"What?"

"Are you asleep?"

"I thought I was."

"Did you think about Keats this afternoon?"

"I didn't even hear his name on the roll. Does he come before King?"

"He was an English poet in the nineteenth century who was also a physician. He wrote a line that goes

> 'I saw their dead lips in the gloam
> With horrid warning gaped wide,
> And I awoke and found me here
> On the cold hill side.'"

There was the pause, almost of embarrassment, that always ensued when Porter recited poetry in the presence of a male.

"No, I didn't think of Keats. What I thought was how hard it's going to be to get along with somebody who tells me to 'remove the integument' when what he means is for me to skin an old dead colored lady who is almost pickled. Quit being romantic and hush and go to sleep."

2 9ross Anatomy was not the only class confronting the freshmen, and the others were not by any stretch of the imagination crip courses. Dr. Willis Jones, the head of the Biochemistry department, had hair the color of taffy and a personality to complement it. He was somewhat fusty, overly patient, totally benign. Never too busy to help a student with a question, he seemed in a detached way to have some genuine concern for individuals and enjoyed respect, even affection, from the class. Had he been a little less dull, not quite such a reserved pedagogue, possessed of more humor, he might even have been loved, colorless as he was. Or had he had a different assistant, he might have achieved that position. That individual, however, captivated and mesmerized every boy who studied Biochemistry. Dr. Angelica Athanopoulos was so vivid that she made her superior seem shadowy, vaguely present but definitely a background figure. She was diminutive to the point of seeming a miniature, perfect in detail but definitely reduced to scale. She moved around the laboratory like a wind-up toy with tightened crank, and her enthusiasm crackled like electricity. So did her intelligence. The line from her widow's peak to the tip of her nose was perfectly straight with no indentation apparent between her thick glistening brows. On first sight Porter was entranced. "Her profile looks just like Aunt Ida Mae's cameo," he marveled.

Within two weeks he was reverently, distantly, hopelessly, safely in love with her. He vowed to memorize all the amino acids until they were commonplace on his tongue and so to manipulate his titration in lab that one-half drop would change his solutions from red to blue and back again on the very first try. Dr. Athanopoulos was so refined, so cosmopolitan, so intellectual, such a lady that Porter felt rural and wormy in her presence. He could earn her approbation only by excelling in Biochemistry; certainly he would never risk her derision by exposing his feelings. He thought it a classic example of Werther and Charlotte and felt deliciously melancholy whenever he had a few moments he could devote to fantasy.

Those moments were rare. In addition to Biochemistry, there was Bacteriology class and lab to attend three times a week. The head of that department was also a female with a Ph.D., and there comparison to Dr. Athanopoulos rested and contrast began. If in Porter's view Dr. Athanopoulos brought romance to the impersonal formulations and reactions of Biochemistry, conversely then Dr. Gabrielle Martell in Bacteriology brought shattering reality to any semblance of romance that may have been inherent in that science. She would have been a big woman even in her youth when she had conceivably been thin, but when Porter knew her, she resembled a load of melons, ungraded for size, all jumbled together and being tumbled to market. Any undergarments she wore were obviously unrestraining, and even long professional lab coats could not conceal the waddling shift of her buttocks nor hold back the precipice of her bosom. Her progress down a hallway was a slipping, sliding passage of flesh that whispered in secret against itself and was probably a little more marvelous to witness from the rear than from the front.

She was red of hair and red of face and she wheezed like a calliope. It was rare to see her without a lighted cigarette, either gripped between her fingers or dangling in eye-squinting insouciance from one corner of her mouth. She consequently moved with little puffs of ashes in her train and always with a layer of them across her bosom and smudges on her white lab coat. She had interest in all men but respect for none. She was the first woman Porter had ever encountered whom he fancied to be completely ribald; he thought her Rabelaisian.

"As all of you know who have bothered to read it, your lesson today is on syphilis. Now I want to begin by saying that it is definitely possible to catch syphilis on a toilet seat, but I am also here to tell you that's one hell of a place to carry your girl."

Conner compulsively was writing every word in his notebook. The rest of the class roared.

On another occasion: "Be aware that you can glean insight into your living fellow men even while buried in the bowels of a Bacteriology lab, which for some reason always seems to be in some goddam basement. I was called last year to culture an abscess in the nostril of one of your professors who thinks he married well and trots around the Piedmont Driving Club like he belongs there. Boys, I want you to know it grew out E. coli." Her face flamed and a wheezing chuckle erupted. "That told me immediately that he had indulged in two activities not condoned in polite society. The moral of this story is that if you're going to pick your nose, do it before you scratch your ass."

Porter was fascinated; indeed, every boy in the class regarded Bacteriology as an oasis of sanity, albeit reminiscent of Alice in Wonderland, the Queen of Hearts more corpulent and bawdy than heretofore imagined. They looked forward to Dr. Martell rather than to the subject she taught, for under her tutelage it was not only permissible to relax and laugh, it was expected. She was not at all devoid of compassion or wary of affection, but she was brilliantly free of illusions. She forgivingly expected the freshmen to behave as adolescents, and with her sharp eye for irony did not anticipate any male growing completely beyond that stage. Ever.

"You have all heard it said in democratic defiance of special privilege that every man puts on his trousers one leg at a time. No one to my knowledge, however, has commented that some do it a lot more often than others and also that the contents may vary. That's what makes life interesting, causes wars, sells newspapers." She paused to light a fresh Camel from the stub of her old one while the class tittered. "Today you are going to learn the difference between the meningococcus and the gonococcus. From the laboratory standpoint, that is. Clinically, you're on your own and will see both of them in profusion when you get to Grady. I'll forewarn you, however, that they both produce terrible diseases, one of the main differences between them being that you don't mind telling your wife that you have meningitis."

Although Bacteriology and Biochemistry in themselves would have constituted a full academic curriculum, they were subservient to the demands and unrelenting pressures of Anatomy; wedged in like inconsequential but balancing pebbles between the boulders of a massive wall. The Butch would flunk a boy out of med school in a heartbeat and they knew it. Sessions phrased it well: "Before we got in this damn war, you could go to summer school at the University of Michigan and make up an F in Biochemistry. Lots of guys, used to, would work so hard passing Gross that they slipped up and got caught on the easier courses. But now he's got us by the short hairs. You flunk now and you're gone. 'This is the Army, Mr. Jones, no private rooms or telephones.' If you don't want your ass shot off in the South Pacific, you better study."

16

If Wingo was aware that his class became sleep-deprived to the point of being zombies, he gave no formal recognition of it. As the days piled up into weeks, the work load and assignments increased. The outside world was forgotten. Japan and Germany were far away. The first pop quiz jolted Porter into the realization that the boys who had been Emory undergraduates were justified in their paranoia; the Butch did pick at least one fourth of his questions from the fine print. Porter studied harder. He memorized trivia that he knew he would forget as soon as the quarter was over. The class, to a man, welcomed the childish doggerel of the mnemonic given them by Dick Faulkner, a medical student who had taken a sabbatical to be an instructor in the Anatomy department. He was already balding, always soft-spoken, a little simian in appearance; kindness exuded from him and he was easily the most supportive person in the department.

"No one is supposed to retain everything by cold intellect alone. You have to know the cranial nerves in their order or Dr. Wingo will give you an F, but it's easy if you first remember, 'On Old Olympus's towering top a Finn and German viewed some hops.' When we get to the extremities and study the wrist, I'll tell you about, 'Never lower Tillie's pants, Mama might come home,' but right now you learn those cranial nerves. All of you look worn out. Why don't you take a couple of hours and go to a movie?"

Porter followed his advice that very afternoon. He and Hutchins and Townsend had the anterior cervical triangle exposed and demonstrated on their compliant and greasy cadaver, the glistening nerves, the rubbery arteries, the thin-walled veins outlined and identified. There were three students at their table, whereas all the others had only two, and this gave them a time advantage in dissection. Porter's tongue was rich with new words — sternocleidomastoid, omohyoid, vagus, scalenus anticus — the pronunciation of all of them carefully confirmed by research in Dorland, their mystery dissipated by visual proof of where they went and whence they sprang. His head was crammed with new directions, precise and scientific.

"Remember when you said somebody was dumb if he didn't know up from down?" asked Walton over a Coca-Cola in the hallway. "Now it's anterior, posterior, superior, inferior, cephalad, caudad, ventral, dorsal, plantar, volar, lateral, medial, proximal, distal, and it's come to the point I can't tell whether I'm coming or going and some days I don't know in from out. I'm all for the movie myself. The Butch keeps telling our table that we have to get oriented. He's talking about that damn scrawny, grimy, stinking neck but I'm thinking about the bigger picture. Let's get a crowd and go."

The crowd turned out to be seven. Everyone else begged off, too much material to study, too few hours before bedtime, too much neglected work to catch up. Conner reviewed everything from the beginning every night just in case. He had figured that pop quizzes would account for twenty-five percent of the total and he intended to be prepared. He responded to their shouted invitation across campus with a frenetic wave and a wagging head as he headed toward his dormitory in a half trot.

Arnold shifted Morris and his clipboard to another hip. "That Thurmond Conner is going to drive me crazy. Everybody ought to have to room with him just one week. He takes ten vitamins four times a day because he says he can't afford to get sick and miss a day. He's determined to make an A in Anatomy—and everything else for that matter. He talks to himself, too. With me sitting right there in the room with him. 'That's the clavicle, the sternocleidomastoid, and the midline fascia, boy,' he yelled the other night. 'The omohyoid divides it into superior and inferior. You got that, Thurmond? You got it? And the origin of the sternocleidomastoid muscle is the mastoid bone and its insertion is on the clavicle and the sternum. Got it now? Got it? Thata boy!' When he gets sleepy he puts his Morris on top of the dresser and stands there barefooted in his drawers to study. This pounding noise woke me up at two o'clock yesterday morning and there's Thurmond spraddled at his dresser, old baggy drawers, hair growing all over his back like a damn monkey. He's slapping his forehead with his palm to stay awake and saying, 'You gotta drive, Conner, you gotta drive! You hear me, boy? You gotta drive.' I told him if he didn't shut up so I could sleep I'd drive his ass straight through that wall. He's crazy but he's got priorities. He's not about to go to a picture show."

By the time the seven had lugged their heavy books to the village theatre and paid their quarters, the feature had begun. They filed into the dimmed theatre and had to split up because it was almost filled. They sat in twos or threes but all managed to find seats about halfway down. Porter could find only a single seat and climbed over three pairs of knees to ensconce himself alone. On the screen, Tyrone Power wore knickers and white stockings, had a scarf tied under his hat and was doing impossible things in a bull ring. Porter immediately became absorbed in the fantasy. The Butch and Dr. Martell and Dr. Athanopoulos were forgotten and so were his responsibilities to them.

He snuggled lower into his seat. Faulkner was right. He needed a couple of hours of escape. No need to feel guilty about wasting time.

Then it began. A silver-haired lady in front of him coughed and leaned sideways to whisper to her blue-haired friend. "Let's move."

Two rows down an older man sitting by Morgan and Roach mumbled something to his wife and they stood and sidled out. To the right and across the aisle, three high school girls arose demurely and moved almost to the back of the theatre, leaving empty seats by Swann and Calloway. For fully five minutes, the shadowy figures of people moving out of their rows and to the back of the theatre distracted Porter's attention from Linda Darnell and Tyrone Power. He heard rustling behind him, the scuff of feet on carpet. The door at the rear admitted punctuating interruptions of light; people were actually leaving this movie before it was well begun. He folded his knees sideways for the couple to his left to move across him. As they passed, the lady leaned back to him and hissed, "If you're 4-F and can't be in uniform where you belong, you could at least bathe before appearing in public." She gave a strangled gasp, held a handkerchief to her nose and fled. Porter sat frozen for moments and then he bolted.

The Butch had told them that the olfactory nerve was weak, that of the human's five senses the one of smell was the most easily fatigued and exhausted; Porter himself was already inured to the stench of the dissecting lab, had even been able to eat with a hearty appetite. He was well aware that no perfumed soap or shampoo could displace or surmount the fragrance of death and rancid fat beneath his fingernails and that formaldehyde clung to skin and hair, moving everywhere with him, but this was the first time he had been out in public around people other than his fellow-sufferers. He was mortified.

As he fled the theatre, he heard Swann's voice above the gallop of Spanish hooves. "Hey, fellows, move to the middle. There are plenty of seats for us to sit together now."

Porter tagged this attitude as the ultimate in *sang-froid* but could not emulate it. All the way across campus his face and ears felt hot. "I'll never do that again," he vowed, "unless we all ring bells and holler 'Unclean.' It's back to old Olympus's towering top for me. What'd that lady mean? I don't look like I'm 4-F."

It was not the olfactory nerve only that became soon overloaded and impervious to insult; the students even became habituated to the terror originally generated by the presence of Dr. Wingo and were able to laugh at gaffes, so long as they were not the victims.

"Simpson, Arthur." It was the first time this student had been in the spotlight of attention before the full class, in the formal setting of the lecture room.

"Yes, sir."

"What is the length of the spinal accessory nerve from its exit from the skull before it sends a branch recurving over the scalp?"

The class held its breath. This was a five-point question. Had Simpson bothered to read it? If so, had he attributed it enough importance to remember it? "Between two to three centimeters, sir, allowing for variations in the individual."

Dr. Wingo's smile was blinding. The class relaxed; more than half of them had not known the answer. They all felt vindicated by Arthur Simpson, who was unduly quiet and prissed when he walked but was proving to be a worthy gladiator in this bloody academic arena.

"Very good, Simpson. Now, tell me, how long is a centimeter?"

"Sir?"

"How many centimeters are there to an inch?"

The boy's ears flamed deep crimson. "I don't know exactly, sir."

"You should not use a term if you're not familiar with its definition, Simpson. If you do not know exactly, then tell me *approximately* how many centimeters there are to an inch."

Simpson shifted in his seat. "Well, sir, I believe there are approximately 2.543."

Dr. Wingo looked at him levelly and hitched the waistband of his trousers up with his wrists, habit engendered by years of protecting his clothing from offensive fingers.

"Simpson, I think a number carried to the third decimal place constitutes an acceptable approximation." The class erupted in glee. They felt that their side had won a point.

They felt a few days later, however, that they had lost some ground, that they might be damned by association with a new gladiator in the arena, that the unwanted searchlight of the eyes of the Butch might be attracted to each of their number like lightning from the crown of a hovering thunderhead, that they might all be judged, might be punished for the miscreant behavior of one. Will Barton was a graduate of Clemson and had obtained his education on a football scholarship. He was the lightning rod. He emitted an aura of physical power and recklessness just in the simple act of walking across the campus. It was not only that his thighs were so muscled he was spraddle-legged, or that his neck was as big as his head; there was a wildness about him that pulsated. He gave the impression that he was furiously revving his motor preparatory to sudden release of his clutch. His tongue was thick with Southern accent and rough with rural syntax but his voice was bold, defiant. At Emory University he was in a foreign land but he bowed not his neck nor bent his knee; he guarded with fierceness his personal space and dared encroachment. His encounter with Dr. Wingo began mildly enough, civilly, without passion.

The papers from the first pop quiz had been returned. Dr. Wingo, leisurely making his supervising rounds among the cadavers, approached Will Barton's table.

"Dr. Wingo, how come you marked off ten points for my description of the clavicle?" He produced the paper violated with red pencil and also now spottily translucent with human oils.

The professor peered through grease-smeared spectacles. "Barton, you overanswered the question. I did not ask for the blood supply of the clavicle nor for the name of every muscle and ligament attached to it, nor for the structures superficial and immediately deep to it. I merely asked for a general description of the bone and Morris states that quite succinctly. 'The clavicle is shaped like the italic letter F.' You failed to mention that. You leaped over the obvious answer into a morass of unrequested information. If you expect to pass this course, you must learn how to take an examination."

That was the trigger. Barton almost leaped over his dissection table, cadaver and all. He hurled his metal probe on the concrete floor and it rang like the gong at a prize fight. The class was as transfixed as if a volcano had erupted.

"What?" he bellowed. "Are you threatening me? Me? I'm not a puny little Emory pussy, one of these Mama's boys. You can't intimidate me by assigning twice as much as anybody could possibly read in one night and then asking picky little questions that don't amount to a tinker's damn. You're dealing with a man here, Dr. Wingo, a real man! Don't hand me any of those veiled threats about not being here at Christmas!"

Dr. Wingo did not raise his voice but he did clear his throat. "Barton, this is an unacceptable exhibition in an inappropriate setting. Let me remind you that I am the final arbiter of who passes and who fails this course and that I can flunk a man as easily as I can a boy. And with as little compunction."

Barton leaned over until his chin almost touched the professor's nose. His eyes were bloodshot and piggish, his face empurpled, the veins in his neck as big as pencils. He could have whispered but still he yelled. "Well, it's a sorry system. You've got no business having interviews and accepting these boys if you're going to flunk 'em out!" He swept an arm to encompass the room. "All these scared little puppies had the grades from college to qualify for your precious med school. You take 'em in here and browbeat them until they're scared to sleep, they're scared to eat, they're scared of their shadows. They're so scared they're pitiful! All because of one little old symbol in the alphabet and it's not in italics like the collarbone, it's a big solid capital F! And you've got it swinging over this bunch as big and terrifying as the sword over the head of whoever that Greek jerk was we had to read about! You wield it like a sceptre! It's not right and it's a piss-poor way to educate somebody! Look at them. They've paid good money to learn to be doctors and you've got them as cowed as flea-bitten, half-starved dogs!"

Dr. Wingo's feet remained planted as stolidly as if they were extensions of the concrete floor, but he had to sway a little backward to avoid actual contact with Barton. Although his voice was still controlled, silky, his throat-clearing was authoritative enough to interrupt the tirade. "Barton, you have wasted enough of the time this class needs for dissection. These students *have* paid their money to learn. They have paid it to Emory. Emory pays me to see that they get their money's worth. To paraphrase Marcus Aurelius, 'I am Emory and I must keep my color.' If the students do not learn to their maximum abilities, I am cheating Emory and them. That little symbol you call my sceptre does not belong to me; it is only in my custody. I award it; I do not wield it. If a student earns it, he gets it." A chilling porcelain smile stirred the brush on his lip, but his eyes were opaque as agates.

"I promise you, Barton, that if you earn yourself an F, I will certainly see that you get it. Your concern for your fellows is stirring, perhaps, but you had better look to your own laurels; you could flunk, too, you know."

"What?" Barton threw back his head and his fury vanished like a whirlwind. His laughter was as loud and maniacal, however, as his anger had been. "You don't know who you're talking to, man! You can't flunk me! Pour it on, give me extra assignments, load me up, give me all you got! I can take it and dish it right back to you! I ain't the least bit scared of you! I can handle this puny little course and learn every fiber and cell in this poor old fat lady even if you didn't bother to get her but about half pickled! And I won't strain myself! You *can't* flunk me, Butch Wingo! Not me!"

He recovered his probe and seated himself on the stool over his cadaver as though nothing had happened. "Very interesting challenge, Barton. We shall see, we shall see." Dr. Wingo moved up the row of tables also as though nothing had happened.

Porter felt strongly that they should all join this pretense that the episode had not occurred. At least for the present. Compulsively, sprightly, he chattered to his partners. "What did y'all think of Dr. Martell's statement that all men are divided into two groups—those that have masturbated and those that are liars?"

Hutchins followed his lead. "Hell, I think she's exactly right. Who's going to take a scientific poll, though, and what difference does it make anyhow?"

Townsend raised his head from the open textbook, the sleeve of his gown resting unnoticed in the gray mass of the dissected neck. "She's not right, either. I never have."

Hutchins snorted. "Don't give us that stuff, Tommy-boy. We automatically think you're lying."

"Well, I'm not. I've tried to a couple of times, but I just can't do it. I cannot physically do it."

Porter's curiosity was salaciously titillated. Here loomed personal confession of unimagined darkness. "Why?" he ventured. "Why can't you?"

"Because," Townsend sweetly replied, "I'm too ticklish."

Porter's spontaneous laugh, albeit quickly stifled, was like a spring breeze across the lab. Everybody relaxed.

Not a student commented on the encounter between Barton and Wingo until the group was not only out of the Anatomy building but well away from it. Even then they looked over their shoulders to be sure no one of consequence could overhear and were thereby as obvious as gossips anywhere.

"He's crazy," Boykin said. "He's crazy, and he's also finished. He might as well pack his suitcase tonight."

"He's got guts, though," said Kinard. "Can you imagine anyone standing up to Dr. Wingo like that? Let alone saying the things he did?"

"I thought the Butch was the one who had guts myself," murmured Teate. "If Barton had been over me like that, I'd have run like a rabbit."

Conner went tearing by, his dissecting gown still hanging and flapping about him, smiling and shaking his head in rejection of the invitation to join the group. "Gotta drive," he laughed. "Gotta drive!"

"He can't stop," Arnold volunteered. "This is the time slot on his schedule for the crapper. He decided he was wasting too much time working up a BM, so he started taking mineral oil. Took too much at first, then too little, but now he's got it titrated just right. It takes him exactly forty-five seconds from pants down to pants up and he's through for the day. That's on one and a half teaspoons of the mineral oil. It has to be taken at six A.M. just before he brushes his teeth and then he gets results at 5:45 P.M. on his way to supper, and he hasn't wasted a second of study time."

"My God," Easley interjected, "Barton was right about us being too scared to sleep or eat, but I'm glad he didn't know about Conner and tell the Butch we were too scared to take a good crap."

Rumble ventured a smile. "Knowing Barton and seeing how mad he was, he might even have violated Dr. Wingo's law about not using slang or coarse expressions and told him we were scared shitless."

Grateful for humor, no matter how innocuous, Porter volunteered, "If y'all think that's funny, let me tell you why Townsend has never masturbated."

"Aw, shut up, Osborne, we know the answer; *nobody's* got time for it. Let's go to supper."

At bedtime, when the taboo of silence in their room could be broken, Porter speculated. "You know, it was right impressive the way Barton went from being so mad about the way Dr. Wingo runs the class to laughing about the challenge to him personally. He may turn out to be a real leader of men. Some lines from a poem kept running through my head while I was studying.

> 'Don John laughing in the brave beard curled,
> Spurning of his stirrups like the thrones of all
>   the world.'

I'm just not all that scared of Dr. Wingo myself and don't feel like I need a champion, but I can't help but admire Barton."

Derrick was quick in response. "As far as Barton is concerned, I think he's crazy as a mad dog and I don't want to be within twenty feet of him. I don't even want to be seen with him; what he's got might be catching. And, Sonnyboy, you better quit letting things like poetry run through your mind when you're supposed to be studying or you might wind up being as scared as anybody else."

He turned off the light and climbed into the lower bunk. "The only poetry that makes any sense to me right now is,

'Do not think you can escape him,
Rise up so early in the morn,
The eyes of Wingo are upon you
Till Gabriel blows his horn.'

Be quiet when you go to breakfast. I'm gonna grab an extra fifteen minutes. Now will you please go to sleep?"

*"We have set the seal of Solomon on all things
    under sun,
Of knowledge and of sorrow and endurance
    of things done."*

3   Over the class there now loomed a new specter, mysterious, imminent, fearsome, a true dreadnaught. Ultimate weapon in Wingo's siege of terror, it was the final crushing blow calculated to impel complete submission in even the most independent student. The class by now was accustomed to pop quizzes, expected them on at least a weekly basis, and had learned to live with nervous systems that had grown as jumpy as those of feral cats. The final examination was scheduled, was at least six weeks away, and fear of it could be deferred. There was, however, a test of merit, of skill, of endurance that was not scheduled but was as certain to come as new moons and death, not as predictable as the former but as undesirable as the latter. It was called "The Practical." Some boys, most of them from south Georgia, soon dropped the article and referred to it as "Practical," thereby bestowing a title that created a mythical monster to compare with Grendel. It terrorized all of them.

"And why not?" said Tootle. "We know it's coming and we know it's gonna run over all us little children that can't get out the way and it's gonna eat some of us alive and crunch our bones. You mighty right I'm scared of Practical, and any you got any sense better be."

Porter prickled in company with his classmates but was really more absorbed in watching their reactions than with any true personal fear. The practical examination in Gross Anatomy consisted of the display of specific structures that the students had dissected themselves; these structures would be flagged and identification demanded. Porter could not imagine enough difficulty in this process to induce the panic that he witnessed now in his older, more sophisticated peers.

"My God, if he'd just tell us when it's going to be! I can't study new material for reviewing the old, and yet if I don't keep up every day, I'll be even that much further behind."

"He's playing with us. That's what he's doing. He knows the day and the hour and he's just playing with us."

"Be sure and check Patz and Chesky's table. They've got an aberrant spinal accessory on the left, and Faulkner says the Butch is hell on anomalies."

"What would we do without Faulkner? He says he can't help us, though, about when the Practical will be. Says Dr. Wingo doesn't let anybody else help prepare it ahead of time and even the staff doesn't know until the day it happens."

"You mean to tell me that the Butch himself ties ribbons around all those little bitty things he wants identified? The head of the department? God, it's obliged to take hours and hours. What a way to spend his time."

"Yeah, and the only time he can do it is at night and it's not ribbons. It's tiny little pieces of red string. One of the sophomores told me he's wise to students checking to see when the lights are on after hours, and for the last two years he does all that work the night before ole Practical comes with nothing but a flashlight. About twice a quarter, he'll leave the lights on all night just to confuse everybody and some of them always fall for it, but for the real Practical he just uses the flashlight."

"That's the truth. Last year the freshmen had volunteers rotating shifts to climb a pine tree behind the building and watch until midnight every night to see if any lights came on. This guy was up there and caught the Butch creeping around among the bodies about eleven o'clock with his flashlight and that green eyeshade on. Nobody was with him but Jessie; he held the light while the Butch tied off the Practical. The boy got so excited he fell out of the tree and broke his ankle, but he spread the word and everybody stayed up all night studying and nobody slept a wink."

"Were the grades any better because of that?" blurted Porter. "If they were, we could do the same thing."

"No, we can't," corrected Anthony. "That tree is gone. The Butch found out about it and took an ax to that tree. Himself. On Thanksgiving morning at daylight, somebody said. I find it hard to believe of the Butch, but they swear it's true. Forget the tree."

"What we need to do is hire Jessie," said Strickland.

"Jessie? Hire him?" asked Porter.

To the casual observer Jessie was the janitor in the Anatomy department. In reality he was much more, an extension of Dr. Wingo, almost his alter ego. He had been hired, trained and indoctrinated by

Dr. Wingo to the extent that some regarded him as made over in the Butch's image. He had the same imperturbable dignity and the same burly physique as the Butch and was reputed not to be above a little spying and tattling. He was only a light milk chocolate in color but his features proclaimed his dominant genes. Porter walked on eggshells around him, with a deference that made up for the fear he lacked for Dr. Wingo.

Jessie was the guardian of the cadavers. As such, he would have appeared in Porter's eyes as a cross between Mr. Micawber and Jerry Cruncher had he been white, but Porter would at least have understood him. As a member of the Negro race, however, he violated every stereotype Porter had conceived through years of living in a farm community with hundreds of adults and growing up in cotton fields and cow-pasture baseball games with their children. All of them would have shunned the Anatomy building and its contents with the dedication of ancient taboo. To see Jessie walking casually through its halls, pipe clenched between his teeth, pushing a gurney with its discreetly shrouded and malodorous burden, the stiffly arched outline proclaiming unmistakable identity to the initiated, separated him, elevated him in Porter's eyes to incomprehensible levels of mystery. He was Othello's spawn, a brooding prince, the vessel of mysterious dark but royal bloodlines. Porter instinctively gave passage to him through hall or doorway; he at least knew eggshells when he saw them.

Jessie was the one who received new specimens and prepared them, it was said, by screwing hooks into their skulls and suspending them in vats of formaldehyde. This was done in the basement, an area off limits to freshmen; it was Jessie's domain.

"Hire Jessie? Strickland, you're crazy."

"No, I'm not. One class swears that's how they found out about the Practical one quarter in time to cram. You have to be delicate about it but it can be done. Bert Fletcher grew up on a shade tobacco farm close to Bainbridge and found out he knew some of Jessie's kin. He took up a dime from nine other guys and caught Jessie one day on the front steps when he knew the Butch was up in the lab. He handed him the dollar and Jessie said, 'What's this for?' Fletcher said, 'That's a fee some of us want to pay you to predict the weather for us, Jessie.' Jessie said, 'I don't know no more about the weather than you do, boy. I get mine on the radio same as everybody.' Bert was cool as a cucumber. 'We're not talking about fancy radio weather, Jessie. We're talking about Practical weather. You know, just from a Practical standpoint. We figure there're only two people who know ahead of time, for a Practical certainty, when it's going to rain. That's what we're interested in. Just Practical knowledge of when it's a Practical fact that it's going to rain.'

"And Jessie said, 'I hear you clucking but I can't quite find your nest. You don't spect me to go behind the man's back for no dollar, do you?' And old Bert Fletcher was slick as owl doodoo. 'Of course not, Jessie, we wouldn't dream of asking you to betray any personal loyalties. That's just a retainer fee; we aim to give you that every week all quarter long, and all we want from you is a little old Practical weather forecast every week.'

"With that, Jessie put the dollar in his pocket and Fletcher knew he was in. Said Jessie told him, 'Don't never use that word round me again, but far as the weather concerned, it's clear, sunny, and dry all this week, not a cloud in the sky.' They anted up their dimes every Monday and Fletcher would tell Jessie, 'Pretty day today, Jessie; what you think the weather's gonna do?' And when the time came, Jessie said, 'Little haze coming up. Might get some thunder and lightning toward the end of the week. Might even be a little hail on Thursday.' It worked like a charm."

"I don't believe it," scoffed Porter. "How could Jessie be sure?"

"Because the Butch had to tell him ahead of time so Jessie wouldn't bail out of here on the nose at six o'clock. Don't forget, he's the only one Dr. Wingo will let help him. Bert Fletcher said Jessie gave him back his dollar the next week, though. Said he could tell Dr. Wingo wasn't enjoying Practical like he used to because none of the boys seemed to be surprised and too many of them had made a good grade. 'Look like it's wearing down his spirit,' he said. Jessie told Fletcher he was plumb out of the weather business from now on and Fletcher would have to commence wearing his galoshes every day, just in case." Porter laughed.

When Practical descended on them, Porter became a convert. The mechanics were simple, almost stark. A sheet of paper with one hundred numbered blanks upon it was given each student. Each structure to be identified was also numbered, and each student started at his own cadaver, advancing around the room in sixty-second increments upon the call of "Time." Touching the specimen was forbidden. Often there would be a deep hole with the red knot of string at the bottom of it the only object Porter could be sure he recognized. He became conscious of his heartbeat. He heard whistling air in the nostrils of fellows passing across from him; Teate swallowed audibly over number forty-nine; Will Barton muttered "sonofabitch" as they passed, but he did it on a whispered breath.

"Time."

"Time."

"Time."

There was a row of separate specimens, bones, pre-dissected exhibitions, examples obviously saved for generations.

"Time."

Because they were rare.

"Time."

Because they were anomalies.

"Time."

Because they were absolutely, totally, sadistically impossible to identify.

"Time."

When it was over, Porter was as drained as if he were not quite recovered from diarrhea, weakened but no longer tense and griping. He felt that he was tottering as he made his way downstairs and joined his fellows for a cigarette.

"What was twenty-nine? I put hypoglossal nerve but it may have been some aberrant branch of the glossopalatine artery."

"What about that foramen in the clavicle on number ninety-four? I didn't have the faintest idea what was supposed to go through that damn hole. It's sure not in the book."

Porter was silent. "What in the hell am I doing here?" he thought. He trudged across campus and almost envied Deacon Chauncey, a former classmate who had been inducted into the Army Air Corps directly from college. A recent brief letter from him stated that he had finished radio school, been promoted to sergeant, and was probably going to be sent to England. Deacon was not one to discourse on feelings but Porter knew that he had hated his science courses and taken only those required for his degree in journalism. How did he feel now about all that science he was obliged to have learned, plus the unaccustomed physical activity he had always eschewed? How did Deacon feel about heading out in an airplane to be shot at? "This is war, too," Porter assured himself, "except we'd have to go through all this even in peacetime. To hell with compartmentalizing, I'm fighting, too." He slung his books on his bunk and headed for the dining hall. "Be damned if the Butch is going to kill this soldier," he vowed.

The next day he was not so sure. Practical had been left intact, a sheet was handed out with the correct answers, and everyone again moved around the room, clocked this time in ten-second slots.

"Time."

"Time."

"Time."

The papers, graded in red, were handed out. Porter's heart sank. He had made fifty-six. He disconsolately approached Faulkner.

"Quit worrying." The voice was soft, inflectionless. "That's not great, it does not reflect brilliance, but it's well within the lower half of the upper third of the class."

Porter digested this hierarchy. "You mean I haven't flunked?"

"My goodness, no. One boy didn't get but eleven answers right."

"Who was that?" gasped Porter.

"You know I'm not going to tell you, Osborne. Any more than I'm going to tell you who made ninety-seven. Keep on working and quit fretting. You're still a decent-sized frog; you're just in a bigger puddle than you've ever known before."

Porter approached his cadaver and his partners with lightened step. "What'd you make, Hutchins?"

"None of your goddam business, but I'm in the upper half of the lower third."

"That's great," said Porter. "So am I. This sure is a big puddle we're crawling around in, isn't it? Even bigger than Northwestern."

4 **T**he summer sun at Emory in 1942 made a hothouse
of the Anatomy laboratory; sweat trickled down spines and thighs and
puddled in grimy saddle oxfords. To the stench of preservatives was
added now a sour odor induced by the moistened cloths wrapped
around the dissection fields every night to prevent desiccation; the
windows were open wide and occasional breezes were welcomed with
silent rejoicing. It was a heavy atmosphere, fecund with decay and heat
and humidity, ripe for hatred to grow like weeds. The freshman
medical class could have become a group of paranoid, suspicious,
competitive boys so hostile to each other, so involved in grade-
grubbing competition that they clawed and scrambled over the backs of
their fellows and plotted throat-cutting ways to advance themselves by
pushing others down. The seeds were there; the soil was fertile; the
climate was ideal; the head gardener nurtured it.

The opposite occurred. The freshman class became a group of
paranoid, suspicious competitive boys so terrified of failure, so
obsessed with grade-grubbing labor for survival that they memorized
everything they could as individuals and then tried to help each other.
Minute or esoteric items were labeled "pearls" and were freely passed
around. No one of them witnessed humiliation of a fellow under the
eyes of Wingo without first feeling relief that it was happening to
someone else and then a rush of compassion for the victim. No one
could know it all. Except Wingo. The devastating display of ignorance
in public could be maneuvered under his expert manipulation to
include any of them. "There but for the grace of God" was the prevailing attitude.

The students, therefore, despite widely divergent backgrounds
and disparate, often conflicting, personalities, became bonded to each
other by the glue of common peril, of shared hardship, of unvoiced

revulsion, of the mortal wounding of hope itself, of the final defiant resistance to despair. They became friends. This moment in time, this explosion of new experiences that was called Gross Anatomy, this servitude under a demanding sultan so unwittingly bound them that they would never escape the memories and only a few of them would sever the ties. They learned compassion, support, pity, understanding of others. They learned it as people before they became doctors. They learned it from each other before they saw their first patient, or entered the subterranean passages of Grady Hospital, or had any courses in psychiatry. They matured to the point of realizing that despite heart-rending pity, no man can answer for another. They did, indeed, become friends. Under the eyes of Wingo. They got their money's worth. Brimming full. Packed down. Running over. As Barton roared one day in lab, "Educated, by God!"

Barton was unique. Everyone walked as stiffly around him as wary dogs, alert to danger, eyes rolling, ready to abandon the pretense of indifference in favor of immediate flight. No one fully understood him, no one particularly wanted to, and no one in the class truly accepted him. Except Porter and Barton's roommate. The roommate was from Illinois and therefore a fish out of water himself. Barton had been his first, his most personal, introduction to the South and consequently became his point of reference, his yardstick of comparison, not only to the region but to its inhabitants. He frequently appeared bewildered.

To Porter, Barton was just another example of the marvelous mortals he found in this new culture which he was resolved to explore and master. All of his fellow students were new and foreign to him; he watched them all, assumed that each had as firm a toehold on the rocky cliffs of knowledge as he and as strong a dedication to surmounting them. Barton, in his eyes, was more than passing strange, but anyone had to be slightly mad to attack Emory University School of Medicine with the fervor the students manifested; most of them had enough eccentricities already to be, in his mind, as strange as Barton. He liked them all. They learned to know each other in bits and pieces, through revelations between classes or at meals, which were about the only occasions they had for inconsequential conversation.

At lunch, Harris said, "Halstrand has a rough schedule. He still keeps his paper route and has to live at home way over in southwest Atlanta. Rides the street car to school and back every day. He's done that for four years through college and says it's not so bad this summer but he dreads having to change cars at Five Points next winter when it's cold and dark. Especially toting all those heavy books, plus his lab gown, and some days even the bone box."

"Yeah," Benton responded, "but it doesn't bother Halstrand. Talk about a positive attitude. He looks at it as an hour's extra study time twice a day on the street car, and he says on lab days he not only has a seat to himself but that folks are standing in the aisle jammed up like sardines to keep from getting close to him. You know he and Inman have that young, real fat woman with the stab wound in her neck. Jessie didn't leave her in the vat long enough; even Butch gags when he gets to that table, but Halstrand says at least he can always get a seat on the street car. He doesn't let anything get him down."

"They say the Butch makes you change cadavers and dissecting partners every quarter," Porter contributed. "I sure do hope I don't get that one. If she stinks that bad on head and neck, just imagine getting up to your elbows in thorax and abdomen. Does Halstrand pack a lunch every day?"

"Shut up, Osborne," Easley admonished, "at least till we finish eating this chicken pie. If Halstrand thinks he's loaded down on that street car now, just wait till next quarter when they make everybody collect twenty-four hour urine specimens for Biochemistry experiments and we all have to lug those two-gallon brown jugs with us everywhere we go and pee in them. Now that will be a load to transfer at Five Points."

"Well, I still want to know if he has to pack a lunch along with all the other paraphernalia or if he can afford a quarter for the cafeteria."

"Shut up, Osborne. Besides, it's thirty-five cents since last week. And no meat on Thursdays. Time to go."

"If he packed hard-boiled eggs or a sweet potato, he'd still have to use his hands to peel . . ."

"Shut up, Osborne!"

"Did y'all notice that Martin's fingernails have grown out? He hasn't bitten them since the first day in Gross."

"Goddammit, Osborne, will you shut up?"

"And have you noticed how Tony Gage keeps picking at his? Even in lectures instead of taking notes? Digs and pushes until the cuticles are almost bleeding, and you know they have to stink."

"Hell, Osborne, I'm walking by myself. You wait and come with Barton and don't even get close to me; I don't want to be seen with either of you."

The summer wore on. The Fourth of July had passed with no acknowledgement of it at all by the medical school as a holiday. Some-

34

one, perhaps it was Barton, maybe Blackman, nobody ever knew for sure, had inserted a small American flag in the penis of one of the cadavers, the wooden staff of sufficient length so that the Stars and Stripes waved upright and festive but startlingly bright in that somber setting. Fortunately, Faulkner was the only faculty member to see it.

"Get that flag out of there and you'd better get it out in a hurry. The one thing Dr. Wingo absolutely will not tolerate is any disrespect for the human body, and we don't have time for a witch hunt right now; you're about two days behind on dissection already."

Porter thought that it was also crude and shocking disrespect for the flag but remained silent for fear of appearing either prudish or naively patriotic. He was learning.

He did not learn, however, that there are times when wisdom dictates silence. He heard during inconsequential conversation in the dissecting lab one day that Armstrong Abernathy's father was history professor in the college of Emory, head of the department by virtue of tenure and, it was assumed, family connections. After all, Dr. Abernathy had married an Armstrong heiress and everybody knew how important the Armstrongs were to Emory and how much endowment they had created through the years. Porter had long since become bored with the social and genealogical structure supporting Emory and the reverence that its graduates manifested for that skeleton. To him it was a tangled maze of Coca-Cola and Georgia Power companies and the families that controlled their charitable contributions. They apparently all lived in lengendary mansions on Ponce de Leon Avenue or some other equally prestigious street in the Druid Hills section of Atlanta. They all belonged to country clubs. They were incredibly wealthy. On top of that, they were all Methodists. Any one of these factors was enough to remove them as far from Porter's comprehension or interest as the Valois line of succession in the French monarchy. He had better things to do with his time; the relationship in his cadaver of the second to the first cervical vertebra was of more vital concern to the citizens of Peabody, Georgia, and to the future physician now preparing himself to serve them than all the important people around whom Emory, Druid Hills, and Atlanta revolved. He, nor anyone else from Peabody, was not likely ever to have any personal contact with them.

As he studied the odontoid process, the conversation of his partners suddenly penetrated his consciousness.

"Armstrong had already been accepted in the Princeton Engineering program for this fall, but when we got in the war, his daddy had him shifted over to Emory Medical School. Armstrong says now he's got a guaranteed three-year deferment, and by the time he's through the war ought to be over."

Porter's head jerked up. "What do you mean, his daddy 'had him shifted' into med school? I thought this school was supposed to be hard to get into and that there was never any politics involved. Also, the absolute deadline for applications, it said in my catalog, was the first of December. I don't believe that about Armstrong. Besides, why would anybody go through all this if he didn't want to be a doctor above anything else in the world? I just don't believe it."

Townsend delicately removed an obscuring morsel of fat from an arterial branch and rolled it between his fingers. "You can believe it. The Armstrongs practically founded Emory, Osborne, and have given millions of dollars to it over the years."

"But that was to the college; this is the med school. You know Dr. Wingo is no respecter of persons. He takes students only on merit."

Townsend shrugged. "Money talks louder than virtue in a lot of places, not just Emory. On top of that, what are you going to tell a fellow faculty member about his only son?"

Porter thought a minute. "Poor Dr. Wingo," he said.

The arresting clang of a probe handle sounded across the lab. Dr. Wingo announced that Merlin and Clayton had dissected an anomaly and that everyone should make a point of dropping by their cadaver and viewing it. It was a seventh cervical rib, and since this was a condition that conceivably could cause clinical symptoms in a living patient, although usually not, each member of the class would be expected to see it. Dr. Wingo cleared his throat and dryly apologized that it had not been available for the recent Practical.

When Porter got to Merlin's cadaver, there was a line. He found himself right behind Armstrong Abernathy, who was holding forth on the hardship of being in Anatomy lab on this beautiful day and missing out on a traditional houseparty at some place called Lake Rabun. Porter had never heard of it, but Armstrong's inflections guaranteed prestige, exclusivity. On impulse, he interrupted. "Armstrong, when did you decide you wanted to be a doctor?"

"On December the seventh of last year about thirty minutes after we learned the Japs had bombed Pearl Harbor." Armstrong had a small mouth with lips that gave the bite of arrogance to his words.

"That was quick."

"You mighty right it was. It made my head swim. My old man was on the telephone before dark and had me at the admissions office almost at daylight on Monday morning. My grades were no problem;

you knew I had already been accepted at Princeton Engineering School, didn't you? The only thing I was lacking was three Chemistry courses, and my old man guaranteed the admissions committee I'd have those before graduation. By lunchtime on December eighth, I was accepted here and had already written Princeton to get my deposit back."

"How did you feel about that?"

"Oh, I was glad enough to go along with it. I didn't much care what I did. Engineering, Medicine, whatever. I was going to Princeton to humor my old man in the first place because that's where he'd gotten his Ph.D. What the hell? As long as you're a professional man, what's the difference in the long run? Except I doubt if engineering school smells this bad."

"Does it bother you that you got the place in class that might have gone to some boy that really wanted to be a doctor?"

"Hell, no. I told you my grades were good. Anybody who might have made the cut at Emory and missed it because of me could sure get in at Augusta. Why should that bother me?"

Porter took a deep breath. "Well, I don't know if I can explain it to you if you don't already see it. It's been bothering me that I got to go on to med school and study to be a doctor, which is what I've wanted to do for as long as I can remember, when I've got friends who are in the Army or Navy just because they wanted to be teachers or lawyers or journalists. They're getting shot at and I'm not."

"That's exactly the point, Osborne. Now we're on the same wave length. Anything beats crawling in mud and getting your ass shot off by a Jap or blown up on a ship in the middle of the ocean by some crazy pilot."

"You don't feel guilty?"

"Guilty? Hell, I'm grateful. Listen, are you trying to preach to me? Derrick says you're a romantic little prig, always quoting poetry and worrying about things that don't matter, but don't you get on my back."

"Don't you call him a prig!" Barton leaned over Porter's shoulder and stooped to eye level with Armstrong. "If there's anything I enjoy it's slapping the snot out of some stuck-up rich kid that's not dry behind the ears. I'm making me a list against the day I have time to do it, and I just put you and Derrick both on it. Tell me, did you get your deposit back from Princeton? It's better to be a romantic prig than a self-serving turd."

Merlin intervened with a weary voice. "Will you guys quit visiting and move on along so I can get back to my dissection? For Christ's sake!"

Porter Osborne was learning.

5 **I**f Practical had been Grendel surrounded by thunder and lightning, then final exams became Apocalypse — inevitable, threatening, terrible; galloping faster and faster through the chaos of Armageddon. No one needed Jessie now for his weather eye. From the Pacific, Tojo had become a household word, more dreaded than Hirohito; from the land of Wagner, Hegel, and Goethe the names of Göring, Goebels, and Rommel were now common titles of infamy. None of these, however, rode like the four horsemen that were sweeping down on the freshmen med students at Emory. The first three horses were Biochemistry, Bacteriology, and an announced Practical; the students armed themselves for combat. Porter had the fantasy that Gabrielle Martell was the rider of a Percheron named Pestilence; Angelica Athanopoulos, lovely and ladylike even in a moment of terror, raced sidesaddle on an Arabian named Famine; Jessie and Faulkner together bestrode War, bareback, clutching each other for balance, galloping with fierceness in the train of the two marvelously unusual women. The fourth horse, however, the pale one, the one named Death, would be the last to come, and no one doubted that Wingo was astride it and no one doubted for an instant that its eyes were red, that its nostrils were filled with flame, or that its hooves were lancinating. Porter forgot the world at war and concentrated on his own personal campaign for survival. He crammed along with everyone else, he reviewed incessantly, he slept less and less. He tumbled into his bunk muttering,

> ". . . They are countless, voiceless, hopeless, like
>   those fallen or fleeing on
> Before the high King's horses in the granite of
>   Babylon."

He refrained, however, from sharing his bedtime thoughts with Derrick.

Arnold gave the group that was still taking time for breakfast a late bulletin on Conner.

"He never sits down now to study; stands up all the time at his dresser, smacking his forehead and lecturing to himself. He set his alarm the other night at three A.M. to wake him up at five so he could study some more, and then he slept through the alarm. You know what he does since then? Drinks a quart of water before he lies down! Says his kidneys can process right at a pint per hour before his bladder gets him up. I tell you, if he ain't crazy, he has sure fooled me."

Porter thought, "And many a one falls witless in his quiet room in hell," but he decided that did not apply to Conner. "Gotta drive, gotta drive!" made a lot of sense now.

They saw it through. They staggered through Monday to the Friday that crowned the week of exams and no one died. The very act of endurance strengthened the bond between them, although at the time they were not aware of it. The Anatomy final was every bit the horror they had anticipated.

There was a discussion question: "A man is eating breakfast and reading his newspaper. He raises his head and asks for a second cup of coffee. Describe in detail all the anatomical structures involved, taking care to list the origin and insertion of each muscle, its innervation, blood supply and function. Be explicit about the derivation of each nerve branch and blood vessel mentioned."

There was one section that was superficially simple but treacherously deceptive, the questions of which covered three pages. The answers were temptingly brief, promising rapid progress and demanding only a check mark under the column of "true" or "false." "The length of the average right internal carotid artery after it leaves the carotid body at the level of the sixth cervical vertebra and before its first bifurcation is slightly more than 3.1 centimeters."

There was a group of multiple choice questions that required concern as careful as plotting a course between Scylla and Charybdis.

There were some questions that transcended Anatomy alone. "Give the root derivation of the term *Galea Aponeurotica* and your opinion of additions or deletions that might more fully pinpoint its position and function."

The post-mortem exchanges were brief.

"The carotid bulb is not at the level of C6, is it?"

"Oh, my God, don't tell me that."

"The platysma is involved in speaking, isn't it? Can you ask for a cup of coffee without changing expression? And it took me forever to get all the nerves to all the ocular muscles, plus I didn't forget the pupil accommodating when he raised his head from reading. I spent two hours on that one question. I know that guy reading that paper and swallowing coffee had to be my cadaver just before he died. The sonofabitch has given me nothing but grief since June."

"Did you remember the atlas rotating on the odontoid, and did you put in the laryngeal muscles?"

"Oh, shit."

"What did you do with that stupid question about the *Galea Aponeurotica*?"

"Hell, I just abandoned caution and went wild on that one. I happened to remember that *galea* in Latin means 'helmet' or 'caul'; so I said we should shorten the term to 'caul' since the structure consists of the frontalis and occipital muscles and the aponeurosis itself, and anybody who took Latin and has goose brains knows that all caul is divided into three parts."

"You're lying; you didn't do that."

"Hell I didn't."

"Oh shit."

Porter was numb as he listened. "I may have just flunked the first final exam in my whole life," he thought. "At least I finished, and some of them didn't do that."

He scampered to his room and stuck his toothbrush in his pocket, not bothering to pack a bag. If he caught the next streetcar at the village, he had a good chance of making it to the bus station downtown in time to get to Brewton County that evening. There was nothing to do in school until Monday. He was going home. He could find a change of underwear when he got there. He was going home.

The streetcar clattered and clacked, the hanging straps swung vigorously to and fro from the ceiling, the few people sitting down the aisle ahead of him swayed rhythmically from side to side. His pulse and breathing settled to normal. The metal wheels screeched on the shining tracks as the car leaned into the right-angle turn on the Byway and hissed to a stop for a group of maids returning to their warrens after a day spent cleaning the homes of Druid Hills. Their dimes rattled musically as the conductor jacked the coins into the change box and handed them each a transfer slip. Porter hardly noticed them as they edged down the aisle to the rear of the car, holding their sacks and bundles aloft to avoid bumping other passengers. He averted his gaze from that of a sternly virile Uncle Sam who pointed his finger from a poster above the window opposite him and thundered in three-inch blue capitals, "I WANT YOU." It was obvious that Uncle Sam's platysma muscles were operative. Bilaterally. Porter leaned his forehead against the window and looked down the gardens toward Lullwater. He was weary of his demons, new and old.

> "They rise in green robes roaring from the
>   green hells of the sea
> Where fallen skies and evil hues and eyeless
>   creatures be,
> On them the sea-valves cluster and the grey
>   sea-forests curl,
> Splashed with a splendid sickness, the sickness
>   of the pearl."

He ventured a covert sniff at his fingers. He could get by if no one was picky. At any rate, he was going home.

His father was waiting at the drugstore which was also the bus station. He twisted his foot to smother the half-smoked cigarette he had tossed onto the tiled floor; his gaze was direct, his handshake firm. Porter's heart leaped. This was safe harbor.

"Hey there, boy! It's good to see you; we've been missing you around here the last three months. You haven't written much the last three or four weeks, either."

"I know," Porter responded defensively; he had forgotten some things about home. "I thought I wrote y'all I was going to be getting ready for finals and would be too busy."

"That's right, you did. Hell, I wasn't fussing. You don't have a bag? Hop in and let's head home; your mother's dying to see you. Everybody else will have eaten, but she'll have saved us out some supper. How were your finals? As I remember, they never were as bad retrospectively as they were in anticipation."

"Even in law school?"

"Especially in law school."

"You've never been to med school, Dad. These were worse. Worse than anything I'd ever dreamed of."

"Well, forget it for this weekend; it's the only time you have between quarters and you need to relax. If any of the girls you like are in town, you can have my car. I can spare enough gas on my ration for

42

you to take one to the picture show if you like. And certainly it doesn't take any gasoline to do a little parking."

Porter regarded the giant red A on the sticker in the windshield. "Thanks, Dad, I'll let you know. How's the war coming? I've been too busy to keep up for the last two weeks."

"Well, of course you know the Philippines are gone. MacArthur said, 'I shall return,' and then got on a boat and left thousands of GI's who had no choice but to surrender. We're getting stories about the death march to Bataan, but it'll be a long time before we know all the details. The Japs are not human beings—they are animals, vicious animals, Son, and we've never been up against an enemy like this before. Things just aren't going well in the Pacific; we need to turn that campaign around and do it quickly. Europe's a little better. Except it was hell when they clobbered the English and French at Dieppe. I don't know what we're going to do about the English Channel. Down in Africa I think Montgomery may be able to handle that Rommel now. He sure beat the butt off the Afrika Corps at Alain Halfa and has come out of Egypt like a wild cat. He's got some American boys and supplies behind him now and we'll make a real difference. This fellow Eisenhower that we've fielded looks like a real winner.

"I'm worried about Russia, though. The Krauts are right at Moscow and if it falls, then the heroism of Stalingrad is nothing. Of course, I don't trust Stalin. He's a Communist and a son of a bitch, but until we've whipped Hitler he's *our* son of a bitch."

Porter leaned out his window into the rushing air of September twilight and filled his chest with familiar air. There was still enough cotton left in the half-picked fields to tease his nostrils with its fragrance—wholesome, flat, warm, a little redolent of the mast of oak forests. It was laced occasionally with the wild and spicy, exciting aroma of muscadines, and he knew that in the dusk they were hanging in ripened clusters, half hidden in a black-purple wonder along the limbs of trees that had been embraced and festooned by the sun-searching vines. The car crossed a creek and there came a whiff of late honeysuckle sweetening the musk of swamp and the faintly fresh promise of a fishing hole. This was the perfume of his childhood; he forgot his fingers, the stench of Anatomy lab; he was home.

"All this island hopping we're doing in the South Pacific is enough to drive you crazy," his father said. "It's going to be a long war, Son. I'd never even heard of Guadalcanal until we landed there last week. The other day I was in the barber shop getting a haircut, and by the way, you could use one, too. Hoss Harp came in and Laurence

Davis said, 'Well, Hoss, what do you think of the status quo?' And Hoss, just as serious as a hog on ice, said, 'I-golly, the Japs'll take it, too, before the week is out.'"

Porter threw his head back and laughed aloud. With his father. He was home.

The welcome at the Big House was effusive. About five dogs gyrated and leaped, too well-trained to jump against him with demanding fore paws but so excited at his appearance that they writhed and tumbled around him in a confusion of yelping, barking, whining and twisting. His mother clasped him close.

"Hello, Son, this is a marvelous day for me. You look tired. Are you hungry? I've got a good supper saved back; there's pork roast and turnip greens and some of the last butterbeans, real young and little bitty like you and your daddy like them." She sniffed and pushed him away. "Why don't you run wash up and come on to the table?"

He made a side trip to his grandmother's room where he assured her that he had been a good boy and had never for a moment forgot who he was. "Where, at times," he murmured, "and why, but never who."

He almost went to sleep at the supper table and fell gratefully into bed soon thereafter. He slept the clock around to find the next morning that his father had already left for town. He roamed the farm all day, revisiting scenes of childhood adventure, surrounded by memories The front porches of the tenant houses were packed with freshly-gathered cotton against the day when it could be carried to gin. The weather now was too ideal for harvest to acknowledge that it was Saturday, and the hands were busily picking, the fields dotted with family groups, the smaller children playing and tending babies around the soft white piles mounded in baskets and spreads on the ground. He watched straining muscles in Jesse Lee's neck and shoulders as he lifted and emptied a cotton basket and wished that his cadaver was as lean and well-delineated. He rubbed his hands in the crumbly red soil and looked at it under his nails and staining his cuticles. "This is as far as you can get from Druid Hills," Porter thought. He watched a grasshopper suspended in autumnal song above the sunbaked clay road. "And I like it." He surveyed the farm from the crown of the big red hill; he could see the roof of the house in the distance. The world was quiet with late September stillness. He spoke aloud into it. "I shall return."

He eschewed the option of a date for the lure of another night's sleep. Home was not changed. Visiting in the kitchen while his mother prepared supper, accepting the probable lateness of his father's return and not waiting for him, he was assured by her, "You're welcome to take my car if you want to go into town, Son; I still have a half tank of gas and about ten more gallons on my card for this month. I'll be glad for you to use it. I try to save my ration for church and the WMS and, of course, I'm still the one to do all the grocery buying and errand running, but I really try to conserve. Everywhere you turn there's one of those signs that says, 'Is this trip necessary?' It's enough to make you feel guilty if you leave home."

"Sort of like that one that says 'Uncle Sam wants you.' It makes you feel guilty if you don't leave home."

"Oh, that's the one that makes your daddy mad. Not guilty, mad. He tried to reenlist and the Army wouldn't have him. He went into a pure pout for at least three weeks, and we still don't talk about it."

"Everybody compartmentalizes, don't they? I won't mention it."

"Speaking of which, you haven't had much to say about med school, young man."

Porter looked around the kitchen and visualized the Anatomy lab at Emory; the smell of fresh hoecake baking on top of the stove blocked out the memory of formaldehyde. Wholesome, comforting. "There's really not much to say, Mother; it's so different from anything I've ever known."

She dried the bread tray. "Put this on top of the safe if you don't mind. Do you like med school, Son?"

Porter hesitated until he could stand her waiting stillness no longer. The question echoed in the room. "Mother," he said, "I feel sometimes like the creature in the poem who is holding his own heart in his hands and eating it. 'I like it,' he said, 'because it is bitter and because it is my heart.' I love it, but I hate it, too. Does that make any sense?"

His mother's pause became almost uncomfortable. She stood holding the dish rag and looking out the east window of the stove room. "Oh, yes," she said softly. "That makes sense. It makes a lot of sense to me."

"Daddy couldn't do it," Porter Osborne, Jr., asserted. "Daddy couldn't do what I'm doing."

His mother looked at him briefly. "Good," she said. "Let me take this hoecake up now while you pour some tea, and we've got supper on the table."

"Mother, you remember reading to us when we were little about how the kangaroo got his legs?"

"Of course I do. 'Make me different from all other animals by four o'clock this afternoon.' I loved Old Man Kangaroo. 'He was gray and he was woolly and his pride was inordinate.' Why do you ask?"

"And remember what happened to him? He stuck out his tail and ran till his hind legs ached so bad that they outgrew his front legs and he could hop. Remember? And do you remember why?"

"Sure I do. 'Still ran Dingo, Yellow Dog Dingo, grinning like a coal scuttle, grinning like a horse collar.' He chased the kangaroo all over the ash beds of Australia until he was completely transformed. Yellow Dog Dingo did it."

"That's it, Mother! Now you know exactly what med school's like. Except you didn't tell us that Yellow Dog Dingo had a Ph.D. in Anatomy." He laughed. "Let's eat. I'm starving."

On Monday he was not laughing. The same tensions resumed after their two-day vacation between quarters. Biochemistry and Bacteriology papers were handed back at the beginning of those classes. Not so Gross Anatomy. In the early afternoon the students endured a droning lecture about the upcoming progression of their dissection into the area of thorax and abdomen. They were to begin with the complexity of the axillary plexus but were not to concern themselves for the present with its effect on the upper extremity. Porter diligently took notes, his mind not even remotely considering the fate of soldiers and sailors at war. He was sweating over finding out what his grade was.

Dr. Wingo ended his lecture. Notebooks closed with a snap. The shuffling noises of departure began.

"Just a moment."

The room stilled. He cleared his throat. The voice was silky; the teeth flashed, in grimace, not smile; the eyes were agate, opaque, passionless.

"Three of you are being dropped from our roll. You failed this course, and two of you failed other courses as well. I will ask the class to remain seated while those three students leave now to turn in their dissection equipment and receive refunds on the balance of their laboratory deposits. The rest of you will be given your exam papers with slips of your final grades in here."

He paused and pushed up his spectacles with the back of his left wrist. He cleared his throat again. The only thing Porter could hear was the swishing of his own blood.

"Jordan. Mitchell. Nichols. Good luck and good-bye."

The victims rose. The face of one was flaming red, of another marble white, that of the third totally expressionless, dazed. Porter first felt a rush of exultation; he had been spared. This was followed swiftly by humiliating pity for Jordan, Mitchell and Nichols, shriveling in the spotlight of peer attention as they walked stiffly from the room. There was a flash of pious reassurance; they were all three known to be poor students; justice had rolled down like a river. Then he felt acute embarrassment that his feelings could be so manipulated. Joy, pity, relief, judgment, anger. All centered on three boys who were now going God knew where, lost to the rest of them forevermore. As the last one cleared the door, Dr. Wingo departed through his private entrance, the hem of his long white coat a flick of the dragon's tail. The room remained for a split second in total silence, thirty faces turned breathlessly toward the closing door. That frozen moment in time was splintered by the voice of Will Barton, defiant but confirming. "Fuck 'em if they can't take a joke."

Faulkner entered at the front of the room and began handing out papers. "Anthony, Arnold, Avery, Barfied, Barton, Benton . . ."

Porter gazed at his own grade slip with concentration excluding any other stimulus. He had a B. He also had a vacuum where his brain ought to be. The tap of a metal probe called the class again to attention. Dr. Wingo had reappeared.

"The other end of the spectrum should be viewed. There were also three A's in this class. They were earned by Barton, Simpson and Conner. You may wish to congratulate them, but knowing the hearts of students, I doubt it."

Any thought of applause was aborted by a crash from the back of the room. Barton had overturned his desk in a rush toward the front. He was waving his paper exultantly in his fist, and he leaned over the desk to shake it in Dr. Wingo's face. His laugh was an exuberant bellow, his hair looked as though electricity were frizzing it.

"What'd I tell you? Didn't I tell you that you couldn't flunk me? Didn't I? Didn't I? Whip up on these pussies all you want, but you never scared me the first time! Pour it on, Butch, pour it on!"

Jordan, Mitchell and Nichols were forgotten. Porter gathered up his books, his only purpose escape from that room. There was a considerable jam at the door.

Headed toward supper in a more tranquil mood, he overheard Richardson. "Almost half the class made D on head and neck. Thank God for Biochemistry and Bacteriology. I figure I'm in the lower eighth of the middle third of the class, and when you figure in the grades of the three who flunked, I'm in the upper fourth of the middle third."

Porter experienced the comfort of smugness.

At bedtime he told Derrick, "I'll admit I was wrong about Barton and you were right. He's no leader. He's crazy.

> 'From evening isles fantastical rings faint the
> Spanish gun,
> And the Lord upon the Golden Horn is
> laughing in the sun.'"

"Let's get one thing straight," said Derrick. "You made a B and I made a D. I've got to study harder this quarter than I did the last one. If you open your mouth with one more line of poetry, I'm moving off campus and getting a new roommate."

6 The class settled into the routine of sharing work again, but there was a difference. Gone was the tension, also the uncertainty. For the former, everyone knew that he had made it and could continue to make it; for the latter, everyone was certain that the Butch would flunk a student in a heartbeat and with no twinge of remorse if his grades did not measure up. The students studied harder and were better organized. Dr. Wingo responded by increasing the workload since they had become more efficient. Porter observed the obsession with grades and decided that he was well content with his B; he had no ambition to emulate Conner and try for an A.

Jordan, Mitchell and Nichols were castoffs, rejected because of inferior performance; no one pitied them any longer. Dr. Wingo might be tough and blunt but no one questioned his fairness. After all, consider the fact that he had given Barton the grade he had earned. Porter self-righteously thought fairness also represented and his own virtue rewarded when he discovered that Abernathy, with all his family connections, had made a C. References to his prior acceptance to Princeton Engineering School fell no more from Abernathy's lips; he now grubbed as humbly and diligently as his fellows, and Porter liked him better. He also liked his new dissecting partner. He missed Townsend but was relieved to be rid of the dogmatic dissertations of Hutchins. Dr. Wingo's policy was to rotate partners every quarter, leaving one student at the same cadaver for continuity but shifting the other in acknowledgment that, with all due respect to the creed of America's founders, all men were not created equal, as evinced by the disparity of the quality of the dissecting material. Porter was pleased with his new cadaver, a heavily muscled and comparatively lean black male who had expired at the age of twenty-eight from a bullet wound to his brain, most certainly a tragic event which had the benefit, however, of leaving his thorax and abdomen completely unviolated. The timing also, regrettably premature though it may have seemed to the victim, was fortuitous for the dedicated medical student, since it provided a specimen of perfect maturity untouched yet by the ravages of age. There was no excess fat to impede dissection, the arteries were still elastic and muscular, the lungs were cleaner and more pliable, and although the odor of formaldehyde was strongly penetrating, the cloying sweet and sour odor was noticeably less. Porter settled into the new quarter with more confidence.

Timothy Lester, his new partner, was a highly intelligent, friendly boy of such fair skin and blond coloring that blushes played over his chubby countenance like sunlight through wind-twisted maple leaves. He had a protective shield of dignity and reserve about him that discouraged personal questions or even crude remarks. Porter thought that he was probably as ticklish as Townsend but was too aware of his dignity to inquire. Lester could discourse on theatre or opera to a degree that may well have been of some depth; Porter was so woefully ignorant of each that he was not qualified to judge. He also used precisely correct grammar so consistently that his statements were subliminally authoritative, certainly lofty. He was well-versed in all aspects of academic politics, Druid Hills social structure, and the myths and legends about medical school, particularly those centering around Dr. Wingo. Porter originally felt a considerable deference for him; he had made a B on head and neck but had come forth with an A in Biochemistry, and in addition to that was a Methodist. All of these qualities made Porter tolerant of his tendency to chatter.

"Let's see, now, I believe I've found it. Read me that part again about the bifurcation of the pancreatic artery. You have to be careful down in here; they say the Butch is real persnickety about your preserving the omental ring, and they say one of the reasons Nichols flunked was that he was too rough with the scalpel and kept cutting structures before they could be identified. You know that he can creep up on you without your knowing it, don't you? Never speaks; just slides up behind you and looks over your shoulder, and the only way you know he's there is that you feel his pot-belly brush against your back."

"I've heard that, but I don't believe it," said Porter. "Watch out for our ductus choledochus there."

"It is most definitely true. It happened to Nelson and he was constipated for a week. It makes you think of the poem about fog.

50

'The Butch comes
On little cat feet.
He sits looking
Over city and harbor.
On silent haunches
And then moves on.'"

Porter was delighted. "You like Sandburg?"

"Not particularly. I just remembered that from American Lit course and it seemed appropriate in this lab."

"Do you know 'La Belle Dame sans Merci' by Keats? That's one that got me."

"No, I don't believe I do."

"How about 'The Congo' by Vachel Lindsey? 'Fat black bucks in a wine-barrel room . . .'"

"Rachel who? Look, I don't know a thing about poetry and I don't really give a rap right now. Read along there and see if I should be worrying about the splanchnic nerve."

Porter felt a little inferior. He wished he had time to learn about operas so that he could show this city sophisticate a thing or two.

Suddenly Lester hissed, "He's coming! He's in the row behind you headed this way. Watch out!" He ostentatiously flipped over a page of his Anatomy book and then applied his attention industriously to the gaping abdomen. His scalp showed scarlet through his blonde hair. "Why, he is literally petrified at the thought of Dr. Wingo," thought Porter.

He leaned over to say a reassuring word to Timothy and then he felt it. Unmistakably. Against his back. Like a dirigible lightly mooring. It rested there and the pressure increased, infinitesimally but definitely. The legend was true. The Butch was present. With clarity, Porter spoke. "I don't think so at all, Lester. I like Dr. Wingo."

His partner gave an agonized gulp; he rolled his eyes upward just long enough to confirm his horror, then he buried his head almost to the ears in the sanctuary of the dissecting field and began flinging particles of fat frantically. His ears and the back of his neck were deep turgid crimson.

Porter felt the Butch's belly shake up and down against his back in silent mirth, and then it did indeed move on. On silent haunches. "Good comparison," thought Porter.

After lab, in the sunlight of Indian summer, he tried to make Lester laugh with him.

"It wasn't funny, Osborne; it wasn't the least bit funny. I'll get you back for it some way. Some day."

Still, Porter was surprised a week later when Barton appeared at his table as his new partner. Faulkner explained that Lester had requested a transfer. Barton impatiently dismissed the incident.

"Fuck him if he can't take a joke. Here, let me show you how to clean those renal arteries. You've got the chance now to watch how a real man dissects."

Porter had much more fear of Barton than he did of the Butch. He spent inconsequential silent moments considering words that might fit a rhyme scheme with Barton's philosophy and decided that the most appropriate one was *luck*. He was a model of behavior for the rest of the quarter.

The days shortened, the nights lengthened, autumn was lovely. Civilian hearts were cheered by the battle of Alamein, the conviction of American competence confirmed by the Allied invasion of North Africa under the leadership of Eisenhower. Stalingrad was still holding out. But so were the Japs in the complexity of the Solomon Islands. All of these were only peripheral items of interest to the freshmen meds who were individually involved in their battle to hang on to the beachhead of class standing thus far acquired and, if possible, to advance it.

Of a sudden, bursting like sunrise, a Medical School dance was announced. Porter had listened idly and without interest to accounts of these events, discounting considerably more than half he heard about behavior there. All medical students, from the lowliest freshman to the lordliest senior, provided he was not on call at the hospital, attended; the house staffs at Grady and Emory Hospitals attended; professors, without exception, attended. Everyone relaxed, drank whiskey, danced, and reveled. Any misbehavior at a dance was immediately forgiven and no sin committed there laid to any student's charge. The success of a dance was apparently in direct proportion to the magnitude of individual and group hangovers the next day. Porter was not a good dancer and felt uncomfortable at the idea of exhibiting his inferior skills before Druid Hills debutantes or Napsonian pinks. In addition, he was still growing and the sleeves of his suit were too short. He vowed that he would sequester himself on the night of the dance and study so diligently that he would, for once, be ahead of all assigned material.

Besides, he didn't drink. For the first time in his life he was confronted with the attitude that this was a social inadequacy. He was not about to go to any med school dance.

He overheard Lester. "This will be a great one. They've got Druid Hills Country Club and it's the night before Thanksgiving; so they can't spring a pop quiz on us the next day. At least we have that one day off."

"They wouldn't do that anyhow," Faulkner assured a group. "It's an unwritten rule that nobody gives a quiz the day after a dance. It's not good form. The professors expect all the boys to relax and let their hair down at med dances. Every one of you should go. You need it and you deserve it."

Abernathy told him, "They'd have done better to get the Driving Club, but Druid Hills will do. You'll really see some good looking girls in some pretty dresses. You want me to get you a date?"

"What do you mean, you're not going?" protested Easley. "Everybody will be there. This is my first med dance, but I've been hearing about them for years; I wouldn't miss it for all the tea in China. This'll probably be the only opportunity you get to see Dr. Wingo through a drunken haze and not be intimidated by him."

"I don't drink and I'm not scared of Dr. Wingo in the first place."

"You're lying. But we'll let that pass. How about Gabe? You can let her see you through a drunken haze."

"Dr. Martell dances?"

"I don't think so. But she always has a table and is free with her liquor."

"Doesn't anybody do anything besides drink at these dances?"

"Naw. I think you have to wait till you're back at the frat house. I imagine Druid Hills Country Club would take a dim view of frigging in those hallowed halls. Most of the guys do dance, you know. At least as long as they can stand up. It's a pity you're not going to make it."

The more Porter heard the more entrenched he was in his resolve. By stealing an academic march on his fellows, he would impress the professors more than he could ever hope to by mingling with them socially. He was a student, a scholar, not a dancing dilettante. His grandmother, he thought fleetingly, would be proud of him; he was remembering.

As he hurried from an errand to the village on Wednesday afternoon, he encountered Dr. Athanopoulos moving busily to her car.

She waved to him and called across the street, "See you at the dance tonight, Osborne."

He sauntered into his room at Dobbs Hall.

"Derrick, do you reckon you and Lon King could drop me off at the dance on the way to pick up your dates? I'll catch a ride back with somebody else."

Nothing that anyone had said could have prepared Porter for the atmosphere of a medical school dance. It was a Bacchanalian revel the likes of which he had never envisioned. The building was crammed with humans, the girls were lovely, the music, when it could be heard, was above average. The noise level, however, set and maintained the mood of the evening. The band played determinedly in the background, the drums underlying the louder instruments and felt in the bones. The music, however, was frequently lost in the cacophony of human voices. Males were yelling, females were shrieking, and they were all doing it at once. Porter had occasionally in the fields of home been overflown by skies full of chattering blackbirds, but they were nothing compared to this. There was no pause, no letup. People shouted into each other's faces and still the major communication was through nods or shakes of the head and eager, blinding smiles. Everyone had a glass; drinks were jostled and dresses were drenched or streaked; no one caviled or whined. Everyone manifested the mad, the frenzied, the unshakable determination to have a good time. This was the end of the world, the last day on earth. Nothing beyond could possibly be of any consequence. "I do believe to my soul," said Porter aloud, since there was no possibility that anyone could hear him, "that this is what they call an orgy."

When the third invitation to have a drink had been yelled into his ear, he procured a glass of Coca-Cola as insurance against explanatory refusals. It worked well and no one questioned it until he came upon Faulkner's table.

Faulkner was surrounded by friends. His fiancée was with him, a lovely Randolph-Macon graduate from LaGrange who masked her sharp intellect and discerning eye behind the heavy drawl of the small-town Southern girl who must be a belle no matter the cost.

"Sit down by me a minute, hon," she mouthed and patted a chair.

"What are you drinking?" shouted Faulkner in his ear.

"Coke."

"Want something in it?"

"No, thanks."

"Why not?"

"I don't drink."

"Why not?"

"Osborne men can't drink."

"Why not?"

Porter deliberately lowered his voice.

> "'He holds a crystal phial with colors like the
> moon;
> He touches and it tingles and he trembles very
> soon.'"

"What did you say?"

"I said my grandmother told me so."

"What does your grandmother know? Have a drink."

"She knows a lot. At least about the Osbornes."

"Hell, Osborne, you're a person in your own right. How do you know what you can or cannot do until you've tried it? Drop that Southern ancestor crap. You've got to be your own person. In every way."

"Thanks for understanding," Porter yelled back into his ear. He kissed the fiancée on her cheek. "Good to see you, Blanche. I'd best move on."

He stopped at Dr. Martell's table. Her back was to a corner and she overflowed her chair in regal abundance, planted for the evening, her evening gown draping and dignifying her corpulence. She had on lipstick, a hint of make-up on her eyes, and she looked every inch a queen. Porter surveyed the ashes of recent cigarettes littering the massive bosom, the butts squashed in the ashtray or resting brown and sodden in the dregs of empty glasses and thought, "A messy queen, but still a queen."

"Have a cigarette, Osborne?"

"I just finished one."

"How about a drink?"

"I don't drink."

"Have a seat?"

"I'll just stand awhile."

"Well, I don't know anything else I could offer you but a piece of pussy. And that wouldn't do any good because I know you're a goddam virgin."

55

As Porter's face grew flaming hot he could see Dr. Martell's mouth open wide, and he knew she was chortling and wheezing into the din surrounding them. He leaned into her ear.

"I am not either a virgin," he yelled defiantly, a bit surprised at his intense loyalty to the memory of Vashti.

She ran fingers through her red hair and lit another Camel from her cigarette; the bosom collected another load. "Yeah? Then let me see you put the moves on that little empty-headed debutante Abernathy brought; they say he's passed out in the john."

"Well, you never know what you can or cannot do until you've tried it, but I am my own person in every way. I don't have to prove I'm not a virgin."

He looked back at her, enthroned in her corner, the incense of tobacco wreathing her head. "Messy. Bawdy. But still a queen. A messy, bawdy queen. And smart as hell," he thought.

Squeezing his way through students and the dates of students and the mentors of students, all of them frenetically having a good time and proving it by shouting and smiling, Porter was careful to hold his glass of Coca-Cola high, hoping that he would be spared the indignity of spoiling the gown of any one of the nameless lovelies, all of whom seemed to have known each other since childhood. The shifting cluster of students around Dr. Wingo's table was composed primarily of upperclassmen now far removed from his power, juniors and seniors safely servile to other mentors in the wards at Grady, sophomores marking time in the comparatively easy limbo of Physiology. Porter listened for awhile to their shouted greetings in Dr. Wingo's ear; most of them were protesting their devotion to him for his unwavering dedication to making them learn Anatomy; most of them were obviously proud that they had manifested the toughness of spirit to finish his course; most of them were also obviously drunk.

"I'll never forget you, Butch; you taught me how to study."

"You're tough, Dr. Wingo, but you prepared us. You taught us that life is tough, but we can take it."

"I thought about you last week at two A.M. when I was helping my attending on a gunshot wound of the abdomen. I'd have been lost in there if you hadn't made me learn about the lesser omentum and the twisting in the embryo."

Through it all the Butch nodded his head and shouted back short replies, his smile growing dimmer or brighter but never fading. He occasionally poured a dollop of Four Roses into a proffered glass but never raised his own to his lips. Porter was close enough to hear the interchange with an upperclassman just ahead of him who swayed over the table and shouted a greeting.

"Good evening, Dr. Horace Wingo!"

Dr. Wingo nudged his good gray wife, sitting solidly corseted in the chair next to him, obviously waiting in patience the hour of departure, tolerantly bored.

"Mrs. Wingo, this is one of my special students, Martin. He made an A for me year before last when more than a third of his class flunked." Porter could not hear him clear his throat and even with him shouting had to strain to register his words. "Have a drink, Martin."

Martin tossed off the shot of Four Roses without adding any mix. His smile was every bit as wide as that of the Butch. He leaned down and bellowed, "I'll never forget what you did year before last." He raised his head slightly and lowered his voice below Dr. Wingo's reception level. Porter, however, at his elbow heard every word. "And I won't ever forget what you did to those twelve poor bastards who flunked." He put his empty glass on the table and his smile grew even wider. "I fuck you very much, you slave-driving old shit-ass."

Dr. Wingo's teeth gleamed brightly; he bowed his head in benevolent acknowledgment.

"Thanks for dropping by, Martin," he shouted. "Keep up the good work."

Martin gave a cavalier wave of his hand and staggered off, making way for another sycophant. Porter followed him and noted that out of Dr. Wingo's view the junior had a much steadier gait.

"This is the most interesting place I've ever been in my life," he said in normal tones to a ravishing blonde who was momentarily pressed against him as she sidled her way to the dance floor in the wake of a tall sophomore. She did not have quite enough red chiffon in her gown to conceal a really impressive cleavage. He took a page from Martin's book and lowered his voice. "Did you know that those beautiful things are just bags of skin filled mostly with fat and that you, including your brain, are more than ninety percent water?"

"Pleased to meet *you*," shrieked the blonde, carmine lips framing an Ipana smile. "Ask me again. I've promised this one to Wade Hampton Boggs."

"But you're still fun!" yelled Porter. He smiled with delight. "What a place, what a place."

At the edge of the dance floor he watched in amazement. It also was crowded, but because its occupants could actually hear the band, the activity there was rhythmic and synchronous. He saw Luten Teate in a frenzy of activity as he most expertly twirled a pretty partner who could jitterbug almost as well as he. Next to him was Cullen Richardson, his classroom seriousness replaced by smiles of revel, dancing almost as well as Lester. Porter was envious.

"If they were giving grades for dancing, I'd be in the bottom sixteenth of the lower third of the class," he muttered. He surveyed his gyrating classmates. "So would Pults and Halden." Those two were disdainful of tempo, of beat, and were revolving slowly in the middle of the floor. One of them was pumping his partner's arm like a well-handle; the other had his head bent so that his cheek rested in his date's hair, and he rocked back and forth with his eyes closed. They were both oblivious to being bumped by jitterbugs; they were in their own world, they were happy.

The band began a new song; the vocalist could be heard only because everyone knew the words.

> "There's a big holiday everywhere,
> For the Jones family has a brand-new heir."

The waves of dancers parted to reveal for a moment a small, proud head, a classic profile. Dr. Athanopoulos was dancing. With a student.

> "He's a joy heaven sent
> And we proudly present
> Mr. Franklin D. Roosevelt Jones."

Porter craned his neck to follow her progress. She was wearing a white evening dress trimmed in places with black lace. Another student broke and whisked her away. Angelica Athanopoulos. What a lovely name. What a lovely lady. Dr. Martell was a queen, but Dr. Athanopoulos was a goddess. Porter's heart yearned, but this piece was too fast.

The music stopped; the dancers puffed and chattered. With an abrupt change of pace, the band began an old tune; unmistakably it had to be "Deep Purple." Even Porter could handle this one. The thought of Pults and Halden gave him courage. He tried to pull his sleeves down to his wrists and took a deep breath.

"May I break?" She was in the circle of his arms, head almost to his clavicle. He had to lean down; she had to stretch up.

"Good evening, Porter Osborne. Are you having a good time?"

"I'm having a marvelous time, Dr. Athanopoulos."

"Have you had enough to drink?"

"I don't drink, Dr. Athanopoulos."

"Really, Osborne? That's interesting in this group. Why not?"

Porter carefully executed a reverse to avoid hitting Silverstein or McGarrity. He discarded his grandmother's philosophy and embraced a new one, formulated tonight. "'Death is in the phial and the end of noble work.'"

She tilted her head back. "'But Don John of Austria has fired upon the Turk.' I was born in Constantinople, and although you may disagree, I have not much compassion for the Turks. Are you the 'last knight of Europe,' Porter?"

His heart lurched, then it sang. She knew Chesterton! He felt a hand on his shoulder.

"May I break?"

He deliberately swept his partner into a turn and gazed into her eyes. "Oh, Dr. Athanopoulos!" he said. "Will you marry me?"

The tap came again. "Break, please."

They stopped. "I mean it. Will you?"

She lifted her arms to her new partner. "Not tonight, Osborne." She turned her head as she moved off in the arms of Armand Hendee. "But thank you for the inquiry. It was interesting."

As Porter stood in the middle of the dance floor, Timothy Lester spoke. "I heard that, Osborne. Are you crazy? Or just that drunk?"

The middle-aged and usually severe librarian for the hospital, bundled into blue crepe and daringly rouged for the evening, danced by in the politely desperate grip of Bud Nelson. Porter broke. As the lady turned to him and smiled, Porter lifted her up supine in his arms and swung to Lester.

"Miss Josten, do you know Timothy Lester? Lester, I'd like to present Miss Mildred Josten to you."

He lurched into Timothy's chest so that the boy had no option other than stretching out his arms, into which Porter deposited the rigid and startled body of the librarian. Without another word, he left.

As he neared the edge of the dance floor, the music abruptly stopped. Its subtraction from the waves of sound washing the ballroom made a noticeable difference in the noise level, and shouted sentence fragments hung painfully audible in the air. Dr. Martell, either too tipsy or too uninhibited to lower her voice at all, finished her conversation. Everyone near her table heard it. ". . . Ole Astenheimer's got the biggest one in Atlanta; I saw it through his scrub suit in the OR."

A voice boomed out beseeching silence and attention. Everyone turned. Martin had appropriated the bandleader's microphone. There was no note of sarcasm in his tone.

"Everyone listen, please. I see that Dr. Wingo is fixing to leave. I don't believe anybody wants that to happen before we sing to him. Let's hear it for the Butch, to whom we all owe so much."

The song began. The band quickly caught on and provided accompaniment. Even non-members of the freshman class and dates from distant home towns joined in.

> "The eyes of Wingo are upon you
> All the live-long day . . ."

Porter sang as lustily as the rest, surprised to note a sentimental tear in the eye of an occasional senior. "Must be pretty full," he thought.

Dr. Wingo rose from his chair and waved his hand overhead, constantly smiling, even through the "Amen." "Exactly like a horse collar. Or a coal scuttle," Porter affirmed.

The crowd immediately returned to its former decibel level. Porter was weary, he wanted to go home. He began fighting his way to the front door, passing a group of drunken freshmen singing in a circle with interlocking arms and heads bowed toward each other, their dates forgotten and perplexed.

> ". . . Gonna lay down my knife and probe
> Down by the niggerside.
> Ain't gonna study Gross no more."

If the waiters in their white coats and black ties took note or offense at these lyrics, Porter could not discover it, but he was more comfortable when he reached the front door.

He descended the U-shaped stairway into the *porte cochere* of the club in time to overhear Dr. Wingo say to his good gray wife, "Of course I am quite aware of what Martin said to me when I gave him a drink. It's only my smell that's gone, not my hearing. The incident gave me no pain at all and probably provided Martin great pleasure and release. He was objectionably servile as a student and is not doing well on clinics, I hear. Perhaps this evening will help him emotionally."

He extracted a quarter from his change purse to give the attendant who was bringing his square black Chevrolet to the steps.

"I've never flunked a student in my life; they've flunked themselves. If it were my sole decision, I would certainly cull more of them; even some of those who lead the class academically are going to be poor and erratic physicians."

On impulse, Porter spoke loudly from the stairway as the man climbed stiffly into the driver's seat. "Dr. Wingo! Do you mind if I catch a ride with you back to campus? Please, sir?"

Minutes later he was not so sure that it had been a provident plea. Dr. Wingo obviously believed that the straight line of his own vision was the shortest distance between two points and consequently took precedence over the center lines painted by the street department on the swooping curves of Clifton Road. In addition, he never exceeded twenty miles per hour and probably averaged fifteen. The trip seemed interminable. The Butch did not let his careful attention to speed completely repress conversation.

"Mrs. Wingo, this is Porter Osborne. Junior, I believe. He is one of the younger members in the current class." He cleared his throat. "Chronologically."

A quarter of a mile and several minutes later he continued, "I remember interviewing Osborne a year ago when he applied for medical school. He told me then that his hobby was watching people. Did you enjoy yourself tonight, Osborne?"

"Oh, yes, sir. At least I guess I enjoyed most of it. It was sort of like school; there was really more material there than I could assimilate in one evening, but I sure learned a lot." Porter could not suppress a rising inflection in his voice as an oncoming car flicked its lights and careened by them in the gutter, its horn blaring indignantly.

"My word, Mrs. Wingo, did you see that? That driver is going entirely too fast. He's dangerous."

"Yes, Dr. Wingo, I saw that. Did you hear him blowing his horn?"

Porter was grateful to be deposited at the corner of Clifton Road and North Druid Hills, although it was still a hike across campus and the hour was late.

"This is as close as I go to your dormitory, Osborne. See you Friday morning."

"Good night, young Osborne," the good gray wife said. "It's always a pleasure to meet one of Dr. Wingo's boys."

Porter's thoughts were varied as he hastened up the dark street from one pool of feeble light to another.

Thank God he knows more about anatomy than driving.

I wonder if King and Derrick are getting any.

Surely she's lying; I don't believe you can see one through a scrub suit. That Otten fellow really has a good tenor voice; I wish I could sing like that.

Thank God she said no; I don't have a dime to my name.

7 **O**n Thanksgiving afternoon Porter and a group of friends went to a movie again, this time in force and this time still clean from their scrubbing for the dance the night before and somewhat fumigated by twenty-four hours away from the Anatomy lab. Porter, nevertheless, sat on his hands through the show; this had become a posture of habit with several of the freshmen.

They were cheered by the newsreel from Europe. The goose-stepping Nazis were being counterattacked by Zhukov at Stalingrad; in North Africa, Alamein and Tobruk were jubilant history and Eisenhower grinned boldly from atop a moving tank. A long-nosed de Gaulle, wearing a hat that in profile reminded Porter of the stewer in which his grandmother cooked rice, saluted stiffly without the hint of a smile. He looked as self-conscious, Porter thought, as anyone should who had been chosen last in a baseball game. Although the Germans had now invaded unoccupied France, proving once again that no treaty was sacred to them, and were bombing Great Britain unmercifully, there was graphic proof on the movie screen that Americans and British were repaying some of it by nighttime raids on Berlin and Hamburg. There was mention of the French resistance. The jungle shots from Guadalcanal were depressing but mercifully brief. Porter thought his father's condemnation of the Japanese as vicious animals fearsomely accurate.

Some of his companions, still disoriented and exhausted from the evening before, "hungover," as Easley remarked, "to the square of the ninth power," slept through Ginger Rogers singing "Jennie Made Her Mind Up," but not Porter Osborne, Jr. He loved the song, fantasized lewdly but vaguely about Ginger Rogers, and was grateful they had not gone farther into town to see Jeanette MacDonald. His thoughts, however, away from the books, free to wander, kept hovering

63

over the last letter he had from Deacon Chauncey. Cryptic, terse, the penmanship typically erratic and occasionally almost indecipherable, written on the transparently thin V-mail paper mandated for air travel and folded on itself to make an envelope, the note was powerful.

Deacon was somewhere in the British Isles, "that's all I can tell you." Most of his work was on the swing shift, ". . . but you know I always did like to stay up late." He did not like what he was doing, "which makes the fact that I'm doing it anyhow a source of satisfaction." He wanted to hear more about home and medical school. "I miss your letters. I know you are busy but please write." Given Deacon's collegiate aura of detachment and lofty independence, Porter perceived this as abject begging and was both complimented and embarrassed. He kept having recall from the newsreel of nocturnal raids, the long tail of light pinpointing bombers falling from the sky, the ack-ack and rapid streaks of tracers from anti-aircraft guns. His friend was in the movies. He's getting shot at, Porter thought; he may even get hit.

"Let's grab the streetcar over to Ponce de Leon and eat fried chicken at the Pig 'n' Whistle."

"There's the car. We'd better run for it. You coming, Osborne?"

"No," Porter replied. He had rapidly calculated that supper at the Pig 'n' Whistle, topped by a hot fudge sundae, plus the streetcar fare required an affluence not covered by his budget. He was still dependent on his father for every dime he spent and he would probably frown at hot fudge sundaes. "Y'all go on. I've got a letter I've been putting off writing too long."

The remainder of the quarter went very rapidly indeed. In Biochemistry they were issued two-gallon glass jugs, dark brown in color to prevent light from producing any chemical change. Each student was required to select one of a series of diets and stay on it rigorously for seventy-two hours. For the twenty-four hours preceding the diet and for the twenty-four hours of the last day of the diet, every drop of urine had to be collected in big brown jugs and then subjected to careful and precise chemical analysis in the laboratory, to demonstrate both content and change. The bottles were a problem. The boys had to carry them everywhere they went because the campus was too large to stash them in one place and rush back when a bladder required emptying. When the med students passed, heads turned and eyebrows went up. The boys felt as conspicuous as if their flies were collectively unbuttoned. It was a rare student who trudged along without regard to what uninitiated spectators might be thinking. It was one more small event to separate them from the herd and make them stand out, it was another strand of remembered indignity to bind them together. Most of them carried the jugs openly by the neck or, as they filled and became heavy, in the crook of an arm. The elite. The select.

"Conner has his in a suitcase that's big enough for a trip to the beach for a week. It hasn't slowed him down a second and he's banging it around like a bull in a china shop."

"Halstrand has to carry his on the streetcar and uses a Rich's shopping bag."

"Roach dropped his first one smack on the second floor of the Anatomy building at two o'clock in the afternoon and had to start all over. That throws him a day behind the rest of us. It smashed to smithereens and sounded like a gun going off. Jessie was mopping piss and mumbling for an hour."

"He's lucky it wasn't the second one; he'd be three days behind us."

"Only two guys picked the meat diet. One of them, of course, is Giddings and we all know he's got the money to buy steak, but the second one is from Alabama, obviously a man of wealth we didn't know about."

"Derrick picked milk and it gave him the scours so bad he's about to die. To top it off, he has to hold the jug between his legs with his deedicle in it every time he sits on the pot. He says he never noticed before that it is absolutely impossible to do number two without doing number one."

"Everybody alive who's ever paid any attention knows that. What are the scours?"

"It's a disease baby calves get; their little bowels run off and they'd die if you didn't take them off milk for a day. I think the word is singular."

"Next thing we know you'll be telling us grits *are*. What you're talking about is diarrhea. Dammit, Osborne, when are you going to forget farm terms and come out of the country? You're going to be a doctor!"

"Well," said Porter with spirit, "I was a farmer a lot longer than I've been a medical student. I'm not a doctor yet, either, and I'll point out that none of us *is*. When I do get to be a doctor, I'm going right back to the country, too."

"Yeah, if you don't get sent to the South Pacific. They say the Japs are using Red Cross armbands for preferential sniper practice, and the medics have had to quit wearing them."

"Hell, relax! Our guys will be in Tokyo before we get out of Grady. We're safe. Speaking of Derrick, he bought a little red wagon and you ought to see him pulling it across campus with all his books and that big brown urine bottle in it. He was headed up North Decatur Road at Oakdale the other day almost causing traffic accidents with folks craning their necks trying to figure it out. He's so reserved I couldn't imagine him with a kid's red wagon, but it was Derrick all right. I believe everybody in this class is a character. What's he doing way off there?"

"He's moved off campus," Porter said.

"Why?"

"Well, for a number of reasons. He thinks it will be a lot quieter than in the dormitory; friends won't be dropping by to interrupt his study and asking if he wants to go for a Coke at ten o'clock; it's a way of forcing himself to get exercise; he doesn't like a whole lot of conversation; it makes him edgy if people recite poetry. He thinks his grades will be better."

"Oh. Why didn't you move with him?"

"Well, for a number of reasons." He tried to sound detached. "It's too far away; it costs ten dollars a month and the dormitory room is already paid for; I like a study break now and then; I sure enjoy visiting with people." He thought of Will Barton's cavalier attitude and shrugged. "Also, he didn't ask me."

He joined the laughter when Easley snorted, "Hell, you can't fault him for that. I hope he doesn't shit his pants before this Biochem experiment is over."

"Dammit, Easley," Porter said, "when are you going to forget sidewalk terms and come up in the world? Don't you know that if you keep working hard and use professional terms like *defecate* you get to be a doctor?"

His learning process continued and soared to new levels.

Anatomical dissection, intellectually objective, coldly and technically revealing, disclosed to him at last the intricacies of the female genitalia, both internal and external, about which he had been filled for years with salacious curiosity. It was much more complicated than he had imagined, especially under the Wingo onus of remembering in detail the innervation, blood supply, and juxtaposition of all structures. He learned and identified, with scientific enlightenment that thankfully did nothing to dispel romantic mystery, about the broad and round ligaments that anchored the uterus in place like mooring lines for an air balloon. He dissected the fimbriated flare of the sal-pinges reaching like tiny fingers for the ovaries; the anterior and posterior fornices; the glands of Skene and also those of Bartholin; the clitoris, indurated by preservatives, standing guard like a hooded monk over the urethra; and the labia, both majoris and minoris. Some modernists called them lips, but Porter preferred the Latin. All the secrets and mysteries inherent in the female anatomy were laid clinically bare before his eyes; he was enthralled by the acquisition of knowledge in this previously taboo area.

He was puzzled, however, by the assertion in lecture that the vagina itself was only a *potential* space. That statement seemed to him akin to the argument that, if no ears are present, a tree falls without noise in a silent forest. He decided to ask Dr. Martell to elucidate on the topic; after all, she had one and should be an expert. It never occurred to him to make inquiry of Dr. Athanopoulos. He received an abun-dance of information beyond anything he either solicited or desired.

"It's that word *potential* that gets you, huh? How does the con-cept of a closed cavity appeal to your awakening intellect? Watch some of those little tweedling twats from Agnes Scott wiggling around throw-ing their pelvises out of joint with every step they take and you'll realize that if there was a fixed chamber in that region, every time they sashay down Peachtree Street, they'd wind up in the infirmary chafed all the way to their little *os innominata*."

Porter blinked. "That's anatomically impossible."

"I'm a Bacteriologist. We're talking conceptual theory now."

"We are?"

"Sure. Don't cloud the issue with facts. My daddy always said that nothing spoils a good story like an eyewitness. You've never seen a living vagina, have you?"

Porter sputtered, "Well, I've certainly never just got down there and looked. No nice girl would put up with that."

She wheezed and chortled. "Spoken like a true male virgin."

"I'm not . . . What's that got to do with concept or theory? And you're the one who said that's what we're discussing."

"You're so forensically correct. Hell, drop the word *space* and use *potential* itself as the noun. This is great; I hadn't considered this before. Every little debutante in Atlanta is blessed with a Potential and she's trained from birth to use her Potential to her advantage. Talk about the velvet trap; a Potential doesn't even have to be baited, it *is* the bait. The hook. The net. She knows how to use it, too. Then she's got a trophy she can have mounted and hung on the wall while she goes about the business of being an aging debutante for the rest of her life."

"Dr. Martell, you're terrible."

"I know it, ain't it wonderful? And I'm cold sober, too. Nobody else in the world like me. Have a cigarette? That should clarify for you the perils of dating a debutante. They all use their Potentials to further their own interests; even withholding the Potential can be an aggressive act if they've got a real live horny med student on the hook. Marriage is the ultimate goal of having a Potential, and all those little Druid Hills gals had rather marry a doctor than go to Rich's."

"Why?"

"Beats hell out of me. Maybe because they think their husbands'll make a lot of money, join the right clubs, and be away from home a lot at night. Then when they are at home they're too worn out to make any cavity be more than a potential."

"Anatomically, Dr. Martell . . ."

"Anatomy be damned. Let me paraphrase Gertrude Stein."

"You mean that freak who wrote

'Pigeons on the grass
Alas.'?"

"That's the one. My, but you're an informed little virgin. A pussy is a pussy is a pussy. Quit fretting."

"I've heard that word all my life, but people who use it don't know that one of them has all these parts I've learned this week. I don't think I can ever say it again except in a mystic sense, and I'll sure think of it with reverence. It's a very complex complexity, a complicated complication."

"Maybe you'll wind up being a Gynecologist and belonging to the Piedmont Driving Club when some little society gal gets to you with her Potential."

"Not a chance. I'm going to be a country doctor. I've got to run; thanks for talking to me."

She wiped the left lens of her spectacles between a thumb and forefinger, her eyes squinted against the cigarette smoldering between her lips. "Osborne, I shouldn't have thrown old Gertie at you. You keep on being an idealist. And a romantic. We need you. But I'd bet my bottom dollar you don't make it back to the country. That's a Potential dream."

"It's real."

"Have you heard this limerick?

'There's a wonderful family named Stein,
There's Gert and there's Ep and there's Ein.
Gert's poetry is bunk,
Ep's sculpture is junk,
And nobody understands Ein.'

Get out of here and study. Put what that old fart Wingo wants to see on an exam paper and save your thoughts for yourself. That's not prostitution, it's just utilization of Potential."

As Porter hurried across campus he considered that Dr. Martell had been little help but she certainly was interesting. She had raised more questions in his mind than she had answered. If he ever got through Gross Anatomy, he might have time to ponder them. "This compartmentalizing is getting a lot of layers and little boxes," he thought.

He had no idea what lay immediately ahead. Dr. Herman Hare was a weedy Yankee, arms and legs like brittle branches, his frame as spare as any winter tree. His wiry hair was long but lifeless, a dried blossom obviously temporary, already thinning along his sagittal suture. The tight scalp gleamed like a glimpse of packed earth through stalks of ripened grain and the promise of baldness was imminent. Porter thought that in a year or two his head would look like a bleached seed pod. His upper incisors were huge and thrust forward so prominently that he was constantly drawing his upper lip down in a vain effort to cover them. This made his nose twinkle and twitch but also imparted a constant cheerfulness to his countenance and was responsible for his nickname among the students of "Happy."

He had earned his doctorate in Anatomy only the year before and was openly enjoying his deferment from military service to teach medical students. Master of the brittle and humorous riposte, he was skittish of any emotional contact, his conversation always shiny, usually superficial.

Early in the second quarter Happy Hare was demonstrating to a sub-group the dissection techniques involved in entering the thorax. He turned to Porter and with polite authority singled him out. "Osborne, run ask Dr. Varner to lend you the rib stretchers."

Without hesitation, Porter hastened docilely across the lab and did his bidding. Dr. Varner, like Faulkner, Dr. Thebault, and Dr.

Wingo, was also instructing a sub-group. He was the only member of the Anatomy staff who had an M.D. The gospel according to Lester was that he had been a brilliant medical student, and in addition, if you will, a football player; that he had married well into Druid Hills affluence and social standing; that he had attempted private practice in a town in Alabama, failed in the effort, and had accepted a position with Dr. Wingo. The salary was not impressive but was of negligible importance compared to professional contentment. After all, he had married an heiress and his wife, Lester said, was generous and supportive. Dr. Varner really didn't have to work at all. Will Barton had contemptuously snorted that obviously he did nothing he didn't have to. Porter thought him occasionally brusque and impatient but more often kindly and affable.

"Dr. Varner, I hate to interrupt, but could I borrow the rib stretchers for a little while?"

"Could you do what?"

"Borrow the rib stretchers. We're having a hard time getting into our thorax."

"Who in the hell told you to ask me that?"

"Dr. Hare did, Dr. Varner. I'll bring them right back."

"I thought so. There's no such thing as a rib stretcher."

"Oh."

"Osborne." The voice was hoarse but firm. "If you don't quit believing everything somebody tells you around here, you're liable not to make it through med school."

Porter blinked and turned away. Dr. Hare and his group of students across the lab were watching attentively.

"And, Osborne."

"Yessir?"

"Try to breathe through your nose and quit going around with your mouth gaping open. It makes you look like a goddam idiot."

On his return, Happy Hare stretched his lip down and then relaxed it; the teeth pointed at Porter, the nose twinkled.

"What'd Dr. Varner say?"

"He said that you knew damn well there's no such thing as a rib stretcher and that if I listened to you I might flunk out of med school."

The group released its pent-up mirth while the instructor shrugged and looked a trifle smug. Everybody liked Happy Hare.

Right after Thanksgiving Dr. Hare was himself the butt of a prank that had far-reaching effect. One of his duties was teaching Anatomy to the first-year nursing students, a short survey course of

70

some three weeks that preceded their introduction to clinical experience. The girls voiced frustration at being restricted to inspection of a skeleton and perusal of charts and pictures in textbooks. Dr. Hare, innovative and enthusiastic, had promised them a trip to the Anatomy lab, the inner sanctum of the medical students. Dr. Wingo, unimpressed by the restructuring zeal of a Yankee immigrant, resistant even to the idea of female students in his Anatomy lab, had refused. Flatly. Finally. The nurses wailed their disappointment.

Dr. Hare compromised, cajoled, promised Dr. Wingo he would exercise good taste, and finally extracted permission from him to transport a dissected specimen, well-shrouded, disguised, female, from the Anatomy building to the nurses' classroom in the hospital. On a Saturday morning. For one hour only. Happy Hare was jubilant.

"Oh, those gorgeous little Georgia peaches are ecstatic! Those nubile Florence Nightingales are just about to cream in their little pink Southern panties; this is the biggest thrill of their sweet sheltered lives and no telling how many dates I'll get out of gratitude for this. I've chosen Morgan and Nelson's cadaver because she's so free of fat and she died before she got a bunch of fibroids or scarring. My little girls particularly want the female pelvis demonstrated to them."

He frisked his brows like Groucho Marx and twitched his nose above grinning teeth. "I may ask some of them to return the courtesy. How I do love this fabled Southland, this fecund backwater of the nation."

When Dr. Hare unveiled the cadaver on the specified Saturday morning, there were the usual inadvertent gasps and protective gulps from the nursing students, reactions automatically displayed by any group viewing a cadaver for the first time. Dr. Hare rapidly pointed out structures of major interest, beginning at the head. With professorial dignity and aplomb he announced, "Now, if you young ladies will gather a little closer and we can get a brighter light, I will demonstrate the female genitalia to you. Let us begin with the vaginal orifice and then the vagina itself . . . What have we here? Apparently a foreign body. . . . Let us remove it . . . Ah, there it is."

Before he had opportunity to identify it himself, he extracted and held aloft the obstructing material. There was no doubt in the mind of even the most naive nurse that the object was a severed human penis and one of mammoth proportions. Happy Hare stood as immobile as Perseus holding aloft the severed head of Medusa. There were shrieks and precipitous exits; some of his students were Baptists.

Happy gathered what shreds of dignity he could muster and declared, "This is by no means to be construed as the cause of death to either party. This intrusion was strictly a post-mortem event."

The classroom was emptying rapidly without formal dismissal. One last and lingering student swayed lissomely and cooed, "Dr. Hare, this was absolutely without the shadow of a doubt the most devastatingly interesting lecture I've ever attended in my whole entire life. Thank you so much. You were simply and absolutely wonderful. I think you are just a marvelous, what do you call it, Anatomastician?"

The irrepressible Happy made an effort to recoup. "Thanks, Toots. What'd you say your name was?"

"Margaret Mae Futrall," she breathed, "but my friends all call me Tweetie. You could call me that. Some time. Any time. Just call me."

"You betcha, Tweetie Mae. Right now I had better get Romeo and Juliet, what's left of both of them, back across the street and prepare for Monday."

He was compelled, irrespective of his wishes, to report what happened. The student nurses, a few of them sophisticated but most of them still innocent enough to be shocked, went running to their supervisor, who invaded the Dean's office on Monday morning demanding an interview with no less a personage than Dr. Wingo. The incident still might have escaped class attention had Barton not been unthinkingly involved.

Barton, on Monday, startled Porter with a roar when he unwrapped their cadaver to resume dissection. "It's gone! By God, Osborne, it's gone! What sonbitch did it? I'll kill him!"

"What's gone, Barton? What are you talking about?"

"My dick! His dick! Our dick! Anyhow, *the* dick! Look! And it was the biggest one in the class!"

Porter gazed in horror. It was their cadaver who had been the donor that routed the nursing class; the mutilation was complete; there was not even the vestige of a stump.

"I'm getting the Butch!" declared Barton. "Where's the Butch when you need him? Somebody's going to pay for this."

"Barton," advised Porter, "say *penis*. Remember urethral meatus, glans, prepuce, frenulum, shaft, corpora cavernosa, all of that. You can even call it *penis in toto* for Dr. Wingo if you like, but I sure would use professional terms. That is, if I were you."

The culprit remained anonymous. Any possibility for confession of sin and subsequent expiation was negated by the prospect of double atonement to both Barton and the Butch. The consequence was too horrible to contemplate and no one ever knew who the criminal was. Easley surveyed the wound and speculated that review of the boys who went into surgery might some day flush him out. Rumble joined in and opined that a list of future Orthopedists might further narrow the field. Barton was not amused. He became obsessed.

"Look at that Callaway across the room watching us. I know he's the one who did it, the smirking son of a bitch."

Thirty minutes later: "It's that goddam Woodall, that's who it is. His daddy is paying tutors all over the place to make him a doctor when he doesn't want to be one and that's who it has to be. It's his sick and twisted form of rebellion."

An hour went by. "It's that Avery. I know it is. Watch how he won't even look at us, and every time I look at him he turns his head."

"Barton, it can't possibly be all those guys. This is like getting an anonymous letter. You suspect a hundred different people and probably never even think of the one who's really guilty. Quit taking it personally. We just happened to have a cadaver that was well-equipped and convenient. Nobody's going to blame us. Put it out of your mind and let's get to work. It's only three weeks until we finish this quarter and get two days off for Christmas — and we've got a Practical and a final to get ready for before then." Porter tried to add a little levity to his tone. "We gotta drive, Barton, we gotta drive."

"I'll get 'em," Barton muttered. "I'll get 'em."

Within the week, the crime was avenged on three innocents. Careful to be off campus, Barton delivered an unexpected blow of his mighty fist that was single, but nonetheless stunning and staggering, to the jaws of Callaway, later Woodall, and finally Avery. He did it with such ferocity and power that there was no opportunity for the victims to retaliate, and Porter reflected that in all likelihood there was little volition in that direction. Class support was solid.

"There's no excuse for it."

"They won't report it because they don't want to spend the time away from Gross it would take."

"If you'll notice, they all three wear glasses."

"So does Barton; that's irrelevant."

"I think they don't report it because they're scared; they're scared of Barton and what he might do next time."

"Hell, wouldn't you be? I am. I'm scared to speak to him and scared not to speak to him. I'm scared to look at him or not to look at him. He'll whip your ass for either reason. They're smart to be scared."

"You're right. I for sure and certain plan to stay out of his way. Aren't you scared of him, Osborne?"

"No. I'm worried about him but not afraid. I always get the feeling that he likes me. At least he's sure I didn't cut off his dick."

"Some day he's going to get his come-uppance, but I don't even want to be in the same town when he does."

At bedtime Porter thought,

> "They rush in red and purple from the red
>   skies of the morn,
> From the temples where the yellow gods shut
>   up their eyes in scorn."

He was a little relieved that Derrick was not present.

The Practical came and went, no less demanding and demeaning than the previous one but washing now in irresistible swell over students so numbed by sleep deprivation and new experiences that they hung suspended in the backwash of mental fatigue, sodden, half-drowned.

On the last afternoon of laboratory, the day before finals began, Faulkner announced the assignment. "Today we go back to the musculature of the posterior thorax. In order to display the complete shoulder girdle plus the serratus anterior, the teres major and teres minor, it will be necessary to remove the latissimus dorsi and the trapezius. Cut away these muscles in their entirety and place them in the large trash containers across the end of the room. Dr. Thebault and Dr. Hare have left early for the holidays and Dr. Varner is sick today; so Dr. Wingo and I will be the only ones to help you. It is, however, a simple dissection. You should not need much assistance."

Nor did they. Porter busied himself at the task, anxious to finish and review for examinations, to be done forever with this particular cadaver. Across the table Barton worked with strong sure fingers, long swift slices with his scalpel keeping him well in advance of his partner.

"It might even have been that Bubba Glass. He's always been so friendly but lately he's real cool, just nods and goes on by. I may just punch him and a couple of others out to be sure I haven't missed anybody. Teach 'em to cut off my dick."

"Barton, I've told you. I sure would feel better if you'd just drop that. Forget it. It's over and done with. Water under the bridge or over the dam or whatever. You sure are good at dissection. I wish you'd help me a little as we go along."

Dr. Wingo was not in the room. Faulkner was bent over Nelson's cadaver, patiently assisting him. Porter heard a whiz and a following splat. Again. And another time. Faulkner briefly straightened and looked around, but all heads were bowed industriously. Porter watched. With a deadpan fake off that would have been the envy of any basketball player, Paul Harper swiftly and unerringly hurled a chunk of gray latissimus dorsi across the room to catch his roommate solidly in the temple. Then he swiftly returned to his task, head bent over his dissection field, a perfect mask of innocence on his face. Porter saw the return shot from Wells Murphy after several lulling minutes. He was scandalized. He remembered Dr. Wingo's flat and final statement on the first day of class distant months ago when the days were still shining and singing and he had been so innocently unaware of the road ahead of him. "If Murphy and Harper get caught, they're out," he thought. "They're playing with dynamite."

If Faulkner had not been impelled to urinate, the class history would probably have been different. He confidently abandoned the laboratory for a few minutes to a group of mature, well-bred, professional young gentlemen who were finishing their second quarter in medical school. Porter never knew whence the missile came or which intrepid soul dared to launch it, but there was a heavy whistling noise by his ear and a piece of muscle weighing well over a quarter of a pound hit Will Barton dead center in the back of his head. Porter had time to notice that the blow dislodged Barton's glasses to the end of his nose. With only a muttered oath, Barton snatched up the trapezius muscle he had laid on the edge of his table and hurled it in its entirety across the room, aimed with vengeance at the completely innocent but invitingly convenient Dick Skinner. The class stood transfixed. Such was the power of the thrower that the muscle unfurled in flight and the edges flapped up and down like a sting-ray swimming in ocean depths. Skinner had enough warning to duck and the trapezius muscle of a male gunshot victim from Auburn Avenue sailed in final glory out an open window, up, up, and over, to land on the steps of the Physiology building. There was a long moment of dead silence. Even Barton's mouth hung open in silent astonishment.

Faulkner's return broke the spell and everyone returned busily to the task at hand. After a safe interval, Porter ventured to Barton, "I'd sure feel better, Will, if you hadn't done that. I need to tell you something. I have a very strong feeling . . ."

Barton hissed, "You're always talking about your feelings. What if I jerked your head off and shit in your neck? How would you feel about that? Don't try to tell me anything. To hell with feelings."

Porter fell prudently silent.

On the way to supper, the babble was intense.

"God, that was a close call. We ain't talking flunking now. We're playing around with surefire and instant expulsion."

"I never could see who was throwing those muscles. They were some more slick."

"Yeah, who started it anyhow?"

"I don't know. But Barton sure as hell ended it."

"He can end anything. Even your life if you're not careful. Who had the guts to hit him anyhow?"

"I don't know, but it for sure and certain wasn't me. I may be a lot of things, but I am definitely not a meat-thrower."

"There you go," snapped Easley. "Off on a tangent again. We don't have time for a course in comparative virtue; I've got to study."

"Drive, Easley, drive!" shouted Richardson. "You gotta drive, boy."

Porter Osborne, Jr., was troubled. Only he had seen the side door open and Dr. Wingo's face peer out as Barton had picked up the trapezius and hurled it like a javelin. Only he had seen the door softly close.

"Is Dr. Wingo afraid of Barton?" he wondered as he studied. "He said positively that anybody would be expelled for that. If he is going to ignore it, what kind of man is he?

"Why did Easley have to make that smart-aleck crack about comparative virtue? Is virtue absolute? Or is it relative?

"What sort of man is Dr. Horace Wingo? Really? When the chips are down?"

76

*"It is he whose loss is laughter when he counts
the wager worth,
Put down your feet upon him, that our peace
be on the earth."*

8 **C**hristmas was filled with wonder, although Porter had not had time to procure gifts nor even enough attention away from his studies to build the usual peak of anticipation that was called in his family "Christmas spirit." When he arrived home on December twenty-third, however, he was immediately caught up in it. The entire family was suffused with love for each other, with gaiety over the impending feast. Daily and petty annoyances fell away and everyone followed the lead of Porter's mother in celebrating the birth of a little Jewish baby who had been destined to save men's individual souls from sin and become known as the Son of the Living God. It was a season of miracles. Porter wondered if anyone else thought Jesus and His Daddy had been remiss, even more than a little negligent, and that it was now up to Roosevelt and Churchill to bail Them out. He had more sense than to voice such heresy, however, and succumbed gladly to the union of place, person, and event that was Christmas in Georgia.

"Sure you won't take a drink with me, Son? You're old enough to, you know, and I imagine fooling around with all those dead folks and studying as hard as you've been, you could use one. Never mind, what do you think of the war?"

"Which war, Dad?" Porter said with guile.

"Why, both of them, now that you mention it, though I usually just think of the Pacific and Europe as 'the war.' But you're right; the fronts are so widely separated they seem like two different worlds."

Porter regarded his own conflict as a possible third front but had no stomach for another lecture on the massive wisdom of military conscription nor discourses on the values of compartmentalizing. "I've been so busy, Dad, that I haven't really kept up. Tell me what you think."

"Well, the Russians are fighting now at Stalingrad like cornered

77

rats." Porter shuddered. "I can't help but think they're going to turn the Huns back; Hitler's got no more sense about Russian winters than Napoleon had. Tobruk was the beginning of the end for Rommel, and we're doing great in North Africa alongside the Limeys. The South Pacific's another story, but I believe we'll eventually run the Japs off Guadalcanal; here, let me show you this map I've got of all the South Pacific Islands. Maybe by spring, we'll be in better shape."

His mother caught him alone for a brief, quiet instant. "Are you more content with med school, Son? How are the kangaroo's legs?"

Porter laughed. "They're long and skinny now, Mother, and they take him up and over all the rough spots." He shrugged. "But I'm worried about Yellow Dog Dingo. He's still grinning like a horse collar, but I'm afraid he's getting old and losing his teeth."

On his return to campus, the freshmen were wheeling and chattering like a flock of feeding starlings. Lester was the center of the horde, twittering with a glut of information that must be shared, quivering with scandalized delight.

"Come here, Osborne. I was just telling them. Did you know Barton's gone?"

"What? You mean he flunked out? He couldn't have."

"Hell, no. He made an A again. In everything. He didn't flunk, he's been expelled. Kicked out. Let me tell y'all the details. I got it straight from somebody in the inner circle who knows all about it but prefers that his name not be mentioned."

"What did Faulkner tell you, Lester?" asked Easley.

"Oh, hush, Easley. It seems that the Butch was looking and saw it with his own eyes on the day that Barton threw the trapezius muscle at Skinner. Didn't see any of the guys before that but was an eyewitness to Barton and sent Jessie to get the muscle back from the steps of the Physiology building.

"Dr. Wingo also heard about all his other wild behavior, and when Barton came back from holidays yesterday afternoon, the security guard on campus, two policemen from DeKalb County and Faulkner walked in on him. They gave him a written notice signed by Dr. Wingo and the Dean saying that he had been permanently expelled from the school, plus an injunction from a judge saying that he had to leave this campus immediately and not come back."

"You don't mean it! What happened?"

"Nothing, really. He's gone and that's that."

"Don't give me that 'nothing really' business. I know Barton. What happened?"

"Well, my source said he got red in the face for just a minute, then turned around without a word and got all his clothes and books and left. Stopped at the door and said, 'Tell the Butch I said thanks for the chance. And also tell him I said fuck him if he can't take a joke.' Then he slammed the door and they could all hear him laughing. You know he's already got a commission because his college was ROTC; so I guess he'll be going to war tomorrow."

"I hope they send him to the South Pacific," said Easley. "We could use him there, and the damn Japs deserve him."

At the conclusion of the Anatomy lecture that afternoon, Dr. Wingo said, "I have just a couple of announcements. Although no one flunked this quarter, there is no guarantee that you are immune for the next three months." The teeth flashed wolfishly. "Your ranks have been thinned by one but it was not because of academic inadequacy. While I do not ordinarily condone gossip and counsel students to disregard it as unfounded and never more than partially true, in this particular instance," he looked levelly at Lester for a moment, "I would say that you can believe every word of it. Will Barton is gone. Remember my admonition and respect your laboratory materials."

Dr. Wingo paused and hitched his trousers up. With his wrists.

"The other announcement is similar. I must inform you that Dr. Hare is no longer with this institution. He married. Rather precipitously. One of the student nurses, a Miss Futrall, I believe, and they moved to Augusta where Dr. Hare has obtained a position in that other medical school. In this instance, pay no attention to gossip; it was a personnel matter and has the privilege of privacy. Mr. Faulkner will pass out your papers and final grades and I will join you later upstairs. Again, I admonish you to respect laboratory material."

Porter looked at his C and felt no compunction or shame.

As he silently apologized to Dr. Wingo, he reflected that Yellow Dog Dingo was still alert and dedicated.

"You gotta drive," he said to Conner. "You gotta drive, fellow."

9 The winter of 1942 was cold but remained fixed in Porter's memory primarily as wet and gray. Dissection of the upper extremity was more mechanical, more architectural, than that of the head, neck, thorax and abdomen. He compared the intricacies of the axillary plexus to the wiring for an apartment building or a department store. Knowledge of the source of energy for each conduit was as important as recognition of which tiny fiber turned on which light. Porter marveled at the fact that in the human body it was indeed an electrical current, infinitesimal but nevertheless electric, that transmitted impulses over the shiny silvery nerves to make fingers curl in acquisition or extend in rejection, to galvanize the muscles of running legs, to maintain like a thermostat the sleeping heart on a schedule of seventy-two beats per minute.

The concept of electricity was a mystery to him, from Ben Franklin to Marconi to Thomas Edison to Alexander Graham Bell, and he had an idea that none of those researchers had anticipated the level of knowledge manifested at Emory University School of Medicine. To him, the entire science still smacked of magic. He dutifully memorized and used the vocabulary appropriately, speaking of anions, cations, polarization and repolarization, but for him it was so much cant. He was, in this respect, like the occasional man who laughs automatically, intellectually perceptive of what his fellows regard as funny but deprived from birth of that innate sense of the ridiculous that is the necessary bedrock of a true sense of humor, a man able to parrot a joke at which others laugh but unable to feel it in his bones. So Porter Osborne faked a knowledge of electricity. Someday, when he had time, he would sit down and make himself understand it. Someday he would do that. For the present it was magic.

He therefore regarded the head of the Neuroanatomy department as a magician, possessed of occult powers, omniscient, almost omnipotent. The physical appearance of Dr. Dewitt Thebault contributed significantly to that fantasy. Porter had never encountered anyone remotely similar to him. He was short but athletically proportioned and moved with the balanced tension of a stalking cat. His face was controlled and careful, without expression, the eyes unblinking and coldly gray, hypnotic when fixed upon a student. When he spoke, he opened his mouth minimally and then moved it only for five consonants and no vowels at all, his upper lip caressing the words with contempt, curled faintly to the right almost in a sneer. His skin was as white as the underbelly of a catfish, Porter thought, and looked to be as thick as flannel. His hair was pondwater brown, combed straight back from a prominent brow that looked as though the brain might be trying to burst out. It was a mature medical student indeed who could meet the reptilian stare of Dewitt Thebault and not feel intellectually off balance.

The judicious and reserved Derrick disliked him. Porter had been present in lab one afternoon when Dr. Thebault appeared silently at the side of Derrick, who was looking intently into his microscope. Startled when he looked up and in the fluster of surprise, Derrick asked the man a question which even Porter realized was not only elementary but made no sense. Dr. Thebault's face was a mask as smooth as enamel, only the unblinking eyes glittering like gray ice. For a long moment his gaze held Derrick's and then he turned in rejecting silence and walked away. From that day on Derrick disliked him.

The eager and exhibitionistic Masters also disliked him. Dr. Thebault concluded a lecture, surveyed the room of industrious, still scribbling students, and intoned through ventriloquist lips, "Are there any questions?" Masters' hand shot up and he began an interrogatory that was like some prayers Porter had heard, convoluted and drawn out, more designed to demonstrate knowledge and erudition than truly to seek answers. Dr. Thebault subjected him for a long moment to the lid-fixed hypnotic stare. The students waited. His upper lip curled ever so slightly, controlled, contemptuous, and he swept the class again with the impersonal, reptilian gaze. "Are there any pertinent questions?" he asked.

Not to be so flouted or summarily ignored, the irrepressible Masters a couple of days later approached Dr. Thebault after class. Winningly and ingratiatingly, his tone implying that they were, after all, congenial men of similar lofty sophistication, he said, "Dr.

Thebault, I have another question for you today, but I do hope you won't think I'm trying to kiss your ass."

Dr. Thebault spared him the condemnatory gray glance but the lip curled instantaneously and the reply was rapid. "I hope you don't think you could," he said and turned on his heel as the hapless student stood with frozen dimples and mouth agape. Masters did not like Dr. Thebault.

Porter asked Lester about him.

"Don't be put off by that insulting way he has. If he gets to liking a student, he's real friendly. They say. Will even ask 'em out to his house for a drink and talk and argue for hours. He's a character all right; likes for a student to use his brains and think, they say."

"You're scared of Dr. Wingo and I'm not, but to tell you the truth, I'm a little scared of Dr. Thebault."

"Oh, he's a real intellectual, he is. No question about it. He did a lot of painstaking research for his doctorate and just keeps on writing papers even now. He's recognized as the world's leading authority on the inner ear of the Rhesus monkey. He's the only man at Emory who has unlimited access to the Yerkes lab, and behind that face his brain is working all the time."

"What's the Yerkes lab?"

"It's the research lab established a couple of years ago farther out on Clifton Road. They have enough money to buy lots of monkeys and even orangutans and chimpanzees. My word, Osborne, don't you know anything?"

Porter thought briefly and replied, "Yes, Lester, I do know a thing or two, but if I knew everything I obviously wouldn't be talking to you, would I?" He might be from the country, but enough was enough. He thought briefly of his grandmother.

Dr. Dewitt Thebault treated the human brain as reverentially as Dr. Wingo did the rest of the body. Six months before, when they had begun their dissection of head and neck, the students, their nostrils filled with the stench of burning bone as the top of the skull was sawed asunder, had gingerly lifted the heavy, still soft and shifting brain from its slickly lined and gleaming sarcophagus. They had tenderly deposited that mysterious dynamo into a Bell jar filled with concentrated formalin. For half a year, those brains, divorced from the robots they had controlled for a lifetime, had been shrinking in the strong marinade, so fragile that extra time was needed before they were conformed to a rubbery consistency that could be handled without destruction of the complex structures embedded so delicately therein.

Handling each brain himself in removal from the Bell jars, Dr. Thebault was like a high priest with a holy reliquary — a solemn druid, set apart, powerful. As he watched the man take a long, thin, unbeveled blade, deliberate, and then slice with one sure stroke through the medulla, pons, mid-brain, and optic chiasma, to halve the sacred object as surely as a melon, Porter's head swam. The expressionless face above the white coat, bloodless lips immobile, head bent in aloof concentration over the gray and buff and glistening white sagittal surface, was a study in monochrome.

> "And his face is as a fungus of a leprous white
>   and gray,
> Like plants in high houses that are shuttered
>   from the day."

Porter decided he was not physically afraid of Dr. Thebault but retained for him considerable intellectual trepidation. As a consequence, he was more than a little flustered one day when the man sat down beside him on the streetcar.

"Mind if I sit here, Osborne?"

"Oh, no, sir. No, sir. Please do."

The streetcar had fewer than ten people aboard, it had just departed from its turnaround point, and it was not the busy time of day. Dr. Thebault kicked the wicker backrest forward and rested his feet on the exposed seat. He stretched and yawned. Porter sat rigidly erect.

"Well, Osborne, how are things going?"

"Oh, fine, sir. Just fine. Yes, sir, just fine." Porter realized that he was babbling, took a breath, and forced himself to speak clearly. "I'm really enjoying Neuroanatomy."

"I had noticed. If I had not recognized that fact I would never have sat down here beside you. The two papers you have turned in reflect that, in addition to your attitude in lab."

Porter ventured a half smile and relaxed. "There's really one thing about it that bothers me, though, and that's the electricity in the nervous system. I've memorized all that business about polarization and repolarization and basement membranes and still I don't understand it."

"What don't you understand, Osborne?"

"Well, where it all comes from in the first place. What generates a thought that in turn produces a resolve that then in turn produces a motor action?"

"That's simple, Osborne. It's magic."

"I beg your pardon, sir?"

"It's magic, I said. In any event, that's what I keep telling myself. That's why I'm doing a lot of research on the living brain over at Yerkes. And I keep running into magic."

Porter swallowed and felt immeasurably better.

"Osborne, some of those chimps I work on have more sense than at least six of the boys in your class. If there's anything I cannot abide, it's somebody who doesn't *think*. At least you're using your brain, albeit an infinitesimal part of it, and not just accepting without question a ration of spoon-fed information, the dreary pap of universities everywhere."

Dr. Thebault nodded at the finger-pointing poster of Uncle Sam above the window opposite them and curled his lip on the side next to Porter. "I wish they'd ban that goddam poster," he muttered.

"Why, Dr. Thebault?"

"Because I am a rational, thinking human creature removed from the hysteria of patriotism that has gripped most of this country but has spared the majority of people with whom I associate to a degree that would make a cynic of me had that not already been accomplished two decades ago."

"Sir?"

"I am forty years old, I have a wife and two small children, I teach in a medical school. Any one of those factors makes me ineligible for military conscription; the combination of them gives me self-righteous immunity. There is something about that goddam poster though that makes me feel guilty because I'm not a buck private in the infantry crawling on my belly through the leeches and snails and snakes and malaria on some God-forsaken island in the Pacific. Hell, I don't even believe in war. I decided that ten years ago drinking Irish whiskey with a Philosophy professor at the University of Chicago."

"Dr. Thebault!" Porter exclaimed with unthinking excitement. "I feel exactly the same way. About the poster, I mean. I feel guilty because I'm not in uniform, because I'm doing exactly what I'd always planned to do, because my friends who didn't want to be doctors are off getting shot at. Some of them killed." He paused. "But I'd feel that way without the poster. Some days I wish I were in uniform and then other days I'm glad I'm safe. That's where my guilt is."

"Well, Osborne, part of your guilt may soon be assuaged. Or intensified. You're quite the idealist, aren't you? So we'll just have to wait and see. I understand that the military forces are going to take over all the medical schools and the students will be inducted. You'll get to wear your uniform."

As Porter opened his mouth to ask a question, Dr. Thebault abruptly changed the subject again.

"Look at that. There is no hope for intellectual advancement in a region that still allows that."

"Allows what, Dr. Thebault? Look at what?"

"Look at that Negro man walking all the way to the back of this car when there are all those empty seats in front."

"Oh. I hadn't noticed."

"I know it. All of you are so entrenched in your customs down here that you think they're all right. If there's anything I can't stand, it's race prejudice."

Porter sat up a little straighter. "Do you feel guilty about that, too?"

"Do I feel guilty? Me? Hell, no. *I* don't have any race prejudice."

"Dr. Thebault," Porter dared, "if you truly didn't have any race prejudice at all, if you were completely free of any taint of it, it seems to me that you would have seen just another person going down the aisle and it wouldn't even have registered on you that he was a Negro."

Dr. Thebault turned the hypnotic stare full on Porter Osborne, the pale gray eyes intent.

"By God, Osborne, you may have a point. Not only are you capable of thinking, you can make me think. I have to get off here."

He rose and looked down at Porter.

"You know, you just might be worth cultivating. We'll have to pursue this conversation over some drinks some time." He shrugged. "Just one word. Drop all that 'sir' and 'doctor' crap. When we're not in class, call me Dewitt."

"Yes, sir, Dr. Thebault. Good-bye. And thanks."

He watched the professor stroll leisurely across Ponce de Leon against the light and thought, "'Good fences make good neighbors.' There's no way I'll ever be able to call him Dewitt."

Two blocks farther, Porter pulled the cord for his stop. "Maybe someday I'll tell him about Buddy when I was a boy or Boston Harbor Jones when I was in college and see if he's had any friends like that."

He stepped down on Peachtree. "But there's no way in hell I'll ever be able to call that man by his first name."

"(Don John of Austria is girt and going forth.)"

10   **a**nother V-mail letter came from Deacon Chauncey, the contents so cryptic in effort to evade censorship, the handwriting so sharply angled and slanted that Porter felt he was deciphering rather than reading. He thought if the world were to be narrowed to individuals for whom the typewriter had been specifically invented, then Deacon would certainly be near the top of the list.

> "I still have the same job except that I got a small promotion and am off the swing shift and working normal hours. My working space is just as cramped as ever, but I nearly got thrown out of it on Tuesday and am not complaining anymore. We are working harder than ever and doing some good. I know that you will be a good doctor, but none of my crowd has needed you so far. If you see anybody I know, tell them hello for me. Please write. You are one of the few I know who can, and about the only one who will. Keep your nose clean. Things are looking good for little Pippa and also for Sweet Alice and Alora. If you can read this, let my folks know what is going on. Billy T. was right, but you don't have to tell them that.
>
> > Fraternally,
> > Deacon."

Porter had taken time to skim the newspapers recently and therefore knew that the Allies had begun the first daylight aerial raids on Berlin and that the Japanese Navy had suffered a significant defeat off the coast of New Guinea in the Bismarck Sea. Otherwise, he would never have figured out that his friend was referring to Japan by allud-

ing to Browning's "Morning's at Seven" in "Pippa Passes" and therefore the East. Germany was implied by his mentioning Alice and Alora
in Longfellow's "The Children's Hour." Poetry had its daily uses so
long as the censors in Great Britain were only fact-oriented officers. It
pleased him to write Deacon's father.

"Dear Mr. Chauncey,

In case Deacon's mail isn't getting through to you
or in case it's overly censored, I thought I'd let you know
I have heard from him. He is delighted by the news from
the Eastern front about the rout of the Germans from
Russia, also by the Japs being driven from Guadalcanal.
Aren't we all? He is still the radioman on his bomber and
has recently been promoted to staff sergeant. His group
has been reassigned to daylight raids on Germany
instead of the night runs. His plane took a hit from anti-
aircraft fire the first week in February, but no one was
hurt bad enough to need medical attention. He is not
complaining and we are not to worry, but he does wish
that everybody he knows would write to him.
I have to study so I had better run.

Sincerely yours,
Porter Osborne, Jr.

P.S. He agrees with Sherman that 'war is hell,' but did not
want to trouble you with that. I really think all of you
should write to him."

"Now, that," he thought, "ought to get Deacon a bushel of mail.
It's a good thing he didn't write to Derrick."

The pace in school did not slacken, but it became calmer on the
surface. The freshmen who had been tossed as precipitously into the
mill race of medicine as a shovelful of new-dredged gravel, rattling
uncontrollably around in the rush of a relentless torrent, were now
considerably further downstream. Their sharp edges had been
blunted not only by sweeping along the bottom of the river bed but also
by rubbing against each other. The gravel had become pebbles and the

shrillness was gone from the bumping passage with their neighbors, was now marked by solid and faceted clicks, polishing, smoothing each other as they rolled over and over toward calmer waters downstream. Soon the freshet would be done with them and they would all be in the safe harbor of the sophomore year. If they could just persevere. If they did as well on lower extremity as they had done on upper extremity. Just a few more weeks.

Porter gave increased concentration to learning the bones of the body. His bone box was large, double-hinged and metal with a snap clasp on either end and a handle on the lid. It was long enough to accommodate a human femur and, with the exception of the skull, contained every bone in the human body, the samples carefully garnered over the years, sacrosanct property of the Anatomy department, meticulously listed on the deposit slips and assigned with care to groups of two students who rotated their custody. The bones gleamed with clear lacquer and were dotted with tiny arrows in India ink which pointed out important sulci, foramina, ridges, and articulating facets. Porter regarded the smaller bones as primitive jewels and the larger, more massive ones as mute testament to the marvels of creation. The skeleton, to him, was the sole relic of a once living, purposeful man, arrogantly and unconsciously supported by this infrastructure, using it daily, never considering the wonder of it. To Porter the bones were a monument to grace, unwitting gifts, a treasure, a perfect example of "The hand that mocked them and the heart that fed."

He visited with Faulkner in lab. "Thanks for 'Never lower Tillie's pants, Mama might come home.' It really saved my life about remembering the wrist bones. You don't have one for the ankle, do you?"

"Nope. You're on your own for that. Just remember the interaction of the talus and calcaneus with the malleoli in the mortice joint; Dr. Wingo is fond of the ankle on finals. Also be sure you remember the blood supply of the tibia down to the last nutrient artery."

"Faulkner, you really have been a help to me this year and I appreciate it. We've been lucky to have one warm human heart beating in the Anatomy department."

"Thank you. How do you feel about yourself now that the freshman year is almost over?"

"Well, I'm not disappointed with my track record. I've always managed to be a big frog in my puddle, but this puddle is the biggest one I've jumped into. I'm used to making A's and being at the top of the class but I've matured to the point I'm proud of a C."

"What do you think of Dr. Wingo?"

"He's weird, but so is everybody else around here, I guess. I've always liked him. Except for one time when I thought he was abandoning his principles. And that turned out to be a misjudgment on my part." Porter thought a minute. "At least I feel like I know Gross Anatomy. Say what they will about him, Dr. Wingo is certainly an effective teacher. I'll never skip fine print in a text again the longest day I live without a sense of fear. What do you think about him?"

Faulkner leaned forward, absent-mindedly stroking the anterior tibial tubercle on Porter's specimen. "I don't hate him anymore," he said, softly, dispassionately.

Porter sucked in his breath but said nothing.

"When I started out as a freshman, I was the organist at Glenn Memorial. Dr. Wingo told me I'd have to give it up, that I couldn't serve two masters, that I must choose between medicine and music, that I couldn't spare the time from my studies it would take to practice."

"And you hated him because you had to quit the organ?"

"I didn't quit, Osborne. I studied Gross every night until twelve or one o'clock and practiced the organ every morning until two or three. I knew that I'd never seen Dr. Wingo at Glenn Memorial in church and that what he didn't know wouldn't hurt him. I'd have gotten away with it if one of my friends hadn't blabbed out in lab one day during second quarter how much he had enjoyed our Christmas program. Wingo overheard him and there he sat the very next Sunday. Right on the front row, with his wife beside him in that gray tweed coat."

Porter could stand being silent no longer. "Don't tell me he flunked you; I wouldn't believe that."

"No. I already had an A on record for my first quarter of Gross Anatomy; he didn't flunk me. He called me in on Monday and asked me why I had disobeyed him. I stammered around and told him I needed the money they paid the organist in order to go to med school. That was only partially true. I think Dr. Wingo knew that, but how do you explain another love to someone who worships only one god and that is Gross Anatomy?"

"What did he do?"

"He grinned a lot and told me he'd be watching my progress in Anatomy closer than he'd ever watched anyone before and that I had better not stumble."

"And did you?"

"Not in Anatomy. But Dr. Wingo started coming to Glenn Memorial. Nearly every Sunday. Always on the front row, always with his wife and her gray coat."

"Grinning like a horse collar?"

"What?"

"Never mind. That's another story. Go ahead."

"I started losing concentration in my music. Even when I was practicing I'd see his face. I began dreaming that he was going to join the Methodist Church, get to be chairman of the board of stewards, and fire me. On the occasional Sunday when he wouldn't come, I'd swivel my neck off searching the congregation to see if he'd changed his seat."

"How'd you do in Gross?"

"Fine. Straight A's. When we finished our finals the last quarter, I had three drinks, unlocked the church òrgan, and played 'Ode to Joy' over and over from midnight till two o'clock. I've never played better. It was great."

"Well, how'd you wind up back here as lab assistant?"

"That's another story, as you say. Or maybe the finale of this one. I did fine in my sophomore year as far as school was concerned. But I kept looking for Dr. Wingo when I was playing the organ, even though he never came back. I kept dreaming about him; a secret Methodist just waiting to pounce. I'd wake up and go over to Glenn Memorial at all the weird hours you can imagine."

"Did you make A's that year?" Porter asked.

"Sure. After Gross and Biochemistry it was a breeze. I knew that when I got to my junior year, I'd be downtown at Grady working on the wards all ungodly hours, and had already told them at Glenn Memorial I'd have to give up being organist. But you know, Osborne, it was a strange thing. The nearer the time came for that, the more confused I got. I kept worrying about my obsession with Wingo; I hadn't seen him for a year and he still hung there like the Cheshire Cat, popping up when you would least expect him."

"Like a coal scuttle," Porter interjected.

"What? I kept remembering what he'd said about serving two masters, and I was actually so ambivalent I felt that I was going to have to make a choice. Either for medicine or for music. That was a real crossroads for me; so I went to see Dr. Wingo and he gave me this year as Anatomy instructor. I decided to saturate myself with Wingo, to get desensitized, so to speak. The dean took me off rotation and is holding my place for me in the junior class. They've been good to me at Glenn

Memorial; they let me keep my key to the organ and I go practice whenever I like, and I serve as substitute for my replacement when she has to miss."

"And what have you decided? Medicine or music?"

"Oh, medicine. Without a doubt. Medicine. Sir William Osler said that medicine is a jealous mistress, you know. In a lot of ways Osler was worse than Wingo, wouldn't let his interns marry or have any sort of normal life. But I will serve that jealous mistress. Gladly. From now on. For the rest of my life."

"What about your music?"

"Music can be my wife. I'll buy her a gray tweed coat and see her when I'm not busy."

"Wow!" said Porter. "I thought I'd had a rough freshman year. I don't see how you did that."

Faulkner laughed. "You gotta drive, Osborne, you gotta drive. You'd better get back to work now."

"I sure do like you, Faulkner."

"Thank you. Why?"

"Because you're human and because you noticed the gray tweed coat."

11   **W**hen the newly promoted sophomores
returned after their hiatus between quarters, Lester was busily spreading new information; Porter was reminded of the involuntary pelvic twisting of a welcoming dog.

"Have you heard? The military has taken over! We register tomorrow and then the next day the entire medical school, seniors and all, goes out to Fort McPherson to get sworn into the Army. Except for the guys who chose the Navy instead. I don't know where they're going. We're going to be called ASTP and the Navy will be V-12 and we're all going to be in uniform and, get this, they pay for all the tuition and books at Emory plus they pay us a salary and on top of that they pay us a boarding allowance for food and shelter of one hundred dollars a month."

"Whoa up, Lester. Slow down and run that by us again. I heard talk of this but didn't expect it this quick."

"It's true! It's true, I tell you! Day after tomorrow we all go out to Fort Mac for physicals and to get sworn in and we spend the night out there and then on Thursday we start classes, except now we'll be in uniform and will get paid for it. They've already got a major and a captain and a sergeant on campus to look after us after we're inducted; they've got an office in Fishburne Building and the major's name is Teufelsdreck. Every Tuesday afternoon we have to spend two hours learning how to march and all like that, but the rest of the time we go on to school like always."

"And they're going to pay us for this?"

"You're mighty right they are. We're being taken in as PFC's instead of buck privates and our salary will be fifty-six dollars a month, but don't forget the one hundred dollars to eat and sleep. This is the most exciting thing I've ever experienced."

Porter did some quick arithmetic. "But I'm not paying but ten dollars a month for my room and thirty-five dollars a month to eat three meals at the fraternity house. That's not right."

"Oh, shut up, Osborne. You get us messed up and we'll kill you. It doesn't make any difference to the government. We're part of the war effort now."

"Oh."

Lester had accurately summed up the situation, but the class was blessed that he had no prescience about the actual process of induction into the United States Army. In addition to the medical students, there were hundreds of other inductees. The scene became in Porter's mind a blur of human flesh, the initial shock of stripping off in the presence of strangers soon dissipated by the anonymity of communal nakedness. There were lines upon lines of tall, short, fat and skinny Americans, all of them shockingly white. All of them with male escutcheons punctuated by penises. Porter soon lost his self-consciousness. Only the administrative personnel wore clothes. They were obviously bored, impersonal in the recitation of instructions so repetitive they were delivered in monotones, objectively intent on guiding these young men like herdsmen supervising a cattle chute.

Porter recognized friends and fellow students in the crowd, but hardly anyone spoke. He spied Lester across the room in a line going the opposite way. "My God, Lester's got titties," he marveled. "Not prominent pectoral muscles, but plain old titties. And a little round belly sort of like Deacon Chauncey's. He sure doesn't talk as much with his clothes off." He felt a little more comfortable about his own bony physique.

The lines moved slowly, stopping at each station for piecemeal examinations. Blood pressure at one place, ears and throat at another, an officer for the important job of listening to the heart, on to another who thumped the back and perfunctorily listened to two respirations. Only two. "Breathe in and out with your mouth open. Again."

"Move on along there."

"Head to the right. Cough. It ain't funny dammit. Cough."

"Bend over and spread your cheeks."

"Move along there, fellow."

An enlisted man put a tourniquet on Porter's left arm, smoothly inserted a bare needle into the antecubital vein, and then deftly slipped a test tube under the hub. It was held in place only by the pledget of cotton and the weight of the needle itself. As Porter watched his blood running out, another enlisted man slapped a glass bottle into his right hand.

"Walk on along and get a urine specimen in this," he instructed in pat phrasing.

"Do what?" Porter was incredulous.

"Piss in the bottle, fellow," came the bored response.

"But I'm bleeding out of my left arm. What if it runs over the test tube?"

"It won't if you'll get the lead out of your ass. We've got it pretty well timed. Move along, will you?"

Just before he got to the long urinal, another corpsman removed the tube of blood, swiftly extracted the needle, and curled Porter's arm over the pledget of cotton without a word spoken or even a glance exchanged. As Porter filled his urine bottle, the man in front of him crumpled at the knees and crashed to the floor. A corporal swiftly pulled him out of line and without raising his voice said, "Need some ammonia for another one here. On the double."

Porter Osborne, Jr., felt that he was still learning a thing or two, at least about timing and organization.

They were fed in shifts in a communal mess hall, herded along by uniformed soldiers. Porter marveled at the metal tray with stamped-out compartments and the indifference with which the food attendants slapped potatoes, rutabagas, meat, bread, and a substance that turned out to be dessert onto the trays. The men who served their food were shirtless because of the heat of the kitchen. They wore khaki undershirts and Porter noted that most of them were middle-aged, fat, and had tufts of hair on their shoulders. They too did not look at the recruits, just at the trays they held. Corporals discouraged mealtime visiting and directed them into another line to scrape their trays into a waste barrel; after all, there were still many men to feed.

Porter found himself ensconced for the night in the barracks that was reserved for the medical students. Members of all four classes were there and he was a little intimidated in the presence of juniors and seniors who walked the wards at Grady, faced splattering blood in the emergency room, rode the ambulances, helped at operations, and even delivered babies. He resolved to listen and not participate.

"God, can you believe this day? I'm glad to get back to a group where people know my name and use it."

"I'm glad to get some clothes on. And for y'all to get some on. Today may not only have disproved the theory that all men are created equal, but also proved beyond the shadow of a doubt that there's nothing in the world uglier than a naked man. I hope I never see another one of you without your pants on."

"There you have it," volunteered Faulkner. "The human body is a thing of beauty, it's just the genitalia that offend us. Which is why Michelangelo and the other artists covered them up or made them proportionately so small."

"Bullshit on proportion," said Giddings. "I've known for years Michelangelo used my privates as a model: I just wondered where he got somebody with all those muscles."

"You guys sound like you've never been in an Anatomy lab. Today wasn't rough."

"I didn't like being checked for a hernia."

"Aw, that's nothing. That's what they mean by a deep-seated cough."

"I didn't like having to bleed and pee at the same time," ventured Porter.

"Well, I didn't like standing there buck naked and getting a shot in each arm at the same time, especially when I didn't know whether that cross-eyed corpsman could aim accurately or whether he knew anything about sterile technique."

"Those recruits were dropping like flies, weren't they? Four fainted dead away in front of me and had to be dragged out of line. The power of suggestion is a powerful thing; I got a little dizzy myself for just a minute, and I've been two years at Grady and seen everything."

"Say what you will, those guys were efficient. They had us all cleared out of there by five o'clock."

"I don't care how efficient they were," Porter muttered. "You just ought not to have to bleed and pee at the same time."

"Cheer up, Osborne. When you graduate and become an officer, maybe you can change these little things that bother you."

"If that day ever comes. Sometimes I wonder."

"Aw, come on, Osborne. If you get by the Butch, it's all clear sailing."

"I haven't worried about flunking since I got back my first Anatomy test. It's just that sometimes I wonder if this is the right time for me to be a doctor."

Britt Gay intervened. "Time? What's time got to do with it? Why did you want to be a doctor in the first place?"

"Well, gee," said Porter defensively, "I guess if you get right down to it, I think it's the best way I know of to help people in my county. Why did you go into medicine?"

"Because I love science. All aspects of it. And medicine is the most fulfilling way I can imagine to utilize it."

Rabbit Rogers was sitting cross-legged on a top bunk, his head bent slightly forward. "My uncle was the doctor in a town in north Florida and I never saw anybody who was respected any more all over town. I guess prestige was part of my motivation."

"Power!" thundered Dickie Cook from the bunk beneath him. "Nobody in our town makes a move without checking if it's all right with Dr. Darcy. They're supposed to be rationing cigars, but the grocery holds out a box for 'the good doctor.' And he gets all the gasoline he wants and drives off to Florida on vacation whenever he takes a notion. He's the only doctor there and folks are scared he won't make house calls or see them at night if they cross him."

"Why don't all of you quit being so high-flown and abstract?" demanded a roly-poly junior. "You all know it's money. Do you know what a surgeon gets for taking out an appendix? Or do you have any idea what a bone cracker charges for a broken hip? I'm going into orthopedics and live on West Paces Ferry Road and drive a Cadillac."

"And marry a Pink who is realizing her Potential," contributed Porter.

"What?"

"Nothing."

Tom Harris spoke out. "You're crazy. Anybody who goes into medicine for the money is going around his elbow to get to his mouth. With the brain power and hard work it takes to get through four years of med school plus five years of residency training, a guy could be a millionaire if he was concentrating on finance instead of medicine. Before he even got off the night shift at Grady."

"Now don't be too rough on him," spoke up a junior named Goodwin. "If you get real honest about this thing, I suspect we all look on medicine as a better way of life. I sure as hell know I do. I grew up on a dairy farm and the biggest reason I'm studying medicine is I've pulled a million miles of cow tits."

"The war." Porter did not have to turn his head to recognize Abernathy's voice. "Don't forget the war. Did y'all see the pictures of the dead GI's on the beaches at New Guinea and on Guadalcanal? I don't want a nickel's worth of that. It makes me love medicine and love this kind of Army life. You know what ASTP stands for, don't you? All Safe Till Peace!"

Curtis Benton changed the subject. "We do get our uniforms tomorrow, don't we? It's going to be a pretty good feeling to walk downtown now and not have people turning their heads and wondering what's wrong with you physically or else what kind of pull you've got with your congressman."

"I know," rejoined Porter. "I'm looking forward to that, too. I'm just the opposite of Miniver Cheevy."

"Who's he? One of the new freshmen?" asked Benton.

"No. A guy in a poem.

'Miniver scorned the commonplace
And eyed a khaki suit with loathing.
He missed the medieval grace
Of iron clothing.'"

"It's time for lights out," said Benton. "We don't want to get in trouble with a sergeant our first night in the service."

"If you think that's bad, you ought to room with him," said Derrick.

Porter lay in the dark and considered the day. He could theoretically identify with each spokesman about the various virtues of med school. Except Abernathy. That stung him as sharply as a sudden thorn under a fingernail. Because it was true? Never.

All Safe Till Peace, indeed.

"Hey, Abernathy?" he called across the darkened barracks.

"Yeah?"

"You kiss my ass!"

"Go to sleep, Osborne. I ain't got romance on my mind tonight."

An authoritative silhouette appeared in the doorway.

"Pipe down in there! No talking after lights out."

Porter slept.

*"Mahound is in his paradise above the
evening star . . ."*

12 The scholastic pace of the first quarter of the sophomore year lacked the paranoia generated in Gross Anatomy but was
nonetheless taxing. The material to be learned was voluminous and
there was always the matter of new vocabulary. There existed in no
student's mind the assumption that this year would be a picnic. For the
first quarter they had Pathology, Clinical Pathology, and Physiology,
with the promise of Pharmacology, Obstetrics, and Physical Diagnosis
to come. Everyone settled with determination into the routine of studying, the fear of flunking lifted forever from their shoulders. By the end
of this year, they would all be going to Grady Hospital and would be
seeing real live patients. They had to be ready. No one wanted to
appear inadequate in the eyes of a piney-rooter patient at Grady.

Their professors were impressive. Pathology was considered the
most difficult course of the current curriculum and the head of the
department contributed to this reputation. Dr. Roy Bracht was a man
nationally known in his field and droned his lectures rather indifferently with the air that he had better things to do with his time than
consort with a bunch of ignorant and unsophisticated medical students. He wore the long white coat that bespoke status and was rarely
seen without a cigarette. His hair was a reassuring salt and pepper
tangle, but his face was awesome, creased and grooved so deeply that it
looked as though it were melting and sliding downward. There were
big puffs beneath his eyes and his upper lids were so heavy that they
threatened to overrun the restraining lashes. He coughed a lot and his
voice was raspy. He was a distant man.

Lester, garrulous again now that he was clothed in khaki, had
the word. "Dr. Bracht is absolutely dedicated to science and has no
human emotions at all, they say. You know his special field is Hematol-
ogy. He's in all The Literature." Porter noted that Lester enunciated

The Literature with the same reverence with which ministers referred to The Old Testament. "He's all wrapped up right now in pernicious anemia, has published papers on intrinsic and extrinsic factors, and is doing a lot of real original research."

Porter could not restrain himself. "What other kind of research is there, Lester?"

"For God's sake, Osborne, do you want to hear about this or not? Dr. Bracht has a whole floor full of nothing but pernicious anemia in the hospital and is searching like mad for something that will cure it. He has a brother who's got it and they say he's dying. He's run a series on feeding these patients raw liver and there seems to be a little indication that it might help."

"I'd sure swear to God I was better," contributed Easley.

"You're getting as bad as Osborne. Just wait till I'm through, will you? I told you he's desperate to find a cure on account of his brother, and guess what? For the last month, he's been feeding his patients raw human liver. Doesn't tell them, of course, and gets the liver fresh from his autopsies. Doesn't tell those families, either."

Porter was big-eyed and completely silent.

"Well, now. I hear through the grapevine, but it comes pretty straight, that he's run head on into University policies about it. Somebody told, and the Bishop is up on his dewclaws about it. They've raised the issue of Methodist policy toward cannibalism and Dr. Bracht is standing firm on scientific research and academic freedom and it's a mess. Hush-hush all over Druid Hills, but still a mess."

"How are the patients doing?" asked Porter.

"Well, now, I hear—I don't know, but from what I can hear— they say that the patients getting the raw human liver are doing better than the controls."

"I told you so, didn't I?" said Easley. "But you're wrong about Dr. Bracht not having any human emotions, Lester. He's got a sense of humor. You know about him handing out a slide for diagnosis a couple of years ago that was camel's blood, don't you? The only way you can tell is that the camel's red cells are oval instead of round. Pratt was the only one who got it right and that's why he's Bracht's assistant."

Porter took a deep breath. "Where did he find a camel?"

"For God's sake, Osborne, I'm like Lester—why don't you just shut up? Maybe he went to Egypt. He's a pretty big shot, you know."

Lester continued, "Now don't y'all tell anybody about this liver ruckus. I'd hate for it to get around that I'd been talking about it and I sure wouldn't want Dr. Bracht to know it."

"You don't have to worry about me, Lester," said Porter.

It was fine with him for Dr. Bracht to be a distant figure, high up and far away.

Camel blood notwithstanding.

Raw liver?

Raw human liver?

Dr. Jules Twyman was also a famous figure academically. His reputation was international, albeit restricted to esoteric scholars. He had pioneered in Electrocardiography and had discovered in the human heart a minor branch in the electrical pathway that now bore his name. Everyone said that Emory was lucky to have him as head of the Physiology department.

Dr. Twyman's lectures were jewels, precisely faceted, polished, glittering. He was Alsatian by birth, European by education, and medievally regal in attitude. He had always required his students to wear coats and ties to class and obviously approved the rigid uniform requirements now instituted by the military presence on campus. Everything about Dr. Twyman smacked of conformity, protocol, and discipline. He was a tiny little man, fine-boned and delicately crafted; he would have looked incompletely assembled without his fastidious hairline mustache. He wore conservative suits, sometimes gray, sometimes navy, always double-breasted; his neckties were expensive and gorgeous; the tonsure around his shining naked pate was always neatly trimmed. He was immaculate and important and had the carriage of a puffin.

The first time Porter saw him he was captivated for life. The door behind the podium opened and a processional began. First to enter was Mr. Enson, lantern-jawed and raw-boned, his suit and tie apparently purchased many years before for a much smaller brother. He carried the pointer for Dr. Twyman, thumped it twice on the floor to ensure silence and attention, and then laid it carefully across the master's long desk in signal for the students to rise. Dr. Twyman marched briskly in, followed by Dr. Russell, the assistant chief in the Department of Physiology, who had not yet managed to surface in The Literature but, according to Lester, had married well and lived on Lullwater Road. When Mr. Enson and Dr. Russell had taken their places in the classroom, Dr. Twyman nodded his head and donned his spectacles. The students sat and he called the roll. Then he closed the roll-book, removed his spectacles, and delivered the most beautiful and well-organized lecture Porter had ever heard.

His speech was spiced with his cradle tongue but every word was comprehensible with never any hesitancy or groping; the delivery was fluid and measured and paced so that note taking was a pleasure. It was obvious that Dr. Twyman would neither suffer fools nor tolerate foolishness. Anywhere. "You vill see in some books and hear from some clinicians dat de human heart repetitively makes de sound of 'lub-dup, lub-dup.' I haf listened to tousands and tousands of hearts, young gentleman, and neffer, not vonce, haff I heard von of dem say 'lub-dup, lub-dup.'" Porter was enchanted and his heart went out to the aloof and perfect Dr. Jules Twyman. He vowed to serve this professor faithfully and earn his approval by being a good student.

The first quarter of the second year settled in, the routine of studying sweetened now with enough time for a date on Saturday night, an occasional movie, an hour or two a week working in the Victory Garden that Rumble had undertaken as a project for the fraternity. Rumble obviously did not know what he was doing. He had, however, visions of bountiful harvests that would not only supplement the fraternity larder but would also be intensely patriotic, tangible proof to everyone from Roosevelt on down that the Emory boys were behind the war effort. Porter longed for a wagon load of manure to enrich the Druid Hills hardpan but helped Rumble anyway.

Porter even found time for occasional visits with Dr. Dewitt Thebault, whom he found still to be a fascinating person. He relished the arrogant contempt the man exhibited for certain revered icons, the mental nimbleness he demanded from a conversationalist, the occasional lidless stare with which he rewarded some sally that stimulated his own thought processes. The emerging friendship was strictly a cautious and intellectual relationship in Porter's eyes, the only one he could manifest for a man who played chess, stuck electrodes into monkeys' brains, painted oil portraits of selected favorites, kept a fierce and strange dog called a Doberman-Pinscher fenced with chain link beside his garage, and was, first and foremost, a nationally renowned Neuroanatomist. He usually felt that he was on brittle pond ice around Dr. Thebault, that a stupid statement would induce threatening cracks in its swaying surface, bring ominous thin creaking sounds to his alert ears, and without careful testing of weight plunge him into the icy water of personal ridicule. He learned early that a dishonest reply above all else could curl that upper lip in shriveling disgust.

"How do you like being in the Army, Osborne?"

"Well, Dr. Thebault, it is an interesting experience."

"Most of your experiences are, Osborne, at least seen through your eyes. What do you mean?"

"I love the uniform. At first some of us went downtown just to walk the streets among all the real soldiers and sailors. I particularly like that because everybody always looked at me before and just assumed I was 4-F."

"Hummm."

"Then there's the money. I have all my expenses paid, every nickel, including books. On top of that they more than pay my living expenses and give me a salary. I wind up with seventy-five or eighty dollars a month that I can spend. I mean just haul off and spend if I want to. I've never seen that much money in my life."

"I don't think many of your fellows have either, Osborne. For the first time I fully appreciate the simile about money and drunken sailors. What are you spending your money on?"

"Not much of anything, really. I don't have a regular girl friend and I don't drink. I go to a movie now and then or to the Pig 'n' Whistle for Sunday supper because the fraternity lets Miss Mattie and Sollie off after dinner, but for the first time ever I have a bank account."

"Really flinging it around, aren't you?"

"Dr. Thebault, do you know what I really can't get used to? For the first time since I was born I'm not costing my daddy a red cent. In college I was on scholarship and worked in the kitchen, at least till I got fired, and tried to help out all I could, but I've always known that my daddy was paying the bulk of my expenses and I've always felt guilty if I spent twenty-five cents I didn't absolutely have to."

"And how do you feel now?"

"I think I understand for the first time how some of our slaves felt after freedom. I miss the chains. I don't know where to go or how to act. Now that my chain of financial dependence has dropped away, I'm having to look at my father and see what else he means to me. What do I do now? Where do I go? Why is he so important to my feeling of security?"

"Osborne, you're an honest little bastard. At least you try to be. Have you read any Freud at all?"

"Not yet, Dr. Thebault. I imagine that comes next year."

"Don't count on it. This school is weak in that department."

"It's almost as though I'd swapped my father for the United States Army. I like the uniform fine but I'm finding out I don't know as much about the Army as I thought I did."

"You leave me there, Osborne. I can't stand uniforms."

Porter paused a moment. "Dr. Thebault, you look pretty comfortable in that long white coat that tells all of us whenever we see it that

102

there goes another important person in this med school. No matter what the shoes underneath it look like."

There was a long silence. The eyes never blinked. The lips parted but barely moved. "As I said, Osborne, you try to be honest. That can be refreshing. Also challenging. How would you like for me to teach you to play chess?"

"Someday. Maybe. When I have time."

There was another pause. "Osborne."

"Sir?"

"You live on a big farm?"

"Fairly big. Close to a thousand acres."

"I have a dog. Fritz. He is a beautiful animal and one of my very close friends."

"I've heard about your dog."

"If I give him to you, will you take him home with you and let him live unfenced and run free?"

"Why, yes, sir, Dr. Thebault. I would love to do that."

"All I ask is that you tell me what he does the first time you turn him loose." He stubbed out a cigarette. "Osborne."

"Sir?"

"This dog is the most muscular, shining black animal you ever saw in your life. He was not born to be a slave. He will not miss his chains."

The Monday following his trip home, Porter found Dr. Thebault in his office at the end of the day.

"Have you got a minute? I found this sentence in the Pathology textbook that doesn't make sense to me and none of the guys in the class can explain it either."

"Hello, Osborne. I don't pretend to be a Pathologist. I doubt if I can help you."

"Here. Under diseases of the lung, it says, 'It is said that the incidence of emphysema is increased in those who play wind instruments, but this may not be true, since one is as likely to beat the drum as play the trombone if one is a member of a band.' Now, Dr. Thebault, I ask you, does that make any sense at all? Especially in a cut-and-dried scientific textbook?"

"It's completely illogical and unintelligible to me. Why don't you ask Dr. Bracht?"

"Dr. Thebault, I'd as soon ask the gatekeeper at a leper colony if I could walk around inside for a few minutes. Dr. Bracht is completely aloof and as cold-blooded as a snake. I think he smokes all those cigarettes just trying to warm his blood."

"Bracht does have an air of *sang-froid* about him. I, myself, wouldn't want to eat dinner with him and I sure as hell hope I never get pernicious anemia as long as I'm at Emory."

"That story's true, isn't it?"

"Yep. And you have to admire the man for having the guts to back up a theory with an effort at proof or disproof. I'm sorry we're losing him."

"Losing him?"

"Yep. They have a little med school in Birmingham and have asked him to be its dean. It's only a two-year institute now, but they've promised to expand it to a four-year university and they've guaranteed him a fabulous amount of research money. That's too good an opportunity to pass up and he's leaving us in the fall."

"Golly! Is it all right to tell this?"

"Sure. Everybody on the faculty knows it. He told us this morning."

"Then I want to catch Lester in a crowd and be the first one to spring that news. He'll want to kill me and I know he'll wet his pants."

"He'll probably squat if he does. Quit playing with me, Osborne. Get to the point."

"Sir?"

"You know damn well what I mean. Tell me about Fritz and the farm."

"Dr. Thebault, you wouldn't believe it. We got out of the car and he nearly jerked me off my feet touring the yard and checking things out. We hadn't been on the ground two minutes before every cat on the place was in the top of the chinaberry tree and our five dogs were under the smoke house, I mean way back under the smoke house.

"Fritz sort of settled down and made another lap or two, sniffing landmarks and heisting his leg. About then Daddy drove up and said, 'Sambo, where in the hell did you get that dog?' And Fritz walked over to him and sniffed his leg. Daddy stood real still and said, 'Don't you piss on me, you devil dog, you.' And Fritz sat back on his butt and looked him straight in the eye and Daddy stuck out his hand and said, 'I'm pleased to meet you.' And Fritz, just as gravely as a deacon, stuck out his paw and they shook hands. You hadn't told me he knew that trick."

"I didn't know that he knew it."

"Anyhow, I told Daddy that I was going to unleash him and see what he would do. We have the largest single and continuous field in the whole county across the road from our house, Dr. Thebault, and when I took that chain off his neck, Fritz didn't even look back. He jumped both ditches and hit that big field. The cotton's about eight inches high now. It's been chopped, run around twice, and hoed; is putting on squares but of course hasn't bloomed yet; you can still see the dirt in the middles. Fritz hunkered down and went like a greased streak, little puffs of dirt kicking up from his hind feet.

"Daddy yelled, 'Look at that magnificent son of a bitch go, Son!' I was nervous and said, 'You reckon he'll come back?' Daddy said, 'What if he doesn't? Look at him *go*!' When you just barely could see him at the edge of the oak woods on the other side, Daddy whistled and yelled, 'Here, Fritz, here.'

"And, Dr. Thebault, old Fritz never slowed or stopped. He made a sharp turn in that cotton patch and came back as fast as he'd gone. He stopped at the mail box at the big road and peed on it, and then he trotted up the driveway sniffing and peeing on every one of Mother's crepe myrtles. Fritz can run faster and has a bigger bladder than any dog I ever saw."

"Did you fence him up then?"

"No, sir. You told me not to. In fact, Daddy made me hang up the leash and choke collar and wouldn't let me put them on him. When I got up on Sunday morning, Fritz was at the back porch step wagging his ass because you cut all his tail off. The other dogs were lined up in a row in front of the smoke house, and the cats were sitting on the wash bench but had their eyes wide open and were closer to the chinaberry tree than to Fritz. Old Simon came along to milk and walked a good fifteen-foot circle around me and Fritz to get to the door.

"When he was through and ready to leave, he said to me, 'Little Cap, what kind of dog is that?' I told him he is a Doberman-Pinscher. And Simon looked at me and said, 'I understand that right enough, but Little Cap, what do he do?'

"That nearly got me for a minute but then I said, 'Simon, I guess you'd say he's a watchdog.' And Simon broke out in a big grin and said, 'Yes suh, I knowed it. I been studying him and that's what he do. He watches. Me and him both. He watch me and I watch him.'"

"He hasn't tried to bite anybody?"

"Oh, no, sir. He's having the time of his life, Dr. Thebault. Thank you for him."

"Thank you, Osborne."

"Yes, sir. I'm going to run. I want to catch Lester."

"Once more, Osborne, when are you going to drop the 'Dr. Thebault'?"

Porter looked back at him. "Why do you always call me by my last name?"

"I'll think about that. When I have time. Osborne, I've never met him but I like your father."

"So do I, sir. So do I. That may be part of my problem."

On his way to supper, before he could say a word, Lester accosted him. "Osborne, you're not going to believe this! Dr. Bracht is leaving us and going to start a medical school for the University of Alabama. We're the last class at Emory that will have him."

Porter kicked a rock on the edge of the sidewalk. "Tell me about it, Lester. Why in the world is he going to do that?"

"Dim drums throbbing, in the hills half
        heard,
Where only on a nameless throne a crownless
        prince has stirred . . ."

13 **I**n July, during laying-by time on the farm, Fritz
further endeared himself to the senior Osborne by biting a boar hog
that was resisting efforts to return him to the barn; the sophomore
medical students at Emory were involved in mid-terms; the Allies
invaded Sicily under the overall command of Dwight D. Eisenhower;
and Porter Osborne, Jr., in the company of Armstrong Abernathy of all
people, got drunk for the first time in his life. Forsaking the wisdom of
the grandmother, he got limber-legged, knee-walking, moon-howling
drunk. Furthermore, he was unrepentant. Looking back. he acknowledged that perhaps the evening was a turning point in his life.

It came about because of his mail. On Wednesday he received a
letter from Mr. Chauncey.

> "We have been alerted by the War Department
> that our son is missing in action. His plane was observed
> crashing two days ago and only two parachutes were
> seen to open. This was due to military action over enemy
> territory, so his mother and I remain hopeful pending
> further notification. We wanted to let you know that we
> appreciate the friendship you have extended him.
>
> Sincerely yours,
> L. D. Chauncey, Sr."

The sky did not darken nor did Porter's head spin. He
repressed recall of Pearl Harbor and his friend Boston Harbor Jones.
He felt detached, numbed and surprisingly analytical. "Mr. Chauncey
is not either the least bit hopeful," he thought as he walked with
normal gait up the sidewalk, "or he wouldn't have added that last
sentence. It's like closing the lid on a coffin. Except that there's no

coffin. It's like that poem by Archibald MacLeish. There's nothing. Nothing. Nothing at all."

He did not even hear greetings from two fellow students across the street. "I'm not the least bit hopeful, either. It took dynamite to get Deacon out of his easy chair when we were in college; there's no way in the world I can imagine him in a parachute. That takes more mental determination plus physical activity than Deacon could possibly muster." He went to his room and began reviewing his notes and Boyd's *Textbook of Pathology*. "You've gotta drive, Osborne," he muttered. "And you've got to compartmentalize. You can mourn later. After exams. When you have the time. Pending further notification."

Late the next afternoon, with two mid-terms accomplished and only one to go, he took the streetcar to Ponce de Leon and walked the short distance to Highland Avenue. He straightened his tie and overseas cap and strode with purpose into the crowded little shop with the falsely cheerful blue and white neon signs flashing.

"Give me a pint of Four Roses, please."

On his return trip, he pulled the cord and dismounted at the last stop before the streetcar swung at a right angle into the Byway, a long dark passage from Briarcliff to Oxford Road, bordered by weeds and not paved for automobile traffic. As he waited for the trolley to move on away, a car came up behind him.

"Osborne! What the hell you doing way out here in the woods this time of night? We've got a test tomorrow."

"I've already studied all I'm going to, Abernathy. I've got other things on my mind."

"I'm through, too. What's up?"

"I'm fixing to get drunk."

"I thought you didn't drink."

"I'm just about to change that."

"Are you serious?"

"As we say in the country, Armstrong, I'm as serious as a hog on ice. You'll have to excuse me."

"Do you mind if I join you?"

"I probably don't have enough liquor for two."

Abernathy got out of his car. "I won't drink, but if you don't mind, I'll just tag along."

There was something in his tone that made Porter conscious of the possibility that even rich boys get lonely.

"Come on then, but if you even mention All Safe Till Peace, I'll jerk your head off." He paused. "And shit in your neck."

He turned the bottle up and swallowed raw whiskey for the first time in his life. Once. Twice. Three times.

There was awe in Abernathy's voice. "I ain't believing this, Osborne. How can you stand it?" Porter forced himself to speak normally around the fire from hell that was searing his throat and blocking his breath. "You don't know everything, Abernathy. This is the way men do it where I come from."

Within thirty minutes, the inhibitory center in Porter Osborne's brain was deadened. The liquor had loosened his tongue, destroyed all reserve and reticence, but done little to suppress his thoughts or expression of them. There was still awe in Armstrong Abernathy's voice. "I can understand you being upset about your friend getting shot down, but maybe he's just captured, and that beats hell out of dying; at least he's all safe till . . . the end of the war."

"You do not understand!" Porter raved. "Nobody understands but me. This guy was cut out to be some quiet and introspective information officer in Washington, D.C., who never took any more exercise than walking to meals. Instead he refused to apply for OCS and went on and took his slot as a radioman in a B-17. Because he didn't want to act like he was better than any other soldier. Because he really believed that this is a land of equal opportunity and not special opportunity. Because he believed that this was truly one time when war is justified and that it is right to kill the enemy or be killed by him. Because in the end the forces of good must and will triumph." With careful attention, Porter resisted slurring his speech.

"He never said all those things out loud to me. He mostly just sniffed and looked at you but he said enough for me to know that's the way he felt. And he made himself jump in the river and ride the current when deep down he's just as scared of dying as me. Or you. Hell, he was almost as scared of dying as you, Abernathy. His plane had already been hit once. It's not fair. It's not fair. God's got no business doing him this way."

Abernathy's voice was now tinged with disapproval as he trailed Porter to the paved crossing of Springdale Road.

"Osborne, you can't question God's will."

"Who the hell says I can't?" screamed Porter.

Abernathy drew back a little. "Well, everybody says that. I've been taught that all my life. God's will is God's will. It sits there like Stone Mountain. You can't move it and you can't change it and you can't even question it. It's a good thing to have, too, when you stop and think about it. Where would we put everything we don't understand if we didn't have God's will to lay it on? Everybody knows that."

Porter stopped and faced him. He stomped his foot and raised a hand toward heaven. "This may be a time when the mind of man has created yet another God. Who the hell is Everybody? We've already got a whole pantheon of lesser gods in America. We worship The Dollar. We worship They. Now here you come with Everybody. Well, I'll let you in on a little secret, Armstrong, old buddy. An Osborne from Brewton County doesn't have to pay any attention to Everybody. I even know old Everybody's last name. It's Else. And, Armstrong, that Else family is pretty big. Everybody has a couple of kid brothers named Anybody and Somebody that he pulls in for things he doesn't want to handle himself. You know where I got this, Armstrong?" Porter blinked with dignity. "I got it from my grandmother. She all the time used to tell me, 'It doesn't matter what Everybody Else is doing, young man,' or, 'Don't try to blame that on Somebody Else.' Or, 'You'll have to do it if you can't find Anybody Else.' Then there's a big mean first cousin in the Else Family. His name's Or and you haven't experienced dread until you hear my grandmother say, 'You'd better mind me, young sprout, Or Else.' So don't throw Everybody at me, Armstrong. One of the Osborne gods is named Who You Are, and we all have to remember that one or the grandmother will know and she'll pass it on back for a thousand years. Who You Are is more important than Everybody Else." In spite of himself, he hiccupped.

"Osborne, you are stark, raving crazy and now you're stark, raving drunk. Come on back to my car and I'll ride you home."

"Not yet, Armstrong, not yet. And don't you leave yet, either. You brought up this business about God's will and I'm not done with it. If all these little gods we've created don't amount to a fart in a whirlwind, as my grandfather used to say, then what about this Big Daddy? This God of Creation? This Father of all mankind? I'm just most deeply and callously not impressed with the way He's doing things."

"Osborne, this is sacriligious. You ought to hush."

"I will not hush. I read somewhere, and it wasn't in Best and Taylor or Morris or Boyd, either, 'In the face of a God, half demagogue, half policeman, I raise my puny voice, I shake my angry fist,' and that's the way I feel right now."

"One thing's for sure, Osborne, your voice isn't puny now. These good people on Springdale Road may hear you."

"I'm not sure *you're* even hearing me, Abernathy. Don't you understand? I don't think any more that God cares. If He does, how come He let the Arizona get sunk? Or pilots in training get killed in P38's? Or Deacon Chauncey get shot down?"

"All right, Osborne, stop right there. Sounds to me like you need to pray."

"Pray? Pray? Armstrong Abernathy, I prayed my ass off for eighteen years. I prayed in the quietness of my heart; I prayed in closets with the door closed; I prayed on bended knee; I spoke to my Father which is in Heaven and I did it in secret with tears in my eyes; I followed every formula I ever heard of." He drew himself up indignantly. "And what did He do? Nothing! Not a damn thing! He's like the lawyers in Luke. He lades men with burdens too grievous to bear and lifts not one finger to help them. I haven't prayed since December 7, 1941, when the Arizona got sunk, and I'm not about to start back because B-17's and P-38's are getting shot down and my friends are getting killed. I'm not about to pray again. It doesn't do a damn bit of good and I'd rather die than ask Him for anything else."

"Maybe that's what you're doing. Remember the Devil tempted Jesus by telling Him to curse God and die."

"What?" Porter's scream was self-righteous. "You Methodists don't know shit about the Bible, Abernathy. That was Job, not Jesus, and it was a group of Job's comforters, not the Devil. I'm not going to curse God and die; I'm going to curse God and live. You hear me? I'm going to live! I'm going to live my own life! I'm going to take charge myself of what I do from now on. 'My head is bloody but unbowed.' Pour it on, God, pour it on; I can take it! I'll show You!"

"Osborne, you're beginning to sound like Barton. That's just liquor talking. Don't you drink any more of that stuff."

"Miss Bunch Brown back home always said, 'What's in there sober comes out drunk.' You want some of it?" Porter swayed a little as he proffered the bottle.

"I don't ordinarily touch anything as sorry as Four Roses, and I'd sure be scared to tackle any of that batch. It might make me talk like you, and I want to stay a good Christian boy."

"Christian?" Porter mouthed the sibilants with care. "You leave Christ out of this. I've got nothing against Him. He can't help what His Daddy does. He got a damn rotten deal Himself, if you ask me, and I don't believe any of that hair-on-your-head crap anymore."

"Osborne, if you won't go back to my car with me and let me drive you back to your room, I'm going to leave you. We've got that test tomorrow and I've got to get some sleep."

Porter's accent was ponderous. "Go on and leave. I'll walk. I'm too drunk to ride."

Abernathy hesitated. "I still don't understand why you're so upset, Osborne. People die every day, and we need to be grateful that we're still alive."

"You sure don't understand, Armstrong. I am grateful. I'm so grateful I feel guilty. And I can't live with that guilt anymore. Now I know what I have to do. And I'm scared."

"What do you have to do?"

"I have to go. I have to stick my neck out. I have to bare my ass. I may even have to get killed; I don't know. But the only choice I have is to take the risk. But I might as well be dead if I can't live with myself."

"You're crazy, Osborne. You're crazy. You need to get back to believing in God."

"I didn't say I don't believe in Him. I've just said I don't approve of the way He's acting. If God can't run a war any better than this, how does He think we're going to believe that He can resurrect all those bodies He's destroying? You saw what we did to our cadavers last year, didn't you? You know damn good and well all those bits and pieces won't ever get reunited, let alone resurrected. I'm not going to worship that God any more, at least not until I understand Him better."

"Good night, Osborne. You're crazy. Lots of luck. Lots of luck with your soul."

"Don't worry about my soul. I'm at least worshipping the minor gods."

"What minor gods?"

"They, Who You Are, and even the Else family."

The two boys turned and walked away from each other in completely opposite directions. On Springdale Road in Druid Hills. In Atlanta, Georgia. It was July of 1943, and Porter Osborne, Jr., felt a million miles from home.

Five blocks later, he mused to himself. "Boston and Deacon are They too, and so in a sense are all the Elses. And that brings you right around to thinking that They may be just another manifestation of God the Father." He stumbled over a curb. His consciousness was not at that moment disturbed by possible reaction on the part of his earthly

112

father to what he planned to do. Porter Osborne, Sr., was impressive enough, but he was not, after all, God.

After the Physiology test, after lunch, after the dissipation of headache, trembling, and queasiness that he assumed were the companions of his first hangover, Porter marched resolutely to Goodrich Hall. He approached the civilian secretary sitting behind the bare-topped desk upon which rested a telephone, an empty wire basket, and a note pad. A pencil was behind her ear.

"Yes?"

Mustering his best manners, Porter smiled at her. "Good afternoon, ma'am. Is Maj. Teufelsdreck in?"

Her answering smile was fleeting. "I can check. Why?"

"Well, if he is, I'd like to see him, please, ma'am."

"Your name?"

"Porter Osborne, Jr."

She was overly industrious, he thought, with the pencil and note pad. "Your rank?"

Porter turned one shoulder toward her to point out the single stripe. "PFC, ma'am."

"Private First Class," she said as she wrote PFC on the pad. "And the purpose of your visit?"

"A personal matter, ma'am."

"Of what nature?"

"Like I said, ma'am, it's personal. I want to speak only to Maj. Teufelsdreck concerning it."

A tiny frown gathered between her brows. "Have you been through channels?"

"Oh, yes, ma'am," Porter beamed. "I was sworn in at Fort Mac a couple of months ago. I'm ASTP, but I'm in the Army same as anybody else. I went through induction and everything just like a real soldier."

"That is not what I mean. In order to procure an interview with the major, an enlisted man is supposed to go first to his noncommissioned officer, who passes the request on up the chain of command. In your case you need to see the sergeant first; then he forwards your request in writing on to the captain, and he reviews it and passes it on to the major. Then the major notifies you when he can see you."

Porter scratched his head, looked extremely bewildered and smiled again, this time with what he hoped was appealing shyness.

"But, ma'am, I'll bet my paycheck all those requests go right through your hands anyhow. Like I said, I'm ASTP and I don't know about channels and all like that, and I need to see the major in the worst way. Couldn't you please help me out and let me see him?"

"He's not in."

Porter carefully suppressed any facial manifestation of exasperation or indignation. "Well, ma'am, I know the sergeant would come to you to get the request typed, then you would take it to the captain to get it stamped, then you would have hold of it again to present it to the major, and then you would be the one to look up his appointments and tell the major when he could see me. So, please, ma'am, just this once couldn't we bypass the channels and get me in to see Maj. Teufelsdreck?"

She looked at him levelly. Porter appeared wistful.

"Is it an emergency then, you would say?"

"Oh, yes, ma'am. To me it is. You know it would have to be or I wouldn't be here. I'm just a PFC and I'm scared to death of majors."

She tapped her teeth with the pencil. "I could set you up for four o'clock on Monday afternoon. But I would absolutely have to put down a reason."

"Thank you, ma'am. You're an angel. Just put down that I am troubled in my soul."

She tugged at a shoulder length curl and arched one eyebrow. "Are you sure you don't need to see a chaplain?"

"Oh, no, ma'am. I've seen so many of them already all my life that I think they may be part of my problem."

"Oh."

"I'll be here at four on Monday. And you'll never know how grateful I am to you. Thank you so much."

"Why, you're welcome. One more thing, Pvt. Osborne."

"Yes, ma'am."

"Be sure your shoes are polished better. The major has a thing about shoes."

"Thanks again."

On Sunday he had become so restive about his upcoming appointment that he called Dr. Thebault and went to see him. They sat in lawn chairs near the chain link fence that had once confined Fritz, its gate now swaying open, unheeded and unneeded. Dr. Thebault sipped at a beer, participation in which activity Porter had declined with a spasm of revulsion he tried to keep from being obvious. He gave the professor the calm and organized presentation that he had rehearsed, concentrating on reasons rather than feelings, proud of his

114

emotionless tone. He summarized with the resolve he had made and then requested that Dr. Thebault accompany him the next day to see the major.

"Not because I expect you to say anything or speak for me, Dr. Thebault. I don't want you to. It's just that I'm new to all this military stuff and I'll feel better if someone is present who understands me and is sympathetic. Somebody to put sand under my feet, as they say at home."

"Sand? Look, Osborne, although I comprehend what you're saying, I'm not at all sure that I understand you. From the standpoint of research, however, if for no other reason, I'll be happy to go. Drop by my office at a quarter till, and I'll walk over with you."

Although Porter had not had precise instruction concerning military courtesy in the weekly sessions his class had with the sergeant, he had been taught to salute.

He had also seen enough movies to have ideas about conduct in the presence of officers. Consequently, when he and Dr. Thebault were led into Maj. Teufelsdreck's office, he clicked his heels loudly, assumed the stiff-spined posture of attention so rigidly and held a salute so tautly that he quivered.

"Private First Class Osborne, sir," he bleated. His voice, he realized, was louder than necessary. He held the salute with desperate resolve.

The major rose from his desk, his jaw slightly agape. He reached for his pipe on the desk top and put it between his teeth. "Well," he exclaimed. "I can't help it. At ease. In other words, for God's sake relax!" He cast a glance at the long white coat, the impassive visage of PFC Osborne's visitor.

"Oh." Porter let his arm fall, started to put his hands in his pockets, then thought better of that. "Major, this is Dr. Dewitt Thebault, head of the Neuroanatomy department at Emory. I asked him to come along because he is familiar with my situation and also with my request. Dr. Thebault, this is Maj. Toofelsdirk."

"Teufelsdreck, Dr. Thebault. But that was close, Osborne. You gentlemen have a seat. What can I do for you, Osborne? One of my duties is to make as smooth a transition as possible for you medical students from civilian to military life. I'm here to help."

With this assurance, Porter abandoned his planned presentation. This was obviously an agreeable, understanding, cooperative and efficient man of the military, truly an officer and a gentleman. No need to waste his time with explanatory preamble. Come straight to the point. Be direct and be done with it.

"I am here to request a transfer, Maj. Tiffelstuck, sir."

The major looked at his watch, pulled a Manila folder toward him, and sighed. "Why don't you just address me as 'Sir,' Osborne? Let me see here. You were in the upper third of your freshman class and, although we do not have the results yet from last week's mid-terms, you are apparently maintaining your class standing this year. Why do you want to leave Emory for another school, Osborne?"

"Oh, I don't, sir. I love Emory. I think it's the best med school in the world. I want to leave Emory for active duty. In a real military unit." He swallowed. "A combat unit."

"Osborne, that is obviously impossible. You still have two more academic years before you are a full-fledged physician and eligible for your commission and 'active duty' as you call it. Why are you bothering me with this visit?"

"Because, sir, you are the only one who can transfer me. I've already researched that. I can't resign from ASTP and re-enlist in the Army as a brand-new recruit; I have to have your permission because you are my commanding officer. You see, sir, I want to interrupt my medical studies and get into this war in a more personal way." Of a sudden his stage fright disappeared; he began pouring his heart out. He laid before this stranger all of the complexities of his feelings, the turmoil and the ambivalence he suffered, the guilt under which he lived. He spoke with artless enthusiasm.

The major removed the empty pipe from his mouth and placed it on his desk. He sat back in his chair, made a tent of his spread fingers, anchored the thumbs under his chin, the index fingers on the point of his nose, and regarded Porter steadily. Porter, in response, talked on and on. He cited names and places but he did not recite any poetry. He also did not tell this all-powerful representative of Uncle Sam about his first view of the Gross Anatomy lab, nor mention any of the personal doubts he had experienced about wanting to be a physician. Those, he felt, were side trails down which there was no reason to scamper for the present.

"So you see, Maj. Teufelsdreck, sir," he concluded in a manly tone, "why this is important enough for me to bother you with this visit."

The major leaned forward, picked up the pipe again, and pointed the stem of it at Porter. "And what about the Army?" he thundered.

"Sir?" Porter automatically shrank backward.

"The Army, Osborne! You stand there bleating like a newborn goat about your own feelings and don't for a moment consider the overall picture. This country needs doctors for the war effort; we have plenty of moronic dog-faces. Do you realize how much your government has already invested in you? Believe me, if we didn't need you as a physician, all this money and manpower would not be squandered in every medical school in the nation to shape you up and pin you down."

"You sound like my father, sir," Porter interrupted. "He was a captain in the first World War."

"Well, I'm sure you must be a great disappointment to him if he's already talked to you. If I were in your situation, I would not mention to him that I had to intrude on the time and attention of a field grade officer with my own personal conflicts and selfish desires. I'd send you to a shrink right now but we've got all of them busy. Hell, you're shell-shocked and never even heard a gun fired. Out of curiosity, Osborne, what branch of the service do you want to get into?"

Porter felt his face flaming; not with embarrassment for once in his life but with fury.

"The paratroopers, sir," he snapped. "The paratroopers. If I'm going to do something, I might as well try to be the best."

The major rose. "Stand at attention, Osborne. If you can."

He walked slowly around the rigid boy. "For all the world like he's buying a mule," Porter thought. The major retired again behind his desk.

"Osborne," he said, and there was contempt in his voice, "you couldn't even bring a parachute to earth. You'd drift up and off instead of down."

Porter swallowed. His face paled. "I weigh one hundred and ten pounds, sir," he defended. The major leaned forward on his knuckles.

"The Army knows what it's doing; I know what I'm doing; and from this moment on I'm going to know what you're doing. You go back to your room and study like you've never studied before. Try to be the best doctor you can possibly be. That's what we need." He took a deep breath, let it out slowly and then yelled so loudly that Porter reflexively jumped. "Now, get your goddam ass out of here!"

As Porter executed the best about-face of which he was capable, Maj. Teufelsdreck spoke in a calmer but still icy voice.

"Don't leave here thinking for a minute that I don't have feelings, too. If I had my way, I'd be in a tank in Sicily right now instead of riding this desk and playing nursemaid," he took a deep breath, "to a

117

bunch of snot-nosed, temperamental, pampered rich kids who parade around like a bunch of pseudo-intellectual mama's darlings. I'm here because the Army put me here, and you had better conform. Or else!"

Dr. Thebault lunged up out of his chair at the back of the room as Porter marched past him. His lip curled around inflectionless words. "Thanks for your time, Major. I'm sure you'll never get hemorrhoids."

On the sidewalk outside they walked in silence for awhile.

"Why did you say that about hemorrhoids, Dr. Thebault?"

"Because, Osborne, that man is without a doubt the most perfect asshole I have ever encountered. Absolutely perfect. Not a hint of hemorrhoids."

Porter mustered a laugh. The professor remained silent.

"Dr. Thebault."

"What?"

"You know me pretty well by now. Do you think I'm a pseudo-intellectual?"

"Not yet, Osborne. But keep working on it and you may get there some day."

Five paces later, Dr. Thebault broke the silence. "What are you going to do now?"

They stopped at the corner. Porter faced his friend and resolutely declared, "I'm taking charge of my life; I'm going to flunk out of school."

Dr. Thebault gave him his lizard look, cautiously still and unblinking. "I can't help you there. You're on your own. Keep in touch."

They stepped off the curb and walked away from each other. But not, Porter felt, in completely opposite directions.

"Don John of Austria is going to the war . . ."

14 **P**orter kept his counsel. He attended class as usual but made only a perfunctory display of taking notes. He went to his labs and enjoyed them because he could not repress interest in the fascinating material presented there; he thought the mucosa of the small bowel, stained red and blue with hematoxylin and eosin, as glowingly beautiful as an illumined manuscript; the slides of thyroid tissue were gorgeous, the patterned cells surrounding the pink colloid material aligned like stones in a retaining wall. He knew what he was doing, he assured himself. There were only four weeks left until finals and there was no need to cause a flurry by making melodramatic announcements to his classmates.

He had read that landing in a parachute was comparable to jumping from a second-story window and should be accomplished with bent knees and a willingness to roll. He practiced, when no one was around, from the roof of the back porch at the fraternity house. He marveled that all of his classmates were so caught up in the frantic pursuit of their own destinies that not one of them manifested more than casual interest in his activities. Certainly no one divined his deeper purpose.

"Osborne, don't tell me you're going to another movie tonight," Bob Waters said. "That's the third one this week. I wish I was a genius and didn't have to study. How'd you do on that Physiology pop quiz this morning? I think I aced that one."

"There goes Osborne again, off for another night on the town. Look at those shoes, will you? He spent hours on them."

"I mean ole Osborne's nigger-rich since he's getting that regular salary, ain't he? Took that student nurse to the Frances and Virginia Tearoom in the middle of the week."

"Sonnyboy, I would ask you why you've checked that book on

operas out of the library, but I'm afraid you'd start singing to me. There's no poetry in it, is there?"

Just three more weeks.

Would he leap bravely into space the first time at Fort Benning or have to be booted in the butt by the jump sergeant?

Just two more weeks.

Would he get hit by a bullet on his way down? Would he have the nerve to grab his gun on impact and kill a German? A Jap?

Just one more week.

Would he have a better chance of surviving to return to Brewton County, to resume his interrupted education, if he was sent to Europe or to the South Pacific?

Just four more days.

The summons came from Maj. Teufelsdreck.

"At ease, Osborne. No, don't head for that chair. You're not going to have time to sit down. Nor are you going to have the least inclination to do so when I get through chewing on you."

"Sir?"

"Osborne, didn't I tell you that I was going to keep a close eye on you and that I would know what you are doing? From now on? Didn't I tell you that the other day?"

"Yes, sir."

"I have grades here on a student who was making B in Pathology and B in Physiology up until three and a half weeks ago. Since that time, you have no grade above fifty. What are you doing, soldier? Are you playing with me?"

"No, sir, Maj. Toofelstoot, sir. I'm not playing."

"Dammit it, Osborne, you know my name as well as I do. Slow down or calm down and pronounce it correctly."

"To answer your question, you refused me a transfer, and I just figured that if the school kicked me out you'd have to send me back to Fort McPherson where you got me in the first place and then I could apply for whatever I wanted. I have decided that I am the only one who can decide what I really want to do and that it is time for me to take charge of my own life. I hear that the paratroopers are almost all volunteers."

"Let me tell you one damn thing. If you think for even a minute you're going to have control of your own destiny in this man's Army, you're a wide-eyed idiot. I can personally see to it that you are permanently and irrevocably assigned to the most menial duties in the medical corps of the United States Army."

120

"Sir?"

"You heard me. If you defy me and flunk out of school, I can promise you that you'll spend the rest of this war gloriously carrying ice water and bedpans to sick sailors and soldiers and jumping to attention every time some lame brain second lieutenant of a nurse enters the room. As for the glamour of the paratroopers, the closest you'll come to that is wiping the butt of some poor bastard who's paralyzed from a jump and can't do it for himself. I'll see to it! Do I make myself plain?"

"Yes, sir."

"Now get out there and study like hell and pull those grades back up where they belong and get all this foolish and romantic trash out of your head. And don't you open your mouth to tell me about your daddy being a captain in World War I; there's not a thing he can do to help you now. Do you understand me?"

"Yes, sir."

"Remember that the dumbest GI in the rank and file learns before he gets out of basic training not to volunteer for anything. One other thing, Osborne. Now that you've relaxed somewhat, let me hear you say my name."

"Teufelsdreck, sir. Teufelsdreck."

"That's right," the major boomed. "I knew you could do it."

"Sir, I looked the word up in the college library the other day. In a German dictionary. When I was checking out a book on opera. Do you know that 'Teufelsdreck' means 'devil's dirt,' sir?"

"I certainly do, Osborne. My family has known that for generations in Pennsylvania, which is why we have never changed the spelling. And of all my brothers, they say I'm the one who lives up to it best. When you get the chance again even to think about opera, read 'Faust' and think of me. Now, get your goddam ass out of here!"

Porter hastened to find Dewitt Thebault. As he poured out the account of his meeting, he was almost whimpering from frustration, indecision, repressed anger, and even dread.

"What in the hell do I do now, Dr. Thebault? He means it. He still hasn't developed any hemorrhoids and he means every word of it. He has singled me out."

The gray eyes impaled him. "Bullshit, Osborne."

"Sir?"

"He hasn't singled you out. You singled yourself out. You dared to act on your convictions and stand out from the herd, and now the major is just reacting to it. In a manner that you could expect from a perfect asshole, I grant you, but it is not a surprising reaction to your action. What are you going to do now?"

"Gosh, I don't know. What would you do?"

"The first thing I would do is tell you damn quick that I would not presume to tell you what to do. Why don't you talk to your father about it?"

The soft suggestion dropped like a stone in a pond, ripples fanning out in larger and larger concentric circles. The silence grew.

Dr. Thebault waited.

Porter considered.

Dr. Thebault waited.

Porter took a shuddering breath and responded.

"I don't have time. The first exam is day after tomorrow. I know what my daddy would say anyhow. He was, after all, a captain. I guess I'd better get busy and do well on those finals. Ice water and bedpans aren't a very exciting way to spend the war."

Dr. Thebault blinked; the bloodless lips moved. "You've got more than a month's work to cover in two nights."

"And the rest of it to review. I haven't cracked the first book last month, but all I have to do is memorize some Boyd, Dr. Thebault. Physiology will be a snap, even if I did quit taking notes. I'm an expert at compartmentalizing. Don't worry."

"With an entirely different meaning, Osborne, I'm going to tell you exactly what the major did; get your goddam ass out of here."

After forty-eight hours of sleeplessness, cramming as he had never crammed before, even during the long watches of the last night smacking his forehead with an open palm and proclaiming aloud, "You gotta drive, Porter, you gotta drive," he thought the actual examinations anticlimactic, fugue-like.

He was rather proud of answering a multitude of questions in Pathology that bordered on academic trivia and discarded concern about retention of material. "I won't hang on to any of this till Halloween."

On the Physiology exam there were only five questions. On one of them, he suffered a complete memory loss and for the first time in his life was compelled to leave a question blank. "Two men named Henle and Malpighii have structures named for them. Describe in anatomical, physiological, and biochemical detail the importance of these structures in maintaining the stability of the human body." Porter thought, "I can't recall Dr. Twyman saying we would have the kidney on this quarter's final exam because we're not quite through with it yet." He had not read one word about the subject. He shrugged. "There go twenty points right there, but I'll still get by in the low seventies. Bless Dr. Twyman's heart, he's going to be disappointed in me. I'll make it up to him next quarter."

He went home, slept without dreams and spent most of the week roaming the fields and woods, Fritz ranging around and in front of him. He dressed carefully in his uniform on several occasions and went to town just to be seen in the courthouse, in the drugstore, on the sidewalks wearing khaki, his part in the war effort visible to all. To his mother's pre-breakfast inquiries he was less than open but stopped short of actually dissembling.

"Oh, yes, Mother, the second year is better than the first. At least I think it's going to be. I've had a little internal conflict about career direction, but Dr. Thebault and the major in charge of our ASTP unit helped me get that straightened out. My grades have probably dropped to the lower third of the class, but I'll pull them on back up next quarter. Golly, that ham smells good."

On Sunday night, back at the fraternity house, Bob Waters came into his room. "I know it's late and you're getting ready for bed, but have you a minute? I don't mean to be meddling, but I think you ought to hear this. You know how Lester always finds out everything before anybody else? Well, he's been telling around campus this evening that five students have flunked out of the class. Says he has it straight. Says all five of them flunked Physiology. Three of them flunked Pathology, and two of them even flunked Clinical Pathology. I told Lester this is one time he's dead wrong. Physiology is supposed to be our crip course for this year; nobody ever flunks Dr. Twyman. On top of that, nobody is supposed to flunk anything after he gets by the Butch."

"I know," said Porter. "And Lester knows. I've heard him say it a hundred times."

"Well, he swears it's true. He also says he has it straight that the major is fit to be tied. Says all five guys are being shipped out to active duty immediately."

Bob Waters shifted his feet, glanced around for an ashtray, carefully groomed his cigarette, and then looked levelly at Porter. "I wouldn't be telling you this, Osborne, except that Lester says you're one of them and that the major is especially mad at you. You're my friend and I didn't want everybody in the class buzzing behind your back and you not to know. Personally, I don't believe a word of it."

Porter met his gaze. "You can believe it, Bob. I don't know about the other four, but you can believe it about me. Have you ever known Lester to miss?"

He reached out and squeezed the other boy's shoulder. "Don't worry about me. We'd better get to bed. Tomorrow promises to be a busy day. Thanks for telling me. At least I'll be prepared for it."

When he crawled between his sheets and flipped off his light, Porter, from old habit in times of crises, opened his heart to prayer. "Our Father," he began. He caught himself and cut it off. He lay for a full minute staring into the dark. "Well, well, well," he said aloud. He turned over and slept like a baby.

In the sunlight of morning he thought that perhaps Lester for once might have garnered and distributed erroneous information. No official had told Porter anything; so he went to class as usual. To inaugurate the second quarter, the sophomores were meeting for the first time in the Emory Hospital Auditorium and were having their first clinical lecture rather than one in basic science. The dogwoods bordering the sidewalk on Clifton Road were beginning to show maroon streaking in their leaves, and their seeds were already shining like red shoe buttons at the end of each twig; Porter thought it altogether too marvelous a day for anything very cataclysmic to occur.

In the waxed and shining corridor outside the auditorium, Lester was talking to a group of four fellow students. He spied Porter, muttered something, the other heads turned toward him, and then the group dispersed in overly nonchalant affectation.

"Lester," called Porter, "wait up a minute. Guess what? You're absolutely not going to believe this. The lecture we're having at eight o'clock this morning is being given by no less a person than Dr. Bertram Glendenning himself. Did you know that he's one of the most successful Obstetricians in town and is so busy he's had to take in a whole stable of partners? Did you know that he's pioneering in giving women in labor something called paraldehyde? It doesn't stop the pain but knocks out the woman's memory completely so that when she wakes up she thinks she didn't hurt. That way the babies are livelier, he says, and since the women think they didn't hurt at all they just rave about him. I know a nurse who comes from the country and she says when you get a bunch of his Druid Hills women in labor at the same time it sounds like a coon hunt in Henry County when every dog in the pack has treed a separate coon. Dr. Glendenning has even had special mattresses made that fold up on the patients so they can't crawl out.

Did you know that? My friend says those ladies go hog wild when they get that paraldehyde and whoop and holler but really don't remember any of it. Isn't that wonderful?"

"Osborne, everybody knows that. Why are you acting like it's fresh news and telling it to me?"

"Why, Lester, I thought maybe you'd been so busy digging out other stuff you might have missed it. And then, too, I thought maybe you'd like an opportunity to rest your voice. We'd better hurry; don't want to be late for Dr. Glendenning, you know."

The Obstetrician was the first physician with a private practice to whom this class had been exposed. He was prosperously plump, sartorially immaculate, and presented an image of ponderous and impenetrable dignity. When he called the roll, Porter answered to his name with some relief. Lester was wrong.

Dr. Glendenning then announced with a fatherly, slightly condescending attitude that this first session would be spent in oral review of the female anatomy, to be followed by a discussion of ovulation, fertilization, and the uterine changes following implantation.

"Let us see how much you boys remember from Dr. Wingo's course last year." His finger went down the roll. "Harper. Valentine Harper. Are you here, Harper?"

Valentine Harper, financially secure in ASTP, had boldly defied student wisdom and married the girl of his dreams in a widely publicized ceremony during the week between quarters, ignoring the admonishments of his peers that he would be responsible for honeymoon performance all through at least the fall quarter and that it would probably wear him out. His neighbor nudged him awake.

"Sir?"

"How long is the clitoris?"

"Sir?"

"The clitoris, Harper. In the average female, how long is the clitoris?"

The class held its breath. Dr. Glendenning, and possibly Harper himself, did not attach personal significance to the question, but every other person in the room was acutely conscious of Valentine's wedding only four days previously.

Valentine Harper shook sleep from his brain. "About six inches, I would say."

When Dr. Glendenning restored order and asked for a volunteer, it was Masters who raised his hand and gave an answer that was such a convoluted, multi-claused statement it could almost qualify as a lecture in itself. With the comforting thought that life in the rabbit hole had really changed very little, Porter drew his clipboard closer and prepared to take notes. "If Valentine Harper is still in the class, there's no way I flunked out. Lester is wrong."

At the conclusion of the period, Dr. Glendenning picked a slip of paper from his roll book. "I have been asked to announce that Calhoun, Flemister, Garrison, Osborne, and Otten are to report to Dean Astenheimer's office at 9:30. The rest of the class will proceed to Dr. Twyman's class as usual. One of my partners, Dr. Calvin, will give your lecture on Thursday, and I will see you next week. Good day, young gentlemen."

Porter felt that a stone had hit his stomach with force enough to make it lurch and sag somewhere in his pelvis. He had not foreseen that something so intensely personal and private to him must inescapably become common knowledge and, at least for its season, fascinating gossip. He thought of Nichols, Mitchell, and Jordan. He thought of Will Barton. Nobody knew where they were now. Nobody cared. He squared his shoulders and cloaked himself in a show of indifference. "Move over, fellows, here I come. Wherever you are. I've sure given everybody something to talk about instead of Valentine Harper." He gathered up his books. "Or, at least, in addition to," he amended.

Lester was waiting at the back of the auditorium, his face alternately flaming and paling, his words as rapid as a waterfall. "Hell, Osborne, I never thought in my wildest dreams it would come to this. I'm sorry as I can be. We've had some differences but I really have come to value your friendship."

Porter clasped the outstretched hand. "Same here, old buddy. I'll see you after the war."

Derrick approached him in the hallway. "I told you I thought you were going to too many movies, Sonnyboy. You want a Coca-Cola? I'll buy you one."

"For God's sake, you don't need to take it that seriously. You go on to class. I'll be all right."

"I told you you were reading too much of that old poetry, too."

Other than Derrick and Lester, no one in the class spoke to him and eye contact was as glancing as that between pedestrians on Peachtree Street. "They're embarrassed," Porter thought. "If Will Barton were here, I'd at least get a proper farewell." He shrugged his shoulders. "I can take a joke."

Waiting in the Dean's office for Dr. Astenheimer, seated in a row of chairs against the wall, he realized that the other four boys still lacked confidence in Lester's infallibility.

"Osborne, you're wrong. I just don't believe it."

"Hell, they can't flunk us. Nobody ever flunks in their sophomore year. We lost four last year, and with our five, that would make right at twenty percent of the class. They can't do it."

"You're right; it would make the whole med school look bad. They're just trying to scare us."

"Wouldn't it make the whole med school look even worse if they passed five guys who really flunked out? And let them go on to be doctors?"

"Shut up, Osborne; what do you know? Calhoun's right; they're just trying to put the fear of God in us."

"It sure is working," interposed Garrison, forcing a laugh.

Porter considered his four companions. Flemister was a soft-spoken, self-effacing boy who, so far, had stayed on the periphery of class attention, a person of rather indeterminate character. He was pasty-faced with a spatter of freckles across his nose and had tightly curled hair that he kept under rigid control by frequent trips to the barber. His palate was so highly arched that it made a V of his upper teeth and gave a near lisp to his speech. He was sitting in the end chair on the row, a seat between himself and Porter, knees spread, hands clasped between them, head bowed, apparently not even listening.

Garrison was an ebullient, gregarious boy with a ready smile. Short of stature, he carried himself with an almost strutting erectness. Active in fraternity projects, ever ready to listen to problems, sympathetic and reassuring, he was popular across the class; everyone opined that you could always count on Buck Garrison.

Although the other two boys were visibly and audibly prominent in the class, Porter considered that he did not really know them as individuals. In his mind, they were like two sides of a coin: it took both of them to make one person. They were from the same home town and had known each other since childhood. They had attended the same junior college, joined the same prestigious fraternity when they moved on to Emory undergraduate school, and the same professional fraternity in medical school. They had known all of the same people for all of their lives, including the debutantes from Druid Hills, and their personalities now had a glittering sameness, at least on the surface. They were constantly together in work and in play, sufficient unto themselves, only superficially noticing, for acceptance or rejection, the other members of the class. They were like near-grown puppies from the same litter, frolicking and running and fighting with each other, absorbed occasionally in chasing their own tails but content in the awareness that the other was always present. Porter, when around them, had felt like an outsider from another kennel, unnoticed, unwormed, and unimportant. He thought he had never known two more self-satisfied extroverts. Even in the dean's office, they still reinforced each other.

"No way I flunked. I'm not worried. They can't do this."

"Right! They're just trying to put the fear of God in us." Griffin Calhoun popped Osborne in the chest with a back-handed slap. "Ain't that right, Sport?"

"I already told you guys," repeated Garrison, "it sure is working."

The door opened and Dr. Astenheimer stuck his head out. "Mr. Flemister. Would you come in, please?"

Osborne and Garrison sat silent in the waiting area, not so the other two.

"Hey, Otten, you reckon old Flemister's been getting much lately? He sure looks awful pale."

"Flemister? Hell, no. I bet he's got lace on his drawers. He's probably pale from bleeding his lizard too much."

"You think that's it, huh? What about you, Sport? You look sorta pale, too." Porter flinched and received another jocular backhand.

After a few minutes the door opened and Flemister came out. He floated trance-like across the room with eyes on distant focus, his freckles glowing like spots on a lamp shade. He looked briefly at Otten. "He said for you to come in next."

Carter Otten entered the dean's office cocksurely rolling on the balls of his feet. Calhoun chased behind the fleeing Flemister only to return in moments. "He acted like he couldn't hear me. Wouldn't even notice me. Almost like he was walking in his sleep. All he'd say was, 'This is going to kill my mother.' What the hell's going on around here, Sport? What? What? Is the whole world going to hell in a bucket? What?"

Porter evaded the backhand. "Well, I think the boys at Messina probably think so. And what's left of them in the Solomon Islands. But here at Emory I think we're just experiencing cause and effect, action and reaction."

"Osborne, I'll bet even your own family thinks you're a little weird! Haw! Ain't that right, Sport? What? What?"

They fell silent as the rumble of voices became audible from the dean's office. Calhoun tiptoed to the door to listen but returned just as cautiously to his seat.

"Can't hear a damn thing. Place too well built. Wall too thick, door too thick, drapes and rugs too thick. If the Candlers and Arkwrights and Woodruffs hadn't spent so damn much money around here, we'd be able to know what's going on in there. Haw! Have to speak to those folks about that. Ain't that right, Sport? What? What?"

Porter was so amazed at this assessment that he accepted the slap on the chest as appropriate punctuation and did not dodge it.

Otten's interview was much longer than Flemister's and was accompanied by the rise and fall of voices. Twice there was unmistakable shouting, the voice obviously Otten's but the words unintelligible. Except for an occasional "What? What?" even Calhoun fell silent. They waited.

When Otten emerged, there was no impression he was sleepwalking. He was in a fury, his black brows scowled completely together. He slammed the door to the dean's office so hard that the two Audubon prints on the solidly built walls of the waiting room tilted. He leveled a finger at Calhoun. "You're next," he snapped. "He wants you now."

Calhoun jerked his litter mate around by the arm. "I'm not going in there till you tell me what happened. What's going on?"

Otten threw off his friend's grip with a powerful twist and hissed, "It's true! It's all true!" He slammed the door to the waiting room and was gone. Calhoun stood motionless and very quiet for the briefest of moments, snapped his head erect, and marched into Dr. Astenheimer's office. It would never occur to a born and bred Methodist who had been to three schools named Emory to keep a dean waiting.

Porter looked at Garrison. "You're in the Navy."

"Looks like I'm going to be. At least sooner than I planned."

"What happened to you?"

"I'm in love with this little girl who just started school at Brenau, and I've been going to see her every weekend and just didn't study enough. If I go to midshipman's school, we may go ahead and get married when I finish."

"Be sure and ask about her clitoris first. You wouldn't want to end up with two things down in that area there six inches long."

"Osborne, you're terrible; she wouldn't know what I was talking about. I felt just real sorry for Val Harper this morning. What happened to you to get you in this room?"

Porter crossed his legs and folded his arms. "I went to a lot of movies."

The door opened and Calhoun popped out. "You're next," he snapped at Garrison. His eyes were small behind his glasses, red-rimmed and glittering. As Porter rose and approached him, he spoke rapidly. "We're gone. All five of us. You and Otten and me are ASTP and we go together. Basic training. Camp Grant. There's no mercy in that dean's heart."

"Camp Grant? Where is that?"

"I didn't know either. Illinois. Somewhere north of Chicago."

"Illinois? Chicago? I'd sooner go straight to the Solomon Islands."

"Quit being funny, Osborne. That may be exactly what we wind up doing. Medical basic training lasts three months and then we're all gone. Somewhere."

"What did you flunk?"

"I didn't flunk, goddammit. I told the dean so. What? They've kicked me out because they're mad about a nasty note I wrote that got into Mr. Enson's hands by mistake. Haw? What! He must have showed it to old Twyman. How Twyman got to Bracht I don't know. Haw? They've been after me and couldn't flunk me so now they've kicked me out. I'll fight it. So will my mama. My family knows some people. Gotta go. Better find Otten and then call my father. Take it easy, Sport."

"When do we leave?"

"This week." He slammed Porter with an open palm to the shoulder. "Haw? What?" He was gone.

Porter sat alone in the waiting room and gathered his thoughts and his feelings. His familiar wariness of new experiences emerged and he recalled his first day at Emory when he had fantasized about Old Man Kangaroo. He acknowledged dread at having to tell his parents what he had done; he had never had to face them before in significant failure. He discarded the tinge of shame, embarrassment, that he might feel in the presence of his classmates; there was no way he could explain to them what had happened inside himself. "They wouldn't believe me anyhow. Especially Masters." What he was not prepared for, particularly in contrast to the reactions of Flemister, Otten, and Calhoun, was the feeling of relief he had. No more cramming and worrying about grades. No longer did he have to make himself learn more than he wanted to know, things he didn't particularly want to know about in the first place. A great sensation of freedom came to him. Whatever was going to happen, he could handle.

As Garrison came out and motioned him without speaking into the dean's office, Porter thought his eyes looked bright with unshed tears. He shook Garrison's hand. "Let's all call Dr. Redwine," he said.

"Who is Dr. Redwine?"

"Never mind. Be happy with that sweet little girl. I'll see you after the war."

Aware as he was of the portentousness of a dean's position and the solemnity of a summons into his presence, Porter Osborne, Jr., faced Dr. Astenheimer with a surprising degree of equanimity. The dean, well into the still vigorous decade past middle age, was first and foremost a gentleman. He was tall and massive, resplendantly bald, soft-spoken, always immaculate in his choice of linen and accessories. Had he not been so huge he would, like Richard Corey, have glittered when he walked, but his hands and feet were so big, his shoulders and chest so thick, that he lumbered; and no one, thought Porter, can glitter when he lumbers. The man's eyes were embedded behind puffed cheeks and were almost obscured by the overhang of his upper lids. His clean-shaven dusky jowls had drooped to such degree that they hung like French shades below the line of his jaw. They quivered with every movement of the great head and served as velvet echo chambers when he spoke. His lips were purplish blubber and so loose that they flapped like a flat tire around the perfect phrases of his conversation. Porter considered in a ludicrous aside that the Dean of the Emory University School of Medicine looked for all the world like a dressed up bloodhound with its ears cropped.

In a flash of levity, recalling the raucous endorsement of Dr. Martell at the med school dance, he ventured an inquisitive glance at the dean's crotch, but the trousers were too tastefully tailored for confirmation. Hoping that he would retrieve intact his own puny fingers from Dr. Astenheimer's engulfing handshake, Porter raised his eyes to meet the grave, the analytical, administrative gaze.

"Have a seat, Mr. Osborne, and talk to me."

"About what, sir?"

"About yourself. About what happened to you on the Physiology final."

"Dr. Astenheimer, I hear by the grapevine that I have failed an unknown number of subjects."

"I see. What else do you hear on the grapevine?"

"I hear that there are five of us who have flunked out of school and that there's no way we can make up the failing grades and stay enrolled." He paused a moment. "I hear that the three of us who are in the Army Special Training Program will be at Camp Grant before the weekend to start medical basic training. I hear that's in Illinois."

"Grapevines are amazingly informative. Back to the Physiology final."

"Would you give me some direct information, Dr. Astenheimer? Exactly what did I flunk?"

"Mr. Osborne, you made a C on each of your Pathology courses. You made forty on the final examination in Physiology, which brought your quarter grade down to the fifties, and you have indeed failed the course. Had you made ten points higher on that final examination, you and I would not be conversing this morning. Now tell me about it."

"What about it, sir?"

"I have listened to four other students this morning, Osborne. Was the examination unduly hard?"

"Well, it obviously was for me, but if I had studied properly it wouldn't have been."

"Was it fair?"

"Of course it was fair."

Dr. Astenheimer's cheeks quivered, his words were soft, they invited confidence. "Have you felt that Dr. Twyman was vengeful or vindictive? That he was aloof, insensitive? Callous, indifferent? Shall I phrase it as a couple of your fellows have, that he didn't give a damn about his students?"

"Oh, no, sir! Dr. Twyman delivers the most well-prepared and finely-tuned lectures you ever heard in your life, Dr. Astenheimer. If he wasn't dedicated to his students and to his subjects, he sure wouldn't go to that much trouble. His lectures are gems of perfection. Why, in the sixteen years I've been going to school I've never had but one teacher who was better, and that was back in high school. Dr. Twyman was born to teach and he's one of the best things Emory has going. He's
. . ."

"That's enough, Mr. Osborne. Dr. Twyman speaks highly of you, also."

"Sir? Me?"

"I have been in conference with him for a little over an hour. Yesterday afternoon. On a Sunday, as a matter of fact. This has been an unsettling affair. He was not surprised at the other boys, he said, but you puzzled him. He thought that you would make a B the first quarter

132

and then advance to an A the second one, but then you failed the final examination and he had no choice but to record, as he said, the grade that you had made for yourself. I asked him in the light of your overall class standing and of your grades in the other two subjects if there were any way he could make an exception and keep you another quarter as a conditional student, pending satisfactory performance."

Porter was touched. "What did he say?"

The dean cleared his throat and his pendulous jaws danced like chandeliers in a mild earthquake. "He declined, and I agreed. You see, young Osborne, Dr. Twyman is a most honest man. He pointed out again that this was a grade you have made for yourself. If he relaxed his rule in your case, then in all honesty he would have to grant the same exception to any other student. Although he conceded that you are a loss, there is another boy who made exactly the same grade you did and we would have to treat him accordingly. Several on the faculty have been waiting for this boy to stub his toe; consensus is that the profession will be better cleansed of aspirants with his attitude. *Ergo*, you are out."

"Yes, sir," acknowledged Porter and rose from his chair.

"Sit back down, Mr. Osborne. You are accepting this event with a calmness, almost a tranquillity, that has been notably absent in the other four boys and truthfully, from your appearance, is the opposite of my anticipation. I am curious." He waited.

"Maybe I was better prepared for it," Porter ventured.

"You mean you expected it?"

"Dean Astenheimer, I planned it. Then I had my mind changed for me at the last minute. By a field-grade officer in the Army. I thought Physiology was going to be the easiest test and relaxed too much about studying for it. Please tell Dr. Twyman I'm sorry I let him down. If I'd known what the outcome was going to be, I'd have flunked Pathology; Dr. Bracht gives lectures like an unmade bed. Dr. Twyman did not deserve a paper like that from me."

Dean Astenheimer shot a glance at the watch fastened by a black band among the thick, shining hairs on his wrist. "Do you want to tell me about it, Porter Osborne, Jr.?"

Of a sudden, Porter decided that he did.

He aped Dr. Twyman's syntax and Dr. Thebault's affect and in concise, well-organized, dispassionate speech displayed his guts to the eyes of the dean. At the conclusion he felt that he had been as objective as Dr. Bracht when ordering the diet for his anemic brother; he might have been talking about someone else.

Dr. Astenheimer again looked at the watch, his lips flapped, his jowls shook. "Amazing. I have to run. I think you could yet become a fine physician. Although I am only the acting dean, I believe I can guarantee you a place in the sophomore class at Emory again. If you ever overcome this desire of yours for active military duty. Lots of luck, Pvt. Osborne."

Porter once again shook hands. As he crossed the waiting room, he marveled at the thickness of the dean's fingers and considered that if other appendages were similarly proportioned, Dr. Martell might well be right. "The biggest one in Atlanta? What an awesome responsibility! I'll bet he doesn't squander it on Dr. Martell. But he should; who does he know who could possibly be more appreciative?"

He put childish thoughts behind him for attention to an urgent duty. Practicing elaborate phrasing in his head, he asked the long distance operator to make his call to Porter Osborne, Sr., person-to-person and collect. When he heard his father's acknowledgment and ready acceptance, all prepared guile deserted him and he said simply, "Daddy? I flunked med school."

The pause on the line grew long enough for Porter to hear the humming of distant wires and wonder anew at electricity. The statement was adequate, all encompassing, self-explanatory. He waited.

Into his ear came the level, directive voice of his father: "Get your things packed and I'll send your mother to get you."

Despite the dismissing click, Porter held the receiver until he heard the nasal and impersonal query. "Operator. Have you finished?" Without reply, he gently hung the receiver back into its hook.

"We have set the seal of Solomon on all things
    under sun,
Of knowledge and of sorrow and endurance of
    things done."

His time at home before departure for the real Army was revealing. It was restorative. Finally, it was challenging.

Nobody cried. His mother's eyes on several occasions grew so big and shiny that he was uncomfortable; he feared the tears might come. On two mornings, as she made biscuits the tip of her patrician nose was suspiciously reddened, but neither of them commented on it. He was grateful for her final farewell. "When I married your daddy in 1917 and he left for France, your grandmother told me, 'Vera, my mother always told me and I'll pass it on to you. "Don't ever let your menfolks see you crying when they leave for war. Send them away with a smile."' Write as often as you can and remember that I love you." He was grateful, especially when he realized that he would probably never be able to appreciate fully the cost to her.

Nobody cursed. Without fanfare his father was home for supper every night and miraculously there evolved leisurely hours alone with him for wandering conversation. In the charm of that communion, Porter bit by bit was able to confide not only events but feelings. When he recounted his conversation with Maj. Teufelsdreck, his father's lips tightened noticeably, but the curses never came.

"You know, son, I've never met him, but I like that Dr. Thebault. If you see him again, tell him if he ever wants to come visit Fritz, we'll be glad to have him."

"Yes, sir, I will."

"You mustn't worry about the Krauts capturing Rome. We're coming up the coast and our boys will root them out before Christmas. With Mussolini out of office, we ought to be able to pick up some help from the Italians. They're like children but nobody likes Germans. Anywhere. The Italians sure don't like them in their country. And the Germans are so arrogant and contemptible they don't care. All they understand is cold steel."

"Yes, sir."

"You know you'll have a chance to apply for OCS if you do well in basic training, which I'm sure you will. You're almost twenty-one and I wouldn't presume to tell you what to do, but my advice would be, if you asked for it, that you'd be more content and more effective as an officer. In the meantime, I'll hang around the office late on Friday afternoons in case you get a chance to call. Make it collect."

"Yes, sir."

On the last day he was home, his mother sent him to the mailbox. "The letter carrier just ran. Would you mind?"

When he dutifully fetched her the *Atlanta Constitution* folded over a small batch of envelopes, she sorted through them swiftly. "Here's something for you. Forwarded from the Emory Post Office."

It was an off-white missive, a little broader than an index card. The return address was the first thing that caught his attention. "What in the world," he said aloud, "is Stalag XIV?"

Incredulously, he read.

"Here I am—high and dry and out of it but at
least safe and sound. Forever. Or certainly till it's all over.

You can send packages to me through the Red Cross. Everybody here says we will need warm clothes, but I would appreciate food. Since you are studying to be a doctor, have you ever heard of anybody having constipated diarrhea? Send food. Also, write!

Fraternally,
Deacon."

"My God!" exclaimed Porter.

"Don't swear, Son," admonished his mother.

"I wasn't," he assured her. "I'll be back before dinner, but I'm going to take Fritz and let him run the Big Red Hill while I think about the definition of irony."

"Irony?"

"Yes, ma'am. And also the real meaning of the old phrase, 'a day late and a dollar short.'"

The next day when he bid his father farewell, there was the exchange of an unusually strong handshake, a long look.

"IFMS."

"Sir?"

"IFMS. When you called me from Emory you said, 'I Flunked Med School.' Some day I hope I'll lift that phone off its hook and hear you say, 'I Found My Self.'"

"Yes, sir. Good-bye, Dad."

From Fort McPherson, Osborne and Calhoun and Otten were delivered, orders in hand, to the Southern Railway Station across Mitchell Street from Rich's. They had tickets for Chicago and Rockford, Illinois. They had vouchers for berths in the Pullman car and meals in the diner. Train travel was a new and novel experience for Porter, and despite the timing he was thrilled. As he struggled to follow Calhoun and Otten aboard, dragging his stiff new duffel bag, he spied a familiar figure with controlled and rolling gait.

"Dr. Thebault! What are you doing here?"

Above the panting, waiting chug of the locomotive, the hiss of escaping steam, the cries of the Red Caps and the cacophony of train-side farewells, the professor was forced to raise his voice, but he opened his lips no wider than usual.

"I was in the neighborhood, Porter, and thought I'd drop by."

Porter considered the time of day, the distance to Emory, and laughed. "Thanks for coming. For 'dropping by.'"

"I had to. I had to see you get on the train and say, 'Look at that magnificent son of a bitch go.'"

Without another word he turned on his heel and was gone.

Porter stooped again to his duffel. "Dr. Thebault called me Porter for the first time."

*"In that enormous silence, tiny and unafraid,
Comes up along a winding road the noise of
the Crusade."*

15 **P**orter Osborne assured himself that he was embarking upon the great adventure of his life. By his own volition, he was going to make an impact in the great war to protect and restore freedom. He ignored his father's assessment that he was acting like a horse that had got the bit between its teeth, its tail over the dashboard, and was running away with the buggy. He was proving to the world that he was no shirker, no coward, that he could put selfish ambitions aside in favor of the common purpose. In his mind, it was not just that someone had to do it; it boiled down to the fact that everyone must do it. *E Pluribus Unum*. If one did not sacrifice some portion of self in this effort, one became only an *Unum*, and it was *Pluribus* that would win this war. He finally felt that he belonged in khaki. He looked forward with eagerness to Camp Grant.

At the same time he acknowledged that in his present circumstances he often felt adrift on a mysterious sea, carried on a tide over which he had no control, forced frequently to tread water, struggling to keep his head above strange currents. Lacking these feelings of insecurity, there would have been no rationale whatever for the friendship and eventual affection that developed between him and Otten and Calhoun. Porter was possessed of enough insight to recognize this and enough candor to refer to the other two as his personal Flotsam and Jetsam. Therefore he clung to them.

On the train from Atlanta to Chicago he discovered just how different they were from him. Sometimes in trivial ways, sometimes in important ways, but frequently different. The identity of a Southern farm boy raised with a grandmother in residence is so positively established that it never occurred to Porter that they might think he was different from them.

"Osborne, you got on last so you have to sit there and ride

backwards. Early bird gets the worm. What? What?"

"Osborne, don't drag that damn duffel bag in here. Leave it in the vestibule and the porter will store it. Our seats are together and we've/got to ride all the way to Illinois, so for God's sake close your mouth and quit staring around like some hick. Ain't you ever been on a train before?"

"As a matter of fact, no. I've heard about troop trains, but they're sending us off in really fine style. I wonder how much this is costing the government. And we're going to ride it all the way to Chicago, Illinois, too."

"For God's sake, Osborne, what does it matter? We've got a Pullman and vouchers for the dining car and the works. We deserve it. And don't say 'Chicago.' I've been talking to some sophisticated people and everybody who lives there and knows bat shit says 'Chio.' Look what's coming down the aisle! Quick, Calhoun, move over there by Osborne so she'll have to sit by me."

As Calhoun automatically obeyed, Porter twisted his head around to observe a smartly attired vision of loveliness looking at her ticket and following the porter.

"Osborne, quit staring and act nonchalant, goddammit. You and Calhoun keep quiet and let me do the talking. You don't know how to talk to sophisticated looking broads. With a little luck, I may get me some company in my bed tonight."

"That's no broad, Otten, that's a lady."

"What do you know, Osborne? They're all sisters under the skin. You haven't learned yet that there's no difference between the colonel's lady and Judy O'Grady. Watch this old pro work. I've been around and I know how to talk to northerners."

"You like Kipling, Otten? I could recite some poetry for her if you want me to."

"You do," Otten hissed, "and I'll break every bone in your back and throw you off this train. Keep quiet and leave this up to me."

Calhoun flashed a grin and pushed his glasses firmly between his brows with a rigid finger. "Hell, Otten, she's at least twenty-six or twenty-seven years old. She's not going to give you the time of day. What? Ain't that right, Sport?"

Porter flinched as Calhoun's backhand caught him in the chest.

Otten's confidence did not falter. "I get along fine with older women. All cats are gray in the dark, you know. Just sit back and follow my lead."

The unsuspecting object of this pre-planned stalking game gave no more than a cursory glance at the three PFC's as she settled into her seat and opened an exclusive magazine. While the train rattled and puffed its way through the maze of tracks that had made Atlanta great, Otten studied her lovely profile and made desultory, beautifully enunciated conversation with his comrades, obviously intended for the ears of his seat companion. Porter wondered if Otten had read *Aeneas Africanus* but decided had he done so his questions would have been more subtle.

"Calhoun, you know what's right over there behind those trees, don't you? West Paces Ferry Road. I'm sure of it." He turned his head and spoke confidentially. "That's the most prestigious street in Atlanta; you wouldn't believe the mansions and the estates."

The lady did not lower her magazine; she acknowledged the intrusion only by a fleeting elevation of her brows and a decidedly disinterested smile.

"Hey, Calhoun, remember the party old Milly Woodall threw at her house the night before her debut?" Again the turn of the head to impel attention. "Her father's Georgia Power and her mother's Coca-Cola."

Again the fleeting lift of the lids in almost imperceptible acknowledgment.

Calhoun joined in. "Yeah, I guess that's the fanciest party I ever went to. Her old man had hired Glen Miller's band but then had to settle for Dean Hudson at the last minute. Party must have cost a fortune, what? Ain't that right, Sport?" He scaled down to a nudge in Porter's short ribs.

"I don't know," said Porter. "I've never been on West Paces Ferry and I've never even seen a debutante that I know of."

"He's not from Atlanta," Otten explained. "Lives way out in the country." The eyes above the magazine leveled for a moment on Porter and returned to reading. "Calhoun, remember ole Tikey Mullins that night? First time he'd ever worn tails and he knocked that Wedgewood vase off the table onto the marble floor. Told Mrs. Woodall he'd replace it at Rich's and then nearly died when she told him he couldn't, that she'd bought it in England forty-five years before on her honeymoon but for him not to worry, she'd been meaning to take it down to the High Museum and leave it with them anyway; it didn't really belong in a house."

"Yeah, that's why he got so drunk and offered to drop out of Chi Phi," contributed Calhoun.

"It may be different where you went to school, but Chi Phi's the most prestigious fraternity on our campus," Otten confided. Porter watched in amazement as he actually batted his eyes at the reluctant young woman.

Calhoun was warming to this subject. "Then remember when the band played the flourish to get everybody quiet and Mr. Woodall waited for everybody to get champagne? And when we drank the toast old Tikey smashed his glass into the back of the fireplace and it turned out to be Fostoria crystal?"

"I thought it was Waterford."

Porter could stand it no longer. "And there were ten fountains in the front yard and twenty-four peacocks on the lawn and forty black slaves just to wait on Milly and her mama."

"Shut up, Osborne. You already said you weren't there." Calhoun raised a hand threateningly. "Old Tikey was so embarrassed then that he got drunker than ever, and when we were dragging him up the steps of the Chi Phi House he even offered to drop out of Emory. What? Remember that, Sport?"

"That's our school," Otten confided into the profile.

The female target sighed and closed her magazine. "You three boys are from Emory?"

"I'm not," said Porter. "I'm from Willingham. I just went to Emory to medical school. It's not the same thing."

"Oh? All three of you are in medical school?"

"Yes. That's where we met Porter Osborne over there. That's Griffin Calhoun sitting next to him. He and I have known each other all our lives. My name, by the way, is Carter Otten, and we're mighty pleased to be traveling with you." His black eyes snapped and sparkled. "It's a long way to Chio. We'll probably be good friends by the time we get there."

"It's not that far; we'll be there right after breakfast tomorrow. What year are you in medical school? Surely, you're too young to have finished."

"That's right. We're in the middle of our sophomore year." Otten's voice was smooth.

"Were," amended Porter.

The lovely lady raised her brows. "I beg your pardon?"

"We were in medical school. We're not any more."

Carter Otten's speech became faster, tenser. He glared at Porter. "We've had a temporary change in career direction. We're taking a sabbatical from academic work and going to Camp Grant for basic training. After that we'll go on active duty until the war is over."

"A sabbatical? In the middle of your sophomore year? That's strange."

"We flunked out," volunteered Porter helpfully.

"Oh," she said. There was the slightest hint of question in the word.

Otten's face became considerably duskier, his neck veins were noticeably distended. He's got beautiful external jugulars, thought Porter.

"No such thing," Otten snapped. "We were kicked out." He turned in his seat and addressed the lady directly.

"We've been most unfairly singled out and mistreated. They didn't like our attitude, they said. I'm too arrogant and cocky and Calhoun over there's too happy-go-lucky, and they kicked us out of medical school as an example to the rest of the class. So they could maintain their death grip of fear on the other boys and keep them so paranoid they're afraid of their own shadows and make them keep on conforming and knuckling under to everybody. Griffin Calhoun's mother was a Cunningham and knows everybody on the north side of Atlanta. She went and talked to her friends and they all admitted that the faculty at Emory is rotten and needs shaking up and that we got a raw deal. She was pulling strings and even twisting arms to get us reinstated, but we were already in uniform and the major in charge shipped us off before we could get a fair investigation. He absolutely refused to discuss it with Griffin's mother. Even when she let him know she used to be a Cunningham and was kin to Richard Russell by blood and Walter George by marriage."

He turned and faced Porter. "We were kicked out! Don't you ever let me hear you tell anybody else we flunked out. You hear me?"

Even in the storm of that unexpected tirade, truth and logic prevailed over caution. Porter looked straight at the lovely lady. "They may have been kicked out but I flunked out. I made an F in Physiology. If they were kicked out it was because their grades were lower than mine. The dean told me so."

Calhoun's backhand caught him so forcefully in the chest that it knocked the breath from him. "You're lying. We were kicked out." He grabbed Porter's arm and twisted it. "Ain't that right, Sport? What? You heard Otten. We were kicked out." He grinned gleefully in Porter's face and twisted harder.

Porter managed to jerk his arm loose. "Whatever makes you feel better, Griffin. I flunked."

The catalyst in the reaction rose and reached directly above Otten to get her purse. The train swayed into a curve, the feminine outline became taut, balancing, most beautifully alluring. The clack of the train was as forceful as Porter's pulse in his ears.

"I think I'll walk down to the club car and stretch a little," she said.

"I'll just go with you," said Otten. "A young girl who is so obviously a lady shouldn't go around unescorted on the way to Chio."

"Come along, then." She moved into the aisle. "But, please . . . Chicago is my home and only gangsters and other hoodlums say 'Chio.' Would you mind?" She turned to Porter. "Watch my coat?" Smoothly but unmistakably she winked at him.

"Griffin," said Porter as Otten hovered his prey down the car, "why didn't you go with them?"

"Don't ever mess with Carter Otten and his women, Osborne. I learned that in high school. If there are two of them along, you can have what's left after he's had his pick, but if there's only one he'll kill. It's what you might call an obsession with him, Sport. Carter's a lot of fun when it's just the fellows. Plays ball, drinks beer, cuts up with everybody, what? He can make a dog laugh. But let some girls come around and he changes before you can bat your eye. Knocks himself out to impress them. He's good at it, too. He likes women and nearly all women like him. What? Most of them fall under his spell right away, especially when he points them like a bird dog and starts batting his eyes at them. If one doesn't, or if one plays hard to get, that nearly drives him crazy and he goes on the prowl like you wouldn't believe. What? What?"

"Otten's got acne scars and his nose goes to hell right on the end, gets flat and pointed at the same time sort of like a mole's snout. He's really not all that good looking."

"Osborne, you know that and I know that and I think Carter may know that, but if you've got the sense God gave a nanny goat, you won't ever tell him so. I'd hate to be wiping what's left of you up off the floor. What? You understand, Sport?"

"I'm going to the restroom. Watch the lady's coat till I get back, will you? I don't believe Otten's going to shoot from taw this time."

Calhoun swung his knees into the aisle and then gave Porter a vicious goose as he stepped over. He cackled loudly when Porter jumped. "Mole's snout? Mole's snout? By God, it does look like a mole's snout. Osborne, did anybody ever tell you you're weird?"

"Now and then, Calhoun. So are you. And so is your litter mate."

In the restroom as he stood wide-spraddled and bent-kneed for balance, determined that he would hit his target neatly, cognizant of the louder sounds of the train wheels coming up through the toilet, Porter appraised his companions. "Maybe they are weird, but so far they're all I've got. I might have to depend on them to save my life from the Japs some day." He rolled with the unanticipated sway of the train but managed to maintain his stream acceptably close to dead center. "On the other hand, they may have to depend on me about the Japs, too."

When he shook himself, he forgave an uncontrolled drop that bounced over the edge as the wheels accommodated a rough joint of track with a definite lurch. All in all he thought his first experience in a moving toilet a competent performance, much easier than the back of an empty wagon when the mules were trotting. He buttoned his fly, washed his hands, and concluded, "I sure hope they teach all of us a lot at Camp Grant, Illinois. Those Japs are hell."

Returning to his seat, he found a glowering Otten and an attentive Calhoun.

". . . and she turned out to be engaged. To some first lieutenant in Artillery and she'd been down to visit him at Benning. That's OK. I've had some sweet times before with an engagement ring at the back of my neck, and say what you will, she's a damn good-looking gal. I think I was really about to make a little time with her, and then you won't believe what happened!"

"You said 'Chio' again and she sent you to the blackboard," Porter said.

"Shut up, Osborne."

"You called her a broad, and she sent you to the office."

"For God's sake, Osborne, will you shut up? This major walked in and came over to our table like he owned the train. 'I'm Maj. Malone,' he says to her. 'Mind if I join you?' He acted like I wasn't even there. Then she, like a proper lady should, says, 'Major, this is Pvt. Otten,' and I, like a proper gentleman should, stood up, held out my hand, and said, 'Pleased to meet you, sir.' And do you know what that base-on-balls, three-strikes-you're-out son of a bitch did?"

"He asked if you were one of the DeKalb County Ottens who went to debutante balls at the Piedmont Driving Club and who was your mother before she married," intervened Porter with glee.

"Osborne, I'm going to kill you and throw you off this train if you open your mouth again."

"Me, too, Sport. I'll help him."

"Well, Otten asked."

"Ain't you ever heard of a goddam rhetorical question? That major looked down at my hand like it was something dirty and then looked me in the eye and says, 'Didn't you know this car is off limits to enlisted men, soldier?' That pompous bastard refused to shake hands with me. Me! Can you imagine that? There was nothing to do but start a fight or leave, so I says to Sybil, 'Are you coming?' and she says, 'No, I think I'll stay awhile. You run along and tell your friends I'll see all of you later.' She went for the brass, she did; she was dazzled by rank! I'm twice the man that pussel-gutted shit-ass of a major is, but she didn't grab the chance to find out!"

"Is Sybil the colonel's lady or Judy O'Grady, Carter?"

"She's a pluperfect, ice-blooded, Yankee bitch," snarled Otten. "Let's go eat. To hell with her."

"What about her coat?" Porter asked. "I promised I'd watch her coat."

"Well, watch it then!" snapped Otten. He grabbed the garment out of the rack, dragged it up the aisle by one sleeve, and flung it through the door of the toilet as he passed on his way to the dining car. "She wants to take up with majors, she can hire herself a butler. Y'all coming?"

"Mighty right," grinned Calhoun. "I'm hungry. She can't treat us like that. Let her hire herself a butler. Ain't that right, Sport?"

Trailing the two, Porter stepped into the toilet, retrieved the coat, and tried to smooth the fur before folding it neatly on the lady's seat. "So her name is Sybil," he thought. "That's appropriate." He started to sit down but then considered that he had never been in a dining car and might not know how to comport himself. He shrugged. "Otten's right, I'm no butler. I wonder if that coat is mink." On his way to join Flotsam and Jetsam, when he crossed the deafening, windy coupling between cars, he said aloud into the clack and rush, "This is going to be an interesting war."

He was glad he had not ventured alone into the dining car. It was easily one of the most elegant environments he had ever seen and he felt almost intimidated by the combination of thick carpet with rich linen. The tables were bedecked with crystal and silver and twinkled in replication of themselves through the dwindling perspective of the length of the car. Warm mahogany paneling covered the ceiling, framed the windows with their ever-changing diorama, and reflected in calming sheen the cocoon that it encompassed. Porter was entranced.

A man came up to him and Porter could not help gaping. He was tall and spare, his hair not nearly so closely clipped as was the fashion in Georgia, definitely woolly and flecked with gray. His face was black and shone as resplendantly as his shoes. His white coat was tailored to him alone, his black trousers had a black satin stripe down each leg, and he bore himself with such assurance that Porter imagined he owned this restaurant, that indeed he might own the entire train. Even in north Atlanta he had never encountered such a personage. He tried to envision him behind a mule, buck dancing for the girls, drunk on Saturday night, eating mullet, starkly stiff in Anatomy lab; he failed on all counts.

When the man inclined his head with exquisitely formal dignity and inquired in beautiful English if the gentleman were dining alone, Porter could not repress the impulsive question. "I bet you never picked a single boll of cotton in your whole life, did you?"

The man paused a moment, recognized the sincerity in Porter's voice, and smiled. "I picked a million pounds of it and plowed ten thousand miles of long straight cotton rows in Mississippi farm land before I was sixteen. And that is the main reason I am where I am today."

"I don't believe a word of it," said Porter.

"It takes fourteen to fifteen hundred pounds weighed up on steelyards in the field to make a five- to six-hundred pound bale. And the ginman takes a toll out of the seed to grind you a few sacks of meal and hulls to feed an old skinny milk cow that has woofs in her back. Now do you believe me, soldier?"

"I do. I know about it, too. And in all honesty that may well be one of the main reasons I am where I am today."

As the man resumed his professional detachment and turned to lead his guest down the car, Porter said to the sculptured back, "But it sure has been a winding road."

When his host made no reply, Porter persisted, "It's not been easy. You know that, don't you?"

146

The man pulled out the chair across from Calhoun. "Indeed, I do. Lots of luck." Otten and Calhoun looked up. "To all of you," he said, and moved on.

To his surprise, Porter found his companions in such a jocular condition they were almost silly. "What are you laughing at? What's funny?"

Calhoun restored his glasses to the bridge of his nose with a jabbing finger, his voice bubbled. "Otten here was raising hell about that officer upstaging him back in the club car and said he hated all the majors in the United States Army. Then all of a sudden he busted out laughing and told me something that got me started. That's the way Otten is, mad enough to kill one minute and then sees something funny and everything blows over. Ain't that right, Sport?" He gave his friend a rabbit punch on the shoulder hard enough to jostle the table and shake a little water out of the glasses. "Oops. 'Bout to make a mess there, what? Tell Osborne what you were telling me, Carter."

Otten leaned across the table toward Porter, who noted that he had once more been maneuvered into riding backwards on this train. He didn't care. He gazed at the transformed Carter Otten who was beaming, poised, confidingly inclusive, his black eyes sparkling. Could this possibly be the same person who minutes before, in petulant tantrum, had snatched a fur coat across the floor and flung it into a public toilet?

"Close your mouth before I tell you a damn thing, Osborne. You look retarded."

"Naw, he doesn't. You see those big ole bug eyes with the blood vessels running all over them, don't you? He looks like Vitamin Flintheart in Dick Tracy. Haw! What? Ain't that right? Old Vitamin himself."

"Shut up, Calhoun. Osborne, I was blowing my stack when we first sat down and I did say I hated all majors everywhere, and then I got to thinking about Old Tootenpoot back at Emory and realized I'd forgotten to tell Calhoun what I heard about him just this morning."

"You mean Maj. Teufelsdreck?"

"That's right, I mean old Stiffneck Limberdick Tootenpoot. Quit interrupting and listen to this. His secretary told me about this when I ran into her on my way to the terminal. I'd buttered her up last week when I had to wait to see the goddam major, and if I were still going to be in Atlanta, I think I could make that. I can tell she's got the hots for me."

"You went to see the major? What for?"

"Because I thought I'd give it a last try to keep us in school. Calhoun's mama had talked to her Emory connections and they'd all told her they couldn't help unless the major waived our Army commitment. She'd been to see him and all she got was a lecture about pampered playboys born with silver spoons in their mouths, and she'd given him a piece of her mind before she left. Your old man had been to see him, too, and that didn't do any good. I sure didn't do any good. He wouldn't even let me sit down and didn't listen to a word I said. I hate his guts."

"My father hasn't been to see Maj. Tootenpoot," said Porter.

"The secretary said he had. How many Porter Osbornes are there in the state of Georgia? She said he was red in the face when he left, too."

"Shut up, Vitamin," interposed Calhoun, "and listen to what's coming next."

"She told me all hell broke loose yesterday. You know that big yellow Packard the major drives? It's his pride and joy; he keeps it shined and polished and is as proud of it as a little nigger is of a big navel. Well, yesterday afternoon it stalled on him right in the middle of the intersection at Ponce de Leon and Briarcliff. It just died. He raised the hood to check it out and developed the biggest traffic jam you ever saw. About the time a policeman showed up to help, here came an Army convoy of at least a hundred trucks and Jeeps up Ponce de Leon, and the officer in charge chewed old Pootentoot's ass out right there in front of everybody, yelled and hollered and pointed a riding crop right at his nose."

"Good!" expostulated Porter. "Sauce for the goose!"

"Shut up, Vitamin. You ain't heard nothing yet. Go on, Otten."

"He got some soldiers to push the Packard into the driveway of that chiropractor on the corner and everything finally cleared out, convoy and all. Pootentoot had to get somebody to tow his Packard. It was dead as a doornail. And guess what? It's going to stay that way. Somebody had put sugar in his gas tank and the whole motor's frozen solid. He didn't have but ten thousand miles on it, but that car's dead and gone forever."

Calhoun gave a chortle. "And he'll play hell getting another car of any sort now. At least till the war is over. What? Ain't that right, Sport?"

"I didn't know sugar would do that," said Porter. "Who in the world you reckon did it?"

"The secretary accused me of it," replied Otten, "or at least of having it done by a cousin or somebody. Said she saw an old pickup without any front fenders and a homemade wooden body painted bright blue parked across from the Packard when she came back from lunch. A white-headed old man was walking across the parking lot toward it. He had on overalls and a wool hat, she said, and hadn't shaved in a week. He was toting a square gallon can, and when she spoke, he tipped his hat and she couldn't help noticing that he didn't have but one finger on his left hand and no right eye at all, just an empty socket. Said he gave her the creeps. I asked her what the hell I'd ever done that made her think I'd have kinfolks that looked like that, and she laughed and backed off. He's the only stranger anybody noticed all day, so Pootentoot figures he's the sinner."

"He sounds very distinctive," said Porter.

"Haw! I wish I could have seen old Pootentoot when that colonel got ahold of him on Ponce de Leon. I'd have asked him if I could loan him my silver spoon to dig that riding crop out of his ass. Serves him right. What goes around comes around; ain't that right, Sport?"

Porter Osborne, Jr., was thinking hard. Ax-handle Chambers was a white-haired, one-eyed bootlegger from the Crossroads Community back home. He had lost three fingers in a sawmill years before and been forced to take up bootlegging to make a living for his sprawling family. He drove a battered blue pickup and always voted for Porter's father. The senior Osborne used his legal skills to keep Ax-handle off the chain gang, and Ax-handle in turn kept the senior Osborne retained with a generous supply of his better runs. The two men were close. The caprice of coincidence could not possibly be great enough to accommodate Ax-handle Chambers having a double.

Porter mechanically forced a laugh. "I can sure sympathize with your dislike for majors, Carter."

"Well, I'm glad to see you agree with me about something. We need some more ice tea. Hey, Boy!"

"Otten," remonstrated Porter, "that man is not a boy. I don't think he would appreciate you calling him that."

"Pipe down, Osborne. What the hell do you know? 'Boy' is a little like saying *garçon* in France; you're supposed to say it. It's a salutation denoting position, not a damn chronological pigeon hole."

"I don't know," persisted Porter. "That's the most impressive black man I ever saw, and I've seen lots more of them than you ever have. It just doesn't seem right to call him 'Boy.'"

"Well, Mister Raised-in-the-country-with-black-folks, what would you call him? If you didn't know his first name?"

Porter regarded the tall figure directing a couple of waiters in the center of the car and reached back into his experience for an honest answer. "My father and grandfather would call him 'Big'un,'" he said.

Calhoun guffawed. Otten leaped on the tiny tone of misgiving in Porter's assertion. "They'd play hell with the music world, too. Can you imagine singing, 'Pardon me, Big'un, is that the Chattanooga choo-choo on track twenty-nine? Well, say, Big'un, you can give me a shine'?"

He caught the maitre'd's eye and unobtrusively half raised his glass. "He really is smooth," thought Porter. A waiter appeared quickly and replenished their glasses. Later the dignified supervisor paused at their table.

"Is everything all right? Fine. You three soldiers are traveling together and seem to know each other well. What is your destination?"

"We're going to Camp Grant in Rockford, Illinois," said Otten. "The meal is excellent and so is the service. You're to be congratulated."

"Thank you. Where did you have your basic training?"

"We're going there for that."

"I see." The man paused. "But all three of you already have a PFC stripe. How did that happen?"

"We were sworn in under the ASTP program and have been two years at Emory University School of Medicine. They take everybody in as a PFC."

"That's interesting. I thought medical school took four years. One of my sons is at Howard University but they have not been approved yet by the military. What happened to you three?"

"To tell you the truth," Otten snapped, "we got kicked out."

"To tell you the truth," Porter remonstrated, "we flunked out." He looked over at Otten who was scowling, flexing his shoulders and threatening to rise from his chair. "But as soon as this war is over we're all three going back to med school." He glanced at Calhoun and added mockingly, "Ain't that right, Sport?"

The tall attendant inclined his head. "I see." He looked at Porter's two companions, both of whom were glaring at Porter. He addressed Porter individually as he departed. "You still have a winding road ahead of you."

"Osborne, haven't I already told you I was going to kill you if you didn't quit saying we flunked out?"

"Yeah, Vitamin Flintheart, you'd better pay attention. You know and I know that Otten won't actually kill you, what? But I promise you this: Every time you say it, I'm going to thump you when you're not looking till you're black and blue, and you and I both know that's the God's truth. Ain't that right? You hear me? You got that?"

"Well, I'll strike a deal with you fellows. If you'll quit saying we got kicked out, I'll quit saying we flunked out."

As Porter lay sequestered behind the curtains in the swaying upper berth that night, his thoughts raced just ahead of sleep.

Sybil's berth was empty. Her coat and magazine were gone when they returned from the diner. Her major must have had more on the ball than old Tootenpoot. Otten was really a smart fellow, intellectually quick and funny. At times. Calhoun was a threat and he had sore spots to prove it. He needed to call his daddy and find out if Ax-handle had really used sugar when it was so rigidly rationed. If he was carrying a gallon can, it probably contained syrup. He was going farther from home every minute. The rhythm of the wheels and the rocking of the car lulled him sound asleep.

*"Strong gongs groaning as the guns boom far,
Don John of Austria is going to the war. . ."*

16 **i**llinois, when he had the opportunity to look at it, amazed Porter. The juggernaut of a prehistoric glacier had advanced relentlessly across this land and leveled it, grinding down its rocks and hills into a billowing quilt. Then, in irresistible and gradual retreat, it had turned around and on its way back smoothed the soil, creating a seedbed that made Yankees out of the people who settled and farmed it.

The trees were nearly all hardwood and gripped the earth, he thought, as though bred to resist the glacier's eventual return. Their trunks were stocky and squat, their bark thick and tight, their branches foreshortened like the arms of dwarves. They were cautious cousins to the profligate Georgia oaks he knew that nourished themselves with abandon and sprawled their branches carelessly in whatever direction they chose. Porter thought the trees in Illinois looked as regimented and artificial as those in a third-grade sand box. No curve, no swell of voluptuous hill, interrupted the progress of the roads through this country. They met and crossed each other in rigidly accurate right angles and then proceeded over lonely miles to form identical squares all across the state of Illinois until it probably looked like a giant checker board. The fields were flat as far as his eye could see, lacking the grace of curving terraces, their rows laid off in straight lines that converged only at the horizon. He reflected how monotonous it would be to plow them.

The soil was unlike any Porter had ever seen, uniformly deep and black and fallow; no glint of ochre or red; no sand nor clay anywhere that he could discern; no rocks to impede a plow. He fancied that could his grandfather have seen this dirt, he would have proclaimed it "as black as Essie's butt." In all probability, he would then have added that it was "rich as six inches up a bull's ass." Porter could envision corn or wheat that would yield a hundred bushels an acre and cotton, could the land be shifted six hundred miles south, that would easily come to a bale or two per acre. But there was a brooding in the vastness of Illinois, a precision of placement and line, that made him feel heavy and earth locked. He could not imagine black folks tilling and hoeing and gathering in this black richness. This was land for white people, for calculating eyes, for tenacity pared down to bones and tendons; land for people inured to weather and contemptuous of glaciers. Porter could sense no singing in these fields, no matter how bountiful the harvest. This was truly the land of Yankees, and Porter felt alien, distrustful.

Reaching for the comfort of poetry, the only fragment he could recall about Illinois was

"When the Norn Mother saw the Hurricane Hour
Greatening and darkening as it hurried on,
She left the Heaven of Heroes and came down . . ."

He rejected it. He was homesick before the train even got to Rockford. He resolved to be guarded and restrained and efficient, an example of earnest dedication, the best basic trainee who ever spent three months in Camp Grant, and he resolved to "get the hell out of Illinois." Flotsam and Jetsam looked dear to him; at least they too knew about the red and rolling hills of Georgia. He could turn to them and they would be his comfort in this environment.

"How come you let them give you that overseas cap, Vitamin? It's two damn sizes too big for you, what? What! Look at him, Otten, it comes almost down to his ears like a damn country hay-seed hick. Ain't that right, what?" A rabbit punch to the shoulder almost made Porter drop his load of newly issued winter clothes. "Get your ass back to the supply room and make them give you another cap. That one's so big and loose it almost covers up those big old Flintheart eyes. Haw! Look! Makes his eyes look like two blubbers in a piss pot. Give us some Shakespeare on the subject, Vitamin. How 'bout that? Ain't that right, Sport?"

Porter assessed Calhoun as a comforter in whom it would be imprudent to confide. Anyone who blustered and guffawed that loudly, he decided, wouldn't recognize homesickness unless it was introduced to him in a tuxedo at the Piedmont Driving Club. Forget Flotsam.

Otten was worse. "Hey fellows, look at old Osborne headed for the showers. You ever see legs like that on anybody before? They're living proof you don't have to have muscles to stand up and walk. They look like two hemp ropes with knots tied in the middle. Hey, Osborne! I admire you; did you know that? It takes raw red courage and blind faith to get up and walk around on those things."

Any confidence entrusted to Otten would probably be broadcast in derision across the barracks for the entertainment of all. Ignore Jetsam. If he will let you. Tread water and keep your nose above the tide. Alone. In only three months you can transfer to the paratroopers.

Porter's storehouse of experience became crammed to overflowing. Camp Grant, near Rockford, Illinois, was anchored on a deep pan of alluvium between the Kishwaukee and Rock rivers and was there for the express purpose of making soldiers and, by inference, men out of the conglomerate of boys gathered in from the far reaches of the United States. It was a specialized facility; it provided Medical Basic Training, and the implication hovered like miasma that its soldiers were somehow not quite good enough for Infantry Basic Training, which preceded transfers to the Artillery, Air Corps, Ordnance, or Air Borne branches of the service. This feeling came from the complete absence of any instruction whatever about firearms. The medics were not even allowed to touch a rifle. Their mission was to save life and limb, not demolish them.

The barracks that housed the initiates were rectangles made of wood and dotted over the prairie in seemingly endless repetition. They were two-story buildings with a balcony on the end to serve as a fire escape and a narrow shed roof between the upper and lower story windows. Porter quickly learned how to live in his barracks and accommodate its depersonalizing lack of privacy. He discovered that what he had known in civilian life as a bathroom had now become a latrine and lay just to the left of the stairs as one entered the building. It contained a row of commodes sitting without partitions across from a line of lavatories beneath stainless steel mirrors. The shower heads were at the end farthest from the door and protruded starkly from the wall without curtain or shielding screen. The floor was covered with segmented platforms called duckboards; at the door and again in front of the showers there was a galvanized pan of purple solution into which one must step before and after bathing. Athlete's foot was the scourge of military existence, and use of the foot baths was mandatory. Every morning after rush hour, a duo of trainees had to scrub the toilets and lavatories, polish the mirrors, take the duckboards outside for scrubbing and rinsing, and mop the floor underneath. Then they refilled the foot tubs with the potassium permanganate solution. If it chanced that no one needed punishing on any particular day, the latrine orderlies were designated at random and at the whim of the first sergeant.

On the door of the latrine was a poster of Uncle Sam with a cautionary shushing forefinger held across his mouth and the warning that a slip of the lip might sink a ship. Porter could not imagine information of that importance being available to Camp Grant trainees but daily assured Uncle Sam that he would be discreet.

Facing the door on the wall between the mirrors was another poster, the portrait of a young girl with smiling blue eyes and soft brown hair. Her head was tilted winsomely, the better to show the sheen of that hair. She displayed the patrician features and tasteful makeup of a lady and looked like the sister of somebody's best friend or at the very least a Phi Mu from Willingham. Across her chest in lurid letters that made the brand on Hester Prynne seem decorous was the alarming caption, "She may look clean, but— — —!" Underneath, in the corner, red capital letters adjured, "Remember V.D." Below that lovely likeness and above a laden tray, a typed list of explicit instructions delineated prophylactic steps to follow in the event one suffered a V.D. memory lapse. As soon as Porter studied that list and the contents of the tray and realized that it involved injecting pungent reddish-brown argyrol into one's own bladder through what he had heretofore regarded as the inviolate entrance to it, he vowed total continence while in this foreign land. He would brush his teeth, shave, urinate, shower, and soak his feet purple, all in the presence of such multitudes that nudity became impersonal, but he would never, ever sink to the level of needing the contents of that tray. Athlete's foot, maybe; V.D., no. Porter learned about latrines quickly.

He also learned that the outspoken and directive Carter Otten was occasionally incorrect in his opinionated pronouncements, the satisfaction of such occasions mitigated by awareness that Otten's way would have been better. On the trip from Chicago to Rockford, he had instructed them. "Y'all might as well be prepared that we'll live our lives at the direction of the bugler. You learn to do everything by the numbers in basic training, and you do it together and there's a different bugle call for everything. 'Reveille' wakes you up and 'Taps' puts you to sleep, and in between they have all sorts of calls for every activity you can imagine."

"Like what?"

"Like meals, retreat, assembly, everything. You've heard 'He's the boogie-woogie bugle boy from Company B,' haven't you? Well, he'll be one of the most important people in our lives for the next three months."

"I'm tone deaf and can't carry a tune in a bucket; you'll have to tell me what the bugle calls mean."

"Hell, Osborne, everybody recognizes 'Taps.' Just remember that 'Reveille' is the first thing you hear every morning. Mess call sounds like 'soupie, soupie, soupie,' and 'Assembly' goes 'There's a soldier in the grass with a bullet up his ass; take it out, Uncle Sam, take it out.' There's a bunch more; as soon as I learn 'em I'll pass 'em on."

"Thanks."

Otten was wrong. The recruits lived their lives by the whistles of sergeants, the bugles at Camp Grant being as distant as bird song and by comparison just as lovely. Those whistles were blown insistently at the whim of whichever sergeant was in charge at any given moment. There were many sergeants and many whistles, but the toughest, meanest, most powerful sergeant in the world was the Master Sergeant of their company. He lived like a troll in a room by himself at the very back of the barracks. The room was off-limits to recruits, spare as a monk's cell, its bed made with blanket as taut as a drum, an inviolable Spartan and holy place. From there the sergeant could bounce forth at any moment, whistle shrilling, shouting orders. Even his whistle seemed more authoritative than that of lesser noncommissioned officers. It looked to be an ordinary heavy-duty chromium-plated whistle, and it hung around the sergeant's neck as constantly as his dog tags. It had a sound, however, unlike any other, and its master was a virtuoso. The whistle could summon or dismiss, direct, alarm, curse, and on rare occasions even purr. Its sound was everywhere and after a few weeks became such an extension of the sergeant's voice that Porter could anticipate the leader's message by the length, the volume, or the ferocity of the whistle blast. He never quite adjusted to the awakening ritual, however, and longed for the melodious Reveille.

Simultaneously with the abrupt blaze of overhead light, three piercing, unbearably loud trills startled him from sleep every morning in predawn darkness. They were followed by electrifying bellows from the throat of Stentor himself.

"Everybody up!"

"Hit the floor! Everybody!"

"Drop your cocks and grab your socks!"

As he scrambled with his fellows for the latrine, a khaki towel over his shoulders, toothbrush in hand, Porter thought wistfully of Miss Dora Snead leading her sixth grade students in song.

156

"We're all in our places with bright shining faces,
Oh, this is the way to start a new day.
Good morning to you, good morning to you,
Good morning, dear teacher, we're glad to see you."

Miss Dora, bless her heart, never wore socks a day in her life and recognized a cock only as a male chicken.

"Everybody out!"

"Roll call!"

"Tenshut!"

"Parade rest!"

"By the numbers. Count off!"

The whistle ruled. Calisthenics. Close-order drill. Double-time to the mess hall. Classes. Mail call. Think what you like, dream as you would, but move with the group like an automaton when the whistle blew. Rake the walkways. Police the grounds.

Police the grounds? Even Otten was subdued.

"Every match stick. Every cigarette butt. Every scrap of paper!"

"Come on, move!"

"I don't want to see anything but assholes and elbows! Bend over and get that trash!"

"Hey, soldier, you want KP the rest of the week? Get the lead out!"

Flag up in the morning. Flag down in the evening.

"Tenshut!"

"Company halt! Hand, Salute!"

It was all right to let the beauty of Taps sink briefly into your soul, but be braced for the peace-shattering blast of the whistle immediately afterwards. How had Deacon Chauncey survived all this? Why had he not described it in his letters? Porter, in the day room, resolved to do better.

"Dear Dr. Thebault, You would not believe what basic training is like." He sat for long minutes staring at the paper, then crumpled and trashed it. "You sure wouldn't," he muttered. "I'm right in the middle of it and I don't believe it myself."

He wrote to his mother. He wrote to his sisters. He wrote to his father. He wrote to three different girls in Georgia. He never, however, wrote to anyone back at medical school. He was reluctant to confess that at increasingly frequent moments he wished he were still there. He hated the secret admission that perhaps Maj. Teufelsdreck and his father had been right about the best way for him to serve his country.

There was no other course presently available to him but to dig in and learn all these maneuvers, so many of which made no sense at all to him. The news was full of the U.S. Fifth Army and its capture of Naples, but his personal participation seemed as distant and inconsequential now as it had at Emory. If war itself was as confusing as his own preparation for it, then God alone knew how it was going to turn out, and Porter Osborne, Jr., still was not speaking to Him. He comforted himself with Houseman.

> "Then keep we must, if keep we can,
> These foreign laws of God and man."

He comforted himself silently. He had no desire whatever to subject himself knowingly to jeers from Otten or Calhoun, and everyone else he had met in his barracks was a Yankee. His resolve to emerge from Camp Grant as an excellent soldier did not waver but became rooted in stubbornness rather than flowing from inspiration. He was learning.

He soon received some reality training. The agenda looked innocuous enough on the cork board by the side of the latrine door. Porter had early decided that when the first sergeant was not blowing his whistle he was typing notices for the bulletin board; he was dedicated to keeping them busy. "Infiltration Course. 1400 hours." "Obstacle Course. 1500 hours." Porter made a quick translation to two o'clock and three o'clock with a note that the military nomenclature really did require a lot of tolerant adjustment. 1400 hours indeed. If that became universal, all clocks and watches would need double faces.

At formation they were loaded into trucks and carried Porter knew not where, only that it was miles and miles across Illinois, well away from the relative security of the barracks, the PX, the mess hall, the chapel. As usual, they listened to graphic instructions. "Crawl on your belly like a snake. Do it like an alligator and you'll get your elbows shot. Do not raise your head to look around while you are crawling. Do not raise your head at all; keep it turned sideways. Pretend you're digging a trench with your head and pushing with your toes. Keep your ass down and your prick in the dirt. Your life depends on it. The machine guns are fixed and will not shoot below thirty inches, but you had damn well better be sure anything you value is below that level. Don't crawl. Slither.".

After twenty minutes of lecture by a fat sergeant and demonstrations by another sergeant who was as wide and thin and hard as a slab of well-cured middling meat, they were led in single file around the periphery of the infiltration course. They passed a grave with a tombstone that had been mounted so close to their path it was impossible to miss reading its inscription: "Here lies Private Head-up Butt-up." Nobody sniggered.

Porter found himself standing before a six-foot parapet of cross ties on a wide platform of stones and earth. Below him and about fifty yards away the Kishwaukee River flowed in silent gray torpor, reflecting the overcast sky with dutiful glint but no sparkle, its progress across this level land unbroken by ripple or foam, its bed too deep for any rocks submerged in it to have the slightest effect on the smoothness of its surface.

On the opposite shore black loam had been bulldozed up into a long mound prevented from sliding into the river by a retaining wall constructed of utility poles and two-by-twelves.

The lean, wide sergeant had them under command. He had stripped to his T-shirt, and Porter reflected that his latissimi were so over-developed they were enviably grotesque and that probably one of them would kill if severed and hurled in anger by Will Barton. He wondered fleetingly where Barton might be.

"First ting you do is turn around and watch dat backboard across the river. I heard some of youse saying dey ain't live ammunition in Uncle Sam's guns dis afternoon. Watch dis!"

He flicked his handkerchief above the parapet and there was the swift rattling response of machine gun fire. Splinters flew in regimented puffs from the timbers across the river. His mouth agape, Porter was positive that the line of fire could be no more than six inches higher than the parapet. He did not for a minute believe that the sergeant had overheard Otten's *sotto voce* comment to him and Calhoun about there being live ammunition in the guns; there must have been some loud-mouthed Yankee voicing the same opinion in the rear ranks. His respect for this sergeant escalated.

"Don't forget da mine fields; stay at least six feet away from da white wires. When one goes off, freeze into da dirt. Dat way you won't getcha nuts blowed off. Remember everting we showed youse and it ought to be all right; we ain't lost but tree GI's in a whole mont now. One of dem panicked halfway tru, jumped up and got cut plumb in half; so stay calm."

Porter glanced at Otten for a disbelieving shrug, possibly even a reassuring wink that would say this was all window dressing designed to scare them into compliance without actually endangering them. Otten was staring raptly at the sergeant. So was Calhoun.

"Awright! Over da top! Pretend dose are Japs and Krauts on dose machine guns and dey want American blood! Any of youse forget what I've showed you, don't worry; we always send da dogtags to da nearest kin."

The company went over the top of the parapet like lines of lizards. The guns began their ferocious barking, and Porter could distinctly hear the whine of bullets above him. Directly above him. He began a frantic wriggle, pushing a shallow trench with the side of his helmet into the earth loosened by the passage of previous trainees, gripping with outstretched fingers and skewed boot toes in a desperate pull and push over this alien terrain. Looking to the side he saw a white wire. Was it six feet away? Suddenly there came a loud and heavy shaking and the dirt behind the wire erupted as though the whole world was blowing up; a black column of soil erupted skyward and hung there for an instant, surmounted by plumes as graceful momentarily as blooms of Pampas grass. Porter felt that every bit of it fell on him. Clods hit his helmet, thudded on his back. Then the loose soil fell; it rained down for what seemed like minutes as he forced himself to lie motionless. He did not realize he was holding his breath until he discovered his mouth and nostrils occluded by heavy, porous soil. As he blew it away he thought, "It really is as black as Essie's butt. And probably formed by one hundred million tons of rotted buffalo carcasses."

He considered wriggling backwards six yards to the haven of the parapet and facing the wrath of the muscular sergeant. That consideration was fleeting. He pushed his body to the right a good two feet and resumed his laborious progress toward the distant finish line. The trip took no more than thirty minutes but seemed like an eon in which new planets could have been created. The machine guns kept up such a constant chatter that they became background noise; it was the unpredictable bursting of mines that tightened sphincters and made muscles rigid. Porter shut his eyes tightly, gritted his teeth, and wriggled forward as rapidly as he could until he felt a solid pressure against his head and heard a laugh. He realized that the machine guns were now behind him, that the exploding mines were more distant, and opening his eyes, discovered that he was some ten yards beyond the finish line and was pinned down by the boot of the fat sergeant.

"On your feet, soldier. You can't go all the way to Georgia on your belly."

Porter scrambled to his feet, dusted his clothes, and asserted, "Right now, Sergeant, I'd be willing to try."

160

He joined his fellows who had finished and watched as Otten and Calhoun slithered to safety, rose, and began dusting their fatigues. Calhoun's face was completely black except where his glasses formed white circles free of dirt. Otten was spitting out gritty black soil and one eye was weeping from a clod hitting it. They looked at Porter and simultaneously pointed in glee.

"My God, Calhoun, look at that. Old Osborne looks just like the tar baby after Br'er Fox jerked Br'er Rabbit off, doesn't he?"

"Haw! Look at those bloodshot eyes. Looks like Vitamin Flintheart fell in the cesspool to me. Ain't that right, what? Besides, Otten, I remember Br'er Fox trying to eat Br'er Rabbit, but I don't remember him ever jerking him off. Haw!"

This sally procured him a shove from Otten, and the entire group joined the three boys from Georgia in riotous laughter. Any remark would have been a triggering excuse for that laughter. They laughed in release, they laughed in youthful high spirits, they laughed in exultation that a hazard had been overcome. On the rich Illinois prairie, under a slate gray sky, gathered in from all over the country, they became warriors for awhile. They laughed at death. Together.

Of a sudden Porter's merriment caught in his throat. Looking over the infiltration course they had just traversed in terror and then in triumph, he saw a crumpled shape in olive green fatigues, a pair of hands clasped over the mound of a helmet, curled in upon itself, motionless. He broke ranks and started running toward it, was stopped in his tracks by the shrill whistle of the fat sergeant.

"Come back here! Stay where you are!"

All voices stilled, all eyes were trained on the scene before them. The wide-chested sergeant vaulted over the parapet and bounded toward the prostrate form. He bent over in swift inspection and then rose to his full height and delivered with all his force a mighty kick with the inner side of his foot, his muscular arms extended in balancing backswing like a sculpture of some athlete. The figure stirred and rose to its knees, then its feet, head hanging. The helmet with its liner rolled off, and the sergeant began kicking it toward the side of the field, at the same time jabbing the tousle-haired soldier in shambling gait ahead of him.

A low murmur rose from some of the company but most of the men were silent. Otten was standing near the fat sergeant.

"What happened?"

"No guts. White feather. Yellow streak. Probably start with the chaplain, from there to the psych ward, wind up with a Section 8."

"Tough," said Otten.

The sergeant gave him a dismissing glance from the side of his eye. "On who? You wanta depend on that whimpering faggot to bring you a stretcher? Or morphine? Or a splint if you laying out there wounded? Companee! Fall in!"

As Porter took his place in the front rank of his platoon, he remembered Nichols, Mitchell, and Jordan. Dr. Wingo. He recalled the similar mixture of pity and embarrassment he had felt then. "If Will Barton were here," he thought, "he'd yell, 'Fuck him if he can't take a joke,' and we would all relax and feel better." Porter Osborne, Jr., stood at attention and stared straight before him. He was as mute as an open grave.

They were loaded again into trucks and carried to the Obstacle Course, although it was only a mile away and Porter felt they could have double-timed there as quickly as they got the trucks loaded, cranked, and turned around. At this installation there was a different set of supervising noncoms who specialized in physical fitness and various tortures designed to demonstrate the lack of it. They were all built like the sergeant on the infiltration course, and there was among them a prevailing contempt for any manifestation of adiposity.

Again the company received instructions. "Run first. Then the hurdles. Don't knock one over or you have to repeat. Run spraddle-legged through the tires and step in the middle of each one. If you miss a tire, Sgt. Mulroney will make you repeat. Grab the rope and swing across the mud pit. If you miss the rope or your hand slips, you go into the mud and it's six feet deep. Sgt. Dundero is there to be sure you keep trying till you make it. On hands and knees through the pipes as fast as you can go. Duck walk under the bridge. Up the net and over that wall and jump on the other side, and you're through. Provided you've done it all in fifteen minutes. Otherwise you can repeat the same exercises next week and the next and the next." At the same time the whistle sounded for the first squad to begin, Porter heard the machine guns begin for another company on the distant infiltration course. He had time only for a brief reflection that there might be more of a challenge to Medical Basic Training in some ways than there was to Emory Medical School, but he could think about that later. After he learned opera and understood electricity. The urgency of the moment was upon him.

He heard Otten laugh behind him. "Ten will get you one, Calhoun, that old Osborne falls in the mud pit. Sinew and bone will only carry you so far."

162

He was off, wind of passage speeding by his ears. He went over the hurdles without mishap, through the pipes, under the barbed wire. He grabbed the knot in the rope on his first leap and, pretending that it was a muscadine vine over the Woolsey Creek swamp back home, swung easily across. He looked down at the mud as he traversed it, knowing beforehand exactly how black it would be. Six feet deep? He dropped safely and lightly at the end of the arc and sped toward the tire casings. A sergeant was roaring at someone behind him.

"Getcha fat ass off the ground! You're moving like a turtle and you gotta jump like a squirrel!" Splat. Slosh. "Awright, get a running start and try again! And get the lead outcha ass this time!"

The tires were placed erratically but Porter went through them rapidly on his first attempt and even earned an off-handed compliment from another sergeant. "Good footwork, Pee-wee." He wanted to tarry long enough to tell the sergeant that it was really not much different from the awkward and rapid dance he had mastered as a child when Auntie had wielded a peach tree switch in peppery keenness against his bare legs. She had uttered, however, the assurance, "I'm going to skin you alive," and had not called him Pee-wee. He resolved that some day he really ought to thank Auntie. After the war.

He sped to the wooden wall that was covered with a heavy hemp netting and scrambled up it like a spider; they hadn't told him this wall was twenty feet high. He pretended he was swarming up the side of an enemy ship. The dull boom of a land mine punctuated the staccato sound of the machine guns in the distance, and he fancied himself exposed openly to a cannon broadside. He scrambled faster and straddled the top of the wall. The deck railing of his conquered ship. He looked back.

The athletic Otten made a misstep, hit a tire casing, and fell sprawling. Porter knew what he must be saying. He searched for Calhoun and discovered him rising through the black slime from the middle of the mud pit. His splattered glasses remained in place, and Porter knew that even when he removed them he would still be blind as a bat. The mud, he noted, came only to Calhoun's knees. The sergeant had lied. Savoring the moment, he heard a corporal below him, "Quit sitting on your scrawny butt and jump. If you do you'll have the quickest time anybody's made so far."

Porter deliberately looked again at Otten dancing furiously through the rings of rubber, at Calhoun holding his glasses in one hand and slinging mud off the other. He had no desire whatever to stand out from the crowd and excel those two in any contest of physical prowess. He knew what they could do. He dawdled as long as he could, then swung his legs slowly over the edge and jumped. On arising he said to the corporal, "There are times when it's dumb to be first."

That night in the Day Room, Porter concluded his letter-writing with one to his father.

"Dear Dad,

Today we finished the infiltration and obstacle courses. At least, most of the company did. I am worn out and it's about time for lights out. I like to be in bed before the first sergeant blows his whistle, so I will close for now. Give Mother and everybody else my love. I have written all the news to Janice and Sara and they will fill you in. Tell Fritz hello and to run the Big Red Hill extra fast for me.
Emory is a long way off. So is home.

Love, Sambo.

P.S. Speaking of the Big Red Hill, would you please mail me a little Bull Durham sack of dirt from there? This dirt is so black up here that I'm beginning to forget how red it is back home. I'd like to have some to refresh my memory. If it's too much trouble, don't bother."

17 **I**n the rigid and unremitting routine that was the lot of the basic trainee, the sergeants and the whistles herded their charges through such inflexible units of time that a budding soldier had barely a minute during daylight hours that he could truly say was his own, free of supervision. They did everything in groups, under watchful eyes, and individuality was not encouraged. Porter participated in all activities with enthusiasm.

At the early morning session of calisthenics, he became proficient at jumping jacks and push-ups, proud that he never manifested the fatigue that some of the burlier guys professed. Paired off with some other GI, he learned to dig a slit trench or a foxhole with the trenching tool, an ingenious device that had both a pick and a shovel on the end.

"Ya spose to be able to get in ya foxhole fiteen minutes after ya start digging! Get the lead out and lemme see da dirt fly!"

"Spose to be shape like a pear or a light bulb! Dig!"

Tweet! "Take a ten-minute break! Smoke if ya got em. If ya ain't, get one from ya buddy."

Porter paid painstaking attention to all instructions, was proud of his finished foxhole. Forget the fifteen-minute myth. Five feet deep and commodious enough to accommodate two soldiers curled up in the bottom while shrapnel and enemy bullets whined and whistled overhead, it took all of an hour to construct, even in the black loam of Illinois. He marveled that they never hit hardpan in their digging. At home there would have been dense clay or even rock before reaching this depth. One of the sergeants gave it his approval on his tour of inspection.

Tweet! "Awright, men, fill 'em up! We gotta double-time back to camp or you'll be late for chow! Come on, get a move on!"

Porter shoveled the dirt back in the hole. He did so with more than a faint feeling of frustration. He realized that you couldn't go off and leave a prairie dotted with holes and you obviously couldn't take one of them with you, but he felt that a small home away from home had been desecrated. He wrote his baby sister about it. "Although the sergeant didn't say so, I'm sure it was absolutely the best foxhole he ever saw in his life. If they give a medal for that, I'm sure to win. Check your local paper."

Porter wrote letters every night. He had very early discovered that in order to get them you had to send them, and he finally understood the frequency of Deacon Chauncey's correspondence. Mail call was the one activity six days a week when a GI was given a little free rein, fifteen minutes off the end of the afternoon before washing up for evening mess. On Saturdays it was just before noon. The guys broke ranks and massed around the sergeant who stood on the barracks steps, bellowing names and waving envelopes. If he came across a pink or blue one that was heavily perfumed, he might even yell out a ribald or jovial remark. The thrill of getting a letter was so deep that the entire day took on a new glow. Somewhere, to someone, every soldier was still an individual, had a definite and distinct identity, and was valued simply because he was who he was. Exultation swelled the throat of the recipient at mail call and produced a shine in the eyes. Shrugs of feigned indifference masked the disconsolate mood when one's name did not resound at mail call. Whatever one did, one did not let real feelings show; not in front of GI's who were being molded into the tough likeness of their sergeants.

The first week of basic, while recruits jockeyed for position, settling and shoving into some sort of living arrangement that everyone could tolerate for the time ahead of them, Calhoun, Osborne and Otten stood out as special, different from the others in several ways. First of all, they had known each other at home and had come into camp together. This gave them an automatic cohesiveness, an aura of superiority because they were assumed to be buddies, the air of being a unit, stronger because of its numbers. Secondly, they were from Georgia, the only representatives in the company from their state. The Yankees were quick to dub them the "three Georgia Peaches," and Porter very early affected a deeper southern accent than he had ever possessed at home, to the delight of the company and the disgust of Otten. Third, they had all three volunteered. This was knowledge disseminated inadvertently and without any boasting on their part; it was acquired by a guy from the Bronx who was noseying around comparing dog tags.

"Osborne, Porter L., Jr. 14143150. Hey, looka here, for Chrissake. What kinda serial number is dis? It starts with a one; dat means dis poor fucker enlisted. He volunteered, for Crissake. Couldn't wait to be drafted like ordinary normal people. What kinda weird hero we got on our hands?"

Porter smoothly pointed out that the other two Georgia Peaches had similar numbers, murmured somewhat loftily that Southerners were always quick to respond to national need when it was called to their attention, that there were some sections of America that produced leaders by heritage, and implied that Georgians had a greater percentage of volunteer serial numbers than any other state in the Union. He was careful not to mention ASTP or the life of special privilege it had entailed; no need to confuse a Yankee unnecessarily.

Otten had already apprised Porter and Carter that it would be to their advantage to keep their med school background secret for the simple reason that ignorance of it made their superior performance in the classroom look even more impressive to the corporals and sergeants who were their instructors. Porter, in turn, had promised not to speak of flunking out so long as the subject never surfaced, a convenient truce that procured the appearance of congeniality. A PFC was at least a token first rung on the ladder of promotion.

"Hey, is dat why youse three guys are all PFC's instead of buck privates like ordinary normal people in dis fucking outfit? Youse are gungo-ho instead of sad sacks!"

"That is a safe assumption, Buster," responded Porter as he winked at Calhoun. The luster of being a Georgia Peach was new and pleasing, a condition to be cultivated, encouraged, even if the New Yorker did pronounce it "Georgie."

Through acceptance rather than effort, Porter had made a new friend. Lamar Betsill was barely eighteen and came from Michigan. He had brought with him into the service, of all things, a guitar, and he took it with him every night to the Day Room. While everyone else read or wrote letters or studied their mimeographed lectures for classes on medicine, Betsill sat in a corner and tuned his guitar. He never actually played it unless someone asked him to or inquired if he knew a particular song. He did not read books, nor did he write letters; he simply sat in the corner, plucking and tightening strings, his ear bent attentively over the instrument. Porter was one of the few of his comrades who did not importune him to silence.

"Stop da fucking noise!"

"For Crissake, Betsill, will you be quiet?"

"You gonna wake up some morning at Reveille and find that music box a bunch of wires and splinters if you don't put it up."

Otten, ever derisive, said, "Betsill, do you pick and sing or just sit and plunk?"

Osborne, increasingly defensive where Otten was concerned, issued the invitation. "Lamar, why don't you play and sing us a song?"

"Whatcha want?"

"Finlandia," snorted Otten.

"Whatever your favorite is," interposed Osborne.

"See if you like this one," said Betsill, with modesty but determination. He struck a chord and crooned nasally.

> "It's a picture of life's other side.
> Somebody has fell by the way.
> Another life has gone out with the tide
> That might have been happy some day.
> Some poor old mother to home
> Is a-waiting and a-watching to hear.
> She's a-waiting to hear
> From her loved one so dear;
> It's a picture of life's other side."

"I like it," said Porter.

"My God!" said Otten.

"I like it, too," said Lamar Betsill. "It's so sweet and so sad. That's just the chorus. It's got several verses. I'll give you a sample.

> First scene is of Sol the gambler,
> Wicked was he toward his wife.
> He whipped out his knife
> Took his own brother's life;
> It's a picture of life's other side."

"My God, Betsill," declaimed Otten. "I always thought country was a term that applied only to a certain class of person in the South. You are the first country Yankee I ever saw in my life. I'm out of here. Anybody with me?"

168

"I'm right behind you, fearless leader," assented Calhoun. "Leave old Vitamin here to sop up culture with his country Yankee. Ain't that right, Sport? Let's go to the PX and find a beer, Otten."

"Don't pay any attention to them," Osborne soothed. "They're always going on with some sort of foolishness; they don't mean a word they say."

"You want I should do you another song?"

"There are some letters I just have to write, Lamar. I tell you what, just pick, don't sing."

The plains and skies of Illinois were seductively sunny by mid-morning, the vast space between earth and heaven filled with air that sparkled and whispered of mysterious thrills to come and was sharply stimulating when sucked into heaving lungs. Indian Summer was upon them. Company B was whipping into shape in close-order drill, beginning to pivot and march in response to barking cadence like a wide millipede whose legs defy understanding. Even Porter Osborne began to feel the satisfaction of proficiency, but he had endured humiliating public instruction on several occasions.

"Hey, soldier, get in step dere! Whassa matter, aintcha got no rhythm?"

"Hey, Sad Sack, quit looking atcha feet. Keep ya eyes on da head of da guy in front of ya!"

Even the first sergeant noticed him. He halted the platoon and held them at attention. "You! Whatcha name! Osborne, dat's it! Quit leaning forward when you're marching! You ain't going to get there any faster than anybody else! No eager beavers in this outfit!"

Otten and Calhoun teased him unmercifully; Porter learned that it is distinctly unpleasant to be singled out for attention in the United States Army.

Lt. Long was kinder. He began to drill the company himself after several weeks of intensive effort by the noncoms. The recruits felt they were the ones being examined and never considered that this was also a test by the lieutenant of the proficiency of their instructors. He stopped the company and shouted, "At ease!" and curled a beckoning forefinger at Porter, who had fancied himself accomplished but unobtrusive in the middle of his platoon. The officer carried him a discreet distance away from his fellows, sunlight glinting from the gold bar on his shoulder.

"What's your name, soldier?"

"Osborne, Suh. Private First Class Porter Osborne, Jr., Suh."

"Relax, soldier. Where are you from?"

"Georgia, Suh. Brewtonton, Georgia, Suh. Route three, Suh."

"Relax, dammit, I'm not planning on writing you a letter." He laid a muscular hand on his rigid shoulder and Porter felt strangely comforted; the tautness lessened.

"Tell me, Osborne, do you have sinus trouble?"

"No, Suh, Lt. Long, Suh."

"Well, I want you to do me a favor."

"Yes, Suh."

"Keep your mouth closed when you're marching. You're making the whole goddam platoon look retarded."

"What'd that shavetail want with you?" Otten queried at the next break.

"He said if I kept on improving I might someday be considered for squad leader," confided Porter, "but don't let it get out. I don't want to make these Yankees jealous."

By intense concentration, Porter eventually learned to coordinate where he put his feet and how he held his body with the commands that assaulted his ears. Soon he began to enjoy close-order drill; he thought it better than digging foxholes that had to be refilled, or being shut up in a classroom pretending to take notes on the primitive first-aid classes that were taught by noncoms he regarded as barely literate. If his attention had not been diverted, he would not have made his greatest *faux pas*, one which made him fleetingly famous in the battalion.

On a Saturday morning in mid October, the parade ground was swarming with the squads, platoons, and companies that made up the battalion, all of them well-separated and spread out over the prairie. The orders of strange and distant sergeants barked to unknown groups of fellow GI's were clearly audible. There was an unspoken feeling of competition and Porter was desirous that the second platoon of Company B appear the best on the field; he wheeled and pivoted. "To the left, Harch. To the right, Harch." He strutted to "Forward, Harch," pranced to "In place, Harch," felt pride in his unit.

Then they came. He heard first the hollow, honking sounds that bugled faintly in the heavens. Then he spotted the unmistakable identifying formation, wavering and shifting but maintaining always a definite V behind the solitary leader that stood out like the point on an arrowhead. Wild geese did not fly over the inland farm of his youth, but he had heard of them, seen pictures of them and recognized them immediately. He was not prepared for the thrill of this unexpected moment, however, and he reveled in wonder as they passed directly overhead, high thin sunlight glinting off outstretched black and white necks. For moments he could hear a constant chatter as the flock gabbled confidentially within itself, the sounds tossed uncaringly into the wind that upheld their wings and sped them southward.

It was the first flock of thousands. They streamed through the skyways at various heights and in varying numbers, determined, indifferent, and altogether splendid, filling the horizon from lip of earth to lip of earth, all of them headed compass-true in one direction. South. Porter Osborne, Jr., was lifted out of himself; he thought this the most important event in the world right now, greater than Cordell Hull being in Moscow for a conference on the war, greater than his own dedication to helping win that war. He realized this was not a thought that would be shared to any degree by the drill sergeant, however, and settled into his familiar discipline of compartmentalizing.

"Hut; hut; hut, two, three, four."

"In cadence, march."

"Hut, two, three, four; hut, two, three, four; hut; hut; hut, two." Pause. "Threefour."

All morning the recruits marched. All morning the geese atavistically traversed the heavens, some formations numbering a hundred or more.

"They're going south," thought Porter as he stared at the busy sky during cigarette break. "Before dark, they're going to see red hills and pine woods and cotton fields. I wish I could fly."

As he answered the command of "Fall in!" and began marching again, he recalled a poem written especially to him years before by Edna Floyd, the indulgent roommate of his indulgent elder sister. He tried to fit its meter to the cadence of the sergeant.

"I love you, little rolling hills
With creeks about your toes.
I love the very mud of you,
The way each pine tree grows.

My friend, the lonely whippoorwill,
Calls me from your heights,
And I answer him with weeping
For lovely summer nights.

I love you for your beauty,
Oh hills where I would be.
Don't think that I am deaf to you,
I hear you calling me."

He became so homesick on that midwestern plain, in broad open daylight, in the presence of thousands of busy soldiers, that he was almost consumed by it. He marched with vigor and professional appearance, never missing a step nor a maneuver, but in an innermost compartment he wallowed in nostalgia.

"Just one little goose, please get lost and fly over my farm in Brewton County. 'Don't think that I am deaf to you; I hear you calling me.'"

In the rear of the column, the last command he remembered hearing was "To the rear! Harch!" He executed it snappily and stepped out in the leading rank. Trained by weeks of humiliating reprimands, he stared rigidly straight ahead. He marched his heart out, thinking of the geese.

Abruptly, he had a sense of aloneness; he was on a direct collision course with another platoon. He heard a distant, "Halt! Halt, godammit!" Feeling like a recalcitrant mule, he did so and looked back. His platoon was a good fifty yards to the rear, his buddies laughing and pointing their fingers. Other platoons, other companies, were wheeling and marching, but all eyes were on him; a maverick had wandered from the herd. Lt. Long was standing in an unmilitary stance, legs wide-spraddled, fists on his hips, his cap at his feet where he had obviously flung it in desperation.

Porter forgot poetry. He dismissed the geese. Resisting the impulse to scamper like a rabbit back to the sheltering haven of his group, he snapped his body rigidly erect, pivoted, and began counting his own cadence, "Hut, two, three, four." With shoulders squared and head held high, he marched straight to the lieutenant, stopped, clicked his heels, saluted and stood at perfect attention.

"PFC Osborne, Suh, reporting for duty!"

Lt. Long's complexion was ruddier than could be explained by exposure to the elements.

"Straighten your glasses, close your lips, and get your scrawny ass back in the ranks. I've decided this whole goddam platoon is retarded and now you're making me look that way."

Porter saluted again, did a perfect about face, and marched back into the midst of his fellows. By the time the morning was over and they could discuss the incident, he had resolved never, ever to mention to anyone either geese or poetry. To his amazement, he became something of a hero.

"Did ya see Little Georgie make a fool out da lieutenant? Dat took guts!"

"Yeh, but what I liked was da military way he marched back to da unit insteada scrambling and running. What a card!"

"Christ, I tought da sergeant and da lieutenant both would shit deyselves; da whole parade ground was laughing."

"I tink he done it a purpose."

Otten and Calhoun were not deceived. Otten, as usual, spoke for both of them. "My God, Osborne, what's the matter with you? You took a broad step this morning, I hope you know; you're no longer a sad sack, you've turned into a first-class fuckup. Nobody will ever make me believe you planned that and did it deliberately."

"But you'll never know for sure, will you, Otten?"

"Haw! 'Old fuckup Vitamin Flintheart' he came to be known as in those days. Ain't that right, Sport?"

At mail call two hours later, the first sergeant himself addressed the situation. "Osborne! You got five letters and one package. One letter got perfume on it and the package feels like candy. Might be fudge. You can pick them up tonight at the company office. Right now you report to the mess hall on the double. You got KP for a week."

That night he was nursing blisters incurred scrubbing not only tabletops but floors with GI soap and a brush. His fatigues were redolent of the grease from a hundred pots he had cleaned of their grime, his hands shriveled from the relatively easy chore of peeling and washing a thousand potatoes. Porter Longstreet Osborne, Jr. retrieved his treasures and staggered upstairs to the Day Room. He refused to whimper; he was planning a letter to Deacon Chauncey in which he would outline new dimensions to war being hell. At the same time his resolve to prepare himself for it was undimmed. The Day Room was empty except for Lamar Betsill, whose solitude was easy to understand; he was singing.

"Whiskey and blood run together
But I didn't hear nobody pray.
I didn't hear nobody pray, dear brother,
I didn't hear nobody pray.
I heard the crash on the highway
But I didn't hear nobody pray."

"Just the music, Lamar. Please. Just the music. Not the lyrics."

"You don't like sweet songs that are sad, do you Porter? How was KP?"

"Not bad at all for a fellow who was raised on a farm and is used to working for a living. They don't believe in ten-minute breaks over there and keep you busy every second, but that way you don't get into trouble. The mess sergeant kept pointing that out to us. I had a job in college waiting tables and washing dishes, and I believe to my soul our dietitian probably trained this mess sergeant; he preaches more than he cooks."

"You sure get a lot of mail."

"I know. I believe I'd die if I didn't. Speaking of which, you don't get any at all, plus I haven't seen you writing the first letter since I've known you. You're not going to get any mail if you don't write to people yourself."

Lamar leaned over his guitar, plucked a string, and attentively tightened it. "Nobody cares what I'm doing. No use to write letters."

"Your folks care. You know they do. You ought to write to them."

"Pop told me when I left I needn't write, that they wouldn't worry about me unless a telegram came."

"A telegram?"

"Yep. They send a telegram if somebody gets killed. Mrs. Muscovy two doors down got one and everbody took her pies and cakes up to two weeks, and she's got a gold star hanging in her window."

Porter thought of his own family, how close to each other they all were, and was disbelieving.

"Lamar Betsill, you ought to be ashamed of yourself. You know your parents would love to get a letter from you."

Lamar laid a deadening palm across the guitar strings. His voice was carefully flat. "Can't neither one of them read."

Porter broke the ensuing pause before it could overwhelm him with embarrassment. "Well, you could write them a letter now and then and a neighbor could read it to them."

"I can read pretty well, but I can't write so good. Mom and Pop and me neither one wouldn't want the neighbors looking at any letter I wrote. I always put things backward or upside down when I try to write. I know when I do it that it looks wrong but I can't help it. I've always done it. My teachers all thought I done it a-purpose, and my fifth grade teacher used to turn red and scream. Something fierce. I made up my mind I wasn't born to stand at no blackboard and be laughed at by little kids and screamed at by a red-faced teacher. So I quit. I never finished the fifth."

"We have a law in Georgia," Porter said, "that you can't quit school till you're sixteen."

"We got that same law in Mitchigan."

Softly, after a long moment, Porter said, "Oh."

Lamar put the guitar aside. "Mom and Pop got pride. They had to leave Arkansas when they got married because Mom wasn't but fourteen. Pop got a job on a barge out of Soo and Mom hasn't never had to do outside work. Nobody in town knows they can't read and they don't want it out. Mom says a soul ain't got to read to know what's going on in this world. She seen the telegram delivered to Mrs. Muscovy's door and knowed right then her gold star was coming, and she got a cake there ahead of that crowd of neighbor women who hang out in the library. My folks do care a lot about me, but facts are facts, Georgie boy. What's in your package?"

Porter jumped. "What? Oh. Let's see."

The package was heavy for its size, it couldn't be candy; his mother didn't do fudge. Removing the wrapping, he saw a cigar box adorned with the likeness of a softly pretty, fat lady who had a puffed hairdo and a baby blue gown that showed an amazing expanse of cleavage. Attached to it was a note in his father's jerking, angular scrawl.

"Here it is. All through life try to hold whatever ground you've gained. Love, Dad."

"I can't believe it!" exclaimed Porter. "All I asked for was a little sack. Some time. And he's already sent it."

"What is it?" urged Lamar. "Go on and open it."

Porter looked around. The Day Room was empty except for a corporal in a distant corner writing a letter with a wallet photograph propped on the table before him.

"Lamar, I know what this is. But before I show you, I want to say part of a poem for you. Except that wherever it says 'England,' I'm thinking 'Georgia.'

'If I should die, think only this of me,
That there's some corner of a foreign field
That is forever England. There shall be
In that rich dust a richer dust concealed;
A dust whom England bred, shaped, made
aware,

Gave, once, her flowers to love, her ways to
  roam,
A body of England's breathing English air,
Washed by her rivers, blest by suns of home.'"

He swung the lid of the cigar box back to reveal a treasure of still-moist loam, stained with the hue of garnets, rubies, and, he had even heard some say, the blood of the Confederacy.

"There! Look! Isn't it beautiful?"

"Looks like dirt to me," said Betsill. "It sure is red."

"It is dirt, Lamar, and it came from the most gorgeous hill in the whole state of Georgia. Right in the middle of our farm. This dirt will grow a bale of cotton or a hundred bushels of corn to the acre, and it'll stain your overalls till you wear out a batter stick on wash day. Isn't it beautiful?"

"You asked for that?"

"You mighty right I did!" exulted Porter.

"What ya plan to do with it?"

"I'm gonna put a little pinch of it in my shoes every morning of the world till this war is over, no matter where it takes me. And I'm gonna walk all over God's Heaven. And I'm going to be blest by suns of home. Even when the wild geese are flying."

"Oh," said Lamar Betsill.

He picked up his guitar and cuddled it, raised his wrist to strum it, and then relaxed.

"Osborne."

"What?"

"You want we should still be buddies?"

"Sure, Lamar. Day Room buddies, anyhow. We're in different groups all day."

"Well, look. I promise I won't sing no more if you won't say poetry no more."

Porter exhaled slowly but thoughtfully. "OK."

"And one more thing. If you won't tell nobody about my writing and my ma's reading, I won't tell nobody about your dirt."

*"They are lost like slaves that swat, and in the
    skies of morning hung,
The stairways of the tallest gods when tyranny
    was young."*

18 **M**indful of the GI who had collapsed on the infiltration course and had vanished nameless into oblivion, Porter accepted toughness as a reasonable requirement for a good soldier. Company B was subjected to various conditioning disciplines intended to harden the spirit as well as muscles. One such discipline, practiced every Friday night, was the "GI party." The first week the sergeant had announced that function, there were recruits gullible enough to assume it meant a social gathering, a quasi-reception perhaps where everyone would mingle over light refreshments, a sort of get-acquainted block party at which compassionate leaders would evince concern for the happiness and satisfaction of their charges.

The leaders were there right enough and so were the charges. The activity, however, consisted of bathing the barracks.

It took hours to satisfy the noncoms. The floors were scoured, light bulbs were dusted, windows upstairs and downstairs were washed and then polished with newspaper until they glistened. The company soon adapted to the awareness that its communal social life would be this weekly preparation for inspection on Saturdays; youthful high spirits prevailed and laughter rang out at unlikely situations and puerile jokes. They even came to enjoy it, although there was not one soldier who would have confessed such. Porter discovered early that the GI credo was to grumble and gripe; God forbid that anything anywhere be deemed completely satisfactory. That would be a sign of softness and they were growing tough.

There was a subculture in the Army centered around grumbling about the food. Troops ate voraciously and their metal trays with stamped-out compartments were amazingly free of residue when carried to the dishwashing line, but the food never suited them. They railed and ranted about Spam and its various ingenious disguises; they

177

fumed about dried eggs and dehydrated potatoes; they sneeringly referred to chipped beef on toast as shit on a shingle, even while they gobbled it down. They grudgingly accepted on good days center cuts of ham, thick steaks, breaded pork chops, mounds of chicken as their just due. Never mind that folks back home were rationing sugar and butter, that civilians were having meatless days each week. Never mind that in every outfit at Camp Grant there were the same few who were first in line at every meal, earning the appellation of "chow hound." Never mind that seconds were encouraged so long as supplies lasted, that Company B glistened from being fed often and well. Army food was awful and that was that. Porter finally joined the grumblers, although in his heart he found the rations wholesome and varied, foreign to his background. The preparation admittedly left something to be desired at times and he missed turnip greens, but all in all, he thought the mess hall a marvel. Nevertheless, one of the things he was learning was never, ever to stand out from the crowd, and he comformingly derided the food while enthusiastically cleaning his tray.

Their first sergeant was adept at mass psychology, and when he judged the professed dissatisfaction with food escalating to an unacceptable level, he announced a fourteen-mile hike. They embarked with bellies full of a hot breakfast that had consisted of chunks of Spam, watery potatoes, and dried eggs scrambled so hard that they rattled. Porter, a little apprehensive about the hike, left the fuming and fussing to his fellows and gorged himself on seconds of milk and toast. The hike, the sergeant said, was in all respects to simulate field conditions.

The company left camp in formation, with full packs towering above their shoulders, including bedrolls, trenching tools, and gas masks. Full canteens and mess kits banged against their hips. The heavy steel helmets covered their heads as completely as a box terrapin's shell, and the straps, unbuckled, swung to and fro with the gait of their march. They marched and marched. Outside of camp the sergeant spread them in ragged single file along each side of the road and they continued to march. After the first five-minute break ("Smoke if you got 'em"), Porter learned that it was easier to lie in a ditch torqued into his pack and half suspended in air by it than to remove it and then shrug it heavily back over aching arms onto weary shoulders when it was time to move on. They marched and marched.

Well into the third hour, some hundred yards off the dirt road they were traveling, they came upon a series of long war tents erected in lonely parallels, their flaps closed, unused, abandoned. A lone Jeep, driverless, was parked nearby. The whistle blared. They were aligned again in formation.

"Aw right! Exercise in survival! I hope you remember your lectures on poison gas because these first two tents, even as we speak, are being filled with either mustard or nerve gas. You are to put on your gas masks and on command will proceed through one of these first two tents. When you emerge on the other side, assuming you do that, remove your masks and proceed through one of the last two tents. They do not have poison gas; they are filled with tear gas. You will go through them on your bellies. Tear gas is not lethal and will not hurt you. It will only give you an idea of what it feels like if you ever get caught without your mask handy. This ain't a case of live and learn, men, this is a case of if you don't learn, you don't live."

Within minutes Company B was transformed into the likeness, Porter thought, of a herd of hump-backed, long-legged armadillos, weak-eyed and wide-goggled; everyone looked as akin to humanity as mechanical robots. One of the creatures approached him and roared in sepulchral tones from within the echo chamber of the mask, "You finally got glasses big enough to cover up those old Vitamin Flintheart eyes, I see." He did not recognize Griffin Calhoun's voice, but the punctuating shove against his back pack sent him staggering off balance for several recovering steps and identity was unmistakable. Porter fell in behind him and ducked through the flap of the first tent.

The light inside was dim, its substance further absorbed by the olive-green mass of regimented bodies. Unmistakably, however, the air itself was visible. It was a dirty yellow, vile and thick. Lying on the ground like a blanket around the shuffling feet, it curled and floated and whispered of death. Porter breathed cavernously and audibly through his mouth into his mask, shuddered, and began sweating. He was in the presence of previously unimagined evil. No one would possibly release such a horror anywhere in the universe. The Germans had done it in World War I, but gas had since been outlawed; not even the Japanese would descend to this level of depravity, of barbaric and indifferent cruelty. He tried to imagine himself on a battlefield, going to the aid of wounded soldiers who had also been gassed. He tried to imagine himself back at Emory, traveling by now from campus to Grady Hospital, intent on becoming a physician and consequently an officer. He tried to remember running on the big red hill with Fritz. He failed on all counts. Nothing in this world was real except this crowded, darkened tent filled with fetid air that would smother life in minutes. Maybe this was just a drill; surely the gas in the tent was not genuine. This was just another Army exercise, like digging the foxholes; they were not truly in any danger.

Bursting through the exit flap into the beautiful expanse of black earth and windy gray sky, he snatched off his helmet and gas mask. As he exultantly sucked in great draughts of pure, invisible air, he caught the faint but unmistakable odor of moldy hay clinging to his clothes and realized that this had not been playtime in the Army; the gas was as real as the bullets on the infiltration course. He shuddered. He pondered whether it would be worse to die suffocated by phosgene or live smothered indefinitely by the claustrophobic gas mask. Carter Otten interrupted this reverie. He came from behind and gave Porter's trenching tool such a vigorous twist that his feet left the ground and he followed the weight of his pack in cumbersome fall. He lay on his back, arms and legs akimbo, thrashing in impotence while Otten and Calhoun gibed hilariously.

"Haw! Look at old Vitamin. Wallowing around like he's sixty years old and can't get off his back. Look at him! Looks for all the world like a damn old box turtle trying to turn himself right side up. Ain't that right, Sport?"

Lamar Betsill extended Porter a hand and jerked him to his feet. Otten laughed.

"You see that, Calhoun? If you got two worms in an apple, sooner or later they'll meet. You ever see two wormier looking soldiers? Hey, Betsill, how come you didn't bring your guitar on the fourteen-mile hike?" He laughed again.

"You Georgie Peaches sure do treat your buddies rough," Lamar said to Porter.

"Yeah, you gotta be tough to grow up in Georgia. Don't pay any attention to Otten and Calhoun. They're like overgrown puppies; all that barking and snapping doesn't mean a thing except frolic and high spirits. Their hearts are in the right place."

"You could have fooled me," murmured Lamar.

A few minutes later the sergeant and corporals were herding them bare-faced through the tent filled with tear gas. They were instructed to crawl through, but their progress was much quicker than through the truly poisonous gas when they had been protected. Porter took a deep breath just before he entered, resolved not to breathe again before he traversed the tent. The stinging gas had him weeping within seconds, however, and halfway through the tent he gave an involuntary inhalation and joined the rest of Company B that was bent double, coughing, choking, crying and stumbling. A corporal who still wore a mask shoved them toward the exit, and they fell out of the tent in a sobbing shambles. Another corporal was outside shouting, "Don't rub ya eyes! Ya hands yet got tear gas on dem and ya just make it worse. Sit facing da wind and give it some time!"

Porter was indignant. Teaching was one thing, he thought, and learning was important, but even Dr. Wingo would not have treated anyone like this. Who the hell did that sergeant think he was anyhow? Sometimes the enemy in this war required a little concentration to define. Unobtrusively he sat on a rock outcropping to the side of Calhoun and turned up his face with its raw and swollen eyelids, praying for the wind to freshen. He heard Otten finish a paroxysm of coughing and spit.

"Goddam, Griffin, can you imagine what the real stuff would be like? As the Presbyterians say, 'Thank God that's over.'"

Calhoun's eyes were streaming, his thick-lensed glasses lying on the rock beside him.

"Hell, I can't quit crying. Haw! You can't either. Reminds me of the day we flunked out of med school. Ain't that right? What?"

"Goddam it, Calhoun, shut up! You've been hanging around that damn Osborne so much you're getting just like him! You know damn good and well we got kicked out of med school. We did not flunk out!"

"Right. Slip of the tongue, slip of the tongue. When you're coughing your guts up and crying your eyes out, you're liable to a little slip of the tongue, what? Ain't that right? Anyhow, doesn't this remind you of the day we got kicked out of med school? Hell, we bawled like babies in back of the Chi Phi house. What?"

"It does not! I don't know what you're talking about! You mention that again and you die. And stop ending everything you say with 'Ain't that right?' If you knew you were right, you wouldn't have to ask, for Christ's sake!"

"Well, you don't have to start talking like a Yankee; you're not perfect yourself. While we're on it, you're cussing worse than ever lately; did you realize that? What? Haw!"

Porter very quietly quit the rock and stole away, aware that he had just witnessed an intimate moment, one that would take him a long time to assess completely. His eyes still stung, but his tears had dried. His cheeks felt stiff.

"I never did cry over that day in med school," he thought. "But then I was prepared for it."

An hour later they shuffled with heads indifferently bowed along the dirt road that trailed in dwindling perspective to a hairline. For no reason Porter could fathom, other than it was an hour later, that man of iron whims, the Master Sergeant, halted them in the midst of the treeless plain that was swallowing them as they traversed it.

"Column halt! Fall out! Remove packs! At ease! We take a thirty-minute break here. Time for your noon chow. Be sure and eat your veggies." Everyone brightened. Porter looked at the Jeep approaching from their rear and envisioned cauldrons of stew, jerry cans full of hot chocolate, great quantities of plain but hearty victuals. He turned up his canteen and took a long pull of flat-tasting water. Lamar Betsill unfastened his mess kit and assembled it; he stuck his fork and spoon into his jacket pocket.

The Jeep stopped beside the sergeant and his noncoms, who pulled canvas bags from the back and began passing out packets to each soldier.

"What the hell?" said Calhoun.

"K-rations, by God," said Otten. "That's all the bastards are going to feed us. See if you can get two," he added.

Porter scrutinized his lunch, a rigid rectangle encased in dark brown paper so heavily waxed that it was not worth the effort trying to read the print beneath it. Heavy in his hand, this was the field ration he had learned about in class that contained vitamins, minerals, and calories devised by the leading nutritionists of the nation and compacted into one bar of chocolate capable of sustaining a GI for twenty-four hours. Easily portable, economical, nutritious, assembled in Hershey, Pennsylvania. He shrugged. Candy was candy and he liked chocolate.

He discovered immediately that he was not dealing with a conventional candy bar. There was no light-reflecting luster here, no creamy texture, no richness on the tongue. This bar was solid and thick, more dull gray than brown. It must have been pressed down for years in the bowels of the earth where rocks were formed, mined by Central European immigrants in wooden shoes, and preserved in airless caves by the United States Government since the War of 1812. In addition to everything else, his lunch had a distinctly medicinal aroma, and Porter, in recall of his grandfather, instinctively knew that it would be invidiously good for him, would build his blood, and inevitably would move his bowels.

He shrugged again and took a bite. Nothing happened. His incisors did not even leave an imprint. He shifted one corner of the bar between his jaw teeth and clamped down like a possum. The resultant shard that splintered off into his mouth swelled and grew the longer he chewed, and he choked with every swallow. Thirty minutes and a canteen of water later, the sergeant's whistle blew. Porter rewrapped the remaining half of his lunch and tucked it in a pocket while he struggled back into his pack.

"Waste not, want not," he said to Betsill, who was restoring his mess kit.

"Damn stuff doesn't fill your belly," groused Otten. "My next crap will be dry as wood chips."

"Crap?" rejoined Calhoun. "That K-bar won't even build a fart. Ain't that right, Sport? What?"

They fell into step and filed back to camp. Halfway there Otten began singing. It was a low-pitched parody and only those right around him caught the words.

> "The first sergeant said it,
> You gotta give him credit,
> For a base-on-balls old son of a bitch is he.
> Kiss my ass but dodge machine gun bullets;
> Kiss my ass but smell the poison gas fumes;
> Kiss my ass but pass the shit-on-a-shingle;
> And you'll all be free."

The tune caught the ear of the entire company, and throughout the ranks arose the correct words of "Praise the Lord and Pass the Ammunition." They were soldiers. They were tough. They were finishing their first fourteen-mile hike and they had survived. Mission accomplished. They were headed back to camp, that haven of hot meals and hot showers. They sang. The sergeant seemed pleased.

Porter looked over at Otten and Calhoun with a cautious affection. "I still can't believe they cried that hard over med school. This is a lot worse, and they're laughing."

They kept on laughing. Porter's puppies, his Flotsam and Jetsam, began laughing at everything and almost everybody.

Most of the time Porter indulgently laughed with them. It was difficult to reconcile the travail and the trivia of preparation in basic training with the war raging through the Pacific and Europe. The newspapers were full of the meeting in Moscow of the foreign ministers of all the Allies. The United States was represented by the genteel and silver-haired Cordell Hull, comfortingly Southern and reassuringly literate. The Germans capitulated at Kiev. Still Porter felt that the scope of this war had progressed to the point that all of the thousands of Americans in the entirety of Camp Grant represented no more than one small, insignificant pawn that could be sacrificed at any play with no effect on the ultimate outcome of a most terrible game. He likened himself to one drop of water in a great river, one fleck of soil on the prairies of the midwest, and he questioned anew the assurance of his Baptist background that every hair on his head was numbered. He assumed that all the other soldiers felt the same way and that they were just as reluctant as he to talk about it. That was why the puppies frolicked, that was reason enough for laughing over little things. Underlying the pleasure of new friendships was the silent awareness of transience, the dawning and sobering knowledge that no human relationship in this man's Army was anything more than fleeting. Loneliness was the vacuum of military life and laughter rushed to fill it.

Porter did not laugh, however, when Otten took to greasing spectacles in the mess hall. Neither did Calhoun. Otten was quick as a striking snake and when no noncom was looking could flick a forefinger through the butter and smear it across both lenses of a bespectacled comrade before any protective reflex could be activated. The resultant mess obscured vision until the victim could find hot water and soap, Otten sniggering and pointing for the entire interval. Porter's solution was to quit wearing his glasses. This was not an option for Calhoun, whose lenses were so crafted that they shrank his eyes as effectively as Pygmy head hunters mummified their trophies; he was helpless without them.

The first two times he got buttered he roared and swore; the third time he landed a punch so solid that it knocked Otten through the water pitchers and mess trays of the table across the aisle and attracted the attention of every sergeant in the building. It took some persuasive lying to blame Otten's flight on being tripped, and thereafter Calhoun was exempt from buttering. Porter Osborne, Jr., prudently put his glasses in his pocket before sitting down to eat.

"Otten," he said with somewhat prim severity, "you're not so damn funny."

Irresistible good humor, however, gave them the ability to acknowledge the ridiculous even when situations seemed most macabre. The redoubtable Otten displayed such when he and Porter were honored for academic achievement. It was approximately six weeks into their period of training, and in one of the afternoon academic sessions, examination papers were actually returned. Osborne and

184

Otten had each made one hundred; Calhoun trailed in underachievement with ninety-eight.

"How'd you manage to miss anything, dumb-ass?" jeered Otten. "Arteries carry blood away from the heart, right? Veins carry blood toward the heart, right? How come you checked the wrong box?"

"Look how faint my copy is," defended Calhoun. "I wish to hell they'd put something besides purple in their damn mimeograph machines. Ain't that right, Sport?"

"Lub-dup, lub-dup, lub-dup," assured Porter. As Calhoun extended his arm in a quick rabbit punch, Porter dodged nimbly and laughed. "You gotta drive, Calhoun, you gotta drive."

"Awright, youse guys, can da chatter!" bellowed their instructor, who had been drafted by Uncle Sam from a secure position in a New Jersey sewer plant a scant two years earlier and had attained through rapid promotions the eminence of tech sergeant. He was entrusted with instructing neophytes in Anatomy and Physiology and was suspicious of any inductee who knew more about the subjects than he. "You, Otten! You, Osborne! In reckanition of a perfect score on ya mid-terms, plus consistent outstanding performance ever since da course started, you have been singled out and selected to go on a secret medical mission. With a real, genuwine, bona fide doctor of medicine. Tink of dat! Da corporal in ya barracks will give ya an early call and youse will fall out at 0300 hours to meet Capt. Randolph Martin, United States Army Medical Corps, who will pick the two of youse up on the back steps of ya barracks. Wear a tie. No helmet. Class dismissed!"

Osborne approached Otten. "This is just like med school. Top of the class and you get to make rounds at Grady with the head of the department. Where you reckon we're going? In dress uniform at three o'clock in the morning?"

"One thing's for sure and certain, it's not any plum he's handed us. If there's one thing I've learned in this man's Army, it's that ripe apples don't fall off the tree at your feet. He's fucking with us."

"You're getting paranoid, Otten. You heard the sergeant; this is a reward for being the two top students."

"You're reverting to childhood, Osborne. There ain't no Santa Claus. Another thing I've learned is that none of these instructors around here cottons to a smart student. That tech sergeant doesn't like us."

"Why?"

"Because our average grade is higher than his damn IQ, that's why."

"So?"

"We're a threat to him. If we catch the lieutenant's eye, he's liable to promote us to be instructors and the sergeant might wind up overseas, and you're the only dimwit in this outfit who thinks that is a goal of choice. That's why. Wake up and smell the coffee."

"Oh."

"I'll kiss Cpl. Fink's ass a little at chow tonight and pick his brain. He thinks I'm pretty hot shit and he'll clue me as to what's going on."

The ploy was successful. "I told you, Osborne, didn't I tell you? We're going on a Short Arm Inspection. That's worse than anything they've got at Grady. Except cleaning the gut at an autopsy."

"What's a Short Arm Inspection?"

"They go in a barracks and roll everybody out of the sack at four o'clock in the morning before they've had a chance to piss and line 'em up to look at their dicks and see if they've got clap or syph they haven't reported."

"What? Why do they need us?"

"Because you always go to a strange outfit where you don't know anybody and can't tip 'em off ahead of time. Don't forget it's a court martial if you have V.D."

"I still don't understand why they need us."

"They have to have a medical officer do the actual looking, but they bring along a couple of dog-faces to hold the flashlight and check off the roster. Also it makes the officers look more important to have an escort."

"I never heard of such. Why do they call it Short Arm Inspection?" Otten leveled a long stare at him. "Oh," said Porter Osborne, Jr.

It was only natural that Otten would volunteer to man the clipboard and check off the names. He stood at Capt. Martin's right shoulder. Porter, at his left shoulder, held the flashlight and shined with perfect aim each individual crotch. A corporal stood directly behind the officer and barked instructions. The officer sat on a stool at the end of the barracks, his hands akimbo on widespread knees while sleep-tousled soldiers shuffled forward one at a time, gave their names to be checked off by Otten, and presented their most private parts on eye-level to the scrutiny of the dutiful captain. No one there had the faintest aspiration on that morning to be an officer.

The corporal seemed to be the only one present who was completely free of embarrassment and, indeed, of any tinge of self-consciousness. He manifested the indifference, the callousness, of habit and long practice, with no hint of either sensitivity or mercy.

"Awright, there! Skin it back and milk it down!"

"Quit hunching backwards and stick it out in the light!"

"Don't be so quick on the draw; hold it there long enough for the captain to look!"

"Whatcha trying to hide? Skin it back! Milk it down, dammit!"

When the ordeal was over and they approached their barracks, it was Otten who began the merriment. "My God, Osborne, I thought I was going to laugh out loud in spite of myself when the captain had to lean forward to see that little bitty thing one guy was trying his dead-level best to stretch out, but it kept getting away from him; looked like a one-eyed newt hiding in a bed of moss. Then the captain had to jerk his head back when the next one in line reeled out a damn fire hose and almost tapped his nose with it. I thought for a minute there we might be called on to treat a whiplash in an officer."

"It was awful," said Porter, "but did you notice how some of those guys couldn't stop chattering? And if one got coy and said, 'Let me see if I can find it,' you knew he was fixing to pull out a big one?"

"Yeah. And there were a couple of boys that had to be from somewhere down South who called it 'my little old goober' and then flashed something that would scare a spreading adder off a rock."

"Well, I hope I never hear 'skin it back' again the longest day I live. The Jews were wrong about Jesus, but they were right on target when Abraham started cutting off foreskins. Some of those ding-dongs just plain stunk even from where I was; I don't know how the captain stood it."

"Don't pull any of that circumcision snobbery on me, Osborne. Anything stinks if you don't keep it clean."

"Kahlil Gibran said, 'In the dew of little things the heart finds its morning and is refreshed,'" responded Porter.

"Kiss my uncircumcised ass," snarled Otten. "Give Betsill that line and maybe he'll make a song out of it. I know what you mean about the captain, though. After fifteen minutes I wanted to yell for the world to hear, 'I didn't want to be a doctor anyhow!'" There was a relaxed tone in his voice that enabled Porter to laugh out loud.

"I've sure learned one thing," he vowed to Otten. "I don't ever want to see that picture again of She-may-look-clean-but. And another thing—I'm not making any more hundreds on tests until I get my ass a thousand miles away from Camp Grant, Illinois."

"You're mighty right," agreed Otten. "Let's keep mum about this experience, though, and see if we can't tutor old Calhoun so he'll be the star next time."

"Arteries carry blood away from the heart; veins carry blood back to the heart," chanted Porter.

"Lub-dup, lub-dup, lub-dup," responded Otten. They threw their heads back and laughed. Together. Camaraderie born of strange union.

They never perpetrated their plan on Calhoun. The next morning while they shivered at assembly despite overcoats and gloves, trying to stand erect and not pull their necks down into their collars, the first sergeant stepped before them with his clipboard. The papers on it fluttered in the mean wind.

"Calhoun!" he bellowed. "Griffin Calhoun, PFC!"

"Present!"

"Front and center."

Griffin Calhoun stepped out of the second rank, cornered to the left, back to the right, again to the right, halted in front of the sergeant, executed a smart left-face, and snapped him a salute. He stood rigidly at attention, one corner of his coat snapping in the wind.

"Your father been sick?" asked the sergeant, his voice still audible throughout the platoon.

"No," responded Calhoun.

"You sure?" pushed the sergeant.

"Yes."

"Well, he's dead." The hand with the frozen finger snatched a yellow paper from the clipboard and proffered it. "Heart attack! Midnight! Here's the telegram, if you want a copy."

Calhoun remained rigidly at attention, not moving a muscle. The wind still blew the corner of his coat.

"Pack your gear; leave it at the company office; pick up your pass for a week's compassionate leave; the Red Cross will carry you to the bus. Dismissed!"

Calhoun executed a perfect about-face and marched off, looking neither to right nor left. The stunned Porter Osborne noted that he was dry-eyed and his face was expressionless. The platoon stood at attention, and the sergeant began announcements. Porter could not bear it. He broke ranks, approached the sergeant, and saluted.

"Osborne, Porter. PFC 14143150. Request permission to speak to 1st Sgt. Fisk!"

"What do you want?"

"Couldn't you send somebody to help Calhoun?"

"He don't need no help to pack a duffel bag!"

"Well, sergeant, somebody just to be with him. This has to be a terrible time for him. Please."

"All right. Permission granted! Go help him pack and then report back on the double!"

"Not me, Sergeant. Send Otten. They've been friends all their lives."

"Otten! Fall out and escort Calhoun to the barracks and then the company office. Report back to duty in thirty minutes! On the double!"

"Thank you, Sergeant," said Porter.

"Osborne!"

Porter looked him full in the face. "Yes?"

"This is the Army. If it's sympathy you're looking for, you'll find it in the dictionary between *shit* and *syphilis*! Have you got that?"

"Yes, sir!" shouted Porter. "Thank you, sir!"

"Sir?" bellowed the sergeant. "As soon as this formation is over, report to the mess hall! You got KP till you can remember how to address a noncommissioned officer!"

"Yes, sir!" persisted Porter and did his about-face.

"He shouldn't oughta have yelled at you," said Lamar Betsill in the Day Room that night. "I can't stand that yelling anymore. This is worse than school. Somebody around here's always yelling, but he's the worst. I'll find some way to fix him. I knowed when I seen that telegram somebody was dead. I told you about them telegrams, didn't I?"

Porter thought of his own father, invincible, vibrant, essential to so many people. He spoke around the lump in his throat. "Lamar, get your guitar and sing 'It's a picture of life's other side,' will you? The time is right for a sweet sad song."

"Won't make you break out in no poetry, will it?" asked Betsill.

"They swell in sapphire smoke out of the blue cracks in the ground. . ."

19 **b**y the time Calhoun returned from the funeral of his father, Osborne had finished the punitive stint of KP, reflecting that gratification afforded by sergeant-baiting was too fleeting to warrant an entire week of heavy pots and spotless floors. His fingers were shriveled and white from GI soap; his hair and skin reeked with the heavy odor of greasy bacon. Nausea was a familiar companion. KP was a torture to be avoided at any cost.

Griffin Calhoun, to Porter's eye, had undergone a strange sea change, had become in the throes of personal tragedy an heroic figure, his habits less irritating because his daddy had died. Porter projected his own feelings had he lost his father. He had learned with horror that the Army gave a soldier compassionate leave upon the death of a parent but none for a sibling or a grandparent. He thought of his frail, dainty little grandmother. Although he still equated prayer with futility and regarded it as a puerile exercise, he found himself occasionally when he was alone saying through clenched teeth, "You'd better not let anything happen to them till I come marching home."

He suffered so much in fantasy that he assumed Calhoun must be experiencing even greater pain in reality, simultaneously manifesting, however, a degree of stoicism that Porter could not have mustered. Suffering produced nobility; Calhoun obviously had to be suffering, although indiscernibly; *ergo* Calhoun was noble. This was a concept that Porter, with delicacy, did not mention, but it was fitting to defer to him; Griffin deserved special consideration. Porter found it incongruous that any figure with the slightest trace of nobility be involved in a Short Arm Inspection, and he thwarted Carter Otten's efforts to entrap their friend.

"Don't make a hundred, Griffin," he said. "Whatever you do, don't make a hundred. On anything."

Calhoun, for his part, gave no indication that he either required or recognized compassion and he apparently confused deference with obsequiousness. He returned to Camp Grant as full of bluff and bluster as ever and the more consideration Porter showed him, the more he badgered Porter. "Vitamin" and "Flintheart" were roared so often and in such glee in the barracks and over the parade ground that they became common nicknames for Osborne with the rest of the company, and his deltoids went from being bruised to callused, trophies of the rabbit punches with which Calhoun punctuated what he regarded as his more penetrating verbal sallies. Porter in charity and tolerance assured himself that this behavior was the inarticulate and rather primitive effort on Calhoun's part to regain his composure and re-establish status quo, and maintained patience. He did, however, develop an agility in twisting and ducking whenever Calhoun opened his mouth that was nothing short of phenomenal and resulted in a large number of Calhoun's meaty assaults swinging impotently and unbalancingly in thin air.

"Why you let him treat you like that?" queried Betsill.

Porter looked loftily at his Sault San Marie friend. "*Ça lui tant de plaisir et à moi si peu de peine.*"

"Huh?"

"I found this book in the Post Library called *The Brothers Karamazov* that's really wonderful after you get through the first hundred pages and figure out who all the characters are. In the middle of it, a young girl is confessing to the priest that she's been screwing yet another man in the village and the priest asks her why she keeps doing this over and over, and that's what she tells him. It's a Russian novel and that's a French quotation, and like it or not, it's the way this guy Dostoyevski wrote it. It means, 'It gives him so much pleasure and me so little pain.' To me it's sort of like the mood in your song about 'It's a picture of life's other side.'"

"You should forget I asked yet," said Lamar. "You wanta go to the PX or not?"

Otten, true to Porter's vision of being the other puppy, did not have an attention span for prolonged grief. He was impatient and imperious. "For God's sake, Osborne, his old man had lived out his life. After all, he was fifty years old. Quit being so melodramatic; you're making a mountain out of a molehill."

Otten had discovered the joys of getting a pass into town and led his two comrades there as frequently as they permitted. It was a ten-minute walk to the front gate of Camp Grant and from there a twenty-minute bus ride to downtown. The Jade Room was the gathering place of choice, its facade decorated with bright green neon, its interior so crammed with boisterous GI's that its walls seemed to bulge, its front door accommodatingly open to allow patrons and canned music to spill out onto the sidewalk and into the night of Rockford, Illinois. It was necessary to turn sideways and push to get through the crush of khaki and the blue cloud of cigarette smoke to the bar. Protocol dictated that a customer scream his request for a beer and then try to plow through the swarm in the hope of meeting one of the girls sitting in booths alongside the walls. Since one of them was unattended no longer than two minutes from entry, this was more often than not a futile undertaking, and the majority of Jade Room clients settled for standing at the bar and swilling beer until happily intoxicated. Otten, obsessed with the goal of feminine conquest, insisted on cruising the walls.

"Hell, you never can tell when I'll stumble onto something choice and get my ashes hauled, and if I don't, I can at least, by God, look," he philosophized.

Night after night, Otten looked and looked. Porter most of the time stayed in camp. Then when Otten returned, he listened and listened.

"God, Osborne, you should have seen what I ran into tonight. The cutest little blonde you ever saw, with a page-boy bob and breasts that stood up and out real proud-like and you could see her ribs outlined below her breasts. I tell you, she was exciting!"

"That's what you call the costal flair," reminded Porter.

"There wasn't anything about her to make you remember a cadaver. This was warm living flesh. Just right. A handful on each side, not too big and not too little. Just right."

"How are your ashes?"

"Aw, a buck sergeant beat me out. If I'd had another sixty seconds to charm her, he wouldn't have stood a chance. These women are fascinated by a Southern accent, but they're still impressed by rank."

"Like the lady on the train," agreed Porter.

"Goddam, Osborne, don't you ever forget anything?"

"Not much. Carlyle said that a nation that forgets history is doomed to repeat it. I try not to forget much; there are a lot of things that have happened to me I don't want to repeat."

"Osborne, you ain't real. You need to get your nose out of those books and smell the coffee. How long have you been reading that thick thing you're on now?"

"Almost two weeks," defended Porter. "It's long and it's slow reading, and in case you haven't noticed, we don't have too much uninterrupted time around this place without sergeants telling us what to do."

"Well, I've heard about guys who read Russian novels. They turn peculiar and have pipe burns on their coats and get scaly and dried up by the time they're forty."

"Well, I will have lived out my life by then, won't I? You reckon you'll have had your ashes hauled by the time I get scaly?"

"Haw!" interposed Calhoun. "Got you a good one then, didn't he? Old Vitamin's on the ball tonight, ain't that right, Flintheart? What? What!"

"Both of you can go to hell," fumed Otten. "I really need y'all to go with me to town because those are nice little girls who go to the Jade Room and they travel in pairs. It's easier for a couple of guys to pick them up than for a single fellow to cut one out from the pack. At least you could go, Griffin. You've got more sense than to be reading things that are good for you."

"Aw, Carter, ease up on us, will you?" said Calhoun. "I never have been any good at meeting girls for the first time and you know it. Besides, when I was home Miss Margaret and I sort of got ourselves engaged. That's the way it is, what?"

Porter assumed that Calhoun was suffering silently again and came to his defense. "That's right, Otten. Lay off. There are those of us who are concerned with things in life other than your ashes and how you manage to dispose of them."

"Osborne, one of these days you're going to run that mouth of yours till it gets you a good ass-beating."

"It's already happened," rejoined Porter. "And at the hands of someone who could pound you into the ground. I'll try to be careful not to let that particular phase of history repeat itself."

> *"Giants and the Genii,*
> *Multiplex of wing and eye. . ."*

20 **a**merican troops soon landed on Bougainville in some place called the Solomon Islands, pinpoints in the Pacific previously undreamt by the average citizen and located only by the most avid geographers, or by ordinary civilians who had purchased globes. The troops were accompanied by daredevil reporters who sent back to the United States graphic stories of the bravery of our boys amidst the gore and horrors of war, complete with photographic proof that Japanese snipers were indeed using the Red Cross armbands of unarmed American medical corpsmen for target practice. One photograph in particular was of a solitary victim; it detailed the limbs-akimbo death sprawl in tall foreign grass, the grotesquely twisted angle of the neck, the identifying armband of international mercy, and, unmistakably, a fly feasting at the corner of a gaping, uncaring mouth. Porter Osborne, Jr., shuddered, considered his own status, denied to himself the sinking feeling in his gut, and compartmentalized vigorously.

Carter Otten gave him unexpected assistance in that activity as he further developed his obsession about dating and sex. He compared it to a military objective and filled Porter's ear with such detail that it took Porter's mind off the war and opened an entirely new compartment for him.

"The admirals and generals aren't the only ones who can plan strategy. Sex is like war: I sight my target, reconnoiter, establish a beachhead, and then penetrate to the interior and accept surrender. It gives me a hard to think about it."

"Carter, I think you're terrible. That's portraying women as the enemy."

"By God, they ain't friends or they'd be meeting my boat waving and smiling and offering their titties like ripe apples. Didn't you read *Mutiny on the Bounty*? Now, those were friendly natives. When some-

194

body has something they're not using themselves but just sit on it and won't let you use it, they're being a dog in the manger and they are an enemy."

"Carter, I don't think that's any sort of adequate corollary; you're using a wild assumption rather than a proven proposition. There are other things in life besides sex."

"Don't hand me any of that learned bullshit, Osborne. We're soldiers now and soldiers are supposed to be horny. Aren't you aware of the proven proposition that if a guy won't fuck, he won't fight?"

"There's a big difference between 'won't' and 'can't', Carter. I realize by now that you'd stick it in anything that squats to pee, but even you can't fuck if there's no opportunity."

"A real man is supposed to make opportunity, Osborne. You can sit in camp on your philosophical butt reading books and babying Calhoun while he moons over Miss Margaret all you want to; I'm going to find me a nice girl and launch a campaign that winds up with me screwing her ears off before we leave this town. Do you realize in only six more weeks basic training will be over for us? If you think I'm leaving Rockford, Illinois, without getting laid, you're crazy. You're supposed to have a girl in every port."

"That's the Navy, Otten; we're not sailors."

"You kiss my ass, Osborne. I'll show you."

Carter Otten kept that promise; he showed his friends. Dedicated to avoiding prostitutes or sluts, he foraged far and wide in search of the beautiful, intelligent girl of resistant virtue who would be a worthy candidate for his assault of Southern charm and overwhelming virility. Girls with that résumé, however, were as isolated by prudence and custom as daughters of wise fathers anywhere; they did not date strange soldiers without at least some semblance of a proper introduction. Otten rose to that challenge.

Diligent research unearthed a fraternity brother still in Georgia who had a sister who was a senior at Northwestern University in Evanston, Illinois. The sister was engaged but succumbed to Otten's combination of charm and outrageous blandishments over the telephone to the point of arranging a blind date with three of her sorority sisters for Otten and his two friends, all of whom were perfect Southern gentlemen, of course. There was safety in numbers, and three was safer than two; one on one was unthinkable among strangers.

"The hell you're not going! I've stood in line with a pocketful of nickels at the damn phone four times this week waiting to call long distance and set this up, and both of you are sure as hell going to back me up. This is the chance of a lifetime. We're going to meet these sophisticated girls from one of the major universities in the country and we're meeting them in the second largest city in America! This could be the beginning of a whole new chapter in all our lives!" He gave Porter a suddenly cautionary look. "They are sophisticated and we are meeting them in Chio, and don't you come up with any of that country bumpkin horseshit you fake at times."

On the bus from Rockford to Chicago, he further admonished, "Osborne, don't you even think about telling these girls we flunked out of med school. You do and I'll break your back when we get back to camp!"

"If you don't mention med school, I sure won't tell them," promised Porter. "How are we going to recognize them?"

"Mine will be wearing a brown hat with a pheasant feather on it, and I imagine they'll be the only three college girls sitting together in the lobby of the Hotel Sherman."

"Hat?" repeated Porter. "Did you say 'hat'?" After a moment he gave a little yelp. "What hotel did you say?"

"The Hotel Sherman, Osborne. It's the finest hotel in Chio; what's the matter with you?"

"Nothing's the matter with me; something's the matter with the damn hotel. You know who it's bound to be named for, and I'm not going to set foot in it. My grandmother would skin me alive if I did."

"Come off that crap, Osborne, and quit acting like a Southern hick. Everybody up here forgot the Civil War a long time ago."

"War between the States," Porter corrected automatically.

"Besides, we're just meeting them there and then we're leaving to go to a restaurant one of them knows about. For God's sake, relax, we won't be in that hotel five minutes."

"I'll wait on the sidewalk while you and Griffin meet the girls and bring them out. There are some things I know ahead of time that I'm not going to do, and entering the door of a hotel named for Sherman is one of them."

They took a cab from the bus terminal and huddled together on the back seat trying to stay warm. Porter expressed outrage when the driver turned onto a wide and busy thoroughfare and he saw the street sign.

"Sheridan Avenue? Can't we ride on some other street?"

"Shut up, Osborne," both of his companions said in unison.

"Whassa matter?" asked the driver. "I tought you want da Hotel Sherman. It's on Sheridan Avenue and we're about dere. Where you guys from? Ever been in Chio before?"

"We're from Georgia," responded Otten. He looked in triumph at Porter. "I told you it was Chio."

On the sidewalk they were buffeted by the meanest, keenest wind Porter had ever encountered. It blew unhindered from the Arctic Circle, grew vicious crossing Lake Michigan, and penetrated relentlessly every garment he wore. With a propitiatory aside to his grandmother, Porter pushed between his friends to seek the shelter of the lobby. "Better to stay alive in the Hotel Sherman than freeze to death on Sheridan Avenue. I haven't forgotten who I am, but you wouldn't believe where we are." Suddenly he held his head high. "I'm not capitulating, I'm invading," he vowed in silence and strode with assurance as a member of the trio.

The main thing he remembered later about their dates was the hats. The pheasant feather was not utilized just as a badge of identification; all three girls were garbed in fashion-magazine style and all three topped off their outfits with hats; not inconspicuous berets or tams but eye-compelling millinery that swooped and swirled and that ladies in Georgia would have worn only to funerals or UDC meetings. Porter took one look and was intimidated; these girls were the most sophisticated creatures he had ever seen. "Poor Otten," he thought. "This is a lost evening for him. They're dressed up like sore thumbs. Whoever heard of getting his ashes hauled by a girl with a hat on?" He was thankful anew for the equalizing appearance of his khaki uniform and grateful that he had expended extra effort shining his shoes.

After the inconsequential chatter of introductions, when it transpired that they were to catch a cab again to go to their restaurant and Porter overheard that it was several blocks over on Stanton Avenue, he excused himself for a moment. Perching on the edge of an easy chair, he removed one of his shoes, tapped it deliberately against his palm, and deposited a small mound of red dirt on an ivory colored portion of the plush and patterned carpet. Replacing his shoe, he carefully twisted his foot and ground the Brewton County soil into the fabric, noting with satisfaction the resultant smudge. The Army could force him to go to Camp Grant, but if he of his own free will was going to roam Sheridan and Stanton avenues and compromise his heritage by chatting in the Hotel Sherman, then he would leave a mark of defiance. He knew from multiple wash days on the farm how difficult it would be to remove that mark.

"What the hell have you been doing, Osborne? The girls and the cab are waiting. Let's go."

> "'In the fell clutch of circumstance
> I winced but did not cry aloud.
> Under the bludgeoning of Fate
> My head is bloody but unbowed.'

Let's go."

"Goddammit, if you let another line of poetry pass your lips tonight, I'm going to break your back twice. You got that?"

"Right," laughed Porter. "No med school, no poetry. Let's go get your ashes hauled. I think it's going to take all three of us."

On the late bus that night for the two-hour trip back to Rockford, Porter rated the evening as an inconsequential encounter with complete strangers, the meal as inferior in quality but better in presentation than one provided by the mess sergeant, the conversation as stylized and stimulating as if all the interchanges between them had been printed on flash cards. Also he was broke. Otten had peremptorily ordered one check from the waiter and decreed to his companions that they could split it equally later. Porter had prudently remembered the contents of his pocket and inspected the right-hand side of the menu. Otten had profligately ordered the most expensive entree available plus an appetizer plus a dessert plus three mixed drinks, and finally a liqueur. When Porter handed over a third of their final bill to Otten, his wallet was empty and he felt swindled.

In the bus, Otten was enthusiastic. "What an evening! I've finally broken the ice and run into some ladies. Life is looking up."

"Otten, you're crazy. It takes those girls an hour to get from Northwestern into town to meet us and us two hours to get there from Camp Grant. Logistics will tell you this was a one-time encounter and they are just ships that pass in the night. A dull and expensive night at that."

"Hell, Osborne, you have a narrow view; you can't see the forest for the trees. I told you I was mapping a campaign, didn't I? The first thing you do is reconnoiter and get all the information you can and then you plot your beachhead. I know as well as you we can't go traipsing back and forth to Chio, but I got the name and phone number of one of their sorority sisters who lives in Rockford and is taking a quarter off from school. This evening was strictly a means to an end; you won't ever learn anything."

"I've learned that from now on I'm going to insist on separate checks," retorted Porter.

"Besides, Osborne," persisted Otten, "these girls were the caliber of the ones back home. You'll have to admit these were the first genteel ladies we've met since we left Atlanta."

"I'm glad to hear you're not calling them 'broads.' And they all three did say 'Chicago,' but I'm not going so far as to say they were ladies."

"What? Girls that looked like that? Who belong to a sorority at Northwestern? That dress like that? You're crazy."

"That's just it," answered Porter. "No lady at home would wear a hat in the evening, especially not out to dinner. And another thing; remember when that wind hit us coming out of the restaurant? It blew the hats off their heads and you and Griffin had to chase them. Well, the reason they lost their hats is that they turned them loose to grab their skirts, and I thought I was finally going to see something to make the evening worthwhile. I'll have you know every one of those girls had on pink flannel baggy drawers that came all the way to their knees. It was a most unappetizing sight."

"What the hell's that got to do with it? That wind was cold as a witch's tit."

"No difference. A real lady is willing to suffer for the sake of appearances. Amalita Hunt would freeze to death before she'd wear drawers like that. I should have known when I saw the hats, but the drawers prove it. Those girls are not ladies."

"Well, smart ass, what are they then?"

"They're ribbon clerks," asserted Porter. "They're pretty, empty-headed Yankee ribbon clerks, and they were as nervous as we were. On top of that, they're going to wind up being old maids. I say, hats and long drawers."

Back at camp, Carter Otten moved quickly to further his own private campaign. Once again he demanded the peripheral support of Porter.

"I don't want any more blind dates, at least not until warm weather," resisted Porter. "I can't afford them in the first place, and besides, I hope I never run into any more of those bloomers or teddies or whatever they call them up here in the north. At least not on girls with hats on."

"Osborne, shut up and be serious. I've gone to a lot of trouble over this date. The first time I called her she stalled but did talk to me for about ten minutes. I laid on the old Southern accent almost as thickly as you do, and she told me to check back with her. When I did she had called her sisters at Northwestern, and it was like stealing candy from a baby; we've got a date this coming Saturday night."

"That's fine. Congratulations. Lots of luck. You don't need me."

"Oh, hell, yes I do. One of her sorority sisters told me that Lenore really loves poetry, so I need you to teach me a poem or two. Nothing like having extra artillery in reserve. All I know is part of 'The Shooting of Dan McGrew.'"

"Well, if you're meeting her in the Jade Room, 'A bunch of the boys were whooping it up in the Malamute Saloon' might be appropriate, but if this girl's name is Lenore, she might not cotton up to 'the lady that's known as Lou.' Why don't you have a couple of stanzas of 'The Raven' on reserve if you need them? Better yet, why don't you just check out a book of poetry from the Post Library for yourself? I don't have any idea what you like or what you need or what you have in mind."

Otten explained to him in explicit detail what he liked, what he needed, and also what he had in mind, the three items being identical. "You've gotta help me, Osborne," he importuned. Porter found him a quick and retentive student and actually enjoyed coaching him on Keats, Dickinson, Housman, Khayyam, and Millay.

"Particularly Millay, Otten. For some reason, all girls like Millay."

"God, I didn't know there was so much pussy in poetry. This is going to be like shooting fish in a barrel. You know what? I like Millay myself.

'I too beneath your moon, almighty Sex,
Go forth at nightfall crying like a cat,'

What an honest woman!"

"And what a dishonest man is memorizing her poems," chided Porter.

"Don John of Austria is hidden in the smoke."

21   **O**tten began dating Lenore regularly and reporting in explicit detail to Porter, whose participation in his campaign was increasingly grudging.

"She really is a great girl, a real beauty, lots of style, and smart as a whip. I'm lucky to have found her. Let's go over that one again about

> 'When I was one-and-twenty
> I heard a wise man say,
> Give crowns and pounds and guineas
> But not your heart away.'

Her Tri-delt sisters were right, she really is a sucker for poetry."

"Is this still a campaign or are you beginning to change your mind about trying to screw such a nice girl?"

"Hell, Osborne, they don't come that nice. Any female is fair game for a hunter, and a really nice one is a gentleman's trophy. The difference is that you have to spend more time plotting and stalking when you're going to bag a nice one. They're gun-shy and wary as hell and you have to creep downwind or on their blind side and be very, very patient, but the hunt is always exhilarating. Hell, yes, the campaign is still on. Pour the poetry to me, old buddy."

Porter finally said, "I'm not feeling good about this, Otten."

"Hell, Osborne, it's going great. I haven't offered to kiss her for these first three dates. That drives them wild, you know. Most girls are schooled to turn you down on the first date or at least to be coy about it, and then when you don't even try, they think either that you're shy and inexperienced or else that they're not attractive or appealing. Then when you finally do make a move they find an unbridled stallion, a fire pit of passion, and the trick is to make them feel responsible for unleashing it. If they feel responsible for causing it, you can make them feel like they ought to do something about it. I laid that stanza on her tonight about

> 'I wouldn't do such 'cause I liked her too much
> But I learned about women from her.'"

"Well, you're going to have to live up to that, I should think."
"Bullshit. Don't forget the last line.

> 'The colonel's lady and Judy O'Grady
> Are sisters under the skin.'

And they are, Osborne. I don't know how I underestimated that poem of Kipling's up until now; it and I were made for each other. I'm gonna have to get you to write it out for me and I'll learn all of it sometime. When I have time. Right now I want you to go over that one again about

> 'Mistake me not—unto my inmost core
> I do desire your kiss upon my mouth;
> They have not craved a cup of water more
> That bleach upon the deserts of the South;'

That kind of fits in with the war and the noble soldier maybe going off to fight in North Africa without me having to spell it out. This is what you call a subtle girl."

"It's not going to work, Otten. Sounds to me like she's got too much sense to fall for this."

"Sense has nothing to do with it; you must be a virgin your own self to talk like that. I've made fifty girls so far and every one of them has been intelligent. Stupid girls bore me to death and it's not worth sticking it in them to put up with trying to talk to them."

Osborne looked incredulous but said nothing.

"Hell, one of those poems by what's-her-face Millay you're so crazy about illustrates that perfectly.

> 'Pity me that the heart is slow to learn
> What the swift mind beholds at every turn.'

I can't use that one and ain't about to learn it, but it sure points up that women are governed by glands as much as we are. Don't talk to me about sense."

"I still say it's not going to work, Otten. But at least you're learning about poetry. You're going to lose this campaign but you'll be a better person for it. And it's Edna St. Vincent Millay. Don't call her what's-her-face. You're bullshitting yourself."

Lamar Betsill was puzzled. "What's going on? Otten treats you like dirt for two months and makes fun of everything you do or say and all of a sudden you're asshole buddies. Don't see one without the other. Got your heads together all the time talk, talk, talking. I heard him on the drill field today during break making you say a verse over and over till he learnt it, and yet he raises hell if I try to play my guitar. I don't get it."

"He won't either, Lamar. Don't worry."

"Huh? Whatcha mean? You Georgie Peaches sure are crazy; I keep telling you that."

Griffin Calhoun was uninterested. He had no inclination at all to listen either to poetry or to recitations of Otten's progress. He was bored because of exposure to previous conquests. "Hell, Osborne, it's the same old story. He raves and rants about whoever he's fallen for at the time till you're sick and tired of hearing about 'em, y'know what I mean? Then once he gets in their britches he drops 'em like a hot potato. I've seen it over and over, what?"

Porter Osborne was scandalized. "You mean every girl he dates he tells all these intimate details to somebody? That's awful."

"Pretty grim, all right. But that's Otten. Take him or leave him. I just say 'uh-huh' and go on about my business. No skin off my ass."

"You do not say 'uh-huh'; you say 'what, what?' I'm afraid that without intending it this is becoming some of my business, maybe even some skin off my ass. I don't see how you can call a guy like that your best friend, Calhoun."

"Who the hell is your best friend, Vitamin?"

"I guess I don't have one."

"Well?"

"Oh."

Carter Otten was excited. "Osborne, it's great. I've got her trust now. She's been hot for my body for the last three dates, but now I've got her trust. The thing is to build to sex so gradually that they begin to think it's their idea. You know they've all been raised not to let you feel around; so I didn't try to grab a tit: I just eased down and kissed one. Drove her wild. That's all I did on that date. The trick is to stop and don't try to push beyond a certain point; then the next time they've got no reason to keep you from going at least that far. The next date I was playing with them like a juggler at the fair."

"I don't want to hear about it."

"Yeah, you do. Let me give you another tip. A nice girl has been taught not to let some nasty old boy put his hand below her waist; they'll tense up and push you away for that every time. But nobody, Mama or Aunt Susie or older sister, ever thought of telling little darling not to play with a boy's pecker; it just never crossed their minds that might be a problem. So what I do is hold hands while I'm laying a hot kiss on her and just casually pull her hand over on my peter. Nine times out of ten she can't resist exploring it, because she's heard about one all her life and all of a sudden here's one she can find out about for herself. Standing up and straining to get out. It really makes 'em hot."

"I told you I don't want to hear about it."

"Shut up, I'm talking. Lenore is about ready for that as her next step, I think. I tell you, Osborne, this is a sweet dish and really a wonderful girl. Another time and another place, I might even get serious about her."

"Are you in love?"

"Sure, Osborne, sure. You said it. For the fifty-first time in my life. You know, I wish I'd met that Millay woman in her youth.

> 'And why you come complaining
> Is more than I can see.
> I loved you Wednesday, — yes — but what
> Is that to me?'

A lot of times she reminds me of myself."

"I'm not going to teach you any more poetry. I'm sick of you. Lenore doesn't deserve to be treated this way."

"What way? A nice well-mannered Georgia boy comes along, recites poetry, teaches her to smooch, relieves her of her cherry and disappears on the battlefield. She gave for her country; she'll remember it all her life."

"She doesn't deserve to be talked about. To anybody. There are some things that are private business. No more poetry, Otten. Don't tell me another word about your progress or your prowess and don't look to me to learn any more poems. I feel dirty."

"Well, aren't you a goddam little prig? I don't need any more out of you. When I say that one to her like you taught me to about

'Love is not all: it is not meat nor drink
Nor slumber nor a roof against the rain;
Nor yet a floating spar to men that sink
And rise and sink and rise and sink again;'

it'll be all over. She'll be hassling in the short rows. When I get to the end of that one, she'll be mine, all mine. I already learned it, I've got it in reserve, and I don't need you anymore. Did anybody ever tell you that you've got serious psychological problems if you think sex is dirty?"

"It's plain as day nobody bothered to teach you the difference between clean and dirty. Did anybody ever tell you that an obsession is a sickness?"

Otten laughed. With true merriment. "Osborne, I ain't believing you. You read all those books, you've got a memory like an elephant, and you seem to be intelligent. Even overly intelligent at times. Yet down underneath you're as innocent as a baby. It's almost as much fun to educate you as it is Lenore."

"Shut up, Otten. No more talking about it."

"I'll talk about what I goddam please."

"I'll tell everybody we flunked out of med school."

The black eyes lost their shine, the brows contorted into an immediate scowl. "You're bucking for a fat lip, Osborne."

"Tell it to the chaplain and get your TS card punched. If we don't talk about med school, we don't talk about your pecker. I mean it."

"You're a hoot, Osborne. You're a real hoot."

Otten's conquest was delayed by an event beyond his control.

"Hell, Osborne, she had on the goddam rag. I'm still saving that last push-'em-to-the-floor sonnet. I acted very mature and understanding and had her almost apologizing for her condition. Next date is it; she's even acknowledged as much. I have her promise."

The next day a longer delay ensued when the first sergeant announced winter maneuvers.

"Ten degrees below zero? Two feet of snow? Fourteen inches of ice solid on the Kishwaukee River? Stay outdoors all day for a week and sleep on the ground every night? You're crazy; even Yankee sergeants and lieutenants wouldn't try to make us do that."

He was wrong. They did. Porter wrote his family not to expect any letters for a week and told them why, being careful to point out that winter maneuvers at Camp Grant, Illinois, constituted no reason for them to slack off on their own writing.

He had recall of reading Jack London and Robert Service and resolved to make this adventure a memorable one, confident that if others could endure it then so could he. All he had to do was pay close attention to directions and remember who he was and that would carry him through.

They were transported in ribbed and tarpaulin-covered trucks that were reminiscent of pioneer wagons, pulled by grunting motors now instead of by horses; they crouched in the back stuffed stiffly in full field equipment. They huddled anonymously near anything or anybody that might provide warmth and a little shelter from the wind. They wore gloves, khaki ski masks under their helmets, long underwear, extra socks, and over everything the heavy woolen overcoats. Still they were cold. They were hauled like cattle, swaying and lurching in those trucks, helpless to maintain their balance at turns and bumps in the road, prevented from falling only by virtue of their tightly packed numbers, constantly sliding and shifting. They went in convoy for miles and miles into a white wilderness punctuated only by bare oak trees, upstretched limbs stark against the snow. They were deposited with their tents, their equipment, their noncoms, and their officers somewhere on the banks of the Kishwaukee River.

As the empty trucks rumbled away and left them, Porter Osborne, Jr., felt abandoned. He promptly forgot who he was. He forgot about Otten and Lenore, he forgot about the Japs and the Germans, he forgot about med school, Brewton County, his family, and Fritz. He compartmentalized as he never had done before; for the first time in his life he faced the prospect that he might be on the verge of death and he concentrated on defeating it. He thought it an imminent probability that he might freeze into the black Illinois mud and not be found before the snow melted. Sometime. Maybe in the spring. Or this might be the beginning of a new glacial age and his body would not surface for eons, not until it had been pushed and ground along with boulders as far south as Tennessee.

He was soon caught up in the battalion's efforts to conquer and tame this frozen vastness. They would establish in the face of ice and wind enough primitive creature comforts to ensure survival. They were American soldiers and they would prevail. They had been trained for this purpose. It was not only their heritage, it was their goal. Civilization, after all, was relative. Porter blindly followed orders, attacking with vigor the pick and shovel labor of digging slit trenches

206

in the frozen earth, contemplating how terrible the stimulus would be to make him hunker at this temperature with bared buttocks in communal evacuation. There were some aspects of civilization that should be absolute rather than relative; maybe he could wait a whole week.

The kitchen crew scraped away snow, suspended a canvas fly between trees, and assembled an efficient kitchen with alacrity, complete with gas burners beneath huge garbage cans of boiling water. The one frothing with soap and with the brush hanging from its rim was for scrubbing the mess kits, the clear bubbling one for rinsing. An army might travel on its stomach, but its progress would be torture if beset with dysentery. Porter approved the sanitary arrangements but noted with awe that the steam from the vats solidified defiantly into rime on twigs and branches not four feet above his head. Mankind was not conquering Nature here, was not accomplishing more than a tenuous truce, and had better watch its step.

This was Porter's initial encounter with a sleeping bag, and his first night in one was unforgettable for both agony and duration. He had shoveled snow away from his sleeping slot, spread his shelter half on the frigid turf as a ground cover, and unrolled the quilted, padded cylinder its full length. He tried to remember all the advice and instructions he had heard. Take your socks off as well as your shoes. Keep the shoes and all other clothing inside the sleeping bag with you. Remove all outer garments. The heat of your body will keep the inside of the bag warm. One of the mess sergeants had even extolled the virtues of lying naked in the sleeping bag as a device for producing radiant heat. Porter considered all these words, gazed briefly at the huge stars suspended in the crisp and crackling air, brushed frozen breath from his ski mask, and squirmed laboriously into his padded coffin, fully clothed in every article of clothing at his command, complete with overcoat and boots. What did mess sergeants know? They were all insulated by at least three inches of lard and had hair on their shoulders and backs as thick as an animal pelt. Porter was as slick and white as any pupa encased in a hibernating cocoon and felt as vulnerable. He put on his helmet liner and helmet, pulled the hood of the bag over his head, and tried to quit shaking. He was encased so tightly that he could not turn over inside his bag; it rolled with him and he dared not move for fear of getting into the snow drift he had made. Eventually he slept, but he could never recall getting warm.

Twice during the crystalline night he had to writhe his way out of the bag and step to the edge of his clearing, discovering first-hand the diuretic effect of combining hard ground, hot chocolate and zero temperatures. When reveille and the shrilling whistle of the first sergeant sounded, he felt that he had not slept a wink but had lain swaddled as rigidly as any mummy awaiting the resurrection. On his way to the chow line, he saw the dyed spots surrounding other sleeping areas, evidence that he was not the only one who had rejected going all the way to the latrine. As he held his chattering mess kit out for two fried eggs and a stack of pancakes, he endorsed the mess sergeant's advice: "Don't eat no yellow snow."

The first few days became blurred in his memory, for he passed them inside tents. Once he was a company aid man administering immediate treatment to walking wounded and returning them to combat. Once he had the responsibility of first aid for serious emergencies and earned kudos from the supervising sergeant for remembering the fluffy ABD pad that was essential for a sucking wound of the chest. Once he was in a larger tent, the Battalion Aid Station, and was given the task of triage under the watchful eye of a lieutenant, a real doctor.

Always he moved quickly, seeking a modicum of warmth through excessive activity, but always he was aware of the monstrous silence waiting just beyond the fragile barrier of his pulsing blood. Waiting, waiting. The snow, the ice, the frost were massive in overwhelming alliance and they would eventually win. He knew that. They were in no rush, were masters of patience, of stealth, so confident that they were frigidly indifferent. They did not even bother yet to creep, they just waited. Porter Osborne, Jr., felt that Yellow Dog Dingo had again entered his life and he ran because he had to. Let whoever would accuse him of being a brown-nosing eager beaver; he looked at the frozen plains of Illinois and he ran because he had to.

The day that his platoon was assigned to play the roles of wounded infantrymen and litter bearers would fade in his mind no quicker than an epitaph newly chiseled in polished granite. Porter was tagged as a land mine victim with a compound fracture of the femur, a wound that was assigned and duly noted by Lt. Long, who instructed Porter that, in the pursuit of realism, he must lie immobile in the snow until transported by litter bearers to the Company Aid Station. The officer also lined out the imperatives for silence and speed.

"You see that frozen river right over there? The Germans are dug in right across it with machine guns trained this way. Don't make a sound that might attract their attention to you or you'll draw fire that'll make your infiltration course look like a tea party. No smoking. Lie still and stay quiet. You got that?"

208

Porter looked at the lieutenant, remembered, and forced himself to breathe through his nose. "Yes, sir!" he snapped.

Within fifteen minutes, the officer with hoarse whispers had supervised a corpsman who wriggled forward on his belly to put a bandage on Porter's thigh before slithering off to another casualty some twenty yards away. Porter lay alone in the snow awaiting rescue and deliverance to the relative warmth of the first aid tent. He hissed at two corpsmen racing by in a crouch, garbed in white overdrapes to indulge the lieutenant's desire for realistic camouflage. They were bent on recovering the farthest victims first and ignored him.

He realized that he could not feel his toes when he curled and straightened them in his boots, fancied that he could feel his blood slowing in his veins. "It's going to set up like Jello and I'll be dead if I don't move," he thought. He looked all around; the lieutenant had disappeared. Porter rose to his feet, dropped the pretense that any Germans were near or that his femur was splintered and began flapping his arms and prancing in place. The corpsmen returned in a half run bearing a lucky victim between them on the bouncing litter.

"Hey," pleaded Porter, "how about picking me up next? I've got a broken leg and am going to freeze to death in this snow."

"No way," said the rear corpsman, after looking around to be sure the officer was not in sight. "We've got at least ten more that are a mile away, and we've got to bring them in first."

"But dammit, I'm going to die from hypothermia."

"We'll call it blood loss and forward your dog tags. It'll be at least an hour and a half before we get to you. We got our orders and Lt. Long is mean as a grizzly bear this morning; must have a big, tight dingleberry pinching and pulling. We're not about to cross him."

Porter reflexively opened his mouth but they were gone. He stamped his feet, hugged his arms, ran in place. An hour and a half? "You shall surely die," he affirmed into the sky.

Suddenly he was filled with resolve. "I'd rather be court-martialed than dead; they'll not get their hands on my dog tags this day." He began briskly marching to the east, away from camp, away from the territory of the lieutenant's rigid rule and his dictatorial supervision.

Within a hundred feet he was challenged. "Where you going, Osborne?"

It was Lamar Betsill, a muslin bandage obscuring half his face.

"I've got a compound comminuted fracture of the femur, and I am going to find a place where I can build a fire and get warm one more time before I find an early death in the snow. I've got at least an hour and a half before they pick me up. You wanta come?"

"I've got a head injury and am unconscious, paralyzed on the right side. The lieutenant told me so. Sure, I'll come. If I'm unconscious I don't know what I'm doing anyhow, and maybe they'll give me a Section 8 if they find me tracking through the snow with a Georgie Peach."

As they moved farther across the countryside, they accumulated five additional wounded who so despaired of being picked up on litters that they also dared to flout the specific orders of the lieutenant.

"Where we going?"

"I don't know yet," said Porter. "Just follow me and be real quiet; don't let the lieutenant hear you. I'll know the place when I find it."

In the sameness of the snow he very nearly missed it, a gully gouged out of the prairie by past rains or melting snows, all sharpness softened now by the thick blanket that padded the rest of the white land. It was at least thirty feet deep, seventy-five feet across. Porter gave one approving look at this hidden hollow, its bowl glistening in the sun, shielded completely from any wind sweeping the prairie, and dropped over the lip to slide down the steep slope to the bottom. Within minutes they had cleared a bare spot and had a fire.

"Only dead dry branches," Porter cautioned.

"Why's that?" asked Lamar.

"No smoke. Back home we hunt lightwood knots to start a fire because we want the smoke; keeps mosquitoes off. But James Fenimore Cooper always said dry dead wood so the Indians can't find your camp. Don't forget we're on maneuvers. We don't want to draw any Germans, Indians, or Japs, and we sure as hell don't want to draw any second lieutenants."

"Jesus Christ, dat fucking fire feels good. I never tought to get my ass warm again in dis life."

"Youse guys realize dis is Christmas Eve?"

"Shut up! You mention dat again we'll roll you in dis snow and talk about your girlfriend shacking up in a feather bed wid some 4-F."

"But we ain't scheduled to get back to camp for two more days. Dat means we spend Christmas Day in dis fucking wilderness. It's da end of de woild."

"Shut up, I'm telling you twice already yet! Jeez, I'm hungry."

Everyone had D bars, but it evolved that most of them also had squirreled away other goodies—crackers, Vienna sausage, candy—

treasures from the PX, tasty remnants of civilization. Betsill even produced three cans of Campbell's tomato soup.

"How'd you get out here with soup in your pack?" marveled Porter.

"Brought it in my gas mask."

"There isn't room."

"I took the guts out of my gas mask and threw them away. Gives you all sorts of room for other things."

"You did what? If we get gassed, you'll die."

"If we get gassed, I wanta die. I decided that on the fourteen-mile hike, smothering behind those goggles and having to suck air like a goldfish. If things get that bad, it's too much trouble to live. There's things worse than dying."

"But that's destroying government property!"

"Right. And if they gas me that's destroying government property. Cause that's all these noncoms and officers think I am anyhow."

"What if you get caught?"

"How's to get caught? You gonna rat on me?"

"Of course not. 'It's a picture of life's other side. Somebody has fell by the way.' Soo San Marie boys are crazy themselves. Tell me, Lamar, do you know what a dingleberry is?"

"Sure, don't you?"

"Never heard of one until a little while ago."

"When a little piece of shit gets caught in the hairs around your ass and keeps twisting up into a little ball for days and days before you find it, that's a dingleberry."

"Oh."

"Why?"

"The lieutenant is supposed to have a whole crop of them," laughed Porter.

They had a picnic; they had a ball. They pooled their resources and feasted on hot chocolate, hot soup, crackers, candy, and canned meat. The combination of sun, fire, and absence of breeze produced a coziness that was unbelievable. They took off their overcoats, used their packs for pillows, and stretched their feet to the glowing embers, as hot and smokeless as charcoal. Exhausted by wakeful nights in cold sleeping bags, inevitably they slept.

Porter awoke and stretched as luxuriously as any cat on a familiar hearth. He fancied that he heard a whistle in the distance. He looked at his six companions, realized that half of them were now sleeping in shadow, and looked at his watch.

He leaped to his feet and yelled. "Wake up! Quick! It's four o'clock! We've got to go! On the double!"

As they scrambled to their feet and struggled hastily into their gear, Porter admonished, "We've got to be sure this fire is completely out. Come on, let's all piss on it; then we can cover it with snow. We've got to hurry."

The fire was immediately surrounded by seven GI's with out-thrust pelvises and hyperextended spines.

"Jeez, I never tought I'd sleep dat warm and sound again. Or be able to go dat long widout getting up to piss."

"Make haste," said Porter. "We've got to get back; they're bound to have missed us by now. I sure hate to face that son of a bitch of a second lieutenant."

He moved his head to avoid the noxious steam arising from their dampened fire and his gaze was drawn upward to the rim of their hideout. Silhouetted against the sky, feet widespread, fists akimbo on his hips, staring down at them was Lt. Long. How long he had been there Porter did not know, but he looked fearsomely greater than life-size. Instinctively, true to his training, he reacted to the unexpected appearance of an officer of the United States Army. He turned loose his penis, saluted, assumed the rapid and rigid position of attention, and shouted, "Ten-shut!"

The buddy to his left gulped. "Whassa matter chew, goddam-mit? You pissed on me!"

At that moment they all followed Porter's gaze, leapt to attention and stood like saluting statues around the steaming remnants of their fire. Lamar Betsill still emitted a stream of urine, but he saluted.

"At ease!" commanded the lieutenant. "Get yourselves dressed and double-time out of there!" He turned and blew his whistle, two short blasts and one long. "I found them!" he shouted across the frozen prairie. Porter heard distant whistles responding and delayed following the scrambling retreat of his comrades up the gully wall long enough to smother the last vestiges of their fire with snow.

"Out of there, soldier!" bellowed the lieutenant. "Up and out of there!"

"Yes, Suh!" Porter shouted and obeyed.

"All right, men. Back to camp. On the double." He turned to Porter. "You walk with me. What's your name?"

"Osborne, Suh! PFC Porter Longstreet Osborne, Jr., Suh! Serial number 14143150, Suh!"

"I thought I knew you. You're the one that marched away from the rest of the company back in October. I thought you wore glasses. Where are they?"

"In the barracks, Suh. I quit wearing them, Suh."

"I tracked you through the snow, and there's no doubt in my mind you started this escapade. What in the hell did you think you were doing?"

"I was fixing to freeze, Suh. I was fixing to freeze and lie dying on the cold Illinois ground with this fractured femur, Suh." He realized that he still sported the bandage on his left thigh as he manfully matched the officer's long stride and remembered that the lieutenant himself had labeled the wound. "This compound, comminuted fracture of the femur, Suh," he added and affected a limp. "I thought I'd move around and find a spot to build a little bitty fire away from everything so it wouldn't mess up the maneuvers, Suh." He gulped, thought of Lamar and added, "I talked the others into going along as I passed them, Suh. The litter bearers said it would be at least an hour or so before they got to me, and we all meant to be back before then, Suh. We just got warm and went to sleep, Suh."

"Quit saying 'Suh' so much; it gets on my nerves."

"Yes, Suh."

"Do you realize that we have been looking for you GI's for over three hours? Orders came down from the general at noon to terminate maneuvers and return to camp. All of a sudden he remembered what day it is and where we were. The battalion gets to spend Christmas Eve and Christmas in camp. We've about got everything loaded on the trucks and your sergeant missed the seven of you at roll call. What do you have to say to that?"

"I'm sorry," he repressed the reflexive "sir" and substituted, "Lieutenant. That is, I'm sorry about slowing everybody up; I'm awfully glad about getting to go back to camp for Christmas. The men will be, too. They wouldn't even talk about it. About it being Christmas, I mean." When there was no immediate reply, he reverted to what he still regarded as the most immediate priority. "I really was fixing to freeze, Lieutenant."

They were approaching camp where activity was frenetic. Everybody was racing to pack equipment into the trucks, waiting in convoy to transport everything back to civilization. The kitchen had disappeared, all the tents had been struck, the snowy prairie had reclaimed its turf. Porter was stricken with the enormity of a full scale search for missing comrades, of the unwitting arrogance of delaying this many people. He felt guilty to the core; he had slowed the war effort.

"What are you going to do to us, Lt. Long, Suh?" he asked in mournful tones.

"I'm not going to do anything to those other six. I haven't decided about you yet. You don't act like a leader, you don't talk like a leader, you don't march like a leader, and you sure as hell don't look like a leader." He took a deep breath. "But I am confronted with incontrovertible evidence that you *are* a leader. Where are you from?"

"Georgia, Suh. I mean Lieutenant."

"Well, listen, PFC Osborne from Georgia. The first thing I'm going to do is have you march twenty paces over there where everybody in camp can see you while they finish loading those trucks. And you are to stand there, at attention, in the snow, in the eyes of the whole battalion until I personally relieve you. You are not to speak to anyone and you are not to move a muscle. I don't care how cold you get, you are not to move out of the position of attention. Do you understand?"

"Yes, Suh!" He saluted, did an about face, and measured off the twenty paces. As the minutes passed, the cold returned. He knew that he was congealing from his feet to his knees, then to his thighs. He held his rigid stance. No Osborne had ever been court-martialed. He knew that was what he faced and his heart constricted with shame. Flunking out of med school had been an onerous burden for his whole family, but to add court-martial to his record was more than he would be able to bear. Without moving his eyes, he watched the companies and platoons assemble in formation before the trucks. He thought probably the simplest solution would be for him to go ahead and freeze. He stood stiffly at attention.

The lieutenant returned. "Osborne, you have been standing here for exactly thirty-seven minutes. At ease. Join your outfit."

He could not move, not yet. "PFC Osborne requests permission to address the lieutenant."

"My God, what now?"

"Are you going to court-martial me, Suh?"

The lieutenant looked levelly in his eyes for a moment and then burst into a laugh. "Not if you wipe that mournful look off your face. Not if you don't tell me anything else about 'fixing to freeze.' Not if you take that fucking bandage off your leg. Not if you learn to pronounce the r in *sir*. If I prepared a court-martial about this incident, I'd never get anybody to believe it. I don't even want to listen to the evidence myself. I don't ever again want to think about seven GI's in a circle standing at attention and saluting me with their cocks flopping in the wind. Get your ass out of here."

As Porter lumbered with his pack to the truck containing his squad, he thought that the lieutenant was not such a bad guy after all and that his dingleberries must have turned loose. Otten reached over the tail gate and helped him aboard. "Osborne, what the hell have you been up to this time? Do you realize that it's a toss-up whether you're the biggest sad sack in the unit or the biggest fuckup?"

"Don't let it bother you Otten; I'm neither. I'm a leader; the lieutenant told me so."

"Leader, my ass. If you don't get a court-martial out of this, you'll at least lose your stripe and get busted down to buck private."

Porter looked at him and affected disdain. "Otten, it has been my experience along life's way that punishment from an authority figure is inversely proportionate to the levity one can induce."

"Oh, kiss my ass, Osborne. If you and your crummy buddies had made this outfit miss Christmas in camp I'd have shown you some levity. Right up your ass. With my boot. Now, tell me what happened. Without any big words."

"Well, once upon a time, way up yonder in the frozen North, in the land of the Eskimo, little children, there was a second lieutenant who got out of his sleeping bag on Christmas Eve with a most terrible, ferocious dingleberry."

Otten shoved him into Calhoun, Calhoun shoved him back into Otten, and they laughed all the way back to camp.

They arrived in time to get showers, clean clothes, a hot meal; then they converged en masse into the PX, scrambling and shoving for a place in the lines before the telephones. Of a sudden, a tall lanky GI climbed on a stool and held outstretched arms over the melee. Everyone instinctively looked at him. Porter recognized him as Pvt. Poole, who had been snatched from his secure position as a history teacher and choir director in an Ohio school. It was an unfair induction because Pvt. Poole was an ancient thirty, married, obviously over the hill, and may have been wrenched from his niche only because he and his wife had no children and he was not in an essential occupation. Porter called him Mister Poole and took care during cigarette breaks to ask him academic questions to make him feel important in the midst of all the youth around him. Now Mister Poole swept his extended arms rhythmically and began singing.

> "Silent night, holy night,
> All is calm, all is bright . . ."

Within seconds, the circle immediately surrounding him joined in; the *a capella* music swept the crowd, pulled in even the soldiers on the periphery, and the harmony filled the room. The hair on Porter's neck tingled; he sang around a lump in his throat.

> "Round yon Virgin mother and child,
> Holy infant so tender and mild . . ."

He noted with astonishment that Nitzberg from Pittsburgh, who had been born a Jew but professed now to be an atheist and a Communist, was singing.

> "Sleep in heavenly peace.
> Sleep in heavenly peace."

Mister Poole was fulfilled in accomplishment. He dried their tears by leading them through "Hark, the Herald Angels Sing," "Joy to the World," and a half hour of other carols, then brought them back to fighting trim with "God Bless America," although the tears of "Silent Night" were still fresh in their hearts.

After lights out, Porter lay in his bunk and made amends. "I'm sorry I got mad at You," he composed silently. "I don't understand, but I know You didn't do it on purpose. No matter what happens, thank You for the Baby Jesus. I almost wish He had never grown up. Watch over my loved ones in Georgia. This is the first Christmas in my life I've not been home."

He washed his pillow with secret tears and slept in heavenly peace.

They began an increased pace of activity, entering now the windup of their basic training, a time filled with written tests covering academic material and grueling practice on the drill field so they would reflect credit on their instructors when passing in review before the general, an exercise which was to serve as their graduation. Shoes were shined to the similitude of mirrors, uniforms were brushed and pressed, the barracks were bathed until they sparkled. Excitement was in the air. Everyone speculated on what would be his personal fate after

216

this, where he would be sent. East coast, west coast, Europe, or the South Pacific? The sudden realization that friendships formed over the last three months were about to be permanently severed induced a tolerance, an intensification of camaraderie.

Otten, never one passively to await announcement of his fate, buttered up to a corporal in the company office. "Guess what? The orders have been cut! We're being sent to Lawson General Hospital to become surgical technicians! How's that for coming out of a sewer smelling like a rose?"

"Where's Lawson General Hospital?"

"In Chamblee, Georgia, that's where."

"Where in the world is Chamblee, Georgia?"

"About ten minutes outside Atlanta, stupid, just the other side of Oglethorpe University. Where they raise cotton and peaches and pecans and there ain't no snow on the ground. You remember Georgia, don't you?"

"What's a surgical technician?"

"A medic that's had so much extra training that he has to be assigned to a general hospital. We'll probably wind up in an operating room somewhere. One thing's for sure and certain, we won't be crawling on our bellies as corpsmen or company aid men; we won't spend the war worrying about sniper fire."

Porter thought a moment. "What would happen if I asked for a transfer to the paratroopers?"

"They'd laugh at you. They're not going to put you through two basic trainings. There's a war on and they're in a hurry."

"Don't the paratroopers have medics that jump with them?"

"I may apply for OCS," interjected Calhoun.

"My dad wants me to do that," said Porter, "but I wrote him that I hadn't seen an officer in this man's Army yet that made me want to be one. On top of that, how in the world are you willing to take the responsibility of bossing the sad sacks that this Army has in it? They'll all get killed and then all your life you'll think it was your fault. I'd rather do my stint as a buck private than be an officer. Plus which, OCS will take at least another six months, and the war might be over before you're really in it."

"Yeah? Keep on talking, Vitamin, you're getting closer to the mark with every breath. Haw!"

"Oh," said Porter.

Otten broke in. "We're shipping out Saturday at noon, I found out, and while I was at it I finagled an overnight pass for Friday night.

I don't have to be back in camp until 0800 hours on Saturday morning. Lenore's picking me up at the front gate on Friday evening at seven in her dad's LaSalle. It's going to be perfect; her folks are going to be in Chio for the weekend; we're going to the Press Club for dinner and then to her house for a bottle of champagne in front of an open fire. I've told her I'm being sent straight to the Solomon Islands and may get killed; so I've got her sympathy aroused for the noble American soldier. While y'all are stuck here in camp, I'll be screwing her ears off on that Oriental rug in front of their fireplace."

"You're dreaming, Otten. She's smarter than that."

"You should have heard her breathing hard into the telephone awhile ago when I told her,

> 'She fed me roots of relish sweet
> And honey wild and manna dew,
> And sure in language strange she said,
> "I love you true."'

She was practically hassling. I tell you, it's a setup that can't miss."

"I told you I didn't want to hear anymore about it. Dr. John Keats would be ashamed of me if he knew I'd taught you part of that poem."

"Who in the hell is Dr. Keats?"

"He is the one who wrote it." Porter waited a second and added, "Stupid!"

Calhoun guffawed. "He got you good that time, ain't that right, Sport? Haw!"

After the parade and review were over, Porter declined an invitation from Calhoun to go to the PX. He started to the Day Room to seek out Lamar Betsill for a farewell visit but was accosted by Otten. "You got any money, Osborne?"

"Three dollars."

"Hell, that's chicken feed. Where's Calhoun?"

"He headed out for the PX a little while ago."

"Maybe I can catch him. I plumb forgot to get any money for my date, I was so busy with last minute strategy." He looked at his watch. "Holy shit, I'm going to be late. Lenore'll be parked at that front gate in just a minute. Do me a favor, Osborne."

"I am not going to hunt down Calhoun at the PX and borrow any money for you."

"No, no. Not that. You know what a LaSalle looks like. Hurry down to the main gate and tell Lenore I got tied up on the telephone with my folks from home and that I'm on my way."

"Carter Otten, I'm not about to get involved in this assault on the fair Lenore. I won't go. I want nothing to do with it."

"Goddam it, don't mess me up now. You're already involved in it. I probably couldn't have made it without your teaching me those poems." He slanted his eyes at Porter and used his most charming tone. "It's going to take me at least ten or fifteen minutes to find Calhoun and dig twenty bucks out of him. Do me this one favor. Please."

Porter capitulated. "OK. Who am I to refuse a good buddy a favor?" He turned and trotted purposefully off.

"She's in a dark green LaSalle, Osborne," Otten yelled at him.

Porter found her with no difficulty.

"Porter Osborne. I've heard a lot about you. Good to finally meet you. I hear you're all being shipped out tomorrow. Where's Carter?"

"He had to go find Griffin at the PX and get some money for his date tonight."

"He didn't have to do that."

"I guess he wants to buy a bottle of champagne to have on the Oriental rug in front of the fireplace at your house while your parents are in Chicago. After y'all eat at the Press Club."

"My, my, you know a lot about Carter's plans, don't you?"

"Down to dotting the i's and crossing the t's, Lenore."

"What do you mean by that?"

"Tell me. What do you think about Carter Otten?"

"I think he's the most fascinating boy I've ever met. He's a very complex character. Just about the time you decide he's a good-looking, arrogant, selfish brute, he shows you a side that is all tenderness and consideration. The way he can quote poetry makes you realize that there's a depth to him you hadn't anticipated, that he's sincere. Really a considerate Southern gentleman."

"Are you in love with him? It sounds like it."

"My, you're an intense little fellow, aren't you? Carter says you're strange. If I'm not in love, Porter Osborne, at least I'm infatuated. What business is it of yours?"

"More than I'd like for it to be, Lenore. I know that he didn't even try to kiss you until the third date, and I know step by step exactly how far the petting went on each successive date, from where he put his hand on down to where he placed your hand. I even know that you were menstruating on your last date."

"What? What in the world are you talking about?"

"I know about the poetry, from Housman to Kipling to Keats to Millay."

"Well, Mr. Know-it-all, how do you know all that?"

"Because I taught it to him."

"Taught him what?"

"The poems. I taught him every one he's ever recited to you."

"I don't believe you."

"You don't have to, but tonight he's planning to spring a sonnet on you that goes

> 'Love is not all: it is not meat nor drink
> Nor slumber nor a roof against the rain;
> Nor yet a floating spar to men that sink
> And rise and sink and rise and sink again;
> Love can not fill the thickened lung with breath,
> Nor cleanse the blood, nor set the fractured
>   bone;
> Yet many a man is making friends with death
> Even as I speak, for lack of love alone.
> It well may be that in a difficult hour,
> Pinned down by pain and moaning for release,
> Or nagged by want past resolution's power,
> I might be driven to sell your love for peace,
> Or trade the memory of this night for food.
> It well may be. I do not think I would.'

I've been worried about you. But I've got to go. I don't want him to catch me telling my guts."

Lenore let out her breath. "What a quaint phrase that is; Southerners really are interesting. Don't worry about me. I think I'm going to do just fine. Haven't you heard that Yankee women are practical and calculating?"

"What I heard was 'cold-blooded,' but I've never known any."

"Well, I can take care of myself. I'll play PFC Carter Otten along and see if I really believe all you told me. By the way, why have you told me all this? When did it become any of your business what goes on in my life?"

Porter stood shivering outside the car. "Because I was tired of seeing a lady treated like an atoll in the Pacific. 'Reconnoiter, establish a beachhead, penetrate to the interior, and conquer.' Because I was raised that a gentleman kisses but never tells."

He met Lenore's calm and waiting gaze and was impelled to greater honesty. "Because I felt guilty for letting Carter flatter me and for teaching him all those wonderful poems when I knew how he was planning to use them. That's when what goes on in your life became some of my business; when I started feeling dirty about Edna St. Vincent Millay. I halfway fell in love with you myself just from listening to Otten. You can do what you want to now, Lenore, but at least I feel better. I think."

She reached her hand through the open window and pulled one of his into the car. Pushing back the woolen glove, she kissed him as lightly as a butterfly just below his wrist. "Good-bye, Porter Osborne, Jr., PFC. I'll never see you again, but have a wonderful war."

"Thanks," Porter grinned. "From now on, Lenore, don't date anybody but officers. Even if they aren't as fascinating as brooding, mistreated Georgia enlisted men. Lots of luck."

It was after midnight when Porter was snatched from a sound sleep and hurled to the floor with bone-jarring abruptness. By the moonlight streaming through a window, he saw Carter Otten belligerently spraddled over him, his face contorted with rage.

"What the hell?" exclaimed Porter. "Are you crazy?"

"Get up from there! I'm going to haul you outside and break every bone in your goddam back!"

"Why?" asked Porter.

"Pipe down, fellows, you're waking everybody up," said Mr. Poole.

Otten ignored him. "What the hell did you tell Lenore, you goddam meddling bastard?"

"I don't know what you mean."

"Oh, yes you do! I had that set up, I know I did. She was mine, all mine! Something happened between the last time I talked to her on the phone and tonight. The only thing I can think of is that you sabotaged me when you met her at the car. It had to be something you said to her! I'm going to kill you!"

He aimed a kick at Porter, who saw it coming and rolled aside.

"Quiet!"

"Shut up!"

"Pipe down, for Crissake!"

Porter saw a figure move in the shadows, recognized Lamar Betsill standing behind Otten in his khaki underwear, and felt supported.

"Otten, you're crazy. What did Lenore say I told her?"

Otten leaned over Porter and lowered his voice. "Nothing! Not a word! But I wasn't born yesterday and I recognize a Quisling or a nigger in my woodpile! It had to be you!"

"What happened?"

"Everything was perfect. She seemed a little quieter, looked at me real steady a whole lot, but I thought she was just sad because this was her last evening. So I kept all the conversation going. After dessert, I leaned over the table and said that last poem I learned, a little earlier than I'd planned but it was a good appropriate time. She squeezed my hand tight all the way through it and looked at me like she could eat me with a spoon. Then she whispered, 'Let's go,' and I drove her home."

"Goddammit, will youse guys shut up? Dis ain't no time for Marie Rose!"

"What happened?" encouraged Porter, wondering if he dared get up off the floor yet.

"We got to her front door, I unlocked it, handed her the keys, and was all ready to pick her up and carry her over the threshold. Instead she turned to me and said that goddam poem about

'I loved you Wednesday, — yes — but what
Is that to me?'

pushed me in the chest, told me to wait on the sidewalk and she'd call a cab, and was in that house and gone! She wouldn't answer the bell and it took the damn cab an hour to come. I nearly froze my nuts off!"

"I know how you felt about that," soothed Porter. "I still don't see why you think I had anything to do with it. I've been telling you all along she was too smart to fall for all that."

"During dinner when I was telling her about going to the South Pacific, she said, 'I thought you three boys were being shipped back to Georgia tomorrow.' There's no way in the world she could have gotten that except from you. What else did you tell her?"

At that moment the barracks blazed with sudden light. Porter Osborne leapt into his bunk and under the blankets as quickly as a startled chipmunk. The first sergeant erupted from his lair and came bellowing between the bunks toward Otten and Betsill, both of whom seemed mesmerized.

"Awright, awright, awready yet! You tink last night in camp you can do what you please? Wake everbody up? Raise hell in da middle da night? Get your clothes off, Otten, and get to bed! Else I'll trow you in da stockade before Reveille! You, Betsill! You dickhead, you! Hit da sack before I trow ya out in da snow in your drawers!" His voice was such a roar that Porter winced and considered pulling his pillow over his head had he dared risk the attention any movement might bring. "You ain't never been and never will be nothing but a fuckup and a goddam dickhead! Good thing you're going to da Pacific, Betsill. Da Japs know what to do wid dickheads! Lights out!"

As he fought to regain sleep, Porter breathed a prayer of gratitude for the innate discretion of Lenore; it had never crossed his mind to request her not to tell. What a lady! Then he mumbled. "Dickhead? How in the world can a human being be a dickhead?"

The next morning excitement over departure took precedence over everything else. Soldiers were so busy exchanging farewells and new addresses that the uproar of the previous night was of only superficial interest. Lamar Betsill came to Porter's bunk as they awaited chow call for their last meal at Camp Grant.

"Thanks, Lamar, for getting out of bed last night to help me if I needed it. I'm sorry the sergeant caught you out and put the blame on you."

"He shouldn't oughta never to have yelled at me," said Betsill. "You can't help what he did and said and you're still the only one in the whole United States Army who's ever called me by my first name. I've told you how I feel about people who yell at me and that first sergeant just shouldn't oughta never to have done it. On top of that, he pushed me."

"We'll see the last of him as soon as we finish chow, pack our duffels, and clean the barracks," soothed Porter. "In a week you'll have forgotten him."

"No, in a week he'll have forgotten us because he'll be yelling at a whole new batch of poor green bastards. I won't forget him any quicker than I have that fifth grade teacher. There's something happens inside me when people yell at me. I won't ever forget."

"Yeah, you will, old buddy. He's not worth fretting over. There's chow call, let's go. You gonna take that gas mask with you to breakfast?"

"Sure. Never can tell when I'll find something I want to hide in there."

In the feeding frenzy of Company B, Porter somehow became separated from Lamar, was carrying his laden tray to a table, and passed him just entering the line for his utensils. He called, "I'll save you a place," and took a seat at the table immediately behind the first sergeant and his staff, who were halfway through their meal.

"I'd really have sorta rather got a table farther back, but I guess this is OK," commented Lamar when he arrived. He seemed to be talking to himself.

"What's the matter with you? One place is as good as another around here; everybody eats like dogs. It's not too bad this morning; the powdered eggs stink but the French toast is pretty good."

Porter's attention was drawn to the table in front of them as the sergeant and his staff pushed back their bench, retrieved their helmet liners from beneath it, and clapped them on their heads as they prepared to leave. Porter distinctly heard the first sergeant say, "What the fuck?" as he hastily jerked the helmet liner off his head. There was not even a momentary doubt in Porter's mind about definition of the malodorous object crowning the first sergeant's crew cut, but there was incredulous conjecture about how it came there. Even as the sergeant raised his hand to investigate, Porter had time to think that he would have been infinitely wiser simply to replace the helmet liner.

"If you don't stir it, it won't stink," he wanted to shout. The first sergeant of Company B flung himself with thundering bellow out of the mess hall, a loathsome load in his hand, his hair smeared revoltingly. Bedlam followed him to the showers. Porter turned to Betsill, who was sopping his French toast in syrup.

"Use your fork, Lamar," he said automatically. He stared until his friend reluctantly met his gaze. "It was in the gas mask, wasn't it?"

"I don't know what you talking about," replied Lamar. "I sure hate to say good-bye to you, Georgie boy. When this war is over, if I come to Georgie and hunt you up, you reckon I could ever get to be a Georgie Peach? Provided neither one of us don't cause no telegrams to get sent?"

"Hell, Lamar, you're a Soo San Marie Georgia Peach right now as far as I'm concerned. Come on back to the barracks and I'm going to split my red dirt with you, and I want some in your shoe from now till you come marching home. Let's go pack."

As they swung across the walkways, Porter tried again. "It was in the gas mask, it had to be. But how you got it in his helmet liner I don't know. I sure didn't see it. That's the worst thing I've heard of since somebody cut off Will Barton's dick."

Lamar's color had returned to normal. "I don't know about Will Barton; you'll have to tell me. I didn't like it even a little bit when the first sergeant yelled at you when Calhoun's daddy died, but like I told you, he shouldn't oughta never to have yelled at me."

Suddenly he laughed. "Tell me, Georgie boy, is it worse to be a dickhead or a turd-top?"

"I hope I never find out," Porter replied. "I've never found out who cut the dick off Will Barton's cadaver and there are some things we're just better off not knowing. Maybe we ought to take the sergeant a dictionary so he can look up *sympathy*; I could sure tell him where to find it. Come on and let me give you my home address and that red Georgia soil. Don't you dare lose either one of them."

". . . whose strong obedience broke the sky . . ."

22 In the winter and spring of 1944, Lawson General
Hospital became to Porter an oasis almost Circean, a land where lotus
was as available as oatmeal, a site where various sirens sang that it was
all right to find pleasure in the midst of war, that postponement of
death on the battlefield was permissible in a man of honor so long as
that man realized that death eventually was inevitable. No one had
stuffed Porter's ears with wax nor lashed him to any mast, and so he
succumbed to the frequent temptations of frivolity, usually with glee.

He found a certain freedom in being an enlisted man of whom
less was expected than he was capable of providing, and he took
puckish pleasure in occasionally testing the mettle of those designated
as his leaders, the noncoms and the officers. With only rare exceptions
they were Yankees, indeed Lawson General Hospital was a Yankee
conclave. It occurred to Porter that all United States military installations were in reality small cities unto themselves, autonomous units of
the Federal Government, and that the main difference between Camp
Grant and Lawson General Hospital was that one was in Illinois and
the other in Georgia.

The minute he set foot outside the gates, however, he knew the
difference. He was back in a land where men removed their hats in
buildings and gave up their seats on streetcars to ladies; where men
were not in such a hurry to speak that they failed to caress the words
that slid across their lips. The feminine gender consisted of women,
girls, or ladies rather than broads, dames, skirts or twists.

Whenever Porter Osborne could finagle a pass and escape the
fenced boundary of Lawson General Hospital, he felt at home. Within a
couple of hours he could even be in Brewton County on the farm. After
the oppressive winter in the brooding land of Illinois, he was exhila-
rated; his assurance and confidence expanded impressively and he

226

went about his chores with a lightened heart. The war was there, it would not be over and done before he dove into it. With guilt that was easily subdued, he enjoyed Lawson General Hospital. "Sufficient unto the day is the evil thereof," he assured himself.

The didactic part of his education was repetitively easy. He lived up to his treaty with Calhoun and Otten to make no mention of their pre-induction medical education and they rapidly attained a reputation for intellectual superiority among their peers. Anyone who had survived Morris's *Gross Anatomy* under the Butch and Boyd's *Textbook of Pathology* had nothing whatever to fear from the unimaginative text entitled *Anatomy and Physiology for Medical and Surgical Trainees, United States Government, Department of the Army. Lawson General Hospital. Technical Sergeant Melvin A. Bass, Instructor, 1944.* It was three inches thick, outlined throughout so tediously that some items were (p) under W, and contained nothing but sentence fragments. In the lectures on this material, Sgt. Bass stood before the class, called out the printed material line by line, inserting subject and predicate to form complete sentences, and then wrote the abbreviated version on the board. Sometimes he wrote with his right hand and erased with his left in order to cover the assignment of the day; always he talked and walked.

Porter had never beheld such a sergeant. This one glistened. He was so swarthy that his fleshy lips had a hint of purple and his teeth in contrast were overly white, as were the sclerae around the deep black of his irises. His eyebrows and the hairs on his fingers shone like shards of obsidian. The nails reflected the lights of the classroom so resplendently there could be no doubt that Sgt. Bass not only visited a manicurist but used nail polish; colorless, yes, but nevertheless polish. In addition, on the fifth finger of his left hand he affected a thick gold ring with a cluster of five diamonds in it. Porter regarded the carefully trimmed and frequently combed curls of Sgt. Bass, recalled his personal observation that ninety-five percent of sergeants in the U.S. Army had hair atop their shoulders, and wondered if Sgt. Bass also combed those and possibly even used Vitalis on them. He swiftly decided not, for grease would have spotted through on his immaculate uniform. Sgt. Bass rejected GI issue with capacious shirt bulging over the beltline as loose as a sack and consulted a tailor as carefully as he did a barber. His shirts were tapered down his lean torso to muscular waist, and his pants fitted so closely that his buttocks were balled in knots when he pranced across the front of the classroom.

His speech in Porter's ears was an auditory assault, so careful of consonants, so rapidly staccato that it whirred fatiguingly. There was a metallic quality to it as if his palate had been hammered from cast iron and every syllable was forced jarringly through his nose. It could have been a cradle tongue only in New Jersey or New York City and caused Porter responsively to exaggerate his leisured, liquid Georgia tones.

"Where the hell does that Sgt. Bass get off? He talks like a Yankee duck, and his tongue swings like a bell clapper," he fumed to Otten and Calhoun. "He's in Georgia now."

"He's a jim-dandy, all right. Did you see that uniform? I'm going to see if I can find somebody to taper my shirts like that; it really dresses a guy up, makes him stand out from the crowd."

"Haw! While you're at it get your pants fixed, too. What? You ain't got enough in the seat to compete with Bass's ass, but I believe you'd poke out more in front. Ain't that right, Sport?"

At first Porter felt grudging respect for Sgt. Bass because of his mimeographed text. A prodigious amount of work had gone into preparing that tome, and the sergeant must therefore be a hardworking, diligent and dedicated, albeit affected, teacher. He must even be learned; not just anyone could write a book. Bass's ass notwithstanding, he was stuck in the backwaters of the war effort, working his head off to train GI's in the foreign terms of medicine; Porter resolved to be a good soldier, to lead Bass's class.

Toward the end of the first week, he awakened to reality. The fastidious sergeant was clattering along with his outline, his tongue and his chalk keeping rapid pace with each other. Porter interrupted by raising his hand.

"Yes, soldier. What's your name?"

"Osborne, Sgt. Bass. Porter Osborne."

"Yes, Osborne? You have a question?"

"Here you have 'blood' listed under 'connective tissue.' I don't understand."

"You don't understand what?"

"I don't understand why it is classified as connective tissue, along with bone, cartilage, muscles and tendons. Why is blood connective tissue?"

Bass gave him a pitying glance, hesitated not one moment, and turned to the blackboard, which he swiftly and emphatically attacked with his chalk. He started a horizontal line across the top of the board, came back with another immediately below and parallel to it and then furiously filled with little circles all the space between the two. "This," he proclaimed, "is a blood vessel." He pointed to the top line. "This is the wall of a blood vessel." He dropped to the second line. "This is the other wall of that blood vessel. Understand?" Then he fingered the stippled area between. "This is blood. It connects one side of the blood vessel to the other side of the blood vessel. Since it is connecting the walls of the blood vessels to each other, it is called 'connective tissue.' It's that simple. Got it?"

Porter opened his mouth but stopped it agape; no sound emerged. "It's me that's simple," he thought, "if I believe that explanation for one second."

After class Calhoun expostulated, "Connecting the walls of the blood vessels? Haw! That noncommissioned Yankee pansy doesn't know his ass from a hole in the ground. And they've got him teaching us. That's a pretty come-off, ain't it, Sport?"

Over the weekend Porter managed to find a textbook.

On Monday he sat on the front row and raised his hand immediately after Sgt. Bass called the roll.

"Yes? I never forget a name, I never forget a face. Osborne, isn't it? Yes, Osborne?"

"About the blood, Sergeant. I should have remembered but I had forgotten. It's classified as connective tissue because of its embryonic origin."

"Say what?"

"You will remember there are three basic types of embryonic tissue after the blastula and morula are formed." Porter had a helpful tone in his voice. "Ectoderm, endoderm, and mesoderm. The blood and all its elements are formed from the mesoderm and that's why it's classified as connective tissue. It has nothing to do with its function. That's what was throwing me off on Friday; I couldn't fathom how blood had any functional relationship to connective tissue."

He became conscious of unusual stillness in the instructor, and his voice tapered off and ended on a note of uncertainty. Sgt. Bass obviously was neither appreciative, impressed, nor amused. He stood as spraddle-legged and commanding as the lieutenant had on the brink of the ravine in Illinois; light glittered from all his twinkling surfaces. His brass belt buckle shone like a mirror, bespeaking vigor with the blitz cloth, and there was not a hint of smudge upon it; his trousers were creased so sharply that Porter wondered if the man had sat down since he put them on. He felt a little chill. Sgt. Bass reflexively snatched the short black comb from his shirt pocket and ran it through his short black curls, the pinky with the diamond extended fastidiously.

"Let me tell you something about the United States Army, Osborne. Most people learn it in basic training but apparently you neglected to do so. All in the world that is expected of a private, even one that's first-class, is to sit back and do as he is told. He is not expected to think; somebody else does that for him. He is not expected to jump forward and act independently. He is a member of a group and the group will move at all times as a unit at the express will and command of officers and noncommissioned officers. A private does not have to worry about a thing in this whole world except doing as he is told when, and only when, he is told to do it. Got that so far?"

Porter nodded his head.

"Good. Remember. Relax. Don't worry, don't think. Obey orders. Never, ever stand out from your unit. That's the reason you got uniforms in this man's Army, so that everybody looks exactly the same and nobody, including you, is any different from or any better than anybody else. A private is not expected to think; just fill in the space, do your job, and take your turn in the chow line, the shower and the latrine. You got any questions?"

Porter shook his head, and the sergeant's daily parade before the blackboard began. PFC Osborne regarded the immaculate uniform, the pinky ring, the bluish cast of the closely shaved chin, the sheen of the carefully maintained hair, the manicured nails; he drew a deep breath and caught a whiff of aftershave lotion blended with Vitalis, talcum powder, and perhaps even perfume. "Bullshit," he muttered.

He settled firmly in his seat, raised his eyes and sought contact with those of his instructor. Through level impersonal gaze he willed the message, "Fuck you, Sgt. William Bass. Fuck your uniform and your hair and your silly finger ring. Most especially fuck your pretentious posturing and your whole goddam attitude. I'm an American soldier; I can make a difference and I will make a difference." He felt considerably better. He knew everything the sergeant had said but resented hearing it.

Porter was waiting for the bus at the hospital gate the following week when Sgt. Bass stopped his car before entering traffic. He looked over and deigned to speak. "Hello, Osborne."

"Hello, Sgt. Bass. Where'd you get that car? You don't see many yellow Packards in these parts."

"I just bought it. Got it for a song from a major who teaches med students over at Emory University. You like it?"

"Sgt. Bass, there's no way in this whole wide world you'll ever know how much I like that car. To tell you the truth, I just plain stomp-down, flat-out love that big old yellow Packard automobile."

With condescension the sergeant leaned over and opened the door. "Well, if you feel that strongly, hop in and I'll give you a lift to Buckhead."

Porter leaned off the curb and closed the door. "No, thanks, Sergeant. I'm going further than that and I'll just take the bus. I want to be sure to get there." He noted with satisfaction the iridescent blue trail from the exhaust pipe as the car moved up the street. "Tell me I can't make a difference in this man's Army!" he said aloud.

He leaped in the door of the bus when it rolled to a stop and its door wheezed open.

"'How far that little candle sheds its beam,'" he said to the driver, who wore a grimy toothpick and a blue-gray cap.

"What?" The toothpick rolled of its own volition to the opposite corner of his mouth.

"All week I've been wanting to see a sergeant screwed, and I just did. A major did it. And Ax-Handle and my daddy and way on down the line I, my own insignificant little old unimportant self, slipped it to the major. Therefore it follows that through an improbable chain of events, I have just fucked the most fancy-pants sergeant in the United States Army. You can't keep a good man down. I have whipped old Bass's ass. I may not be in the paratroopers but I'm sure helping win the war. 'Brighten the corner where you are.' Notify the general that I am due a medal!"

"I'm due fifteen cents. Hand it here or I'll notify the MP's." The toothpick rolled again; it looked tired. "You act like you drunk already and you ain't even got to town yet. You sure you in shape to leave the post, let alone get back on it?"

"I am in better shape than anybody you've seen all week! Follow that car!"

"You follow that aisle and set down; make room for somebody else."

*"The North is full of tangled things and texts
and aching eyes. . ."*

23 **I**n the raw and slushy latter days of January, fifty thousand Allied troops, American and British combined, landed on the beaches at Anzio, only thirty miles south of Rome. Atlanta had grown accustomed to victorious invasions at Salerno and Naples, had been cheered when the Germans abandoned Corsica and Sicily, had assumed that within only a few days the juggernaut of the Allies would crush the retreating Krauts in Italy. Apprehension recaptured America when the Germans instead dug in and repulsed the Allies three times at Cassino. Across the world, Hideki Tojo had been elevated to military dictator of Japan, but the Marines were wrestling unpronounceable communities from his warriors in the Marshall Islands. In Brewtonton, Georgia, Porter Osborne, Sr., assured his son that there would be plenty of war left for him when he finished his stint at Lawson General. Young Porter felt that, after all he had brought on himself, he would feel ashamed if he did not at least get overseas. At the same time he reflected that he might well die from bullets if he did. He mentioned these conflicting feelings to no one, least of all his father.

He wanted no homily on the nobility of medicine, for the more he became involved in its everyday delivery, the more seriously he doubted the validity of such a concept. He immersed himself in the superficial hilarity that prevailed among his comrades.

Their lives were still regimented at Lawson, but there was not the constant watchdog supervision, the harassment they had experienced at Camp Grant. These trainees were all from the top of their basic training groups, and their superiors had a much more relaxed attitude, even assuming that they were possessed of a semblance of intelligence and occasionally knew what they were doing. "Dickhead" and "fuckup" had been left behind along with the snow and ice of Illinois. They still had calisthenics every day, followed by classes until mid-afternoon and then close-order drill and hikes, but the noncoms were overseers for three or four barracks, and the first sergeant slept in one far down the hill. The corporal assigned to Barracks C was a disinterested military man with a new wife from Pittsburgh who had followed him south and was ensconced in an apartment down the road between Oglethorpe University and Buckhead, near Hospital 48, an institution for WWI veterans with tuberculosis. His interest lay in the bed of his bride, and he fled the post every chance he got. His attitude toward his charges proclaimed make no waves, don't rock the boat, you scratch my back and I'll scratch yours. The privates covered for him when the first sergeant might have noted his unauthorized absences, and a small cadre of co-conspirators, of whom Otten was a prominent member, had his phone number at home and could call him for quick return if discovery seemed imminent. Cpl. Daley, in gratitude, was more than generous in arranging extra passes into town for his favorites.

Otten was in his glory. He had no interest in beds or brides, but he was obsessed with automobiles. He regaled his platoon with tales of one-night exploits on the back seat, even occasionally the front seat, of various motor vehicles. The girls were of a sameness, always beautiful, always wealthy, smitten with his charm, bored with dating the officers and gentlemen their social status in Atlanta decreed for them. The cars they drove were the true indices of their worthiness, and he described them in almost as much detail as the girls. The more prestigious the make, the greater the gloating. LaSalles, Packards, DeSotos, Buicks, Hudsons, and Chryslers were expected transport for him. The occasional Cadillac would induce ecstasy and he would even comment on the color and texture of the upholstery. If he were ever reduced to riding in Fords, Chevrolets, or Plymouths, they were always convertibles with leather seats and had been purchased as a toy for some idle daughter of the mighty rich. All these girls were pristine in their innocence, and he gave exultant accounts of their education at his hands, with occasional allusion to some hapless neophyte's wonderment at the mystery of his genitalia.

"There we were in her driveway on Lullwater thrashing around in the front seat when I pulled it out of my pants and put her hand on it."

"Jesus Christ, Otten, whatcha doing on the front seat? Don't the fucking gear shift get in ya way?"

"Naw, she went for the big one."

Otten had a strong proclivity for center stage wherever he was, was possessed of an overabundance of energy, and contributed to the high jinks that went on in Company C when the troops were left unsupervised. Porter decided that, except for his invidious obsession with women, this comrade who had been thrust on him by the vagaries of war and the finesse of fate was really not so objectionable after all. Since Otten was no longer singling him out for help and making him feel like a traitorous Cyrano, Porter shrugged his shoulders about the Atlanta girls and assumed that Otten was their luck of the draw.

His arrogance, impatience, and narcissism were compensated by his quick intelligence and ribald sense of humor, his aggressive playfulness, and Porter began to comprehend why Calhoun was so bound to him. The puppies frolicked furiously on the second floor of Barracks C, and occasionally most of the soldiers, including Osborne, would join them, albeit peripherally and always briefly. Nobody but Calhoun had the stomach nor the endurance for a whole lot of Otten.

It was Otten who started the run on GI underwear. His bunk was near the top of the stairs, and every soldier on second floor passed by on his way to the showers. Standard practice was to strip to one's drawers, drape a towel around one's neck, and sally forth with soap dish and toothbrush in hand. The drawers were khaki boxer shorts with three buttons in front and were so much a part of their uniform that no one felt the least immodest parading across the barracks in them. Otten discovered in a scuffle with Calhoun that a quick and vigorous yank on the exact center of the back of the waistband not only exploded the buttons off but actually rent the garment asunder so that it came away in the hand of the perpetrator like a trophy in Capture the Flag. Otten was delighted. He became a master at the new sport.

He would feign inattention to some hapless passer-by, sneak behind him, rip his drawers away, and hold them aloft while laughing uproariously. The victim was always helpless. To be suddenly standing naked before your fellows, all of whom were laughing and clothed, generated more the impulse to flight than to fight, and a large majority of the soldiers so assaulted yielded reflexively to the impulsive youthful gesture of covering the crotch with shielding hands. To evince anger only provoked more mirth from the spectators, and the standard response was to pretend, however sheepishly, to accept the indignity as a joke.

Vince Pietrini was slight of stature, had a tendency to be cross-eyed, and was endowed with a nose that made him look like Walt Disney's caricature of a parrot. He was from Chicago, filled with zest for new experiences, and hungered so desperately to be accepted in his new outfit and to belong to some cohesive group that he attached himself like a leech to the three Georgia Peaches and willingly became a buffoon.

"Jesus Christ, Otten. How da hell you do dat?" he wheezed admiringly through his nose.

"Nothing to it, Pietrini. It's like snapping a rattlesnake's head off or kissing a duck's ass without getting feathers in your mouth; you gotta be quick."

"Don't fuck wit my brain, Georgie boy. I ain't stoopid and I ain't fresh off no boat. Me and you neider one never seen no rattlesnake nor yet kissed no duck's ass. I gotta learn dat trick."

And he did. Long after Otten and others abandoned the practice because of subliminal awareness of the time a joke goes stale, Pietrini persisted in it. In his effort to attain popularity by emulation, he became a nuisance. Inconspicuous because of his size, he was able to sneak up behind soldiers, denude them, and scamper nimbly away before anyone could grab him. Men were having to dig into their own pockets to buy underwear at the PX because no one wanted to face the ire of the supply sergeant, let alone squeal on one of their own. This was neither an anticipated nor welcome addition to anyone's budget, and Pietrini's annoyance index soared precipitously.

Bernie Friedman was a homesick soldier from the Midwest who wanted to return after the war to graduate school at De Pauw University and get his Master's degree in English. He was picture-book handsome with jet black hair, startlingly deep blue eyes, and perfect teeth. He smiled a lot and was so overly nice to everyone that at first he grated on Porter's nerves. Pietrini mistook politeness for obsequiousness and persisted in pestering him.

"Pietrini, if you don't stop that I'm going to do something terrible to you."

A wheezing laugh bounded from Pietrini's high palate and rattled through the awesome arch of his nose.

"Whatcha gonna do, Jew-baby? You ain't fast enough to catch no Guinea outa Chicago."

"I'll get somebody to help me pen you up. How about it, Osborne?"

"Any time, Friedman. Are you Jewish?"

The smile froze, framing the beautiful teeth; a faint shadow deepened the blue of the eyes. "Yeah. Why?"

"I haven't met many Jews, and I never saw one with blue eyes before."

"You may have met more than you realize; we come in all shapes, sizes, and colors."

"Osborne, you sure innocent to be so smart. Where you tink a handle like Friedman with a first name of Bernie come from if it ain't from the bosom of Abraham? It sure ain't no good Dago moniker."

"Well, there wasn't but one Jewish family in our town and that was Mr. and Mrs. Rosenbloom. They were both about five feet tall and had brown eyes. Everybody in town loved them. Mr. Rosenbloom gave a little something to every kid who ever came in his store, and we'd have all gone to his funeral except they hauled him off to somewhere in Atlanta and nobody could get there. Sort of shut us out."

Friedman's eyes relaxed; the smile was fluid and easy. "I know the feeling. You gonna help me get Pietrini if he snatches my shorts off again?"

"Sure," laughed Porter. "Pietrini, you see that fire extinguisher hanging on that post right there? If you mess with Bernie's drawers again, we're going to give you an enema with it."

"Yeah, Georgie boy? The two of you ain't man enough. You can't threaten a true Wop and get nowhere." His glee matched his cockiness and was just as genuine. They all laughed.

Porter had determined that the fire extinguishers in their barracks were really nothing except gussied-up sprayers similar to the one his uncle used on the beans and potatoes in his garden. They were not charged with chemicals, contained only water, and pressure had to be built up by pumping the handle in the top.

When Pietrini again sneaked behind Friedman in defiance and ripped off his underwear, Bernie abandoned any pretense at modesty and chased him across the barracks.

"Grab him, Osborne! He's headed your way!"

Porter tackled and held the writhing Pietrini, who was overcome with weakness induced by his own laughter. When Friedman, without benefit of lubricant, inserted the metal tip of the fire extinguisher appropriately, Pietrini's eyes widened in astonishment, but he still tried to maintain good humor. He laughed and yelled, "Watch it, you clumsy Hymie! If you ain't careful you gonna stick that ting right up my ass!"

Friedman laughed louder than anyone and began pumping vigorously. Pietrini's eyes bulged. "Hey, you fucking Kike, dat stuff's going in! Lay off, will you? You gonna bust me wide open."

Porter maintained his hammerlock but considered the perils of water under pressure in a human colon. He shared Pietrini's concern and cautioned, "Maybe we'd better quit, Friedman."

Bernie Friedman laughed and pushed the plunger down again. "You going to leave my shorts alone?"

Pietrini was not laughing. "For God's sake, yes! Mother of God! Please stop!"

Porter released him and Pietrini frantically rolled away from the nozzle, which spurted in disengaged misdirection across the two nearest bunks.

Pietrini bounced to his feet, his normally flat abdomen as swollen as a term pregnancy and protruding far beyond the nose above it or the appendage beneath it.

Suddenly he burst out laughing. "Dat's what you call da Dago water torture. I hope I can make it to da latrine, you goddam Christ-killer."

As he bounded spraddle-legged down the stairs to everyone's applauding mirth, Porter turned to the flushed Friedman. "He called you some pretty rough names."

The bright smile was accompanied by a shrug. "I've heard them all before."

"It didn't make you mad?"

"Coming from you, it would have. But not from a little guy who refers to himself as a Wop, a Dago, or a Guinea. And laughing. I imagine he thinks we're in the same boat about some things."

"Oh," said Porter, then he nodded his head. "The colored folks back on our farm can joke around and call each other 'nigger,' but it pokes their lips out if one of us says it. That's what you mean?"

Friedman's face became stilled and solemn, the eyes as cold as a northern sea. "Not exactly," he said dryly. Sunshine reappeared with his smile and the edges of his eyes crinkled with warmth again. "But you're getting there, Osborne. Keep it up and someday you may make it."

"He called you Christ Killer, but the Jews didn't kill Jesus," Porter said. "The Romans did. An Italian who's descended from those Romans ought not to be blaming someone else."

"Good point. Spread it around up north, will you?"

"Friedman, what's a Kike? I never heard that before."

"It's a particularly dirty word. That's why I gave the plunger an extra push even after you told me to quit."

"Oh."

Pietrini reappeared and approached them with exuberant laughter. "Cheez, youse guys sure go da limit to make ya point! Truce, huh? Truce! I don't touch no more underwear and in return I don't get no more fire plugs rammed up my ass. Christ, I'll be sore for a mont, and I got no desire to take a crap for da rest of my life."

Friedman smiled, Pietrini laughed, and Osborne felt momentarily lonely as he watched the two soldiers shaking hands, oblivious to the fact that they were both stark naked. There were some things he was unsure he wanted to understand completely, but there was no doubt in his mind that this was becoming for him an ever more interesting war. He mused on the differences between "buddy" and "friend," decided the former was less demanding and certainly more fleeting than the latter, and accepted Pietrini and Friedman as his Lawson General buddies.

He tried to learn from them.

"Pietrini, explain to me this business of the Rosary."

"It's what you pray wit."

"I know that. But why do you pull a little bead through your hands and say the same thing over and over and then wind up kissing the cross when you get around to that?"

"Because da priest tells you how many 'Hail Marys' and 'Our Fadders' to say after ya been to confession and told him how bad ya fucked up dis week, dat's why."

"You're talking about sinning and forgiveness? Through penance?"

"Yeh, dat's what I said. Fucking up and making up."

"Why does it have to be at the direction of the priest?"

"Because he's delegated by da Bishop and da Bishop answers to da Archbishop and da Archbishop gets his orders straight from da Holy Fadder and passes all of it on down da line. See, in da last word da priest gets his marching orders funneled down from da Holy Fadder himself and all us little Guineas got to do is what we're told."

"You believe all that, Pietrini?"

"Sure. Why not? Dat's our way."

"I had a roommate in college who was Catholic and that's what he said when I tried to learn something about y'all's church. 'Dat's our way.'"

"Yeh. What's wrong wit dat?"

"I'm serious. That's no reasonable answer."

"I'm serious, too. Ya spose to have faith, don't you know dat? Faith! How you gonna explain faith except to say, 'Dat's our way'?"

"OK. OK. Do you go to confession and mass every week?"

"Hell, no. I ain't been since Christmas. What da hell? Way I look at it, it's always dere if I get in trouble, and if I ain't in trouble, Osborne, to tell ya da truth, sometimes it's just too much a bunch of shit to bodder wit."

"Oh."

"It makes ya feel good at Christmas, though, and it makes ya mama happy to see ya at mass." He shrugged his shoulders. "I keep telling ya, Osborne; for Chrissake, dat's just our way."

On one of those days that come to Georgia in February, when the sky is blue, the wind is stilled, jonquils are blooming, a fuzz of green is on the earth, and the peepers are promising immediate deliverance from winter, on one of those days that Georgians take for granted but that northern newcomers regard as a miraculous suspension of universal laws, Porter found Friedman behind the barracks without his shirt, his face turned up to the warm sun.

He plopped down beside him and in a wondering voice said, "Tell me about being a Jew, Bernie."

Friedman stiffened ever so slightly. "What about it?"

"Well, I've read the Old Testament all the way through. Twice. Once I didn't even skip the begats when I was doing it as my end of a bargain I'd made, but I don't really know a thing about Jews since the days of Jesus. I know Saturday is their Sunday and they don't eat pork, but the Seventh Day Adventists don't do that. I know Jews don't believe Jesus is the Messiah, and they still make a fuss and a big deal out of being circumcised, but what do they believe besides that?"

Friedman leaned back and shut his eyes against the sun, a faint smile on his lips. "That about covers it, Osborne. Throw in Bar Mitzvah and bagels with cream cheese and lox and that's all there is to being a Jew in America right now."

"Aw, Friedman, don't bullshit me; I'm serious. Hitler has come along and the whole world's focused on Jews, and furthermore he's got all of us on their side. You know there's more to a religion than what you're describing."

"Osborne, maybe being a Jew is now just a cultural condition and has nothing to do with religion."

"That's bull, Friedman; even I know better than that. Y'all had plumb lost ten tribes out of twelve by the time Jesus came along; the Northern Kingdom dropped out of sight and nobody knows what became of them; they gave up their religion. That means that the two tribes of Judah and Benjamin have existed in this world without a homeland of any sort for over two thousand years and still remain a distinct entity and nothing but religion has done that for them. Cultural attitudes would have had them assimilated in less than three generations. Like the Confederates who emigrated to Brazil and now speak only Portuguese. Or the Huguenots who came to South Carolina and forgot their French. It's their religion that's kept them distinct. What do Jews believe in?"

"You'll have to ask somebody who knows, Osborne. I'm not Orthodox, I'm Reformed. We eat shrimp and ham at cocktail parties and we hang out on Saturday night and drink beer like good Christians and try not to think about being Jews."

"I thought y'all believed in Jehovah and kept all the laws and covenants and were still looking for the Messiah to come."

"Messiah? Next thing I know you'll be talking about life after death and Santa Claus."

"You don't believe in a Messiah? Somebody to save your race?"

Friedman sat up and looked at the sky. His eyes were the same blue and almost as distant. "If I do, it's not some poverty-loving philosopher who lets a bunch of *goy-kopfs* hang him on a cross. It may not be a person at all but more a concept. A united push by people who have, by God, had enough and are finally going to reclaim their homeland and establish a new nation."

"What? Where?"

"Aw, come on, Osborne. You're well-read enough to have heard of the Zionist movement."

"Nobody takes it seriously, Bernie."

"You'd be surprised."

"You can't just go in and take over Jerusalem and gouge out a country. Other people have owned it for a thousand years or more."

"Why not? We've got good precedents. What about the Crusades? Didn't all of Western civilization band together to wrest its holy land from the Infidel? If a good Christian can do something, why can't a dedicated Jew?"

"Hell, don't flare up at me. I'm a Baptist and every one of us regards the book of Exodus as a quitclaim deed to Palestine and Canaan. Are you really a Zionist?"

"Osborne, I'm not really anything. My oldest brother, the good-looking one in the family, married an Episcopalian debutante. Now he's fighting Germans in Italy, and my mother is trying to smile when her grandchildren come by after Sunday School and talk about Jesus, and then my father asks Mama if getting on the Symphony Board was really worth it."

"I see what he means. I don't personally know any Episcopalians, but we all know they got started so Henry VIII could keep on marrying, and they drink real wine at Communion and let their priests marry and screw, like somebody. What does your daddy do?"

"He runs the department store that our grandfather started and owns most of it. He gets along well with my sister-in-law; tells her his favorite song at Christmas is 'What a Friend We Have in Jesus.' My mama smiles and then when my sister-in-law leaves, she tells my daddy that she is sick unto death of Jesus and knows what Rebekah meant about the daughters of Heth."

"They didn't get along at all," said Porter.

"Right! You really have read it, haven't you? Then my daddy tells my mama if she had spent more time in the synagogue with the children and less time running around in society, we wouldn't have Christian grandchildren under our feet and in our hearts, and that she can forget trying to get my baby sister on the debutante list, no matter how much money she gives to the Symphony Board and the Museum. Then they both get to yelling and slamming doors and that's Sunday at my house."

"Why can't your sister be a debutante? I can't for the life of me see why your mama wants her to, but what's the hindrance?"

"You're either thicker or more innocent than I can believe, Osborne. That's what we've been talking about. We're Jewish."

"Well, I can't help it; don't get up on your dew-claws about it with me. Why are you so self-conscious and defensive anyhow?"

"Self-conscious? You don't know anything about self-conscious. I'm locked into being a Jew all my life. Forever. I never enter a room without looking around and wondering how many people in there are Jewish too, and how many of them who aren't know that I am and are going to reject me."

"Reject you from what, for Heaven's sake?"

"From their consciousness, goddammit. I can stand the clubs and the neighborhoods and the college fraternities—we have our own; but as soon as they hear my name, their eyes glaze over and they get an indifferent tone in their voices and I'm on the trash pile, the dung-hill, as Chaucer would have put it. I have to keep my guard up and smile and pretend I don't notice it and that I still have the hope that they will accept me. If I'm polite, use good table manners, eat what's put before me, and smile, they'll think I'm one of them. At least for a little while."

"Gosh, Bernie, I'm sorry. I didn't mean to stir all that up. You're a helluva nice guy, and as far as I'm concerned, you *are* one of us."

"That's OK, Osborne. I've never let that out before, but then I've never had anybody be that candid and direct with me before. I really think it doesn't matter to you."

"That you don't believe in Jesus?"

"No! That I'm a Jew. And I do believe in Jesus. I've already told you we make our living off of Christmas, and that has his name in it. Our Easter sales aren't bad either. Then look at the calendar, dammit. The whole world everywhere counts days and months and years in his name; we went along fine before his birth and then stopped time and started counting all over again." He laughed. "Of course I believe in Jesus. He's everywhere. You can't get away from him. He sure as hell existed. I don't necessarily approve of him, but you can't help believing in him."

"That's sort of the way I'm feeling about God the Father for over a year now," Porter rejoined. His voice lightened. "Don't resent the calendar, Friedman. What if the world used Moses as a starting point for time? B.M.? Nobody would take that seriously. A.M.? Come on! You know B.C. and A.D. are better."

When Friedman laughed, Porter waited a moment. "You said you always look around in a room to see if anybody else is Jewish. Can you tell by looking?"

"Ninety percent of the time. Make that ninety-nine for me; I'm perceptive."

"Well, I sure can't tell. Who else around here is one?"

"Katz. Solomon. Novick; you can't miss him. Hell, Sgt. Bass! I know you know him."

"Bass? Are you sure? Have you asked him?"

"You don't have to ask, I'm telling you."

"OK. OK." He paused. "Bernie, Melvin Bass is what Pietrini calls a Kike, isn't he?"

Friedman jumped, then laughed. "Guess if there has to be one, he's as good a candidate as any." His teeth faded away in solemnity. "But when you get right down to it and strip off all the flashiness and the obnoxious veneer, I suspect that Sgt. Melvin Bass is just as far from home and lonesome as the rest of us."

Porter thought for a moment about his public dressing down by the sergeant. "Friedman, you may not realize it, but you are probably a better Christian than I am." He laughed. "I'll tell you one thing. I don't know how far from home Bass is, but if he tries to drive there, he'd better get set to do a heap of hitchhiking. The son of a bitch!"

"Don John's hunting, and his hounds have bayed —
Booms away past Italy the rumor of his raid."

24 **f**arther and farther removed from basic training, the boys in Barracks C became irrepressible, felt freedom to reassert themselves as individuals. Otten and Calhoun each developed to an art form the ability to kick the instep of the comrade marching in formation just ahead so that the victim's foot shot upward but cadence was not lost. It made a sound like a pistol shot, and the sergeant would whirl around, interrupt his count to peer suspiciously along the ranks of the platoon, and then resume close-order drill with lateral gaze worthy of a pitcher watching a man on first. Nobody ever changed expression and no one ever told. It gave purpose to their hours of close-order drill.

Pietrini had a natural rhythm to match his ebullience and also a snappy swagger. After a few weeks, he was elevated without any increase in either rank or pay to the position of drill master. Following his encounter with the fire extinguisher, he had become the unofficial mascot of Barracks C, their court jester as surely as if he had worn a long cap with bells on it. He earned a lifelong niche in their memory by demonstrating on the drill field that he could prance along and fart loudly in cadence for a full four beats, at will and recurrently. These exhibitions, of course, were always at times when the sergeant had entrusted the platoon to him alone, and that puzzled worthy would come rushing out onto the parade ground to ascertain why his group was marching in perfect formation and shaking with laughter. Nobody ever told, but nobody ever forgot Pietrini.

In the classroom they learned how to make beds to hospital specifications, and then they learned how to change linens and remake the same bed when it contained a patient. They learned that it was unacceptable to tuck a pillow under one's chin while applying the pillow case, an enlightenment that Porter restrained himself from

244

passing on to the womenfolk in his family as prudently as he did mention about mitered corners for sheets and blankets. They learned that it was strictly forbidden to sit on a patient's bed at any time, whether conversing with him or not, and Porter recalled the doctors of his youth making house calls all across the county and at all hours of the night devoid of this dictum of professionalism. He believed in germs right enough and that doctors and nurses should neither harbor them nor transport them, but too much worship of sterility, he thought, could breed aloofness and distrust. He remembered the directives of Sgt. Bass, shrugged his shoulders, and did as he was told. Privates were not supposed to think.

They were sent across the road to the hospital, ostensibly to learn, but found themselves also potential prey for opportunistic ward clerks and orderlies who sought to ease their own loads by shifting work onto the shoulders of these neophytes. Porter did not mind. The first day he was assigned to the wards, he found himself pressed into attending a soldier who had barely survived a Jeep accident and was now suspended in a maze of wires and pulleys that made of him a helpless automaton; he was rigged for action but dependent on some puppeteer. Porter recalled Maj. Teufelsdreck's prophecy that he would wind up the war carrying ice water and bedpans to sick soldiers and sailors. "The damn war's not over yet," he asserted, and carried the bedpan with resolve and some degree of cheer.

The hospital was a sprawl of one-story rectangles fronting on a series of four parallel corridors that were almost a mile long and were crisscrossed at intervals by connecting side corridors. It had been conceived, designed and erected with the same fervor characterizing many installations that sprang up across the country after Roosevelt sounded the death knell of isolationism and began the draft. Some engineer, in unwitting collaboration with hasty bulldozer operators, had not prepared the building site prior to construction so that it was level, and the long corridors at Lawson slanted downhill. It was easy for a corpsman to transport a wheelchair patient from Ward 32-B down to X-ray, which was housed in Building 2-C; one had to hold back to prevent the chair from careening in unguided flight. It took hard work and sweat, however, to push him back after the X-rays were done.

Occasionally, when the corridors were empty, attendants would conquer boredom by relenting to the pull of gravity and would actually run, hurtling pell-mell behind the handles of the chairs in races with each other. Officers who happened to step unsuspectingly out of the cross corridors at their peril thundered disapproval, but the patients who were passengers loved it.

Porter easily defeated the short-legged Pietrini every time they competed but was never able to tease Friedman into a contest.

"I'm not saying I'll never get court-martialed before I get out of this man's Army, but if I do it certainly won't be for drag-racing wheelchairs. You're crazy! You're both crazy!"

On the wards, Porter acquired a reputation for efficiency, for speed in performing tasks. The patients jokingly called him an eager beaver but requested his services.

One day he was returning from noonday chow and passed the open door of one of the officers' wards. He overheard argumentative voices and instinctively slowed. One of the voices was beyond being loud; it was a yell. The other was definitely female.

"Lieutenant, you are rapidly transgressing the bounds of any semblance of gentlemanly conduct. You will calm down immediately and remember that you are an officer and a gentleman, or I shall be forced to report you. I am only obeying the orders of your medical officer, and he has written on your chart that you are not to be discharged back to your unit until the first of the month."

"If the son of a bitch is going to write orders like that, he ought not to take a three-day pass without consulting me. I'll stuff those captain's bars of his where the sun don't shine if he doesn't get me out of here this week. I tell you, I'm going crazy sitting around this bunch of goldbricks and I'm ready for active duty."

"My God," said Porter. "The world just couldn't be that small."

The voice continued, but not in a very mollifying tone. "I really don't need any PT, nurse; the cast is off and the X-rays are good, and I'll lose this limp in a month anyway. I tell you I'm hauling my hairy tail out of here to Italy and joining my unit before it jumps behind Cassino. Somebody has to hold on so that goddam stupid Gen. Lucas can finally bring his troops up and take the Monastery; he's been fiddling and farting around long enough. If they hadn't moved Ike out, we'd already be in Rome. They need me over there to kick some butt and kill some Germans. I'm out of here, I tell you!"

"Lieutenant, I really do take exception to your language!"

"Yeah? Well, I've got something else I'll, by God, let you take exception to. If you're interested, come on back to my cubicle after lights out. If you're not interested, you can kiss my ass."

"Lieutenant!"

246

"All right, all right, it was just an invitation; you don't have to do it. I wish you Army nurses would make up your minds whether you're women or soldiers. I'm damned if I can treat you like both. I'm off to the PX. If Eisenhower or Roosevelt either one calls, take a message."

"Don't forget your crutches."

"Fuck the crutches. I'll be jumping out of an airplane at Anzio next week. You can have them as a souvenir."

"Lieutenant!"

He limped into the corridor as Porter stood transfixed. He had already identified the speaker by voice and by speech content, but the sight of his old classmate in the standard blue pajamas and maroon bathrobe of Lawson General Hospital made him a little dizzy. "It's a small world, Will Barton," he volunteered.

"My God! It's Osborne! What are you doing here? Where are your glasses?"

"I left them in Illinois. I'm carrying ice water and bedpans to sick soldiers and sailors."

"You're a fucking orderly? For God's sake, why?"

"I flunked out of med school."

"You're shitting me."

"No, I'm not."

"I can't believe the Butch got you; you weren't a meat thrower."

"He didn't. Physiology got me. Last fall. What about you? Where have you been since you got banned from the campus at Emory?"

"Jump school at Fort Benning. North Africa. Sicily. Salerno. Bullet in the thigh that hit the femur, three weeks in a field hospital and evacuated to Lawson. Now I'm headed back to Italy to move Lucas off his dead ass and get the good old U.S. dogfaces into Rome, where they can enjoy the liquor and pussy us paratroopers haven't appropriated by the time they get there."

"Same old Barton. I heard you talking to that poor nurse. It makes me feel . . ."

"Makes you feel what, asshole? How'd you feel if . . ."

"I know," interrupted Porter. "I know. How'd I feel if you jerked my head off and shit in my neck. Like I said, you haven't changed a bit."

In the corridor they laughed so uproariously that passers-by gawked at a first lieutenant and a PFC slapping each other on the back.

"Come on in and visit with me, Osborne. I'm going stir crazy in this place. All the guys on my ward act like a bunch of goddam lotus eaters, happy to sit on their asses and let somebody else fight the war just because they've had a little wound or two. Then they get their bowels in an uproar when I tell 'em they're goldbricking."

"Gosh, Barton, I'd love to, but I'm late getting back to my ward now. Besides, we've been told about fraternizing with officers."

"Fraternizing, my ass! You can't let the Army twist you into something you don't want to be. Meet me in the PX when you get off duty. That's an order, Pvt. Osborne."

"Yes, Suh," laughed Porter and snapped a salute.

Will Barton had shed the robe and pajamas of the invalid by afternoon and was in uniform. He was impeccable in tie and Eisenhower jacket, and his silver bars glistened. Porter's eyes, however, were drawn compellingly to his boots. There lay the drama and the glamour of the airborne branch of the service. Those boots bespoke it all; the extra toughness of their training, the pay subsidy for jumping into combat from airplanes and swinging down from heaven as a target for snipers, the death-defying hell-for-leather mind cast instilled in all of them until MP's everywhere shuddered when paratroopers had passes. Those beautiful boots, shined to the perfection of fine mahogany, came only one-third of the way up the leg, their tops obscured by the blousing of the trousers; they were flauntingly arrogant. The size of the foot and the ballooning of the pants made the tightly-laced ankle in between look as sinewy but dainty as that of a race horse, massive muscles and mighty heart ready to spring forward on improbably thin supports. The boots of the paratroopers put any member of another branch of the service on guard, conscious of being excluded from the meanest fraternity on earth, therefore as envious as a prepubescent little brother. Porter thought it appropriate that Will Barton was not only a paratrooper but also an officer in their ranks.

"How long you been a first lieutenant, Barton?" he asked.

"About two months this time. Went in as a shavetail, overseas as a first looie, got a battlefield promotion to captain, then busted down to shavetail and then another battlefield boot to first looie just before I took that bullet in the leg."

"What'd you get busted for?"

"For slapping the living dogshit out of an English major who tried to act snotty and look down his long nose at me in an officers' club in Algiers. He didn't say anything, it was just the way he looked. He needed slapping and I was handy; so I did it. Turned out he was a cousin to Monty's chief aide and there were witnesses, and I got busted."

"Like the Butch seeing you chunk that trapezius."

"Sort of. How is that old bastard? I'd like to see him."

"I don't hear anything about him, but then I don't go around Emory or see any of the guys since I got back from Camp Grant. They're all down at Grady now I should think. Why do you want to see Butch? He's too old for you to slap the dogshit out of."

"Hey, I got nothing against the Butch. He lives by his rules, and if you break 'em you pay the price. I understand guys like that; it's the wishy-washy candy asses that frost my balls. I wanta see the Butch about getting back in med school."

"What? You're crazy."

"All my life, Osborne, all my life. So what else is new? This war's not going to last forever, and I still want to be a doctor."

"If you don't get killed first jumping out of an airplane or shot to pieces by some German."

"Me? Hell, Osborne, they can't kill me. You ain't talking to some mama's darling, you're talking to Will Barton! The German ain't been born can kill me."

"Sounds like what you said to Butch in Anatomy lab. Tell me, Will, why do you still want to be a doctor?"

"Damned if I know; it's complicated. When I figure it out, I'll let you know. Tell me why you flunked out of med school."

"I wanted to be in the paratroopers."

"Bullshit. Why'd you want to do that?"

"Damned if I know; it's complicated," Porter rejoined. He remembered the vacillating feelings he had experienced from the day of Pearl Harbor to the present. "When I figure it out, I'll let you know."

He thought of the dicta of Sgt. Bass and felt stifled. Oppressed. Privates are not supposed to think. He looked at the boots of Will Barton, primly laced but as insolent and dangerous as the neck of a copperhead. He threw all caution to the winds. "Will, do me a favor. Do you think there's any string you could pull, any arm you could twist, to get me transferred to the paratroopers?"

"Are you serious?"

"I'm dead serious. Can you do it, Will? I'm sick of sitting out this war letting other people, who don't have half as much sense as I do, decide where I'm going to go and what I'm going to do."

"Sounds suspiciously like you're growing up, Osborne. Hell, you might even be a real man some day. You're goddam right I can get you transferred. Don't say it if you don't mean it."

"I mean it, Will. They're obliged to need airborne medics, and I'd rather get shot jumping out of the sky than be safely bored to death in the States. I mean it, all right."

"I can do it. Tell me the real reason you want the transfer, though."

Porter opened his mouth to recount his emotions, caught Barton's steady gaze, and remembered that person's explosive attitude toward feelings. He thrust his head forward until his nose was only inches away from Barton's, stared unwaveringly into his eyes, and yelled, "I want to get myself a pair of those goddam boots!"

Will Barton erupted with laughter. "That's good enough for me. I'm dressed up like this because a buddy who's a light colonel in Personnel is picking me up and we're going to the naval officers' club. We go a long way back and he owes me. He's a Yankee from Pennsylvania but hard as nails and a good man to have at your back. I'm going to get him to have orders cut to get me out of this hospital before that captain gets back from his little pussy pass, and there's no problem about getting a PFC transferred to jump school. Here, write down your full name, address, and serial number. Check by the ward in the morning. No, I plan to be hung over in the morning. Check with me on the ward tomorrow afternoon."

Porter was so excited he could not pace the dreams he had that night. The next morning he endured chow, calisthenics, two hours of class, and an hour of close-order drill. While his comrades were preparing for a Saturday afternoon pass into town, he hurried across the road to the hospital. On the officer's ward he accosted a corpsman.

"Would you tell Lt. Will Barton he's got a visitor?"

"Lt. Barton? He shipped outa here tree hours ago."

"What? Where?"

"Beats the shit outa me. You never heard so much yelling and cussing in ya life. At least outside a psycho ward. You a friend of his?"

"Well, sort of. At least, I thought I was."

"To tell you da trut, I'm gonna miss him. Ever nurse on da ward, including da ones dat float and relieve, was ready to slit his troat or cut his nuts off. He kept something stirring all da time."

"I know. Did he leave any message?"

250

The corpsman shrugged. "Not wit me." He stopped another private returning from Central Supply. "Hey, Baker. Did Wild and Wicked Will leave a message for anybody dat you know of?"

The man fished a slip of paper from a pocket. "Your name Porter Osborne?"

"That's me."

"Lt. Barton said tell you he's off for Italy and didn't have time to wait to see you. Said tell you he'd write."

"That's it?"

"You got it."

"I sure have," replied Porter. He turned disconsolately away, repressing a stirring of elation that he would not be shot out of the sky after all. The letter came on Tuesday.

"Dear Osborne,

The next thing you know we'll be out of Anzio and in Rome. Barton's on his way!

Bad news for you. My buddy brought his brother with him the other night. They're the Teufelsdreck boys from Pennsylvania and are meaner than nine-day-old cat shit. The brother knows you. He does not like you. In fact, he hates your guts. He thinks you had something to do with freezing up the motor in his car. The only place he could find a new motor was some place called 'Hawg Man's Junk Yard' out in Brewton County, and it turned out to have a hairline crack in the block. He had to unload the whole car on some New York Jew, and he is headed for the Marshall Islands. The man damn near cried about that car.

He foamed at the mouth at the idea of your getting in the Airborne. Said if I saw you to tell you to keep those bedpans and ice water coming—and do it on the double. I tried and tried, but I couldn't overpersuade him nor bypass him to his brother. In fact, I was lucky to get Number One looked after.

Keep a high head and a hurricane ass. Have a good war. Maybe I'll see you again at Emory when it's over. It'll move now.

From your sky-diving, butt-kicking buddy—
Killer of Krauts and saviour of the Allies—Will Barton

P.S. Osborne, I tried. Don't feel bad. Fuck him if he can't take a joke.

P.P.S. I'll bring you some boots when I come home. I really did try."

Porter read the note twice and then shrugged his shoulders. "I tried, too," he said.

He read it a third time. "What in the world is a hurricane ass?" he said. Then he began laughing. "God bless Hawg Man, and God bless Ax-Handle, and God bless my daddy. This is a sure enough small world, at least on this side of the water." He musingly kicked a rock ahead of him all the way across the road and up the hill to Barracks C. "And don't leave out old Sgt. Connective-tissue Bass. Bless him, too."

Porter led his class academically, and all but the lower third were automatically promoted without request for permission into the increased mysteries of *Advanced Medical-Surgical Technician Training Program, Dept. of the Army, Lawson General Hospital, Chamblee, Georgia. Melvin A. Bass, Technical Sergeant, Medical Corps.* Porter felt like chattel.

Spring came singing in over the hills and rivers of Georgia; tantalizing breezes cleared the skies and teased new leaves from the swollen tree tips. Porter relaxed his attention to the war enough to be excited by renascence of the earth. If he had been assigned to the supervision of Lt. Katie Albert in any other season of the year, he might not have been so captivated by her. All other enlisted men feared her frown and resented her hostile approach to teaching, indeed, to life in general. Friedman comforted Porter when their ward assignments were posted.

"My God, Osborne, Bass must have had a hand in this because of the mesoderm lecture you gave him. Lt. Albert is supposed to be GI to the bone and has never been known to smile. Even the other nurses are scared of her. Rumor goes that the Colonel put her in charge of the PW wards because she's tough as nails and nobody can put anything over on her. Lots of luck."

Two wards came under her purview and Porter worked on each of them. Both were locked and he was admitted and released by an armed sentinel, an arrangement that made his work seem sometimes authoritarian and sometimes conspiratorial. He had never been locked up before. One ward was occupied by Italians, the other by Germans. All patients wore pajamas and robes with POW stenciled on them in black, and there the similarities between the wards stopped.

The Italians were a rollicking group that burst into unexpected and sometimes inappropriate song. They immediately accepted Porter. They made frequent allusions in both sign language and labored English to the surrender of Italy the previous fall. Their ebullient implication was that the Italians and the Americans were allies and that their own incarceration was the result of slow paperwork on the part of diplomats and bureaucracies, to be shrugged off not even as an embarrassment, merely a temporary inconvenience. Every one of them loved America, hated Mussolini, had not borne arms in North Africa, and those who were old enough to have served in Ethiopia had all been cooks or postal clerks. They could swear in the presence of the Holy Mother Herself that they had never lifted a rifle against an American. It was Porter's first introduction to the universal and cohesive innocence of all prisoners everywhere, and he was a willing participant in the web of deceit they wove.

Pietrini snorted at Porter's naive accounts. "Don't believe even half the goddam lies them Guineas tell you. They a bunch of con artists and would sneak the coins off their grandma's dead eyes. Every one of them is in there with a war wound, ain't they? Unless they half-killed each other rushing to surrender. I wish they'd put me on that ward for a week; I'd straighten the lily-livered cocksuckers out in a hurry."

"I don't care what you say. They're a bunch of nice guys and they're a long way from home and lonesome," Porter assured Pietrini and then lectured him that his entire attitude toward life had been hopelessly tainted by being raised in Chicago. "I'd rather be a Guinea than a Yankee," Porter said. They laughed together, but Porter meant it.

The first thing he noted about the German POW ward was the strict regimentation of the inmates. The officers on the Italian ward were mixed willy-nilly among the enlisted men in relaxed camaraderie. On the German ward, there was rigid segregation according to rank and an atmosphere of tense watchfulness. There was little laughter and no singing at all. Every time Porter engaged one of the prisoners in an exchange that appeared to be approaching a level of cordiality, a terse and unintelligible sentence fragment would erupt from another prisoner and the individual would immediately break eye contact, shift his feet, and retreat into formal indifference. Porter noted this, was puzzled by it, but was edified by Lt. Katie Albert.

"That goddam Prussian colonel has got all those people terrorized. Holed up in his section of the side porch and being waited on hand and foot by these German enlisted men who are scared to death not to jump every time he coughs. He's got this whole gaggle of German enlisted men organized like a goddam Gestapo unit, and you know what? He hates them. He hates them and he hates us and he hates losing this war and he hates being a prisoner of war. I hope he leaves here soon, but before he does, I hope he gets hemorrhoids so I can put turpentine on them. The Nazi sonofabitch."

Porter soon adored Lt. Albert. There were other nurses in the United States Army who commanded respect because of their ability and dedication to their profession, and there may even have been another nurse who could swear as naturally and expertly as she, and there may have been another nurse who was physically as beautiful as she, and there may have been another nurse somewhere who was as unselfconsciously open and frank as she, but he knew before he had worked under her direction for a week that there was no other female anywhere who embodied all of these characteristics. Lt. Katie Albert was unique. Porter Osborne, Jr., had sense enough to realize it, and he became fascinated by her; he could hardly wait to get to work on the wards every day.

Her form was as pliant and smooth as a hickory sapling along a winter trail, clean-limbed and free, oblivious to crowding from other trees, queening its space. Her skin was smooth and tanned, her eyes were green, her hair was red, and she wore her beauty effortlessly, as though it had been added as an afterthought, an inconsequential accessory. She moved with a litheness that encompassed both power and grace and inspired Pietrini to remark, "You can take one look at her heading down the corridor and know she don't take no shit off nobody."

Pietrini was right.

"Osborne, you are to follow me every morning when I make rounds, and I will give you instructions for the day. If you don't finish them, you go on report. If you don't do them well, you do them over. No fraternizing with these patients. Remember they are prisoners and enemies. Treat them professionally but don't take out personal hostilities on them. Don't let me catch you sitting on a bed or anywhere else for that matter. The best surgeon I ever worked with told his interns that it was all right for them to pee in the sink but never to sit on the desk. There is nothing about your ass that can be regarded as a sterile surface. You understand all this? Wipe that sick-calf look off your face, and I hope to hell you can work faster than you talk."

Porter could, but as soon as he found how much his Southern accent annoyed Lt. Albert, it became more pronounced. He prided himself on being the best assistant she had ever had on any ward anywhere, as hardworking and dedicated as she, but he also began dredging up phrases and figures of speech that would set her green eyes snapping. She soon realized what he was doing and for the most part would ignore the sallies, only occasionally giving in to inquisitive comments or to impatient outbursts. He was able to find out about her only in bits and pieces, snatches of information garnered between patients when they made rounds every morning.

"How are you, Giovanni? *Male* this morning or *bene*? Where the hell are you *male*? OK, we'll get medicine for you. Osborne, write down that his cast is off and there is no local edema, but that the malingering sonofabitch claims to be constipated and I'm giving him two teacups of castor oil."

"'Cast checked. No edema. MO ounces one half h.s., per request of patient.' I hear you're from Nevada, ma'am."

"It's not 'Nevahda'; it's 'Nevada', for God's sake. I am from there, and if I'd thought I was going to spend my war effort listening to POWs whine and having my ears assaulted by mush-mouthed Georgia enlisted men, you can bet your sweet ass I'd still be there. Move on to the next patient. Alberto. are you *male* or *bene* this morning?"

As Porter recorded Alberto's response and the lieutenant's assessment of his condition, he ventured another overture.

"I know how you feel about Nevada, Miz Albert. I was so home-sick in Illinois I thought I'd plumb give up and die."

"For God's sake, I'm not homesick. I'm too mature for that. I miss my horse, that's what. And don't call me Mrs. Albert. Let alone 'Miz'. I'm 'Lieutenant' and don't you forget it."

"Yes, ma'am. I thought you were married; I see your wedding band every day."

"I am married. Which is part of my goddam problem. But that's no business of yours. 'No fraternizing with enlisted men' is one of the first goddam sermons they preached us when I joined this benighted group of nincompoops they call the Medical Corps."

"Yes, ma'am. 'Scuse me. I sure meant no disrespect to a lady. It's just that 'Lieutenant' doesn't seem to do you justice. I can sure understand about your horse. I've got a dog at home that I think about every day."

"What kind?"

"A Doberman-Pinscher. He's registered. A friend gave him to me. His name is Fritz. The dog, not the friend, Lieutenant."

"If he's registered, he is not a 'dawg', for the love of God. Can't you say 'dog'?"

"I'd have to work at it so hard it wouldn't be worth the effort, and then I'd have to change again soon as I got home, Lieutenant. What kind of horse do you have?"

"A Palomino. A Palomino stallion. He's registered, too." Her voice became a little less nasal, the tone not quite so gritty. "If you'll put an R in the word and not make two syllables out of 'horse', I'll show you a picture of him."

"I can for sure and certain try, but you'll have to be patient with me. Golly, Lieutenant, I never saw a Palomino before. That is some more fancy animal. His mane and tail are white as snow. What's his name?"

"Sultan. As you noticed, his color is outstanding, even for a Palomino. His coat looks like honey in contrast to the platinum of his tail and mane, and he wins blue ribbons every time I ride him in a show. I get five hundred dollars stud fee for the magnificent bastard. Look how he arches that neck."

"He's beautiful."

"Thank you. Do you have a picture of Fritz?"

"No'm, but I have one of my three sisters I'd be glad to show you."

"God in Heaven, I'm not believing this. Do they have on hats and hoop shirts?"

"No'm, but I do believe that their mammy saw to it they had on pantaloons before she let them go to the photographer. You don't have to look at them."

"I wasn't trying to insult you, Osborne. Here, let me see. They're pretty girls; don't look the least bit rural or Southern."

"I can assure you, Lieutenant, they are both. Born and bred. From time immemorial. Ladies, each and all."

"Well, that's enough personal stuff. Back to work. Where's the dressing cart? And if you tell me one more time that it's right over yonder, I'll wring your goddam Southern neck. Just get it and let's change those bandages."

Although she never gave the slightest semblance of being happy, Lt. Albert seemed actually angry on the German ward in contrast to her attitude on the Italian ward. She masked it behind increased formality. "Good morning, Herr Colonel," she said icily on the side porch. "The wounds are healing nicely. Did you have a bowel movement this morning? Describe it, please." She then scribbled busily on her clipboard. "Hard? Soft? What color? Brown? Green? Any gas with it? Any pain?"

Porter was puzzled. "Lieutenant, why do you ask him about his BM every morning and then fuss when the other prisoners complain about theirs?"

"Because he's such an arrogant and haughty SS bastard. He thinks women are as inferior as he does Jews, and it chaps his ass to admit in front of the German enlisted men that he's human enough to have to take a crap like everybody else, let alone describe it in detail." She cut her eyes at him. "And that to a good-looking militant *fraulein* who's writing it down. If he thinks about it, and you can be sure he thinks about everything, he's bound to assume that my nurse's notes, with all that detail about his excrement, portray him as a big pile of shit."

"Golly, Lt. Albert, why do you go to all that trouble instead of just cussing him out and putting him on bread and water?"

"Because this is a war of nerves, Osborne, and that sonofabitch knows the Geneva Convention better than I know Merck's Manual. He came on this ward pulling rank and making demands and even reported me to the CO for insolent and insubordinate behavior. He may know protocol and the rules of war, but I know men better than he'll ever know women if he studied day and night for the next forty years in a whorehouse. Me! Insubordinate to a goddam Kraut prisoner! Can you imagine?"

"Gosh, Lieutenant, I sure would hate to cross you."

"Good. That's the way I like it. You be careful around that colonel, though. He understands every word you say and speaks English as well as I do. That means he speaks it better than you. Come on, we're running behind."

"Yes, ma'am. If you ever decide Herr Colonel needs an enema, Miz Albert, I can bring in a friend who'd do a plumb bang-up job. And he'd be right down happy to do it. He's Jewish."

"I told you to call me 'Lieutenant,' dammit. And why do you have to say 'plumb bang-up' and 'right down happy'? The words don't mean anything. If I don't get away from Atlanta, I'm going crazy."

"Yes, ma'am. I had a buddy from Soo San Marie when I was in basic training who would have been handy with the colonel, too. I think he's somewhere in the South Pacific. He's not Jewish, but he sure is inventive."

Both sets of prisoners, bobbing and eddying through the uncontrollable currents of war and washed up now into its backwaters, were subject to the stifling ennui of captivity and were for the most part as apathetic as caged animals. They welcomed any diversion. Porter remembered Deacon Chauncy and made an effort to be kind to each of them, hoping that by some mystical transference Deacon's captors might therefore befriend him. The prisoners, watchful as birds, were well aware that their head nurse was spending more time with this particular corpsman than she ever had with any of his predecessors. They puzzled over and observed the relationship.

"She like you, yes?"

"Today she not like you, no?"

Porter was almost as ambivalent as they.

"Miz Albert, I mean Lieutenant, scuse me again, but I just keep on forgetting, you've told me about Sultan but you haven't told me a word about your husband."

"Perhaps that's because it's none of your goddam business."

"Yes'm, I know that. I was just interested. I sure didn't mean to be prying or pert."

"For God's sake, Osborne, it's no secret. Every officer on the post knows I'm chasing the sonofabitch all around the world; I can see no reason why you shouldn't."

"Ma'am?"

"You heard me. He's an Orthopedic surgeon, the best hands I ever scrubbed with when he came through our hospital in San Francisco as an intern. I've always been damned proud of his professional ability, and I've never looked at another man since he turned those big blue eyes on me. I'd have followed him to Timbuktu, but instead he followed me back to Nevada and we married and settled in. People loved him, patients and doctors. You never saw such a practice nor such a good-looking, happy couple."

"I can imagine."

"I had a miscarriage. That's when he gave me Sultan. He loved horses as much as I; I could never have married a man who didn't. You should have seen Himmy ride!"

"Himmy?"

"Yes, Himmy. That's my pet name for him. He was forever reading, and he called me She after some stupid romance novel by H. Rider Haggard. I never read the goddam book, but he said I was his flame-haired goddess and he'd been searching for me all his life; so I called him my little Himmy. He said my syntax was off but we laughed a lot about things sillier than that. It was a wonderful life."

"Gosh, it sure sounds like it."

"Then this goddam war erupted and the entire world will be changed forevermore. Do you know what that inconsiderate sonofabitch did to me?"

"No'm."

"Hand me that roll of tape. He came home one night and announced out of the blue that he had enlisted and was off to the war! What I am telling you is that he had all the paper work, his commission, his orders cut, and was gone two days after he told me. He'd been planning it for weeks and hadn't told me one word about it. Said he didn't want to upset me and ruin our last few weeks together. I turned my red hair loose and gave him hell and shinola till breakfast time. Then I spent the next day and a half giving him enough loving to remember through the rest of the war. God, Osborne, you should have seen that goddam patriotic, good-looking sonofabitch in his uniform."

Porter could think of nothing to say and concentrated on trying to breathe through his nose.

"Enough of that. Fetch the cart and let me show you how I want this spika trimmed. You're learning a lot."

"Yes, ma'am, Lt. Albert. I sure am. I'm learning a lot from you."

Later that day, Gionini sidled up to him. "She like you today? Yes? No?" He crossed himself.

"She likes nobody today. B'rer Rabbit, he lay low!"

"Me no spika de English so good, yes?"

"You speak English fine, Gionini. You wouldn't understand this if you were fluent."

A few days later Lt. Albert resumed the conversation with no prompting from Porter. Although the POW's could understand only occasional words, they eavesdropped intently, well aware that this was unusual conduct on the part of the dictatorial lieutenant.

"Osborne, I was absolutely distraught when Himmy went marching off to war and left me stranded on the ranch and with everything about the practice to look after, too. I cleaned house, shifted patients, closed the office, packed his clothes in mothballs, and did everything he should have done himself before he left. I'd have gone crazy if I hadn't had Sultan. I fretted for two weeks and then I decided that what's good enough for the goddam gallivanting gander is good enough for the goose also. I was sick and goddam tired of pretending to be civilized and sitting down by myself to eat. I'd never been lonely before in my life. I got so mad I enlisted! Put Sultan in good hands and I've been chasing Himmy ever since. Whenever he's moved to a new base, I put in for transfer as soon as I know where he's going to be."

"Are you close to catching him?"

"Hell, no. I'm exactly three months behind him. You wouldn't believe how unresponsive the brass in this Army can be."

"Yes, ma'am, I'd believe it."

"Paper work, paper work. It'll drive you crazy. Hurry up and wait. If the Germans are organized at all, we'll never win this war. I thought I'd finally caught up with Himmy. He was here at Lawson for three months and that's the only reason I applied to come here. So what happens? One week before I ship in, he ships out. I'm beginning to take it personally."

Porter pushed the medicine cart along and withheld comment.

"Dammit, I'm going to get him. He chased me all over the western United States before he got me, and I'll get him if I chase him all over the world to do it. He's in Italy now, working his ass off in a general hospital, and I'm stuck here tending the people who caused all this disruption in the first place. I know I can't get in the same unit he's in, but I've applied for overseas duty in the ETO and the CO has approved it. At least I'll be on the same continent with him. Someday before this year is out, I'm going to walk up unexpectedly on Maj. Sylvester J. Albert III and say, 'Now I've got you, you sonofabitch!' Is he ever going to be surprised. He'd better be alone when it happens, too."

"I'm sure he'll be delighted, Miz Albert. You know he's got to be as lonesome as you are."

Katie Albert snorted. "How naive can you get, Osborne? He's not lonely. Men love war. They get as excited as little boys about proving how tough they are and trying to outguess and outfight the other side. And Southern men are the worst of all. They all think they were born to be soldiers and that their goddam honor will be sullied if they're not in the thick of it."

"Not all of them, Miz Albert. Is your husband a Southerner?"

"Hell, yes. He was 'bawn and raised' in old Virginney. 'Down where the cotton and the corn and taters grow.' Down in the 'aboot the hoose' section of the state. And that's twice you've failed to call me Lieutenant. Don't you think for one minute I've let my guard down. That's where Himmy got all that charm. He's absolutely irresistible. All my friends told me ahead of time that Southern men are the world's best lovers and worst husbands."

"I've never heard that."

"You've never been anywhere to hear anything. There's a lot you're going to learn before you get out of this Army. Before you're married, a Southern man waits on you hand and foot, and after you're married, he expects the process to be exactly reversed. I'd just about whipped Himmy into shape though when this goddam war came along and he got out on his own. Now it'll all be to do over again."

"Why?"

"Because of the damned Red Cross."

"The Red Cross, Lt. Albert?"

"Yes. The goddammed holier-than-thou, supercilious Red damned Cross. They've pulled all those college graduates with their big blinking eyes and their perfect make-up and those darling little uniforms into the Red Cross and just turned them loose to run wild in the officers' clubs. They've never carried a bedpan or helped drain a lung abscess or scrubbed on a hemorrhoid case or given an enema or washed a filthy butt. They have never, ever let their little hands get all poo-poo over anything. In fact, they've never touched anything nastier than Jergen's Lotion. I've been watching them ever since I joined up, and you can be sure they're passing out a lot more than coffee and doughnuts to our boys in uniform."

"Lieutenant, anybody who looks like you can't possibly be jealous."

"Jealous? I'm not jealous; I'm a realist. My man is human, no one knows that better than I. If he gets desperate and bangs a nurse occasionally just for release, I can handle that, but I promise you if he gets himself mired up with one of those Red Cross pseudo-debutantes, I'll hack his goddam balls off with my bandage scissors. One at a time!"

Porter gulped. "Yes, ma'am. We'd better move along, I guess, Lt. Albert."

"You're right. Good morning, Herr Colonel. How do you feel today. *Gute? Nicht gute?*"

"Good morning, Lieutenant. Today I am thinking that I show some improvement. A little pain in the side, but only once last night did I have to request the pill for pain."

"*Nicht gute*," she responded. "And the bowel movement, Colonel? How many? What color? Hard or soft? Any mucus? Any blood? Round? Or square?"

As the Herr Colonel answered with cold face and through rigid lips, Katie Albert scribbled busily on her clipboard. The enlisted men within earshot looked furtively askance and Porter Osborne, Jr., kept a solemn look on his face.

For minutes after the colonel stopped speaking, the nurse continued to write, her brow creased in concentration. When the silence grew uncomfortable, she stabbed a period in place and looked coolly through the colonel at the window beyond.

"*Danke*," she said impersonally and moved on with Porter in her train. He was, indeed, learning a lot.

Porter triggered an outburst from her a few days later that left him openmouthed and awe-struck. Lt. Albert was unusually tense and abrasive and had taken no notice whatever of Porter during their rounds, refraining from comment on chores which had obviously required extra effort on his part.

"You feel awright this morning, ma'am?" he inquired with respectful concern.

"I feel fine," she snapped. "I have never felt 'aw'right' in my life nor do I intend to. There are two *l*'s and no *w* in 'all right.' And there's no *w* in 'morning,' either. My God, you're mush-mouthed today; you must have stuffed your gut with those goddam grits at breakfast."

"No'm, our cook is a Yankee and we have hash browns instead. I'd sure like some grits, though."

She sniffed disdainfully and said nothing. Porter considered the situation, realized that he had done nothing to offend anyone and decided that his chief nurse must be menstruating. Ingratiatingly he said, "I'm all caught up with my assignments, Lt. Albert, and am fixing to get ready to go to the PX for some of the prisoners. Can I bring you anything?"

She whirled on him in a rustle of white starched uniform, green eyes flashing, red hair flaming.

"You are doing no such a goddam thing. Forget that 'fixing to'! You are not 'fixing to' do anything. *Fix* means *to repair*. And while I'm at it, why are you forever saying 'listen at' somebody or something instead of 'listen to'? I can put up with that 'y'all' crap as a regional eccentricity, but, my God, you Southerners are butchering and desecrating the King's own English. 'Fixing to get ready to' is an abomination. You could just use 'going' and save all that verbal garbage. I'm sick and tired of your 'ma'am' this and 'ma'am' that with that soft as flannel, long drawn out accent. I'm so sick of Atlanta, Georgia, and this fake magnolia-blossom, butter-wouldn't-melt-in-your-mouth atmosphere all of you project that I could scream!"

Porter prudently refrained from pointing out that she was already screaming. He stood before her in submissive silence.

"Oh, get out of here. I'm tongue-lashing you when it's not your fault. My orders still haven't come through and look what I got in the mail this morning instead."

She flung a snapshot on the desk. It was a group picture of seven smiling figures before a ward tent, three of them male officers, the other four female. Unmistakably the woman on the left with the widest smile wore a Red Cross uniform. Porter raised a questioning look to Lt. Albert.

"Yes, that's Himmy. The major in the middle with the big cigar, grinning like a Cheshire cat and draped all over those two nurses. They look like a couple of comfortable pigs, but you see what's waiting in the wings ready to pounce, don't you? Get your deep South ass on to the PX. I reckon I'm fixing to get ready to feel awright by Saridy mawning. You heah me, ole Pvt. Osborne, sugar?" She turned abruptly and stalked away, defiantly erect in immaculate white.

Before the approaching prisoner could open his mouth, Porter said to him, "No feel good today, Gionini, no? Yes. I've got to come up with something to get Lt. Albert's mind off her problem." He looked speculatively at the friendly Italian. "You want to help? Lt. Albert just thinks she's tired of my Southern accent."

He spent Friday afternoon and all of the weekend on the two locked wards, persuasively utilizing the men who spoke the better English as interpreters. Even the Germans, having received taciturn consent from their guardian dragon, joined in the project with enthusiasm. On Monday morning they all stood by their bedsides at a semblance of attention if they were able, or lay expectantly beneath pristine linen if they were not ambulatory.

Lt. Albert swept through the locked gates of the Italian ward ready for rounds, all business, very professional, every inch the no-nonsense director of this corner of the universe. In quick appraisal, she glanced down the ward.

"Well, it looks as though this bunch of carefree prisoners is finally learning some discipline. Good work, Osborne. Hand me my clipboard and come along."

Porter had, as she said, done good work. So had the prisoners. Porter had reached back into his past and pulled forward the answer of the older, the rural, the unsophisticated men and women of his youth when greeted with the polite but perfunctory, "How are you feeling?" The prisoners had been good pupils and had learned the words and the accent to perfection. They were delighted with their accomplishment and also with their inclusion. Lt. Albert stepped smartly forward, crisp and starched, braced for a brand-new week.

"Good morning, Alberto. How are you feeling this morning?"

The man drew himself up as correctly as a hero on review and looked with military precision straight ahead. "Jes' tol'able, ma'am," he drawled.

"What did you say?"

"Jes' tol'able, ma'am. Jes' tol'able." The accent of rural Georgia was incongruously but authentically on the lips of the prisoner who had been born in Sicily and was seeing more of the world than he had ever wanted to.

Lt. Albert tried again. "Not *male* this morning, Alberto? You get no medicine if you're not *male*."

"Jes' tol'able, ma'am," he repeated with pluck.

Lt. Albert moved to the next patient, who actually snapped his heels even though he wore washable terry cloth slippers.

"All right, Gianini. How are you feeling?"

"Fair to middling, ma'am. Jes' fair to middling."

"Gianini, you're forever saying, 'No spika da English.' How the hell are you feeling?"

"Fair to middling, ma'am."

Lt. Albert trained a piercing glare on Porter Osborne. Porter was looking with intense concentration at the baseboard, so puffed up with feigned innocence that he was about to burst. Now was no time to meet Katie Albert's eye. There was the very faintest of snickers from a bed halfway down the ward; otherwise the silence was pulsating. They moved on.

The answers alternated as they progressed from bed to bed. Halfway through rounds the indomitable lieutenant with the Palomino thoroughbred in Nevada and the Virginia thoroughbred in the trenches of Italy, both probably standing at stud, abandoned her concerns about each and conquered the moment.

"All right, Bosi. Middling or tolerable?" She snapped, but Porter thought one corner of her mouth twitched.

"Pacetti, good morning. Tolerable? Middling?" Something was definitely causing the corners of her mouth to twitch; there was an almost audible sigh of relaxation across the ranks of the prisoners. Katie Albert wielded the clipboard like a sceptre, but she was not writing on it. Her passage remained regal but became more rapid. They finished their rounds and not one prisoner had muffed his lines.

"Come along, Osborne," she snapped, and they marched back up the ward to the nurses' office. As they waited for the guard to unlock the gate, Lt. Albert turned and surveyed the Italians, but not a one of them had moved. She stuck one hip voluptuously akimbo, posed a hand in her red curls, and spoke with burlesque exaggeration. "You boys been mighty sweet this mawning. Get busy with your little ole jobs now, and I'll be back to see y'all first chance I get, you heah? Bye, now."

The subsequent sound was explosive and almost deafening, the mixture of laughter and applause punctuated by "Bravo!" erupting exultantly from joyful throats. They could still hear it as they made their way down to the German ward. Porter felt it would be improper protocol for him to initiate speech between them, and Lt. Katie Albert said not one word. She marched. Porter trailed behind her, atwitter with mixed apprehension and titillation.

The German ward was a repetition of the Italian experience. Porter had been nothing if not thorough. The prisoners were well-coached, the accents passable. Lt. Albert moved hastily but methodically through their ranks. At the entrance to the side porch, she stopped. "I think I'll skip Herr Colonel this morning. If I ask him about his BM and he tells me it's fair to middling or jes' tol'able, I'll smack him with this clipboard. Come with me, Osborne."

In the corridor outside the ward, the laughter of the Germans still in their ears, she turned to Porter. "That is a world record for making rounds without a bunch of insignificant complaints, but don't you think for one minute you can get away with it again." She looked at her watch. "We are exactly one hour and twenty-five minutes ahead of schedule. You get this bunch of prisoners straightened out in that time and I won't report you for fraternizing with the enemy."

"Yes, ma'am."

"I'll be back at precisely ten-fifteen and we'll change dressings at that time. Understand? *Verstehen-sie? Comprende?*"

"Yes, ma'am. Where will you be if I need to find you before then, ma'am?"

"In my quarters. Writing letters. I am most certainly going to write Himmy about this, and if I have time I may even drop a line to Sultan."

Suddenly she laughed. Porter was transfixed and joined in. "Her teeth are perfect when you get to see them," he thought.

"Since there are no witnesses to this conversation, and the word of an officer is always accepted over that of an enlisted man, let me tell you, PFC Porter Osborne, Jr., that you are the most unpredictable, irresistible, fascinating little bastard I've run across since I've been in the Army."

"Why, thank you, Miz Albert, ma'am. I think."

"Lt. Albert, soldier. Halfway through Italian rounds I had to exercise rigid control to keep from laughing and hugging your neck."

Porter gazed at her in surprise.

"And then slapping the everlasting shit out of you. Carry on." She turned on her heel and moved with majesty up the hall.

> *"Don John calling through the blast and the*
> *eclipse,*
> *Crying with the trumpet, with the trumpet to*
> *his lips. . ."*

25 **h**e returned to the wards as something of a hero. When Gianini approached him, Porter grinned in anticipation.

"She lika me today, Gianini, yes. Most definitely yes." Then he grinned and flashed the V for Victory sign. The prisoners broke into cheers and pounded his back, gleefully and nonsensically repeating "jes' tol'able" and "fair to middling."

"Never say those words again to the Lieutenant. Understand? Not funny any more. *Comprende?*"

On the German ward his reception was more reserved but definitely friendly. "I'm fraternizing," he thought but shrugged and forgave himself. He wandered out on the side porch, nodded to the Herr Colonel and walked to the end. It was early May and a faint breeze came through the open windows. Outside, a black civilian glistened as he pushed a lawnmower through rich rank grass, the sun already warm enough to produce sweat on his forehead and his exposed forearms. The fragrance of the new-cut grass was sweet. A carpenter bee hovered beneath the window, sunlight glinting on its black carapace and white head, tinting the busy wings with iridescent prisms. Its hum was a comforting drone. Porter drew a deep breath of satisfaction.

A voice came over his shoulder. "You have more intelligence than most of the American soldiers."

The identity of the speaker was certain, but it was the most pleasant tone Porter had ever heard in that accented voice. He turned his head and beheld at his elbow the Herr Colonel on crutches. Surprise delayed any response.

"You have perhaps a cigarette?"

In silence Porter drew a package of Camels from his pocket, proffered them, and then held his khaki-colored Zippo lighter for the colonel. He remembered Lt. Albert's early admonition about this man and was guarded, cautious.

"*Danke*," said the colonel as he blew a twin cloud of smoke through his nostrils, a gesture which did nothing to increase his appeal. Porter aspired to that sophisticated refinement of the art of smoking but had never been able to express smoke through anything but his right nostril; the left was always frustratingly occluded.

"Sure," Porter said. He knew nothing of the Geneva Convention but for safety added, "Sir."

"I confess that the American tobacco is superior and the morning today is most pleasant. I confess also that I enjoyed the demonstration you organized and directed this morning. I gave my approval for the German soldiers to participate."

"*Danke*," Porter murmured and shifted to his other foot.

"The *fraulein* with the red hair, she takes so seriously her duties as a nurse and also her rank as an officer. We have no women as officers in the German army. This Lt. Albert, she deserved the charade you imposed upon her this morning."

Porter's hackles rose a bit, but he said nothing. The colonel's tone changed, included a conspiratorial touch commingled with just a little off-handed supplication. "Those notes she makes at my bedside every morning. You have access to them because I see you always are reading them before you prepare the medicines for the patients. Yes."

"Yes?" said Porter. He omitted, "Sir."

"Could you, *bitte*, would you read the notes on my chart and inform me what they say?"

Porter shifted again. "Herr Colonel, I'm not at all sure that is allowed. I'll have to ask Lt. Albert."

"No, no, no, no. *Nein*. It is nothing. It is her notes that are of interest to me. I have already reported on one occasion to the Red Cross the attitude of the Lt. Albert toward a superior officer, and I have suspicion that those notes might be grounds for yet another complaint, yes. It is a nothing. Do not mention it to her."

Porter swung his gaze back to the outdoors, the lawn mower, the increasing expanse of freshly trimmed grass. The territorial bee zoomed off like a bullet in pursuit of an intruder. "I won't."

The colonel moved to his side, stood a moment, and gave a small chuckle. "The American press does not agree with our idea of a master race. It condemns our *Fuhrer* for being honest about the Jews and for having the courage to, how you say, follow through on his convictions."

"I know," said Porter.

"Aha," said the colonel. "But look at that."

"Look at what?"

"Look at that man cutting the grass out there in the sunlight in the uniform of the labor corps while you perform more highly trained services inside."

"That man is a civilian. He's not in uniform."

The colonel's tone reflected a note of condescension. "Ah, so? Why then do I see from my window all the black men, the Negroes, wear the blue clothes, the overall, I think you call it, and the other men, the white ones who drive them in the truck, wear trousers? That is not a uniform?"

"Colonel, those are working clothes. For outdoors. Lots of white folks wear them, especially on the farm. I wore them myself when I was a little boy." He remembered in a flash that he had never seen his father, his grandfather, or any of his uncles in overalls and fell silent. Maybe overalls were a uniform of sorts. What did this haughty foreign man know? Why could he make him feel defensive?

"You are intelligent. You are honest. You know in your heart that man in the grass is not so good as you." The voice was smooth. "Of course you are better than he is. You were born better than he is. There is living example before your eyes of an inferior race. Everyone knows it, but is not polite to acknowledge, yes?"

Porter was stricken dumb by the horror that there was a modicum of agreement in his soul with what the man was saying.

"You know. Good. Is better to know. Also you have not to me quoted that all men are created equal. That also is good." As Porter stirred, he added, "Oh, do not think I have failed to study your document called 'The Declaration of Independence' that Americans worship as blind truth. No two men are ever created equal in all respects. If they were, those Negroes would not let you treat them as slaves. You know your Bible, yes? 'For what is man that Thou art mindful of him? For Thou hast made him a little higher than the animals.'"

"Lower than the angels," Porter corrected automatically.

The colonel looked at the ash on his cigarette. "Really? They have then a caste system also in the ranks of the angels?"

Porter took a deep breath. "My grandmother says that even the devil can quote scripture to his own purpose."

The colonel smiled. "Ah, your grandmother. *Die grossemutter*. How innocent you are, my young friend. And what tells you your grandmother about these Negroes? These black people?"

"She tells me to be nice," flashed Porter without thinking. Suddenly he was swamped with recall of the Negroes with whom he had grown up on the farm, all of whom he had accepted as extensions of the family, most of whom he had loved. He had a swirl of recollections of Buddy, of Boston Harbor Jones who had befriended him in college, of the Negro doctor who had treated him as an alien, of the porter on the train in Illinois. He whirled to face the colonel.

"Perhaps you are correct that I am innocent. There is a difference between innocence and ignorance, and the destruction of one may abolish the other. I'm going to have to think about that. Conversely, one of the two may grow when the other is destroyed. I don't know. But this I do know. I know who I am. My grandmother taught me that, too, Herr Colonel. And I know who that man cutting the grass is, too. And that's more than you know. We fought seventy-five years ago to keep him in slavery, but we have learned a little since then. We are fighting now to keep him free.

"And you know what, Colonel? I know who you are also. I know what you represent. And I reject it. That Negro man cutting the grass is an infinitely better person than you are. In my eyes, and I hope in the eyes of the Lord. He and I are fighting you and we're going to win. If you were truly a master race, you wouldn't have a leader that looks like he escaped from a mouse trap."

"Ah, what a fervor! Be careful, young man, that you do not transgress protocol to the point of insubordination." His eyes narrowed. "You will not win. We have now a new weapon that will make England an ash heap, and everyone will surrender to *der Fuhrer*. They will have to. I have seen myself the plans. It will be ready. Soon. You will see."

A chill ran over Porter. The man obviously believed what he was saying. He threw it off.

"I do not pretend to know the rules of the Geneva Convention as well as you, Herr Colonel, but I am very familiar with the gulf between enlisted men and officers. I strongly believe that you are as guilty of fraternizing with an enlisted man as I am of insubordination to an officer. Sir."

"You displease me. I misjudged you."

"Indeed you did. Which should tell you something but probably won't. But let me give you one little piece of information. Lt. Albert has not misjudged you. You asked about the nurse's notes. I will tell you about those notes. They reflect voluminously that you are obsessed with your own excretion. To the exclusion of almost anything else. Page

270

after page after page. While everyone else is fighting and dying, you lie in an American ward and talk about your excrement. And you know what, Colonel? You should. That's the most important thing about you. Tell me, how was your bowel movement this morning? Hard? Soft? Did it stink? Or today, Herr Colonel, did you manage to shit a pretzel?"

"Out!" the Colonel roared. "Out of my sight! Neffer enter my room again! Understand?"

Porter turned on his heel; the heads of two German prisoners vanished back into their ward.

"Vait!" The bellow was more heavily accented. Porter turned. The Colonel drew himself rigidly to attention and dropped his crutches. He stretched out his right arm in full extension. "Heil Hitler!" he thundered.

Porter snapped his heels with a smart click, responded with the same salute. "Heil Roosevelt!" he retorted.

As the Colonel held his frozen stance, purpled to the roots of his crew cut, Porter pumped his arm again and again.

"Heil Jefferson Davis! Heil Robert E. Lee! And while we're at it, Heil George Washington Carver and Booker T. Washington, too!" Under his breath, he muttered, "And up your wazoo, you arrogant Nazi shitass." He gave one final salute. "Heil Bernie Friedman!" he shouted.

As he went up the ward through total silence, a couple of the prisoners, after looking to each side, very furtively slipped him a wink. Porter began laughing. "They may like Hitler," he thought, "but they don't like that colonel any better than I do."

"Could you unlock the gate for me?" he said to the guard. "I'll be right back, but I just want to be sure I can still get in and out. All of a sudden freedom is a real puzzle and I've got to think about it. And thank my grandmother."

He walked down to a side corridor, found a door to the outside, and strode directly into the path of the lawnmower. When it stopped, he spoke to the operator. "Good morning, Big'un. You got a cigarette?"

The black man tugged a wrinkled package of Lucky Strikes from his bib pocket. "Just happen to have a little old tailor-made here."

"Thanks. Got a light?"

The man snapped a match alight with an expert thumb nail.

"Thanks. How 'bout facing toward that ward over there and both of us showing them the Victory sign? One of those German prisoners needs a picture."

Porter draped an arm nonchalantly over the compliant man's shoulder. Each of them dangling a cigarette from his mouth, they raised their hands in Churchill's famous V and then Porter Osborne, Jr., slowly curled his index finger under.

"That should have done it," he said. He reached out and shook the laborer's hand in farewell. "You just struck a blow for democracy," he said.

"Say I did?"

"You did. 'They also serve who only stand and wait'," Porter said.

"You crazy, white boy. You ain't what they call shellshocked, is you?"

He was working industriously on the Italian ward that afternoon when Lt. Albert went off duty.

"Osborne, come here," she called to him from the nurses' office. Her face was impassive, her voice as full of gravel as ever.

"Yes, ma'am?"

"Close the door." She looked at him intently. "Now. Where are you really from?"

"Ma'am?"

"You heard me. Where do you live? Tell me the truth."

Porter looked at her in bewilderment, thought for a brief moment, and said dreamily, "Forty miles and a hundred years from this very spot."

"Goddammit, don't get philosophical on me. What's the name of the town?"

Porter was having fun. "Well, Miz Albert, ma'am, we haul our cotton to Peabody but we get our mail out of Brewtonton. Why?"

"Because I think you're a big fat fake, that's why. I heard every word of that interchange between you and that Gestapo bastard this morning, and I have to admit I'm wrong. He does not speak better English than you. You speak absolutely perfect English, in addition to which I applaud the content. The point is that you had absolutely no trace of a Southern accent when you were talking to him. None. You might have been an orator from Washington or New York or Illinois."

Porter winced. "Not Illinois, Lt. Albert. Not Illinois."

"Oh, can the crap. The point I'm making is that you speak two languages. You wallow around in all that grits and magnolia and backwoods mush and then you can snap out of it and speak as precisely as an English teacher. Where did you learn it?"

"Which way, ma'am?"

"Both."

"Well, I learned the proper way from our mother." He thought a moment. "And our daddy. The other I learned from listening to everybody else."

"Why in the living hell don't you speak properly all the time then?"

Porter had not considered this in depth before. "I guess you feel like it's sort of putting on airs at certain times and in certain places. It's fun to relax with the language, and as you say 'wallow around' in it. Kind of like taking off your tie after church and then your shoes and at last your socks. It feels good." He paused and then pushed his luck. "Why do you curse all the time, Lt. Albert, if it's not to turn loose and relax? That's not proper English, either."

"Osborne, I do not . . ." she began and then raised her eyebrows. "You're right. I guess I do. And it's such a habit I'm not even conscious of it. I picked it up from running with one of the nurses where I trained. Now she was afflicted; that poor thing couldn't open her goddam mouth without a swear word falling out."

"Yes, ma'am. Poor thing," Porter responded so quickly that they both laughed.

"The reason I was asking about where you live, Osborne, is that I would like to go there."

"Ma'am?"

"You heard me. I want to see your town, your farm, the house where you grew up, and I want to meet your family. The few civilians I've met here at some of these official officers' club functions are just generic human beings and most of them snobs just like anyone else in the United States who has mounted the social ladder."

"Snobs, Lt. Albert?"

"Yes, snobs. The minute they find out you're not kin to someone they know and that in addition you're a registered nurse, they immediately assume you're socially inferior and have risen above yourself. You can almost hear them holding their skirts aside to avoid contamination and then you get the sweetly patronizing tone in their goddam voices."

"Maybe they just ain't used to ladies cussing, Miz Albert."

"'Lieutenant,' goddammit, and don't say 'ain't.' It's not cute. Anyhow, Osborne, I want to visit your mother. I've an idea that she's a genuine Southern lady and I want to be able to say I met at least one before I ship out of Georgia. Can you arrange it? Maybe get a pass for Saturday afternoon?"

"I can try," Porter said slowly. "We don't have a telephone at home, but I can call my father in town at his office. If Mother's not tied up and has enough gas coupons left over, maybe she can come get us. I'll try."

"My God, Osborne, don't bother your mother with that. I have gas coupons running out of my ears. God knows I've been working so hard I've not had time to use any of them. I'll pick you up in my car."

"Your car? Oh. I didn't know you had one. You mean you're going to carry me home?"

"Hell, no, Osborne. I am not going to 'carry' you home. You are not a sack of horse feed to be 'carried' anywhere. I am going to 'take' you home. I heard you speaking to that colonel, remember? Get back to proper English."

"That was just diction you were listening at, Lt. Albert. My mama says 'carry'."

"Well, I'm sure she does it with charm. Now, get your ass on that telephone."

"Yes'm."

"You know, Osborne, you really got under the Prussian's skin. He was so stuck in that Heil Hitler posture I thought he was getting catatonic and I might have to move his arm down for him. Then when he saw you and that black man laughing together, he started Kussmaul respiration and I had to shove a wheelchair under his butt. I am putting a memo in your record that you are extremely thorough in follow-through on patients."

"Thank you, Lt. Albert. You're the best nurse I ever met." He stuck his head back in the door. "And far and away the best officer."

He reached his father with facility, was assured that his mother had nothing planned that she would not of course be happy to postpone for the opportunity of a visit with her son. The father himself might cut short his Saturday afternoon and evening in town to meet such a marvelous woman as Porter described.

"That's great, Dad," he assured him. "Just remember she looks like a queen and talks like a sailor."

"I can handle it, young man. Just bring her on down."

274

Porter reflected that he could not yet even talk to his father on the telephone without feeling inexperienced, even callow. It was the abrupt and imperious tone, he decided, for there no longer existed in his heart the faintest doubt that his father loved him. "Comes from being an officer all those years," he said and abandoned the thought.

When Lt. Albert arrived at their rendezvous the next day, Porter was awe-struck. He had realized she would not be in nurse's whites and assumed she would be wearing the khaki uniform with straight skirt and sensible shoes. Instead she wore sand-colored whipcord jodhpurs, carefully tended soft riding boots, and a bright yellow blouse with neckline full of promise. A yellow silk scarf was tied carelessly through her red curls. He was also not prepared for her to be at the wheel of a white Cadillac convertible with red leather upholstery and the top down.

"Well, for God's sake, quit standing there gawking and puffing like a goddam goldfish and get in."

Porter obliged with alacrity and hoped that the heavens would decree that Carter Otten chance along to behold this vision. If he had been Elijah pretentiously entering a chariot to transport him to Heaven without the indignity of death, he could not have felt more select or unreal. His head swam a little as he resisted the impulse to wave at all the soldiers waiting for the bus.

"This is my buddy, Lt. O'Brien," Katie Albert explained as Porter took notice of a person in the back seat. "Flossie O'Brien. I decided if there were three of us no officer could accuse us of fraternizing if he saw us out together, and I was sure your mother wouldn't mind an extra visitor."

Porter surveyed the tiny woman with close-cropped hair and small black eyes set more than a trifle too close together. Her breasts were incongruously the size of small melons and threatened to pop buttons from her white shirt. They did, however, draw the eye away from a prehensile harelip, the scar of its less than perfect repair shining white through a speckle of the same downy black hair that framed her face in sideburns.

"Of course my mother won't mind," Porter said. "And you're right as usual, Lt. Albert. No one can accuse us of fraternizing." With care he refused to meet Katie Albert's swift glance. "I'm pleased to meet you, Lt. O'Brien."

"Just call me Flossie. We're not on the wards. We're not even in that God-forsaken hospital for the rest of the afternoon and evening."

There was a lilt in her voice and a cheer in her eyes that made one momentarily forget her face in repose. Responding to her good-natured sally, Porter said, "Where you from, Ms. O'Brien? Flossie?"

"Ah, listen to him, Katie Albert. Don't you love that Southern accent? I'm from Massachusetts. South Boston to be exact, 'way up yonder in the frozen North.' And here I am in Katie Albert's convertible with a good-looking Georgia boy heading out for a taste of the Old South. Just like *Gone With the Wind.*"

"Oh, Flossie, don't get your hopes up. It's not quite like that. Hollywood overglamorized the book. The houses don't look like that; they're certainly not furnished like that."

As her face stilled, he let his eyes fall from her lip to her bosom and then self-consciously jerked them back upwards as he realized he was staring. "We do live in the part of the country Margaret Mitchell wrote about, though," he reassured her hastily. "In fact, her mother's people were all raised on a farm just across Flint River about seven miles from our house. In the part of Clayton County called the Panhandle. Close to Bumblehook. The family was named Fitzgerald and they're buried in the cemetery in our town. It's the only Catholic plot in the graveyard and it's fun to go and read the names. Some of them tie in with the book, too."

"I never read the book," said Flossie, "but I loved the movie."

"Oh," said Porter.

"Well, I read the book," interposed Katie Albert. "And I think this is fascinating. Maybe we'll have time to run by that cemetery this afternoon."

Porter envisioned the impact of his appearance in the cemetery with this duo and in this automobile. "I'd like that," he said. "There are three infant sons buried there, a black woman who must have been Mammy, and it says right on the tombstone that Mr. Fitzgerald was born in Ireland."

"Big deal," snorted Flossie O'Brien. "So was my old man. I don't want to spend a beautiful day like this grubbing around a cemetery. I didn't come south to consort with dead people."

"Are you Catholic, Lt. O'Brien? Flossie?"

"Am I Catholic? Me Irish? Me from South Boston? My old man in hock to every ward heeler in town? And one of them, by the way, is also named Fitzgerald; it's a small world, ain't it? Of course I'm Catholic!"

"You went to Catholic schools?"

276

"Of course I did. From first grade through high school and then all the way through nursing school. I'm as Catholic as you can get and be a woman. Unless you're a nun. And that's not for little old Flossie, no siree."

"Why not, Floss?" asked Katie Albert in a teasing tone.

"With these knockers, for Christ's sake?" shrieked her friend. "It takes a lot of hormones to produce a pair like this, girl, and I'm not about to tie them down under a nun's habit and waste them." She caught the startled look on Porter's face and laughed. "Oh, relax. I've seen you watching them ever since you got in the car. Everybody does. They're my greatest asset."

Porter swallowed and said nothing. "Knockers?" he thought. "My God, Yankee women are crude."

"When I was a student nurse, the cardinal himself had a brother who was a surgeon on staff at the hospital where I trained. When I got assigned to the OR and had to scrub with him, I was scared to death, I was. You know what I mean? Afraid I'd do something so stupid I'd disgrace myself. Then the sister who was head nurse said the great doctor was requesting me to scrub on his cases and I was so flattered I got goose bumps. I'm that short I had to stand on a stool, but it was some more thrill for a poor lass like me to be such a good nurse that a famous doctor would notice me and me still only a student."

"I guess so," murmured Porter.

"All the girls were jealous. I had a wonderful future, they said. I told Ma and she told Pa and all the neighbors. It was great. Then I began noticing that when I'd be leaning over the sterile field to hold a retractor or to snip a suture, his elbow would always be pressed into my breast. 'No, Floss,' I said to myself, I said. 'You've always been a great one to imagine things.' So I put up with it. Then one day I heard him when he was at the scrub sink with one of the interns. 'I always ask Sister for the short one with the big tits,' he said. Plain as day he said it. I heard it with my own ears, I did. The intern and I were helping him with a gallbladder that day and, sure enough, here came the elbow, again and again. I kept trying to move away. Then he nudges me a good one. 'Kocher clamp,' he says and so help me, Holy Mother, winks at that intern. He did, too. I saw it with my own eyes. I already had the clamp ready. For God's sake I'd done enough gallbladders by then to know that's what he needed next."

"You are a good nurse," said Porter.

"Well, sir, I lost my temper. I'm not Irish for nothing, I'm not. I rapped him so hard on his knuckles with that heavy clamp that the crack made the intern jump and the great white surgeon yells, 'Ow, that hurt! Be careful!' And nudged me again! I was off guard and he got me right across the nipple. I whacked him another one and said, 'You're the one to be careful, sir, and kindly keep your elbows at your own sides or I'll break scrub and scratch your eyes out. I'm a good girl, I am.' 'What's the matter with you?' he said. 'Sister! Can you scrub in and dismiss this student? She's irrational, she's disoriented.'"

"I can't believe that, Flossie," said Porter.

"You can believe it, Georgia boy," said Katie Albert. "It's a big bad world out there, and a girl on her own has to be on guard every minute."

"'Disoriented, am I?' I says to him. 'My father is Big John O'Brien himself who works the docks for twenty years and you'll be unconscious yourself, you will, if I tell him somebody's been playing tiddly winks with his baby daughter behind the masks and sterile drapes of the surgical suite. On top of that my oldest brother is Terrible Tim O'Brien who bit the nose off that Hunky in a saloon last year and is a sweet and lovable lad to his family but gets terribly mean when he's mad, he does.' 'Go to your room, O'Brien,' says Sister, 'and wait for me.'"

"What'd she do?"

"Took me off surgery and put me on probation for the rest of the year."

"What? What'd she do to the doctor? Kick him off staff?"

"Are you kidding? 'Flossie,' she says to me, 'you know you're distraught and imagining things.' I told her about the intern and I told her about the wink if she wanted more proof than my own word and she says, 'Well, men are coarse creatures, Flossie, and you must remember this is the Cardinal's brother, and we wouldn't want our hospital to get a bad reputation in the Church, would we?' 'So I should get cancer of the breast,' says I to her, 'because he's the Cardinal's brother? And be a martyr in the Church like Saint Theresa or Saint Genevieve or somebody? I don't want to be no saint, not I, but what about my reputation? I'm a good girl, Sister. My dad is John O'Brien and he raised us all to be good, even including my oldest brother who just happens to be Terrible Tim O'Brien and gets mean when he gets mad.' 'I know who your father is, Flossie,' she says to me, she says, just as cool as you please, 'and also your brother. That's the only reason we're not expelling you. You must understand that we have to do what is in the best interest for the greater good of the Church as a whole.' Then she patted me and said, 'I know you're a good girl and you keep on being a good girl. Just try not to be so explosive about it. And unpredictable. And maybe a little more selective, when you do explode.'"

Porter had been laughing, but he interrupted with indignation. "What? And you're still a Catholic?"

Flossie laughed. "Of course I am. I'm a damn good Catholic. I go to Confession every week. Don't I, Katie Albert?"

"I guess that's where you go. You leave the nursing quarters with that announcement. I'm not your goddam chaperone."

"I don't know much about Catholics. What do you confess?"

"My sins, baby."

"Oh."

"I'm driving the priest crazy. He's obviously of English extraction and has no sense of humor at all. Nobody's got any business in the priesthood anyhow, as far as I'm concerned, except the Irish and the Italians, maybe an occasional Polack. Certainly not an Englishman. I told him I'd joined the Army and come South because I heard the men were such smooth lovers and I wanted to find me one. One who'd never heard of Big John O'Brien. Let alone Terrible Tim."

"You told him that?"

"To be sure I did. And now every week I say to him, 'Father, I have not sinned. I hate to waste your time, but nothing has happened. Yet. See you next week. Pray for me.'"

Even Katie Albert laughed aloud. Porter observed the flashing wit in Flossie O'Brien's beady little eyes, the wind whipping the scarf in Katie Albert's hair, and decided he was having one of the great times of his life. Of a sudden he stiffened.

"Flossie."

"What?"

"Don't tell my grandmother you're Catholic, hear? She wouldn't understand."

"I won't. But I bet she would."

"I promise you she wouldn't. And I'm not going to tell her you're from Massachusetts," Porter laughed. "Just to be on the safe side."

"Now, I'll go along with you there, Georgia boy."

They were off Stewart Avenue, headed for Jonesboro on Highway 41. Porter noted that Katie Albert drove as smoothly and rapidly as she worked.

"My God, Floss, with all these restrictions on us in this foreign land, maybe we'd better letter POW on our shirt. Osborne, see if I remembered to put that package for your mother under the seat."

Porter groped obediently under the red leather. "There's a package here all right. It's for my mother?"

"Sure. Just a little visitor's gift for her being nice enough to have us in her home today."

"Oh, Miz Albert, you shouldn't do that. It's not necessary."

"Well, it certainly is necessary. You don't understand women. It's not anything much, just a bottle of Sauterne."

"Isn't that wine?"

"Of course it's wine, you ninny. White wine. Not a great one, but good."

Porter listened to the singing of the automobile tires for a minute. "Lt. Albert."

"You don't have to call me 'Lieutenant' when we're not on post."

"Yes'm. About that gift for my mother. I told you it wasn't necessary, but let me rephrase that. It is most unnecessary."

"Why?"

"Because it's wine."

"Whatever in the hell do you mean?"

"My mother and grandmother are such tight Baptists they squeak, and they're the biggest teetotalers you ever heard of. My grandmother has told me all my life that Osborne men can't drink. My mother sure backs her up on it, and there's never been any alcohol served in their house."

"What?"

"The menfolks have to go outdoors or down to the barn to sneak a toddy on Christmas Day. You just don't understand, Miz Albert."

The tires sang again for a moment.

"Maybe I understand more than you give me credit for. I can assure you that your mother is not going to be offended by a goddam insignificant bottle of white wine. I'll tell her she can cook with it."

Porter listened again to the tires and thought for a moment.

"Cook what, Miz Albert?"

"Oh, Osborne, for God's sake! I don't worry about inconsequentials. Chicken, fish, veal, I don't know what all. She can slosh it up the goddam turkey's butt if nothing else."

Porter could not help laughing. "Can you cook turnip greens in it?"

"Yuck," contributed Flossie O'Brien, and they all laughed.

"Osborne, you just relax. Your mother and I are going to get along beautifully. You just don't understand women."

280

At the sound of the same dictum under cover of which males universally seek absolution, Porter fell silent, but he could not help repeating her own phrase. "Maybe I understand more than you give me credit for."

"What'd you say, Georgia boy?" Flossie called. "I can hardly hear you with the wind blowing like this, I can't."

"I just said we're coming into Brewtonton. Slow down when we go by the courthouse and the drugstore and let me see if my daddy's car is still in town. Don't worry, Floss, we're not going by the cemetery today."

On the dirt road for the last six miles of his impromptu home-coming, Porter felt tension mount within him. How would his home, the sentimental core of his entire being, appear to these sophisticated women who were also Army officers, one of whom already derided his provincialism, who made several inspection tours weekly of the house-keeping under her command? Quaint? What would they say to each other if they caught his grandmother with her snuff? At that thought he relaxed; nobody except closest family had ever been privileged to witness that ritual nor had any strangers ever appeared so precipitously that she was not able to wipe her mouth and pocket her little snuff box before greeting them. On the other hand, how would his family accept and greet his friends? Would they be formal, shy, stand-offish? Or warm and genuine, as they were if they liked someone.

"I haven't told y'all, but my grandmother and her brother plus my aunt and uncle live in the house with us."

"Plus your parents and your three sisters? That's almost a squad you grew up with. Life in the goddam barracks must be a piece of cake for you."

"More like dry unleavened bread," Porter responded. "Here's where our land starts, and around that curve and over the hill you'll see our house."

"I've been wondering why your ancestors came way out here to live, I have," said Flossie, "but I've got it! They went as far as they could possibly go and had to stop. I've never been this far off a paved road in my life, I haven't."

"This distance is nothing," assured Katie Albert. "You should come out West. What I can't get used to is the soft rain and all the beautiful goddam trees. What's that green stuff in the fields?"

"Cotton," said Porter. "Already chopped, run around once, and hoed. And over yonder is corn."

"Your accent is getting thicker than molasses," she snapped. "Where are the taters?"

"Taters?" puzzled Porter.

"Yes, the goddam taters. You've heard that song Himmy drives me crazy with. 'Carry me back to old Virginny, that's where the cotton and the corn and taters grow.' That's it, Osborne, your mother can cook the wine with the goddam taters."

"I'll let you be the one to tell her, Lt. Albert. Lots of luck."

"So that's your house, is it? It's big enough. Does all this land belong with it?"

"As far as you can see from the upstairs porch."

"I'm impressed, Osborne. I thought you had been exaggerating."

"Why?"

"Because all Southern men do. Don't forget I'm married to one."

"It's not just Southern, Katie," interposed Flossie. "I'm not even married and I already know, I do, that all men exaggerate. You have to take them like you find them, you do. The problem is finding them."

Porter had not taken Fritz into account in his fret about greetings. When he stepped from the car, the dog recognized him and checked his suspicious advance. He hurled himself forward, cropped rump writhing frantically, leaping so high with joy and abandon that he threatened to topple backward in descent, lean muscles taut, great tongue caressing. Unable to contain himself, he ran in circles around them and then unleashed the straining power within him by racing across the ditches and the cotton field, belly thinned and low to the ground, headed for the horizon.

"My God," said Katie Albert from Nevada, "look at that magnificent son of a bitch go."

"My sentiments exactly, ma'am," said a cultured voice behind her. They turned to the figure dressed in white from top to toe.

"You must be Porter Osborne, Sr. I'm Katie Albert, and this is my friend, Flossie O'Brien."

"My pleasure, ladies. Won't you come in?"

Porter's mother awaited them on the porch at the top of the steps, a welcoming smile so sweet on her face that Porter's heart swelled. What if no one else in the whole world liked it? This was home and it was his. He went through introductions with pride.

"Mrs. Osborne, it's so nice to meet you. What a lovely home you have. It's absolutely beautiful. And such a lovely yard and flowers. I want to tell you what an intelligent and inventive son you have; he's a great credit to you." Porter's jaw dropped. Could this be Lt. Katie Albert, the vitriolic scourge of the POW wards? "Now who's being mush-mouthed?" he wanted to ask.

"Thank you, Katie. I hope he's doing a good job."

"She's seeing to that," Porter interjected.

They both ignored him. "I brought along a little something I thought you might enjoy in your home."

"Why thank you, Katie. You shouldn't have done that; it's not necessary. How sweet and thoughtful of you."

"It's nothing, just a bottle of wine." She shrugged. "You can cook with it or whatever; I always think a little Sauterne adds flavor. To fish, especially."

His mother's smile neither faltered nor dimmed. "I'm not much of a fancy cook, Katie, but I'll treasure this because it's from you. We'll save it for very special occasions. Thank you again. Come on in and meet the rest of the family and then let me get you girls some ice tea."

Katie Albert shot Porter a triumphant glance which he smoothly deflected. Sauterne cooked with fried bream? With fried catfish? With occasional fried mullet when the store at Peabody could procure a barrel of them from Florida, packed in stiffened death between layers of ice that preserved like glass the shining stars of sightless eyes? The lieutenant, gorgeous and confident, might well know who she was, but she sure didn't know exactly where she was. Sauterne, indeed. He was willing to bet that bottle would be emptied down the sink as soon as their visit was over.

The two nurses were delighted with the old house and, to them, the strange people who inhabited it. Porter's family was enthralled by the Yankee and the Westerner who had appeared so precipitously among them and who expounded so enthusiastically over any reliquary which attracted their comment.

"Katie, let me carry you and Flossie in to meet Sambo's grandmother. Her father was from Ireland and he built this house, almost a hundred years ago."

"Came over from Ireland, did he now? Well, Osborne, we've got something in common, we have. You never told me that," chattered Lt. O'Brien.

"Sambo?" queried Lt. Albert and raised one brow but not the other.

"Yes," beamed Porter's mother. "His daddy nicknamed him that when he was just a baby and it stuck. Don't call him that in front of his grandmother, though; she doesn't approve of it."

"I wouldn't dream of it," assured Katie Albert."

"I'm not going to open my mouth in front of her at all, I'm not," asserted Flossie O'Brien. "I've been told not to."

"Did her father own slaves?" asked Katie.

"Mercy, yes. You don't think he built this big old house all by himself, do you? I was raised in Bartow County and my folks didn't own slaves, but the Osbornes and the Porters did."

Porter Osborne, Sr., joined in. "Grandpa was older than Grandma. He was coming through this part of the country on horseback with just his body servant, had business in Columbus or near there, and stopped to ask for a drink of water. Grandma was the Widow Roberts then with three little children hanging on her coattails and she had just drawn a fresh bucket from the well. She gave Grandpa water and then asked, 'Would your man like some, too? There's a trough over there for your horses if you like.' When they rode on, Grandpa told his slave, 'Jason, soon as we get done in Columbus I'm coming back here and marry that lady and we're going to settle down.'

"And they did. Bought up this land and cleared it for cotton, cut the timbers for the house right on the spot. The sills are oak twelve-by-twelves and the studs are four-by-eights, put together with wooden pegs. These twelve-inch boards in the hall are heart pine and you can tell they're hand planed. See the little ridges where the slaves didn't quite get them smooth? See the old square nails?"

"How fascinating. This house has a lot of history."

"A lot of memories, ma'am. My mother was born in that room over there and so were all her children and then all of my children."

"I'm surprised the house survived the Civil War."

"It very nearly didn't. Sherman's forces didn't get any closer than Lovejoy and then headed east after the battle of Atlanta, but a foraging party came across the river into this part of the county. The darkies came running through the woods and told Grandma the Yankees were coming. She sent the cow to the deep woods with Aunt Tabby, had the children and the pickaninnies catch all the chickens and go hide, and made Old John Tom turn the hogs loose and ride the one horse they had left as far as he could out an old field road. She had been giving shelter to three or four Confederates while they got over their wounds and they slipped out and hid in the woods down at the crossroads. They shot in the air when the Yankees came in sight and

284

made so much fuss with Rebel yells that they sounded like an entire company, and the Yankees were glad to turn their horses around and gallop back to Lovejoy."

The litany of this history was so familiar to Porter that he turned to Flossie and said, "Come out on the back porch and sit in the swing with Uncle Bung. He's older than my grandmother and remembers the Yankees well."

"You be sure and tell him I'm Irish, you do. I can understand those Yankees running; I told you your ancestors had gone as far as they could before they built this house, didn't I?"

"Don't worry, Flossie. We have a couple of cousins who married Yankees. Came about because of sending them to West Point for an education. One of them's even a Catholic. My grandmother has accepted it, she just doesn't allow anyone to mention it when we're eating. You'll like Uncle Bung. Don't forget he's half Irish. He was too young to go to the War."

Flossie stopped abruptly. "Uncle who?" Then she laughed. "I never thought the day would turn out like this when Katie Albert asked me if I wanted to go to ride. Now you know this is more fun than a cemetery! How are you feeling, Uncle Bung?"

"Jest tol'able, I reckon, young lady. Jest tol'able."

"Oh, shit," said Lt. Flossie O'Brien.

"What'd you say, young lady? I'm a little hard of hearing. Sit here by me."

"I said, 'It's a beautiful day,' I did."

Porter left the two side by side in the swing. He noted that the feet of neither touched the floor. He also noted that Uncle Bung was staring straight ahead of him as stiffly as though he had a crick in his neck and that the imperiled buttons on Flossie's blouse were still holding. "They'll entertain each other," he thought.

His father joined him. "Let's sit on the front porch, son. The ladies have gone in your grandmother's room. They'll entertain each other. That's a real live pair you're traveling with."

The heavy oak rockers, their backs and seats contoured by three generations of human backs and seats, creaked reassuringly of comfort and stability and gave momentary promise that nothing, after all, had changed, not on that high, sun-kissed, breeze-swept front porch in middle Georgia. They listened to the bold and demanding three-note whistle of the bobwhite and the secretive two notes of his nesting mate's response and felt initiated, bound to each other. They spoke of war and the strategies of generals, they moved globally from New Guinea to China to India to France to North Africa to Italy.

Inevitably their subject narrowed. Ed Travis, Miss Mary Green's only child, was now at Anzio, having survived Sicily, Salerno, and Naples. His mother wanted people to pray for him.

"I'll write Miss Mary Green a letter," evaded Porter; religion was not a topic he discussed with his father. Preacher Turner's youngest boy, Alvin, had shipped out to England, where Eisenhower was sure to find use for him on the day he invaded France. Custard Mize had been separated from his unit in Italy and had evaded German capture by hiding beneath a hog pen for three days and nights. Joseph Ballard had been shipped out; his wife and baby were living on the farm of his younger brother who had an agricultural deferment. All six of Miss Nell and Mr. John Ambrose Burch's boys were in uniform and every one of them either overseas or on the seas.

"I couldn't get in the paratroopers, Dad. I tried."

"The hell you did."

"Yessir. I'm blackballed for that. Old Maj. Triplepoot did it. By the way, I found out he's headed for the South Pacific."

"Good. He's so fond of yellow he ought to enjoy the Japs."

"He sold that car to a sergeant. For a song, the sergeant said."

"Well, the supercilious snot-headed son of a bitch may get shot in the back by his own men if he doesn't change his tune. He'll not be dealing with a bunch of college gentlemen now." He shifted his rocker a little. "You could still apply for OCS."

"Griffin Calhoun is doing that." A cow lowed from behind the barn. "I'm going to apply for overseas duty as soon as I finish at Lawson."

His father flipped a half-spent cigarette into the yard and immediately lit another. "You be careful. This county needs you to come back and be a doctor when this is over."

"We'll decide about that later," Porter demurred and shifted the talk to crops, the scarcity of sugar, black market gas coupons, and local profiteers. It was a very satisfactory visit.

They began preparing to depart.

"Are you sure y'all can't stay for supper? We have lots of new potatoes and English peas and it won't take but a minute to kill a chicken. There are plenty of graham biscuits left over from dinner."

"No, Mrs. Osborne, we have to get back. Tell me, though, about this little chair here. I've never seen one like it."

286

"That's a nursing rocker, Katie. See? It has no arms to it. My great-grandfather made it for my grandmother when she was expecting her first child. My mother and all her brothers and sisters were rocked in it, then I and all my family, and then all four of my children. It's about worn out, but I'm saving it for my grandchildren."

"How precious. It's just darling."

"Thank you. If you are sure you won't stay for supper, wait just a few minutes and let me fix you up a little sack of my bread-and-butter pickles and some fresh dewberry jelly."

"Sambo, come here," called the twinkling silver-haired non-agenarian from the swing.

"Yes, Uncle Bung?"

Covering his mustache behind a funeral home fan he had been plying, the old man said *sotto voce*, "You give that Yankee heifer a little more cotton seed meal on her hulls and I expect you can get three gallons of milk and a pound of butter a day. Them tits make me wish I was two years younger." He cackled soundlessly and hit Porter with the fan. "Better make that five years, I guess."

"Uncle Bung, you're awful."

His father crooked a forefinger at him, beckoning him to his side. "Boy, you be careful. That red-haired one is a tiger and possibly more than you could handle, but both of them are officers and you're not. You be careful."

Porter thought about Terrible Tim O'Brien's teeth and Katie Albert's bandage scissors. "Dad, I promise you this is purely a platonic outing."

"Yeah, I'll bet. Like I said, you be careful."

To Porter's surprise, when his parents followed the trio to the car in hospitable farewell, Katie Albert went into his mother's arms in a clinging embrace, his mother patting her gently on the back. Both women's eyes were moist. Then they were off. Fritz leveled himself alongside the car in silent speed until they accelerated enough to leave him. He sat in the middle of the big road, watching them until they were out of sight. Porter quit looking.

After a mile, Flossie began chattering. What a marvelous house, what a great group of people, what a swell guy his dad was, how sorry she was his sisters weren't home, how cute Uncle Bung was once you got him relaxed and talking, how wonderful it must have been to grow up on this farm, how lucky Porter Osborne was.

Porter interrupted. "Lt. Katie Albert, you said I was a fake with my Southern accent. Well, I think you're the same kind of fake. I haven't heard you use a cuss word all afternoon."

"They weren't necessary, Osborne, nor appropriate."

"How about that 'precious' and 'darling' over a beat-up old rocking chair? I didn't know those words were in your vocabulary; I certainly never expected to hear them cross your lips." He waited for a reply, then pursued. "You said you wanted to meet my mother. What did you think? It looked to me like you really took to each other."

"We did." She looked at her watch. "Although she's probably pouring that bottle of Sauterne down the sink right this minute."

Porter gulped. "You're right about one thing; I just don't understand women."

"Of course you don't. And any of us who has a dab of sense will keep you that way. All your life."

"What did you talk about in my grandmother's room?"

"Well, let's see now. I asked your grandmother about the war as she remembered it and if it was really as bad as I've heard after Sherman came through. That took awhile. She's still very bitter. Said what Sherman did to the countryside took a whole generation to get over. Two years after Appomattox they were still digging dirt from under the smokehouse and boiling it to get salt. There wasn't any to be had, she said, even if they'd had any money to buy any."

"I've heard those stories all my life. Did she tell you about giving the silver to the slave to bury two days before he fell out of the barn loft and broke his neck? I spent half my childhood hunting that silver."

"We didn't get around to that. I told her and your mother about Himmy and how I'm trying to catch up with him."

"What'd they say?"

"Your mother told me about being pregnant with your older sister when your daddy shipped overseas and how hard it was to see him leave and not know if she'd ever get him back. Believe me, I could relate to that. Then she told me the hardest part to do was listen to your grandmother's advice and send him away with a smile. And your grandmother said she got that from her mother, that you should always let your man's last memory of you be one of a smiling face. War is so horrible and lonely, she said, that memories are the most important thing a soldier has to carry him through and protect him."

"My grandmother's pretty smart."

"Your grandmother goes further than being smart. She's wise. There's a big difference. Did you know she got married when she was sixteen?"

"Of course I knew it. And my grandfather was only seventeen."

"I said something dumb about dropping out of school and she said, 'Young lady, there were no schools. We were concerned about something to eat and a roof over our heads.' Before I thought I pulled out a cigarette and lit it. She looked at me so hard I started to apologize and put it out, and then she said something to your aunt and got a little can of snuff out of her pocket and rolled a little twig in it and popped it in her mouth. Then she told me to sit down."

"I can't believe it. What did you do?"

"I sat down, you ninny. Then I heard about how determined she had been that all her children get an education, that it was the only hope for the South, that she had watched the men work harder and the land get poorer and she knew in her heart that farming would never again be a life for a gentleman. She sold butter and eggs and took in boarders to help pay for her children to go to school, and she is so proud of your father it shows when she mentions his name."

"Well, you ladies certainly had a visit. You got into the inner circle quicker than anybody I've ever seen before."

"Uncle Bung and I had a good visit, too, we did," said Flossie O'Brien.

"Shut up, Floss. We'll hear about that later. All of a sudden it got so quiet I could hear that old clock ticking on the mantle and I turned to your mother and said, 'Mrs. Osborne, my husband's last memory of me is yelling and giving him what for. Pray that I catch up with him before it's too late.' And she said, 'I've been praying for you ever since you told me about following him, Katie. Given the same circumstances I'd be doing exactly what you are. Thanks for being nice to my boy.' I told her I had not by any stretch of the imagination been nice to her boy or anybody else for the last year and a half."

"But . . ." interjected Porter.

"Be quiet. I'm not through. Your mother stood up and stroked my hair and said, 'Katie, I don't think you're a mean girl and if I don't, you surely haven't fooled the good Lord. I'll pray for you every night, but the important thing is that you pray for yourself.'"

"Oh, my God," said Porter. "I carry a couple of Army nurses home for a drop-in visit and my whole family jumps naked. Then starts missionary work."

"You just shut up, Porter Osborne, Jr. You don't know how lucky you are to have a mother like that."

"Well, you told me before we started out that you particularly wanted to meet my mother. Now you have."

"Yes. And one of the reasons is that my mother was killed in a wreck when I was fourteen and I needed to meet a real one again. One who would tell me to smile."

Her tone precluded any reply. Even Flossie was mute. After a moment, Katie Albert resumed. "You were right about the distance. It's forty miles and a hundred years. We've learned how to pave roads and make automobiles and airplanes, but we've forgotten a lot of other things. I have a lot of remembering to catch up on."

"That's beautiful," said Porter. "Why in the world did you ask my grandmother about the War in the first place?"

"Because I'd never talked to anyone who lived through it before. At least not in Georgia. Especially not in this section of Georgia."

"But why is that important to you?"

"Because," she took a deep breath and stared straight ahead, "before I got married my name was Katie Grant Sherman."

Porter took himself a deep breath. "You mean . . . ?"

"Absolutely. Where do you think the red hair came from? And why do you think Himmy's mother disinherited him and won't even speak to him? Let alone to me."

From the back seat Flossie chirped, "Did you know that Uncle Bung's wife is still living at ninety-one? That he left home and came to live with your grandparents after seventy years of marriage, he did, because he couldn't stand her nagging any longer?"

Oblivious to Army rank or the protocol of manners, Porter snapped, "For God's sake, Floss, shut up."

They rode in silence for awhile. Heading north from Buckhead and Oglethorpe, Porter volunteered, "Katie Grant Sherman Albert. You missed the mark a little when you said I don't understand women. I'm not real sure at this moment I understand a single goddam thing in the whole goddam universe."

She laughed and the sound was sweet. "Don't swear or I'll put you on report. Where in the world did your father come up with a nickname like 'Sambo' for you?"

"I'm not sure, but I've always been grateful."

"You like it?"

"With a name like Porter Longstreet Osborne, Jr.? Come on. I could have fared a lot worse. I don't have to live up to anything to be 'Sambo.' It's all mine and only mine."

She slanted a glance at him. "You may be off the mark yourself there. We all establish a reputation and make our own name mean something. I enjoyed the afternoon. You never told me you'd finished a year and a quarter of medical school."

Quickly and lightly, Porter answered, "You never asked. It's not important."

"Maybe that'll be part of what your name comes to mean. We take everything we do along with us."

Porter stilled a moment. "I guess you're right, Mrs. Himmy Albert. I'll be careful."

She laughed again. "I'll believe that when I see it."

"Thanks. I'll get out right over there. I enjoyed the afternoon, too. I'm very glad to have met you, Lt. O'Brien, and I'll see you Monday on the wards, Lt. Albert."

He closed the heavy door carefully, wishing that Otten were watching.

"No, you won't. My orders are in and I'm shipping out Monday at 0800 hours for England. You're on your own with the Herr Colonel and all the others." She laughed. "Don't panic."

Porter stood in the center of the street and watched the white convertible until it turned the corner. Neither of its occupants looked back. He shrugged and started up the duckwalk to Barracks C, hoping that either Pietrini or Friedman was there and digesting the fact that he would never see Himmy Albert's beautiful wife again.

"But Don John of Austria has burst the battle-line!"

26 **P**orter had been planning to call Dr. Thebault ever since his arrival at Lawson and perhaps go visit him at Emory should he be invited. Realizing that his remaining time in Atlanta was now very brief, he called him at home that night.

"Dewitt? This is Porter Osborne." He found it relatively easy to use his ex-professor's Christian name when not visually confronted by his stony gaze and tightened lips. "I'm winding up a course out at Lawson General Hospital in advanced surgical training and will be leaving in a week or two . . . Well, I've been meaning to and they've kept us so busy I just haven't had the time. I called to let you know how Fritz is doing. He is lord of all he surveys. Everybody loves him, even the women folks, and he has taken control of that entire section of Brewton County . . . Not at all. We are the ones who are grateful to you for letting us give him a good home. How are things with you? And Emory? . . . Hell, no, I didn't know that Dr. Martell had started medical school. And she's still teaching Bacteriology until she starts down at Grady? Wow! That's one big break in tradition for Emory; she's the first female medical student they've ever admitted . . . They plan to accept more if she does well? You'd better get ready; that old lady will go through the Butch like Grant through Richmond . . . I know, I know. 'Lady' is a generic term. What do you want me to call her? A Mesopotamian fertility goddess? When you see her, tell her I'm jooging the Potentials of debutantes in pay toilets all over Peachtree Street and haven't caught syphilis yet . . . Naw, it's an inside joke. Also, tell her when she scrubs with Dean Astenheimer to keep her hands to herself, that is, if you'd like to see her blush . . . I know that's a lot of flesh to turn red, but that's what she'll tell you about the dean, too . . . Yes, I heard that the perfect asshole had left Emory. He's headed for the South Pacific, I hear . . . Yessir, I heard about his car, too. In fact, I

292

saw it, although come to think about it, I haven't seen it lately . . . No, sir, I was in Illinois. Remember? You saw me off at the station? I couldn't possibly have messed with that car. Besides, I don't know anything about machinery . . . I've seen Barton. He's in the paratroopers and in Italy now. He's already been wounded twice but hasn't changed a bit. The German hasn't been born who can kill him. Says he wants to go back to med school when the war is over; so y'all get ready . . . I appreciate that, Dr. Thebault, but I'm not thinking that far ahead yet. I may not even want to study medicine if and when I get out. I sure haven't worked with any doctors yet who make me want to be one . . . Yessir, I still have the guarantee from the dean — or at least my daddy does. He got it in writing and gave it to my mother and told her to put it in the big red trunk . . . Well, I've got to run. A couple of buddies and I are going out on the town to eat spaghetti and lox and turnip greens; this Army is an education for everybody. Tell any of my old class you see that I said 'hello' and I'll look you up when I get back from overseas. Dr. Thebault, do one favor for me. Tell Dr. Twyman that I'm doing well and that I apologize for flunking his class . . . What? . . . Oh, yes, I see them both. Calhoun is going to OCS, but Otten says he hasn't got time for that foolishness . . . Sir? . . . I know what you mean, but Otten would make a great major, and he would sure raise hell around the officers' club till he got promoted that far. I've got to run. Thanks for talking to me. Tell Dr. Athanopoulos that I still love her. And so does everybody. Bye."

On May 25, the Germans finally yielded the Italian coastline, all of it, and the Allies began their push toward Rome. All of America was joyous, prayerful now about the monstrous build-up in Britain. The island must be bursting at the seams, but Ike would pull it off. Speculations flew about the place and, with more tension, about the time of that assault. Calhoun, Osborne, and Otten finished their training at Lawson General Hospital, graduated, and received three-day passes. Porter bade his friends, the Italian with strabismus and the Jew with gentian eyes, the farewell he was learning to accept as a necessary part of military life.

"You guys have a good war. I'll see you around."

"Yeah, you too."

"Pietrini, don't you mess with nobody's drawers. Wherever you go."

"You know I won't. Christ, I've just now got my pucker string back in tune."

"Bernie Friedman, you be careful. Maybe I'll see you in Jerusalem after the war. I've learned a lot from you."

"Keep your nose clean and your powder dry, Osborne. I've learned a lot from you, too. Better luck with the Second Coming than you had with the first."

"Kiss my ass. At least my sister hasn't married an Episcopalian."

"So long."

"So long."

"So long."

Don't get too close and don't care too much, for tomorrow it is over. He wondered where Lamar Betsill was and how he might be faring.

After his pass, aware now that he was being sent away with a conscious smile by his womenfolk, unsure of his genuine response to this, he shouldered his duffel bag and boarded the train once again on a military ticket. No Pullman this time, he noted, and a limit on ration expenses in the dining car. His coach seemed tawdry compared to the memory of his first train ride. He shrugged. "*C'est la guerre*," he murmured and surveyed the aisle. Carter Otten was the only soul on the train that he knew; he swung his duffel overhead and seated himself.

"Hello, Osborne," Carter snapped.

"Good morning, Otten. What's wrong with you? You get up on the wrong side of the bed or have you got a dingleberry?"

"Sit down and shut up. Why in the hell is the fucking Army sending us all the way back to Chio and Camp Grant to sit around with our fingers up our butts when they know and we know that we're going overseas? Why couldn't they ship us out from Lawson and save all this time and money?"

"For God's sake, Otten, we're being put into a medical pool to await assignment and deployment. You heard the sergeant briefing us before we went on pass. Ain't you learned no Army words yet?"

"Shut up, Osborne."

"We're just privates. We're not supposed to think. We're just supposed to do as we're told. Hurry up and wait. Dig those foxholes. Fill 'em up. Take a ten-minute break. Smoke if you got 'em. If you ain't got 'em, bum one from your buddy. This is the Army, Mr. Jones; no private rooms or telephones."

"If you don't shut up, Osborne, I'm going to throw your ass down the aisle like a bowling ball."

The train began creaking, moving ever so slowly out of Atlanta. Porter wagged his head sagaciously. "All the signs and symptoms; it must be a dingleberry."

"Jesus Christ! Will you shut up?"

"Talking like a Yankee is part of the symptoms, too. Diagnosis confirmed. Dingleberry, stage IV. Probably inoperable. Nurse! I'll prep and drape the patient for surgery. Would you see if there's a doctor in the officers' club who's still able to stand? Any officer will do. The patient is only a PFC."

Otten grudgingly laughed. "Osborne, somebody some day is going to whip the living shit out of you about your wise mouth."

"I've told you before; they already have. It didn't help a bit. You'll have to devise some other treatment modality."

The train picked up enough speed for the car to sway and its wheels to begin rhythmic clacking. Otten looked out the window with his forehead resting against the glass. Telegraph poles whipped by, their interspaces shortened; the near landscape became blurred. Atlanta fell behind them. Atlanta was in the past.

Porter mused for awhile. "Last time we made this trip, Calhoun was with us."

Otten kept his head resolutely against the glass, made no response.

"And now, what do you know? He's headed off to OCS and then he's going to marry Miss Margaret when he graduates. His life is over as far as we're concerned. He was a good old guy; I'm going to miss him. Conversations now will be so sane. I won't have anybody to holler 'What? What?', or call me Vitamin Flintheart, or slam me around till I'm black and blue."

Carter Otten jerked his head around, his overseas cap askew. Unmistakably he stuck the tip of his tongue out first one corner of his mouth and then the other and intercepted a tear as it trickled down the groove beside his nose. He gave a sniff. His eyes were brimming full, but they were also shining with fury.

"Osborne, don't sit here and prattle like a child about something you couldn't possibly understand."

Porter was so astonished that he inanely blurted, "Otten, you're crying! Whatever for?"

"I am not crying, you nosey little son of a bitch. And if I were it's none of your goddam business."

"Well, excuse me. You're always telling me I'm from the country and ignorant, so I'm sure you can overlook the fact that I mistook all that salt water and snot and red nose for weeping. Your shirt collar's wet."

In response to that pragmatic aside, Otten automatically procured his handkerchief and dabbed at his shirt. Then he blew his nose. The tension was broken and Porter dared to relax. "I'm sorry, Carter, for whatever I said that upset you."

"You didn't say anything. You have nothing to do with this. You wouldn't understand."

Porter could not help himself. "Carter Otten, you are above average intelligence and so am I. I have read *Hamlet*, *The Brothers Karamazo*, and all of Aesop's *Fables*. If you are capable of explaining something, I can sure as hell understand it. Don't hand me that bullshit."

The train went into a curve and each of them swayed with it. Otten took such a deep breath through his nose that it whistled. "Osborne, I was just thinking. Except for maybe a month or two in the summertime, Griffin and I have never really been separated since we started school in the first grade. We graduated together from grammar school. We learned to drive together on a beat up Chevrolet that his old man had junked. Double-dated together, finished high school, went to Emory at Oxford together, graduated from there together, went on to Big Emory, roomed together and graduated from there, went to med school," he cut an eye at Porter, "got kicked out of there together and then graduated from basic training and Lawson together. We've gone into and out of more things together than anybody else I know of, and for a minute there it got to me. It's nothing."

Porter made no response but looked steadily at Otten's profile. The silence grew.

"Well, say something, goddammit. One minute you're chattering like a chipmunk and the next you're sitting there as solemn and quiet as a fucking owl."

"Maybe that's why they say 'Who'," tossed in Porter compulsively. "You've been telling me to shut up ever since I met you, and now you're telling me to talk. Maybe I'm like the guy you yourself told me about who didn't know whether to shit or go blind, and so he spent all his time blinking his eyes and farting."

Otten settled into his seat. "Osborne, you could make a dog laugh. That may be the only asset you have; so hang onto it. I'm sorry I let down like that, it's just that all of a sudden I realized how much I was going to miss old Griffin."

"I know. I was thinking the other day how over and over in this war you have to say good-bye to buddies and know you'll most probably never see them again."

"See? I told you you wouldn't understand. Griffin Calhoun is not my buddy. He's my friend. I've had lots of buddies. I'll have lots more. Griffin is the only friend I've ever had." His black brows contracted into a scowl. "Or will ever have."

"Oh," said Porter. Then he added, "You're right, Otten. I don't understand."

Otten was so long responding that Porter thought he had let the matter drop. "You're right about one thing, Osborne, much as it chaps my ass to admit it. He is headed off to OCS and he is going to marry Miss Margaret and his life is over as far as we're concerned. A friend is never the same after he's married." He took a breath. "And you're right about something else. He is a good old guy and we are going to miss him. Let me out. I've got to go to the can."

Porter listened to the train wheels, heard the whistle blow for a crossing, its sound streaming back over him, and in the midst of rushing activity was lonely. He thought of all the people he knew outside of his kin that were special to him. Were they friends? Were they buddies? He decided it didn't matter because it would be a miracle if he and Otten wound up as either. He shrugged, said, "*C'est la guerre,*" again, and felt mature.

In Chicago, making their way from the railway station to the bus terminal, they learned that the Germans had withdrawn from Rome and abandoned the city to Allied occupation. They had done so without harming any of its treasured structures or the Vatican itself. Every church bell in Chicago was ringing, an overture of joy above which the scream of taxis and the rattling roar of the El gave reassurance that it was a work day and that Illinois would conduct business as usual. Porter traversed the streets with pride that he was in uniform but with shame that he was still in the USA. It was June 4th; he had been in the Army for more than a year.

He had assumed that his return to Camp Grant would involve the same type of barracks living to which he had grown accustomed. Instead he found himself ensconced in a square squad tent, one unit in a welter of perfectly aligned rows and blocks of such tents, the distance between them precisely measured. There was duckboard for flooring and also for sidewalks outside. Each of them had an identifying number and held six folding canvas cots. The side flaps were rolled up and tied, providing ventilation at the expense of privacy. The latrines and showers were in buildings at regimented intervals through that city of tents, and there was a central mess hall that seemed a half mile away.

"Where's the PX?" Porter inquired. "Where's the library?"

"Oh, shit," said Otten and carried his duffel bag down the row and around the corner to a tent as far removed from Porter as he could arrange. Porter's relief was tainted with annoyance. "Beat me to it," he thought.

The corporal in charge spoke in a loud, impersonal monotone. "Map on the bulletin board. Check the board daily 0900 hours and 1500 hours for assignments. Tents must be ready for inspection every morning, cots made up and squared. Listen for your names on the bullhorn. Be ready at all times for departure within one hour of notice. Don't send out no dry cleaning. Next chow in two hours. Dismissed."

The atmosphere in his tent was torpid. Interchange between its six occupants was not quite as personal as that between strangers on a bus, each aware that the others might dismount at the next stop, insulated against intrusion behind newspapers or the fixed unseeing gaze of studied indifference.

"My name's Osborne," he announced. One soldier twitched a brief glance from polishing his belt buckle. "Porter Osborne," he persisted. "My name is Porter Osborne."

A burly private with a long jaw, shortened forehead, and the clipped flatness of New England responded. "We can't help it," he said.

No one else gave any indication that sound waves had invaded that tent, and Porter thought again of the dictum proclaiming if a tree fell in the wilderness far enough from any tympanic membrane it would fall silently. He also thought of Ulysses stumbling among the Lotophagi, of a Chinese opium den. These were American soldiers. He looked with bewilderment at the private, whose tone had been detached but not sarcastic, and noted that the closely shaven jaw and lip were puffed like a pillow by vibrant black whiskers straining to escape.

"You Yankee son of a bitch," he thought, but kept his counsel.

"Take that cot over there, since it's the only one left," the soldier relented.

"Thanks," said Porter, and felt that he should tiptoe.

The amplified roar of the bullhorn intruded. "Pendergraft! Ronald J. Pendergraft! Report to the company office."

The soldier polishing the belt buckle packed away his blitz cloth, ran his belt through the trouser loops, checked his shirt collar in a mirror hanging on the center pole of the tent beneath the one naked light bulb, and departed. If anyone else noticed the activity, he gave no sign of it, but Porter stepped through the tent flap and watched him stride down the duck walk past the bulletin board. He had forgot how flat the land of Illinois was. He felt lonely but not homesick. This was a transient, insignificant pause in his progress. He would be assigned to a unit and shipped out within a day or two. There was no need to develop even a cursory relationship with anyone here.

He found his way to the PX, where groups of soldiers chatted excitedly about the accession of Rome and speculated over the invasion of Europe, referring occasionally to the painful successes of island-hopping in the Pacific, but when he returned to his tent no one spoke. Camaraderie stopped at the tent flap.

When he entered the tent after breakfast on June fifth, Ronald J. Pendergraft's cot had been stripped, the blanket folded beneath the naked pillow. When he returned from obediently checking the bulletin board at 0900 hours, he sat on his cot and looked intently between his feet at the duckboard, noting that the black soil visible through the cracks had a drying glaze of grayness to it. A shadow fell across his vision, and a voice proclaimed, "Hello, fellows. My name is Campbell. Will Campbell."

Porter detected the twang of Tennessee in the newcomer's voice, answered, "Take the empty cot over there," but studied the graying earth as though it were on the stage of a microscope and refrained from looking up. Eye contact would be too personal.

By 0400 hours two more of the tent mates had responded to individual summons on the bullhorn, shouldered their duffel bags, and departed for assignments. Porter could not help wondering where each was going, could not resist an effort at farewell, no matter how fleeting and shallow their association had been, regardless of the apathy that was so *de rigeur* in this chamber of waiting.

"So long," he said to the first one, and "Good luck," to the other some thirty minutes later. Each responded with a widening of the eyes and a temporary hesitation in pace, but neither looked directly at him. "Yeah," answered the first one; the second one only shrugged.

Porter rose and stretched, angled his overseas cap defiantly on his head, and proclaimed, "What a war! This tent has a turnover rate that makes Butch Wingo look like an amateur; I should be out of here tomorrow. Hold my calls! I'll be in conference with the camp comman-dant and his staff at the PX for the next hour. If Secretary Stinson rings, tell him I'll get back to him tomorrow. If it's Eleanor Roosevelt, tell her I'm downtown drunk."

He strode down the duck walk with the affectation of purpose in his bearing and said, "I wonder if I'll get sent to the Pacific or the ETO; I can't take much of this waiting."

On June 6, the music of Reveille floated in the new air of morning while the early-rising Porter Osborne, Jr., was in the latrine. It was immediately replaced by the strident amplification of the bullhorn.

"Attention!" bellowed an anonymous noncom. "Attention, all troops!"

Porter was brushing his teeth and paused so he would not miss his name. "They're real eager beavers about their assignments this morning," he thought.

"May I have your attention? This is it! I am authorized to announce that the Allied Forces under General Dwight D. Eisenhower have begun the assault on the coast of Normandy! The invasion to free Europe is on! This is D-Day!"

Porter froze while bent over the sink, stared for a moment into his own startled eyes reflected from the stainless steel mirror, and then bolted outdoors, his mouth spewing with Ipana like foam on a hydrophobic dog. The squad tents seemed to be dancing, soldiers in various stages of array pouring from them like ants departing a violated hill, frenzied, hurried, tumbling over each other. The early sun shone aslant on bare gilded arms and rosy faces, the air filled with screaming.

"Where?" "How?" "How many?" "Where?" "Paratroopers?" "Any Marines?" "Where?" "Beachhead?" "Germans?" "Where?" "Casualties?" "Goddam Germans!" "To hell with Hitler!" "Goddammit, where?"

This unit of soldiers, medics all, trained to support, to rescue, to sustain, to restore, totally innocent of any training whatsoever with firearms, jumped and yelled like Indian braves transforming themselves into warriors. They pounded each other on the back, punched the air with their fists. The apathy of waiting, the lethargy of the tents, evaporated. They were primed for invasion; at that moment they would have charged Kraut machineguns in their underwear, have overrun them with nothing more than tooth and nail, then have roared in fullthroated blood lust. Porter watched with mouth agape. In the hysterical unreality of this jubilation, around a bulletin board in a tent city in

Illinois, for the first time he plumbed the reality of war. His heart felt tight. And cold.

Carter Otten swung him around by an elbow. His face was somber, his eyes small. His hair stirred in scrambled disarray. "Get your shirt on and let's go to chow before this mob decides to go."

Porter nodded, glad to see Otten.

"And wipe your fucking mouth."

"Good idea. And you comb your fucking hair."

After stacks of pancakes and rashers of uneven bacon, they tarried in the mess hall, elbows sprawled, slouched over steaming canteen cups. Coffee for Otten, hot chocolate for Osborne.

"God, Osborne, this is exciting. I can't believe we're finally going in."

"I know. Do you feel relieved but also a little guilty that you're not over there this morning?"

"Hell, no. We're over-trained for that sort of thing. They'll ship us out to a battalion aid station at the very least or more probably to a general hospital. Hell, no, I don't feel guilty. Don't start analyzing everything this morning and looking under the surface of everything. Give your fucking soul a rest and accept things as they are. When you grow up, you'll start liking coffee and quit swilling that damn hot chocolate like a blinking Boy Scout on his first campout."

"If you're so big on accepting things as they are, why do you have trouble with me liking hot chocolate?"

"Osborne, do you realize that we can't be together for more than five minutes without arguing? I'm fixing to say that this is the sorriest, greasiest goddam bacon I've ever seen; it's burned on one end and damn near raw on the other; I'm going to say that the Army cooks can fuck up even a dead pig. And I'll bet you have some smart-ass comeback for that."

"Well," replied Porter judiciously, "there's plenty of it. You could either bite off the crisp end or suck on the fat end and throw the rest away according to your individual preference, couldn't you? It's probably due to the way it was sliced before the cooks ever got hold of it. At least we're not getting flour with weevils in it or being issued shoes with pasteboard soles like the soldiers in the War between the States. And maybe the reason we argue all the time is that I won't let your opinionated bullshit pass as truth by giving it the assent of silence. Besides, I like hot chocolate. What's that got to do with the invasion of Normandy and the beachheads we're fighting for? I wonder why they named them

Utah and Omaha. Even after all that digression you so skillfully maneuvered, I still feel guilty. Let's go find a radio."

They checked the bulletin board, went to the PX, huddled around any radio they could find, their thirst for news insatiable. Paratroopers and gliders had landed inland at places previously undreamt and presently unpronounceable, were fighting to make contact with the Allied forces storming the beaches. Americans, British, Canadians, and Free French were swarming ashore in concerted assault of Virtue over Evil, bound together in the most dedicated thrust since the Holy Land had been wrested from the Saracens. Porter felt small and insignificant and very, very safe. He and Otten stayed together all day. For the most part they were congenial.

"You know, Osborne, you're not so bad in small doses, especially when you're not always trying to disagree with me or make some major issue out of everything I say. I think I'll see if I can't move my duffel into your tent until we get moved out of this dump. We might even get to be buddies."

Porter's mind abandoned Normandy for a moment. "Neither one of us is that desperate," he said. "Yet.

> 'Something there is that doesn't love a wall,
> That sends its boulders sprawling in the sun,
> Leaving gaps that even two can pass abreast,'

Naw. You stay where you are. We can check on each other every day but maybe the reason we've gotten along today is that we haven't been together before. You were right when you chose separate tents. Leave it that way."

"But my tent mates drive me crazy. They sit around and do nothing and say nothing and act like they're waiting for those carts to carry them off to the guillotine."

"Tumbrils," said Porter.

"Thanks. I tell you, living in that tent is like wading around in three thousand pounds of wet chicken feathers."

"I know," said Porter; then he affirmed, "'Good fences make good neighbors.'"

"There you go with that fucking poetry. You almost made it through a day without any. Don't you think I know Robert Frost? You don't have to preach to me."

"Well, do you know Kahlil Gibran? 'Let there be spaces in your togetherness; for the willow cannot grow in the shade of the oak.' You stay where you are and we can escape the chicken feathers in the daytime."

Before lights out, the firm announcement had come from Washington that the beachheads in France had been secured. Omaha, Utah, Sword, Juno, and Gold. Infantry troops had worked their way several miles inland and joined with the Airborne. Soldiers and supplies were being amassed on the Carentan Peninsula from the vastest armada ever assembled. "Let us pause and give thanks," American leaders proclaimed, "for the gallant men who have given their lives this day that others might someday soon be free."

Porter paused and dutifully gave thanks. He paused again and considered that he would almost certainly be assigned to some unit and shipped overseas immediately. He realized that he had not even thought of his box of Georgia soil since repacking his duffel to leave Lawson. In the event of peril, Anteus had best be armored; he would put a pinch of dirt into each shoe before he slept this night.

By feeling from the outside, he located the cigar box near the bottom of his bag, groped through layers to extract it, placed it on his cot and untied it. Some of his dirt had been removed, was replaced by a package and an envelope.

"What the hell?" he said, feeling violated. He opened the envelope. A silver chain fell out.

"Osborne. I put some of your Georgia in my shoes. It's been great knowing you. Here is St. Christopher. My mama gave it to me. She had our priest bless it. If you are away from home, he will keep you safe. She told me so. Don't ask me how. It's just our way.

Your buddy,
Pietrini

P.S. I think it will also protect you from Kikes."

Hastily Porter undid the roughly wrapped package beneath the envelope. The brass nozzle of a fire extinguisher rolled out. He read the accompanying note.

"Dear Osborne,

I should have found a Star of David for you so that Pietrini would be neutralized, but the enclosed, as we have found out previously, will take care of him nicely.

Thanks for giving me a true picture of the South. You have made me think, and one never forgets anybody who does that.

Until Jerusalem,
Bernie Friedman

P.S. I read Pietrini's note. You can regard my gift as a Wop Whopper, a Guinea Gouger, or just simply a Dago Douche. Don't forget us."

Porter laughed. Then he blew his nose. Slowly he slipped the chain over his head; the medal nestled easily between his dog tags. He put the nozzle in his right pants pocket. "I hope to hell it's not the one we used," he thought. Then he added, "Poor Otten has no idea what a buddy is."

Drifting off to sleep he recalled a line from Service.

> "Around his neck he wore
> The maid Utrulda's charm,
> The little silver crucifix
> That keeps a man from harm."

Suddenly he thought of his grandmother, her distrust of Catholics and Yankees. He removed the St. Christopher medal and pushed it under the pillow. Next morning, he put it in his left pants pocket and sought out Otten for breakfast. He was free of chicken feathers and he was ready. Porter Osborne, Jr., knew with certainty who he was. His country needed him and he was prepared to die for her if need be.

*"And he strides among the treetops and is
taller than the trees."*

27 **P**orter watched soldiers come and soldiers go, none
of them staying more than two or at most three days at a time; some of
them not needing to delve into their duffels for more than a diddy bag
for one morning's toilette, their stay not long enough to require a
change of clothes. They moved in and out like birds halting to roost,
migration suspended for darkness and brief rest, impersonal, unnotic-
ing, uncaring. Porter held himself perpetually in readiness, prepared
to join them in flight, brimming with purpose. The days passed him
by. Time moved on, he stood still.

D plus two. D plus ten. The stories of unbelievable heroism in
France dominated the news. Photographs and documentation of the
carnage on Omaha Beach filled Porter with horror, with wonder, until
he was numbed. Had he not been sent to Lawson for advanced training, he might have been a corpsman in that first wave, he might have
been cut in two by German fire or dragged down by heavy gear to
drown in the crimson seas that bathed that beach. He felt that he was
alive at the expense of others, that every breath he drew was a gift he
did not deserve from a fortune he did not comprehend.

"We'll never get out of these chicken feathers," he fumed to
Otten. "I feel like Patrick Henry: 'Our brethren are already in arms;
why stand we here idle? Is life so dear or peace so sweet as to be
purchased at the price of chains and slavery?' I can hear my children
and grandchildren now. 'Where were you on D-Day, Daddy? Granddaddy?' And what do I tell them? 'Oh, little children, I was in the
latrine at a dangerously imperiled military installation called Camp
Grant. I was bravely brushing my teeth after having accomplished a
truly formidable crap when I heard the news that we had landed at
Omaha Beach. I survived a withering burst of Nazi machinegun fire
aimed at me from three thousand miles away and sheltered myself

behind the bodies of ten thousand dead buddies until nightfall. Only thus did I live to sire you: so do not despair that the blood of a coward courses sluggishly but fortuitously in your veins.'"

Otten snorted, "For God's sake, Osborne, cut the shit! You keep on like that, I'm going to send for the chaplain and then a shrink and get your ass kicked out on a Section 8. I'm tired of listening to it! It's not our fault we haven't been assigned to a unit."

"Do you realize that yesterday the First Army reached some place called St. Lo and that it's already D plus forty-three? We're going to spend the rest of the war right here. I can feel it in my bones. And I didn't like Illinois the first time I saw it."

"Damn it, Osborne, you're obsessed. It's not D plus forty-three; it's July 19. The USO is giving a dance tonight. Let's go see if we can get laid."

"It's D plus forty-three," said Osborne, "and I wish I knew Friedman's address so I could write him that a new calendar is begun and he can finally get away from Jesus. You go on to the dance if you like, but don't count on any favors except from Old Lady Thumb and her four daughters. I've got a book to read."

"You've always got a book to read, you little pissant. You're going to put your goddam eyes out and wind up the war blind as a bat."

"I'd rather lose my vision that way than by consorting with Mrs. Thumb's daughters," said Porter loftily. "Lots of luck."

Otten was right; Porter Osborne did indeed constantly have a book to read. He felt no contrition about it, however; it was his salvation, his escape. Only thus could he lull himself into temporary forgetfulness of the war and his entrapment in the backwaters of bureaucracy. He lay on his cot and read all day and then returned to his cot and read until lights out. He had memorized the hours of the Post Library and also how many steps it took him to walk there; that was his exercise.

Porter read and read and read. D plus fifty.

Ten days later, Otten accosted him. "Osborne, while you've been lying on that cot with your nose in a book and your finger up your ass, I've gotten myself assigned to a unit and we'll be heading out for Europe in another week. Looks like I may get there before the war's over, after all."

"What? How'd you manage that?"

"I kept prowling around and asking questions, and I found out about a brand-new general hospital that's being formed. A guy I met at the PX had been assigned to it, and he's only been in this hell-hole of a staging area for two weeks. I went charging into headquarters to find out why I'd been passed over, and guess what? They'd mislaid our fucking papers! They didn't have me and you on any roster for any assignment."

"What?"

"So help me, God! We could have stayed here till we got soft peters and died of old age."

"Damn! That really gets my goat."

"I went across camp and found the office for that new hospital. Took me half an afternoon. Talked to a sergeant, then the first sergeant, then a lieutenant in the MAC, then finally in to the CO himself. He's a lieutenant colonel and this is his first command. He's from Texas and is real gung-ho about organizing a first-rate hospital. He's a fine man. I volunteered on the spot and he jumped at the chance to get an advanced surgical tech who has a background in medical school and is also a Southern gentleman."

"What?" repeated Porter.

"Those were his words, not mine."

"I suppose you told him you got kicked out of med school instead of flunking out?"

"Let's not whip that damn horse again, Osborne. I told him I'd temporarily interrupted my formal education in favor of active military duty and that I'd be honored to serve in his unit. The whole point is that I told him about you, and if you hurry I think he'll take you, too. He's still got a couple of vacancies in his Operating Room."

Porter jumped off his cot. "Let's go, Otten! Come show me where this is and introduce me to that colonel. Which hospital is it?"

"It's the 816th and so far it's only on paper. I've already told Col. Draughan I'd send you by this afternoon; he's expecting you."

"Thanks, Otten. You're a buddy, after all."

"Osborne."

"What?"

"Don't you tell him we flunked out."

"I promise I won't."

"Osborne."

"What?"

"Paris has been surrendered by the Krauts. I heard it an hour ago."

"Oh, boy! 'What were you doing on D plus eighty, Daddy?' 'Hell, son, I had taken root in Camp Grant, Illinois, where I was heroically and with considerable disdain for my own welfare attending the mangled troops who had just liberated Paris. The authorities interrupted me in conference with a colonel to seek my expert help.' *Heil Hitler*, Otten. *Seig heil!*"

"We're going to have to hurry if we get there before it's over."

"I'll not be the one to slow us down. I'm on my way."

Col. Otto Draughan was not quite so tall as Porter Osborne, Jr., but he was twice as wide and three times as thick. His face was almost a cube and, with the unlit cigar he affected in jaunty slant, was reminiscent of a bite of cheese impaled on a toothpick. His uniform was so meticulously tailored that Porter remembered Sgt. Bass and was tempted to turn and flee. Instead, he snapped and held a salute and in properly crisp tones announced, "PFC Porter Osborne requests permission to speak to the colonel."

The colonel beamed, and leaving the cigar in his mouth substituted a cursory upward flick of his right forefinger for an answer to Porter's salute.

"At ease," he barked. "I already know about you. Your buddy was here an hour ago and said he was going to send you. You're from Georgia, too, aren't you? Fine state, fine state. Lots of Georgians settled in Texas in '65 and '66. Good sense, good sense. Wish I could staff all my unit with Texans and Georgians. Fine unit, fine unit. We'll have the best general hospital in Europe. You're ready for a little overseas action, I hear. Is that right? What's your background?"

Porter had momentary recall of Calhoun's speech patterns but realized it was too late to flee. "Medical basic training, Camp Grant; medical surgical and advanced surgical training, Lawson General Hospital, sir."

The colonel's countenance was as steadily beaming, Porter thought, as a flashlight with new batteries. "No, no, no. Before that. Where you grew up. Went to school. How much school. Things like that."

"Oh," said Porter. "Georgia cotton farm. Brewtonton High School. A. B. Willingham University. One year Emory University School of Medicine. United States Army Medical Corps." He could not resist adding in staccato emulation. "Fine medical corps, sir, fine medical corps."

"Medical school, eh? Why'd you leave medical school at the end of one year? Army needs doctors."

308

Porter glanced at the colonel's chest jutting in apparent permanence and as prominently as a pouter pigeon's. He remembered his promise to Otten; after all, Col. Draughan was Otten's discovery. He met the officer's gaze and addressed the cigar like a microphone.

"I temporarily interrupted my formal medical education in favor of active military duty, sir," he barked back.

"Good man, Osborne, good man. I tell you what, I've got space for one more surgical tech in my Operating Room, and I'm going to take you aboard."

"Thank you, sir. I'll try not to let you down."

"No worry about that. No worry at all. Always glad to get a Southern gentleman who is a volunteer." He grabbed his cigar and pointed with it. "See my first sergeant in the tent next door and he'll take care of the paper work; assign you to quarters. See you in Berlin." He slammed the cigar back in its socket; the chest never wavered.

"Yes, sir. Thank you, sir." Porter executed a perfect about-face and marched next door.

"I believe to my soul Col. Otto Draughan wears a corset," he thought. "He beams and barks and puffs and struts and is as full of shit as a Christmas turkey, but at least you're on your way, Porter Osborne."

Later, leaving his interview with Sgt. Milton Lagerpiel, who was also, it evolved, from Texas, Porter paused behind the tent flap as two officers passed. The Humpty-Dumpty silhouette was unmistakable; the cigar was proof positive.

"You know, Smith, I have just about filled my Operating Room with med school flunk-outs and fuckups. Ought to give that Anesthesiologist from Chicago who went to Harvard a fit. Ought to give him a running fit. Army pushed him on me and I had to make him Chief of the OR, but I believe between Georgia and Texas we'll be able to control his sophisticated, snobbish, Jewish ass."

Porter stood immobile for a long moment. That night he wrote his parents a long letter and added a P.S. "This is really getting to be an interesting war."

"Don John of Austria is riding to the sea."

28 **T**he 816th General Hospital was born on paper at Camp Grant, Illinois, in the summer of '44, its members gathered in from whatever human chaff and grain were available. With the exception of Otten and Osborne, no two people in the hospital had worked together before, nor even known each other prior to this assignment.

Porter dedicated himself to learning the organization of the operating room and the names of people on its roster; after all, he was now a member of a permanent unit in the United States Army, devoted to saving the lives and limbs of noble American soldiers wounded and mutilated in the defense of democracy and their homes. This hospital was poised for departure to the war zone, would soon be involved in human succor under the thunder of enemy guns. Apathy evaporated. Porter was afire with enthusiasm. He would do whatever was in his power to make the operating room of the 816th the best surgical facility in the European Theater of Operations.

Col. Draughan's ambition was for the 816th to be such a model of organization and administration that it would shine forth like a full moon, and eventually the upper echelons in the Army would recognize that it reflected light emanating from the sun that was Otto Draughan himself. He had no military training prior to Pearl Harbor, felt inferior to graduates of the Point, and had attained his present position by two capricious turns of fate.

First, bored by the practice of medicine and frustrated by marital ennui in a rather shabby Texas town, he had stepped boldly forward and volunteered for military service, abandoning his practice for the duration of the war to midwives and one doddering homeopath. His acceptance in the Army medical corps had been based on his length of civilian practice, heedless of the quality of that practice, and he was offered the rank of major, an example of bureaucratic myopia unnoted in the flurry of an army preparing for war. It was then in mimicry of MacArthur and Churchill that he had adopted the cigar. His swagger was individualistic and no affectation. It was part and parcel of being born a short man in Texas.

Second, by a rectifying caprice, he came under the direct surveillance of a full colonel who happened to love Medicine better than life itself. That good man looked at the new medical officer assigned him and appraised him as a possible Surgeon, Internist, Gynecologist, even Dermatologist. He then directed him into Administration. He did this with dedication to the medical profession. He utilized the authority his position afforded by growling to his personnel officer, "I don't believe that over-stuffed, sawed-off son of a bitch can do anything but grin and strut. I wouldn't let him doctor a dog in civilian life, but they've made him a major and we have to do something with him. Put his laced-up, puffed-out ass in Administration, and we'll at least keep him away from sick soldiers."

Otto Draughan had found his niche. He willingly abandoned any pretense to medical expertise and became instead an expert on Army rules and regulations. Within three months he was put in charge of indoctrinating newly recruited physicians into all aspects of military protocol, from proper dress to how to conduct themselves in the presence of enlisted men. He was entrusted with turning groups of shambling, shuffling doctors into smartly stepping, briskly saluting officers and thereby gentlemen. Within six months he had personally organized and outfitted three new officers' clubs on as many bases and been grudgingly promoted to lieutenant colonel. It was then that he had added the bark to the swagger, the cigar and the beam. It was then that he had been given command of his own general hospital by orders from a new CO who spoke to the same competent personnel officer: "Get him the hell out of my sight. Get him the hell out of this country."

Thus did the paths of Lt. Col. Otto Draughan and PFC Porter Osborne, Jr., converge, both of them dedicated to the success of the 816th General Hospital, the one as a means of personal fulfillment through the Holy Grail of overseas service, the other as the next logical step toward gaining eagles for his shoulders, perhaps even the lone star of a Brigadier before this war was over. Porter thought the vagaries of Fate unpredictable; she had certainly smiled on him thus far. He amended his original impression of Col. Draughan to regard him as an able leader and would have followed him to hell, provided Europe lay along the fiery path. Otto Draughan did not think of Porter Osborne at all; he had not at that point discovered that Fate can snicker as well as smile.

Within a week the hospital had been transported by rail to Camp Kilmer, New Jersey, giant port of embarkation where troops were spewed into boats like wheat straw from a thrashing machine and shipped eastward across the Atlantic. Here the 816th, amid the scramble and chaos of the Kilmer staging area, was organized into its component units; faces and names were assigned to people by matching them with typed lists. Otten and Osborne were indeed delegated to the Operating Room, met in a squad tent with their supervising NCO, Sgt. Oliver Crowder, and were introduced to other strangers who would henceforth be their working comrades.

"Wait until we git over there and git ourselves set up and then I'll assign everbody to they duties. This is jest a git-acquainted session, not what you'd call a proper orientation meeting."

"Sergeant, where are we going?"

"That there's classified information."

"Do you know?"

"Not at the present time, not exactly, but if I did know exactly it would still be classified. You got no need to worry about that."

"When do we ship out?"

"When the colonel tells us to; you got no need to worry about that neither. I'll let you know when the time comes. Just do as you're told."

Otten nudged Osborne. "Oh, shit," he muttered.

"That there's potty talk," Porter replied. "How far do you think our new sergeant got in school? And where do you think he's from? I hope it's not Georgia; I'd hate to take credit for that accent, let alone that level of literacy."

Kilmer was a scramble, a babble, an exciting confusion. Porter, in his bewilderment, hoped fervently that someone in authority knew what was going on and where they were going. He recalled Sgt. Bass and blindly did what he was told. He caught an occasional glimpse of Col. Draughan, dressed in perfectly tailored pinks and Eisenhower jacket, moving with apparent purpose, barking orders aggressively to a train of officers and noncoms, and felt reassured. They would ship out when Col. Otto Draughan told them to; in the meantime, they would hurry up and wait. Again. As for sergeants, he felt that they could be called Fisk, Bass, or Crowder; be Yankee, Jewish, or Cracker; appear rough, dandified, or ignorant; there was a sameness to them, and he could maneuver around them wherever he was sent. He had become a soldier.

The excitement of their time at Camp Kilmer hinged directly on its designation as a POE; it was here they departed the familiar and faced the unknown. The Atlantic Ocean was imperiled by German submarines prowling its depths with periscopes and torpedoes, such a scourge that Allied troop ships crossed the ocean in zig-zag patterns calculated to confuse the wolf pack. Perishing at sea was not something Porter had previously considered, and the idea made his neck prickle. Now that the die had been cast, he was impatient to cross his individual Rubicon and chafed at the postponements they encountered; but when he visualized a sinking ship, contemplated his ineptness as a swimmer, he ambivalently welcomed the reprieve. They had compulsory assemblies for boat drill where they were lectured on techniques for survival. Otten knew about six verses of "The Great Ship Titanic" and, with sardonic perversity, insisted on singing them. Porter stood in almost endless lines for use of a telephone and called his father four times within a week to bid a soldier's farewell.

"You haven't left yet?"

"No, sir. Any day now, they tell us. As a matter of fact, it was supposed to have been day before yesterday."

"Well, I appreciate your calling. Anything new with you?"

"No sir. The folks still all right?"

"Yep, nothing new here."

"Well, I guess I'll let you go. I just wanted to touch base. Give everybody my love again."

"I'll do it. We have your APO number and your mother has already written you three letters. They'll catch up with you somewhere. Take care of yourself."

"Yes, sir. You, too. Bye, Dad."

"Sambo?"

"Yes, sir?"

"If you still haven't shipped out by this time next week, call me again."

"Yes, sir. I will. Bye."

"Good-bye. Keep a level head and your feet on the ground."

"Yes, sir, I will. I don't know about my head but I have the right ground under my feet; I gave my shoes another dose last night."

"Atta boy. Good-bye, Son."

"Good-bye, Dad."

As the days wore on and the fever of expectancy, of urgency, subsided into the norm of boredom, Col. Draughan decreed that his troops who wished one be granted a six-hour pass into New York City. Buses were arranged. The men were cautioned again that a slip of the lip may sink a ship, a futile exercise in Porter's mind, since he had not the faintest idea where, when, or how they were going. He had begun to doubt that they would ever move before the war was over. Corporals and sergeants were assigned different groups for the visit to the city. Their destination was the USO and only the USO, they were informed. Porter was reminded of grammar school but welcomed the outing with much the same spirit as a third grader on Memorial Day going to place flowers on the graves of Confederate veterans. Any change from routine was exhilarating, regardless of whether he was being herded by a spinster teacher or a bored sergeant.

"Pull your goddam head back in the bus, Osborne, and quit rubbernecking straight up like a fucking hayseed."

"Shut up, Carter. That's the Empire State Building, and I'll rubberneck all I please. We may never see it again, and after all, it's the tallest building in the world and this is the biggest city in the world, and anybody who doesn't live here is considered a hayseed by the inhabitants anyhow. It makes you dizzy to look up at those buildings."

"You were born dizzy and been having relapses ever since."

"But Carter, this is exciting. Look at the crowds on the sidewalk, everybody hurrying. Nobody knows anybody else. Every nationality in the world in their faces. Even the air seems electric. This is New York!"

"The air isn't electric to me; all I get out of it is gasoline fumes. You're forever reading more into something than is there. We're not doing anything but going on another trip to another goddam USO where they'll have free doughnuts and cigarettes and nothing but nice girls and we won't stand a snowball's chance in hell of getting drunk or laid. Calm down."

"OK. OK."

"And keep your goddam head inside the bus."

An hour later Porter thought that Carter Otten might be mistaken, that unless he was completely misjudging events, he was, himself, caught up in what must be at least the initial steps of getting laid, and that right on the dance floor of the USO in the vertical position. He had been pressed against the stage on the periphery of the closely packed mass of GI's twisting and roiling upon itself like whipped cream growing turgid between the rotors of an eggbeater. The blueness of cigarette haze was a scant two feet above their heads and moved even more heavily than the people who produced it. He was sipping his second Coca-Cola and watching Carter Otten as he charmed his third dance partner. Porter was one of the minority that heard the announcer on the edge of the stage.

"And now I give you the little lady who has come all the way from Russia itself to entertain us with her twin guitars! The queen of the nightclub circuit, fresh from a triumphant performance as a classical guitarist on Broadway! Let's give a big hand to Miss Maria Nirova!"

Porter had turned amidst the smattering of applause, placed his cup of Coca-Cola on the low stage and politely clapped. That was when he met the gaze of the performer. She was every inch, he thought, a glamorous mistress of the stage, resplendent in form-fitting silver sequins and heavy make-up. Her wide Slavic mouth was a slash of red. Her eyes nestled in exotic slant between her pointed cheek bones and were so framed by mascara that they glittered green as phosphorescent surf on a midnight sea. She did indeed bear two guitars and perched herself atop a small stepladder with one knee upthrust provocatively through the thigh-length slit of her twinkling skirt. She carefully propped one guitar on the floor and cradled the other to her breast, never releasing Porter's eyes from her luminous stare. She spoke into the din of the USO, but Porter could have been the only person present. He was mesmerized. Never had he even dreamt of such a creature.

"I haff for you not one but two gifts tonight. I haff my guitars. I bring them for you. They are twins. This one is name Ivan. This one is name Petro. They have different voices. I play for you first on Petro. Then after, I put him down and play for you on Ivan. You will luff them also. They sing to you from Russia."

Few soldiers heard her and from those who did only cursory interest emanated. Porter felt socially obligated; he was impaled on her gaze and knew uncomfortably that it would be rude if he shifted his eyes first. She went through a repertoire on Petro and then on Ivan, moving her body so that the sequined dress reflected light like scales on a sensuous snake, but never unlocking her glittering eyes from Porter's. He felt that she was plumbing his soul and thrilled to the coincidence of this foreign goddess singling him out. This had to be high romance; of a sudden all his dreams, his poetic fantasies, had come together in a crowded New York dance hall where two unconventional individuals had happened to meet and recognize each other as special, set apart from the rest of humanity. He was enthralled.

He hoped fervently, however, that she could not read his mind, for he was filled suddenly with memories of Lamar Betsill and reflected that in his unprofessional Georgia-boy opinion, Maria Nirova did not pick nearly so well as his buddy from basic training, although she did have the good taste not to sing. He acknowledged that he had not yet learned opera or classical music and that his opinion might therefore be inferior, but he did hope that Lamar was safe wherever he was, that no one was making the mistake of yelling at him, and most of all that his mother had not yet received a telegram. He forced his thoughts back to Maria Nirova and sent his admiration for her through the hypnotic channel they had established.

When she concluded her performance, the group applause at best was perfunctory, but Porter clapped loudly and fast, stared into Maria's eyes, and for the first time in his life yelled, "Bravo!" He felt sophisticated. She moved slowly toward him, extended both be-ringed hands, and he lifted her down to his level.

"You are young. You are sensetiff. You are passhnut. You have a soul not like other men. You are buteful. So much I learn already from your eyes in fife minutes. Also you are lonely, far from home. Like me. Now we dance."

Amidst the mob on the dance floor, they were an isolated unit, oblivious to anything but themselves, breathing information into each other's ears.

"Ah. Porter Osborne. What a luffly name. And from Georgia. Somehow I know at vonce that you would be from the South. A luffly name for a luffly man from a luffly country. I cannot tell you how much already I luff America."

Porter answered every question she asked and responded with some of his own.

Maria Nirova was an artiste; she was in the United States as a performer, having had a most successful year in London; her soul was in her music; her heart, which she professed to be still as tender and vulnerable as a child's, had until tonight belonged to Russia, but she was prepared now to entrust it to Porter Osborne. He would, she knew, be kind, be gentle. Porter realized that he was beset with a fulminating erection and politely danced with hyperextended pelvis. Maria, she said, was older than Porter and at age twenty-six had already been married twice. These were the only two men she had ever known, if Porter knew what she meant, for despite all the invitations she had received from ardent suitors, she was a good girl. Her tender young heart had been bruised, devastated, by her marriages. The first one was to a Russian and had lasted less than three months, for he was a brute, a nothing; she had already forgotten him. The second had been to an Englishman and she had endured it for a year, awaiting the answering spark from him to the embers of passion that had glowed in her own soul. When this was not forthcoming, she had reluctantly divorced him, for it was obvious that he was, "how you say in America, a cold fish."

"I know, Porter Osborne, that you are not a cold fish. I can tell by your eyes. I read eyes well."

At that moment a violent bump in the buttocks from a couple attempting to jitterbug removed the concealment of his condition from Porter's control. Maria gave a gasp and then welded her body to him from knee to torso.

"Aha! I know it! Maria is always right about the eyes. You are no cold fish. Maria knows about luff." She wiggled her pelvis. Porter reflexively wiggled back.

"Ah, *Babouschka*. That is what we call the one we luff in Russia. You are my *babouschka*. Can you say it? Aha, already I teach you Russian language, yes? I teach you much more. I promise."

"*Babouschka*," repeated Porter and gripped her tightly.

"*Ya lubla tenia*," said Maria.

"*Ya lubla tenia*," Porter prattled mindlessly.

"Iss good. Mean 'I luff you.' Let us go where we can talk. You want to be married?"

"Sure," said Porter, "Someday. If I live through this war, I want to get married."

"Hush, *Babouschka*. Do not mention dying or Maria will weep. I cannot stand the idea of losing you now that I have found you. Remember, my heart is tender; you will make my mascara fade over my face, and Maria could not stand for you to see her like that. In Russia the women send their soldiers to war with a smile. The gallant noble Russian women hide their suffering soul behind a smile. You like to marry with me, yes?"

Of a sudden, Porter's nether regions no longer afflicted him. His brain whirled in a wash of memories. Katie Albert talking to his mother. His father's story about the black parishioner who assured the preacher that indeed she did want to go to heaven but not if he was getting up a busload tonight. Strongest, however, was the recall of dancing with Dr. Angelica Athanopoulos and, retrospectively, how kind and considerate that lady had been.

"Gosh, Maria, what red-blooded American boy wouldn't like to marry you? It's out of the question for me now; I'm shipping out most any day."

"Here iss my address. Giff me your name and number and I will write to you. You will not be lonely when you get my letters. And Maria will wait for you. Ivan and Petro will sing of Russia to the soldiers still, but Maria does not look again into anyone's eyes until they are yours."

"Well, sure, Maria, let's write to each other and who knows, after the war something may work out." He struggled to regain his feeling of sophistication. "*C'est la vie*, you know." Then he managed a shrug and mumbled, "*C'est la guerre*."

The loud shrill of a whistle split the air. A sergeant leaped on the little stage.

"All right! Attention! All members of the 816th General Hospital report to your buses. On the double! I say again, all members of the 816th General Hospital . . ."

Porter turned to Maria. "This is it, Maria. I'm off at last!"

"Ah, *Babouschka*! Hold me tight! For one last moment there are no two people on earth safe us."

She drew him into such a prolonged embrace, accompanied by such a convoluted kiss, that the issue of the cold fish was once again resolved. A hand grabbed Porter by the shoulder and jerked him around. Otten bellowed, "Up and at 'em, Osborne! Grab your socks! We're out of here!"

"I am smiling, *Babouschka*!" Maria called. "Remember me smiling from a heart full of pain! My luff will keep you warm! *Ya lubla tenia*! Foreffer!"

On the sidewalk, stumbling over each other to get on the bus, Otten snorted, "Jesus Christ, what's the matter with you! Dry fucking on the dance floor like a high school kid! Smooching that old broad who's old enough to be your mother! You look like your face is bleeding; wipe your fucking mouth."

"Quit talking like a Yankee," said Porter Osborne, Jr., "and I'll tell you about it on the bus."

Bumping back to Kilmer, Carter Otten laughed until the tears ran. "God, Osborne, I can't believe you! I'm glad nobody's selling the Brooklyn Bridge tonight or you'd be buying it to take home. Either she was a Russian spy or she wanted American citizenship or she wanted to hustle you into marriage so she could collect your GI insurance. Wake up and smell the coffee!"

"You have no soul, Otten," sniffed Porter. He gazed out the window and tried to remember all the lines of a poem he cherished.

"That lovely lady had hair as pale
As French champagne or finest ale . . .
Sometimes she'd scream like a cockatoo
And swear wonderful oaths that nobody knew . . .
Her low-cut gown showed a dove on its nest
In blue tattooing across her breast . . .
No one in all the countryside
Has forgotten those men and that beautiful bride."

"*Babouschka*," he murmured.

Otten snorted. "God, Osborne, you're so young and innocent you need a keeper."

"I am not innocent," retorted Porter. After a moment he said, "And I'm not as young as I used to be."

Their area of Kilmer was aswarm; no soldier so blasé he did not manifest excitement. They were actually moving; they were going to Europe. No one wanted to be the one to slow the process; no one wanted to be stranded in Camp Kilmer, New Jersey. Everyone assembled his gear, lugged it to the departure point, and then waited again.

"I expected this. It takes time to arrange a convoy."

"We're not going in a convoy."

"What you talking about? Of course we are."

"Nah. I got it straight from a private who is a clerk at Headquarters and he heard the colonel telling the first sergeant. This is gospel: We're going on the *Queen Mary*."

"The *Queen Mary*? You're shitting me! We'll still be in convoy."

"Dummy, the *Queen Mary* never sails in convoy. She's so fast she always goes straight across. No zigging and zagging for us. We won't be in the North Atlantic more than four or five days. This is a picnic. A cruise to Europe on the second biggest luxury ship afloat!"

"Wow, we came up smelling like a rose. This is great! I hope you're right."

Porter listened as the rumor spread but any elation he might have felt was overshadowed by a sense of doom. Everyone knew that the two *Queens* had been stripped down and outfitted as troop carriers and had transported hundreds of thousands of GI's to Europe. So far, without mishap. Everyone also knew that the German submarine fleet was deadly and vicious, wreaking havoc on all Allied shipping. What better prize than to torpedo the *Queen Mary* and send it to the bottom of the ocean with thirty thousand or so American soldiers and Porter Osborne, Jr.? No sub, it was said, could overtake or outrun this ship, but the Germans were bound to know her whereabouts, and she was not equipped with depth charges. Who could say she could not be intercepted? Some German U-boat, he became convinced, was even now submerged in the Atlantic awaiting Porter's approach with deadly purpose.

By the time he had boarded one of the trucks to ride to the harbor, he was certain that he was approaching his doom. The luck of the *Queen Mary* had run out and it was his fault. With his propensity for being singled out by fate, this would be not only the end of the *Queen Mary* but a watery grave for Porter. The anonymity of being submerged forever with twenty or thirty thousand other GI's depressed him. He remembered the Arizona. He felt for his dog tags. So life does go out, not with a bang but a whimper, he thought. He reached in his pocket and rubbed Pietrini's Saint Christopher. He squinched his toes and fancied he could feel his fresh pinch of Georgia soil. "If I should die, think only this of me," he began in a whisper.

He was jolted by a thump between his shoulders. "By God, Osborne, ain't you glad I told you about the 816th? If it hadn't been for me, you'd probably still be reading your ass off in Camp Grant."

"Yeah, thanks, Otten. 'Full fathom five the coral lies.' I wish I could call home."

"Well, you can't. And this ain't no time for any of that Shakespeare shit. We're on our way."

"I won't recite poetry if you won't sing, because I'll tell you right now that if you start on 'It was sad when that great ship went down,' they'll discover your dead body on the pier after we leave."

Porter never felt that he had an opportunity to appreciate the magnificence of the fabled ocean liner to which he entrusted his life. It was like trying to look at the Empire State Building only from its entrance way. There was no way he could see all of it that close. The ship was bigger than any building in Atlanta or Macon, and it was jam-packed with soldiers. After more tedious waiting on the pier, the 816th was herded aboard, its enlisted men overriding each other like cattle. Porter glimpsed the railing and assumed that he was finally off American soil for the first time in his life. He also assumed that the wood of the railing was either teak or mahogany and briefly considered how many years of submersion would be required for it to rot.

All of the luxurious appointments of the *Queen Mary* had been stripped away when she was prepared for a troop ship. The carpets, chandeliers, paintings, sconces, and even paneling had been stored for protection from the massive wear or possible vandalism of crude American soldiers. Only the huge art deco mirror above the landing, where the grand staircase converged, remained in place as proof of previous grandeur. Porter observed iron walls, covered with so many layers of chipping white or gray paint that they looked puffed, narrow corridors like tunnels in an ant hill, steep stairwells that led interminably down, down, down. The ship was crowded with hordes of soldiers everywhere he tried to move or look. He struggled patiently through the din and anticipated the tranquility ahead, for he had heard that they from the 816th were to be quartered on a deck with larger staterooms.

He assumed this was true but never explored the boat enough to prove it. He had no desire to behold anything anywhere that might be more cramped or crowded than the quarters to which he was assigned. What once may have been a stateroom for two in the days of sun and glory was now a box-like space, its porthole sealed and painted over to assure blackout on the seas, its sole illumination a naked bulb behind a grid in the ceiling. Its floor clanged underfoot. the metal showing through gray paint in patches around the table that was bolted to it directly beneath the light bulb. The space was taken up with built-in beds, two bunks wide and four bunks high. There were three of these units along each wall, their sagging mesh springs covered with mattresses that were one inch thick in some spots and bunched into three inches elsewhere, dismal and lumpy evidence that others had preceded them here.

Otten took one look, punched Osborne in the back and advised, "Scramble for the top one, closest to the door. You grab the inside and I'll take the outside."

Squeezed against the wall, unable to sit up without his neck and shoulders pressed against the roof, Porter listened to Otten crow about appropriating unto himself the best accommodations available in this newest home away from home.

"At least I won't have somebody stepping in my face every time they climb to their bunk, although you'll have to crawl over me to get to your bunk if I'm the first one in. I hope to hell you don't get up to piss every night."

"How do we get air in here?" Porter asked.

"They've got ventilator ducts all through the ship, stupid. They work when we're moving."

"When are we going to move?"

"I heard a sergeant tell a captain a stairway or two back that we sail as soon as we're loaded and some VIP we're waiting on gets aboard."

"How long will that take? I can't breathe good."

"How the hell should I know how long it will take? I'm no goddam sailor. They must be trying to pack a million men along on this trip; it takes hours even to march them all aboard. Look, if we change ends in the bunk, we'll be able to get enough light to read. This is even better than being on the bottom bunk next to the bulkhead."

"Bulkhead?"

"Yeah. That's Navy talk for 'wall.' You've got to say 'fore' and 'aft,' too. Also 'starboard,' 'port,' 'windward,' and 'leeward.'"

"I thought you weren't a sailor."

"I'm not, but I don't want to look like a goddam ignoramus, either."

"I'm worried about the air," said Porter. "It's too thick to breathe."

"Probably just a touch of claustrophobia. Relax and think about something else. Take a nap or something, for God's sake."

"Do you realize," mused Porter, "that there are forty-eight human beings in this room? That's forty-eight mouths with unbrushed teeth every morning."

"It's also forty-eight assholes," snapped Otten. "We'll all just have to sleep with our pants on."

"It's ninety-six armpits," said Porter.

"We'll keep our shirts on, then."

"And," pursued Porter, "that counts up to four hundred and eighty toes in this one little bitty room, and every one of them is going to stink. Will they let us sleep with our shoes on?"

"Shut up, Osborne, you depress me. I wonder when they'll call us to mess."

"When they do I sure hope they don't feed us beans or sweet potatoes and then send us back down here to digest them. Could you call it something besides 'mess'? At least till we get back in the open air?"

"Shut up."

"I've read about the slave ships; they were a hundred times this bad. No wonder they were ready to pick cotton when they got to Georgia. Anything would be better than this."

Porter paused for Otten's punctuating order. When it did not come, he continued. "Carter, if we get a torpedo, we're going to the bottom of the ocean in this sarcophagus. There's no way we could get out of here. Is this thing moving?"

"I'm not sure. This boat's so big and smooth it's hard to tell. Wear your life jacket and at least you'll float to the ceiling. Now will you turn off your devious mind and shut your everlasting mouth?"

"I will if you will, Carter Otten, but I ain't going to like it."

Porter's fears were well-founded on one score. When they were finally herded to the great dining salon, there were no sweet potatoes but there were beans, white navy beans served with corned beef that was congealed in tallow to the shape of the can from which it had been turned. In addition to dismay over the food, Porter was puzzled by the smell of the place. The spicy fragrance of corned beef was easily identifiable but it floated only transiently on the surface of a heavy underlying odor that was all pervasive and threatened to cling to clothes and hair. He thought briefly of the Anatomy lab at Emory, but it was not that bad. He defined the flat clean smell of soap or scouring compound, but there was an elusive memory in the air of some habitual food that did not stimulate an appetite. He was, however, impressed by the room and its appointments.

It was a great cavern with boarded, darkened windows which must previously have afforded magnificent vistas of the seas and bathed the salon in sparkling light. Illumination now came only from naked bulbs that flickered synchronously with occasional stutters pulsing from some emboweled dynamo, causing the deck to throb faintly underfoot. There were rows upon rows of benches bolted to the underside of great racks suspended by rods from the ceiling. The upper shelves were crammed with stores, every inch of space utilized in compact efficiency. The bottom shelf of each rack was the dining surface, covered with well-scrubbed tin and bordered all around with an upturned lip of metal. Each unit swayed in unison with the roll of the ship, and although Porter felt that it was like eating on a Ferris wheel, he admired the engineering that had thus reduced spillage to a minimum.

American noncoms directed the soldiers speedily in and out of the mess, but it was the British sailors who rushed to and fro with the bully beef and beans, admonishing the diners, "Let's speed it up a bit there, shall we, matey?" It was his first experience with Anglo-American cooperation in the war effort, and Porter participated willingly although he resented being rushed out to make room for others while he was still chewing and swallowing. There were thousands to feed and they were fed. Three times a day. The racks made Porter remember the long feeding trough in the mule barn at home, and the sameness of the menu recalled the rasher of ten ears of corn and two bundles of fodder allocated to each working animal on the farm. This was war and he was in it, and be damned if he would grumble like the Israelites in the wilderness for lack of leeks and garlic.

At breakfast he very nearly recanted. The odor of the dining salon was definitively labeled, the perfume of the *Queen Mary* permanently imprinted; it was a blend of oatmeal, condensed milk, and hard-boiled eggs. Confronting the impingement of reality on romance, Porter conceded that this erstwhile luxury liner smelled throughout of boiled eggs and oatmeal and downscaled his opinion of the British. The eggs were presented in galvanized buckets at intervals along the feeding troughs, and Porter thereafter, whenever he smelled one, would recall the pitch and roll, the massive plunge and wallow of a giant ocean liner. He would hear the whine of great screws as the bow dropped and the stern rose into shallower water, feel the shudder and the throatily comforting thrust as it settled back into more efficient depth and hurled the *Queen Mary* straight and true across the Atlantic directly at the throat of Hitler. Hurrah for King George and boiled eggs; death to Adolf and oatmeal.

At midmorning they were allowed a rotation on deck. Porter was grateful. He saw wide gray sky cupping the bluest water he had ever imagined; he breathed an infinity of fresh air. He forced his way to the railing and was finally cognizant of the size of the Leviathan carrying them. He looked down and the height made him dizzy; so did the speed with which the great ship was moving through the mighty blue hills below. Porter was bemused. He compared the giant keel of the boat to the point of a two-horse turner ripping through fallow earth on the farm of his youth, tossing waves of soil aside in curling abandon, the hiss of its passage rewarding the ear, the opened furrow a witness of accomplishment. Surely this boat was one of the marvels of the ages. He was filled with elation and yelled above the wind of their passage into Otten's ear. "Damn the torpedoes! Full speed ahead! We'd have a chance if we got hit now while we're on deck instead of crammed in that cell below."

324

"There won't be any torpedoes," Otten yelled back. "Look at all the boats escorting us! I count seven on this side alone and two of them, unless I'm sadly mistaken, are destroyers; they're really determined nothing will happen to this ship."

They moved away from the rail into the lee of a bulkhead, and Otten began speaking in normal tones. His words were interrupted by the metallic squawk of the loudspeaker. "Now hear this. Now hear this. All personnel! In fifteen minutes the right Honorable Winston Churchill will briefly address all troops who gather around B deck amidships. I say again — —"

In the immediate babble from a thousand throats around them, Osborne and Otten looked into each other's startled eyes and simultaneously mouthed, "Winston Churchill?" Any sound they made was lost in the great growling roar that swelled from American throats, and they hurled their bodies into the massive human wave pushing toward B deck.

They very nearly missed him, for they had to scramble and shove among their fellows even to approach the midship deck. Otten was bigger and stronger and bulled his way through with no apology. The lightweight Porter Osborne was tossed like flume from a massive wave and wound up three decks above the great man looking down on top of his head. Porter heard not one word he said, for he spoke without amplification, but he knew with certainty that the cigar, the twinkling cane, the black derby could belong to no one except the Lion of England, the leader of the British Empire. In response to the applause and cheers that erupted at his concluding word, the celebrated figure removed his hat, held it in the hand with his cane and cigar, and raised his right hand in the personalized and defiant, challenging and reassuring V for Victory. The cheers swelled louder, and Winston Churchill held his salute while he rotated full circle amid the throng of admirers. Porter Osborne, even from his telescoped view, identified beyond doubt the bulldog jaw, the snub nose, the bulging brow of one of the leaders of the Allies.

"He's finished that meeting with Roosevelt in Canada," he thought. "Of course they sent the *Queen Mary* to fetch him home. All the rest of us are along just to make a full load in the wagon." A wave of exultation immersed him. "The whole world will keep any harm from him, and there's no way the Germans can get me without getting him, too." His thrill was abated by an inconsequential thought. "Winston Churchill is as bald as a baby's butt when you see him from above. I wonder if he eats hard-boiled eggs." Elation swelled again within him. "I wish I could call home," he said aloud. Nobody heard him.

He and Otten found each other again on main deck.

"Wasn't that great, Carter?"

"I couldn't hear a fucking word he said," replied Otten, "but it's good to know he's aboard. He's as cocky as a banty rooster but you can't help liking the old son of a bitch. I reckon you've relaxed about the submarines now."

"You bet I have. Except for the food, I'm having a good time. We're headed for England on a luxury liner, and I can't wait to see the sights in London."

"Fat chance. I talked to a corporal who had it straight from a sergeant that we're landing in Scotland, catching a train to Liverpool and shipping straight across the Channel. We'll have less than twenty-four hours in the British Isles."

"Oh."

"We're not going to be on this luxury liner long, either. This whole trip is going to take only four and a half days. There's no bad weather reported and we're doing a steady thirty knots."

"How fast is a knot?"

"That's just more Navy talk so we don't look dumb. Who gives a damn how fast it is? To tell you the truth, Osborne, I'm relieved myself to know that Churchill is on board."

He cut a mischievous glance at Porter and a grin pulled his mouth askew. Then he began singing.

"'Oh, they were off old Bengal land and
    headed for the sea,
And the band struck up with "Nearer My God
    to Thee."
They thought they'd send a wire
But the wire was on fire.
It was sad when that great ship went down.'"

Porter laughed and joined in the chorus.

"'Oh it was sad (it was sad)
It was sad (Hallelujah)'"

"Harmonize, goddammit, Osborne." Otten draped an arm across Porter's shoulder and leaned his head closer.

"'It was sad when that great ship went down,
   (hit the bottom).
There were husbands and wives,
Little bitty children lost their lives.
It was sad when that great ship went down.'"

Amid the throng of crowded GI's and oblivious to their stares, Porter Osborne and Carter Otten raised their faces to the scudding clouds and laughed and laughed.

Otten, Porter decided, was not going to be a completely intolerable buddy after all.

"Carter," he said, "I'm glad we're going to get there quick. I don't know how much longer I can fight that oatmeal and those hard-boiled eggs. Let alone the navy beans and corned beef. Wouldn't you love a good mess of turnip greens along about now?"

"Shut up or you'll make me homesick. Quit bitching about the food. If you don't start turning your butt to the bulkhead when you fart, you ain't going to live to eat another breakfast."

They laughed again.

"St. Michael's on his Mountain in the searoads
of the north...
He shakes his lance of iron and he claps his
wings of stone;
The noise is gone through Normandy; the
noise is gone alone..."

29   **f**reed from fear of a watery grave, Porter spent his
waking moments exploring all areas of the *Queen Mary* available to him,
even sneaking occasionally into zones clearly marked "Off Limits."
British sailors, he decided, regarded Americans at best as mildly
moronic, and he found that his proclivity for mouth breathing, combined with a wide-eyed stare and an exaggeration of his Southern
drawl, induced them to forgive him much. He was shooed away from
the engine rooms, but not before he had thrilled to the mighty throb of
the great dynamo that drove this ship. He was scatted out of the
spacious kitchen where the eggs and oatmeal and beef were boiled to
death, but only after he had discovered that British cooks did not skin
down to their undershirts to work and that they were considerably less
hairy than the ones to whom he had grown accustomed. He got part
way up a steep ladder to the bridge before he was apprehended.

"'ere, where do you think you're going and what are you up to?
Back to your mates, you hear? Hi say, aren't you the little blighter I
plucked off the bow? Lost again, are you? 'Ow we'll win this war is a
great question with the Yanks sending us the likes of you."

"I sure am much obliged to you, sir. I keep getting myself
turned around on this big ole boat. I sure don't mean to be any trouble
to anybody."

"All right, all right. Off with you now. Hi've work to do. If you
just remember to stay behind the ropes you'll be all right. Don't take it
so hard."

He managed to secrete himself in solitude behind a stanchion
on the poop deck where he hunkered undetected for half of an afternoon, suspended over the Atlantic Ocean. The turbulent white froth
spewed from the stern and then fanned out to cover the wide flattened
track with foam as soft and rich as lace on a shawl. The great wake

streamed out behind him as far as his eye could see, flung in a straight line that joined him to the horizon like the securing strand of an adventurous spider. The mighty ship rapidly, tirelessly replenished and extended that line, and Porter Osborne, Jr., overcome with awe, felt that he was in the presence of a miracle. The waves tossed in from either side and the returning swell of the ocean would not be denied, but the wake was unmistakably visible, and for hours afterwards that train of majesty would proclaim that a Queen had passed this way.

"I finally know how Masefield felt," he said, and recited aloud,

> "'I must down to the seas again, to the lonely
>   sea and the sky,
> And all I ask is a tall ship and a star to steer
>   her by,
> And the wheel's kick and the wind's song and
>   white sails shaking,
> And a gray mist on the sea's face and a gray
>   dawn breaking.'

But, for God's sake, let us all be thankful for the Right Honorable Winston Churchill."

Cramped and chilled, he deserted his sanctuary in the fresh air and descended through the stale air to his quarters.

"What's up, Otten?"

"That squawk box has been going 'Now hear this' like crazy. We land at Greenock at dawn, and we've set a speed record for crossing. Where've you been?"

"I've been helping them set the record. The English sure know something about boats. Where's Greenock?"

"In Scotland, by God. Close to Glasgow, they say. By this time tomorrow, we'll be on foreign soil."

"Not all that foreign, Otten, not all that foreign. Way back yonder we're kin to all these folks. Move over and let me in my bunk."

"Tail to the wall, Osborne, tail to the wall."

It was raining when they disembarked unceremoniously on the concrete pier that had replaced Scottish soil. Hustling along with his fellows, Porter had time for only brief backward glances at the soaring wall of the *Queen Mary* as she disgorged them. He caught sight of a roly-poly figure in derby hat and upturned collar, cigar in place, being bustled under umbrellas into a gleaming limousine but gave no more

329

than cursory attention to it. He was eager for what lay ahead. By dint of calculated timing, ruthless use of elbows, and actually leaping over fellow soldiers, Otten ensconced himself in a window seat on the train, one facing forward.

"Might as well do your foreign travel in style, Osborne. If you can't go first-class, you better stay home, I always say."

Porter meekly trailed him and gave only fleeting consideration to the place of good manners in foreign travel. The crammed train picked up speed; water bathed the windows so that vision through them was as blurred as peering through ground glass. Otten was excited.

"This is bonnie Scotland, Osborne! Home of Robert Burns and Sir Walter Raleigh. We're riding through history!"

"Sir Walter Raleigh?"

"Yeah. You know. Wrote *Ivanhoe* that you had to report on in the eighth grade."

"I think that was Sir Walter Scott."

"Quit nit-picking. What the fuck's the difference? Anyhow it's the home of Heathcliff. Did you see that movie? Laurence Olivier reminds me of myself sometimes."

Porter looked at his buddy in amazement, hoped that he was jesting, and pulled his cap over his eyes for a nap.

Their trip through the British Isles was not so rapid that it was not educational, although it was less than comprehensive. The train sped through a countryside obscured by the lowering clouds and the water-swept windows. It stopped in London. They knew it was London because a sign in the railway station proclaimed it. They were detained for long minutes under a shed and had a clear view of their side of the terminal and the activities on the dock. Everything was in varying shades of gray, including the clothing of the workers. Porter peered intently but could see nothing beyond except other trains.

"Wow, Otten, this is a city for you. Parliament, Buckingham Palace, Westminster Abbey, Old Ben, the Tower, St. Paul's. I wish they'd let us off the train for an hour."

"Hell, they haven't even opened the doors. We're waiting for a clear track to Liverpool and we're gone. What's that man selling over there?"

"Beats me," said Porter. "Looks like apple pies."

Otten let down his window. "Hey, Mac! What you got?"

"Pies, Yank. Pies."

"What kind?"

"Meat pies. Mutton. Steak and kidney. Want one?"

"How much?"

"Two shillings."

"I don't have any English money. How about a quarter?"

"Not on your life. I'll take a dollar."

"Gimme a dollar, Osborne."

"Not on your life," parroted Porter.

"Goddammit, Osborne, this is London. Home of Dickens, who wrote about Little Nell and all that stuff. We can't get off the train to see it but we can at least explore it a little. I know I remember reading about steak and kidney pie. Where's your cultural curiosity? Gimme a goddam dollar!"

"Not on your life," repeated Porter. He liked the sound of it.

"Come on, Osborne. The train's beginning to move."

"I'll lend you a dollar."

"All right, all right. Here you go, Mac."

"Lots of luck, Yank." He offered up with grimy hand a brown unwrapped orb of dough.

The train pulled out of the station into the rain again. Otten held up his prize. "My first purchase in a foreign land. You want first bite?"

Porter recalled the hand and clothes of the vendor. "No thanks. And you owe me a dollar."

"You're a chinche little bastard; you know that?"

"You still owe me a dollar. Besides, I don't think it's going to taste very good."

Otten replaced the dubious stare with which he had begun regarding the pie with a lordly glance at Porter. "What the hell do you know?" he scoffed. "You're such a provincial hayseed you'll never get out of the backwoods and become a cosmopolite. Open yourself to new experiences. When in Rome, do as the Romans do!"

His dissertation had attracted the attention of their seatmates, and four other sets of eyes joined Porter's as Otten took a massive bite, slowed his chewing gradually to a standstill, and then swallowed with a gulp that reminded Porter of a hound dog on a shivering hungry morning.

There was a long moment of silence.

"Is it good?" said Porter.

Otten's gaze dodged around among the waiting eyes. "Not bad," he answered and opened wide his mouth for the second bite. Suddenly he snatched the window down, hurled the steak and kidney pie into the rain, and looked with defiance directly at the GI across from him. "It's tough and it tastes like pee," he roared and then joined in the ensuing laughter.

"Carter, I'll cancel the dollar if you'll keep your mouth turned to the window till you brush your teeth." Porter thought for a few minutes and said, "We've just been through one of the greatest cities in the world and all I'll be able to write home about it is that it's gray and grimy and smells like pee."

Liverpool was no better but his expectations had not been so high. They were guided directly off the train onto a wharf with speed and precision that made Porter feel the train crew was gratified to be shed of them. The recently organized 816th General Hospital was then assigned to a ship of its own to cross the English Channel, and by dint of a kind of free-floating authority emanating from unsure noncoms in such a new outfit, they boarded the *Star of India*.

This boat was not reminiscent of the *Queen Mary*. Rather than being stripped down for the purpose of carrying troops, it had been upgraded, a process which did not extend to cleaning or painting. It was of such a size that it moved a little every time a GI added new weight to the deck. Rust was prevalent, with dripping streaks of it delineating every screw on the bulkheads. The deck was wood, sorely in need of repainting, and the railing twisted slightly under Porter's hand, attesting to rot somewhere along its course. He hoped that the crew had paid better attention to the hull but decided that he would not go through that cycle of fear again. He turned to Otten, who was crowding behind him, and sang softly with off-key bravado.

> "'They built the ship *Titanic* and when they
> had got through
> They said they had a boat that the water would
> never get through.'"

"Shut up, Osborne," came the reply. "You're not funny worth a shit. You can get your goddam ass drowned in a scuttled fishing boat in fifty feet of water as easy as you can in the middle of the ocean. I can't imagine the British certifying this tub in their fleet. It makes me nervous."

"If you can't go first-class, you ought to stay at home," offered Porter.

"You got that right," sniffed Otten. "This is one piss-poor way to see the world. They call this the British Navy?"

"I don't think so," observed Porter. He had been regarding the crew members, who were sleek of hair and spoke to each other in unintelligible phrases. Their dark brown skins had mauve undertones and their features were certainly not Negroid. "I think this is a family-owned relic from some far-flung reach of the Empire, pressed into service for the glory of the Queen."

"Queen? What Queen?"

"Victoria, you idiot. Don't you read Kipling? The name of this boat is no romantic title; I think we're on an East Indian ship. It came all the way from Calcutta to help the war effort and has not been scraped or painted or scrubbed since Dunkirk. It is et up with rust and dry rot, but they're doing their bit."

"Shut up, Osborne. I'm already convinced that it leaks. Have you noticed how low we're sitting in the water? You worried about crossing the Atlantic; now I'm scared we're going to sink in the goddam English Channel."

They stacked their gear in corners below deck and settled onto benches in one large room.

"What's that odor?" queried Porter. "I thought boiled eggs and oatmeal were bad, but this is unbelievable."

"You and your goddam nose," snapped Otten. "I wouldn't notice it if you wouldn't talk about it. I think it is a blend of sweat and curry laced with Hindu toe jam, but any way you look at it, I am sick and tired of the British Empire."

"We've been moving for half an hour, and you certainly didn't see much of it. Like Miss Phronie back home used to say, we were in and out like 'a pore horse's ass.' Do you realize that we never really set foot on English soil? They've paved it all. Rupert Brook would have to rewrite his poem and say he's six feet of English concrete."

"Will you quit babbling? Look, they're serving supper. I'm so hungry I could eat a bear."

Their exotic hosts handed out tin pans and forks along the benches. Others came with rice and others followed to ladle a rich dark stew atop it. The steam was pungent.

"You were right, Otten. It's curry."

"What the hell's the meat? I never saw anything that looked quite that dead."

"I think it's mutton. Or else Big Billy Goat Gruff. It's not too bad if you have your own teeth. It's got so much stuff on it you can't really tell what it is, but at least it's not steak and kidney pie."

The *Star of India* lurched and wallowed; soldiers reflexively held their plates up to prevent spilling as they swayed against each other.

Otten rose. "I'm not hungry after all. I'm going topside for a little fresh air."

Porter scraped his plate and some minutes later followed. He found Otten forward, leaning back against the rail.

"This is exciting, Carter. Running the English Channel with no lights at all. It sure smells better out here. This is salt water and diesel fuel but at least there's no curry smell except what's on my clothes. You don't reckon we've got a leak in an oil line, do you?"

Otten had his face turned forward into the wind and said nothing.

"Look at the moon, Carter. I realize it's really not moving, that what's causing that impression is the way we're slipping and sliding around in the water, but it looks like the moon is jumping across the sky and then skipping back to where it started from. I have the conviction that the moon itself is dancing back and forth up there. Isn't that fascinating?"

Carter Otten was bent over the rail, retching until he choked. Porter stared in amazement.

"Are you seasick? You must be. It couldn't be anything you ate because all you've had since breakfast was that one bite of steak and kidney pie. Look at the moon; it'll take your mind off your stomach."

Otten's buttocks tightened and fresh spasms erupted.

"I don't understand. You didn't have any trouble on the *Queen Mary* when we were busting twenty-foot waves wide open, and now it makes you sick when we're just sort of lurching around through these little old choppy swells."

Otten turned his streaming face toward Osborne but did not push away from the railing.

"There wasn't enough room on the fucking *Queen Mary* to get sick. I told you already how I feel about the British and all the boats in their Empire. Will you, for God's sake, get your ass below and let me puke in peace?"

What sleep the men of the 816th got that night was on the benches in the belly of the *Star of India*, propped upright against each other. Breakfast was an insult rather than a surprise. They expected the boiled eggs, but the oatmeal had been cooked so long it had congealed and could be eaten like a cake if one desired.

"It still smells like curry in here," Porter remarked, "and that jam you were talking about."

"Shut up, Osborne," whimpered Carter Otten. "We're unloading on Omaha Beach in thirty minutes."

"Omaha Beach?"

"Yep. We're going over the side and wading ashore."

"With all our clothes on?"

"For God's sake, what do you think this is, a houseparty at St. Simon's? I'd rather break my neck diving into the beach than stay on this godforsaken tub another hour."

An hour later Porter was pressed against the rail between GI's whose faces had become familiar but whose names he had not yet learned. The *Star of India* had backed as near the shore as she could without scraping bottom. The lightest of drizzles was wetting their clothing, and what Porter could see of France through the mist appeared like somber piles of deeper darkness layered upon each other beneath a brooding sky. Nearer at hand, he regarded the tilted concrete crosses embedded in the sand to impale boats approaching France, recognized them as "Hitler's toothpicks", and shivered. His imagination peopled the cliffs ahead with entrenched German soldiers, machine guns at ready, all of them aimed at the *Star of India*. He thought of home and his family, of Fritz.

"This is why they make you wear your dog tags all the time. I'm going to be in the first wave ashore. Be with me, God."

"Aw right, you guys. This is it! Over the side!"

"It's still too deep," demurred Porter. "Can't they get us a little closer?"

"First ones in make a chain and we'll toss the duffel bags down. Pass 'em along and make a pile on the beach. Stay inside the ropes on shore and you won't get in no mine fields. After you've caught three bags, move ashore with one. Over the side!"

This was no landing craft, Porter discovered. No great hinged metal pathway was lowered into the surf upon which they could go racing ashore. He clambered over the railing, looked for a moment into the murky water beneath and dropped. The water came up to his chin. By determined bobbing on his toes against the weight of his pack, he managed to push himself into chest-high shallows and turned obediently back toward the boat, hands upstretched. The smack of a loaded duffel bag knocked him completely under water, but he regained his footing and passed it on. He noted the lettering on the side. "Dalrymple, Allen O. 2nd Lt."

"Don't get those duffel bags wet," roared the sergeant.

"Up your ass," breathed Porter. "I believe to my soul, Lt. Dalrymple is in his own duffel bag. It's heavy enough for that."

The excitement of new experience, coupled with gratitude that there were now no guns on Omaha Beach and relief at having survived passage on the *Star*, filled everyone with good cheer. Laughter rang out above the curses as the enlisted men of the 816th General Hospital unloaded its gear by hand and relayed it to dry land.

"Morale, I would say, is high among the troops today," said Porter to Carter.

"And I sure as hell don't know why," huffed his buddy. "Nobody in this whole outfit knows what the fuck he's doing. If we'd gone to OCS with Calhoun, we'd have dry butts and some dogface would be toting our baggage. Hey, look out!"

Porter dodged backward as a wooden chest with rope handles was hurled at him.

"Don't let it get wet," yelled the GI from the deck. "It's some kind of records."

The chest was floating beyond Osborne's reach. He called to a tall red-haired PFC with exaggerated prognathous profile, "Hey, grab that chest and push it back this way. It's full of important papers."

The redhead turned, over-reached for the floating chest, and floundered into deeper water. Righting himself, he looked at Porter and spoke with unmistakable tongue of the South.

"Hell, let the sonofabitch go. I didn't come over here to be a goddam Red Cap." He turned and with deliberate fingertip shoved the chest into deeper water. His freckles shone. "I've already sent two officers' bags out to sea. Who do they think they are?"

Porter watched the chest bob into the current and sweep beyond the bow of the *Star of India*.

"I know who I am," he said. "Porter Osborne. Who are you?"

"Roger Jewel, from Commerce, Georgia. Let's move on up the line. I'll never get my ass dry again."

They slogged ashore with duffels on their shoulders and shrugged them onto the mound growing ever higher on the beach. A few of them, Porter noted, were dry. He looked across the shelf of sand with coils of half-buried barbed wire still barring passage except in cleared areas. The precipitous cliff that ringed this beach drew his eye upward and he gasped when he spied the concrete bunkers that overlooked and threatened the spot where he stood. The hair rose on his neck.

"How did we ever manage to do it?" he said in a low tone to Otten.

"I know what you mean," came the reply in uncharacteristically studied response. "This is almost holy ground." He turned to Porter. "You know something? Right this minute I'm glad they kicked us out of med school. I wouldn't be back in that ivory palace for anything while all this is going on."

"Shit," said Roger Jewel. He sat down, pulled off a shoe and poured water from it. "We didn't get here till they'd put down sidewalks. Can you imagine those poor fuckers crawling through mine fields under machine gun fire? I'm ready to go home. Now."

"Sidewalks?" said Porter.

"Mighty near it," responded Roger Jewel. "You see those yellow ribbons zig-zagging up that hill? That's a path that's been cleared of mines. Stay on it and you won't get your nuts blown off. If that ain't a sidewalk, I'll kiss your ass." He wrung out a sock and pulled it back on. "If it is, you can kiss mine."

"Oh," said Porter. It was such a common invitation in the Army that he did not take it personally.

"I tell y'all one thing, though," continued Jewel, "that path is so huffing puffing steep I bet a dollar they find some way to ride those pussel-gutted officers to the top."

"Sidewalks," accepted Porter. "This is D plus one hundred and six. I guess you could expect sidewalks if you're that late setting foot on French soil."

"One hundred and six? French soil?" repeated Jewel.

"Yeah. At least it's not paved." He pulled off one of his own shoes. The water that poured out of it was undeniably red. He reached into his pocket and extracted a small brass nozzle. Digging a hole in the sand, he dropped it in and emptied the water from his other shoe upon it before covering it.

"What the fuck are you doing, Osborne?" asked Otten.

"It's September 19, 1944, Anno Domini," said Porter. "And I'm sending Private Bernie Friedman back to Jesus. Forever. I'm tired of counting."

He stamped the sand flat.

"Ain't your buddy crazy as a fucking bed bug?" asked Roger Jewel.

"You got that straight," assented Otten, "but you don't know nothing yet. Wait till he starts throwing poetry at you."

"Poetry?"

"I'm afraid so."

"Is he queer?"

"Nah. Just crazy. It's OK to turn your back on him. It's just that you never know what his fiendish little mind is working on."

"To hell with both of you," said Porter Osborne, Jr. He faced the cliff, stared defiantly at the grim bunkers and saluted.

"*Lafayette, nous sommes ici*," he proclaimed.

"See what I mean?" said Otten.

"I just be goddammed," said Roger Jewel.

"One hundred and six," said Porter.

". . . Holding his head up for a flag of all the free . . ."

30   Porter was glad he had not bet with his new acquaintance. The enlisted men were guided by their sergeants like a straggling flock of goats up the roped-off gully that Roger Jewel had earlier compared to a sidewalk. Near the top, he looked backward and downward. The *Star of India* was headed west. Its deck rose now considerably higher; its stern, rid of its burden of soldiers, seemed to toss and cavort in its own wake like the hind legs of a young calf in spring pasture.

"Empty wagon going back for another load," said Porter. He surveyed the beach. Canvas-covered trucks had appeared from somewhere off to the left and duffels were being piled aboard. "Thank God we're not having to lug those suckers up this hill," he said to Roger Jewel, who was just ahead of him. "My pack's heavy enough."

"Thank God we've got a path that's been cleared of mines," said Jewel. "You remember those things blowing up the infiltration course in Basic, don't you?"

"Yeah," called Otten. "This gives 'Between the Ribbons' a whole new meaning. This is for real. Look at that bunker over there."

"I still can't believe what those guys did on June 6," said Porter.

"Move along back there!" yelled a sergeant. "Get the lead out!"

"Up yours," muttered Jewel and Osborne in unison. Then Roger Jewel said, "Look at those damn officers and nurses climbing into trucks. What'd I tell you, goddammit?"

Porter smiled and shrugged. "*C'est la guerre.* Don't let it get to you." For a moment he felt worldly.

At the top of the cliff in a small village called Vierville-sur-mer, the drizzle turned into a steady light rain.

"Get your rain gear on," yelled the sergeant. "We wait here. I just got word that Col. Draughan has procured trucks to take us to our bivouac area."

"Col. Draughan is a good guy," said Porter. "He's looking after his men. Somebody down on the beach told me it was at least six miles to wherever it is we're going."

"Good old guy, my ass," growled Roger Jewel. "They're going to send the trucks back for us when the officers get done with them. You don't see any commissioned officers standing out here in this fucking rain with us, do you? That colonel's thinking about his own hide, he's not worrying about you one minute."

"Well, everything I've seen about Col. Draughan makes him look like a good leader, but then I only saw him for the first time a couple of months ago." A note of primness invaded his voice. "Where did you have so much contact with him and get to know him so well?"

Roger Jewel, looking faintly like a monk in the billowing raincoat, turned his hooded face toward Porter. "I don't know the son-bitch from Adam's off-ox," he admitted, "but I've been in the Army long enough to know that everybody in it is looking after Number One. That includes me, by God, and if it doesn't include you yet, I promise you that it will. The other thing I've learned is that you don't have to get to know each officer personally, you can just take it for granted that every one of them is a pluperfect, dyed-in-the-wool shitass, and you better not expect anything from them."

"Oh," said Osborne.

"Hey, Jewel," contributed Otten. "Why don't you come on out and tell us how you really feel about authority figures? You can trust us, we won't rat on you."

"Yaah, fuck you both," said Roger Jewel and moved away.

"He's from Commerce, Georgia," said Porter.

"What the hell's that got to do with it?" said Otten. "He's probably right about Number One, you know."

"Not yet," said Porter. "Not yet, Carter Otten. Here come the trucks. We're finally going to get our hospital set up and running."

They were carried over narrow roads with so many turns and changes in direction that Porter was never able to retrace them, even in his mind. He never forgot the puddles and the bumps, however, that threatened to toss him from the back of the truck. He peered intently through the rain at the landscape, divided geometrically into plots by lines of trees that were adorned at their tops by gnarled bulges with sprouting branches.

"Those are the hedgerows of Normandy," he informed his fellows packed behind him, who were restricted to tunnel vision and could see little but the road behind. "I really never thought I'd live to see them."

"You better hope you live to see the last of them," a voice came from the front. "I had a neighbor from home who landed with the Airborne and saw his buddies caught in the branches of those damn trees. The German snipers picked them off like chickens. Don't tell me about Normandy hedgerows. They're all mined. He had to watch his best buddy get gut shot and leave him hanging there. Couldn't do a damn thing to help him or even get his body down."

"Why do they prune the tops of the trees like that?" a voice asked in a lighter tone.

"For firewood," answered Porter. "That's the way they get their faggots."

Another voice with definite Brooklyn accent broke in. "Christ, I never would have believed they grow them on trees, even in France."

The ensuing laughter re-established the level of thought with which the group was comfortable.

Porter lowered his voice and spoke only to Otten. "See those big black and white cows? I had a professor once who called them the 'great gentle kine of Normandy' and ate cheese made from their milk. I still remember it; it was terrible."

"Hell, Osborne, you don't know what you're talking about. With all that reading you were doing back at Camp Grant, looks like you'd have found out that France is famous for its cheeses and that every region has its own special cheese just like it does wine. You weren't cut out to be a connoisseur. When in Rome, do as the Romans do. I can't wait for a chance to try some of the local cheese. They call it *fromage* over here."

"I know that. I also remember a line from a poem about the sycophantic fox and the gullible raven where the fox got the raven's cheese:

> 'J'admire,' said he, 'ton beau plumage'
> (The which was simply persiflage.)'"

"What the hell does 'persiflage' mean in French?"

"I don't know," replied Porter, "but in English it means 'bullshit.'"

"Osborne, I'll never quit wondering why I even bother to talk to you."

"Christ, I was tinking the same ting myself," said the voice from Brooklyn.

They went through a hamlet. "That's Ste. Marie du Mont," murmured Otten. "It's not far from here we're supposed to bivouac."

Porter thought briefly of Lamar Betsill and even more briefly of Maria Nerova. "Not Soo San Marie du Mont, is it? We're getting to be world travelers, Otten. Three countries in less than twenty-four hours we've seen now." He looked at the lonely countryside, the rainy skies, the gray road. "But we sure ain't going first-class. Maybe you should've stayed at home."

Several miles later the truck turned off the road, bumped for fifteen minutes down a rutted lane, and then turned into a pasture and stopped. "Everybody out! Fall in over here!"

They jack-knifed out of their trucks and assembled in a shrouded hodge-podge in front of a hedgerow. The rain had stopped and they threw their hoods back. Otten headed for the mountain of duffels to rummage and find his own.

"Over here, soldier! You're out of line. The colonel says nobody moves from this spot even for a piss call till you've all signed a duty roster!"

Porter fell into line just in front of Roger Jewel. "Duty roster? They've got a dozen already from Grant and Kilmer. What's going on?"

A short, black-eyed, ivory-skinned GI just ahead of him spoke over his shoulder. "I understand they've misplaced the company records. It's not a duty roster they want; this is a human inventory. They can't find any list of personnel anywhere." His words had the cultured cadence and accent of collegiate New England.

"Where you from? Bawston?" Porter volunteered.

"New Bedford." His glance was a little reminiscent of Katie Albert's. "What about you?"

Porter felt impelled to speak properly. "What about me?" he answered defensively with a hint of defiance.

The eyes flickered. "Where are you from?"

"Brewtonton."

"I never heard of it."

"We're even. I never heard of New Bedford."

"Touché."

"Is it in Massachusetts?"

"Yes. It's a pre-Revolutionary whaling port. Forgive me. I thought everyone had heard of it because of that. Where is Brewtonton?"

"In Georgia. It's an antebellum cotton, corn and tater village, and nobody who wasn't born there ever heard of it."

The boy laughed and Porter felt accepted.

"I was at Lawson General for three months. Just left there in August."

"Did you have Sgt. Bass?"

"You mean Sound and Fury, Tight-assed, Availeth Nothing Melvin Bass? Certainly. He's to Lawson what the infiltration course is to Camp Grant — a lot of futile noise and gunpowder and the only thing you learn is to look after yourself."

"What'd I tell you?" said Roger Jewel, and punched Porter in the back.

Porter ignored him. "We've been a lot of the same places. How'd you like Atlanta?" He expected approbation.

"I've never encountered so many queers anywhere east of the Jade Room in Rockford, Illinois."

"What?" squawked Porter. "I've been both places and never saw a one. I don't believe you."

"You can believe him," assured Roger Jewel. "If you never ran into one, you were either blind or lucky. I made my spending money baiting, trolling, and rolling."

"What are you talking about?"

"It's easy. You walk in any bar by yourself and when some guy starts looking at you, you sort of rub your crotch and the next thing you know you're being propositioned. Then you knock his head against the wall in the closest alley and empty his wallet." He looked down on the Massachusetts guy. "What do you do with them, Blue-belly? You're mighty slight to roll one."

The New Englander looked at him cooly. "I just say, 'No, thank you,' and keep on smiling. I'm not a homophobe and I don't need much spending money. They can't help it, you know."

Porter squirmed at the direction of this conversation. "We didn't have them where I come from. I forgot to tell you I get my mail at Brewtonton, Georgia, route three, but we haul our cotton to Peabody."

When they both laughed, he added, "I wonder what happened to our records." Porter felt a steadily pressing finger in his back and added with innocence, "I sure hope nobody has accidentally misplaced my duffel bag. Or any of the officers'." The pressure increased. "We haven't been in the field half a day and already we have to make up for accidents."

Roger Jewel removed his prodding finger, but Porter could hear him breathing through his teeth.

"All we want is your name, rank, and serial number!" called a sergeant. "Make two lines here and let's speed this up. Last name, first name, middle initial, rank, and serial number. You know the process! Move along!"

As the boy from New Bedford bent over the makeshift table to sign his name, he turned to Porter at his elbow. "Watch this: I'm ambidextrous," he said.

"Does that mean you can live on land or in water?" Porter was flippant. "If it keeps on raining, that'll come in handy."

"Pay attention to this; I can write as well with my left hand as with my right."

Beneath his own signature he scrawled another name. "Now, let's give this new guy a serial number," he said, "and really confuse somebody. For a few minutes, at least."

Porter followed him, picked up the pencil, and bent over the pad. He was as curious about the real name as the pseudonym.

"Kostas, Stevens P., Pvt.," he read.

Beneath it, in an obviously different handwriting, was registered, "Farbecker, Daniel D., PFC."

"I wonder which one is real," said Roger Jewel. He looked steadily at Porter Osborne. "And I wonder where in the hell our records are."

Porter returned the gaze without expression. "There's really no telling. They ought to check LeHavre or Cherbourg or maybe even Lisbon, Portugal. With grappling irons and a straining net. The officers in this Army can really get things screwed up. They're probably not ever going to find those records."

Neither one of the boys smiled as an unlikely bond was formed. Porter looked across from his own name to that of his new friend.

"Jewel, Sherman R., Pvt."

"Hey," he exclaimed. "I thought you said your name was Roger."

"It is. At least that's what they call me back home. My daddy never would let anybody call me Sherman; that came from somewhere back on my mother's side. The Army always wants your first name, you know."

Another sergeant was bellowing at them. "All right! Get a buddy and two other guys, fan out, and put up your pup tent! Soon as that's done and you ditch them good, come claim your duffel!"

"You wanta team up?" asked Jewel.

"I better wait for Otten," said Porter. "I'm all he's got."

"He from your home town?"

"Nah, I knew him in school and we've been together ever since. Sorry."

"Don't matter. It was just an idea. Did anybody ever tell you that you might be just a little bit what they call weird?"

"Come to think of it, on occasion there does arise an oafish and unperceptive bastard who mentions that possibility." He watched Otten approaching. "Here comes one of them now. See you around. I really am all he's got."

"Lots of luck," said Roger Jewel. "Look after Number One."

Otten had procured two burly men with flattened Slavic faces as their tent mates. They growled at each other in accents that were so thickly unintelligible on initial utterance and so devoid of interesting content on repetition that Porter soon abandoned any effort at conversation. He did not bother to learn their names. All four of them spread their shelter halves on the wet grass and, after a few fumbling trials, managed to button them together properly.

Otten was in peak form as self-appointed director.

"Not that way, Mack. If the buttons are on the outside, it'll leak like a sieve. Slant that pole more, Jack, or it'll pull out of the ground when you tighten the string. We don't want the damn thing collapsing on us in the middle of the night." A note of almost imperious impatience was detectable in his voice. "No, no, no. Let's turn it this way. You want to stay wet all night? Goddammit, Osborne, dig that trench deeper on the upper side of the tent and drain it downhill so you're not damming up a pond for our sleeping bags to float in."

Porter observed the massive necks and shoulders of their temporary roommates and was conscious of increasingly sullen scowls. He sought to erase them by pointing to Otten and with tolerant disdain announcing, "I think this brilliant, eager-beaver son of a bitch is bucking for sergeant, don't you?"

"Get off my back, Osborne," hissed Otten. "Don't you start on me."

"Well, you back off," replied Porter. He lowered his voice. "Do you realize we've got to be cramped up in this canvas chicken coop all night for no telling how long with these two Neanderthals? I'd rather have the tent collapse in the rain than for Mack and Jack to strangle you in your sleep. Be nice."

"Hell, we're only going to be here for one night, at the most two. I heard on the grapevine that they're not even planning to set up our hospital here. We're headed for St. Lo, and they need us there quick."

Porter thought of his long weeks at Camp Grant. His records had been lost there, too, but he felt no urge to enlighten Otten. He surveyed the oil-impregnated double trapezoid that was a little over knee high and heard the rain pattering on his helmet. "I really think we should look on this as our little home away from home, Carter, and be as considerate of each other as possible."

They searched out their duffel bags to stash them in the tent. At a gap in the hedgerow that separated two pastures, a lone figure was hammering with a stone a hand-lettered sign into the soggy earth. "Reserved for Officers," it read.

"Big deal," muttered Otten.

"Lots of luck," added Osborne.

The figure straightened. His raincoat had cloth captain's bars sewed on each shoulder. Even his rain hood had two parallel white bars painted on it. The drawstring was pulled snugly so that the cowl framed a face distinguished by a bulbous nose and cheeks pocked with craters of old acne. Rain misted his brows and glistened on his skin.

He spoke to a hooded figure hastening by. "Hey, soldier. Come in here and help me put up my tent."

There was no hesitation in answer, no halt to purposeful step. "No, thank you." Porter was sure that he recognized the nonchalant, dismissing voice of Stevens P. Kostas.

The captain hailed another. "Hey, soldier. I need some help with my tent. Come across the hedgerow and put it up for me."

"Hell, no. Do it yourself."

"Halt!" ordered the captain. "Stop and listen when I'm talking to you! What's your name, soldier?"

That GI also never paused but he answered, "Farbecker, Daniel D."

"I can't hear you. What did you say?"

"I said, 'Fuck you.'"

"Do you realize you're talking to an officer? I'll court-martial you! Come back here!"

The figure disappeared in the rain before the captain could pursue, but Porter had no difficulty at all in recognizing the voice of Roger Jewel. When he and Otten had distanced themselves from the attention of the belligerent captain, he said, "No guns yet. No wounded yet. No contact with the enemy yet. But, Otten, this is sure as hell one interesting war."

"You're weird, Osborne. That damn captain is so GI his balls salute every time his pecker stands up. I sure as hell hope we don't see much of him."

They unrolled their sleeping bags in the tent and carefully placed their duffel bags in the center to form a bulwark between them and their Yankee neighbors, who had already deposited theirs and departed.

"Don't let anything touch the tent from the inside," warned Otten. "You'll have water draining in like a faucet. I never saw so damn much rain."

"I wonder where Mack and Jack are," said Porter.

"Who cares? There's lots more room when they aren't here, and you can bet the air is better. This is worse than the *Queen Mary*."

"I'm not so sure. It's just as crowded, but at least we're on *terra firma*."

"It's not going to stay firm long if this rain doesn't let up. These tents weren't designed for anything but sleeping. You can't hope to sit up in here unless you're a spraddled-legged, hunchbacked dwarf. If we're going to get along in what you call our little home away from home, we've got to have some house rules around here. First one is no farting in the tent. Even if it is raining outside."

"Good idea," assented Porter. He thought a moment. "I nominate you as house mother and you can tell Mack and Jack. If you do well with this assignment, I'll recommend you to Capt. Scarface for a promotion."

Otten was easily diverted. "I checked, and every man in the Operating Room should be at least a sergeant, with the ranking non-com being a master sergeant. That ignoramus from Arkansas we've got as our chief in the OR is just a regular sergeant, and you know if he goes up, we will too. I plan to have three stripes and two bars by this time next year."

"Why do you want them?"

"More money, stupid."

"Where are you going to spend it? The Army provides our every need."

"There's also the prestige."

"Who are you going to impress? Don't forget I am with you always, so to speak, and I knew you when."

"Ah, kiss my ass, Osborne. Shut up and read a book."

"I think I hear Mack and Jack coming," said Porter. "Or it may be Jack and Mack. I'm not sure which one is which. Don't forget to give them your farting lecture."

Their tent mates were in apparent good humor, making noises between themselves that Porter assumed constituted laughter.

"Hi, fellows," said Otten. "Where you been?"

As they crawled in the tent, there followed a spate of gutterals to which Otten responded, "Tough luck." That produced another burst of sputtering syllables, followed by braying wheezes, and Otten began laughing also. "That took balls," he said. "You two have really got guts."

Regardless of their proximity, Porter understood not one word they uttered. "What happened?" he asked Otten *sotto voce.* "Where did they say they've been?"

"They've been putting up a tent for some officers."

Porter lowered his voice even more. "Poor dummies. Was Scarface one of them?"

"He's the one who sucked them in."

"What in the world are they laughing about? At least, I think they're laughing."

"They buttoned the shelter halves backwards. That tent will never shed rain."

"You'd better straighten them out," advised Porter. "You're not going to make sergeant like that."

"On top of that, when they trenched it they patted the divots against the sides of the tent. It looks good, but within a couple of hours water'll be running across the bottom of that tent like Peachtree Creek. It's going to be a long night, and that captain is going to be sleeping in the middle of a sponge."

"And Mack and Jack can get away with it by playing dumb ignorant enlisted men?" laughed Porter in admiration.

"You were right, Osborne. This is going to be an interesting war."

"Yep," said Porter. "Especially in the 816th General Hospital. Where some battle lines are being drawn that I had not really expected." After a pause, he added, "I didn't hear you tell them about the farting."

"After reviewing the situation, I decided that's not such an important issue after all."

Porter laughed again. "Now you're getting smart. Maybe you'll make sergeant after all."

They hunkered in their tent and peered through the end flaps at the veils of soft rain drifting across the skies.

"So this is Normandy," said Porter. "It's as gray as England and Scotland."

"This is it," echoed Otten. "You know, Osborne, I've figured out how to predict weather here."

"You have?"

"Yep. If you can see the hedgerows, it's fixing to rain. If you can't see them, then it is raining."

From the other end of the tent came a laugh and a burst of staccato words.

"What'd they say?" asked Porter helplessly as Mack and Jack crawled out of the tent.

"They said chow in thirty minutes. I'm damn glad to hear that; I was afraid they were going to forget to feed us. I can sure use something in my stomach."

They put on their wet shoes, donned their rain gear, and sloshed across the meadow toward the prominence that had been designated the central gathering area. A canvas fly identical to the one used on maneuvers at Camp Grant had been erected as a mess tent. They remembered the steaming cauldrons from that snowy landscape and hastened toward it. The lines moved rapidly before the mess sergeants, who were behind a counter. Porter extracted his mess gear from its canvas cover and assembled it, his canteen cup on the ready.

"I hope they've got hot chocolate," he said.

They had D-bars. One sergeant was handing them out like an experienced card player dealing a new deck. Porter looked at him in surprise. It was Mack. For once he understood what he was saying.

"One to a customer. Only one to a customer. Let's move along there."

The other sergeant was pouring water from a Jerry can and Porter recognized him also. The odor of chlorine was so strong it was almost palpable.

"Goddam, Jack" said Otten. "We're starving to death and you guys give us hard dry chocolate and a cold cup of halazone tea. How many of those tablets did you drop in that bucket? We could have done that good for ourselves. Have a heart, at least give us an extra D-bar."

Once again, Porter could not decipher the answer. "What'd he say?"

"Dammit, Osborne, what's wrong with your ears? He said he'd bring some extras back to the tent, and that they're setting up to give us hot breakfast in the morning, and that somebody has already put up latrine tents right across the lane, one for the officers and one for the enlisted men."

"Mustn't have any fraternizing, you know. Don't get them mixed up. How'd you like to hold a salute all the way through a crap?"

"If they don't feed us any better than this, we won't be able to take one," grumbled Otten. "All we'll need to wipe ourselves will be a whisk broom."

"Quit bitching," laughed Porter. "You see those hedgerows? That means it's fixing to rain. Let's head for the tent."

If anyone in the 816th General Hospital ever forgot the first night spent on French soil in the service of God and country, he was blessed with a healing memory. The damp, hard ground beneath them, the whisper of listing rain on the succulent roof a scant three feet above their heads, the water they had drunk to wash down their D-bars all merged into an irresistible urge to urinate at two-hour intervals. Some bigger bladders and more determined sleepers made it for three, but their slumber was fitful. Normandy was awash from above and below. The sounds of muttered fretting marked the hours.

"Dammit, Osborne, and you, too, Mack and Jack, point downhill or we might as well have stayed inside and pissed in our sleeping bags."

"You're getting closer to making sergeant every minute," murmured Porter.

At morning he stirred in his sleeping bag. "What's that fuss?"

"Somebody has found a bugle and somebody else has found somebody who can almost blow it. I think it's 'Assembly,' but the bugler is either hiccupping or blowing under water. Let's go."

"Line up!" directed the sergeant. "Don't worry about formation! Just line up for roll call and then we'll break for chow! Listen close because we don't have the roll in alphabetical order. When you hear your name, sound off!"

"Roll call? In this weather? How damn GI can you get?" protested Carter Otten.

"Discipline depends on organization and regimentation," comforted Porter. "It's bad enough to be out here but it would be horrible if the powers that be didn't know we are. Be thankful Col. Draughan is on the ball."

"Kostas!" he heard the sergeant yell.

"Here."

350

"Farbecker!"

There was not even a pause. "Here!" called a different voice.

"Osborne!"

"Here."

"Jewel!"

"Here."

At the finish, Porter sought out Kostas.

"What the hell's going on? You better get that name erased."

Kostas looked coolly at his left forefinger and replied. "Behold the fickle finger of fate. Yesterday it created a new human being and today I have breathed life into him. Let's see how long he will live and what he will accomplish."

"What? You're crazy."

"Not true, but that would probably help." He raised his eyebrows. "Do you have anything better to do?"

"Well, no. I guess not."

"Good. War is so boring. Since you were present at Farbecker's birth, I'll regard you as being in the inner circle, but the fewer who know him, the longer he will live."

"Gotcha. Long live Daniel D."

Farbecker could never have existed in a seasoned unit where the majority of officers, noncoms, and enlisted men knew each other; he could have flourished only in a group that was so unfamiliar with its members, so chary of intimacy, so unwilling to approach each other as individuals that privacy was guarded as a treasure. Porter later thought that the name of Daniel D. Farbecker would never have been accepted and placed on the permanent roll of the 816th General Hospital had its first sergeant not been named Milton P. Lagerpiel.

Accepted it was, however. Someone found paper, typewriter, and folding tables and a company office was soon established. Organization was once again asserted, albeit from a squad tent with a dirt floor in the middle of a Normandy cow pasture. The ritual of roll call opened the activities of each day, and Porter decided that a sergeant would as lief be caught without his stripes or his pants as be seen without his clipboard. They stood under wet gray skies every morning and bellowed "Here" when their names were called. Someone always answered for Farbecker, the inner circle being careful that the response came each morning from a different person and a different sector of the assembly, lest some diligent noncom associate the name with a specific face.

Otten's proclamation that they would move immediately to St. Lo proved false. After a week, boredom became a bigger problem than the lack of creature comforts. They were frequently warned that their bivouac was the only ground in the region cleared of mines and that anyone who strayed beyond the designated areas of safety would incur sudden death, dismemberment, and court-martial; the implication being that the latter was the more serious of the three.

Days went by. They fumed about the rain, the mud, the cramped and malodorous dampness of their pup tents. They marked the exclusivity of officers who by now were sheltered in squad tents erected by details of enlisted men and furnished with cots that rescued, as Jewel phrased it, "their high and mighty commissioned butts from the cold wet ground." The kitchen was still housed under a simple canvas fly, and the ground before it became a sucking, pulling quagmire comparable to the February cow lot of Porter Osborne's youth. Disgruntled soldiers lined up with mess gear in one hand to receive dehydrated potatoes or eggs and slices of Spam cooked so rapidly that the upturned edges cradled puddles of grease. The other hand grasped steaming canteen cups of coffee ladled from a garbage can mounted over a gas burner. They grumbled about the heavy mud that daily grew deeper in the chow line and threatened to tug the boots from their feet. Sherman R. Jewel, with both hands laden, reddened in outrage when the same pocked captain encountered him and snapped, "Aren't you going to salute a superior officer?"

"If you'll hold my mess kit and not spill any of it in this mud, I'll be glad to."

"That is not acceptable."

"Then come back in half an hour when I'm done eating and you can pick up your salute, sir."

"That's insubordination. What's your name?"

"Farbecker, Daniel D."

"I'll report you to your sergeant."

"Yes, sir."

A notice went up on the bulletin board that strict military courtesy was to be observed except in the living area of the enlisted men. It could be relaxed, however, in the vicinity of any work area if both hands were encumbered. The inner circle opined that the GI captain had encountered Regular Army Sgt. Lagerpiel and that a remnant of reason had prevailed. Respect for Lagerpiel mounted, nor was it mitigated by the separate announcement on the bulletin board that PFC Daniel D. Farbecker would report for KP duty on three successive shifts.

Kostas shrugged. "Compromise is essential to civilization. Lagerpiel did well. KP around here amounts to nothing more than opening cans and boiling water. Three of us will split the assignment."

"What?"

"Sure. You go for breakfast, I'll take noon, and Kragel can pull the evening shift. They're changing sergeants every meal anyhow; haven't you noticed? We don't want anybody to get a clear idea of what Daniel D. really looks like, do we?"

"What about Jewel? He's the one who ran his mouth and got us into this."

"That adds to the confusion in case anyone ever gets to comparing notes with the captain. The guilty must at all costs appear completely innocent."

"Have you ever read Lewis Carroll?"

"Do you think me illiterate? You can be the White Rabbit and try to decide if I'm the Hatter or the Jabberwock."

"Long live Daniel D.," said Porter.

"Precisely," agreed Kostas.

Porter tolerated inactivity as long as he could. On the day that they were issued a Jerry can of hot water, he hastened to his tent and bathed in his helmet.

"I don't believe my toes ever felt this good before in my whole life," he told Otten. "Cover me in case anybody looks for me in the next hour or two; I'm going to walk."

"You're crazy. You won't get past the guards at the gate. We might as well be in a goddam stockade."

"I'm not going close to the gate. I'm going to cut across the next pasture and hit that back road we can see over yonder when it's only fixing to rain."

"You're nuts. You know about the mines."

"So do these French farmers. They wouldn't have three cows loose in that pasture if it were mined. I've been watching them for a week, and they'd have been blown to smithereens before now if there were mines next door. I'm going to explore Normandy a little bit before I go stir-crazy."

"You'll get court-martialed if they catch you."

"I'll risk it. If you act stupid enough, a strange officer will believe anything you tell him."

"Well, if you're going, take some of those D-bars with you."

"For what?"

"In case you find something to buy, dumbass. You can trade. You sure as hell don't have any French money."

"What's to buy way out here?"

"Whatever you find. Liquor. Perfume. Pussy. Bring me some cheese if you can find some."

"No pussy?"

"I'll wait and shop for my own; I don't think you could handle that."

"I can hear it now. 'Little children, on D-plus one hundred and thirty your father went on a foraging mission in the midst of heavily mined enemy territory and procured emergency supplies for his comrade who professed a stronger preference for exotic food than he did for sex, a reversal of tastes on his part that raised the suspicion that he had suffered a complete personality reversal and might even be afflicted with a severe case of non-battle fatigue induced by cowering for all of his sleeping and most of his waking hours in a fetid pup tent cultivating mold and mildew.' Listen out for me, pardner, and if I'm not back by 10:30, send the sheriff 'cause it means trouble."

Otten sailed a boot at him. "I almost hope you don't come back. Don't forget the cheese."

Porter did not return for five hours.

"Where the hell have you been, you little bastard? I was about to decide you were dead."

"I'm not real sure where I've been. Anybody looking for me?"

"Naw. That New England snob you've been hob-nobbing with came by, but nobody else. Tell me where you've been."

"Well, I found a little town about three miles or so down the road, but I couldn't find a name for it. These people can understand my French but I can't understand theirs. I'd gone by several farm houses and, Otten, they have the cows right in the house with the people. You can smell the urine from the road. The people are all wearing big wooden shoes and they leave them at the door and go inside the house with felt slippers on. There's a big pile of apples in every barnyard along the road and chickens pecking around just like home. I didn't see any hogs, though."

"Had a real exciting time, didn't you, Osborne?"

"Well, yes, I did. It's all so different. When I got into the town it smelled better and the little yards were neat, and I found sort of a cafe or something that was open. The people are real friendly. One man gave me some cider to drink. They call it *seedrah*. And they call their shoes *les sabots du bois*. I had a real good time."

"Big deal."

"And I didn't forget you. Those D-bars are good as gold. I traded some of them for some black bread and a box of *fromage* that I'm not real sure about. It stinks to the high heavens, but you say that doesn't matter."

"Osborne, you're turning out to be OK after all. The worse cheese smells, the better it is to a real connoisseur. Hand it here!"

"It's pretty runny. Be sure you don't spill any in the tent or I might throw up. The cheese smells to me like somebody already has."

"Shut up, Osborne." He removed the lid of the little round wooden box. "This is good cheese."

Porter gagged.

"Good cheese," Otten reaffirmed. "What do you think you know?" He cut a piece of bread, smeared it with the faintly greenish cream from the box, and popped it into his mouth.

He chewed twice, his cheeks ballooned precipitously, and he crawled rapidly to the tent fly and spat. It had begun raining again, but Otten stood upright in the weather and looked backward at Porter in the tent.

"*Good* cheese," he repeated and sailed the box with all his might as far from their home away from home as he could. Then he crawled back and they laughed for at least ten minutes.

"Was it as good as the steak and kidney pie, Carter?"

"Not quite as subtle a flavor. The pie tasted like piss, the cheese tasted like shit."

"You really are a connoisseur, Otten."

"If you tell it, I'll kill you."

"I traded for something else. I had to give six D-bars for this." Porter reached into his raincoat and pulled out a corked bottle of liquid as clear and colorless as water.

"What is it?"

"Something they call Calvados. I think they make it from apples. This is real fresh."

"Very good, Osborne. You've raided a moonshine still. If that ain't rot-gut, I'll kiss your ass."

"Not with that cheese on your breath, you won't."

"Hand it here!" He pulled the cork, turned the bottle up for a tentative swallow, and shuddered.

"Does it taste as good as the cheese?" Porter ventured.

"Worse. But it burns real good, all the way from the top of your head plumb to your asshole. Let's see if Mack and Jack can get us some lemonade powder to cut it with. France is getting brighter by the minute."

Porter could no more drink the Calvados than he could eat the cheese, but Otten, Mack and Jack finished the bottle before bedtime. One of the bleary-eyed cooks, whom he assumed to be Mack, assured Porter the next morning while they were simultaneously pointing downhill in the pre-dawn camaraderie of burgeoning bladders that he would furnish an unlimited supply of D-bars if Porter would promise repetition of his bartering spree.

As the man shook himself before jerking his hips backward, he spoke slowly, "Ain't you the one I seen coming off KP the other day when I was coming on?"

"Pardon?" said Porter. "What did you say?"

"Was you on KP Tuesday?" the giant repeated carefully.

Porter nonchalantly buttoned his fly. "Not me, Jack. I've been a good boy."

"What's your name?"

"Pardon?"

"What is your name? I can't hardly never understand a fucking word you say."

"Osborne. Porter Osborne, Jr." His tone brightened. "See? I can understand you real good when you speak slowly like that. Let's grab another nap before roll call. You get me those D-bars and I'll see what I can do."

Porter sneaked out of camp the next day with his fatigues and his raincoat so laden that he waddled. He also left with the assurance that for the time being at least, the deception by Kostas was secure.

"I checked our rosters at the kitchen, and you was right. The one I seen was some fuckup named Farbecker what caught the duty for smarting off to some cock-sucking officer."

"Pardon?"

"I said, it wasn't you on KP I seen. It was some guy named Farbecker."

"Oh. I told you so, didn't I?"

"Sure as hell looked like you, though."

Porter spoke rapidly. "At times along life's way there arises an occasion when the appearance of innocence is greatly to be preferred over innocence itself; also there is more in heaven and earth than thine own judgment, Horatio."

"Huh? For Crissake, slow down. I didn't understand a mother-fucking word you said."

"I said all these bars of chocolate are great and I'm glad you brought some packets of instant coffee and the bars of soap and the Spam. I'll be back by dark. See you, Jack."

"I ain't named Jack."

"Pardon?"

"My name ain't Jack."

"Oh. What is it?"

"Miclazewski. Stanislas Miclazewski."

"Oh. Of course you're not Jack. You're Mack. Scuse me."

It was well after dark when Porter returned, but by good fortune the skies had cleared and he had been able to navigate by starshine. His tent mates were tumultuous in their welcome. Carter Otten was the most vocal.

"Where in the hell have you been this time, Osborne, and what in the hell took you so long? Do you realize that I didn't have the faintest idea where to come looking for you? I thought maybe you'd stepped on a mine or else had your goddam throat slit by some Frog, you sonofabitch."

"Otten! All these months and I never knew you cared!"

"Oh, kiss my ass. What'd you bring?"

"Yeh," said Mack. "What'd you bring?" Jack echoed them both.

"I'll have you know this has been a great afternoon. I've met the most nice folks and learned some more French and have even been inside one of those farm houses for a meal. The cow stall doesn't stink inside because they shovel it out twice a day; it's the compost pile at the corner of the house that you smell from the road. I felt like Heidi staying with her grandfather. Did you know that the French word for horse shit is *pomme de rue*? That means 'apple of the street.'"

"What'd he say?" queried Mack.

"He hasn't said a mumbling word that amounts to a flying fuck," said Otten. "What did you bring back, asshole?" He gave Porter a reprimanding push.

"Easy, there! I ought to be stamped 'Fragile. Handle With Care.' I'm as loaded as Ax-Handle Chambers's car going through Cross Roads Community in Brewton County, Georgia, and these bottles may break. I've been clanking so loud when I walk that coming across the pasture I got mistaken for a bell cow and had an escort all the way to the fence. Did you know the French call cows *les vaches*?"

By the time he unloaded his pockets, there were eight unlabeled bottles of Calvados lined up on his bed roll. Mack and Jack were ecstatic.

"Half and half, right? That's four bottles for me and four for you."

"You have the soul of a sharecropper, Mack. I know you furnished the seed and the fertilizer, but I furnished the mule and did all the work."

"Pardon?"

"I said, doesn't Jack get anything?"

"You're right. He's my buddy. I'll give him one."

"Well, Otten's my buddy. I'll give him one for worrying about me."

"I was not worried about you."

"You want the liquor or not?"

"Hell, yeah. Long as I don't have to eat cheese with it."

"You were worried."

"Maybe a little. Gimme the bottle."

Porter eyed him innocently. "In a minute. First I want to tell you about this little old lady feeding me. She lives in one of those little houses with a wall out front, and when I went by she was putting her cow in the house. She had on a black dress and a white apron and a red scarf on her head and was so tiny she looked like that story about a redheaded woodpecker in the third-grade *Elson Reader*. Even her little legs were birdy; her stockings were wrinkled and they looked like toothpicks in those big wooden shoes. I asked her if she'd like some chocolate, and she invited me in, and of course, I'd been dying to see inside one of those houses anyhow. I gave her a bar of GI soap and some coffee. She's not had any coffee for three years. They've been grinding up acorns instead. I gave her all the coffee I had and she about had a hissy fit."

"What's he saying?" interrupted Mack.

"Nothing yet," laughed Otten. "I'll let you know."

Porter sniffed. "Well, I won't bore you bastards with details, if that's the way you feel about it. She's a poor widow and we got to visiting, and I milked the cow for her while she cooked the best meat and potatoes I ever put in my mouth. I hadn't milked a cow in years, but I still remember how. Do you know how they say a blessing over here? They make a cross on the loaf of bread with the knife before they cut it. I was trying to learn French and kept asking what the meat was and she kept saying *lapin* and I thought she was saying *la pain*, which

358

means 'bread,' and we got to yelling at each other about bread and meat till she finally carried me out back and showed me her rabbit pen. *Lapin* is French for 'rabbit.' I had a good time drinking fresh milk, which they call *lait*, and eating *Monsieur Lapin* and trying to tell Granny about B'rer Rabbit back in Georgia."

"Did he say he got laid?" Mack asked.

"Not unless he tipped Granny up," whooped Otten. "You can't ever tell what this weird little bastard is up to. I'll let you know."

"Well, she helped me get the Calvados and says she can get us all we want if we've got coffee and lard to trade. Also tobacco. She doesn't smoke herself but says she can get *beaucoup des sous* for American cigarettes."

"Hey, Mack, nothing happened yet," called Otten. "For God's sake, give me that bottle, Osborne, and let's all take a drink."

Porter passed the bottle over. "'Drink' is *buvez*, and do you know how they say 'I'm hungry'? *J'ai faim*, which really translates out 'I have hunger'."

"Aw, shut up. We ain't interested in that. You have to talk too funny if you're going to speak French."

"He speaks French?" asked Mack.

"I can cull cheese and find calvados," rejoined Porter.

"Now who's a connoisseur?" laughed Otten. He held his bottle up. "Here's to France."

"*La belle France*," said Porter, "*et aussi nous bouvons a la Normandie*."

"Son of a bitch," said Mack. "He does speak French."

Thus, thought Porter, myths are born.

He never saw Granny again. He tried but he was intercepted by a corporal in a Jeep shortly after he leaped a soggy ditch onto the road, his pockets stuffed with cigarettes.

"Where you think you're going, soldier?

"Just walking."

"What outfit you with?"

"816th General Hospital."

"How the hell you get way back here?"

"Through that pasture right there."

"Don't you know about mines?"

"Ain't no mines where there's cows."

"You got a pass?"

"A pass? Just to go to walk?" Porter let his mouth gape and tried to sound puzzled.

"Hell, yeah. Any time you off post you supposed to have a pass. Else you AWOL."

"Golly, I sure wouldn't want to be AWOL. That's bad. I sure thank you for telling me. I'll go right on back."

"I'd take you, but I'm on an errand for the captain. Some sergeant told him there was a place down this road you can buy brandy."

"I'm sure much obliged to you for telling me about AWOL. I'll get right on back."

"Watch out for mines."

"Oh, I will."

"Wait a minute. What's your name?"

Without a moment's hesitation, Porter widened his eyes and identified himself. "Farbecker, Daniel D."

"How do you spell it?"

"D-A-N-I-E-L."

"Are you stupid? I mean your last name."

"Oh. Scuse me. F-A-R-B-E-C-K-E-R."

"Yeah. I think I heard your name at roll call. You watch out for them mines."

"The ass-kissing son of a bitch reported me," Porter fumed to Kostas as they read on the bulletin board a notice that anyone leaving the confines of the bivouac area without a pass, except on official business, would be absent without leave. Beneath that proclamation was the assignment of Daniel D. Farbecker to latrine duty for the following day. "What are we going to do?"

"No problem. Summon your friend Jewel. It's his turn."

It took some persuasion to elicit Sherman Roger Jewel's cooperation.

"What do you care? You've nothing else to do but lie on your ass in your tent and listen to it rain."

"Latrine duty can't amount to much out here, anyhow. There are no duckboards to wash and no running water. It probably doesn't amount to anything except being sure there's dry toilet paper in the cans on the benches."

"You really have no choice," Kostas pointed out. "We covered for you, and Capt. Scarface Smith would certainly recognize you if Farbecker failed to show up for latrine duty and it came to his attention. We just need to avoid positive identification."

He and Porter were never able to convince Jewel that they had been genuinely ignorant of the details of latrine duty in Normandy. When next they encountered him, his face had reddened in rage to match his hair.

"I'm through with both of you! I'm through with Farbecker! I'm through with the whole goddam United States Army and this shit-sucking, godforsaken hospital in particular!"

"What's bugging you, Roger?"

"You're bugging me, that's what! You knew what they were going to make me do and you set me up!"

"Calm down. I don't know what you're talking about. Tell me."

"You ever heard of 'honey buckets'?"

"No."

"Well, I spent the morning loading honey buckets on the back of a truck and then riding with them till we got to a field where we could empty them, scared to death the dumb goddam driver was going to hit a bump any minute and slosh them all over me."

"What's a honey bucket? What ... Oh, no, Roger, you mean those ten-gallon galvanized buckets under the holes in the latrine benches? Oh, no. Honest to God, I didn't know ... Why do they call them honey buckets? Never mind, I can imagine. I'm sorry, Roger. Honest I am."

"You damn well better be! I'm worn out with this Farbecker crap. I've a good notion to go to Lagerpiel and tell him the whole story."

Porter tried to imitate the insouciance of Kostas, although he could not affect the Boston accent. "Sherman Roger Jewel, the man who deliberately floated the records of the 816th General Hospital into the English Channel at Omaha Beach on D plus 106? How would Capt. Smith and Col. Draughan react to that information, I wonder?"

Jewel's chin jutted out so far that his lower teeth were visible. "You wouldn't."

Porter curled his fingers in and studied his nails. "Don't bet on it."

Sherman R. Jewel swallowed audibly and then said resolutely, "In that case, long live Daniel D. Farbecker."

"Amen," said Porter. "Come on over to my tent. I've got a bottle I want to give you for outstanding performance over and beyond the call of duty." He sniffed. "You didn't get any honey on you, did you?"

Later that day Porter crouched in his tent and composed a dutiful letter to his father.

"Sorry I haven't written sooner, but things have been a little confusing. I'm not allowed to tell where we are, which is just as well because I'm not real sure myself. I can tell you that I'm safe and occasionally I'm dry.

I can also tell you that I'm still learning a lot. Every day. Everywhere I turn. Some day I will get the chance to fill you in. Give my love to everybody and keep plenty for yourself.

Sambo

P.S. One of the things I am learning is that you do not have to be an officer or noncom to lead. I'll discuss that with you, too. A lot of it depends on what the leader has in mind."

*"For that which was our trouble comes again
out of the west."*

31 **b**y the time the 816th General Hospital moved in field-hardened convoy from its muddy bivouac area, the Allies had invaded the Netherlands, the Russians had penetrated Czechoslovakia, and the Warsaw Resistance Army had surrendered to the Germans. These events, however, were, to his self-acknowledged shame, of less concern to Porter Osborne, Jr., than whether he might ever again get an all over bath, sleep in a bed, or wash his clothes in something besides a helmet. In addition, there had been no mail call and he hungered for news from home. He felt that in this foreign land and in the midst of these strange comrades, he was in desperate need of reaffirmation of identity. He knew who he was right enough, but no one else did, and he had a growing suspicion that no one cared.

He rode near the tail gate of a covered truck next to Sherman Roger Jewel as they moved deeper into Normandy. Try as they would, they could see no building along their route through Caen that was not shambles; the rubble of ruined masonry outlined the streets as they rumbled through. They were slack-jawed with wonder when they approached St. Lo. The trees stood in splintered shards and the little tiled roadside shrines were pocked by bullet scars. A church in the town was missing its roof. Nearby stood the remains of a tower, the gaping absence of an entire wall bleak reminder that this town had not been given over lightly but had been wrested from the Germans in cataclysm. Porter became keenly aware that beneath the bombs and the shells and the machine guns and tanks that had left this devastated real estate lay the true currency of war, and that this place short weeks before had been purchased by shattered bone and coursing blood and the screams of dying men. He removed his helmet.

"What the hell you doing?" growled Jewel. "That fucking sergeant catch you riding bareheaded, he'll clean your ass from here to kingdom come and have you toting honey buckets. You better put that helmet back on your head."

"I will in a minute; this is hallowed ground."

"You're so weird, Osborne, that your goddam head may be hallowed next. See if I care."

"Look after Number One. Right, Jewel?"

"Fucking aye."

"No matter how many guys died here so that we can ride through without getting shot?"

"That's their job. No big deal." He looked around. "What I can't figure out after getting over here is what the hell we're fighting about anyhow. This is the most godforsaken country I ever saw, and who the hell wants it? The Germans can have it."

"'Ours not to reason why,
Ours but to do or die.
Into the valley of death rode the six hundred.'

Bickety-bickety-bick."

"Will you put your goddam helmet on and shut up?"

Porter reflected that if he shut his eyes he would be hard put to distinguish between Carter Otten and Rufus Jewel. Of a sudden, Jewel broke the silence.

"Did Farbecker get on one of the trucks?"

"Fucking aye," said Porter.

"Good. We don't want to lose old Daniel D."

The 816th General Hospital first became a functioning unit in an expanse of cow pasture well westward of St. Lo near a small town called Isigny, soon dubbed Easy Knee by the linguistically handicapped but phonetically nimble Americans. Col. Draughan appeared everywhere; beaming, strutting, swaggering. His presence spurred his troops to concerted and dedicated effort, and the hospital in tents took form overnight.

A quadrangle of war tents faced each other with Medical, Surgical, and Orthopedic designation. Three war tents in combination became the operating suite. Two more downhill from the wards were the enlisted men's mess and kitchen. A single tent beyond the common kitchen served as the officers' mess. Just as the swarms of enlisted men finished erecting their own quarters, a weak and watery sun shone forth. Porter regarded it as a good omen, only slightly more radiant than the countenance of Col. Draughan as he surveyed his new domain, pointing out one moment with his cigar some item on the site plan to Sgt. Lagerpiel and the next strutting through work details tossing out right and left an affable, "Good job. Good job."

Porter noted Capt. Smith striding with purpose, carrying two signs under his arm. He appropriated a hapless private and within minutes of construction of the 816th General Hospital, one sign was pounded into the soggy sub-soil. "Officers' Quarters," it announced.

The other was posted before the nurses' tents. Its message was terse and authoritative. "Off Limits," it proclaimed.

"Son of a bitch,' said Carter Otten.

"Is Capt. Smith a doctor or just an officer?" asked Porter.

Kostas was standing nearby. "I understand that he was a general surgeon before the war but had his operating privileges suspended. He and Col. Draughan are reputed to have known each other in civilian life, and he is second-in-command in this outfit. To answer your question, he is both a doctor and an officer, but not an exemplary manifestation of either."

Porter noted with admiration the absence of any profanity in the New England voice. "Well, there's nothing about him that makes me want to be either."

Kostas raised an eyebrow. "Who would?"

"Well, I did," Porter defended. "Want to be a doctor, that is. I still may do that when the war is over. I've never wanted to be an officer."

"I should hope not," replied Kostas.

"My father was an officer. In World War I," Porter felt moved to confide.

"No need to apologize. You can't help it."

Porter smiled because he felt he was supposed to. "He was wounded twice and all his men loved him. They gave him a scroll at a reunion in Raleigh, North Carolina, one time that says it all. We have it framed and on the wall in our parlor." He swallowed. "He's been wanting me to be an officer ever since I got in the Army."

"That's not surprising." The tone was aloof. "You mustn't take it personally. Caste systems historically tend to perpetuate themselves."

"Caste systems?"

"Certainly. Look at this compound. There are enough people here to populate a village. We have the ruling class, its harem, the solid noncommissioned burghers and then the peasants. Of course your father wanted you to be an officer."

"Cut the crap and let's get through so we can go to chow and mail call," said Carter.

"Was your father an officer?" Kostas asked Otten.

"No. He was a doctor." Otten snugged a rope around a tent peg. "He has always wanted me to be one, too."

Kostas raised an eyebrow. "You see?"

Porter decided he did not want to consider all the ramifications unfolding before him. "*C'est la vie*," he said. "*Enfin, c'est la guerre*." He asked Kostas with considerable composure, "What does your daddy do?"

"He makes candy and sells it."

"And?"

"He wants me to get an education. In the United States of America, a caste system does not have to be self-perpetuating."

"Oh," said Porter Osborne.

"America has already changed history, or rather the direction in which history was going. Our experiment with democracy may well turn out to be far better than its prototype in Greece. Only time will tell."

"Oh," repeated Porter innanely. "Let's go to chow."

"Right," said Otten. "I'm not going to forget, though, how that old son of a bitch had the nurses posted off-limits before we ate or had mail call." He looked over his shoulder as they left Kostas. "God, Osborne, you can pick up the strangest characters. Where'd you find that blue-bellied Yankee that sounds like he went to Harvard?"

"Same place you found Mack and Jack. And he went to Brown. I asked."

"Where the fuck is that?"

"I don't know. He sounded like everybody was supposed to know; so I didn't ask." He looked at Otten. "Have you noticed that he doesn't cuss? That's a refreshing change."

"Have you noticed that he talks like a history professor? Caste system, democracy, Greece, America, prototypes, yesterday's bowel movement. We're going to miss chow if we don't get the lead out our ass."

They did not miss chow. As the colonel had promised, it was hot. It also consisted of beef stew with real onions in it. They were too elated to complain about the dehydrated potatoes or the glutinous tapioca pudding.

"That Col. Draughan is a real leader and a great officer," enthused Porter. "He looks after his men ahead of anyone else."

"Is that so?" said Otten. "If you ain't going to touch that pudding, give it to me."

"Sure. I know it's better than cheese, but I'm full."

Mail call was unforgettable. They had eaten, cleaned their mess kits, and were swinging them dry when the whistle sounded and the stampede toward Lagerpiel's office ensued. Everyone had mail. It had taken weeks to catch up to them and there were even rumors that Col. Draughan had sent a special envoy by Jeep to Cherbourg to fetch it, but mail from home had finally arrived. Jubilation was boundless. A tranquility settled over the tents that was never repeated.

Porter had twenty-one letters from his mother, a dozen from his three sisters, and two from his father. He sat on the edge of his cot in the big tent that housed the enlisted men from the operating room and forgot his surroundings and the multitude of odd new acquaintances who formed the community to which he was currently committed. For an hour he was transported back to Brewton County, Georgia, his consciousness suffused with nostalgia.

Otten was seated on his cot across the dirt aisle, similarly occupied. His bundle of mail was smaller.

"Hey, Carter, my older sister had her baby. It's a girl. Want to see her picture? I can't believe all that's going on and I missed it."

"Let me see the picture. Griffin has already married Miss Margaret and they had a big reception at the Driving Club. I can't believe I missed all that. Want to see a snapshot of them?"

"Sure. Pretty bride."

"Pretty baby."

"Thanks."

Porter was feeling very friendly toward Carter Otten, now the only link to his past and not such a bad egg after all.

"My dad's letters are one page long and pretty terse, but I've never known him to write any personal letters before. He says my dog is doing fine."

"I know what you mean. My dad doesn't write at all. Your dog's that Doberman that goddam Neuroanatomy professor gave you, isn't it?"

"Yep. He doesn't bark but he'll eat your ass off."

"That figures. Look who raised him."

"Carter."

"What?"

"You remember that guitar player I met at the USO in New York?"

"You mean old Mother Russia with the mascara and pancaked face who was so hot for your body on the dance floor? Sure. Why?"

"Well, I have six letters from her and a whole bunch of pictures."

"Lemme see. God, I'd never have recognized her. These must have been made ten years and fifteen pounds ago. Look at those legs. Look at those tits. Hell, Osborne, these are publicity glossies that were made in a studio, and she's written across every one of them. 'To my darling Porter, with one thousand kisses, Maria Nirova.' My God, Osborne, you've landed a pin-up girl. Look at this one with the skirt slit up to her ass holding two guitars. 'Ivan and Petro sing always of Maria's love for Porter.' Hell, if all I had to go by were these pictures and didn't remember what she looked like in the living flesh, I'd swear she was a beautiful woman. Look at this one where she's looking back over her shoulder. 'To my own *Babouschka*, who is definitely not a cold fish,' And here's one with a fucking rose between her teeth. This ain't real. Hot damn, Osborne, you've turned from a country Georgia boy into a real live sophisticated cocksman." He exploded into laughter.

"I have not any such thing. Get serious for a minute, Carter."

"It's going to take longer than a minute."

"Carter."

"What?"

"Quit laughing and listen to me. In her first letter she talks about us getting married. By the sixth she's talking like it's a settled fact and has already told her friends. Quit rolling on that damn cot and kicking your heels like a three-year-old. What am I going to do?"

Carter Otten wiped his eyes. "I'll write her a note and tell her you were killed by a German sniper at Omaha Beach."

"She'll know better than that. D plus one hundred and six? She can count, Otten."

"I'll tell her you were strangled in your tent in Normandy by a drunk Hungarian cook who mistook you for a French pig and fixed you for supper."

"Otten, get serious."

"I'll tell her you were court-martialed and executed by rifle fire at sunrise under orders of Capt. Smith for failure to salute in the chow line."

"Now that might be credible. If you leave out the part about the sunrise. Nobody who's been to Normandy would believe they ever have one." He unwillingly also began laughing. Suddenly he stopped. "Otten."

"What?"

"Why are you hell-bent on killing me off in all those excuses? You son of a bitch."

"You want to marry that Russian broad? Believe me, Osborne, there are some things worse than dying. Give me those pictures; I'm going to pin them on the side of the tent."

"Over my dead body, you will."

"Now who's killing you off?"

They laughed and slapped each other on the back.

They had cots now on which to sleep, a permanent kitchen with rough tables at which to eat, capacious tents for shelter, a detail of German prisoners under guard who daily came on trucks called "honey wagons" to attend the latrines. To top the list of blessings, the sun shone forth for several days and the earth dried out a little. Indian Summer had not bypassed Normandy after all. Morale in the 816th General Hospital was high as they settled in and began receiving and treating patients.

Activity in the Operating Room required so much concentration that days went by before Porter encountered Kostas.

"Whatever became of Daniel D. Farbecker?"

"He's doing very well since he got over the sulks about being the only man in the outfit who didn't get any mail from home. I'm thinking of having some people I know write him."

"I saw on the bulletin board that he's been assigned to night duty on the Orthopedic ward. There must have been hell to pay when he didn't show up for work."

"Are you kidding? Daniel D. would never miss work. You think he's some kind of gold brick or something? He's the only enlisted man on Orthopedics at night right now. They're not very busy, and all he has to do is pass out a few urinals and sleeping pills and then goof off and run errands for the nurse the rest of the night."

"Stevens P. Kostas, do you mean you're working on your medical ward all day and then running over to the Orthopedic tent every night?"

"Certainly not. What do you take me for? An eager beaver? We all get one day a week off, right? Nobody's permitted to leave the compound, and so all you can do on your day off is sit in your tent and write letters or read, right? All I do is keep a secret little Farbecker roster and assign a man to Orthopedics on the night before his day off. It's very simple, really. A little organizational ability, a little imagination, a little pressure here and there, a dash of *sang-froid*, and there you are. Daniel D. lives and is doing well."

"How many guys know about him?"

"Eight, in addition to you and me."

"Ten people? That's not a secret anymore. That's a conspiracy. Or at the very least a fraternity. Aren't you afraid it'll get out?"

"Absolutely not. The eight boys besides you and Rufus Jewel who know about it are all Wafflebacks. They'd die before they'd tell."

"Wafflebacks? What the hell is that?"

"The Wafflebacks, I'll have you know, are the inner circle of the inner circle. The rococo of the rococo."

"Cut that elitist crap, Kostas. What are you talking about?

"There were eight of us crammed in a broom closet coming over on the *Queen Mary*. It was hot as blazes down there and we all went without shirts. Some idiot of a sergeant came by and got extremely annoyed because we were lying on our bunks all day and made us roll up the mattresses every morning. Therefore, as soon as he would leave, we'd lie on the naked springs all day, which left the print of the springs on our backs. We named ourselves the Wafflebacks and became blood brothers."

"And what's the purpose of this group?"

"To do our duty for God and for country and to uphold the Waffleback rules."

"Which are?"

"The first one is live and let live."

"That's all?"

"Oh, no. The second one is to recognize the old Army runaround whenever we see it and not be impressed by it. And to look at all officers, both commissioned and noncommissioned, and see what we would think of them as civilians. After all, this is a citizens' Army."

"Are there any other rules?"

"Yes, a third, but it's phrased rather crudely. One of our members is an Irishman from the lower Bronx who's had two years as an English major at Columbia, and he formulated it."

"Well, quit apologizing. What is it?"

"You dick me now, I'll get you with the big one later."

Porter grinned. "Sounds like my kind of group. That's a variant of Sherman Jewel's 'Look out for Number One.' By the way, if you have any problem with Jewel, let me know. I can apply a little pressure there."

"Problem?" Kostas raised an eyebrow. "That cynic from Commerce, Georgia, has become a pussy cat. The night nurse on Orthopedics with him comes from Iowa, and they sing hymns with each other all night when they're not working."

"Better not let Capt. Smith catch them. That's fraternizing."

"Not at all. It's harmonizing. They're really quite good, if you have a taste for that kind of music."

"Have the nurses tumbled to Farbecker's identity?"

"Heavens, no. If one inquires, we just tell her Farbecker's sick and we're a substitute. Nobody knows very many people in this unit yet."

"What about the doctor?"

"He's not a doctor. He's an Orthopedic Surgeon, and all he cares about is getting through rounds and not being called out from the Officers' Club after hours. He addresses all enlisted men as 'you' and has never been known to look one in the eye."

"Come on, Kostas. Orthopedic Surgeons are very highly trained doctors."

"You're the one who was asking if Capt. Smith was a doctor or just an officer, aren't you? Well, I work with a real doctor. He's an internist from Oklahoma who stays up all night if somebody needs him. He's not the least bit impressed with all this military hierarchy, even if he is a major. He told me that a good rule of thumb in medical school is that if you review the lower third of the group of guys who wind up in surgical residencies, those who can bench-press two hundred pounds go into Orthopedics and the rest into Ob-Gyn."

"Now that," laughed Porter, "is what I would call the inner circle of the inner circle. What's his name?"

"Pierce. Maj. Bartholomew Pierce. The nurses call him Buster and would die for him. So would all of us."

"Well, I haven't run into one like that in the operating room yet. I've got to go. Tell Farbecker if he needs a substitute, I'll be available."

"I'll tell him, but the Wafflebacks have the situation well in hand."

"I'll look forward to meeting them," said Porter.

"All in good time," responded Kostas. "But you can never be one."

"*C'est la vie*," smiled Porter. "Look out for Number One. Long live the rococo of the rococo, whatever the hell that is."

While Daniel D. Farbecker, the cherished ward of the Waf-flebacks, appeared nightly and as unobtrusively as possible in the guise of a corpsman on Orthopedics, Porter Osborne and Carter Otten worked efficiently and at top speed in the newly organized Operating Room.

"Hit it hard right at first, Osborne, and let's establish a reputation for excellence with these doctors and nurses that will live forever. We'll just step in there and razzle-dazzle them with superior intelligence, skill, and attitude till they're charmed right out of their tree. I ought to be a corporal in a month and a sergeant by Christmas."

"Carter, I don't mind working hard. In fact, if I'm going to be anywhere I'd rather be working than lolling around and goofing off. Nothing wears me out more than waiting; I'd rather be busy. But I still don't understand why you're so gung-ho on getting promoted. I haven't yet met a sergeant I regard as any sort of ideal."

"Like I said, stupid, it means more money."

"And like I said, where are you planning on spending it? We're confined to post."

"Listen, you goddam, fucked-up dickhead. What about recognition for endeavor and accomplishment? That's what those stripes mean."

"'Virtue is its own reward,'" quoted Porter. "But you may be right. You're talking like a sergeant already. A Yankee sergeant. Lots of luck."

"Recognition is what I want, by God! When I'm a sergeant, everybody will know who I am."

Porter looked at him and spoke softly. "Except you."

"Now what the hell is that supposed to mean, O cryptic and poetic sage?"

"Just exactly what it says, Carter Otten. You don't know who you are. I'm about to decide that I know you better than you know yourself. Even on much shorter acquaintance. In the first place, what you're talking about accomplishing will require some major-league dedicated ass-kissing, and you ain't got an ass-kissing gene in your make-up. They were all displaced at birth by your arrogant genes. You won't be in that Operating Room a week before you're telling some captain what he did wrong.

"In the second place, it would require some down-home politicking and maneuvering, for which you are totally unqualified. You were born an emperor maybe, but you're a piss-poor politician. The officer in charge is not going to recommend you for a promotion until your supervising NCO does, and you can just forget that step."

"Why?"

"Because that's Sgt. Oliver Crowder, and in case you haven't noticed it, Carter Otten, he hates our guts already."

"By God, we're the best men he's got."

"That may be part of the problem. Remember what you told me at Camp Grant when we made a hundred on that quiz? We're a threat to him. He's jealous."

"Bullshit. There's no way we could bounce him out of his job. Why should he be jealous?"

"Because of the caste system Kostas was talking about."

"Hell, he's on top. He's above us."

"Bullshit yourself. He may out rank us, but he knows that we're really on top."

"Why do you say that?"

"Because we're above him back home and he'll never escape that. We're smarter, younger, better-looking, but above all we're better educated. I'll bet you a dollar there were ten kids in his family and that his daddy moved all over Arkansas from one farm to another and never owned a foot of land himself. I'll bet you that Oliver Crowder dropped out of school in the seventh grade to pick cotton and that being a staff sergeant in the United States Army is higher than he ever thought he'd climb. He hates us because we're gentry and he's gully-dirt po' white trash."

"Hell, I'd never hold that against him."

"Nor would I. I'd be proud of him for getting this far, if he'd let me, but he'll look at us and say if his paw had had the money he'd have been able to do better his own self. He won't forgive himself, and you can be sure that he won't forgive us. You watch. Let me see you politic your way around Sgt. Crowder and then kiss enough magnificent officer ass to get promoted. Otten, you think you want something when you look at it on the surface, but you won't have the dedication for the long haul, I promise you. I think that's what happened to you in med school. You'll never make sergeant as long as you're in this outfit. If you do, I'll be the first to congratulate you. Now do you see why I say you don't know who you are?"

"I hear a lot of philosophical drivel, smart-ass. Do you think you know who you are?"

"You're mighty right I do."

"Osborne, do you realize you're a snob? I don't know what about, but you're a goddam snob."

"Of course I realize it. And I know what about."

"Well, I'm not! I'm going to bust my ass, and Crowder and the captain won't dare overlook me for promotion! Who do they think they are?"

"You see what I mean? That's arrogance, not politics. It's not even diplomacy. It's worthy of Coriolanus, but it won't get you anywhere. 'They have ears and they hear not,'" He laughed and gave Otten a Griffin Calhoun punch. "Ain't that right, Sport? What? What! Let's go razzle and dazzle those officers and nurses with our superior intelligence, wit, and charm. Way to go, boy! Right! What? What!"

Otten laughed. "You kiss my ass, Osborne!"

"Might as well. You're going to be so busy at it yourself, yours will be in convenient position. If you'll take Crowder's, I'll take yours. Any day."

"Who the fuck is Coriolanus?"

"Was, Carter. He was a soldier, too. But he was also an officer. Among other things he was right."

The hospital was too far removed from Patton's advances to receive many fresh wounds and injuries, but there was a huge census of soldiers requiring rehabilitation and nonemergency surgery. They came in a steady stream of box-like ambulances rolling daily into the compound to deposit patients from all over the western sector of France. Col. Draughan's outfit quickly established a reputation for excellence of medical care, in large part because of the speed and efficiency with which his Operating Room functioned. They worked furiously at their tasks. Otten goaded and pushed the other corpsmen to follow his example, proving himself a leader worthy of emulation from below and accolade from above. He astutely never mentioned promotion. He worked harder, scowled and muttered to himself as he rushed to and fro. Sgt. Crowder watched with suspicion but he never broached the subject of promotion either.

The OR was housed in dark canvas, and even the surgical lights, fed by a special generator, seemed weak and dim in the cave-like space between dirt floor and olive green ceiling. Responsive to the grumblings of her surgeons, the chief nurse and the Operating Room supervisor sought the condescending approval of Capt. Ballas, the detached, pipe-smoking Anesthesiologist from New England who was chief officer of the Operating Room. With his assent she requisitioned extra sheets, and the enlisted men draped them as a double ceiling all along the two war tents that contained the actual operating cubicles. They were festooned, Porter thought, like ornamentation in medieval tournaments, and they billowed with every breeze, but they reflected light efficiently and raised the mood of everyone.

The corpsmen were everywhere, always under the supervising eyes of nurses and the dour Sgt. Crowder. They wrapped drapes, instruments and sponges for specific operations and then autoclaved them in the cubicle set aside for sterilizing. They scrubbed dirtied instruments with green soap and short-bristled brushes until the metal in them should have thinned. They emptied buckets of bloodied sponges after each operation. They cleansed the operating tables and changed the sheets on them between surgeries. They raced to the wards to bring patients on litters at their appointed time on the schedule. They washed rubber gloves by the hundreds, turned them, washed them again, dried them on racks and then powdered them, folded down the cuffs, inserted them into cloth pockets and autoclaved them.

The nurses were as busy and overworked as the corpsmen. Their chief function was to scrub on operations, sometimes even as first assistant, smoothly anticipating the next step in each procedure and slapping the appropriate instrument into the outstretched palm of the surgeon. They bustled furiously around when they functioned as circulators, often attending two or three operating cubicles simultaneously. They rushed to obey orders from the doctors and at the same time were charged with supervising the activities of the enlisted men, taking care that none of them violated sterile technique or otherwise strayed from protocol. They could be compared to angels, hovering well below the throne of the Almighty themselves, but constantly directing earthly activities far beneath either the concern or attention of Godhead. No one in the world could have manifested more professional dedication, Porter thought, than the Operating Room nurses in the 816th General Hospital; he strove to follow their lead and earn their approbation. The surgeons were as aloof as minor gods but the nurses did not seem to be aware of their own commissioned condition. They had work to do attending patients and placating doctors, and they were absorbed in those duties. And in that order.

The surgeons also worked hard, but it was in spurts. Between cases they sat in the back tent drinking coffee and smoking cigarettes. The doctors chafed and grumbled because their schedules did not move faster.

"Waiting is always harder than working. We could handle twice the case load we have if we had more nurses," Maj. Emmons was heard to complain.

Capt. Ballas poured condensed milk into his canteen cup of coffee. "They're not to be found, Jim. I've requested them but there are just no more nurses to be spared in the whole ETO. You'll have to be patient and carry on with the status quo."

Thirty minutes later Porter overheard Carter Otten as he industriously assembled laparotomy packs and prepared them for sterilizing. "Captain, I couldn't help hearing what Maj. Emmons said, and I have an idea."

"What's that, Otten?"

"POW's, sir."

"POW's? Prisoners of war?"

"Yes, sir. I know there's a stockade somewhere around here because they bring a truckload of Germans every day on the honey wagons. If they would bring in German prisoners to help with the scut work here — like carrying litters, emptying kick buckets, changing sheets and things like that — it would free us up to work as advanced surgical technicians. That's what all of us have been trained to do, you know. We could circulate and scrub, always under your supervision, of course, and only on the less complicated cases until you're sure of our competence. We did all of that back at Lawson General Hospital in the States; that's part of our training. They're obliged to have our counterparts in the German army, and it's a shame not to pull them out and use free labor if it's available."

"Hmmm," said the captain and blew a puff of pipe smoke reflectively into his coffee.

"That way you'd be utilizing your noncoms to the max, and we'd catch up with the back load of cases we have."

"I don't know about that, Otten."

"The noncoms wouldn't be replacing the nurses, Captain. We'd just be an extension of them."

"I'll think about that."

"We noncoms will do anything you say, Captain, but we've got the capabilities. It's a shame to waste noncom potential on little piddling chores that anybody who can walk upright and count to three could be doing."

"Don't say anything about this to anyone else, Otten, and I'll think about it."

Three days later, six German prisoners were delivered to the operating tent and were utilized exactly as Carter Otten had suggested.

"Hot ziggety goddam," he chortled to Osborne. "You laughed at me."

"I'm not laughing. I told you a week wouldn't be out before you'd be telling some captain what to do."

"Yeah, but he's doing it! I'll be a sergeant by Christmas."

"Good strategy, Otten, but poor politics."

"What do you mean?"

"You should have gone through Crowder and let him present it to Capt. Ballas. That way Crowder would have looked good and felt in control and have been more inclined to recommend you for promotion. All he's going to do now is look on you as competition, and he's maneuvered around in this man's Army a lot longer than both of us put together. I thought if you said 'noncom' one more time to Ballas I'd laugh out loud."

"Well, I want the son of a bitch to know that we expect to be promoted. He's so blind you have to rub his nose in something before he can see it."

"I still say you shouldn't have by-passed Crowder."

"Dammit, Osborne, I'm good. I'm good and I'm intelligent. I don't have to go through the Virgin Mary to approach God the Father. I ain't no Catholic."

"You ain't no noncommissioned officer either. Lots of luck," laughed Porter.

Three days later Col. Otto Draughan himself strutted through the Operating Room, flanked by Capt. Scarface Smith. The colonel held an unlit cigar, the captain held a clipboard. They arrived in the work room after a hectic day of surgery. The cases had all been finished ahead of schedule, the surgeons had departed, the nurses and corpsmen were busily preparing for the morrow. Otten was painstakingly patching rubber gloves that were salvageable and Osborne was sharpening needles.

"Ten-shun!" bellowed Sgt. Crowder, his back ramrod straight, his arms rigid at his sides.

"At ease, at ease," beamed Col. Draughan. "Capt. Ballas, I came by to tell you that requesting prisoners of war to work in appropriate situations was a master stroke. I've already been commended for it at headquarters and we're going to use them all over the entire hospital. God knows they're in plentiful supply. Headquarters, mind you. Commended at headquarters. I believe in giving credit where credit is due. Yes, I do. I do indeed. How did you come up with the idea?"

"Observation and analysis of the situation, sir, made it obvious. I did no more than my duty."

"Commendable, Ballas, commendable. You men can take pride in the fact that your unit in the last week has topped the record for the number of surgical cases completed per day for the entire ETO. I'll see that Smith gets this on your record, Ballas."

When they left for chow, Porter was not laughing. Neither was Carter. "Goddam, goddam, goddam," he said. They walked a step or two further and Otten kicked a pebble so hard it whined in flight. "Goddam, goddam, goddam, goddam."

Porter Osborne, for once, remained discreetly silent. He thought it interesting, however, that in times of stress Carter Otten reverted to his heritage and did not talk at all like a Yankee.

Such was Col. Draughan's new-found pride in his OR and the prestige it reflected on him that he ordered a concrete floor poured immediately adjacent to it. The night before they were to erect the tents on the new pad, it was cold and blustery. Capt. Ballas had been called back around midnight to administer anesthesia for an emergency appendectomy. When it was done and the patient, swathed in blankets against the chilling wind, was carried back to his bed in the recovery ward, the captain dawdled in the work room ostensibly to have a last cup of coffee. The two corpsmen on duty, PFC Porter Osborne, Jr., and Cpl. Bosi, thought it more than coincidence that he hovered with his pipe in the close vicinity of Lt. Johanna Bordillon. He murmured inconsequentially about the weather, the previous case, the upcoming improvement for the next day when they would finally have a true floor beneath their feet, an accomplishment that in all due modesty must be assigned to his credit. He interspersed these lofty pronouncements with personal questions about Lt. Bordillon's past: Where she was born, where she went to nursing school, her marital state, how long had she been married, where was her husband, how long had it been since she had seen him, did she feel lonely in Normandy.

Lt. Bordillon was dark-eyed, olive-skinned, and possessed of the most regular features and gorgeous mouth Porter Osborne had ever seen except on a movie screen. She was well aware of her beauty but did not capitalize on it. She was also well aware of its effect on males, but her decorum and aloofness disclaimed their response and consequent problems as any concern of hers. Porter had exclaimed when he first saw her in scrub suit, "She moves in beauty like the night," and had fallen completely but respectfully in love with her.

He had discovered that she was born in rural Louisiana, had gone to nursing school at Charity Hospital in New Orleans, and spoke what she called "a brand of French." "Have you read *Evangeline*?" he asked.

She had not and her tone held an indifference that relegated Henry Wadsworth Longfellow to the dust bin of literature for Porter. Persisting over weeks of working side by side, he learned that she was Catholic and was married. Comporting himself as he should in the presence of a goddess who was four years older than he, a commissioned officer in the United States Army, a married woman, and above all obviously a lady, Porter had earned her trust sufficiently for her to confide in him that her husband was an enlisted man, an instructor in ordinance at Fort Benning, whom she had to marry in secret and meet on the sly. She had little patience for married officers who used the separation of the Atlantic Ocean and the circumstances of war as an excuse for philandering.

Bosi was a short, blond, blue-eyed Italian from Chicago, his physiognomy an educational experience for Porter who had previously assumed they were all swarthy. "Christ," he muttered to Porter as he watched Capt. Ballas lean ingratiatingly over the work table. "You see that captain putting the moves on our nurse? You think we should maybe disappear to the latrine or somewhere so he can score?"

"Stay put, Bosi, and fear thou not. That captain from Harvard will have the worst case of blue balls in France. He's up against a Southern lady and doesn't stand a snowball's chance in hell."

He surreptitiously admired the feline grace of Lt. Bordillon as she moved around Capt. Ballas as though he were a piece of furniture inappropriately placed in her path, mildly annoying but of no great consequence. Her answers were all monosyllabic, and she occasionally interrupted his conversation with level and impersonal instructions to Bosi and Osborne. She deftly packed instruments and sponges between surgical drapes and folded a layer of huck towels and gowns on top of them while Capt. Ballas toyed with his cold pipe and directed a particularly lengthy and convoluted question into her lovely ear. At its conclusion she raised her eyes and looked at him as she would have an intrusive stranger on a street corner.

"Were you speaking to me?" she inquired politely.

Porter had more self-control than to snigger, but Bosi did not.

Capt. Ballas whirled and snapped, "Osborne, build up the fire in that stove. It's getting too cold for comfort in here."

Porter had a lifetime of experience with wood stoves. "Captain, it's the wind that's making it seem so cold. I just checked the stove and it doesn't really need any more wood. I wouldn't do anything to make that stove pipe get any hotter, if I were you."

"I didn't ask for your opinion or your advice. Put some more wood in the stove. Immediately. That's an order."

"Yes, sir. I recognize one when I hear one. But, Captain, the way those sheets are flapping around up there under the ceiling and with the wind as high as it is, I think it's dangerous."

"You are disobeying a direct order! Bosi!"

"Yes, sir!"

"Put some wood in that stove!"

"Yes, sir!"

Lt. Bordillon's voice was languid and beautifully detached. "Osborne is right, Captain."

"What do women know about fires?" he snapped.

"Well, Captain, some women know how to start them and some women know how to put them out. And some women just let them burn."

"Bosi!"

"Yes, sir, Captain! I'm doing it."

When the billowing sheets ignited near the top of the stove pipe and the flames went racing the length of the OR suite, Lt. Bordillon calmly gathered as many instruments and sterile packs as she could load on a gurney and rolled it out the back of the tent. She was a person of some composure.

The entire sky was swiftly lit by the burning Operating Room. Everyone in camp hurried to the fire. Otten raced up in his undershirt to discover Capt. Ballas sloshing the contents of the coffee pot against a widening burn in the side of the work tent, while Bosi and Osborne trundled operating tables frantically into the night.

"Hey, fellows! It's all going! Get the oxygen tanks out or they'll explode! Too late! Too late! It's out of control! Leave the tanks alone! Everybody stand back!"

Even Sgt. Lagerpiel and Col. Draughan obeyed Otten. The fire raced toward the end of the tent, engulfed the area where the heavy oxygen tents were rolled for storage at the end of schedule every day, burned furiously over and around them, and died. The tanks of oxygen stood as stark and unmoved in the smoldering aftermath as the pillars of Stonehenge.

Otten took a deep breath and there was disappointment in his voice. "Goddam. I thought sure they'd explode and burn."

Col. Draughan stood well behind him. "So did I, son; so did I. How did this damn thing start?"

"I'll look into it, Colonel," said Sgt. Crowder. "You fellows git clear of that far ahd be here at daylight! We got to git us some tents up and everthing going. Our first case is at eight o'clock."

"If you're going to pull that off," snapped Otten, "we'd better not go to bed. See if the Colonel can order some lights rigged up and we'll start now. Our new floor is ready and waiting!"

Col. Draughan beamed. "See to it," he barked at Capt. Smith. He turned to Crowder. "Sergeant, you're to be commended for having organized a group that displays such dedication and willingness to sacrifice. I'll see that this goes on your record. Don't concern yourself about how it started. They'll have to send a fire marshall from Battalion to investigate that anyhow. You stay with your men and supervise them. Carry on!"

Porter admired the swift salute Sgt. Crowder tossed off his eyebrow to the colonel, thinking it truly snappy for an Arkansas linthead. He also admired the discretion Carter Otten exhibited by waiting until they were out of earshot.

"Goddam, goddam, goddam," he said.

"I know what you mean," replied Porter. "Amen."

The investigation from Battalion level was three days coming and the OR crew was busily ensconced in new quarters when the strange lieutenant arrived. He interrogated Capt. Ballas first, and from the questions he later asked Bosi and Osborne it was apparent that in no way did he consider the good captain to be at fault. Porter realized that the captain could never indict him for disobeying a direct order without making Porter under the circumstances look like a hero and the captain himself an inept and rigid fool. He was content to let sleeping dogs lie.

Lt. Bordillon, however, calmly and dispassionately recited every word of the encounter preceding the conflagration, all of which the lieutenant duly recorded and included in his report. When Col. Draughan received a copy, he did not await the end of a working day nor summon Capt. Ballas to the privacy of his office. He erupted into the work area in mid-afternoon, empurpled and passionate.

"You enlisted men and nurses clear out of here! Out of here! Out of here!" he roared, an order which was promptly obeyed but did not serve his purpose. They could hear his every word through the walls of the tent. "Ballas, you dandified, blue-bellied jackass! I ought to bust you down to first lieutenant for this caper! You've made my outfit look bad all through the European theater. Whenever an officer tries to cover something up, it stinks; but when he outright lies about it, it's a felony. This goes on your record and you'll never get another promotion as long as I've got a breath in my body! You'd better thank God for your devoted enlisted men. Crowder and Otten do your work for you, and Bosi and Osborne cover your ass. But don't forget, I'll be watching you from now on! I'm watching! I'm watching!"

Bosi commented, "The colonel's pissed because he won't never get his eagles now on account of the fucked-up report about Capt. Sparky."

Otten's face was full of glee. "Hot damn!" he said. "I mean *hot* damn!"

Sgt. Crowder's eyebrows slanted plaintively down to the sides and he sighed. "He's gone. Y'all git back to work, you hear me?"

"*C'est la vie*," contributed Porter. "*C'est la guerre*."

"Shut up, Osborne," said Otten. "Hot *damn!*"

Later, when Porter was busily assembling hemostats and sponge forceps for a laparotomy pack, Lt. Bordillon glided past him with queenly dignity. "The French word for 'shit' is *merde*," she murmured in his ear.

From that day on Capt. Ballas was referred to behind his back as "Sparky," but only rarely with any degree of affection. Porter Osborne, Jr., on the other hand, felt that he was learning something new every day and becoming ever more worldly. He now had a marvelous substitute for "*C'est la vie*," and when one considered nuances, it meant exactly the same thing,

Carter Otten's campaign for the stripes of noncommissioned status was no more self-aggrandizing than Otto Draughan's pursuit of eagles for his shoulders. The two were definitely on parallel courses, although the one had greater resources at his command than the other. Otten was restricted to his individual efforts and machinations; Draughan had every warm body in the hospital subservient to his command. The phoenix of the Operating Room rose in splendor greater than before the fire, more smoothly functional on its concrete floor, encased now in a Niessan hut of corrugated metal rather than tents. Its daily caseload of patients impressively increased as the corpsmen, nurses, and surgeons settled into cooperative dedication to become the best surgical center in the ETO. Col. Draughan orchestrated a move to obtain recognition and consequent promotion.

Porter was perplexed. "Why are they whitewashing the trunks of all the trees along the entrance?" he queried.

"I hear that Gen. Lee is coming," said Kostas.

"Oh."

A few days later he noted more activity. "Why are they painting the little posts and guide wires along the paths between the wards white?" he asked.

"Gen. Lee is coming," answered Sherman Jewel.

"Good idea. I was forever tripping over them because I couldn't see them."

On that same day he remarked at chow, "They've finally put duckboards in the latrines and sprinkled lime around the honey buckets. It's about time."

"Yeah," said Otten, "and have you noticed how they've got the POW's raking leaves and polishing garbage cans until they shine? I wish you wouldn't mention honey buckets while I'm eating."

"Well, I was just remarking on progress, that's all. I'm glad they did it."

"They only did it because Gen. Lee is coming."

"All I've heard for a week is that Gen. Lee is coming. Who the hell is he, Carter? The only one I ever heard of was Marse Robert."

"Gen. Lee," explained Otten with uncharacteristic patience, "is Inspector General for the ETO. He is the meanest, crabbiest, most GI and most uptight old shitass in the whole world. He marches through and inspects an outfit, and then it's his recommendation that determines whether or not the CO of that outfit gets a commendation and promotion. He's hell on wheels. Remember Saturday inspections in Basic when the shavetail would run his fingers above the door frames looking for dust? Well, this guy is ten times that bad."

"Why?"

"Hell, it's his job. He's Regular Army, finished at the Point, and is extra tough on new units, I hear. He's famous for taking the lid off the garbage can when he's inspecting a kitchen, looking in, pulling out a scrap of something and nibbling it. Then he yells and hollers at the mess sergeant and gives him unshirted hell. 'Sergeant, military rules require that food becomes garbage only when it is inedible! As I have just proven, this is obviously edible!' Then he gets right in his face and yells, 'What in the name of all that's holy is it doing in this garbage can?' That's where he got his nickname of 'Holy Lee.' He's a real son of a bitch."

"That's why Sparky has us restacking all the packs in Central Supply and washing the bottoms of the operating table."

"Right. And Crowder told me that we're not scheduling any surgery for the day that he comes; we'll only be available for emergencies. The Operating Room has got to be spic and span."

"He's coming through the Operating Room? No wonder Sparky is so nervous."

"We assume he will," corrected Otten. "They say he goes through an outfit, including the company records, in less than an hour, but every ward and every department has to be prepared for him. Just in case he breezes through."

"Has he ever done anything that amounted to anything?" asked Porter.

"Goddam, Porter, what sort of question is that? After all, he's a two-star general in the United States Army!"

"I know that," retorted Porter. "But has he *done* anything? Like kill a German or Jap. Or lead troops into battle. Or give a patient an enema. What has he ever *accomplished*? All this hullabaloo over inspection is worse than a wedding. Work, work, work for weeks beforehand. Spend a lot of money unnecessarily and decorate everything to a faretheewell. And then you have a fifteen-minute ceremony and it's all over. What's the point?"

"I've explained the point. Col. Draughan wants a promotion. If he gets one, it stands to reason everybody will get one. If he doesn't get one, nobody will. I'm not going to philosophize about cold, hard facts. I'm going to bust my ass!"

"Well, I'm not," said Porter. "Capt. Sparky is our CO, and the colonel has already said in public that he'll never get a promotion; so it stands to reason by your own statement that we'll never get a promotion."

"I'm going to be so good and so indispensable that I'll attract the notice of the colonel, himself, and he'll by-God order me a promotion."

Porter reflected for only a moment. "Carter Otten, if there is one thing that I have learned over and over in this man's Army, it is that you do not ever want to attract attention from an officer. I think this inspection is tacky and I'm not going to do any more than I'm absolutely told to do. The very idea of deferring surgery cases just because

384

an inspector general might appear on the scene! It's downright tacky, I tell you."

It was Carter Otten who had the inspiration and the temerity to approach the colonel and point out that the soft coal being burned in the stoves around camp was producing an unsightly amount of soot and dust. Two days before Gen. Lee's advent, the order went out that all fires would be extinguished at midnight, the patients issued extra blankets if necessary, and every stove in the 816th General Hospital would be polished by 0900 hours. Porter grumbled. Carter smirked.

"What'd I tell you, Osborne? This is going to be the most gussied-up, best looking field hospital in Europe on inspection day."

"And the most poorly functioning."

"What the hell? Gen. Lee has never had fires put out in his honor before, I'll bet. I'm going to make sergeant yet because we're going to get us a chicken colonel."

"Well, Sgt. Otten, your honor, sir, we're also going to have chicken shit instead of chicken salad. I just heard that we're getting nothing but K-rations and coffee for breakfast that morning because the kitchen is under direct orders to have the garbage cans cleaned, polished, and empty."

"K-rations? Goddam! The colonel better make Chicken!"

Fate did indeed decree that they had an emergency case in the Operating Room on the morning of the inspection. It was a patient that Maj. Buster Pierce insisted could not wait for attention until after Gen. Lee's departure. Porter observed the confrontation between Capt. Ballas and the major with interest and restored respect for physicians.

"Dammit, Ballas, I know Gen. Lee's coming. Every idiot in camp knows it if he's not blind, deaf, and stupid. I also know my main job is to look after sick soldiers, and this boy is sick. I've already told you he has trench foot with dry gangrene. His right foot is completely dead, black and mummified. I've been called on consult for Ortho, and he's already getting a red streak. He's got to have disarticulation or he'll lose a whole leg instead of the foot. He can't wait the four hours you're suggesting. I've already talked to Maj. Emmons, and he's standing by to do the surgery. It won't take twenty minutes after he's anesthetized. I've personally given this boy his pre-op injection and I'm bringing him over here in twenty minutes, and you'd better have an Anesthetist and a surgical team ready and waiting. You got that? If you don't, I'll file charges against you for disobeying an order from a

385

superior officer, and in addition to that, I'll personally kick your butt right in front of the general when he does arrive. You got that?"

He whirled to Porter, who had been making a valiant effort to be inconspicuous but at the same time not to miss a word.

"You! What's your name?"

"Osborne, sir."

"What do you do around here?"

Porter rapidly assessed the question. He had carried litters, bed pans, urinals; he had folded drapes, assembled packs, washed gloves; he had, since the advent of their German prisoners, circulated, scrubbed on cases, assisted surgeons, even on two occasions pushed pentothal under the direction of the nurse anesthetist. He drew himself proudly erect.

"Everything, sir." He considered for one brief moment. "And well!"

"Good! You help Capt. Ballas here get ready for my patient. And do it on the double! You understand?"

"Yes, sir!"

When Maj. Pierce marched off, Capt. Ballas lit his pipe and with level voice directed, "I'll give the anesthesia myself, you scrub, and tell Otten to circulate. Maj. Emmons is already here. Let's move. You heard the major."

"I didn't hear all of it, Capt. Ballas. Honest I didn't. I didn't hear that part about kicking your butt, and I also didn't hear that part about disobeying a superior officer."

The captain gave an aloof smile. "Neither did I, Osborne. A good Anesthesiologist learns very soon how to deal with irate physicians and placate them. He also learns to ignore things they say that they'll either regret or choose to forget later. He spoke intemperately in a moment of stress. You mustn't take it personally."

Porter recalled fleetingly the confrontation over the stove. "Oh, I didn't, Captain. I didn't. I'll go get Otten."

As he left he thought, "Was that his way of apologizing? Don't tell me I'm going to wind up this war liking old Sparky. But I should have known when Kostas told me about him that I was going to like any major who's named Buster. I guess it takes different things to produce stress in different folks."

While the nurses bustled like hens in an early morning barnyard and straightened, tucked, and smoothed everything in sight in one last opportunity for spit and polish in honor of the general, the operation in the farthest cubicle went smoothly and well. The patient was dispatched to his ward, Maj. Emmons dressed in his uniform and departed, and Porter busied himself helping Otten clean up after the surgery.

"Hey, Carter, what you want to do with this foot?"

"Oh, my God, give it here quick and I'll run it over to the incinerator."

"You ain't got time," advised Sgt. Crowder. "The general's Jeep just turned in at the front gate, and Col. Draughan has gave a direct order for not nere an enlisted man to leave his post twell the general leaves. He give demerits to one outfit cause he seen enlisted men walking around the compound when he said they oughta been working."

"Oh, shit," said Otten. "What am I going to do with it? We can't let the general find it in here."

He wrapped the dismembered specimen in a huck towel and called, "Shorty! Come here! Quick!"

Shorty was a gnome-like, middle-aged German prisoner of war with bandy legs encased in frayed leggins whom Carter Otten had adopted as his own personal servant. Slow-witted but unfailingly affable, the man knew almost as little English as Otten knew German, and it amused Otten to instruct him about his chores, much as he would have adopted a stray dog and patiently taught him tricks.

"Shorty, *foos. Verstehen-sie?* Foot. *Foos.*"

"*Ya, ya. Foos, das foos.*"

"Right. Go out back door, Shorty. Don't let general see you. Take *foos*, Shorty. Put *foos* in incinerator. Open incinerator. Put *foos* in. Close incinerator. Come back here. *Verstehen-sie?*"

"*Bitte?*"

"*Bitte*, hell! *Foos*, Shorty. *Gehen-sie*. Quick! Quick!"

Otten's assumption that any lack of comprehension could be overcome by innovative gestures and increased loudness was rewarded by Shorty trotting obediently out the back, obviously impressed with the need for speed. Otten, on Shortly's return, approved him.

"Good boy, Shorty. *Gute. Sehr gute.*"

"*Ya. Shorty gute.*"

"Did the general see you?"

"*Ya. Ya.*"

"Oh, my God! General? *Grosse* officer? See you? General *siehen* Shorty?"

"*Nein, nein. Shorty siehen general. General nein siehen Shorty.*" He beamed. "Nobody *siehen* Shorty. *Ist gute, ya?*"

"*Sehr gute*, Shorty. You, good man." He clapped him on the back. "Me get you promotion to *oberleutenant*. Good boy, Shorty."

He turned to Porter. "You see, Osborne? One sign of a good leader is the ability to delegate duties to subordinates. The relegation of authority."

"Quiet down over there," commanded Crowder. "If you're done with your relegating and delegating, all y'all be ready to snap to when I holler attention. The general oughta make it by the OR in about ten minutes, the way I got it figured."

They waited through tense, slow-dragging minutes, but Gen. Holy Lee never set foot in the Operating Room of the 816th General Hospital. In fact, his entire time at that installation from arrival to departure was something under twenty minutes. The visit established several records that were never exceeded, the most inconsequential of which was the brevity of it. Sgt. Lagerpiel, who remained at Col. Draughan's elbow throughout, drawled later that he thought from the minute the general dismounted from his Jeep that he was in a bad humor. He gave a desultory flick of the finger in response to the colonel's virile salute and ignored the warm smile of welcome.

"Let's get on with it, Vaughan," he snapped.

"Draughan, sir. It's Draughan."

"All right, Draughan. Whatever you say. You ought to know."

"Where do you want to start, Gen. Lee?"

"We'll start by letting you get rid of that cigar, Vaughan."

"Draughan, sir. It's not lit."

"Get rid of it, Vaughan."

"Yes, sir. It's Draughan." He handed the cigar to Lagerpiel, who looked around and then stuck it in his shirt pocket. The general fixed him with such a stare that the sergeant moved it to his pants pocket, and then the general said, "Let's start with the kitchen. I can always get a good idea about an outfit by checking its kitchen and mess hall."

Col. Draughan slipped Sgt. Lagerpiel a wink and responded with hospitable assurance, "Right this way, General. We're proud of our kitchen."

So were all the enlisted personnel. When the general's entourage entered their tent, they jerked to perfect attention and remained there, since he gave no order of "At ease." The general prowled up and down the aisles between the spotless tables, felt the tops of the cold and polished stoves, and then moved to the trio of covered garbage pails, gleaming like pewter at the end of the serving area. He put his hand on the lid of the nearest one, glared at the mess sergeant and delivered his dictum.

"Sergeant, regulations require that no food be discarded as garbage if it can be classified as edible. Are you prepared for me to inspect these garbage cans?"

"Yes, sir," replied the sergeant and winked at Lagerpiel as the general removed the lid and peeped inside. Sgt. Lagerpiel relayed the wink to Col. Draughan.

"Empty," said the general. "Clean and dry and empty. Humph."

He reached for the lid of the middle can. "Did no one have breakfast here this morning?"

The colonel looked smug and made no reply.

"Aha, what have we here?" barked Gen. Holy Lee and reached into the bottom of the can. He straightened and held up before everyone's startled gaze a wizened, blackened foot. "What in the name of all that's holy is this?" he thundered.

The mess sergeant was downwind and retched. Col. Draughan's eyes bulged but he was speechless. Only Sgt. Lagerpiel, who had six hashmarks and was imperturbable, had the presence to respond.

"A foot?" he said.

"You're very observant, Sergeant! Of course, it's a foot! What I want to know is how in the name of all that's holy did it get in the garbage can in this kitchen!"

He thrust the object into Col. Draughan's unresisting grasp. "On second thought, that's the last thing I want to know!" He turned to the captain who trailed him with a clip board and to the sergeant who was his driver. "Get me out of here, men!"

The skin that festooned his thin neck was wrinkled into diamond shapes in the back and was a colorful contrast to his white tonsure, but it was no redder than Col. Draughan's face. "As for you, Draughan, I'll have my report on your desk in two days!"

Col. Otto Draughan lifted his stunned gaze from the foot he was holding like a new-born baby. "Vaughan, sir," he said. "Vaughan!"

"Whatever you say! You ought to know!" the general barked and was gone.

Col. Draughan was without speech for only a short while. "Where's my goddam cigar?" he bellowed.

In the Operating Room, the unsuspecting personnel were mystified. Sgt. Crowder was spying through a tent flap.

"There goes the general outa here in his Jeep. He never even come by here atall." He sniffed and sighed. "And after all that work I done." He looked again. "Here comes Col. Draughan, though, and he's headed straight for us. Git ready."

The door banged open and Col. Draughan burst in; the force of his passing seeming to suck Sgt. Lagerpiel in his wake.

"Ten-shun!" yelled Sgt. Crowder.

Col. Otto Draughan waved the foot. "How in the name of the deepest pit in Hell did this wretched thing find its way into an empty garbage can in my kitchen where Gen. Lee was sure to find it? Ballas!" he yelled.

Capt. Ballas wiped his glasses in disbelief. "Crowder!" he yelled.

Sgt. Crowder did not even look around. "Otten!" he yelled.

Otten did look around but he did not raise his voice. "Shorty," he called, "Shorty! *Kommen-sie hier*, Shorty. That's a good boy, Shorty. Good boy. *Sie kommt, ya*? Here, Colonel, let me take that specimen for you; I've been looking for it everywhere."

When Col. Draughan, his dream of promotion dashed, left the OR, Carter Otten, his aspirations trimmed drastically by the scissors of reality, a furious scowl on his face, did not request permission from Sgt. Crowder. He proclaimed to him, "Sergeant, I'll dispose of that foot properly and then I'm going to take Shorty and dig the holes for those posts you've been wanting out back." He did not even glance at Porter as he stormed out of the tent.

Everyone resolutely resumed normal duties, but the air was electric under the strict and monitoring gaze of Capt. Ballas and Sgt. Oliver Crowder. No one dared speak except in low and level tones and then only of impersonal details. It was forced, but it was business as usual.

Lt. Bordillon glided by Porter, who was popping gloves inside out for further drying. "*C'est la vie,*' she murmured.

"*Merde,*" he responded.

"*C'est la guerre,*" she countered, but neither of them dared an open smile.

Time came for the POW's to be carried back to their stockade and Shorty came back into the tent. Sgt. Crowder made way for him by the stove. "Git warm before you go, Shorty. It's raw out there today."

Shorty pulled off his gloves with the ragged holes in the fingers and held his thickened red hands near the stove pipe, splintered nails rimmed in black. "*Danke,*" he said and sniffed through a soupy nose.

"Where's Otten at?" asked Crowder.

"*Bitte?*"

"Otten?" Crowder raised his voice. "Where is Otten? *Wo ist Otten?* American soldier. *Wo ist him.*"

"Ah," came the comprehending response. He pointed to the outdoors. "*Das. Arbeiten. Ya.*" Shorty was obviously pleased to be able to communicate. His features contracted in puzzled concentration and he looked at Porter. "Soldier *arbeit. Wie heisen-sie dis* goddam?" he inquired.

That was the spark. From the captain through the nurses to the last enlisted man, releasing laughter washed through the tent of the OR. They were a team.

"There is laughter like the fountains. . ."

32 The days shortened. The rains returned and the penetrating cold of Normandy increased Porters's work load in the Operating Room. He grew hardened to the increasing incidence of amputation due to trench foot. The patients were all drugged beyond caring by preoperative doses of morphine, atropine, and scopolamine before he ever saw them, were still in the deep sleep of anesthesia when they departed his attention; and so he was aware of them primarily as cases and not people.

"My daddy and an uncle were both officers over here in the first war," he confided conversationally to Lt. Hormley while he held a limb in position for him to saw through the lower tibia. "They kept telling me to watch my feet and keep them dry, and be sure to take my shoes off and rub my toes every day and powder them so I wouldn't get trench foot; and somehow I got the idea it was something like athlete's foot. I never knew it could come to this."

Lt. Hormley had been two years into private practice in Omaha with every intention of returning to Creighton Medical School and specializing in Dermatology as soon as he had paid down his educational loan and hoarded enough savings to finance his venture. Pearl Harbor, the draft, and Col. Otto Draughan had changed his goals. Presently, all he wanted from life was for the war to end so that he could once more be a civilian and shed what he regarded as the double stigmata of being an officer in the United States Army and, in addition, one spuriously designated as an Orthopedic Surgeon. He was a rail-thin refugee from a corn farm in Nebraska, with sharp-edged planes to his face, overly large teeth, and such a high palatine arch that his spoken word was a confusing mixture of the nasal and the sepulchral.

As soon as the enlisted men had realized that his perpetual scowl was not an aggressive replica of Capt. Smith's, adopted to keep them satisfactorily subordinate, but was rather the banner of conflict with his own entrenched morals, which were strong enough to embrace the ideals of good medicine, they respected him. They would have even come to love him had he ever relaxed his self-castigating attitude or evinced any spark of interest in others.

"How do you think I feel?" he responded to Porter. "I never heard of it before either and I'm a doctor. I'm charged with the responsibility of treating these cases, and I had to get a book to find out first of all what it was and then what to do about it, and how, and when. In fact, Miller, I wouldn't know how to treat the simplest fracture if I hadn't bought a set of Watson-Jones out of my own pocket and brought it with me to France. Maj. Emmons is a wonderful General Surgeon and he advises me. I wouldn't know what to do if it weren't for him and my Watson-Jones. Don't you feel bad because you didn't know what trench foot was, Miller." The lieutenant's voice sounded as though it was coming from the bottom of an empty churn.

"Miller?" Porter thought. "No, sir, I won't," he said aloud.

"I was training to be a Dermatologist, and I hate Orthopedics. I hate all this mutilation and having to watch these boys wake up without their feet. It's a brutal branch of medicine; I hate it, but somebody has to do it. Hold that foot a little higher."

"Can you bench press two hundred pounds, Lieutenant?"

"I seriously doubt it; I never tried. Why?"

"Then you are absolutely right, you weren't meant to be in Orthopedics," Porter asserted with consoling confidence. "And besides that, the war is soon going to be over. I hear Gen. Patton has got his tail over the dashboard and the bit in his teeth and is running away with the buggy, headed for the Rhine so fast nobody can stop him. Cheer up, sir."

"Miller, you're a fine boy, I'm sure, and probably a joy to your mother, but do people ever think maybe you're a little strange?"

"Not that I've noticed, sir. Of course, if they did, no one would be rude enough to mention it to me, would they? Have you thought about specializing in Ob-Gyn?"

"Never. That's worse than Orthopedics about blood and mess and odors. Deliver me from Obstetrics."

Porter raised his eyes in hope but discovered that Lt. Hormley still wore an introspective scowl and was unaware of his pun. He sighed. "I guess you're right, Lieutenant; Dermatology is the place for you. I heard a doctor say in Chattanooga once that it's a good life because your patients never get well, never quit coming, and never wake you up at night."

Lt. Hormley was stripping off his gloves and turning for the circulator to untie his gown. "Look, Miller, I've heard that old saw before. Have you ever heard that if somebody knows the diseases of the skin, he knows all of medicine? No doctor ever refers a patient to a Dermatologist until he's tried everything he knows and it didn't work. I wanted to be a Dermatologist when I was a peaceful civilian and minding my own business. Nobody is here because he wants to be, including you; the war has gathered us all together and probably changed us forever. I don't know what I'll want to do when I get back; I may even want to be a missionary."

"You gotta drive, sir. You've gotta drive."

"What do you want to be, Miller?"

Porter gulped and decided that this had gone far enough. "A fireman, sir," he replied, "or else a railroad conductor. Thank you for talking to me, Lieutenant, sir. You've really made me think about some things I'd never thought about before."

"Are you crazy, Osborne?" Carter Otten demanded. "You're the one who was telling me not to attract the attention of an officer, and then I heard you deliberately gigging Lt. Hormley when I passed by your cubicle."

"I know it. For a minute there my compartments started running together, but I couldn't resist; he's so morose it'll be good for him. If he's gone, I'll take off my cap and mask now. He thinks I'm somebody named Miller from Tennessee, and I'll be safe if he ever asks Crowder or Capt. Ballas about a scrub tech named Miller. He'll think he's the one who's strange. Especially since he works on the Orthopedic ward with Daniel Farbecker."

"Who is this Farbecker I keep hearing people mention? Do you know him?"

"Not exactly." Porter became very still. "Why?"

"Every time I get around that crowd that hangs out with your buddy Kostas and somebody starts bitching about an assignment, one of them always says, 'Let Farbecker do it,' and they all laugh. He must be some sort of gullible patsy if he's letting them dump on him all the time."

"Could be," assented Porter. "I'm not real sure which one he is."

"Well, that's not what I grabbed you for. I talked to Sgt. Lagerpiel and to Sgt. Crowder, and I've got both of us an overnight pass."

"An overnight pass? What the hell are we going to do with it, put up a tent in Isigny?"

"We're going to spend the night in Bayeux."

"You're crazy. That's too far to walk."

"I know that. I've made friends with a corporal from the motor pool. He's got to make an overnight haul to Cherbourg for supplies, and we're catching a ride in the back of his truck. Bayeux is on the way and has just this week been approved for R and R. I talked our sergeants into giving us a pass, and I've even got a voucher for a hotel room. Change into dress uniform, bring your diddy bag, and we're out of here at 0200 hours. We've been working so hard we need a change in pace; we've had to help on so many amputations we need a change of scenery; we've accumulated so much stress level we've got to get off post for a few hours."

"That's bullshit."

"I know it, but it's what I fed Lagerpiel and Crowder and they bought it." Otten gave him a feral grin. "We're going to get laid."

"Oh, God, not that again," groaned Porter.

"No mistake this time, Osborne. These French girls are hot, they tell me, and I've even learned how to approach them. '*Couchez avec moi, Mademoiselle*' is the polite way to put it. *Zig-zig* is the basic word if you can't make 'em understand anything else. We may need something to trade, so be sure to bring any extra cigarettes or D-bars you've been saving."

"You be sure to bring Old Lady Thumb and her four daughters," laughed Porter. "You may need them."

When the truck swung out of the hospital gates, Porter experienced a rush of elation. It was the first time he had been out of fatigues and in dress uniform since leaving the USO in New York. He had held no girl in his arms since he danced with Maria Nirova. The nurses were wonderful but off-limits; you could look at them and even speak to them, if you managed it discreetly, but it was unthinkable that you touch one. Not under the suspicious eye of the ever watchful Capt. Smith. Who knows? he thought. Old Carter may be right this time. He remembered a saying from his past and said aloud, "Even an old blind hog stumbles up on an acorn now and then."

"What the hell are you thinking about now, O sage of the barnyard?" asked Otten. His features were impish, his eyes danced with inner light. His affect was definitely one of glee, and when in that mood Carter Otten was irresistibly charming. Porter saw no reason to ruin that mood.

"Nothing," he replied. "What the hell have you got in that laundry bag? You told me to bring just my diddy bag."

"This is my bank. I've got four cartons of cigarettes, two dozen D-bars, twelve bars of GI soap, two pounds of lard, and a package of coffee."

"Lard? Whatever for?"

"I went by the mess hall to beg old Mack and Jack out of a few supplies. I told 'em we were going on pussy prowl, and they're the ones who suggested the lard. The motor pool boys are bartering for everything in Normandy, and they told Mack and Jack that lard is a hotter item than cigarettes or chocolate. The only thing the French like better is American dollars. Joe Lamar went out with a pound of lard, Mack says, and came back with two ounces of Chanel No. 5."

"That's perfume. I thought we were after pussy, O stalwart leader."

"You don't think I'd stoop to paying for that, do you? I might pass out a few gifts in appreciation for favors received, but these supplies are for shopping."

"Oh," said Porter and gave his attention to the passing countryside and to maintaining his balance in the back of the empty truck.

Bayeux was convalescing from wounds suffered when the Allies forced the Germans to relinquish its streets and buildings and had resumed a semblance of municipal activity. Some streets were neatly lined with stacks of freshly cleaned building stones, while the curbs of others were still cluttered with the spill of fallen rubble. There were pedestrians going in and out of nondescript shops, but motor traffic consisted only of Jeeps and trucks of the American military. The overall feeling was the somber one of poverty, but the gray day and the gray town and the gray mud underfoot were not enough to darken the spirits of Carter Otten and Porter Osborne.

Their truck driver pulled over and they swung out in front of their hotel.

"See youse guys in the morning. No later than 0930. If yez late, I leave yez."

Porter surveyed his surroundings. This street had escaped shelling. The hotel stood flush with the narrow cobbled sidewalk, a small sign by the side of the door inconspicuously identifying its function. To its left stretched an eight-foot stone wall behind which the crowns of leafless trees could be seen. Everything seemed closed in and secretive to Porter.

"Hey, Otten, look at that wall. It's got sharp glass and broken bottles stuck in concrete all along the top of it."

"Quit pointing. That's to keep prowlers and thieves out. Let's check in and go shopping."

The lobby of the hotel was no larger than the average-sized parlor of Brewton County, but its fifteen-foot ceiling gave the illusion of space. It was dominated by a graceful staircase with intricately designed wrought iron railing and marble steps, the lips of the treads smoothly indented by years of traffic. The reception desk was under the stairs, tidy and efficient but with a lack of pretension that obliged a customer to search for it. A metal chandelier with electric candles illumined the lobby, the wattage of its bulbs assuring that light would never be crude in here. A straight-backed sofa with bold stripes was against one wall, and facing it was the strangest clock Porter had ever seen. The pendulum was exposed and hung free of any casing. It was fashioned of heavy white china adorned with garlands of pink china roses and some tiny blue flowers Porter did not recognize. The pendulum, he thought, was fashioned like a fat-bottomed child and probably weighed just as much. It swung ponderously to and fro, producing deep resonating clicks that notched inescapably the progression of time, but, with mesmerizing repetition, gave the comfort and assurance that there was always more time to come if one relaxed and had the patience to listen. He looked down at the parquet floor that creaked beneath his feet. "At last I am in France," he thought.

A door at the rear opened and a tall woman with a graying bun of black hair precisely centered on the nape of her long thin neck entered. She gave no notice of their presence until she seated herself on a stool behind the desk and folded her hands on the counter. Then she looked with composure at them and spoke. "*Messieurs?*"

"What'd she say?" said Carter Otten.

"I think she said, 'What can I do to help you?' or else, 'Is there something you want?' or maybe, 'This is my house and what are you doing in it?' but the word itself just means 'gentlemen.' You want me to try to talk to her?"

"Hell, no. You keep your countrified mouth out of this and let me handle it. You don't have to talk to do business."

"Be sure to say 'please' and 'thank you,'" said Porter.

"*Bonjour, Madame,*" ventured Otten.

"*M'sieu,*" responded Madame.

"Two rooms." He held up two fingers. "Two rooms." He pointed to himself and to Porter. "Me. One. Him. One. Two rooms."

"*S'il vous plaît*," contributed Porter.

Otten produced the voucher and presented it. "Two rooms. All paid. Shut up, Osborne."

The lady raised her spectacles which swung from a chain around her neck and inspected the document. She slid the register toward them and when they had signed, she produced two keys and handed them to Otten. She pointed one finger upward and delivered in a lovely contralto a rapid-fire and prolonged spate of instructions of which neither soldier understood one word. Then she inclined her head and regally turned to the door from which she had entered.

"*Merci, Madame*," Porter called to her back. "*Je vous remercie beaucoup.*"

"What'd she say?" asked Otten.

"I think she said our rooms are upstairs," replied Porter.

He would have dawdled longer inspecting their rooms, the real beds, windows with draperies, rugs on the floor, washstands with bowls and flowered ewers for water, but Otten was impatient.

"Put on your raincoat and let's hit the street," he said from Porter's open door.

"What's your hurry? Where's the bathroom? I want to see a real bathtub one more time in my life."

"End of the hall. The crapper, too. Everybody uses the same one. Will you, for Christ's sake, put on your raincoat and let's go?"

"It's not raining."

"Well, this is still Normandy; so it's going to rain. What does that matter? Here, carry these cigarettes for me."

When Porter looked up, he discovered why Carter Otten was insisting that they wear their raincoats. He stood there like a snowman swathed in khaki. Every pocket he had was stuffed and crammed with articles for trade. His raincoat would hardly button around him, and even the pockets of it were bulging.

Porter laughed. "Hell, Otten, you're going to waddle instead of walk. Why should I carry your cigarettes for you?"

"Because, goddammit, I can't get more than half of them in my pockets; they're full of soap and lard and D-bars. The least you can do is carry some of the cigarettes."

Porter reached for his raincoat and laughed again. "OK, hand them here and let's go."

By the time they walked the streets, most of the shops were closed. The small ones that remained open had a dearth of merchandise and the ladies who ran them were interested in nothing but cash.

They found one shop still open that had a variety of objects on display. Porter explored and Otten fumed.

"There's no perfume left in this whole town, Osborne. I believe every goddam truck driver who ever rode through Bayeux has raided the place, and these women won't swap anything they've got for cigarettes. It's just as well, because everything they have in here is china. It's expensive, and you couldn't get it back to the States without breaking to save your soul. I'm hot as a bull in a ginger mill under this raincoat. Let's go."

On a shelf behind an elegant array of Limoges plates stood a figurine that caught Porter's eye. It was out of place, an earthy, almost utilitarian presence in its surroundings. Porter pointed to it. "*S'il vous plaît?*" he asked the clerk.

When he held it in his hands, he was enchanted. It was a young girl in peasant dress with bared head and feet, holding a lute. Across the base was stamped the word "Mignonne." It was a piece of limited charm, but what endeared it to Porter was that it was fashioned of red clay. Baked and fired, rough under his fingers, definitely red clay.

"How much?" he asked, remembered where he was and struggled with the tongue. "*Combien?*" He hastily added, "*S'il vous plaît?*" Into the staccato burst of French that erupted, he smiled and wagged his head to denote lack of comprehension. The saleslady wrote on a shred of paper, "270 f."

"No wonder I didn't understand," thought Porter. "No francs," he said aloud. "I have no French money." He reached in his pocket. "American money? Dollars? Two American dollars?" He remembered to smile. "*S'il vous plaît?*"

"*Ah, non, non, non, non, non, M'sieu,*" responded the clerk in chiding tones.

Porter handed back the figurine and bowed. "*Merci beaucoup, Madame.*" He turned to follow Otten.

"*Un moment, M'sieu,*" She frowned, smiled, gestured, waved Mignonne in the air and all the while spoke so rapidly that Porter could not space sentences, let alone discern individual words. Finally she held out her hand in unmistakable gesture, and Porter laid two one-dollar bills across her palm. She clucked and wrapped Mignonne securely in newspaper before handing her over.

"*Merci, M'sieu,*" The phrase had a musical ring, an upward lilt.

Porter could not recall the words for "You're welcome," bowed low, and said, "*Au revoir, Madame.*"

"*Au 'voir, M'sieu, au 'voir,*" she practically sang.

"*S'il vous plaît*," proclaimed Porter and carried his prize to the street.

"What the hell you think you're going to do with that goddam statue?" demanded Otten.

"I'm going to mail it home. To my mother."

"Hell, it's twelve inches high and brittle as an eggshell. It'll be nothing but dust when it gets there. You're totally impractical. Let's find some place to eat and see if we can get some girls. The shopping's shot to hell."

"I haven't seen any girls. Just old ladies. I think they heard you were coming to town and locked up all the young girls."

"Here's a cafe. Let's eat."

Despite the wartime restrictions and the impoverished menu, they were able to dine. The cafe was small, was apparently more a bar than a restaurant, and was presided over by two men obviously beyond the age of military service. One of them, in fact, had only a stub for one arm. Otten and Osborne seated themselves at a table and by dint of smiles, signs, and fractured phrases were served a clear soup with something resembling a collard leaf floating in it, a loaf of heavy black bread, and a segment of meat stewed with onions and potatoes past identity.

"At least it ain't kidney," Otten said. "I'll vouch for that."

"*Lapin?*" Porter asked the waiter.

"*Voici, c'est le pain,*" responded the waiter, the tray tucked under his stump, and pointed to the loaf.

"Forget it," said Porter. "*Merci beaucoup.*"

"*Du vin?*" asked the man.

"What'd he say?" asked Otten.

"I think he wants to know if we want some wine."

Otten tilted back his chair, flashed an impish grin, and spoke directly to the waiter. "This little piggy cried '*Oui, oui, oui*' all the way home."

Porter was in position to see their wine drawn from a wooden barrel behind the bar into a thick carafe. He thought it tart and a little like fresh buttermilk to his palate but recognized that he was certainly no connoisseur and freely assigned his share to Carter Otten.

When they had finished eating and Otten had emphatically declined the invitation of "*Fromage?*", they paid their bill in dollars. Otten directed Porter, "Ask him about girls."

"I don't know how," protested Porter.

"Hell, Osborne, I thought you knew some French. I'll do it. Hey, *garçon!*"

Their waiter shambled over.

"*Mademoiselles?* You know any *mademoiselles?* We want to meet some girls. *Compris mademoiselles?*"

"*Oui, m'sieu. Non, m'sieu. Pas demoiselles ici.*"

"What'd he say?"

"I think," Porter said, "that he said there aren't any girls here."

"Well, hell, I can see that. I ain't blind." He looked at Porter in frustration. "I remember something from a detective story, by God." He turned again to the waiter. "*Cherchez la femme,*" he commanded in triumph. "*Cherchez la femme.*"

The waiter looked extremely puzzled. Porter tried not to stare at the man's little chicken wing of an arm while wondering if he managed to tie his apron himself or had to have help doing it.

Otten reached into a pocket, held out two packages of Camels and lowered his voice. "*Zig-zig, monsieur.* You *compris* zig-zig?"

At this point the man behind the bar loosed an unintelligible string of words and jerked his head toward the window. Their waiter bowed, pocketed the cigarettes, stepped to the door and called something into the darkness, obviously to an unseen passer-by. Then he returned to their table and announced with a placating smile, "*Tout de suite, messieurs, tout de suite.*"

"What'd he say?" demanded Otten.

"I think that means 'Right away,'" said Porter with confidence.

"Goddammit, Osborne, I know toot sweet when I hear it and everybody knows what it means. What I'm talking about is what'd he say out the door?"

"Your guess is as good as mine," said Porter and put his hand over his wine glass to decline a refill.

The door opened and their waiter escorted two women to their table, pulled out chairs for them while speaking with animation, and then departed. Osborne and Otten had risen at their approach and automatically held their chairs and seated them. While Porter tried not to stare, Carter Otten recovered his poise.

"You speak English?" he asked.

"*Non, m'sieu,*" they replied in unison.

"Thank God," said Otten. "Thank God for small favors. *Vin,*" he called to the waiter. "More *vin. Beaucoup* more *vin!* Osborne, we are in the middle of a mess."

Porter looked at the women. Both were heavily rouged, wore coats that had outlasted many winters, and they reeked of conflicting perfumes. Their shoes were scuffed pumps, run over at the heels, and their bare legs were chapped and scaly. The woman who was seated at his side had dyed blonde hair, crow's feet around puffed eyelids and was at least, he estimated, eight months pregnant. In reflexive response to his upbringing, he avoided looking at her stomach, but her eyes, he thought, were sad.

Otten's partner was of even more interest to Porter. Unmistakably, with no evidence of hanky-panky in her ancestry, she was a Negro. He leaned forward and looked intently into her muddy eyes. "Are you real sure you don't speak any English?" he asked.

She directed her gaze to Porter but left her hand on Carter Otten's arm. "*Pardon, m'sieu?*"

"*Parlez-vous anglais?*" He groped for elaboration. "*Un petit peu? Peut-être?*"

Her mouth was wide and darkly painted, her teeth splayed and strongly defined by interspaces. "*Non, m'sieu.* No Engleesh. *Pas de tout.*"

"I'll just be goddammed," said Porter Osborne, Jr., giving no thought at all to who or even where he was.

With the comfort of chitchat lost as an introductory option, he filled the awkward moment by proffering and lighting cigarettes. Otten poured them each a glass of wine. His partner ever so fleetingly brushed her hand across his thigh.

"Say something, Osborne," he ordered. "Speak some French, for God's sake."

"What do you want to say? I can't remember any."

"Anything, anything at all. I tell you we're in the middle of a mess. If you can't talk to them and distract them, it's going to get worse. This one's headed for my pecker, sure as gun's iron."

"Well, you wanted to get laid."

"Not by a whore, dammit."

"They aren't whores, stupid."

"You're crazy as hell."

"I am not. I never heard of a whore being pregnant, and this one's liable to deliver any minute. I also never heard of one being black. Certainly not if she's educated enough to speak fluent French. Both of them are old enough to be our mothers, and I think we should be nice."

"So do I. I think we should be nice enough to get the hell out of here without a lot of fuss or even getting into a fight. No telling what they've got in their purses in the way of knives or shillelaghs, and those guys behind the bar are at our backs. Speak some French till we can maneuver out of this."

At that moment Porter unmistakably felt a hand come softly to rest on the inner surface of his thigh. "You're right, Carter," he acknowledged. "They're whores." He turned to his companion, smiled brilliantly, and voiced the only full sentence in French that he could remember. "*Le crayon de ma grandmere est sur la table,*" he said.

"*Pardon?*" The hand moved.

"What the hell did you say, Osborne?"

"I said, 'My grandmother's pencil is on the table.' I learned it in the tenth grade."

Otten broke into sudden laughter.

"It's not that funny, Carter. It was all I could remember."

Otten laughed harder.

"What the hell's that funny, Otten?" The women had both hands busy now with cigarettes and wine glasses. They exchanged glances and shrugged.

Otten wiped his eyes. "I got to analyzing the situation we're in and decided that in the event we had to fuck instead of fight, you'd be in a worse fix than me. I got a picture of you sticking it to that old gal and that baby in her belly wondering what the hell that was come crowding in on him, and I could just hear him saying, 'Get outa here. Get outa here and leave me alone.'" He whooped and made short slapping motions with both hands. "'Get outa here, get on outa here.'"

Porter sat straighter and spoke with asperity. "I'm not about to either fuck or fight. I'm giving each of these women two packs of cigarettes and you hand over some D-bars, and we're out of here. Right now. Quit braying like a jackass and do as I say."

He rose, bowed politely, said, "*Au revoir,*" "*Merci,*" and "*S'il vous plaît,*" repeatedly, and they departed.

Alone on the street, Carter Otten started laughing again. "Just wait till I write Griffin Calhoun that old Osborne took up with a pregnant whore whose unborn baby was hollering, 'Get outa here. Get outa here.' What a cocksman."

"You do and I'll write him that you had one that grinned like a picket fence and was black as Essie's butt." They laughed together. "But it sure was fascinating to hear her speaking French."

"They felt the same way about you. You should've seen their faces when you told them your grandmother's pencil was on the table.

Honest to God, Osborne, you're crazy. I never know what you're going to do next."

"Neither do I, Carter, a lot of times. So many things come up on short notice. But let me point out that you don't get very far when you go to the trouble of planning. We still ain't been laid. And I don't believe you're going to find any girls in Bayeux."

Otten's festive mood was not to be dimmed. "No problem," he declared airily. "We'll go back to the hotel and I'll fuck the chambermaid."

"Chambermaid? I didn't see any chambermaid."

"Well, they're in every French hotel. And they expect to be seduced by traveling Englishmen."

"How do you know?"

"Goddammit, Osborne, ain't you ever read *The Scarlet Pimpernel*?"

"No, I haven't. And besides, we're not Englishmen."

"Hell, these Frogs can't tell the difference."

Porter considered only briefly. "They can tell," he stated.

"Will you, by God, let me do the talking? I'll never ask you to speak French again."

To Porter's surprise, they did indeed have a chambermaid. Or concierge. Or housemother. All this was new to him. When they found the door to the hotel locked, he was perturbed.

"We don't have a key."

Otten pressed a white enamel button in the wall. "That's why they have a chambermaid. To let swashbucklers and Englishmen in after hours."

"Nobody's coming."

"She will." He played shave-and-a-haircut on the bell. "Don't worry."

Porter heard a high feminine voice beyond the door but could distinguish no words. Then a heavy key turned in the lock and the tall door swung open.

"*Entrez, messieurs.*"

"What'd I tell you?" gloated Otten. "Not bad, either, and dressed for beddy-bye already, too."

The young woman attending them was indeed in her night clothes, but most chastely so. A long flannel nightgown swaddled her from neck to ankles and a cloak swung from her shoulders. Her hair was tucked into a nightcap that had a little ruffle around it, framing small features and plump pink cheeks. She was short, chubby rather than tiny; her small hands had dimples where the bones of knuckles should have shone. She met Otten's provocative grin and raised eyebrows with a demure half-smile and lowered lids; amiable good will emanated from her.

"What's your name?"

"*Pardon, m'sieu?*"

"You." He pointed. "Your name. What's your name?"

"Ah! Name. My name. My name is Suzie."

"OK. Suzie it is. Well, *bonsoir*, Suzie."

"*Bonsoir, m'sieu.*" She started for the stairs.

Otten blocked her path. His mouth was pulled into a half grin, his eyes danced and they danced only for her. "Suzie, *couchez avec moi?*"

"Me no speak English, *m'sieu.*"

"That wasn't English, goddammit. That was French." Porter sniggered. "Shut up, Osborne." He twinkled down at Suzie. "Let's see if you understand this. You *zig-zig* with me?"

Suzie drew herself up and raised her chin. Her mouth and her eyes were equally round, her voice an octave deeper than before, resonant with surprise. "*Ah, non, m'sieu.* Suzie no *zig-zig* wiz you."

Otten maintained his puckish charm; he tilted his cap rakishly over one eye and reached into a pocket. "You *zig-zig* for chock-a-lot?" He put four D-bars on the table by the sofa.

Suzie's eyes flickered. "Suzie no *zig-zig* for *chocolat, m'sieu.*"

"Cigarettes?" A carton of Camels and one of Lucky Strikes appeared. "You *zig-zig* for cigarettes?"

"*Non, m'sieu.* Me no *zig-zig* for cigarettes."

The game went on. Porter tumbled to awareness that this diminutive French girl was neither insulted nor afraid. She was possessed of unbelievable poise and was playing the charismatic Otten like a fish on the line. Her good nature was astounding but contagious. He fancied she was enjoying herself.

Two sacks of coffee joined the chocolate and cigarettes.

"*Non, m'sieu,* Suzie no *zig-zig* for coffee."

Otten emptied the pockets of the raincoat and held up two cartons. "How you say lard in French, Osborne?"

"Leave me out of this, O great Pimpernel. Besides, I don't know. I do know that *lard* means *bacon*, so don't try that word."

"*Grease!*" proclaimed the innovative Otten in wolfish triumph. "You *zig-zig* for grease, mademoiselle? Watch this, Osborne. They go crazy over shortening, I'm told."

The girl did not look beyond Carter's snapping eyes. There was, Porter thought, a lilt of amusement in her voice, the provocative suggestion that the goal was not unobtainable.

"Suzie no *zig-zig* for grease."

Otten pulled both pants pockets out. "Money? Five, six, seven, eight, nine, ten American dollars? You *zig-zig* for money?"

At this, Suzie stiffened her shoulders and a frown appeared. She wagged a tiny finger under Carter's nose and answered indignantly, "Suzie no *zig-zig* for money. Never!"

Otten retreated a step, still smiling, still intent. He draped one arm over the newel post and leaned into her face, trying his best to look like a cross between Tyrone Power, Clark Gable, and Humphrey Bogart. "Well, goddammit, sweetheart, what *will* you *zig-zig* for?"

Suzie raised one arm, forefinger pointing to the heavens, and spoke with invincible pride. "Suzie *zig-zig* for love! Only for love."

The irrepressible Otten laughed aloud, spread both arms wide in welcome, and trumpeted, "OK. OK. For love! Why didn't you say so? We *zig-zig* for love!"

Suzie pulled her cloak about her and spoke with dignity and amused finality. "But, *m'sieu*, me no love you."

Quick as a flash she evaded his lunge and was up the stairs. There was a long moment of silence and immobility, and then Porter doubled up with laughter.

"Touché," he announced.

"Shut up, Osborne."

"Maybe she could tell we weren't Englishmen. I'd hate to think it was because your pimpernel wasn't scarlet. Wait'll I tell Griffin about this!"

"You breathe a word of this to a living soul and I'll break every bone in your back." He aimed a kick at Porter and stormed up the stairs. When Porter heard his door close, he mounted the stairs himself. The clock with the exposed pendulum ponderously asserted that it was ll:45. It would be good, he thought, to sleep in a real bed. Besides, this was the first time in his life he had spent the night in a hotel.

As he turned down the corridor on the second floor, he heard "Psst" behind him. Turning, he saw Suzie, leaning around the corner of the steeper, narrower stairs that led to the floors above. She beckoned to him and, when he approached, grasped his hand and led him on tip-toe up two more floors to her own room that was tucked under the roof as efficiently as the reception desk beneath the stairs below.

Porter's sense of presence was shaken. "Why me, Lord?" he thought. He watched as she shed her cloak, stepped out of the night-gown, and with a downward toss of her head freed her tawny hair of the nightcap. He gazed in awe at the mounds of her breasts and belly and revised his thinking. "For Pete's sake, why not me?" he exulted and held out his arms.

Holding a finger to her lips to mandate silence, she went into his embrace without reservation, helped him undress, and then pulled him into the feather bed. Porter learned by application the full meaning of *zig-zig* although no words passed between them during the active intervals between cat naps. At dawn she pushed him from the bed, indicated by signs that he should return very quietly to his room below, and gave him one last lingering kiss.

"*Merci, Suzie. Je vous remercie beaucoup. S'il vous plaît,*" he whispered.

She gave him a little squeeze and a smothered giggle. "*Au 'voir,*" she whispered.

On the way back to camp that morning, Otten was grouchy. "How in the hell do you keep going to sleep in this damn bouncing truck? You're going to fall out and break your fucking neck. Didn't you sleep last night?"

"Not much. My bed was lumpy, and besides, I was too excited about being away from camp all on my own in a strange French city to sleep. That's the very first time I ever spent the night in a hotel."

"Are you kidding? You really are country, aren't you? How do you think you're going to get that damn figurine back to the States without it busting?"

"I've got it all figured out. I'm going to wrap it in wads of cotton sheeting and then put it in a plaster cast before I mail it."

"Hey, that might work."

"Sure, it'll work. What I wish is that I could have bought that clock in the hotel, but it's too heavy to tote, let alone wrap in plaster and mail."

"Who in the world would you mail it to."

"My dad."

"Your dad? Why, for God's sake?"

"Because he'd shit, that's why. He's never in his life seen one like it, and for once he'd be caught completely by surprise."

"You know, Osborne, I've never met him, but I can't help liking him."

"Everybody likes him. Even his enemies."

"Well, he sure deserves better than you for a son."

"Kiss my ass, Otten. I sure wish I could give him that clock as a souvenir of that hotel."

"Goddammit, Osborne, that was a third-rate crummy flea bag of a hotel. The chambermaid wouldn't even fuck. Forget it."

"As far as I'm concerned, Carter Otten, that is the finest hotel in the world, and I'll never forget it. Now will you shut up and let me sleep?"

A week later Porter realized that he was tortured by the urge to scratch himself, even when he was scrubbed on a case in the Operating Room. A surreptitious examination revealed a host of little visitors. With aplomb, he sprinkled himself with DDT powder, saturated his sleeping bag with it, and continued to remember Suzie with favor.

"Dear Dad," he wrote. "They censor my mail and I can't tell you where I am, but I have had my first overnight pass and enjoyed it immensely. When I get home and we are by ourselves, remind me to tell you about it and to describe this clock that I saw in the hotel. That will bring it all back to mind. I have sure had it reinforced to me that good manners pay off."

*"It is he who saith not Kismet,
It is he who knows not fate."*

33 **O**n Monday at dusk the train blew up; not all of it, just the car that was loaded with explosives. It had sat on a siding at a crossroads two kilometers from the hospital, had been there for a week, and had attracted desultory notice because American MP's occasionally checked on it. No one was ever sure of the cause, but the explosion shook the earth for several miles and produced pandemonium.

Lulled by the information that Gen. Patton was wreaking havoc miles ahead of them in the German lines, the personnel of the 816th had adapted to the tame existence of life in the rear. Porter had accomodated himself to the probability of never being involved in combat, never having to prove heroism or the lack of it under fire. When the boxcar blew up and they felt the rumble, heard the deep roar, saw the blaze in the sky, they immediately assumed that it was military action. Reaction was varied.

The explosion interrupted the evening meal; Porter had washed his mess gear and was headed back to the OR. He heard the nurses' involuntary screams over in the officers' mess and heard the mess sergeant bellow, "Hit the dirt!" Exultation washed over Porter in a flood. This was the moment of truth. The chips were down. This was his chance to respond to the accumulation of generations of fighting genes that had pooled in his veins. He would not cower in the mud. His duty lay in the OR where thousands of wounded would shortly require care, and he would be there, disregarding the hail of German bullets and facing violent onslaught. Osborne men did not back away from danger. He would be true to them. He knew who he was.

Raising his mess gear above his head and swinging it like a saber, he went charging up the hill yelling at the top of his voice, "The Yankees are coming! The Yankees are coming! Yeee-ah!"

One of the figures lying prone on the wet earth turned its head. "Osborne, this is not the Civil War! Hit the dirt!"

He recognized Capt. Smith even with mud on his nose and paused for a second. "Right you are, sir. It's easy to get confused. They say wars are all alike." He leaped over the captain's buttocks and raced away, yelling, "The Redcoats are coming! The Redcoats are coming! 'One if by land and two if by sea!'"

"Dammit, Osborne, this is also not the Revolution! Hit the dirt! That's an order!"

"No sweat, sir!" Porter yelled over his shoulder. "'When duty whispers low "Thou must," the youth replies "I can."' I'll see you later. Have a good war!"

"Ignore him," Capt. Ballas said to Capt. Smith. "He's obviously shellshocked."

"He's crazy as hell," responded Capt. Smith and spit out a blob of mud.

Consternation dwindled when news came of the nature of the explosion. Expectation dulled into boredom when no casualties appeared and all the OR personnel were sent back to quarters except the emergency crew. The news spread that an American major had been thrown from his Jeep when it collided with a cart drawn by a rearing horse frightened by the explosion. The man driving the cart was unhurt, but his wife was cut across her forehead. The horse was killed, and the American had a fractured femur. A French civilian who had been riding in the Jeep with the major had been decapitated in the wreck.

The ambulance driver was defensive with Capt. Ballas. He spoke above the screams of the French woman. "I know the rules, sir. I know we're not supposed to transport civilians and I know you're not supposed to treat civilians in this facility, but there's no French doctor anywhere around here, and that American major refused to let us pick him up until we brought this lady here. Said the wreck was his fault and he wanted this lady looked after first." Capt. Bloom jerked his head at Porter and they began attending the hysterical woman. Capt. Ballas pursued protocol. The ambulance driver was adamant.

"I understand what you're saying, sir, and I apologize. But that major does outrank you, and frankly, sir, I don't believe even you would like to cross him. He's a wild man."

"Osborne, you know any French?" Capt. Bloom demanded. "Talk to this woman and get her quiet. She's yelling so I can't thread my needle, and all she's going to need is about ten stitches and we'll be through. But if she keeps snatching her head around and screaming like a banshee, we'll be here all night."

Porter grabbed a pocket dictionary of French phrases. "Try '*Reste tranquille,*' sir."

"*Reste tranquille!*" roared Capt. Bloom. "*Reste tranquille!* Goddammit, woman, shut up!"

"We can't accept this woman officially . . ." Porter heard Capt. Ballas telling the ambulance driver.

"With all due respect, sir, the major . . ."

The woman's screams drowned out the rest of the sentence. In desperation, Porter put his lips against the woman's ear and spoke. "*Le crayon de ma grandmere est sur la table,*" he proclaimed.

She stilled. "*Pardon?*"

"*Le crayon de ma grandmere est sur la table.*"

"*Qu'est-ce-que dit, m'sieu?*"

Porter repeated it. Over and over.

"Good job, Osborne. One more stitch and I'm through. Give her T.A.T. and you put the bandage on."

Capt. Ballas was still explaining to the ambulance driver that U.S. rules and regulations prohibited his Operating Room receiving or treating any French civilians.

"I'm sorry, sir. I truly am. But with all due respect, I'd rather face a court-martial from you than to run into that major again if I disobeyed him. You should have heard him."

"What exactly did he say to you?"

"Well, sir, for openers, he told me he'd jerk my head off and shit in my neck. He meant it, too."

Porter fumbled and almost dropped the roll of bandage. "I didn't know Will Barton was a major," he said to his patient.

"*Pardon, m'sieu?*"

"*Le crayon de ma grandmere . . .*" Porter began, but was interrupted.

"*Non, non, m'sieu. Pas de plus. Reste tranquille.*"

Capt. Ballas looked at the neatly bandaged lady, puffed on his pipe and told the ambulance driver, "There is absolutely no way that I am going to receive this woman and treat her in my Operating Room, Corporal, and that is final."

The corporal also surveyed the woman. "In that case, sir, I'll just transport her right on out of here and see if I can find where she lives. Their horse is dead and I'll have to take them home." He saluted and the captain returned it.

Porter said to Capt. Bloom, "You're my kind of doctor, sir," and followed the corporal to the ambulance. "Where is that major? Are you bringing him here?"

"No. He told the other driver to take him directly to the Orthopedic ward. Nobody disobeys him tonight. The windshield to his Jeep was broken and cut off that Frenchman's head, and he just grabbed it and tossed it in the back seat like it was an old shoe or something. I wasn't about to argue with him."

"You are one more smart corporal," Porter assured him.

When he re-entered the OR, Capt. Ballas had departed. Porter told the nurse on duty, "I'm going to run up to Orthopedics a minute. Holler if you need me."

He found Will Barton so drugged with morphine that he was almost unresponsive. It was not his femur that was fractured, it was both bones in his leg about four inches above the ankle. Near the knee was a small gaping hole that was oozing dark greasy blood. Lt. Hormley was irrigating the wound with an Asepto syringe and sterile saline. He had on gloves, a mask, and a scrub jacket but no gown. His arms were as thin and as hairy to the shoulders as an orangutan's. The enlisted man holding the foot stable while Lt. Hormley packed the puncture wound with sulfa crystals looked up. So, briefly and disinterestedly, did Lt. Hormley.

"Hello, Kostas," said Porter.

"I thought you were Farbecker," the lieutenant said with detachment.

"So I am, sir," responded Kostas. "Hello, Osborne."

The lieutenant looked up again. "I thought you were Miller."

"Who, sir?"

"Miller. Works in the OR. Your name's not Miller?"

"No, sir. I'm Osborne. I work in the OR, too, but I don't know anybody there named Miller."

"Well, you sure look like him and he sure as hell looks enough like you to be your brother, and I know he works there, for he scrubbed on a case with me not a week ago."

"My name's Osborne, sir."

"Well, you could have fooled me. That's the trouble with this outfit; they pulled a bunch of strangers together and expect them to function as a unit. I'll never learn everybody's name." He removed a piece of fat with thumb forceps.

"I know, Lieutenant," soothed Porter. "All enlisted men look alike." He did not dare meet the eyes of Kostas.

412

"I never had thought of that before, but you know, you may be right. Long as you're here, turn the page on this book for me and Farbecker won't have to break scrub."

The copy of Watson-Jones, Vol. II, was spread on a Mayo stand beneath the light bulb, immediately adjacent to the tray of sterile instruments. It was opened to fractures of the lower extremity. Porter obediently turned to the section on tibia and held it up while the lieutenant perused it like a cook book. He muttered as he read.

"Two-bone break. Junction distal and middle third. Poor blood supply. Now hold up the x-ray. Yep, that's it! Two bad you're not Miller. He's quite a philosopher in a homespun way. Seems to be fairly well educated, too. For a Southerner, that is. He's from Tennessee. Know what he told me? Said, 'You gotta drive, Lieutenant, you gotta drive.' It's been sort of a challenge ringing in my ears ever since, and I've been working my tail off. Good man, Miller. Turn the next page."

Lt. Hormley studied the recipe in Watson-Jones carefully. "Aha! Just as I thought. The cast has to go to mid-thigh with the knee bent and the ankle flexed to stabilize the fracture. Farbecker, put in a half dozen rolls of six-inch plaster; this patient is a big man."

"What are you going to do about that puncture wound, Lieutenant? It looks pretty nasty."

"I know, but there's nothing else to do. There's nothing to suture; it's just a hole. I've lavaged and debrided it and packed it with sulfa. We'll put on a sterile dressing and incorporate it in the cast. You already gave him a tetanus booster, didn't you, Farbecker?"

"Yes, sir," replied Kostas. "At the same time the nurse gave him that last dose of MS."

"Good man. Let's move with that plaster. Long as you're here, Osborne, you might as well squeeze out the rolls and hand them to me, and we won't have to pull the nurse off rounds on the next ward. Not too dry, now, but also not too wet. Good man, Osborne."

From the head of the table came a voice, thick and slowed by narcotics but definitely the voice of Will Barton. "Don't tell me I've run into that wall-eyed little bastard named Porter Osborne again."

Lt. Hormley flicked a glance away from the cast he was building. "You know this patient?"

"Yes, sir. We were in school together back in Atlanta. Before we went in the Army."

"Why is he a major and you're just a PFC?"

Porter did not even hesitate. "It's a long story, Lieutenant, and you wouldn't believe a lot of it. I don't myself."

Barton's voice was stronger. "Why don't you quit pussyfooting around, Osborne, and just tell the son of a bitch it's none of his goddam business?"

"There, there, Major. Don't excite yourself. This GI a friend of yours?"

"Friend? Hell, we're asshole buddies! He's one of the few people I know who's been as fucked over as I have and still kept fighting back. I want permanent permission for him to visit me at any hour while I'm in this hospital, or I'll jerk one of those long hairy arms of yours out of the socket and beat the living shit out of you with it. And then report you to Gen. George Patton, who is a personal friend of mine. You got that straight?"

Lt. Hormley's voice changed in pitch so that it sounded more like it came from a large cave than from a tomb, but it was perfectly level and free of any inflection. "I understand perfectly, Major. Consider it done. We're almost through here. I'm going to order you another shot for pain and you try to relax. You need to get plenty of rest to heal a wound like this."

"Look, Sonny, don't tell me how to get well; I've had more broken bones than you've had pieces of ass. Get me some crutches tomorrow, skip the morphine, and I'll be back with my unit in a week."

"There, there," said Lt. Hormley. "You just relax. Everything's going to be all right. Have you noticed, Farbecker, how interesting Southerners are?"

"Not yet, Lieutenant; I've been too busy." Kostas met Porter's eyes briefly. "But I'll start noticing. I've always thought them regionally dense and very provincial."

"You kiss my ass," murmured Porter as Lt. Hormley left. "You blue-bellied Massachusetts Yankee. I'll be back to see you, Will, every chance I get. Let me help Farbecker here put you to bed."

By Tuesday, Will Barton was an exciting change in Porter's routine. He made multiple visits to him, rushing over to the Orthopedic ward every time he had a break.

"By God, Osborne, I'm glad to see you. This leg hurts like hell, but I'm not letting them give me any more morphine. You help me watch them. I've collected four purple hearts already, and I've learned that you get well faster and back on your feet quicker if you just pop a few APC's and stay away from that poppy juice. It gets you where you don't give a good goddam; it'll make a pussy cat out of a Bengal tiger. I just barely remember seeing you last night. Tell me what you've been up to."

"Not much, Will, not much. I kept on trying but I've just about resigned myself to marking time till the war's over. As you can tell, I never got in the paratroopers. I lay on my ass in a damn medical pool at Camp Grant for three months after I ran into you at Lawson, and it damn near broke my spirit. D-day came and went and I finally got over here on D plus 106 after Otten found an outfit coming over and we both begged a place in it. I've been working high and dry in the Operating Room ever since. Or let's put it this way: I've been safe and secure well behind Patton's Army. There ain't no high and there ain't no dry in Normandy."

"Otten? Carter Otten? Is he in this outfit?"

"Sure is. Works in the OR with me. Keeps the sore head and stays pissed off all the time about not getting promoted, but he's here."

"I always meant to slap the shit out of him some time when the opportunity arose, but I left Emory before I got around to it. It's funny how you change. I don't even want to anymore."

"What'd you have a run-in with Otten about?"

"I didn't have a run-in; he's still able-bodied, ain't he? I just didn't like the arrogant way he went around like a damn social butterfly and didn't take med school seriously. Seemed to accept his position there as a God-given right instead of a splendid opportunity. I didn't know him well at all, but I always figured it would do him whole bunches of good for somebody to slap the living dog shit out of him."

Porter laughed. "I know the feeling, but they say war makes strange bedfellows and he's my buddy now. I'll tell him you want to see him, but you tell me what's happened to you since I saw you."

"I told you I had to get out of Lawson and go clean up Italy for them, didn't I? Well, by God, I did! I got to drinking one night with a colonel who had the general's ear, and he finally came around in his thinking and let us jump behind the lines and prove there wasn't a single German left in that damn monastery at Cassino. I'd been telling them that. We chased their butts all the way to Rome. I picked up a bullet and had to spend a week in the hospital but got back on line in time for the liberation of Florence. Now there, Osborne, is a town. I'd worked back up to captain by then and had two days I'll never forget. And nights. Then my men jumped on the fifteenth of August just east of Toulon. It was messy but I've seen worse. Marseilles was wild. Toughest town I've ever been in. Had to stay there a while. Every other

415

trooper I had caught the damn clap, it looked like, and two of them got knifed by civilians. Rough town, Marseilles. Stay out of it.

"I made Paris about a week after the liberation and have been quartered there off and on ever since. Went on special assignment for a couple of weeks to Brussels at the special request of Gen. Dempsey to help the Limeys clean it up, but most of the time I've been in and out of Paris."

"When did you make major?"

"A couple of weeks after I got back from Brussels. I impressed the hell out of Dempsey, the British general, and he recommended me for a promotion. I hadn't stayed long enough to piss him off. My promotions have gone up and down like a yoyo, Osborne, but by God I'm still Will Barton."

"I can tell. I don't understand why they're keeping paratroopers in Paris right now, though."

"You don't have to understand, you fucking little PFC. I've been taken off jump status and am on temporary assignment to Intelligence."

"Intelligence? You? Doing what?"

"None of your goddam business. And you don't even know that, understand? If you so much as open your mouth, I'll jerk your head . . ."

"I know, I know," intervened Porter. "Fear and trembling seal my lips, Maj. Will Barton. You sure I can't get you a little morphine before I go?"

"You trying to turn me into a candy ass, Osborne? Give me a drink of water and come back as soon as you can. I'll tell you one thing, though. The Germans ain't through yet. Those V2 rockets are playing hell in England."

"I met a German colonel at Lawson who scared me about a weapon they were working on. I guess that was it. I don't see how they could come up with anything worse."

"There is something worse, Osborne, but I don't think they have it. Yet. We need to beat their ass as quick as possible. Pray for Patton. He's the son of a bitch who can save us."

"Son of a bitch?"

"Hell, yeah. When you're in a fight, you need a son of a bitch. Not a saint. But in my mind Patton is both. Now, get outa here."

Porter spent the afternoon scrubbed on cases in the OR, but his thoughts were with Will Barton. "He's a damn hero," he mused, "and who would ever have thought it?"

Otten went by to visit but reported, "You have the strangest tastes, Osborne. That guy is a damn Neanderthal maniac, and how he ever got those gold leaves beats the living shit out of me."

"You better be glad that's already tended to." Porter was smug.

"Now what the hell is that cryptic statement supposed to mean, you pompous little bastard? You go see him all you want to, but include me out. You're both just as crazy as hell and deserve each other. 'Birds of a feather' and 'Water seeks its level.'"

"Kiss old Rusty, Otten."

"Up yours, Osborne."

At Will Barton's inviolable command, Porter was allowed to sit at his bedside all through the long hours of Tuesday evening.

"Anything to keep him quiet," Lt. Hormley informed the nurse.

"Right," she responded. "That doesn't quite do it, but it's better than nothing."

"What are you going to do after the war, Osborne?" Will Barton inquired.

"I had assumed I'd go back to med school; my dad's got a letter from the Dean guaranteeing it. But lately I've had my doubts."

"What do you mean, doubts?"

"I'm not real sure I want to be a doctor any more, Will. To tell you the truth, I'm not sure at times why I ever wanted to be one in the first place. I always had this picture of going back to my home town and helping people, and people would love me like I love them and life would be wonderful. Then I went to med school and found out how hard it was and how grim most of it is. On top of that, I've been around a lot of doctors since I got in the Army and most of them are not very noble role models. On top of that, nearly everything you do for some-body smells bad, and I just plain don't know how I feel about med school any more."

Will Barton folded his hands calmly on his belly on the outside of the blanket. "You were terribly young," he said.

"What are you talking about? You're not but three years older than I am."

"Screw you. I was at least twenty years older than you when we were at Emory, and now I'm fifty or more."

"In that sense we were all younger than you."

417

"You got that right. And by the time this war is over, you're going to feel that you're older than a lot of people your own age. Some folks, like old Otten, develop a case of arrested development and don't ever grow any more after they get old enough to smell their own piss."

Porter grinned. "I'll remember to tell him that at some appropriate time down the road. What do you plan to do after the war, Will?"

"Hell, I'm going back to med school. I'm going to be a doctor. I'm no wishy-washy candy ass. I know what I want to do."

"Why? Why do you want to be a doctor?"

"Osborne, get this straight. There are two kinds of people in this world: those who give to other people and those who spend all their lives taking. Or planning to take. Either by bulling around on one end of the economic scale or whining on the other. I'm not a taker, Osborne, I'm a giver. Some folks were born to serve and others to be looked after. I'm Will Barton. I was born to give and to serve, and the world had goddam well better know it and get ready. There's no better place to do it than in medicine. I'm going to be a doctor."

Porter had a swift vision of Will Barton with an interview committee. "Where do you plan to go to med school, Will?"

The man looked at him in surprise. "Emory, of course."

"Emory?"

"You're damn right. It's the best med school in the world. I told you I'd been in hospitals over and over since I got in this fracas. I'm a connoisseur of hospitals, by God. The Emory unit is the best hospital the United States has put in the field. A surgeon named Dan Elkin is head of it, and he's got mostly Emory doctors staffing it and they're the best doctors I've run across anywhere. I've been around doctors from Harvard, Yale, Duke, Vanderbilt, California; you name it; and the ones from Emory top them all. I'm going back to Emory, by God."

"How are you going to get accepted?" asked Porter with skepticism. "Dr. Wingo is still there. You think you can suck up to him?"

"Shit, Osborne! I told you you were young. None of y'all ever understood the Butch. If I went back and told him, 'Father, I have sinned before heaven and before thee,' and begged to be taken back, he'd gag like he was watching maggots work in a dead dog. Horace Wingo is tough, but what none of y'all ever realized is that he's fair, and, by God, he's a man's man. I'll tell him I'm still not scared of him and that he can't flunk me. I'll tell him to pour it on, that I can take all he's got. Just like I told him before. Then I'll tell him I'm ready to settle down and not lose my temper with little baby-faced pissants and that

I'm going to be the best goddam doctor who ever took Gross Anatomy twice. He'll be glad to see me. The Butch gets bored, too, you know."

Porter recalled the grizzled, pale-eyed visage of Horace Wingo. "Barton, are you sure you haven't just had a shot of morphine? You'd be the only one who ever had the Butch twice."

"See? See what I mean? You're still in awe of him. You're not ever going to grow up till you get over being scared shitless by authority figures and see them as ordinary walking-around men underneath all the trappings they've surrounded themselves with. Besides," he added with a wink, "none other than Dan Elkin and a dozen of the most influential doctors at Grady Hospital and Piedmont and Emory have pledged to help me get past the Butch. You'd be surprised how many settled physicians can remember back to when they were either meat throwers themselves or were tempted to be. At least when they run across somebody who's up front about why he got booted out of med school. Everybody in the world has fucked up at some time or other in his life, Osborne. I'm going back to Emory."

"Lots of luck," said Porter. He looked up as Sherman Roger Jewel walked by. "Hi, Farbecker," he greeted.

"Farbecker?" Will Barton scowled. "That's a name I never heard before, and all of a sudden I'm hearing it all around me."

"It's a common name up north." Porter was glib.

"Maybe so, but how the hell many Farbeckers you got in this one unit?"

Porter leaned over and stared him in the eye. "None of your goddam business," he quoted.

Will Barton returned the look, unblinking through a moment of silence. "Gotcha," he said. "Gimme an APC and get your ass out of here so I can get some sleep. See you tomorrow."

Barton was still sleeping when Porter went by in the early morning. The nurse on duty was the fresh-faced girl from Iowa who was humming, "God Bless America" as she went about her work. "Don't you wake him," she said.

When he went by at noon, she broke off humming "Everybody Ought to Love Jesus" and said, "I'm glad you've come. He's got a temperature and he's a little subdued, too quiet to suit me. He's been asking for you."

Everybody in the whole wide world has a temperature, Porter thought, and wondered where she had gone to nursing school.

"Hey, Barton," he said, "you better marry that lieutenant; she worries when you're quiet."

"When I get a little better, I may just have to tend to her before I ship out. She's a pretty little country girl and has a beautiful voice, but I wish she knew something besides those goddam hymns she's always humming."

"She knows 'God Bless America;' I heard her this morning when you were still asleep."

"That's a fucking hymn, too, Osborne. You mark my words, the Baptists will sing it in church for years to come and long after Kate Smith is dead and rotten. It'll be right up there with 'The Battle Hymn of the Republic.'"

"That's a Yankee song, Barton, but you're right. It sure caught on, didn't it? How do you feel?"

"I'm puzzled. I've had a dozen broken bones worse than this, even ran fever with some of them, and I never felt like this before. I'm weak and my vision is a little blurry. I'm aching like people say they do when they have flu, although I've never had it myself. There hasn't been a germ invented that had the balls to invade Will Barton's blood stream. My leg is throbbing and not where the break is. Take a look at my toes, will you? It may be that I've just got some swelling and the cast is too tight."

Porter dutifully raised the covers. "The toes are swollen and a little dusky, but they sure aren't black. Can you wiggle them? Can you feel this?" He pinched a toe and then ran his hand up the hard smooth cast. "Hey, this cast is wet." He bent closer. "Up here around the knee it's soaked through and through. And it stinks, too. That puncture wound must be infected and draining. Let me go get Lt. Hormley."

He found Lt. Hormley in the next tent in the plaster room. He was just beginning to apply an airplane spica for a fractured shoulder. He listened to Porter's recital and then directed, "Cut a window in the cast. You're probably right about infection. Cut a window and clean the wound and I'll be along as soon as I finish here. Don't be afraid to cut a good sized window."

"Yes, sir," Porter replied.

"You let that saw slip and cut me," Barton advised, "and I'll ram it up your ass all the way to the cecum and drag your appendix out from below, coupled with the lesser and greater omentum and the superior and inferior mesenteric arteries."

"Damn it, Barton, forget you made an A under the Butch and relax. I've done this dozens of times. Your leg'll feel better as soon as we get some pressure off it."

"And the cisterna chyli and the splanchnic nerve. I might even knock on your prostate when I rip through the levator ani. Get on with it, Osborne. What are you waiting for?"

When he lifted out the rectangle of soggy plaster, Porter could not immediately see the puncture wound, for it was obscured by slimy, frothing pus. As he cleansed it away with sterile four-by-fours, the odor was so offensive that he went into paroxysms of coughing to keep from vomiting. With watering eyes he gasped, "I told you everything in medicine stinks if you get close enough to it. You still want to be a doctor?"

"Cut the shit, Osborne. What does it look like?"

Porter surveyed the swollen, macerated flesh he had exposed; the green, yellow, fiery red and purple surrounding the wet blackened strip that now was awash with pus and stretched away from the original small puncture. "It looks like a rainbow against a thunder cloud," he marveled, "but it smells like a hog pen."

"Goddam, Osborne, you'll never make a living as a poet. Get medical! I can't see into that damn little hole for myself."

"Well, there is definitely a large area of blackened, necrotic tissue spreading up at least as far as your knee. If your toes weren't all right, I'd say gangrene had set in." Porter pressed around the wound with a flat. "It feels crunchy and bubbly and makes a crackling noise. I think it's what they call 'crepitation.'"

"Oh, shit," whispered Barton. "*Clostridium welchii.*"

"What?"

"Gas gangrene, Osborne. Don't you remember that fat red-headed broad in Bacteriology? *Clostridium welchii.* First cousin to tetanus and twice as dangerous because we don't have a shot to prevent it. Anaerobic bacillus. Survival depends on early diagnosis, aeration and amputation." He laid his head back on the pillow and stared into the tent above him for a moment. Then he raised himself on both elbows and roared, "Cut the rest of that fucking cast off and get that pinch-nosed lieutenant in here! Where's that 'When-the-roll-is-called-up-yonder-I'll-be-there' nurse? Farbecker! Everybody! Front and center! On the goddam double! Get the lead out of your goddam flabby asses! Move, goddammit!"

"What's going on here?" inquired Lt. Hormley. "Now." he added.

"Maj. Barton thinks he has gas gangrene, Lieutenant."

Lt. Hormley held a flat over his nose and studied the wound. "I'll be back in a minute," he said.

Will Barton grabbed him by the arm. "Where the fuck you think you're going?"

"I'm going to get Maj. Pierce and Maj. Emmons. The best internist and the best surgeon on the post. Just as soon as you turn me loose, sir. Osborne, get him a fourth of morphine, stat."

"Yes, sir," said Porter.

"Where'd he go to school, Osborne? You can forget that fucking morphine."

"Creighton. It's in Nebraska. I never heard of it before. He's not much of an Orthopedist. He was a GP studying to be a Dermatologist before he got drafted."

"Don't put him down to me. The first sign of a good doctor is that he gets help when he needs it from somebody who knows more than he does. Goddam one who stands around with his finger up his butt and worries about his image. Honesty is all right."

Porter was terrified. "Are you hurting? You sure you don't need that shot?"

"I need to think." He beckoned. "Get close so you can hear what I'm saying. If I pull through this, which I have every intention of doing, you forget every damn word I'm telling you. If I don't, you remember every damn word and do what I tell you."

"OK, Will. I promise."

"First chance you get, go to Paris. Go to Pig Alley. That's the whorehouse district. Go to the Moulin Rouge. That's a cafe with a red windmill for a sign. Ask for Mimi Labotte. Got that? She's a whore. You're going to have to fuck her, Osborne. That's part of the I.D. trail. When she uses the word 'frog,' you tell her you've got to see La Petite. Got that?"

"Pig Alley. Moulin Rouge. Fuck Mimi. When she says 'frog,' I say 'La Petite.' Will, are you all right?"

"La Petite is the one you've got to find, and Mimi is her only contact. La Petite's not a whore. She won't fuck. She's a double or triple agent, I'm not sure which. Keeps her head shaved to pretend she was a collaboratrice. Which she never was. We've been on a hot chase together and she needs to know what happened."

Porter was round-eyed and silent.

"There's a whole bunch of questions she'll ask to prove your identity but you don't have time to learn those. Or any business learning them. Just use my name and she'll listen. You with me so far?"

Porter nodded.

"Tell her she can sleep at night now. Tell her The Barber is dead."

"The Barber?"

"Right."

"The Barber is dead. Who is La Petite, Will? What's her real name?"

"She never told me, but if I live I'm going to marry her. She's like that woman Jack London wrote about in *Martin Eden*; she's big enough for me. You tell her so."

"OK, Will. I'll do it."

"Aw, hell, Osborne, while you're at it tell her how The Barber died, too. Tell her I broke my leg in a Jeep wreck hurrying him back to her, and he was about to get away again. I smashed the windshield and jerked his neck down on it and cut his fucking head clean off. She'll like that."

Porter, if his survival had been at stake, could not suppress the question. "I've got to know, Will—did you shit in his neck?"

"What are you two laughing at?" asked the nurse.

"Inside joke, sister. Wanta come back tonight and climb in the sack with me?" He winked at Porter and Porter winked back, but his brain was spinning.

Maj. Emmons and Maj. Pierce confirmed Barton's suspicions and gave instructions to Lt. Hormley. "Try to get some antitoxin for *welchii* in him if they make it and if they've got any anywhere in the ETO. In the meantime, skin test him and start an IV drip of tetanus antitoxin in case there might be some collateral benefit. Round up any penicillin you can find and let's load him with that. There've been no reports on it, but anything is worth trying. Get the OR ready. I want Ballas for anesthesia and Bordillon as scrub nurse. Get me Otten to circulate. Stat!"

Maj. Emmons turned to Will Barton. "Major, I'm Jim Emmons, FACS. I hate to tell you, but we need to amputate."

"I know that, Major. Get on with it."

"Major, I'm Buster Pierce, General Internist. You know we're talking about taking your leg off, don't you? There's an infection in it that will kill you if it spreads."

"I know all that. Take the damn thing off."

"You've already decided? That quick?"

"Do I look like a rosy-cheeked pussyboy, Buster? Of course I've decided. George Patton said he's going to beat the fucking Russians to the Rhine and piss in it, and I aim to live to see it. A one-legged man can see water flowing as good as anybody. Let's go!"

The nurse from Iowa put her hand on Will Barton's forehead. "You want I should call the chaplain?"

"What in the hell for?"

"To pray before you go to surgery."

"Hell, no. I don't need him, and furthermore, I don't want him."

She spoke with resolute pluck. "Are you saved, Maj. Barton?"

Will Barton raised his head. "That, Lt. Florence Nightingale, is privileged information between me and my Maker. Are you Baptist?"

"As a matter of fact, yes. How did you know?"

"It figures. Let me tell you one thing, Toots. I've never saved anything in my life. As soon as I generate anything, I spend it. And the more I've spent, the more I've generated. Saving implies hoarding and there ain't a miserly bone in my body. Try that on for size."

Her eyes filled, but she persisted. "Do you believe in Jesus, Major?"

"What kind of dumb-ass question is that? Of course I believe in Jesus! Who in the hell is stupid enough not to believe in Him? I don't give much credibility to that namby-pamby sissy britches associate of little old ladies and trembling virgins. That's a personality they fashioned for themselves. I believe in the tough Jew who said 'No' to the Devil himself in the wilderness and then when they hung his ass on the cross and he was hurting like hell wouldn't knuckle under. He didn't take morphine, did He? You mighty right I believe in Him! He was one hell of a man, and if He was a god, he was my kind of God." He considered the nurse's trembling chin and patted her hand. "Don't pay any attention to me, Little Sis. You're a sweetheart and a joy to the whole frigging world. But," his voice rose again, "don't you sic any chaplain on me. Give my left boot to old Osborne, here; he's already sold his soul for a pair. But save the right one for me. I'll be walking day after tomorrow. Out of here, Osborne! Let's go!"

As he helped the POW's carry the litter, Porter said, "What in the world do you think I'll do with one paratrooper boot, Barton? Especially yours. It'll be too big for me."

"Bronze the fucker, Osborne. Bronze it and put daisies in it when the war is over."

Capt. Ballas helped place Will Barton on the operating table while Maj. Emmons and Lt. Hormley were scrubbing. Lt. Bordillon was already gowned and was arranging her instrument table. Carter Otten was fetching supplies at her command. Maj. Pierce stood in the background.

"Hi, Otten," said Will Barton. "Don't pick your nose till you're through with this case."

"Hi, Barton. Sorry about the leg."

"Thanks. It's just one of those things." He looked up at Capt. Ballas. "Where'd you go to med school, Captain?"

"Harvard. Trained at Mass General."

"What about Emmons?"

"Yale. Head resident at Peter Bent Brigham. President of Connecticut Surgical Society before his induction."

Will Barton looked over at Maj. Pierce. "What about you, Buster?"

"George Washington. Barnes."

"And you, nurse?"

Johanna Bordillon did not pause in rewrapping catgut around rolls of flats. "Charity in New Orleans."

"And Hormley is from Creighton. Hot damn," exclaimed Will Barton, "that's quite a team." He tried to lick his dry lips. "Especially when you add three forgotten fuckups from Emory. Otten, you and Osborne watch those educated bastards for me while I'm asleep; they never even heard of Grady and may need a little supervision."

"Major!" remonstrated Capt. Ballas. "I realize you've had your pre-op medication and you're a little out of control, but you really must watch your language in front of our nurses."

Porter refrained from telling him that the patient had received only the atropine and had refused the morphine. The patient looked at the nurse. "Toots, if I said anything you haven't heard before, there's a bridge in New York I want to sell you when this war is over."

"You relax, Major. I told you I'm from Charity. I scrubbed on at least a hundred cases worse than this before I ever joined the Army, and I'll keep an eye on every one of these *canailles*. You just relax and go to sleep."

"Way to go, baby. I feel better already. The goddam Yankees think we raised nothing but baby doll debutantes in the South; they don't know what a really strong woman is. Let's go!"

Emmons and Hormley came from the scrub sink with upraised dripping forearms and were gowned and gloved by Otten and Lt.

Bordillon. Capt. Ballas had an IV in place and an ampule of pentothal at the ready. "Shall I put him under?"

"Any time you're ready," Maj. Emmons said. "Keep him light as you can until we see how much trouble we're in."

"Wait a minute," ordered Barton.

"Yes?"

"This is it? You're fixing to put me to sleep?"

"Yes. I want you to start counting to ten and breathe slowly and deeply."

"I ain't about to count. I don't want to go to sleep listening just to the sound of my own goddam voice. Otten!"

"I'm right here, Will."

"You always sounded like a fucking angel back at Emory. You and Osborne help me sing it while I go under."

"Sing what, Will?"

"What? You know what!" Will Barton began the tune.

Otten looked across at Osborne. "Harmonize, Osborne. For God's sake, harmonize."

The operating team looked at each other with rotating heads as the voices rose in unison.

> "The eyes of Wingo are upon you
> All the live-long day . . ."

When they slowed for "Till Gabriel blows his horn," Porter nudged Capt. Ballas and he gently pressed the plunger. Will Barton's voice faded completely out on "Amen," and he gave a last snoring breath as he went to sleep.

The world immediately became a frozen one of white linen and sterile steel under the glittering light of the operating lamp. The team worked smoothly, efficiently, and very rapidly. All the world now focused, Porter thought, on the surgical field that Will Barton's leg had become.

"No need even to think about anything below mid-thigh, Hormley. We've got to get proximal to the gas or we haven't accomplished anything. This looks like healthy tissue. Let's remove right here and at least get the lower leg out of the way. Saw. Ligature. Sponge. Let off the tourniquet now."

"Blood pressure is falling, Major."

"Bag him. Start plasma. I wish we had blood. How's it look, Hormley?"

426

"Feel here, sir. There's crepitance in the femoral tissue, I think."

"Bring another lap pack," Johanna Bordillon instructed Otten. "Quick."

"Scrub in, Osborne," directed Maj. Emmons. "I need another pair of hands for retraction. We're going to have to disarticulate at the hip."

"Let Otten do it, sir. I just can't scrub on this."

"Why not?"

"I'm just this minute finding out how much I love the bastard, sir. I'll circulate."

They worked as one fast and furious juggernaut, guided by the eyes and hands and brain of Jim Emmons. Sweat poured off the surgeon's forehead and Porter dutifully mopped it. They worked so hard and so fast and so long that it seemed to Porter everything had geared down to slow motion.

"He's in shock, Major."

"More plasma. Pump it. Increase the oxygen. Bag it. We'll leave the wound open. Saline for lavage."

"There are gas bubbles coming out around the common iliac, Major. See them?"

"I see them. We were too late."

Capt. Irving Ballas spoke softly without inflection, "He's dead."

"Shit," said Lt. Johanna Bordillon.

Everything stilled. All shoulders drooped in complete exhaustion. No one moved and no one spoke. The very air was drained. Porter felt a hand squeeze his shoulder and Maj. Buster Pierce said in a low voice, "I don't know what to say, Porter Osborne."

"I do," said Porter and raised his head. He looked with wide dry eyes across at Carter Otten, shrugged, and spoke through tightened lips. "Fuck him if he can't take a joke."

"Don John of Austria
Has loosed the cannonade."

34   **P**orter did not go near the Orthopedic ward. Two days later the Waffleback who had served as Farbecker the night before visited him in his tent.

"The nurse on Ortho said give you these boots and tell you they'd shipped all your buddy's personals home."

"Thanks, Levek."

"She said for me to be sure and tell you that your friend is in a better place and that's she's praying for you."

"I knew she was going to say that. That's why I didn't go get the boots myself."

"She wanted I should give you some other messages yet, but I told her my rabbi wouldn't be able to handle my mama's hysterics if she found out I'd mentioned Jesus to anybody."

Porter smiled. "That was sticking your head in the lion's jaws, Levek. She'll regard you as a challenge from now on. She's a Baptist."

"She was crying and smiling at the same time." Arthur Levek had only two inches of forehead separating thick eyebrows from his heavy thatch of unruly hair, and it was furrowed in perplexity. "What's the story? She sweet on you? What's to smile when somebody kicks off? Even if he was a major?"

Porter had recall of Pietrini at Lawson. "That's just our way, Levek. Don't worry. By the time you're Farbecker again, she'll be smiling and humming."

"That's for sure and certain. She has a pretty voice, though."

"Thanks for the boots, Levek."

"No sweat. There's dried blood caked all over them. You want I should help you clean them? They look too big for you."

"No. That's a job I need to do myself. But I sure thank you for offering. You're right. I couldn't fill these boots. I was dreaming."

428

Porter spent an hour cleaning the boots and then polishing them until they glistened and winked. That was all The Barber's blood, he thought, for Will Barton didn't put out enough from the little hole that killed him to make that kind of mess.

The boots sat under his cot and he looked at them for two more days. Then he found a rare period of solitude, rummaged through his duffel bag for his cigar box, and poured all the remaining red soil into the two boots. He went behind a tent as near the officers' quarters as he could sneak and dug a hole. Carefully arranging the boots in it, he removed his helmet and held it over his chest.

"Rest in peace, Will Barton. I ain't about to bronze those fuckers." He dropped in Petrini's Saint Christopher medal, tamped the black soil back in place and replaced the divot he had reserved. "But I swear by the red earth of Brewton County I'll find La Petite first chance I get."

That night he wrote his father.

"Dear Dad,

Sorry I haven't written sooner, but things have been pretty hectic around here. I am following Mother's advice and only writing on one side of the paper. Now when the censors cut holes, at least they won't ruin what's on the other side.

I am well and safe, and that is about all I can tell you. If you will save my letters, though, they will remind me of what I really want you to know when I get back.

I did away with all my dirt from the big red hill. It had gotten to be pretty heavy in my duffel and on my heart, and I didn't really need it as much as someone else did. I know where I'm from still and am grateful for my family every day.

I am also grateful that I did not get transferred to the paratroopers. I might have been assigned to an officer who was more of a challenge than I could have handled. As one of our nurses says, 'The Lord knows best.'

I am getting closer to being a man every day, and I may be about as close as I want to get. For a while anyhow.

Otten and I still have not been promoted, but neither has anyone else. I have decided that our outfit

429

has the best doctors available, and it is a privilege to work with most of them. If I told you about a few who still act more like officers than they do doctors, it would be sure to get cut out. Like I said, nobody has been promoted yet.

The last three days I have been thinking about a poem by Edwin Markham that I had to memorize a long time ago when Mother made me take Expression lessons. It's called 'Lincoln, the Man of the People,' and it's the last four lines that I've been remembering this week.

'And when he fell in whirlwind, he went down
As when a lordly cedar, green with boughs,
Goes down with a great shout upon the hills,
And leaves a lonesome place against the sky.'

If you run into my old Expression teacher, tell her I said 'Thanks,' which is not something I'd ever thought I would want to say before. I have not cried since last Christmas.

Be sure and hang on to my letter from Dean Astenheimer. I just might still want to be a doctor when I grow up.

Give my love to Mother and the girls and tell them I appreciate each and every letter they write. This particular one had to be special to you.

Sambo."

A week after Will Barton's death, Porter and the Wafflebacks lost Daniel D. Farbecker.

Madison Lucetti was the unwitting catalyst who began the chain reaction that led to that event. He worked in the OR and enjoyed respect from all his fellows and a strong, albeit distant, affection from Porter. He was older than his comrades by six or seven years, and went about his work with solemn mien and an individual dignity that made him a little aloof from everyone.

He was ivory-skinned but his eyes, hair and close-shaven cheeks made him also swarthy. His eyebrows met in a straight bush above his nose and were so rank that he frequently had to remove his steel-rimmed spectacles and polish the skim from them, a habit that gave the impression he was a dedicated scholar, as wise as an owl. He was lithe rather than thin, and moved always with a speed and strength that intimated he was not bowlegged after all but that his legs, like spring steel, would pop into alignment as soon as he stood still.

Porter had assumed from his appearance and name that he was Italian and Catholic and from his speech that he was a Yankee—a collection of attributes that made him less than the ideal companion. The fact that he pulled a New Testament from his breast pocket and read it on break rather than joining in group banter and repartee was a further isolating characteristic in the eyes of the other OR personnel but was a titillating inconsistency to Porter. Very early after meeting him, he had approached Lucetti with what he regarded as the proper amount of diffidence.

"I thought Catholics weren't allowed to read the Bible for themselves."

"I wouldn't know about that." Madison Lucetti courteously closed the Testament over a forefinger to maintain his place in the Gospel according to John. "I'm a Methodist."

"Oh," said Porter. "I don't believe I ever met a Methodist from up north before."

"Nor have you now." His tone was patient, the inflection even and calm.

"Oh. Where you from?"

"West Palm."

"I beg your pardon?"

"West Palm Beach. It also is in Florida. Nearly everyone has heard of Palm Beach, and so I always just say 'West Palm' so nobody will think I'm putting on airs, pretending to be one of the rich people."

"You folks from South Florida all sound a little bit like Yankees. I didn't mean any offense."

"Nor did I take any."

"What did you do before you got in the Army?"

"I am an attorney."

"I don't believe I ever met a lawyer before who was always reading the Bible."

"You have now. It's very important to me."

"How did a lawyer wind up as a surgical tech working in an Operating Room?"

"I pray nightly about enlightenment on that point. Every time I've ever been moved, I've applied for transfer to the Adjutant-General's department, but one thing kept leading to another and here I am."

"Toting litters and reading the Bible in a cow pasture in Normandy."

"Exactly."

"Gosh, that's got to be frustrating."

"'The Lord moves in mysterious ways His wonders to perform.' I'm living to do my job and get home to my wife and baby."

"You have a baby?"

"Yep. Want to see his picture? He was born just before I shipped out, and I got to see him on my last leave."

The picture of his infant son gave further isolation to Madison Lucetti from his boisterous younger companions. He was set apart. It was obvious to Porter that he preferred it that way. It never occurred to him that this frustrated young lawyer would do anything of secular interest.

"What are you writing, Lucetti?"

"A formal demand for back pay. Do you realize that we have not had a pay roll in almost three months?"

"Big deal. The records were lost at Omaha. We'll get it eventually. There's no place to spend money now anyway."

"I know. But my wife is not receiving her allotment check, and she needs it to make ends meet. I got another letter today."

"You think you can make them pay us?"

"I think I can. I'm sending a copy of this report to Gen. Lee and also to AG headquarters in Washington. At least I'm making a note on the bottom of this complaint that I am, and I think that will be sufficient goad to make Col. Draughan wake up and order a payroll for us."

He was right. Within two weeks there was notice to pick up checks for current and back pay at the company office. Payroll was not so popular as mail call and not as well attended. After four days, Assembly was called for Sgt. Lagerpiel to define stragglers and personally deliver their checks.

"Farbecker! Daniel D."

Porter nudged Kostas. "Who's going to pick up his check?"

"Whose check?"

"Daniel D. Farbecker's, dummy."

"Who?"

"Farbecker, Kostas. Can't you hear?"

"I believe I've heard that name around for the last couple of months, Osborne, but do you know I've never laid eyes on the guy?"

Porter ruminated awhile. "Gotcha." When there was no answer forthcoming, he persisted. "Why?"

"You know that storage tent behind the plaster room? Meet me there in ten minutes. Right now I'm leaving here and we shouldn't be seen together. That sergeant's pretending not to, but he's watching us like a hawk."

Porter felt a little like a character in *Penrod and Sam*, but he waited around as he was told. He decided that his friend was not paranoid, for he noticed that Sgt. Lagerpiel's eyes did indeed follow Kostas as he strolled away, nonchalant and unconcerned, stopping to chat briefly with an occasional acquaintance.

Behind the plaster tent, Kostas told him in low tones that the Wafflebacks in solemn conference assembled had decided that none of them was brave enough to risk Leavenworth by signing for a check made out to another soldier. They had, after careful consideration of all details, including the fact that everyone was getting to know everyone else the longer the hospital worked together, decided that they were lucky for no one to have tumbled to the truth so far. Despite emotional harangues from a couple of the Wafflebacks and several totally preposterous suggestions from the Irishman who had formulated their motto, they had agreed reluctantly to let Daniel D. Farbecker die. Indeed, they had pledged to assert complete innocence of his existence and had finally sworn by the sacred bed springs of the *Queen Mary* from which their identity had sprung that they would deny and deny and deny and even undergo disciplinary action rather than admit to any knowledge of another's association with Daniel D. Farbecker.

Porter was awed, as he always was in the presence of Kostas, but thought him overly cautious.

"Everybody will think it's funny. Why not just tell the whole story? If Lucetti hadn't petitioned for it, we wouldn't have had a payroll until the copy of our official records caught up with us from Washington anyhow. Nobody will care."

"Porter Osborne, you are still so naive you blink in the twilight. Do you realize how many sergeants, nurses, and officers are going to feel stupid if they ever find out how badly they've been fooled for the last three months? Have you ever noticed how an officer behaves and treats enlisted men when something happens that makes him look stupid? Daniel D. has got to go, but I really am going to miss him."

"So am I. When does he go? Where is he going?"

"Who?"

"What's the matter with you, Kostas? Daniel D. Farbecker, of course."

"I'm sorry. I don't know who you're talking about. Maybe whoever it is has already disappeared."

Porter slapped him on the shoulder. "Gotcha."

Daniel D. Farbecker's failure to show up for his assignment on Orthopedics that night engendered more activity than Kostas had anticipated. The nurse from Iowa had two wards to cover. Both of them were full, and she had to request emergency coverage from Reserve Medical Pool. When this was reported to Sgt. Lagerpiel, he went on a search for the missing private. To his surprise, there was no record anywhere of which tent had served as Farbecker's living quarters and there was consequently no point from which to begin his quest, other than the Orthopedics ward itself. The lass from Iowa gave a description that fitted Sherman Roger Jewel, but that stalwart faced her down that he had never worked Orthopedics except once as a favor to some guy he thought was named "Woodpecker" who claimed to be sick. Jewell produced dog-tags to prove his identity. His sputtering indignation at being falsely identified, plus his anger at Farbecker who had never bothered to thank him or, come to think of it, ever shown his face again, lent credence to his statements. So did the fact that the other nurses questioned gave conflicting descriptions.

"He was definitely a blond with a Bronx accent."

"He was from Illinois, I'm sure. He always stayed sort of in the background, if you know what I mean."

"He has a definite New England accent as I remember. You know, Sergeant, 'Pock your caaar in the yaaahd' kind of talk. Sort of high-toned and long-nosed. That didn't fake me off, though. I had the distinct impression that he was, you know, Jewish?"

Sgt. Lagerpiel got no more solid help from Lt. Hormley, who was reading Watson-Jones and mumbling to himself and did not seem truly interested in the problem. "Farbecker? Oh, yes, I've worked with him. In the OR, I think. Scrubbed on a case with me. Wants to be a fireman when he gets out. Seems like he's from Tennessee. Or was that Miller? I can't remember. Is it really important? You know, Sergeant, I believe to my soul he's the one who told me all enlisted men look alike. There's a lot of truth in that, Sergeant, a lot of truth. Good man, Farbecker. Yes."

Lagerpiel followed the faint trail to the Operating Room where Sgt. Crowder dampened his hopes. "I ain't even got no man from Tennessee works here. Couple from Georgie and some from Texas, but most of the rest of 'em's Yankees. You can't pay no attention to Lt. Hormley, Milton, he ain't got syrup between all his pancakes, if you know what I mean. For awhile there, he kept requesting somebody named Miller to scrub with him, and I ain't never had nobody named Miller on my roster. I sure as hell ain't had no Farbecker."

"Goddammit, Oliver," snapped Sgt. Milton Lagerpiel, "he's got to be somewhere. I've got records where he's been on Orthopedics, done time on the honey wagon, even worked KP with those two Polack mess sergeants. There's a check waiting for him in the company office. Where is he? I can't find anybody who can even give me a description of Daniel D. Farbecker. He must be a real loner."

"Come to think of it, Milton," drawled Crowder, "I have heerd from time to time ever now and then one of my men say, 'Let Farbecker do it.' I knowed when you ast that name sounded familiar, and now I recollect that's where I heerd it."

"Which one of your men?"

"Osborne. He's off duty now. You might could find him in his tent. All my men bunk in tent number seven."

"Thanks. I'll look him up. At least it's a lead."

"Milton."

"What, Oliver?"

"Don't expect too much. Dealing with Osborne is like messing with a pile of stove wood."

"You mean he's shy a stick or two?"

"Naw." Sgt. Crowder tongued his cigarette deftly to the other side of his mouth. "If anything, he's got a few sticks extra. But ain't none of it stacked. You can't never tell what's going to come falling out on you. He ain't been the same since a major he knew in civilian life died here in the OR close on a week ago."

"I can handle Osborne," said Lagerpiel. "I know him and like him. You oughta be recommending him and Otten for promotion."

"Effen you can tend to your job, Milton, I reckon I can handle mine. It's important to teach a mule to walk between the traces before you slack up on the bit and give him his head."

Bosi overheard the interchange and relayed most of it to Porter, who was lying on his cot reading when Sgt. Lagerpiel sought him out.

"Don't get up, Osborne. You should have learned by now you don't have to come to attention for a noncom." He sat down on the empty cot next to Porter's.

"I know, Sergeant, but I was so lost in this book I didn't even know where I was."

"You know somebody named Farbecker?" Lagerpiel affected an off-handed manner.

"Sure, Sergeant. Daniel D. That's his name. Daniel D. Farbecker."

"What's he look like?"

"Oh, he's about average, I would say. Just the average GI you see everywhere."

"What kind of build?"

"His build? Oh, yes. He's not tall, but he's not what you'd call short, either. He's definitely not skinny like me, but on the other hand, he's not as heavy-set as you. I guess he's like I say, average. It's hard to say about his build because every time I've ever seen him he's had on his raincoat and, tell you the truth, I think the quartermaster goofed and gave him one too big for him. The sleeves come down to the very tip ends of his fingers. That's one thing I've noticed about Farbecker. You could never see his hands. Just the very tips of his fingers. And, tell the truth, Sergeant, not all of his fingers. That raincoat is definitely too big for Farbecker. I don't know why he's so attracted to it."

"Osborne, what color hair does he have?"

"Hair? Come to think of it, I'm not sure. He always wore his helmet liner, even in the mess hall. You're obliged to have noticed him. There aren't many guys who wear their raincoats and helmet liners while they're eating. It makes you a little leery of sitting by them. I don't believe, to tell you the honest truth, now that you bring it up, that I've ever seen Farbecker's hair. Seems like maybe it ought to be dark brown. But then I've noticed what ought to be is not always the order of the day or the way things are in this old world, Sergeant."

"Dammit, Osborne, what color are Farbecker's eyes?"

"His eyes? Golly, Sergeant, I never noticed. Sometimes he wears glasses, I think, and then sometimes he doesn't. I never paid the first bit of attention to his eyes. I guess I'm not interested in eyes. Come to think of it, though, Lt. Bordillon has brown eyes, doesn't she? And Lt. Curry has the prettiest blue eyes I ever saw. I guess I'm just not observant about men's eyes. Maybe it's because I don't care. Sorry I can't help you there."

"Goddammit, Osborne, you're the first enlisted man I've met who even remembers seeing Farbecker, and all the nurses are giving me conflicting descriptions. Now settle down and remember. Think, dammit, think. Were his eyes black, brown, blue, green or gray?"

"Of course."

"Of course, what?"

"They were either black, brown, blue, green or gray. What else is there? Wait a minute. You left out hazel. They might have been hazel. My grandmother always said she had hazel eyes. That's sort of between blue and gray. Yep, Sergeant, I suspect you've got it. I'll bet Farbecker's eyes are hazel."

Sgt. Lagerpiel narrowed his eyes. "Oliver Crowder says he's heard you say 'Let Farbecker do it.' Now that sounds to me like you know him better than you are claiming. How come you say that?"

"Oh, that. It's just sort of a saying. Like the little drawing you see everywhere that says 'Kilroy was here.' It's just sort of a saying, Sergeant, that you come out with when somebody tells you to do something at a time, you know, when you're too busy to do another single thing and you come out with 'Let Farbecker do it.' I don't know, but maybe it stems from him being sort of a goof-up or something."

Sgt. Lagerpiel gritted his teeth and stood with arms akimbo. "Let's try this, Osborne. His voice. What does Farbecker's voice sound like when he talks."

Porter brightened. "Now there I can be more definite, Sergeant. He sounds like either a Yankee, you know, somebody from up north, maybe from Chicago or New York City or Minneapolis or some place like that. Not Boston. You know what I mean? Or else he sounds like a North Georgia hillbilly."

Lagerpiel's face was definitely red, Porter noticed. "Osborne, how in the name of hell can a person sound like both a Yankee and a Georgia cracker?"

"Oh, it's simple, Sergeant. You see, Farbecker is not one who does much talking. I think he's what an intelligent person might call a loner. Don't get the idea I'm what you'd call his buddy or anything like that. Like I said, he's not what I would, by any stretch of the imagination, call a conversationalist. In fact, to tell you the truth of the matter, I've never heard him open his mouth and say a mumbling word except two times. One was in the chow line when somebody cut in front of him, and I can't for the life of me recollect who it was, but Farbecker was standing right in front of me and I plainly heard him say, and you'll have to forgive me, Sergeant, but I'm sure you want me to be accurate. I plainly heard with my own two ears Daniel D. Farbecker say, 'You dick me now, I'll get you with the big one later.' He did. He said it. That's when he sounded like a Yankee, Sergeant."

Lagerpiel took a deep breath. "Osborne . . ." he began.

Porter held up a hand. "Wait just a minute, Sergeant, I've not yet finished answering your question. The other time I heard Farbecker say something was also in the chow line when he nudged another guy out of line and said, 'Tough shit. You have to look after Number One.' That, to my shame, is when he sounded like a North Georgia hillbilly."

"Osborne, you are an eyewitness. I'm supposed to go out of here on your description and look for a raincoat and helmet liner over what may be brown hair and hazel eyes and somebody with either a Southern or Northern accent. I can't believe that I told Sgt. Crowder not a half hour ago that you merited a promotion. I'll for sure and certain have to correct that error in judgment. My God!"

Porter dared to wag a finger. "Don't forget, Sergeant. He's a loner, too. Farbecker's a loner. Look for a guy who creeps around by himself in a helmet liner and a raincoat and hardly ever talks at all. Gosh, when you describe him like that, it makes me feel bad. He sounds like somebody who has problems and more than likely needs a friend, doesn't he, Sergeant? I feel guilty that I haven't paid him any more attention than I have. In fact, to tell you the truth, I think I've actually shunned Daniel D. Farbecker. When you find him, Sergeant, tell him I'm looking for him too, will you? I'll try to make it up to him."

Sgt. Lagerpiel's voice was tight and a noticeable octave higher. The volume was also greater. "Osborne, I don't think I can take another stick of stovewood this turn."

"I beg your pardon?"

"Never mind." Sgt. Lagerpiel headed for the tent flap.

"Sergeant," Porter said with innocence, "next time I see him, I'll tell him you're looking for him. And, Sergeant, when you talk to Sgt. Crowder, be sure and tell him I'm perfectly happy to do my duty right where I am. I haven't seen anything yet that makes me want to be a sergeant. I don't see how you guys stand it."

When he was sure the first sergeant was out of earshot, Porter spoke softly into the empty tent. "Will Barton would love it." Then he laughed for the first time in a week. "So will Kostas." He swung his legs off the side of the cot and went in search of the Wafflebacks.

Kostas was standing by Osborne at the bulletin board two days later when the announcement was posted that PFC Daniel D. Farbecker had been declared absent without leave and that anyone who saw him or had any knowledge of his whereabouts should report it immediately. He gave Porter a cool look and remarked dispassionately, "Ah, isn't this the guy Sgt. Lagerpiel was looking for? I'm so glad that he's only AWOL; I had become convinced that he must be dead. It takes ingenuity to go AWOL from this outfit. Those Mexican sentries from Brownsville, Texas, are quite good, you know. It would be easier to get out of a convent than the 816th Hospital."

"Kostas, you know everything. All I knew about the guards was that they're the only ones with rifles and they speak with a funny accent. Maybe they saw this Farbecker fellow leaving and reported him to the sergeant. I sure hope old Daniel D. decides to come back; I'd like to get to know him better."

They moved away and Kostas dared to laugh. "I feel great, Osborne! Like Zeus, who's had one of his creatures survive great perils and still live."

"Or God," Porter amended.

"Like I said, Zeus."

Porter persisted. "Or Jesus?"

"Really, Osborne. Keep it clean, will you?" He cocked an eyebrow. "Of course, we all realize that Daniel D's days are numbered. When the permanent records catch up with us and his name is not on them, they'll all realize that they've been duped. The Wafflebacks will have to arrange some sort of proper burial service for Farbecker. We'll include you and Jewel, of course."

"I'm not sure I want to come to any service where Zeus is the god."

"Lighten up, Porter, lighten up. Haven't you learned yet not to take anything seriously? At least anything I say? In the Wafflebacks, we have a Jew, a couple of Catholics, a Congregationalist, a Greek Orthodox, a Baptist, one idiot who swears he's an atheist, and a Unitarian, whatever that is. I doubt if he knows himself. We certainly don't get into religious discussions. Lighten up and get ready to mourn Daniel D. Farbecker."

"Gotcha," said Porter.

The issue never arose and there was never a burial service, for Farbecker did not suffer demise. Arthur Levek and George Kragel were hanging around the company office when the copies of permanent records arrived one week later. They reported the frenzied conversation they overheard between Sgt. Lagerpiel and his immediate assistant, Sgt. Blanchard, who came from Maine, was picture-book handsome, sported a dark pencil-line mustache and whom Kragel labeled a Canuck.

"Hey, Blanchard, look here! That Farbecker fuckup isn't on this roll."

"What do you make of that, Milton?"

Lagerpiel slapped the sheaf of papers. "Hell, he never was assigned to our outfit in the first place! He never was one of my men and there never was any need for me to be worrying myself sick about him!"

"How'd his name get on our roll? How'd he get in this outfit, Milton?"

"He drifted in and joined us when we first landed, Blanchard. That has to be it! We know he was with us right after Omaha because we have a signature on the duty roster and we've got records that he was on KP and latrine duty for smarting off. He really fooled us good, but he couldn't have done it if we hadn't lost our records. It's fate, that's what it is. Hell, he was AWOL from some other outfit when he signed on with us."

"Humm," said Blanchard.

Lagerpiel became even more excited. "Hell, Blanchard, as long as this has been, he's no longer AWOL; he's a damn deserter!"

"I guess you're right," acceded Blanchard. "What are you going to do?"

"Do? Do? I'll do what I have to, of course. I'll notify SHAEF and they'll be on the prowl for PFC Daniel D. Farbecker all over the ETO. I'll teach him to make a fool of me!"

"I resent that," commented Kostas when he received the report. "Daniel D. didn't make a fool out of him; he merely reaffirmed what the good Lord had already accomplished." He raised an imaginary glass. "Here's to Daniel D. Farbecker! Long may he live!"

"Amen," said Porter Osborne. "What's a Canuck?"

35 With an increasing sense of urgency about his
vow to Barton, Porter approached Sgt. Lagerpiel.

"I asked Sgt. Crowder and he said it was all right with him if I
could talk you into giving me a three-day pass on the next truck the
Red Cross sends out."

"And where do you propose to go, Osborne?"

"Paris, Sergeant."

"Paris? Do you realize there are only six enlisted men and no
more than a dozen officers in this outfit who have been to Paris so far? I
haven't been myself. Why should I give you a pass to go?"

"Because I'm such a hard worker, Sergeant. And because I hear
they've opened the *Jeu de Paume* again, at least part of it."

"What the hell's that?"

"It's that famous museum in Paris, Sergeant, close to the
Louvre. I've always wanted to see it." When Sgt. Lagerpiel looked
down and began writing again, Porter persisted. "And the Cathedral of
Notre Dame, Sergeant. It's world famous. I know you've heard of that."

There was no response from the busy man.

"And *Sacre Coeur*, that's another church that's famous. I need to
see that. And perfume, Sergeant. The GI's have about bought up all
the perfume in every town in Normandy, but I hear there's plenty in
Paris. Christmas is less than a month away and I'd like to get some
perfume to send back to my mama and sisters for Christmas presents.
I could bring you some back, too, if you want me to."

Lagerpiel apparently did not hear him.

"And the Folies Bergere. One of the truck drivers told me that's
a real classy show. With lots of beautiful women."

Lagerpiel raised his head. "And half of them buck naked too, I
hear. Now, Osborne, you're getting close to making me believe why you

want to go to Paris. But not quite."

Porter decided that he had already lost this proposal and that he might as well have a little fun.

"Sergeant," he confided, "this business about Daniel D. Farbecker has been weighing on my mind. If you were an enlisted man and a loner and you were AWOL and loose in Europe, where would you head? Paris. Of course. Now I know that's a big city and you could stay lost there for a hundred years if you knew French. But Farbecker doesn't. He's going to go where soldiers congregate so he won't look suspicious and stand out like a sore thumb. I thought since I'm apparently one of the few who knows what he looks like that I could prowl around in the popular places and maybe spot him."

Lagerpiel pushed his camp stool back. "Osborne, you're the most unusual soldier I've got in this outfit, I've decided. I'm going to give you that pass just to hush you up. Plus I think it's past time you did a little growing up. But don't think for a minute I believe a word you're saying. I can see through you like a glass of water."

"Oh, thank you, Sergeant. I really appreciate it."

"On one condition. You report back to me when you return and tell me what Paris is really like. I don't for a split second think you have a snowball's chance in hell of finding Farbecker, but if you do, I promise I'll look after you."

"Oh, thank you again, Sergeant. You already do look after me. I mean, I really feel like you're a father figure to all the guys."

"In that case, Osborne, cut the bullshit. And when you get to Pig Alley, be damn sure you have some rubbers."

Porter was open mouthed.

"And go to the Pro station. And watch your step."

Porter gulped. "Sergeant."

"I don't want you to come back here with a French knife in your back or French pox on your pecker. Get your ass out of here and see me when you get back."

"The son of a bitch really can see through me," said Porter when he left. He change-stepped. "But not all the way. Nobody can do that." He swallowed. "Not even me."

On Saturday, the Moulin Rouge in La Place Pigalle was crowded, glaringly lit, and noisy with music from a jukebox that could have been made in America but played unfamiliar tunes. The place was filled with soldiers and brightly painted girls who added to the din with shrieks of forced laughter and equally forced English. Couples went in

442

and out from the street in a rapid turnover, oblivious of the wintry day. The bar was busy, the air thick with tobacco smoke. Porter stood awkwardly to one side of the door.

A bright young blonde swayed provocatively before him. "You lonesome, babee?"

Porter reddened. "I'm looking for Mimi, ma'am. You know which one is Mimi? Mimi Labotte," he repeated.

"*Mimi*," she pouted. "*Toujours Mimi. Merde*."

Porter forced a beaming smile. "And the same to you, I'm sure, lady."

She shrugged and flounced away.

He stepped over to the bar and waited for the attention of an older man who seemed to be directing the other waiters.

"*M'sieu?*"

"Mimi," said Porter as he slid an unopened package of Camels across the bar. "I'm looking for a girl named Mimi Labotte. Do you know Mimi? *S'il vous plaît*."

The man looked around the room. "Mimi!" he called.

He was answered by rapid-fire conversation from a waiter at the other end of the bar. "Mimi," he told Porter, "busy. Mimi *toujours* busy. Mimi be back. You wait, no? Yes? Mimi be back."

"I wait," affirmed Porter. "*Merci, beaucoup. S'il vous plaît*."

"*Du boire?*" the man asked. "A drink? You want?"

"*Non*," said Porter. "Mimi. I want Mimi. No drink. I wait." He bowed. "*Merci. S'il vous plaît*."

He waited and waited, smiling fatuously when any girl eyed him and then nervously averting his gaze. "They can't all be whores," he thought. "Some of these girls are as pretty as Phi Mu's or ADPi's at Willingham University. But the way they're going in and out of this place like bees in a hive, I guess they are." He noted several of the women had very short hair still, a signal that they had slept with the Bosche such a short time ago that their hair had not yet had time to grow out completely. None of the other girls was speaking to them. "This sure is France," he marveled.

He was so absorbed in watching the human kaleidoscope around him that he failed to see Mimi's approach.

"You want Mimi?" a suggestive voice said in his ear.

He tried to control his startled response but knew that he gave a little jump. "Yes. *Oui*. At least I think so. *Oui, Mademoiselle. Merci beaucoup*. Yes, yes. *Oui. S'il vous plaît*. Are you Mimi?"

"*Mais certainment, mon cher.*" She put a hand on his arm. "I am Mimi. *Mimi du Moulin Rouge.* You like?"

Her makeup was assertive but not garish; her hair bounced in soft brown curls on her shoulders. She was dressed in a suit, high heels and stockings as though ready for shopping. She even wore a tiny pillbox of a hat with a wisp of veiling across her forehead, and her tiny hands were sheathed in kid gloves. He looked into her dark blue eyes accentuated with just the right amount of mascara, observed her thin lips with no smudge of the lipstick as artifice to make them seem fuller, and thought, "Will Barton was wrong. You ain't no whore."

"I like," he said aloud. "Yes, ma'am. *Oui. Oui.* I like *très beaucoup. Comment t'allez-vous?*"

"*Ah,*" Mimi smiled. "*Vous parlez très bien le français, Monsieur.*" She rattled into French that completely escaped Porter's comprehension.

"*Non, non,*" he protested. "*Un peu. Un petite peu. Non compris beaucoup.*"

"*Alors.* We speak English, but Mimi not *très* good at English. You buy me a drink, yes?"

"*Mais certainment,*" Porter blustered in French and then corrected himself to avert another unintelligible torrent. "I mean, yes, ma'am. I'd be happy to buy you a drink."

"Good. We sit, *oui?* Mimi have need of a cigarette."

"Yes, ma'am. Have one of mine." Porter busied himself with the ritual of smoking. "Just keep the pack, Mimi. I have plenty."

"*Garçon,*" she called. "*Champagne ici. Pour deux.*"

Porter looked at his watch. Three o'clock. "You drink mine, too, Mimi. It's a little early in the day for me."

She took a sip from her glass. "We go now, yes? I only buy the drink to keep happy *le proprieteur.* You want to go with Mimi now?"

"Yes, ma'am." Porter paid the waiter and rose behind the woman. "At least I want to talk with you, and I've been told this is not the place to do it."

"You have two hundred francs?"

"Oh, yes, ma'am. I have lots more than that if we need it."

Mimi smiled and took his arm and they emerged on the sidewalk. "Two hundred francs is fair price. Mimi not cheat. Fair play for everybody, she always say. Especial American *soldat.* Mimi always fair play." She smiled coquettishly. "You also have fifty francs for ze room? I get very nice especial room for fifty francs."

"Oh, yes, ma'am. That's no problem. Here."

"Good. You nice. You *très gentil*. Mimi give you good time."

She led him through a maze of narrow side streets closed in by shuttered windows and finally knocked on a nondescript weathered door. It was opened immediately by a bent little woman with frayed sweater, white apron, and a tight bun of gray hair. She could, Porter thought, be almost anybody's grandmother. She stepped back to let them enter and immediately held out her hand. Mimi just as immediately handed her off a twenty-franc note.

"*Pas un longtemp pour ce petit moineau*," she cooed rapidly. "*Pas de plus dix minuits. Peut-être seulement cinq ou sept. Complet.*"

She moved rapidly up the steep stairs, looked over her shoulder at Porter. "*Vite, vite*," she said. "Come along."

With the door securely locked behind them, Porter had little time to survey his surroundings, for Mimi removed her coat and then her blouse. Porter could not keep his eyes from her breasts.

"You like, yes?"

"Oh, yes, ma'am. *Oui*."

"Good. Come here." She rubbed against him. Porter remembered Buckalew Tarpley's advice never to kiss a whore and adroitly hung his chin over her shoulder.

"Aha. You ready, babee?"

"Mimi, look," said Porter. "I don't want to operate under false pretenses here."

"You pay first, babee? Business is business. Some *soldats* leave and no pay. Fair play for everybody, Mimi always say. You pay first?"

"Sure." Porter handed over two one-hundred-franc notes which Mimi promptly and efficiently placed in the toe of a shoe.

She moved in again.

"Look, Mimi. You don't have to sell me your body. What I really want from you is some information. Do you know an American officer named Will Barton?"

She put a finger across his lips. "Mimi not know any names. You pay Mimi two hundred francs and Mimi *zig-zig* with you. *Compris*? Fair play is fair play and is fair play for everybody. After, we talk. No tickee, no washee. *Compris*?"

Of a sudden Porter relaxed and laughed. "That's Chinese, Mimi, and not quite logical, but let's go. To hell with Will Barton."

As they tumbled onto the bed, Porter remembered Sgt. Lagerpiel's advice and followed it. He also remembered the picture of the girl in the latrine at Camp Grant. "She may look clean, but . . ." he murmured and abandoned himself to vigorous physical exertion completely devoid of emotion.

Mimi patted him on the shoulder. "You *fini* soon, babee?"

"Sure. Soon," grunted Porter. "*A bientôt*," he ventured.

A little later she patted him again. "Mimi very busy, babee. You *fini vite*, yes?"

Porter was doing his utmost to oblige his hostess and was finally accomplishing it when he heard an unmistakable giggle beneath him. "*Regardez-vous*," said Mimi. "Look. *La petite grenouille*."

Porter paused. "I beg your pardon?"

"Look. Look up."

He craned his neck and looked over his shoulder where she was pointing. A small silvered globe hung from the ceiling, and unmistakably mirrored in it was the backside of his own skinny figure sprawled whitely in the embrace of the amused Mimi, whose legs were extended in the air. He noted that she still had on her shoes, and that they, being nearest the rounded mirror, were disproportionately large and framed his spraddled backside.

"What the hell?" he expostulated.

Mimi laughed. "*La petite grenouille*," she spluttered. "You look like a little frog . . ."

"Frog?" The word refocused Porter's attention. "La Petite!" he said to Mimi. "I must see La Petite. Will Barton told me when you used the word *frog* that I could ask you about La Petite. Can you find her for me?"

Mimi rolled off the bed and busied herself at the washstand. She tossed Porter a wet towel. "We see. For why you want La Petite?"

"I want to talk with her. That's all you need to know."

Mimi shrugged and picked up her hat. "May be. Like I say before, Mimi almost never know name of her customers, but I tell you zis. When you say Weel Barton to me, I should know already you take long time and make Mimi work extra hard. Come. I take you to La Petite."

Porter extended another hundred franc note. "Here, Mimi. You were great. I really wasn't expecting to enjoy the mechanics of this outing so much."

When she began to shake her head, Porter clasped her gloved fingers over the money. "Fair play for everybody, Mimi. *Vous avez, toi-même, dit la même chose*. Let's go find La Petite."

Mimi tucked the note through an opening in her blouse. "I take; you *très gentil*. I tell you two things about La Petite. First of all, she not, how you say, fuck. No *zig-zig* La Petite."

"I already know that," Porter said. "Will Barton told me. I'm not expecting it."

Mimi turned from the step below him and wagged a finger under his nose. "The other thing. La Petite speak very good Engleesh. Do not speak your French with her. She spit on the French the *soldats américains* try to speak."

"I'll remember that, too," promised Porter. His heart was racing.

Mimi had another rapid conversation with the old woman in the apron, who appeared with outstretched palm. Another twenty francs changed ownership, and Mimi repeated to Porter, "Fair play for everybody." Then she led him beyond the stairs to a long narrow room that had been furnished as a parlor in the rear of the building. It was so filled with overstuffed chairs and its walls so heavily draped that sound was muffled.

"Mimi never ask name. La Petite different. La Petite always ask name. You write? She no come if she not know who."

"Sure," said Porter and took the proffered card. "She won't know me from Adam's off-ox," he explained to Mimi, and under his own name he also printed, "For Will Barton."

Mimi discreetly did not look at the card. "You wait, yes? You have watch. If La Petite not come in thirty minutes, you leave, yes? You *compris*?"

Porter nodded. "If she's not here in thirty minutes I am to leave. *Oui. Je compris.* Do I pay twenty francs to Granny to get out of here? Fair play for everybody?"

Mimi's laugh was a tinny tinkle in the muted room. "*Non, non, non.* Business is business for all people, but *sortie* is free. Mimi not see you again unless at Le Moulin Rouge, but if you come back she be glad. Ask for Mimi some more, yes?"

"If I do, is next time free?"

"*Ah, non, M'sieu Tard.*" She wagged her finger again. "Mimi very busy. Next time is three hundred francs. You *très gentil* but business is business. *Au 'voir.*"

Porter held out his hand, then impulsively tilted Mimi's face up, said, "To hell with it," and kissed her very lightly on the lips. "You are *très gentil aussi*, Mimi, and *je vous remercie beaucoup.*"

"*Très gentille*," Mimi corrected. "No French to La Petite. Remember? '*Voir*.'"

Porter was glad he had his watch and even so listened several times to be sure it was still running. He thought of all the people he had known, from E. V. Derrick to Carter Otten, who had pronounced Will Barton crazy. He agreed wholeheartedly with all of them. At the end of twenty slow-moving minutes, as he finished his third toe-to-heel measurement of the length of the room, he turned and gasped in surprise. He had heard no sound but standing at the other end of the room with folded arms was a statuesque and immobile figure swathed like a monk in a black cloak, the hood of which obscured shadowy features.

"You wish to see me?" The voice was deep and throaty, the English words spiced with tantalizing accent.

"No, sir," said Porter. "I'm waiting for a lady."

The figure did not move. "You are waiting, I presume, for La Petite?"

"Yes, sir," stammered Porter. "*Oui, monsieur*."

The figure stretched out its arms and tossed the cloak aside. Porter could not muster another breath to gasp. Standing before him was a woman so dramatic, so unlikely in appearance, that his imagination was stunned as completely as his senses. Her gown stretched from ankle to neck to wrist, its form-fitting lines interrupted by the strong planes of rib cage and bony pelvis. Only the faintest swelling indicated breasts, and there was no sign of anything but the flattest of abdomen. The dress was exactly the crimson of her wide mouth. Her cheeks were sunken and the lips looked incongruously voluptuous in contrast. Her large dark eyes were heavily made up, but the truly startling feature was the slickly shaved scalp. Even her eyebrows had been shaved. The smoothly molded pate and her cadaverous thinness gave the visual impact of a death's head that had been decorated. Only the lips and the glittering eyes manifested life. It was an altogether fascinating and impelling vision, and for one insane moment Porter wanted to rush forward and kiss those sensual, convoluted lips, even though he would have to stand tiptoe to do it. He heard Will Barton's voice, "She won't fuck."

"Thank God," prayed Porter. "You," he said aloud. "You are La Petite?"

"Yes. The name for me is droll, is it not?"

"Yes, ma'am, it is. No offense intended."

"And none taken. Relax. You need come no nearer. Seat yourself there. I shall stand. You are Mr. Osborne, I presume, but you have also written the name of Will Barton, one which is of great importance to me."

"Yes, ma'am. He would be glad to know that. He told me that if he lived he planned to marry you some day."

"Will Barton? Marry? Me?" The eyes widened ever so faintly and the ridges where the eyebrows should have been rose slightly. "Will Barton is a wild man, a passionate man, a fierce man. A lover? Yes. A husband? No. For an occasional weekend, he might be a magnificent challenge. He has no gentleness in him. Where is he?"

"He is dead, Miss La Petite," Porter said simply.

She did not move nor did her voice change. "Do not use saluting titles with nicknames, Mr. Osborne. You American soldiers cannot speak well even your own language. Address me simply as La Petite. How did Will Barton die?"

"Well," Porter replied. "Will died well, La Petite, and you are wrong about the gentleness. There was a streak of it in him. He died, as far as he knew, with a song on his lips. He was singing when he went to sleep. Did you know that he wanted to be a doctor?"

"I knew. Tell me about his death. Were you there?"

"Yes, ma'am." Porter poured out the saga of the wreck, the ensuing gas gangrene, the frantic activity in the Operating Room. He edited the language for the ears of this improbable creature and purposely made no allusion to the boots. That was an extremely personal experience and might seem childish to this female of mythological aura.

"Do you know where he was going?" The question was carefully off-hand. Of a sudden Porter felt that he was being used.

"No, ma'am. Will Barton never told me. In fact, he refused to tell me much of anything about what a major in the paratroopers with all his combat experience was doing driving a Jeep himself on a backwoods road in Normandy. I asked but he told me it was none of my business. He did say it was a special assignment and had something to do with intelligence."

The figure did not move. Porter thought she stood before the somber drapes like a tall Christmas candle tipped with a white flame, for it seemed the skull emanated light rather than reflecting it.

"He didn't even tell me how to find you by seeking out Mimi until he knew he had gas gangrene and what his chances were. He told me if I ever mentioned it to another soul, he'd jerk my head off."

La Petite bowed her head a millimeter or two. "I know the rest of the threat. I have on a few occasions heard him use it. Most effectively, I concede, even to the terrified souls who understood not one word of English. Will Barton's passion and fierceness and wildness have been most useful on occasion. What did he tell you about me? I want every word of it."

"Why?" asked Porter. He was beginning to feel less cowed. "He's dead and you say you would never have married him anyhow. So why do you want to know what he said about you?"

"It is very important to me. Every word. Begin." The tone was so imperious that it stimulated in Porter a feeling of defiance.

"The very first thing he said about you was, 'She won't fuck'," he said daringly and stopped for reaction.

The only indication that she moved was the increased accentuation of her collar bones beneath the red satin. Her voice was impersonal. "How did he know? He never tried."

Porter was not feeling completely comfortable, but he had made considerable progress in that direction. "It gets around on a girl, La Petite," he said. "All over the world."

The faint shrug was just enough to make the satin tremble. "This is a childish and inconsequential digression, a technique at which I imagine you are quite skilled. Back to basics, Porter Osborne."

"He told me you kept your head shaved so people would think you were a *collaborateur* but it was just part of your cover, that you hate the Germans."

"I do not believe you."

"Honest."

"No."

"Why not?"

"I many times drilled into Will Barton that the word is *la collaboratrice*. I do not believe he would make such a shoddy reversion into American misuse of French."

Porter gulped, once more in awe of the woman's majesty. "You're absolutely right, La Petite. That is what he said. I'm the one who never was any good at French."

"I know. Another reason I shave my head is that during this war I have spent much time literally underground with comrades in the Catacombs. I came to think the skulls stacked there more beautiful than the heads of living Germans and French traitors we worked so hard to neutralize. When Paris was liberated and the patriots shaved the heads of the compliant whores, I followed suit. It is a diverting and confusing signal to the ones we now seek, and also I like it. What else has Will Barton told you about me from his death bed after swearing you to secrecy?"

"He said you were a big woman like Jack London described in *Martin Eden* and that he was going to marry you."

"Yes, yes. You said that already. Do not waste La Petite's time. Repetition is an insult to intelligence. I will read the book some day if I ever have leisure again."

"Are you sure you wouldn't have married him, La Petite?"

"I am married. Forever." The voice was deep. There was a pause in which each waited for the other to say something. "*Il est mort.*" Her dignity was awesome. "My husband is dead. I live. I live and I shall triumph, and I shall be married only to him. Forever."

Porter dared to pry. "How did he die, La Petite? Can I know?"

"Protecting me." Her eyes were dry but they glittered. "He was older than I and not so physically active. He could not participate in all the activities that impelled me. He was a professor and had also not the zest for revenge that filled my belly. We lived simply in Toulon, and after the Allied invasion I was on a mission to Lyons tracking down the Quislings that had tormented us during the occupation. When I returned, I found him dead."

"I'm sorry."

"You ask how he died. He was murdered. There is a very gross traitor to France who protects himself by killing all who know him or get close on his trail. We call him The Barber because one of his techniques is to cut off the ears of his victims with a razor to extract everything they know before they die. My husband died because even under torture he would not tell where I was. The Barber was after me, do you understand? My husband died that I might live. My only passion now is to find The Barber."

"And Will Barton was helping you?"

"Yes. I had been of assistance to him on a special mission he had to Belgium and came to trust him. He took a week of personal leave and promised to bring him to me. Did he mention The Barber?"

"Yes. I'm coming to that. But tell me, how did The Barber kill all the people who knew about him?"

"With a gun. After he tortured them. He did not, *sal bête*, have to waste one of his bullets on my husband, however. Jean's heart gave out. The ears were neatly lined on his desk and nine fingernails were scattered on the rug where Jean lay. His heart had stopped before the tenth nail could be pulled. The lamb had died for me. I live to avenge him."

Porter swallowed hard. "La Petite, it has been done."

"Tell it! Quickly."

"Will Barton had caught him and was bringing him back to you in that Jeep. When they had the wreck and Will broke his leg, he said he realized The Barber might get away, and so he kicked out the windshield with his good foot and rammed The Barber's neck down on the broken glass. The ambulance driver who brought a French woman in told me he saw the major toss the man's head in the back of the Jeep, but nobody knows that Will himself had cut the head off. He did it for you." He paused. "I will love him all my life."

The gaunt figure was as still as the room itself. Porter could hear the busy little ticking of the watch on his wrist and the steady thump of a pulse in his ears. He rose from his chair.

"Stay where you are! Do not dare to touch me! So shall I love Will Barton. And I shall love Porter Osborne. Both of them. All my life. But from a distance. As always. I have many other things to do now. You may go. I have many connections I must pursue. If you ever tell any of this, one of them will track you down and jerk your head off, and you know the rest." For the first time she smiled.

Porter grinned. "Only Will Barton could catch B'rer Rabbit and do that. I'll never tell a word. Good-bye, La Petite. I don't know anything to say but God bless you."

La Petite donned her cloak, pulled the hood over her shiny head and became again the shrouded monk. The light in the room was noticeably dimmer. Porter shivered.

"We will never see each other again, but whenever you think of me, you may know that *le Bon Dieu* has most richly blessed me. And that you are one of my blessings."

As Porter closed the door, he heard the beautiful low-pitched contralto. "*Au revoir*, Sambo."

He was nodding to the bent concierge at the front door before he wondered how she knew his nickname. "Will Barton must have told her." he shrugged. "She's so mysterious I was lucky to get any information at all out of her."

Disoriented without the guiding hand of Mimi, he managed to retrace his path to La Place Pigalle after several false starts down blind alleys. Something kept nagging at his mind. He stopped in the middle of the sidewalk and let GI's with their girls walk around him.

"Naw. It couldn't be. Besides, I'd never in six months find that house again by myself."

He took one more step and stopped again. "You've got too active an imagination. You know that marvelous woman never pooted in class."

Nevertheless he was still shaking his head when he entered Le Moulin Rouge. He walked directly to the bar. "Mimi," he said to the bartender. "*Mimi ici?*"

"*Mimi? Ah, non. Mimi parti. Tout fini aujourd'hui. Beaucoup fatigué.* Tomorrow, perhaps."

The driver from the Red Cross hailed him. "God, what took you so long? I was about to leave you. We've got to get out of here and head back to camp."

"For God's sake, let me take a leak," Porter said.

On the wall coming out of the toilet he noted a poster in one corner of which someone had drawn a little baldheaded, beady-eyed man with a big nose peering over a fence. "Kilroy was here," it proclaimed. He carefully removed it and tucked it in his pocket.

When he returned to the hospital, he sought out Kostas and held out his trophy. "Sign under this with your left hand," he instructed.

"How do you want me to sign it?"

"How else?"

"Gotcha."

Porter found Sgt. Lagerpiel alone. "How was the museum, Osborne? And the cathedrals?" A note of smugness tinged his speech.

"Just fine, Sergeant, just fine. I sure recommend them."

"How was Pig Alley, Osborne?"

"Just fine, Sergeant, just fine. There's a place there, sort of a cafe like, with a lot of benches and chairs and tables and girls. It's called the Moulin Rouge, has a windmill lit up with red neon. I recommend it."

"Did you use a rubber?"

"Sure did, Sergeant. I recommend that, too."

"Glad you're back, Osborne."

"Sergeant."

"What?"

"Look what I found on a poster near the pisser."

"A Kilroy drawing? They're everywhere."

"Look at the signature underneath. I nearly fell over when I saw it. I thought maybe you could compare it for authenticity."

"Good godamighty! I don't have to compare it; I've memorized that signature! I can't believe this! Where'd you say you found it? I'm going to Paris next week, by God!"

"Lots of luck, Sergeant. Thanks for the pass. When you go in the Moulin Rouge, be sure and ask for Mimi. Mimi Labotte. She'll take it from there. When she says 'frog' ask her if she knows Daniel D. Farbecker. Between the two of us, we may find that sucker yet."

> *"And death is in the phial and the end of
>   noble work,*
> *But Don John of Austria has fired upon
>   the Turk."*

36   The workload in the Operating Room leveled off.
Surgeons, nurses, technicians, and corpsmen settled into a smoothly
efficient routine. They had grown to know and, for the most part, to
like each other, but affection was manifestly superficial.

The soldiers on whom they operated were reclusive and impersonal. Sometimes, on impulse, they confided in some of the medical
techs; Kostas, Jewel and the Wafflebacks were privy occasionally to
battlefield accounts and graphic descriptions of how wounds had been
incurred. The members of the OR crew, however, were treated as elite
strangers, specialists who performed repetitively like perfect robots.
Porter had learned to work mechanically and saw only trench foot,
revision of stump, debridement, secondary closure, drainage of lung
abscess, exploratory laparotomy, gunshot wound of the abdomen,
removal of shrapnel, sucking wounds of the chest. He forgot names
and faces on a daily basis, and he learned never, ever to look into the
eyes of his patients when he prepared them for anesthesia. His memory, therefore, became a palimpsest of various wounds to which he had
paid detailed attention to avoid the faces, the searching eyes.

Never mind. Patton was on his way, this war would be over soon,
Porter would then be sent to Japan, and eventually he would see
Brewton County again. Mark time, Osborne, mark time. Compartmentalize, work like hell, give the officers and sergeants appropriate
stimulation when you can get away with it, don't think about what's
happening to all those wounded guys, laugh whenever you get the
chance, and whatever you do, compartmentalize, goddammit. Don't
let anybody see even a flash of your soft underbelly. He would have
been highly indignant if anyone had pointed out to him that he was
inching up on Sherman Roger Jewel. "Look out for Number One."

In late November he became a true specialist. This was not a position he had sought. Indeed, it was one which every enlisted man in the Operating Room would have avoided at all costs. He had specialization conferred upon him by fiat—by direct orders from both Sgt. Oliver Crowder and Capt. Irving Ballas. He became the first functioning anesthetist in the ETO with the rank of PFC.

When the OR had increased its number of cases by utilizing enlisted men as scrub nurses and circulators, the demand for anesthesia had proportionately increased. Capt. Ballas was an Anesthesiologist, and he had only one Nurse Anesthetist to help him. The captain had lost his break times for pipe smoking and often was supervising two operations simultaneously. The harassed and bedeviled Nurse Anesthetist became increasingly fractious and on some days rushed around as aimlessly hysterical as a mother hen whose flock of biddies has been dispersed. It was this nurse who was responsible for Porter's elevation.

She was older than anyone else in the OR and in the early days of the unit had freely disseminated information about herself. Both the information and the dissemination were overly lofty, and the initial respect she had commanded, because despite her age she had requested overseas duty, soon faded into tolerance and then degenerated into derision. She was a first lieutenant, a higher rank than any other nurse in the outfit enjoyed, with the exception of the Operating Room supervisor.

Her name was Corinne Zeiderheusen, and she was of Dutch descent; "not recently, mind you." Her ancestors had migrated to America and settled New Amsterdam on the Hudson River, where they had "made just scads and scads, don't you know?" in the fur trade before moving with their fortune to Maryland, "where I was born, reared, and made my debut." From this pinnacle of heritage she early sought dominance of her fellow nurses in the 816th by reminding them daily that back home she enjoyed special advantages professionally, educationally, materially, and, of course, socially.

When everyone else in the ETO eschewed any jewelry other than wedding bands and wrist watches, she wore a diamond ring, obviously antique. It gleamed like a light on her finger, securely fastened in a platinum mount that pivoted under the weight of its stone round her bony finger, shifting with her jerky motions like a weather vane in a high wind. She wore the ring with careless, almost heedless arrogance, and it was that diamond that mesmerized other females and lent credence in their eyes to her personal mythology.

She was slight and wiry and scampered through the Operating Room in her fatigues and leggings like a hurried goat. Her hair was honey colored, as fine and sparse as corn silk, and did absolutely nothing except cover her pate. Her eyes were green and might have been beautiful had they not been divided by a nose like a tomahawk blade, its bridge so prominent that it made the eyes seem a little crossed when she was looking at near objects and wonderingly unfocused for distance. Her lips were thin with a straggling of hairs at the corners that she neglected to pluck completely. Her chin was pointed and sharp and her neck a column so festooned with sagging skin that she carried her head uplifted like a chicken drinking water, thus temporarily obliterating the wrinkles.

"On top of all that," Carter Otten had early commented, "she ain't got no tits atall."

The litanies of her life in Maryland, and even her efforts to be chummy, smacked of condescension. "Just call me Z," she twinkled at everyone. "All that old Army rank doesn't matter to anybody who counts. I know who I am and you know who I am. Just call me Z."

She chattered constantly. Daddy was a doctor. Mama, of course, had been a debutante. Daddy taught at Hopkins in his spare time. Daddy loved his baby girl better than anything in the world. Mama had been upset about her going to nursing school, but Daddy stood up for her. If little Z made her debut like a good girl to please Mama, then she should be allowed to be a nurse if that's what she wanted. Daddy's name at Hopkins would insure that everyone treated his little girl with respect. She had loved her Daddy more than anything in the world, and it nearly killed her when he died. That had been when she started wearing his mother's engagement ring and had gone on to Nurse Anesthetist school. Then when the war broke out, she just had to leave her settled life in Baltimore, board up her house, and try to do something to help the soldiers. That's the way her daddy would have reacted, and she had to fulfill the Zeiderheusen tradition.

It was the enlisted men who first began avoiding her. She would grab one as he sped by on an assignment and divert him. "Be a lamb for Z. Run to Central Supply and bring her a doobobby, will you?"

No one but Z had the glimmering of an idea about the identity of a doobobby. Neither did they know what she was talking about when she demanded a "thingamajig," or a "whatchamaycallit." When pressed for definition, she sputtered and fumed and complained about the ignorance of enlisted men and the woeful inadequacies of military medical training. The men shunned her whenever they could.

457

Porter rather liked her. She had at least the comfort of familiarity. He had grown up accustomed to superannuated spinsters who were arrested permanently in time as daddy's little darlings and clothed their loneliness in good works and harmless delusions. At home, their sentences frequently began with, "Before the War," and what they could not experience in passion or romance they sought in self-denial. Porter understood the rules and endeared himself to the lieutenant by calling her "Miss Z."

"How quaint. How sweet. You are obviously a boy of some breeding. Southerners are such dears. My mother had Southern connections in her background, a grandmother from Mobile. That's in Alabama. Be a sweetheart and run bring Z a doobobby, will you? She can't possibly leave this patient."

Porter further endeared himself to Z by not challenging her for definitions or specifics when she asked him to fetch things for her. He was accustomed to the vagaries of maiden aunts and cousins in all the families at home and understood that all hens were more pleasant if their feathers were not ruffled. He studied her equipment tray, put a supply of adaptors, screw clamps, and other movable pieces in the pockets of his fatigues, and was thus able to proffer a palmful of choices for her selection.

The nurses soon followed the example of the enlisted men in avoiding Z whenever possible. Porter enjoyed overhearing their comments.

Lt. Martha Hisel was a work horse regarded as a ball of fire at the operating table. She was from Missouri and difficult to impress. "If that old biddy doesn't stay out of my way when I'm setting up for a case, I may have to slap her clean to Texas. I'm here to do a job and not to listen to her chatter."

Lt. Maureen Curry was from Beaumont. "Don't slap her our way, Hisel. We got troubles enough already."

Lt. Shirley Toomay was a plump and dimpled Jewish woman from New York. "Another thing. Do you girls really believe all the things she tells you about how perfect a life she has led? I can't help but think she has to be exaggerating. No one could have had all those advantages."

Lt. Allen Dalrymple was a flat-nosed, dark-skinned giantess from San Antonio who had been given a surname by her English father but nothing else. Porter had been surprised to find a female with that name but swiftly forgave her the heavy duffel bag at Omaha Beach. Her accent was a song in Porter's ears. "She may be as full of it as the Christmas turkey. We don't know, do we? I don't believe it is because she love her daddy she have never marry. I think it is the nose. And she may or she may not have the big house and the sterling silver for big parties that she talk about. She may be rich as Croesus or poor as church mice, but you can't get around that diamond ring. It is there for all to see and I, for one, will have to say it is the biggest one in all the world that I have ever seen."

"*Merde*," muttered Lt. Johanna Bordillon and glanced at Porter.

"You're right," said Hisel. "You can't get around that big ring. How big is the sucker anyhow? I'd die before I asked."

"It's a little over five carats," volunteered Shirley Toomay. "I had little enough intelligence to inquire in a very tasteful way how big it is and got a lecture that it's gauche to judge a stone by size. You are supposed to judge it by weight, and the unit of weight for a gemstone is the carat. Hers is 5.25 carats. 'Gauche,' indeed. I never expected to encounter that word in the Army. You're right, Dalrymple. You can't get around that diamond ring. It's there. Always."

"Like Jesus," murmured Porter to Johanna Bordillon.

"*Merde*," she replied and did not even look up.

As Z scampered around the OR from one case to another, becoming busier and busier, she approached Capt. Ballas and then Sgt. Crowder. The other nurses, she complained, had their responsibility and work load lifted by enlisted men taking over some of their duties. Anesthesia had become a bottleneck in the department. Why could she not have an enlisted man assigned to her? Just for her own personal use? To fetch and carry only for her and not be sent off by some other nurse on some other errand? And she just might teach him to give just a teeny-weeny bit of pentothal. "Just on minor, unimportant cases, don't you know?"

She met two stone walls. "Neither your work load nor your rank justifies the lateral transfer of personnel solely for your individual attendance," Capt. Ballas said and lit his pipe in dismissal. To Crowder he was later more open. "An enlisted man giving anesthesia? Talk about putting my ass in a crack!"

"Lt. Z," Sgt. Crowder told her, "I just ain't got no extry man I can spare right now. With all due respect, that request of your'n don't fit no job description I can think of for the OR nohow. Scuse me, I gotta go see how Osborne's doing back yonder. There's a war to be won, you know." For Capt. Ballas's ears he was more freely indignant. "The very idee! I never heerd of such," he proclaimed in masculine camaraderie.

Stone walls did not faze Z. She regarded them as temporary stumbling blocks in the pathway of her will and launched a single-handed campaign that would have shamed Joshua. She approached Crowder and Ballas as her personal Jericho. She danced in circles around them, she followed them everywhere they went, she walked backward before them so she could shake her finger under their noses. She nattered incessantly. She nagged, complained, whined, cajoled, fumed, stormed, threatened, and occasionally wept.

At the end of only three days of her constant bombardment, the walls came tumbling down.

"For God's sake, Crowder, give her what she wants! Just don't put it in writing. If it's not written down, it didn't happen. But appease that woman and get her off my tail. If I didn't know better, and if her nose was a different shape, I'd swear she was a Jewish mother. Do whatever it takes to shut her up."

"Yes, sir, Captain. My sentiments exactly."

"See if you can get an enlisted man to volunteer, although I cannot, by the wildest stretch of my imagination, foresee one of them doing it."

"With all due respect, sir, I think I've got that little problem licked. I'm gonna order Osborne to do it and not give him no choice."

"Osborne? Why Osborne?"

"Well, sir, every now and then I catch him looking at me like he's fixing to get too big for his britches. He don't say nothing but his eyes sorta look like he wants to, if you know what I mean. I think this will be a good learning experience for PFC Osborne and will keep him in the traces and learn him to appreciate what he's got."

"Huuum. Brilliant, Crowder, brilliant. I know the look of which you speak."

"On top of that, old Z requested him. He's got the breeding and social background she's comfortable with, she says."

"Indeed," mused Ballas.

"On top of that, sir, she says he's the only one in the outfit got sense enough to recognize a doobobby."

"Doobobby, Sergeant?"

"Don't ask me, Captain," Sgt. Crowder sighed. "I ain't got the faintest idee. I'm like you, sir, I just want to shut the woman up."

"Osborne it is," smiled Ballas. "Good job, Crowder, good job."

Z patted Porter on the shoulder. He could hear the ring rattling around on her finger. "You're all mine, you understand? At least every morning until the cases are finished. Sgt. Crowder, that wretched

peasant who is only minimally articulate, says you still have to do your
regular duties in the afternoons. If it means you have to extend your
work day a little, don't you worry. Z will look after you. I'm going to
teach you so much about anesthesia your parents will be proud, and
old Z will stick up for her enlisted man and see that he gets a promotion. What kind of sergeant do you want to be?"

"Ma'am? You have to be a corporal first."

"Do you want one of those plain three-stripe whatchamaycallits
or one with a rocker underneath? Or maybe two, even. I don't personally care for the one with three above and three below; it looks too
cluttered on a soldier's arm for my own personal preference. Hand me
that doobobby and watch me closely now."

"Yes, ma'am." Porter's heart was leaden.

"The trick is to have your pentothal diluted in this 50 cc.
syringe and push it ever so slowly and gradually like a little slow snail
crawling up a rose bush or like the long steady minute hand on your
watch. That way your patient doesn't get a sudden jolt and run the risk
of laryngospasm. You'll never see one of Z's cases getting
laryngospasm. Oh, dear, I forgot to bring a thingamajig. Run fetch
one. Quickly. Quickly."

"Yes, ma'am."

Otten laughed until his cheeks were wet. "Goddam, Osborne,
you've shit in your mess kit now. You and Z! That's the funniest pair of
fuckups in the whole U.S. Army."

Porter sniffed. "It'll be a real learning experience, Carter Otten.
You can't ever tell when it'll come in handy to know how to give
anesthesia."

"Learning experience? Learning experience? You've learned
the difference between a doobobby and a thingamajig and a what-
yamaycallit, I know. But I heard her tell you to bring her a hickeybob.
What the hell is a hickeybob?"

Porter mustered what dignity he could. "She's promised to get
me promoted straight to sergeant. What do you think of that?"

"That old bat can't do anything like that. A promotion would
still have to go through Crowder and Ballas, and you can forget it.
Sergeant?" he scoffed. "Sergeant? Hell, Osborne, you're not going to
be a sergeant. You're just going to be Z's nigger. 'What did you do in
the war, daddy?' 'Why, son, way I recollect I fetched and carried for ole
Miss. Sho' nuff, now, I did. I waited on Ole Miss hand and foot all the
way across Europe. That's how come I like watermelon so much. Ole

Miss use to feed me that along with a whole heap of promises.' You're going to be her nigger, Osborne." Otten laughed until he coughed.

"You kiss my ass, Carter Otten," Porter said. Defiance was in his tone, but belief that Otten was probably right made it lifeless.

Porter worked as he was bid. He became proficient at smooth induction with sodium pentothal and tried to ignore the indignities that accrued.

"That's right, Ozzy. Hold the head back and the chin up and as soon as you hear him give that little gasp, he's gone. That's when you slip this little curved metal whingdilly down his throat and strap the mask over his face. See?"

"Yes, ma'am." Ozzy? "My God!" thought Porter.

"Then you hook the mask up to the GOE machine and he's all yours. You watch his pupils like this, you breathe for him, and you check his pulse right here in the neck. These gauges and doobobbies down here tell you how much oxygen or gas or ether you're giving him. Remember gas and ether are slower than pentothal, and if you think he's getting too light, just creep on in with a teensy little push of the pentothal. But not too much. Never too much. Z has never had a respiratory arrest and you mustn't either."

"Miss Z, I'm happy to bring you things and save you some steps, but I don't think I ever want to do this. It's too complicated and too dangerous. I could kill somebody."

"Nonsense, Ozzy. You learn the technique and a few simple rules, and all you have to do is sit at the head and watch. My daddy used to tell me, 'Little Z, baby, a man is supposed to be ruled by his mind. You control his mind and you control him.' That's why I went into Anesthesia. That and the fact that the surgeons are absolutely useless until you get the patient ready for them. They may not like you, Ozzy baby, but they sure can't do a thing without you. You really control their minds, too; they just don't know it. You relax and do what I tell you. Hand me a piece of Dentyne, will you? I don't smoke but I sure like a fresh piece of gum now and then."

He managed to maneuver daily around the little-girl coquettishness and perform the tasks to which she assigned him, but he became unduly sensitive to the jibes of his fellows.

"Hey, Ozzy, baby," said Bosi, "Otten tells me you're Z's slave. Is that right?"

"That's not what Otten told you I was and I know it, but let me tell you something. You call me Ozzy again and I'll whip your tail till the Pope hollers calf-rope."

"All right, all right, already yet. I didn't mean to get your ass up on your shoulder. I thought you could take a joke."

"I thought so too, Bosi, until all of a sudden it seems that most of the time everything in life is a joke of one kind or another on somebody, and all the time on me. I'm about laughed out." He lightened his tone. "I didn't mean to insult the Pope; I'll only whip your tail till the parish priest tells me to stop." He shut his eyes briefly. "But don't you call me Ozzy."

He worked. He learned. He endured. He fought boredom any way that he could. Capt. Smith, of a sudden, decided that the camaraderie manifest between the nurses in the OR and the hard working enlisted men serving under their direction must surely be an indication of forbidden relationships. He became paranoid about fraternization. This grew in large part from the fact that some of the nurses would not date nor even converse in the club with some of the officers who were so randy that their hormone urges had overwhelmed their marriage vows, men who could not comprehend the perseverance of simple virtue in the midst of war and the uncertainty of their present existence. They consequently assumed that common human appetites must dictate that everyone was banging someone. *Ergo*, it followed that if a nurse was impervious to the wiles of an officer and a gentleman, she must have established a liaison with someone else, and who was more readily available than those charming Southern boys who were college graduates and med school drop outs? Indeed, some of them had even been seen talking for long minutes to those boys on the walkways outside the OR or on the way to the mess hall. Capt. Smith assigned himself as not only the honor guard but also the bird dog.

Lt. June Fitzgerald, who hailed from Colorado but could bat her eyes like a New Orleans debutante, was a symphony of fluid feminine efficiency in the midst of surgery. She was also undeniably cuddlesome in her scrub suit. She warned Otten about the situation. "We mustn't even speak to each other outside the line of business for awhile. Old Scarface is on the warpath."

"You mean I can't meet you behind the oxygen tent tonight?"

"Right, Carter. Somebody has seen us and Smith knows about it. He told old Sparky that he was highly suspicious of me and you and that if there was anything to it he'd catch us for sure. He's actually got somebody following all of us."

"Well, I wouldn't do anything in the world to hurt a hair of your head, Fitz, but if this war is ever over, I'm going to kill that captain. Let me know when the heat is off. I think of you all the time."

The eyelids lowered. She sighed, "Me, too. My girlfriend also heard him say that he knows Bordillon is sweet on Osborne but that Osborne so far has been too slick for him to catch. Can you imagine? All that because Johanna Bordillon is faithful to her husband and won't go near the officers' club unless she's with a bunch of girls. Then when some guy tries to be friendly and strike up a conversation with her, she won't even talk. Scarface says the only word she knows is 'Really?' and she says that like she's bored to death."

Otten recounted this to Osborne, whose reaction was quick. "Believe me, that's not the only word she knows. Those officers don't know when they're well off."

Later that afternoon, when Porter had cleaned all of Z's equipment, washed and dried the rubber bladders on the GOE machine, and finished the other chores that Crowder had heaped upon him, he approached the long work table where Lt. Bordillon was deftly assembling lap packs. Capt. Ballas and Capt. Smith were sipping coffee from canteen cups and watching the lovely light on her long bare arms. Porter dawdled. He drew a finger aimlessly along the work table edge. He even twisted a toe for a moment, rolled his eyes upward, whistled faintly beneath his breath. He obviously waited. The captains stilled their talk. Lt. Bordillon finally raised her eyes, Porter leaned forward and spoke with the sultriest voice he could muster.

"Same place?" he breathed.

She did not falter for one second, and if there was a flicker of surprise in her deep dark eyes, only Porter detected it.

"Why not?" she murmured in a low private voice. As he turned away, she added, "Same time?"

Porter was out of the tent in a flash and did not permit himself a smile until he left the mess hall and huddled with Otten in their quarters to plot strategy.

"You go west beyond the oak tree where that big gully drops off real sharp. Don't use your flash light and maybe whoever follows you will fall in and break his neck if you move fast enough that he won't be watching his step too close. I'm going to cut off through the pasture behind Orthopedics where that Frenchman has had cows grazing for a week. I'm a country boy and can spot a fresh meadow muffin in the dark, but the ground is covered with them. Let's keep 'em busy for a couple of hours."

It worked. Sherman Roger Jewel encountered Capt. Smith at the latrine, grimly trying to clean his boots and trousers with sticks and toilet paper. He reported to Porter with deadpanned solemnity.

"He sure was snappish and ill. All I said was, 'What you doing in the enlisted men's latrine, Captain? You sick, sir, or did you just miss the hole?' and he told me to shut up and asked if I knew where you were. I told him that when I left to come to the crapper, you were on your cot reading a book with a flashlight and looked like you'd been there a right smart while."

Jewel shook his head. "He sure is interested in you, Osborne. Asked me if I'd seen anybody go in that goddam cow pasture with you tonight, and of course I told him, 'No, sir.' Then he wanted to know what you were doing over there in the first place because it's off the post and therefore off-limits." .

Porter was equally solemn. "Yes?"

"I told him the only thing I could figure out was that maybe you had a crush on one of them heifers, since everybody knew you were a real country boy."

"Thanks a lot, Jewel. I'll help you out some time, if you ever need a character reference."

"Not atall; think nothing of it. That's when he commenced yelling. 'Not even Osborne would stoop to that,' he said. And I said, 'Way I've heard tell, Captain, you don't stoop; you have to stand on a stump.' And he really hollered then. 'Goddammit, you know what I mean! I'm going to find something to court martial that Osborne about yet!'"

"What an attitude. I'm trying to be the best soldier I know how. Did you tell the Captain that?"

"Come to think of it, I didn't. What I told him was not to worry, that I was pretty certain none of them cows was commissioned. That's when he cussed and stomped out and I was finally able to set my butt down and take a crap in peace."

"I mean it about the character reference, Jewel. I'll swear to anybody that you're a real character."

"I'll keep it in mind. You watch your step."

"Oh, I do, Jewel, I do. You don't see any shit on my shoes, do you?"

Somehow the nurses were apprised of the events of the evening prior to appearing for work the next morning. There was much surreptitious smiling, even occasional mischievous winks. When Capt. Irving Ballas walked in with a long flamboyant scratch down one cheek and a blue bruise on his forehead, Lt. Fitzpatrick blinked alluringly and softly cooed, "Whatever happened to you, Captain? Did you fall in a ditch or something?" That was the first time Porter ever saw Lt.

Bordillon laugh aloud, and he thought her teeth were the whitest, most even he had ever seen, although her gums, he thought, were purple enough to make him just a little suspicious of her bloodlines.

It was the beginning of a lasting friendship between June Fitzgerald from the mountains of Colorado and Johanna Bordillon from the swamps of Louisiana, who might not otherwise have found much in common. It also generated a stiff-legged, on-guard attitude of Capt. Smith toward Porter Osborne, who pretended that he did not notice it at all. If there was one thing he had learned, it was always to respect superior officers.

The tedium of routine was startlingly destroyed by uncon-firmed rumors of ominous events at the front. The confident assump-tion that the Germans were on the run and that their total defeat was only a matter of time was destroyed by the fearful news that the fleeing dog had turned on its attacker and had him down in the snow and was shaking him by the throat. The German POW's still went capably about their duties but were guarded and withdrawn, avoiding looking directly at their captors.

"Where is Bastogne?" Porter asked.

"Who the hell knows? Help me move this guy to the litter. We've got them stacked up like cordwood and all of these are fresh wounds. God! It's awful. Let's move it!"

Everybody in the hospital doubled up and worked at fever pitch. The OR personnel immediately went to sixteen-hour days, and the night team was as busy as the day crew had previously been. The surgeons worked to exhaustion, but there was no griping. Everyone Porter knew submerged any forebodings about enemy reversal in the dedicated care of the wounded Americans who were fighting so fiercely to prevent it. Porter saw gallantry underlying every mutilated soldier he attended. He welcomed fatigue, embraced extra duties. He pushed concern about Allied defeat, even the possibility of his own death, to the back of his mind, and exulted that in his own way he was fighting back. Carter Otten surprised him by voicing similar feelings.

Porter was giving pentothal to two GI's simultaneously, their heads approximated so that he could monitor both. Otten was dashing by to re-gown himself for another operation and paused only long enough to say, "Goddammit, Osborne, this is worth flunking out of med school."

Porter nodded, startled that Carter, for the first time, had not protested that he was kicked out. He refrained from reference to it but from then on he felt closer to Carter Otten.

Z was everywhere. Her voice became shriller, she muttered to herself, she constantly bumped into people hastening with purpose on chores of their own. Sometimes when she bustled along with no one near her, she would twirl several times in a circle, look confused, and prate of doobobbies, thingamajigs, and hickeybobs. The demanding cry of "Ozzy" rang so frequently through the OR that the other nurses adopted the nickname. Porter gritted his teeth and took it. After all, Miss Z was old and spoiled and pampered and should not be expected to stand up well to the stress under which they all presently labored. He catered to her whims the best he could but was drawn to Capt. Ballas for direction.

"Osborne, you well know that I have never approved of an enlisted man giving anesthesia and, to tell you the truth, gave in to Lt. Zeiderheusen's request as much to test your mettle as anything else. I've watched closely, however, and you have proved yourself an able student, quick to learn but cautious and conservative in application. We are in a tight and the lieutenant is going to pieces on me. You and Lt. Toomay are going to have to accept an official schedule of anesthesia cases in order for us to look after all these wounded patients."

Osborne hesitated. "You mean a PFC is going to be giving anesthetics on his own? What if I goof up? What if I get an arrest? Or a laryngospasm? Capt. Ballas, I can't handle that much responsibility. I'm just an enlisted man."

"I'll supervise you when I can. And don't be shy about asking questions. I'll help. Those goddam Germans are slaughtering us, and I can't stand it if one of our boys makes it back this far and then we lose him because we don't have personnel to get him operated. We're a team, Osborne, and we don't have but one purpose."

"Yes, sir. I'll do my best. But I would sure feel bad for one of our boys to have made it back this far and then we lose him because an untrained PFC was sleeping him."

"Don't fret about that, Osborne. If we pull through this crisis, I'll address Sgt. Crowder recommending you for promotion."

"That's not what I meant, Captain." There was a note of indignation in Porter's voice. "I don't give a tinker's damn about making Sergeant. But," he added craftily, "Otten does. Have you noticed how he's busting his balls and what a good job he's doing?"

Capt. Ballas pushed his glasses up and rubbed his sleepless eyes. "Have you noticed how arrogant he remains? You tend to this Anesthesia department and discard any other concerns."

Over the next two weeks Porter Osborne and Capt. Irving Ballas vied with each other to see who had the greater powers of endurance, who could put service more constantly ahead of self, who could respond more to the call of duty than to the goad of fatigue. Lt. Zeiderheusen was left in the backwater to putter along with a normal work load while the captain from Harvard and the private from Georgia frantically but efficiently kept the torrent from engulfing them all. Respect between them grew but it was not warmed by any glow of affection. Try as he might, PFC Porter Osborne, Jr., could not bring himself to like Capt. Irving Ballas.

"He's a good Anesthesiologist," he conceded to himself, "but he's a piss-poor person. Talk about being arrogant, he's twice as much so as Carter and with much less justification. On top of that, he's pompous as hell. I have had a bellyful of Harvard, and old Sparky Ballas from upper state New York, wherever that is, is a plumb stomp-down double-dyed shitass."

He felt better and worked even harder.

Everyone thrilled when Gen. McAuliffe defiantly answered "Nuts!" to the imperious German call for surrender; then they waited in suspense to see if Patton could bail him out and make the taunt valid. They redoubled their efforts to repair the wounds of the American soldiers whose personal sacrifices of life and limb made the achievements of the generals possible; knowledge which reinforced that everyone was an essential part of this conflict.

Amid the resultant intensity, both emotional and physical, hardly anyone took much note of Z's departure. One day she was there and the next, very simply, she was not. Capt. Ballas, Lt. Toomay and Porter absorbed her work load without even sighing.

Bosi chattered as he circulated. "What happened to Lt. Doobobby? I hear she got orders last night to ship back to the States and bailed out on a truck this morning before day with all her duffel. What gives?"

"We'll have no disrespect for superior officers here; her name is Lt. Zeiderheusen," reproved Capt. Ballas.

Lt. Hisel was scrubbed on an abdominal exploratory, standing on a stool so she could peer over the shoulders of the surgeons to anticipate their needs. "I saw her last night right after she got the orders. She was white as a sheet and was thumbing that ring till it rattled around her finger like a windmill in a prairie storm. Said she didn't want to go home. I told her if she'd give me her ring, I'd swap places with her. She didn't even laugh, said that ring had been her shield and defender ever since her daddy died, and she wouldn't part with it for twice what it's worth. She's weird, but I was worried about the old girl. We'll never see her again."

Porter spoke from the head of the table. "You mean she's gone for good?"

"Sure is, Ozzy."

Lt. Dalrymple further enlightened him, although he really had no time to listen. "Hisel is right. The old one was upset. I came upon her in the latrine, and she was crying with both her eyes and a whole box of Kleenex. I pat her on the shoulder and ask her what is the matter, and she tell me that I would not understand. I tell her that I am just as intelligent as she is and if she is capable of explaining it, I am qualify to understand."

"Believe me, Lt. Dalrymple," interposed Porter, "that does not always hold true. I know."

"You are right. She cry some more and say her daddy would come back up from out his grave if he know how they treating his baby girl. Say that he have not raise her to be humiliated. He have certainly not raise her to be poor. She have not hurt a living e-soul in all her life, she say, and all she try to do is look after herself in the e-style her daddy teach her. I listen and listen. I have patience and I listen and pat. I listen to daddy this and daddy that and what a wonderful life in Baltimore. Finally I pat her one last time and tell her she was right in the first place; I do not understand. Hisel is right also, Ozzy, about her being weird."

Because of the caseload, everyone had a staggered lunch break. Lt. Toomay padded up to Porter. "Mind if I walk to chow with you?" she asked. "We're the last two to go."

"No, ma'am," Porter replied. "Long as Capt. Smith doesn't get the idea we're fraternizing."

She dimpled prettily. "Even Capt. Smith wouldn't think that of me; nobody dates short fat girls. Besides, everybody is so busy now, including Capt. Smith, that he's temporarily had to abandon that witch hunt."

"Good. I sure hope our boys are going to beat them back at Bastogne. One of the guys I slept this morning said the snow is lots worse there than here and they went four days on nothing but

K-rations. I've got to rush; Capt. Ballas has me down for an amputation in thirty minutes."

"I know. Me, too. Ozzy, I want to tell you how proud I am of the way all you enlisted men are knocking yourselves out on double duty. Everybody's pitching in and not grumbling and it's a good feeling, even in the middle of all this worry and sadness."

"I know, Miss Toomay. I suspect that's why Miss Z was so upset about being sent home; she probably feels cheated out of her part in the war."

Shirley Toomay's voice was calm and small. "Why do you think Z was ordered home so precipitously, Ozzy?"

"Why, I assume it's because of her age. She told me, and swore me to secrecy, that she lied about her age when she enlisted and that she's really five years older than it shows on her papers. I figured that when they checked records somebody finally tumbled to that like they did to Farbecker being AWOL, and that she's being transferred Stateside to less strenuous duty. Isn't that it?"

"No."

"You sound like you know something no one else does."

"Capt. Ballas knows."

"What?"

"Z is going to be met at the boat by the military police and faces court-martial and dishonorable discharge."

"What are you talking about? Whatever for?"

"For stealing, Ozzy. For theft and conversion."

"What's to steal, for God's sake?"

"You remember that dentist, Lt. Hyman Finkle, who was ordered home a month ago?"

"I didn't know him but I heard it was because his wife was sick and dying."

"That's the tale he put out. He was shipping government equipment home and his cousin was bootlegging it to civilian hospitals. He went so far as to ship a brand-new dental chair that had never even been uncrated, and now he's in Leavenworth. My sister is in the same synagogue with him and says his mama has almost had two heart attacks and a small stroke."

Porter took a deep breath but waited.

"Z was in cahoots with him, hand and glove. You remember those three new anesthesia machines that disappeared the night of the fire? You remember all the instruments that kept disappearing? Z was funneling them to Finkle and he was splitting with her."

"I can't believe this. How did they find out?"

"I got suspicious and told Irving Ballas, and we both watched and set little traps and he reported her."

"My God!" remonstrated Porter. "We've got boys fighting their guts out and getting blown to kingdom come, and I've been working my heart out under an old crow with a diamond ring who's stealing from the government and feathering her own nest. We ain't ever going to win this war."

"Don't say that, Ozzy," reproved Shirley Toomay. "There are enough of us pulling together in the system to make it work. There's no way we can let those terrible Germans win. We shall prevail."

"There sure are some rotten apples in the barrel, Miss Toomay."

"I had some training in Anesthesia at Bellevue and Capt. Ballas has been working to refresh me. You'll be working under me from now on, Ozzy."

Porter looked down at her and thought she might be attractive if she lost thirty pounds, grew two inches, and started using lipstick. "You mean that from now on you're going to be Old Missy to me? Did Capt. Ballas promise you a promotion, Lieutenant?"

"He did mention it, Ozzy."

"Well, Ole Missy, let's get one thing straight from the start. I don't mean any disrespect, but I keep finding out you have to look after Number One in this outfit. I'll work real good under you on one condition."

"What's that, Ozzy?"

"That you listen real close to what I'm about to say and enforce it with all the other nurses in this outfit. There is not the slightest doubt in my mind who I am. I am Porter Osborne, Jr., PFC, United States Army Medical Corps."

"What do you mean?"

"Just what I say." He threw his head back, clenched his fists, and howled at the top of his voice. "Don't call me Ozzy!"

Lt. Toomay stood and looked at him with no show of emotion whatever. "All right, PFC Osborne. I can arrange that. Provided that you never refer to me again as 'Ole Missy.' To a person of my background, that is repugnant. I also know who I am."

Porter gulped, stood briefly at attention, only his mess kit preventing him from saluting on the spot. "Yes, ma'am," he said. He felt a little dizzy.

They had all been so absorbed with the Battle of the Bulge and its casualties that Christmas Eve had crept upon them with no official notice and little personal attention. Of a sudden, with sunshine brilliant against the snow, the day was there. They were cheered by news that the American Air Force was utilizing the crystal skies of the improved weather to battle the Germans and that McAuliffe's defenses had been adequately supplied by airlift. They were resolved not to let sentiment breach their interpersonal barricades; no one spoke of home. No one used first names that day, and everyone chattered of official duties and news of the war. They avoided each other's eyes. Lt. Dalrymple cut a small tree that was devoid of leaves but covered with thorns. She mounted it on a table in the work room of the OR and proceeded to decorate it with cotton balls she had soaked in merthiolate or gentian violet or even weak iodine solution. Its appearance was festive enough to provide smiles but was so far removed from any remembrance of Christmas Porter could summon that it evoked no nostalgia in him. He worked with resolution and pushed back thoughts of Brewton County and the temptation to envision what the various members of his family might be doing at some particular moment. He dismissed the tightness in his throat as an indication that he might be trying to come down with a cold.

At noon the ambulances quit running. By mid-afternoon they finished the last scheduled operation for the day. By dusk they had cleared the OR suite and had everything prepared for the morning. Capt. Ballas announced that no evening surgery had been scheduled and that only the skeleton crew responsible for emergencies need remain on duty. Strangely, no one seemed eager to leave.

"What you reading over there in the corner all by yourself, Lucetti?" asked Sherman Jewel.

The lawyer from Florida did not look up. "Luke," he replied.

"I'm sorry you told me."

"I wouldn't if you hadn't asked."

"Anybody want to sing 'Jingle Bells'?" Lt. Dalrymple interposed archly. "There is plenty of e-snow outside that we could go dashing through. I have not ever seen something like this in San Antonio."

"Nice try, Dal," snapped Lt. Hisel. "Can it."

Capt. Ballas stretched. "I think I'll go on to chow." He surveyed the nurses and tried not to let his gaze linger too obviously on Lt. Bordillon. "There's a get-together tonight at the officers' club; a truck came in with a new allotment of whiskey. I guess I'll see you there."

Lt. Bordillon did not indicate she heard him, but as she turned to place a stack of sterile gloves, she looked briefly across the room at Porter. Soundlessly but simultaneously their lips mouthed *merde* and her glance slid smoothly on. None of the other nurses responded either, and the silence in which Capt. Ballas departed was decidedly awkward.

"I wonder where Z is," said Lt. Fitzgerald.

"I hope McAuliffe breaks through tomorrow," said Lt. Bordillon.

"I hear they're going to start evacuating casualties straight to England and we won't be so swamped," said Lt. Hisel.

"I think it is a shame that the enlisted men do not have a club to go to and do not get some whiskey to drink on Christmas Eve," said Lt. Dalrymple. "Don't that make you feel e-sad and lonely, Ozzy?"

"Don't call him Ozzy," said Lt. Toomay.

"All of you quit clucking around like a bunch of old hens," advised Lt. Ruth Neilson in crisp tones. She was the chief nurse of the Operating Room, a native of Wisconsin who manifested her Norse heritage in summary rejection of indolence or incompetence. Everyone respected her, and she gave no indication that it mattered to her one whit if anyone liked her. Her attitude was one of "get your job done and do it well with as little nonsense as possible." Porter was a little bit afraid of her. "Stop your blathering and either get to work or get out. I would advise all of you girls, however, to make at least an appearance at the officers' club tonight. Col. Draughan has announced that everyone will be in dress uniform."

Johanna Bordillon did not look at Porter but he distinctly saw her lips meet in the letter M.

Enlisted men sat or lay on their cots that evening without the stimuli of work and activity to divert their thoughts. Try as he would, Porter could not concentrate on reading nor ignore the fact that this was indeed, ready or not, Christmas Eve. He considered that this was the second one in a row he had missed being at home and drifted into speculation on how many more might pass him by before his life returned to normal. He chastened himself then for self-pity and tried to dwell on how much better his situation tonight was than that of the Battered Bastards of Bastogne. This produced the old quiver of guilt by contrast, as he thought there was hardly a one of them who was looking after Number One.

From the tent that housed the officers' club, the sound of revelry pealed across the night in sporadic bursts, so muted by distance that words and individual voices could not be distinguished, so unmistakably accompanied by laughter, however, that it was excludingly elite, incomprehensibly foreign to the wistful mood in the enlisted quarters. A significant amount of the laughter was musically feminine and was audible confirmation that in the choice of worlds, commissioned officers would always occupy the better one, for who had the women and whiskey tonight? One by one the GI's drifted aimlessly up the hill, away from the noise of celebration, drawn to the further removed and familiar wards where they worked.

Bosi came in from the latrine. "What you reading, Lucetti?"

The steel-rimmed glasses glittered but Lucetti's head remained bowed. "Matthew," he said.

"I think I'll mosey up the hill and see what the guys on duty are doing," said Porter.

"Goddam," said Carter Otten.

Porter found most of the Wafflebacks huddled around the stove in the office area of a Medicine ward, their conversation disappointingly desultory and stilted. He wandered from OR to General Surgery to Orthopedics, unwilling to settle long in one place, resolved not to return to his quarters until the boisterous officers had retired to theirs. He stood on the periphery of a group of twelve or more in the Orthopedic tent, a lone light bulb fighting the gloom of olive green walls and ceiling, faces shining starkly white and flat as they floated in and out of darkness. Everyone awaited the approach of midnight but they spoke of other things. If they spoke at all.

Lt. Barbara Short burst into that assemblage from out of the night as startlingly disruptive as a creature from another planet. She was an OR nurse as eye-catching as any drawing by Petty or Varga. Porter had watched doctors meeting her for the first time become suddenly motionless and ogle, so transfixed before physical perfection that they were temporarily bereft of speech or motor skills. She had only to open her mouth, however, to restore normal functions in most men. She was possessed of an East Texas accent and limited vocabulary that made all but the more illiterate wince. Porter was convinced that her cranial vault had the capacity of a Dominecker chicken's and wondered how she had finished nursing school, a concern that apparently motivated Lt. Ruth Neilsen when she assigned Barbara Short the simplest of tasks and arranged even those to shield her as much as possible from the vision of males.

Intelligence had little to do with male perception of this vision on Christmas Eve of 1944. She came in giggling, her platinum hair uncovered, her blue eyes sparkling, her milky skin and reddened lips a blaze of color in the darkness of the tent. In each hand she held an opened bottle.

"Merry Christmas, fellows," she chortled. "I am the Christmas fairy, and Santa sent me to bring every enlisted man on duty tonight a drink of liquor and a kiss. To hell with all those officers getting drunker by the minute and not thinking of nobody but theyselves. To hell with all those old military rules that, to tell you the truth, I ain't never bothered to learn anyhow."

She raised a bottle before their gawking faces. "Well, for pity's sake, line up and let's go! I got a heap of rounds to make tonight. Every fellow gets two swallows and one kiss. Keep your hands to yourself, though. If I was gonna put up with grabby-feely, I would have stayed in the officers' club."

Galvanized into previously unimagined activity, the enlisted men responded with delight. Their comrades poured in from the night. The line grew longer. There was jostling but no shoving.

"Two swallows and a kiss?" said Kostas. "What an unusual communion service."

"Beats grape juice and crackers," said Porter and held his position in line.

"Best Twelve Stations of the Cross I ever witnessed," Ted Kelly responded.

"Merry Christmas!" said Barbara Short to the recipient she was attending.

The boy just ahead of Porter was Marvin Scott, a shy corpsman from Oregon who smiled secretively when in groups but never had much to say. When he stepped up, overcoming embarrassment, he looked into Lt. Short's eyes, turned beet red, and Porter heard him say, "I don't drink, Lieutenant, but I sure will appreciate the kiss."

Barbara Short raised her arms so that her breasts stretched upward as she stepped closely against Pvt. Scott. "You get two, baby, cause you got lonesome, hungry eyes."

The entire group was so intent on the ensuing embrace that no one noticed the tent flap part and the new arrival step in. Porter was the one who looked up and saw Capt. John Smith with Sgt. Lagerpiel and Lt. Ruth Neilson right behind him. They were staring open-mouthed at the couple beneath the light bulb.

"Ten-shut!" bellowed Porter.

Lt. Short turned her head. "Hush your mouth, Porter Osborne; everybody knows what a devil you are. You scared me to death there for a minute thinking maybe that old Capt. Scarface had tracked me down. The horny old married fool's been chasing me all evening." She followed Porter's gaze. "Oh, shit," she said.

"*Merde*," whispered Porter and for the first time in his life felt like crossing himself.

Barbara Short pushed her two bottles into Pvt. Scott's hands, leaned up and kissed him again very softly, patted his cheek, and said, "Merry Christmas." Then she faced Lt. Neilson, whom Capt. Smith had pushed ahead of him, and saluted. That white-faced lady returned the salute and then put an arm around the miscreant's shoulders. Barbara Short looked at the soldiers and sang out, "Good-bye, y'all." Tears shone brightly in her eyes.

Capt. Smith stepped toward Scott and reached for the bottles. "I'll just take those. Hand them here," he said. Instead, Marvin Scott handed the bottles off to Kostas, who immediately passed them on to Porter as though they were too hot to handle, and Porter relayed them swiftly without even looking. The bottles were gone.

"You disobeyed an order," Capt. Smith said, but in the sullen silence his voice sounded ineffectual.

Pvt. Scott drew himself up and looked straight into Capt. Smith's face. He did not salute but incredibly began singing. He sang softly in perfect pitch and everyone present immediately joined in.

> "God bless America,
> Land that I love.
> Stand beside her
> And guide her
> Through the night with the light from above."

Their voices trailed Capt. Smith in chastening harmony out of the tent and floated over him down the hill. Porter was almost positive that he heard Sgt. Lagerpiel's voice briefly join them in the song before he disappeared behind the captain into the night. Porter left for his tent. "If they sing 'Silent Night' on top of that, I'll cry like a baby and be up all night," he thought.

"What you reading, Lucetti?" he asked.

Lucetti looked up. "Mark," he said. "Merry Christmas. Where have you been?"

"Singing hymns. Merry Christmas to you."

"If I'd known you were going to do that, I'd have gone with you."

Porter slid between his blankets, considered the evening, wondered briefly where the whiskey bottles were. "You were better off reading," he assured Lucetti. "Good night."

As he drifted into sleep Porter could not help thinking, "If I'm not compartmentalized by now, sweet Baby Jesus, I'm not ever going to make it. Happy Birthday."

No one in the 816th ever heard from Lt. Barbara Short again; she was notorious for not writing letters. No one ever heard from Pvt. Marvin Scott; there was really no one for him to write. There was not a nurse or an enlisted man, however, who ever encountered Capt. John Smith thereafter without at least fleetingly remembering both of them. On the day after Christmas, the Americans fought through the German lines besieging Bastogne and "Nuts!" became enshrined forever as a victorious battle cry. The population of patients in the 816th General Hospital changed precipitously from wounded GI's to wounded prisoners of war. The wards and the Operating Room were swamped with Germans.

Porter watched the prisoners eat butter, canned turkey, ham, and all the sugar they wanted for their coffee. He remembered the civilians in the United States enduring rationing and going without meat, thought further that these same Germans only short days previously had been killing GI's or at the very least causing them to get trench foot and lose their toes.

"This is a crazy damn war and not worth flunking out of med school," he said to Otten.

"I got kicked out," responded Carter. "Goose this one with a little more pentothal, will you? He's beginning to wiggle."

In the press of patient overload, overwhelmed by the hordes of PW's needing attention, Carter Otten had been elevated in effect from surgical technician to the level of a functioning surgeon. He was entrusted with debriding wounds and performing secondary closures on cases of some magnitude, and these without supervision. The real surgeons were exhaustingly utilized on major cases. Carter was still only a PFC but he still harbored aspirations.

Porter was giving anesthesia under the much more loosely supervising eye of Capt. Ballas and was being ordered to give it to increasingly complicated cases. He, like Otten, became more and more proficient in his assignments, but Porter Osborne harbored no aspirations. He still listened and learned, however. The surgeons were interesting.

Lt. Hormley, never able to remember names, was apparently oblivious to the nationality or political persuasion of his current patients. He still brought both volumes of Watson-Jones with him to the Operating Room and did a lot of muttering and earnest frowning as he scrubbed. He still vaguely addressed enlisted men as "Miller" or "Farbecker" when he bothered to address them at all. Lt. Hormley was comfortingly consistent.

Capt. Bloom was a passionate and intense man even on a mild day, and he loosed occasional tirades to Capt. Ballas. "My God, Irving, what have they done to us? Us, of all people? After the way these goddam Germans have been treating Jews for the last ten years, how do Otto Draughan and the United States Government dare expect us to be physicians for them? Some of these bastards are arrogant as hell, and I keep fantasizing about letting my knife slip."

Capt. Ballas had often referred to being a Harvard man, but he had never flatly proclaimed himself a Jew; he squirmed a little and looked over his shoulder to see if Maj. Emmons was listening. "Calm down, Walter, calm down. Sit on your emotions and just do your job. If we weren't winning, we wouldn't have this many prisoners to work on; two other hospitals in the area are getting nothing but German admissions either. The 168th, on the other hand, has been designated for Americans only."

"How can I get out of this outfit? By God, I'll ask Otto Draughan for a transfer before I kill somebody!"

"Calm down, Walter. You're not commissioned in this Army as a Jew. You're commissioned as a Surgeon. And you're a very good one. Just put the lid on and dissociate. Do what is before you and dissociate. As our ancestors have for centuries. Relax, man."

"Relax, hell!" shouted Walter Bloom. "I'm sick and tired of us being shoved around, and this is the supreme insult! They rob us, beat us, jail us, and probably kill us in Germany, and then we're expected to operate on them and save their lives! Next thing you know we'll be asked to blow their noses and wipe their asses. What's the matter with you, Irving? Don't you feel insulted?"

"Maybe I've developed a thicker skin than you, Walter. I also have cousins who have disappeared in Germany without a trace. I realize that these patients are also our enemies, but I am not insulted. I confess that I have relaxed about Osborne giving general anesthesia and would not be upset if he caused our mortality rate to rise at the present time, but, by God, Walter, you have to be a Surgeon first and Jewish second. Dissociate, man, dissociate."

Porter listened in amazement. "Why, the insolent, overbearing, commissioned shitass," he thought. "He'd actually let me slip up and kill somebody out of my own ignorance as long as it wasn't laid at his door step. Sparky ain't ever going to change." He became even more cautious and watchful about the mixtures he used and frequently consulted Lt. Toomay.

He even very occasionally asked her a non-medical question. "I don't mean any harm, Miss Toomay, but is *dissociate* more a Jewish or a Harvard term?"

"I'm sure I wouldn't know, Osborne. I've never even thought about it. In what sense are you using it?"

"Oh, I don't use it, Miss Toomay. I say *compartmentalize*."

"You have a strange but interesting mind, Osborne. Hand me that flow-meter, will you? And you'd better get busy; we're running an hour behind."

The patrician Maj. Emmons was as imperturbable as usual. "I am amazed at the number of physicians and medical technicians we've captured. A German surgeon even asked me the other day when I was changing his dressing if it would be possible to let him do some cases. He's bored to death in the stockade and volunteered his services."

"I wouldn't want a Kraut operating on me," said Capt. Smith.

"He was speaking of operating on fellow Germans, of course," replied Maj. Emmons. He looked coolly at the captain. "You realize, don't you, that if you required surgery right now you'd be shipped over to the 168th? Do you know anyone over there?"

"Did we capture any Anesthetists?" ventured Porter.

He never knew where the idea germinated or how it spread to upper echelon ears. During the week of January seventeenth, after the news that the Germans had been routed from Bastogne and that finally the Battle of the Bulge was an heroic and hard-won triumph for the Allies, the 816th Hospital was singled out for unique assignment. Three general hospitals in Normandy would now have no patients except German prisoners of war. These three hospitals would be staffed and operated by German medical personnel selected from the ever swelling ranks within the stockades. The American staff from two of the hospitals would move nearer the front that Patton was daily extending. The Americans who comprised the 816th would be divided among the three newly-formed POW hospitals, and their jobs would be to supervise their German counterparts.

479

Col. Draughan orated, "This is a signal honor that has been bestowed upon us in recognition of superior performance and excellent administrative capability. It is a high privilege for which I shall expect each and every one of you to manifest worthiness by your usual exemplary dedication to duty. High privilege. High privilege. The eyes of the ETO are upon us, and we will measure up to the trust that has been placed in our ability by the higher command. I am certain that in due course this new venture will lead to recognition and promotion for every member of this outfit. Every member. Entire outfit. Let us hope so. Good opportunity. Good opportunity."

With that he jammed the cigar between his lips and strutted off in the direction of the officers' club.

"Goddam, goddam, goddam," said Carter Otten.

"Holy flying dog shit," said Sherman Roger Jewel.

"I wonder who wrote that speech for him," said Stevens Kostas.

"I think the last sentence was original; you could tell it was spoken from the heart," said Porter Osborne.

Reaction in the Operating Room was varied.

"I reckon I'll be shuttling backwards and forwards between the three units supervising the enlisted men who are supervising the German enlisted men," sighed Oliver Crowder and took a great sucking sip of coffee. "My aching back," he added.

"They don't have any German nurses in the stockades," advised Lt. Ruth Neilson. "You girls will be split up among the three hospitals to teach their techs to scrub or else scrub for the German surgeons yourselves."

"It will be interesting to travel on the trucks every day to a new outfit and meet new faces and people. I will volunteer to rotate if you want me to," said Lt. Dalrymple.

"I wonder if those suckers are any good as surgeons," contributed Lt. Hisel. "We don't have to take any stuff off them, do we?"

"Osborne, I'm going to leave you in charge of Anesthesia here; Lt. Toomay and I will each have to take one of the new units. You think you can handle it?" asked Capt. Ballas.

"'He who setteth his hand to the plow and looketh back is not worthy of the Kingdom of Heaven,'" said Porter, obviously quoting.

"Who said that?" asked the captain.

"Henry Wadsworth Longfellow, I think, sir. Or it may have been Sidney Lanier; I keep getting them mixed up. I'm sure it was not Algernon Charles Swineburn. Perhaps it was Governor Cincinnatis Lucius Lamar."

"You should forget I asked," said Capt. Ballas. "Do what you're told."

"I always do, sir," murmured Porter.

"Irving," blustered Capt. Bloom, "this is the last straw! I will not tolerate it! This is the supreme insult! I'll be damned if I'll consort daily with these arrogant Prussian bastards and help them look after their misbegotten underlings. I'm going to tell Otto Draughan I want a transfer out of this outfit. I'd rather tell my rabbi I'd eaten a ham than that I'd been civil to these animals who've been persecuting our people."

"'Love your enemies; do good unto those who persecute you; pray for those who despitefully use you; be ye kind one to another,'" murmured Lucetti.

"Who in the hell is responsible for that mouthful of drivel?" demanded Capt. Walter Bloom.

"Pvt. Madison Lucetti, sir," intervened Porter with alacrity. "I thought you knew him by now."

"Goddam, goddam, goddam," said Carter Otten.

"This should be an interesting diversion," said Maj. Emmons, "and not nearly so demanding as our schedule for the last four weeks. We should look on everything in life as a learning experience."

Lt. Johanna Bordillon looked at Porter, shrugged, and they simultaneously said their word.

The effort was a shambles. With its personnel fragmented among three hospital units, there was no longer any sense of unity or cohesiveness. With its patient load now one exclusively of PW's, the high purpose and dedication that had sustained the 816th through the Battle of the Bulge evaporated. When all actual work was performed by PW's and the duties of Americans restricted to supervision alone, many of them shed responsibility.

"Hell," said Sherman Jewel, "if they start chewing your ass out about something, you can always lay it on the fucking PW you're trying to train."

"Right," said Porter Osborne. "There's always a dog under the table to kick."

"Goddam, goddam, goddam," said PFC Carter Otten.

"You Southerners truly are interesting," said Stevens Kostas. "Osborne, do you realize that you are probably the only PFC in the ETO who spends his working day looking over the shoulders of German medical officers and criticizing them?"

481

Morale plummeted. Christmas mail caught up with them and spirits temporarily brightened. Porter saved a letter from his father till last.

"Dear Son,

I am assuming from the account of your peregrinations you have managed so ingeniously to slip by the censors that you are still in Normandy and have not been anywhere near the Ardennes. I pray that is true and that you are safe.

I am also assuming from the cryptic tone of your last letter and the elusiveness of it that you have probably had to come to terms with death; that perhaps you even lost a buddy who was very near to you. You are not becoming a man, you are a man. One, I might add, whom, despite occasional differences of opinion between us, I am extremely proud to call my son.

Because it would be more difficult for you if we dissembled and protected you now, only for you to learn the truth later, I write to tell you that Fritz is dead. You said in your letter that you had not wept since last Christmas. You do not need to do so now, for I have done it for both of us.

Fritz was the most noble animal since Bob, Son of Battle. No stray dog dared approach the premises, and the livestock so dreaded him that a pig, cow, or mule would no longer walk through an open gate if Fritz was anywhere around.

He died without pain. Steve Mann is sawmilling on the Stubbs place. His muffler was gone and your mother complained about the noise. It was almost as though Fritz understood her, for it infuriated him for the logging truck to come down the big road. I yelled and yelled at him, but he thought it his duty to chase the truck. Yesterday he caught it. He didn't even yelp. We buried him behind the barn.

Your mother sends love. She is crazy about the statue you sent her, but we had to take it to town for Dr. Seawright to open it with his cast cutters. I already have a clock but I appreciate your thinking of me. If you decide you want any more red dirt, I have plenty available.

Love,
Your Dad.

P.S. I am sorry about Fritz and I am sorry to have to tell you. I have been where you are, however, and I remember that it is hard to trust someone after you once find out he withheld information from you. When that happens your imagination takes over and that is always more dreadful than truth. That is a sword that cuts both ways, so keep me informed."

He folded the letter and felt an almost irresistible urge to fall on his cot and sob. Instead he whirled through the tent flap and began running. He ran beyond the mess tent and company headquarters to the long driveway that served as an allee for the hospital. Down that road he sped with bared head, the wind of his own passage loud in his ears. When he approached the sentry station, he reversed himself and sped back. His thoughts were fleeter than his feet. "My class in med school is three months from graduation. I have just spent my second Christmas away from home. Deacon Chauncey is still a PW in Germany. I'm up to my ass in German PW's. Will Barton is dead. I have fucked a whore. My old missy turned out to be a thief. I can give as smooth an Anesthesia as Capt. Irving Ballas, who is a Jew from Harvard and for some reason doesn't like any of us enlisted men. My sister had a baby back home. I am stuck here with Sgt. Crowder who is a tenant farmer from Arkansas and likes fewer people than Capt. Ballas. Now Fritz is dead." The latter phrase took over his consciousness and he ran to the pounding rhythm of "Fritz is dead, Fritz is dead, Fritz is dead."

He staggered back into the tent and collapsed on his cot, chest heaving, heart galloping. Carter Otten stood over him.

"What in the living hell is wrong with you? Tearing out of here without your helmet liner and sprinting down the road with all the goddam Germans staring at you? Have you lost your fucking mind? What got into you?"

Porter's heart still threatened to break through his chest wall, but he mustered enough breath to reply. "You wouldn't understand."

Otten kicked the end of the cot. "I challenged you with that once. Try me."

Porter sat up. "I was suddenly overcome with an urge to check out a line from Kipling."

"Which line?"

"'If you can fill the unforgiving minute
With sixty seconds worth of distance run,
Then yours is the earth and everything that's in it,
And, which is more, you'll be a man, my son.'"

"You're wrong, Osborne," said Carter Otten. "I understand that perfectly. I've been thinking about it off and on myself ever since they turned us into a branch of the Nazi army. What triggered your unforgiving minute?"

Porter decided to trust him. "Fritz is dead."

"Fritz? You mean that goddam dog of Dr. Thebault's?"

"Yes."

"Why in the hell did that stimulate you to think about Kipling and bolt out of here like Glenn Cunningham?"

"I lied, Carter. I wasn't thinking about Kipling. I was thinking about Fritz. He loved to run. I ran in his honor."

Otten shook his head. "Like you said to me on the train, 'You were right the first time. I don't understand.'" He paused and kicked the cot again. "Thank God. If you want sympathy, it's still in the dictionary between shit and syphilis. Remember? Grab your mess kit and let's go to chow."

Two days later Otten excitedly interrupted Porter in midafternoon. "Guess what? Griffin Calhoun is here! Second Lieutenant in MAC, has his own Jeep and driver and two quarts of bourbon! He tracked me down over at the branch hospital and has wangled two twenty-four hour passes for me and you. Change into dress uniform as soon as you can and we're out of here! Our luck has turned."

"Worm," said Porter.

"What?"

"Luck changes. Worms turn. You have to say either our luck has changed or our worm has turned."

"You goddam half-assed scholar. Do you want to go or not?"

"Sure," said Porter. "Nobody's called me Vitamin Flintheart in a hundred years."

His presence was no more than background to Otten and Calhoun's reunion; he was reminded again of two giant puppies frisking

484

and cavorting. Calhoun looked strange and elegant in his officer's uniform, his gold bars twinkling impressively, but Porter had the impression that he was deferring to him and Otten.

"How long you fellows been in France, what, what? Sorry you had to win the Battle of the Bulge without me, but I got here soon as I could. We all serve where we're told, ain't that right, Sport? OCS was tough, but I knew you guys were having it rougher than me. How 'bout that, Sport?"

Otten poured out questions about Calhoun's wedding, the welfare of Miss Margaret, home front news about people Porter had never heard of. Then he spewed out answers to Calhoun's inquiries about their adventures. Calhoun guffawed loudly at Otten's version of their encounter in Bayeux with the two ladies of the night. "'Get out of here! Get out of here! What's this poking around up in here with me?' Goddam, Osborne, I ain't believing you were studding around with a pregnant French whore. Haw! Can't ever get the country out of a real hayseed, can you? What? What?"

Porter thought of Suzie, smiled enigmatically, and kept his counsel. Anything that Carter Otten and Griffin Calhoun did not know was unlikely to cause him discomfort, whereas he had ample experience of the reverse.

"Don't pay any attention to Carter. I was just trotting in his train. The only thing he's been trying harder to do than get a piece of pussy since we got here is to get a promotion. So far you can call him Bon Ami on both fronts; he hasn't scratched yet."

"Shut up, Osborne, or I'll break every bone in your back."

"Haw! Same old Otten, same old Osborne. A-feuding and a-fussing and a-fighting. Ain't that right, Sport? Nothing's changed, what?"

"Speaking of which," Otten grinned as he spoke, "and now that you've brought the subject up, where are we going to spend the night? You're an officer, you ought to be able to scare us up some women. Even some that are good looking. How 'bout it?"

"No dice," said Calhoun quickly. "I'm married now. Remember? What, what?"

"Hell, I know you're married, but goddam, you're not dead. A little piece of strange never hurt anybody, and a soldier this far from home is not expected to stay in the pasture. Be a sport. I'll never tell."

"Are you going to lay this on *The Scarlet Pimpernel*, too?" interrupted Porter.

"Kiss my ass, Osborne. I'm talking to Calhoun."

"Go on and talk to him. He can tell bullshit when he hears it. He's known you longer than I have, and he's sure you wouldn't tell anybody but our fifty most intimate friends."

"Stop the Jeep! I want to whip his butt right now!" yelled Otten. "Calhoun, don't pay any attention to old bug-eyed Vitamin Flintheart here; you know he lives in another world half the time anyhow. Let's find some women."

Griffin Calhoun responded with more dignity than Porter had ever seen him exhibit. "Forget it, Carter. I made some promises that you haven't made yet, and I'll keep those promises till the day I die."

"And not talk about it," approved Porter. "Welcome to my world."

"You're both cold-codded," snapped Otten. He recovered his aplomb and twinkled charmingly. "How do you feel about promotion?"

They all responded with laughter and were friends again.

Griffin Calhoun showed them a new world. They found the hotel in Granville that he said was recommended for officers. The lobby was grand enough to induce awe. The elegant dining room had parquet floors, old paintings in massive gold frames, and a lofty ceiling decorated with murals. The linens and service surpassed anything Porter had experienced since the dining car en route to Camp Grant.

"So this is the way officers live," he observed. "They won't court martial you for fraternizing with lowly enlisted men, will they?"

"Tell me why you goddam guys haven't at least made sergeant by now," said Calhoun. "You're not a couple of fuckup dickheads, are you? What? What? Haw!"

An hour later they were down to the last quarter of the second bottle of bourbon, and Otten was still answering the question.

"Hell, Carter, if I could get you transferred to my command, I'd have three stripes for you in a week, what? I've got a position open that calls for that rank to start off with, ain't that right, Sport?" Calhoun asked no one in particular. "Only trouble is the damn paper work. It takes months to get anything done in the Army because you have to fill out forms and get permission. Ain't that right? What?"

"I'd give my eye teeth and one nut to get out of that chickenshit 816th and into an outfit with you," said Carter.

Porter was under the influence of much less than his due share of the bourbon. "Otten, if you'll quit bitching and y'all listen to me, I can tell you how to pull it off."

He expounded until bedtime and coached them next day all the way back to camp. They lied like Trojans and went through channels. Crowder and Ballas agreed, and Calhoun went to Lagerpiel.

"Lieutenant, I can hardly believe that the government is actually about to catch up with that Daniel D. Farbecker, and God knows, I'll do everything I can to help you with your special assignment. He's made a monkey out of everbody he comes in contact with. I've yet got a paycheck laying in this desk we weren't able to deliver to him. But if what you need out of me is an enlisted man who knows him, tell me, how come you don't request Osborne?"

Unrehearsed on this particular question, Calhoun Griffin spontaneously responded, "I'd rather die."

Sgt. Lagerpiel nodded his head. "I know what you mean."

"I've worked with Otten before on assignment, Sergeant, which is why I tracked him down and am requesting his transfer. I need a man of his discretion and intrepid daring. If you know what I mean. What? What? Time is of the essence." He looked at his watch. "I need to be back at SHAEF with him by noon tomorrow. We don't want the trail to get cold, do we? What?"

"I'm typing TDY orders fast as I can, Lieutenant, and I'll follow them with permanent transfer tomorrow. Let me step down to the officers' club and get Col. Draughan's signature. This time of day he'll sign anything, long as you don't pester him too much. If you know what I mean."

When he handed the papers to Lt. Calhoun, Sgt. Lagerpiel offered some advice. "I still think you ought to at least talk to Osborne, Lieutenant. He found Farbecker's name on a toilet wall in Pig Alley in Paris and came back to sic me onto a woman named Mimi LaBotte. I didn't get nothing out of her but an embarrassment that I sure wouldn't recommend to no commissioned officer, but maybe Otten could get farther with her than I did if Osborne coached him right. She wears the biggest shoes you ever saw in your life."

Porter went with Carter to their tent and helped him pack his duffel.

"My God, I can't believe this worked. Just on the off chance I ever run across this Farbecker guy somewhere, what the hell does he really look like?"

"Don't worry about it, Otten. You'll never run across him."

"Well, I sure thank you for dreaming up this plan. Things are finally looking up for me."

"I sure hope so, Carter. I hope you don't look back on this and cuss me."

"Why would I do that? You finally did something right for a change."

"Because," said Porter reflectively, "you were on my ass about being Z's nigger, and all of a sudden you're about to become Griffin Calhoun's nigger, and I don't know how you'll react to bowing and shuffling to Ole Massa. I sure didn't do well with Ole Missy."

"Don't fret, Osborne. Always whatever has been Calhoun's has been mine; I can maneuver with no trouble. I'm used to it."

"I don't know," said Porter. "I had a good friend I haven't heard from since Pearl Harbor who said what was wrong with our country was Ole Massa."

"What the hell did he mean by that?"

"He meant we're supposed to earn what we get and not pull strings to get handouts. It's a matter of pride."

"I got plenty of pride, Osborne." He held out his hand. "So long and good luck."

Porter clasped the hand. "So long, Sgt. Otten. The same to you." As Otten left with his duffel on his shoulder, Porter called after him, "Keep it in your knickers!"

The last he saw of Carter Otten in the ETO was a hand held high over his head with the middle finger hyperextended.

> *"The hidden room in man's house where God*
> *sits all the year,*
> *The secret window whence the world looks*
> *small and very dear."*

37 he war was going well. The Russian Bear had recovered from its near mortal wounds sufficiently to rampage with fierceness into Eastern Europe. It devoured Warsaw and a scant ten days later drove the Germans from Lithuania and gobbled up all the Baltic states. The provisional government in Austria signed a treaty with the Allies. Churchill and Roosevelt met in Anglo-American huddle at the island of Malta in preparation for a conference the next week in Yalta with Stalin. In the Pacific, fulfilling MacArthur's vow to return, U.S. troops marched into Manila.

All these events were faithfully reported in the *Stars and Stripes* and Porter Osborne took fleeting note of them. From duty he always scanned the headlines, but there was really no need for him to read war news, for it was on the lips of every GI in the outfit, was digested, analyzed, repeated, projected until his senses were dulled. Porter was trapped in the belly of the Beast of War, had no control over the digestive process of that beast, and could do little but wait in his compartmentalized cocoon until he was spewed forth. It was unclear to him from which end of the beast he would eventually emerge, but he knew he had little control over that either. He personally had observed so many gaffes in his own outfit and had heard of so many blunders in various military encounters that he became cynical about American efficiency. This had to be a holy war, he decided, and God had to be on their side if they were winning, for the Germans could not possibly be goofing up as much as the Americans. He had no necessity to ask what the capitals SNAFU meant when he first saw them joined in print; he had frequently heard the phrase they represented and acquiesced to the philosophy they expressed. He wallowed therefore in the belly of the beast, the stench of boredom alleviated sporadically by the acid wash of fear, and he waited. "Run in place and mark time," he muttered to himself. "That's what they call it; I'm just marking time. I'm also dissociating."

His work became his escape. With Carter Otten gone, there was no one who saw anything about him other than the face he chose to present. No one remembered Emory; no one was close enough to him to get angry and threaten to beat his ass. Number 14143150 missed Carter Otten tremendously, but Porter Osborne, Jr., did not. He was completely on his own, free to choose his own companions without caustic comment, a stripling youth pushed suddenly from the shadow of a bigger brother. He hung out with Jewel, Kostas, Lucetti, and some of the Wafflebacks and he continued to learn.

"Osborne, have you noticed how friendly and smiling all the PW's have gotten lately? Just in the last few days?"

"I hadn't paid any attention, Kostas, but now that you mention it, they have been grinning like a bunch of jackasses eating briers. You hobnob with those peckerwoods more than I do; I don't like them, and since Bastogne I sure as hell don't trust them. If any of those Kraut noncoms were nurses, Capt. Smith would already have court-martialed you for fraternizing."

"Ignore Capt. Smith. It drives an officer crazy to be ignored. And you are really too intelligent to be so locked into attitudes about people who have been labeled enemies and about beating them into the dust that you miss opportunities to know them as individuals." Kostas spoke so off-handedly, as though tossing off an inconsequential aside, that Porter declined to take offense.

He responded in a dry tone, "Believe me, Kostas, I don't. Remember? I'm from Georgia and haven't missed the opportunity to know a Massachusetts Yankee, have I?"

Kostas waved a hand in dismissal. "You Southerners can't get past the Civil War, can you? I'm a Greek immigrant's son and you can't hold Sherman's march against me; I'm not a Yankee."

"You talk like one," said Porter. "You talk like a dyed-in-the-wool Yankee."

"A regional and insular perception, Osborne. You should have risen above that by now. At least you don't have any Mediterranean prejudice that I've been able to detect."

"What the hell is it?" said Porter. "How could I have it? I never even heard of it."

"It's prevalent in New England. They look down on people there from countries that border on the Mediterranean. Greeks, Italians, Spanish, Portuguese."

"Portugal's not on the Mediterranean."

"New Englanders don't know that." There was another dismissing wave. "Or, if they do, they don't choose to make a distinction."

"It must be terrible to live all your life in a place where people don't accept you because of your race," said Porter.

"You ought to know," smiled Kostas, his tone still light. "There are a lot of people like that in Georgia, I hear."

Porter was nettled. "That's different." He sniffed. "Tell me how you feel about the Turks and how many of them you know as individuals."

"Touché," answered Kostas and raised both eyebrows mockingly. "I will proclaim to the world that Turks are underhanded, lying, cruel and inferior barbarians who cannot be trusted even while you are looking at them. I've never met one, but my mother and father have told me about them."

"No wonder I like you," laughed Porter. "Now that we've rambled all over half the world, let's get back to why the PW's seem happy."

"Yes, the Germans. Surely you've noticed how all of them are smiling and speaking to the GI's the last couple of days. Even the officers are acting friendly. I found out from talking to Hans on one of my wards that the rumor is all over the stockade that as soon as the Americans reach the Rhine, we're going to free all the prisoners of war and arm them, and then we're going to fight the Russians together and march all the way to Moscow. 'Ve vill be comrades,' Hans said."

"What?" expostulated Porter. "That's the silliest thing I ever heard of. The Germans are our enemies; the Russians are our friends."

"Hans and everybody else in the stockade say it's the other way around and that finally the Americans have realized it. I tell you they're convinced it's going to happen."

"Don't they know we have a treaty with the Russians?"

"They know they had one, too. Every one of the PW's apparently knows another soldier who has a brother or a cousin in the high ranks of the German army who had told someone they know that Roosevelt has given the nod to Secretary Byrnes to work out the details. They're going to depose Hitler and conquer Russia. It is the only way Europe or America will be safe, Hans says. He says their officers in the stockade have told them this is true. They say this is the reason Roosevelt and Churchill met at Malta without Stalin, they're going to put the screws to him."

"Did you tell him that the Germans have fallen for propaganda so long they hunt lies to believe in because that's all they're comfortable with? The only purpose of the conference at Yalta was to decide how to divide up Europe after we win, and you can bet your ass Uncle Joe had a big voice in that."

"Osborne, I didn't tell him anything. I found out a long time ago that you never learn while you're talking. You learn by listening. I wanted to know why the PW's were all of a sudden so happy, and I found out. Hans told me. He'd have told me nothing if I'd filled his ears with moralizing lectures." Kostas shrugged. "It's not my duty to change anyone. I either accept them as they are or avoid them. I enjoy Hans just as he is for the short time I'll know him."

"You enjoy him? A German PW?"

"Sure. Why not? He's interesting. He has a different perspective."

"I had a nurse at Lawson," said Porter, "who would have cleaned his greens by now, plus yours. And both of you would have found her interesting. I also have a buddy who's an American PW somewhere in Germany. You sure are different, Kostas, from anybody I've run into before."

"Everybody's different. That's what makes people interesting. And at the same time everybody's the same. That's what makes living in this world a challenge. Hans may be right, you know."

"About what?"

"That the only way the world will be safe is if we defeat the Russians while we're over here."

"You're crazy. What else have you learned from Hans?"

"I learned why he wears a wedding ring."

"Hell, I should think it's because he's married."

"So are a great many of the PW's, in fact most of them. I remarked to Hans that he was the only enlisted PW I'd seen with a wedding band on and wondered why. He said most of them wore rings when they were captured but that some of the American soldiers collect them. Rings and watches or anything of value. Sometimes, if their sergeants weren't looking, even at gunpoint."

"That's awful," said Porter.

"Tell me," responded Kostas. "Hans stood his ground and backed them down every time he was threatened. He says most GI's don't understand the Geneva Convention but they're intimidated by the threat of it."

"My God, Kostas, we're over here to overthrow tyrants and bring freedom to Europe and some of our soldiers are thieves? It makes me sick."

"Relax. You see what I mean by everybody being different but everybody being the same? You can't change the world, Osborne."

"Maybe not," said Porter, "but I'd like to think occasionally that some of us somewhere had made a little dent in it. You gotta drive, Steve Kostas, you gotta drive."

"Why did you smack your forehead and laugh like a loon while you said that, Porter Osborne?"

"Oh, I guess it's a matter of 'This do in memory of me,' and I sure have memories of a lot of people."

"Have I ever told you that Southerners are even more interesting than German PW's?"

"And probably than Turks if you really check us out. Ask Hans if he's ever had constipated diarrhea, will you?"

"I wouldn't think of it. See you around."

The day after the *Stars and Stripes* displayed on its front page the thrilling photograph, triumphant but chilling, of U.S. Marines planting their flag atop a mountain in Iwo Jima, the 816th itself was swept by rumor that rapidly proved to be true. They abandoned the three hospitals they were supervising and shipped out as a single unit once again for undisclosed destination nearer the front. Gen. Patton needed them. Victory was only a scant time in the future. Their expert service would be utilized once more in caring for wounded Americans. The PW's could look after themselves. Porter Osborne, Jr., was resuming his pathway to war. He thrilled with expectation, wondered fleetingly how Otten might be faring under the patronage of Calhoun, and in his exultation felt no remorse whatever at departing Normandy.

They left in trucks, an impressive convoy of them. They carried only their duffel, leaving the tents and Niessen huts to whatever successors might appear. As they drove out the gate, Porter noted that Col. Draughan's white paint had flecked off the wires around the walkways and that the tree trunks had become scabrous and needed retouching. He also noted that no eagles yet perched on the colonel's shoulders and that he had heard of no one in the entire outfit receiving a promotion. "*C'est la guerre*," he said in farewell and faced toward the front of his truck.

"They're just carrying us to the train in these trucks," Sherman Jewel announced, "and I'm sure glad. I hear tell we're going all the way across France, and I don't believe my aching back could take this bouncing truck for long."

"You haven't seen the train yet," said Lucetti. "It's a little narrow-gauge railroad and we're going to pack into forty-and-eights. I don't imagine that's going to be very good on any of our backs."

"Forty-and-eight?" said Porter. "I've heard my daddy and uncle talk about them. Those are boxcars they had in the first World War, fellows, that carried forty men and eight horses, and they say that was sure enough a crowd. You know they don't have the same cars still hanging around and they're sure not using horses anymore. That must just be the name they've held onto for any form of military transportation on the railroad."

The only thing correct about his observation was the absence of the horses. The narrow tracks of the French railroad necessitated smaller cars than Americans built and their perspective immediately recalled toy trains. Porter even thought of the Toonerville Trolley.

"We ain't riding in that thing, are we?" remonstrated Levek. "It don't look safe to me; I'd rather sit out what's left of the war at St. Lo."

Porter considered that option, looked again at the train, and said, "Quit trying to talk like a Southerner, Levek.

> 'My heart is warm with the friends I make,
> And better friends I'll not be knowing;
> Yet there isn't a train I wouldn't take,
> No matter where it's going.'"

"Cut the bullshit, Osborne. You don't know what you're talking about."

"Yeah, I do. I just keep forgetting who I'm talking to."

The cars were not ramshackle; they were merely old. Anyone who ever rode one with forty men, tucked at night into sleeping bags like so many pupae, rolling on the straw-littered floor with every start and stop, absorbing through his back the bump and jolt of iron wheels crossing every joint of track, was likely to remember the experience for the rest of his life.

"This is worse than the *Star of India*," Porter told Jewel when their sleeping bags bumped into each other during the night. "You don't suppose they call this train *La Gloire de France*, do you?"

"If they do, it just goes to prove what I been knowing for a long time. No matter what that long-nosed deGaulle says, France ain't got no goddam *gloire*. They've put a honey bucket with a lid on it in every car; how the hell they expect us to use the damn thing without it sloshing everywhere when this fucking train is jerking us ever which a way?"

"Relax," soothed Porter. "All we've got to eat until we get there are D-bars and K-rations. You know that'll bind us up; maybe we won't have to go at all. I hear it's going to take only two days and three nights on the train anyhow."

"Did you see the cars they put on the front of the train for the officers and nurses? They got seats on them that make out into berths at night, and you can bet your sweet ass they ain't sleeping on the floor."

"Neither are we," observed Porter. "We're not sleeping at all. We've got to look after Number One; so let's keep on trying."

The next morning, with raucous screeching of iron on iron, the laden train slowed to a stop. GI's slid open the heavy doors to their cars, and multiple heads poked out the apertures like those of chickens in a crate.

"Stay in your cars!" yelled the sergeants striding up and down the shoulder. "We've just pulled up to let a supply train go by! We'll only be here a few minutes. Stay in your cars!"

"Where are we?"

"All I can see is another railroad track and open fields. I can't even see any hedgerows."

"That means it's raining."

"That only applies in Normandy. What I mean is there ain't any hedgerows. We're in a foreign land."

"Close the door. It's cold in here."

"Leave the door open. It's dark in here."

"Right. And it stinks worse when the door is closed. Leave the fucker open."

"Stay in your cars!" yelled the sergeant. "We'll only be a few more minutes. Stay in your cars!"

"That's what he said two hours ago. Where's that other train?"

Finally it came, roaring by within inches of the 816th General Hospital, so fast and so close that it rocked their cars, spewing dust and cinders so heedlessly that they slid their doors fast shut and waited in darkness at noonday, the noise so great they could communicate only by shouting.

When it faded away up the track and they began chugging onward again, Porter spoke with some indignation. "Side tracked for a supply train! That sure doesn't make us look very important."

"Don't take it personally. Patton's Army needs those supplies worse that it does us; he's moving fast."

"That train's moving fast, too. Between it and those trucks on the Red Ball Express coming out of Cherbourg like bats out of hell, Patton ought to be up to his pecker in provisions by now."

"Where are we going? Has anybody found out for sure?"

"I ran into Lemon early this morning and he said Bosi told him that Crowder had told him that Lagerpiel had told him that Capt. Ballas had heard we were headed for a town called Metz. But that's classified; so don't repeat it."

"With that chain of communication," Levek remarked, "it doesn't need to be classified; nobody would believe it anyhow. What I want to know is what day it is and when this train ride is going to be over."

"It's March seventh" Lucetti said, "and we ought to get to Metz or wherever we're going tomorrow or at the latest by the next day. Sgt. Lagerpiel told us we wouldn't be en route more than two or, at the most, three nights."

"What you reading, Lucetti?"

"Revelations."

"That figures. You'll believe anything, won't you?"

"Lay off," said Porter. "It's a free country. Fair play for everybody. Does it feel to y'all like this train's stopping again?"

Indeed it was. This time they were routed slowly along sidings into a depot of sorts, although it was apparently nowhere near any town or village. There were dozens of tracks thronged with idle trains, debris along some rails testimony that the cars had been sitting unmoved for days or even weeks. The 816th puffed slowly alongside one of them and came to rest with such jarring jolts that Porter gave thanks there were no horses sharing their shackled cars. Sergeants again walked up and down outside the train bellowing instructions. The men were to be allowed out of their cars for short periods of exercise. They would be on this siding until morning in order to clear the main tracks during the night for supply trains headed for the front. Everybody should pick a buddy and not go wandering off alone. Do not make any fires. Do not walk further than fifteen minutes in any direction.

"Where are we, Sergeant?"

"Close to some town named Courville. About five kilometers outside it."

"Where is Courville?"

496

"Damn if I know. But it don't make no difference. It's off-limits."

"Where we headed, Sergeant?"

"East."

"What place?"

"I hear tell it's some town called Metz."

"Where is that?"

"Damn if I know."

"Is this going to slow us down, Sergeant?"

"What kinda question is that? How can a train stop without slowing down?"

"How far behind is this going to throw us?"

"Damn if I know. But it don't make no difference. Ain't nobody gonna get there before nobody else nohow. Don't worry and do as you're told."

Porter was rereading an Agatha Christie pocketbook, paying little attention to his surroundings.

"I want to go walk. How aboot being my buddy?"

The speaker was a gangling, crudely assembled GI who was nearly Porter's age but looked to be trapped in perpetual adolescence, his face given to uncontrollable perfusions of pink when singled out for notice and punctuated by periodic crops of pimples. He was not the only guy in the outfit from Virginia but he was the only one who said "aboot" and "hoose." Because of this idiosyncrasy of speech, which gave titillating recall of Katie Albert and her husband, Porter had initially cultivated the boy but had abandoned the effort when he found him dull. He was innocent of any experience beyond the pale of strict conformity inherent in the proscriptions of maiden aunts who had raised him; he was prone to reminisce about his mother who had died when he was ten. Mention of a mother, even a live one, was nearly always taboo in military circles, and this boy from Virginia made Porter uncomfortable. His name was Walter Stinson, but he had been awarded the nickname of 'Stinky' by his stateroom companions on the *Queen Mary*, not from any effort at alliteration but in recognition of the exaggerated reaction of his alimentary canal to the diet of oatmeal, boiled eggs, and bully beef.

"Sure, Stinky. I could use a walk. Let's go."

They strolled along the siding, remarking that the winter bushes along the roadcut looked like winter bushes anywhere and were not distinctive of France. Stinky looked at his watch.

"It's been aboot fifteen minutes. I guess we'd best turn around."

"Well, for Pete's sake, let's don't just retrace our steps. Let's cut across three or four tracks and walk between different trains. We'll at least get a change of scenery."

That was how they discovered the wine cars.

"Look at those great big wooden barrels up ahead. I wonder what they are."

"I don't know, but there's sure a bunch of them coupled together. Like oil tankers on the trains back home. Except they don't look very well balanced on these little narrow wheels."

"And nobody would haul oil in wooden casks. Look here, Stinky. They've got *Vin* stenciled on them. And they've got those tremendous wooden stoppers halfway up the side blocking bung holes. I'll bet this is the way the French ship their wine."

"Well, we'll never know. It's been aboot fifteen more minutes. We'd better turn around."

"Hell, Stinky, we're at the beginning of our time leash; our train is straight over yonder. And we will know what's in these barrels in just a minute. Hand me that spike over there and hold it while I knock a hole through this wood."

"I'm not sure I feel right aboot doing this."

"How'd you feel if I jerked your head off, Stinky? Hold that damn spike straight; this rock's heavy." Porter felt that he knew how to handle panty-waists from Virginia.

The wood of the giant cask was oak, but he persevered and finally felt the spike plunge through. When he wiggled it out, he was rewarded by a crimson jet arcing in a glittering spiral that bespoke enormous pressure. He hung his lips sideways and caught a mouthful.

"We were right, Stinky, it's wine!" He smacked his lips and captured another mouthful. "Not bad wine, either."

"It's pouring oot on the ground."

"If you're going to say 'oot,'" Porter said coolly, "you should be consistent and also say 'groond.'" He stuck his thumb over the hole and was surprised at the pressure required to staunch the stream. He released his thumb, watched the steady fountain erupt again, and spoke in bemusement. "This is the blood of France, Stinky. Which, by the way, is also shed for many. We can't possibly drink all this wine by ourselves; we'll have to share."

"I never drink wine except at communion. My aunts always said Stinson men can't drink."

"Yeah. I heard that same thing all my life way down in Georgia. Pay no attention to them. I'm sure they're nice ladies, but what do aunts know about soldiering?"

Stinky's tone was both dubious and defensive. "My aunts are pretty wise. They'd think this episode ootrageous and reprehensible."

"They're probably opposed to pussy, too," scoffed Porter. "You can't run your life by what a bunch of aunts decree. You hold your thumb over this hole, and I'll be back in a minute."

"Where are you going?"

"Over to our train and get something to catch some of this wine."

"I can't stay here by myself. What if a French policeman comes along?"

"Engage him in conversation. I'll only be a minute."

"I don't know any French."

"Say, *Le crayon de ma grandmere est sur la table*. That always gets their attention. You can also say *merde*. Don't mention *zig-zig*. For God's sake, Stinky, quit whining and enjoy this caper! You'll never have an opportunity like it again if you live to be a hundred. There's nothing to be scared of."

"I'm not scared. I'm terrified."

"*Le crayon de ma grandmere est sur la table*. I'll be back in a minute. Remember the little Dutch boy and keep your finger in the dyke; even your aunts would approve of that."

Porter went due north under four lines of freight cars and quickly found his train. In each car there was stacked a row of twenty jerry cans, each filled with five gallons of water, calculated as ample supply for drinking and for minimal ablutions until they arrived at their destination. They had all been warned of the pestilential horrors awaiting them should they drink any untreated water in France. The men in his car had already emptied three of their cans in their twenty-four-hour sojourn and Porter, his horizons expanding, decided to take all three of them back to his rendezvous with Stinky Stinson. The car was deserted, everyone out for a stroll, but he encountered Sherman Jewel.

"Where you going with those jerry cans?" the redhead asked above his outthrust underjaw.

"I found a wine shop right around the corner and thought I'd lay in a supply for our journey. If you'll furnish the candle light and violins, I'll bring the wine and we'll dine in style tonight."

"Get real, Osborne. Don't dick with me. This is the most fucked up outfit in the ETO. Nobody's got the faintest fucking idea what's going on or when we're going to get to wherever it is we're going. I ain't in no humor to be jacked around."

When Porter explained his mission, Jewel became ecstatic. "You tapped into a wine tanker? Way out here in this god-forsaken wilderness? Christ, I ain't believing it! There's hope for you yet. Wait a minute and I'll go with you."

He leaped into their car and began dragging out jerry cans, which he rapidly emptied. "Trouble with you and most GI's, Osborne, is you don't think big enough. Let's go."

"You've poured out all our water."

"You're fucking aye. Let's go."

Stinky's relief at their arrival was soon replaced with misgivings. "I have doots aboot this being legal," he remonstrated.

"Don't worry," Porter soothed. "This is war time and soldiers are expected to forage around and live off the land."

"But if we fill all the cans in our car with wine, what are we going to do for water?"

"Look, Stinky," Porter chortled with enthusiasm, "I've told you this is a once-in-a-lifetime experience. I'm reminded of a poem that says,

> 'I don't care where the water goes
> If it doesn't get into the wine.'

Think how all the fellows are going to thank us for this when we hit the road again."

"I'm thinking aboot what the sergeant and the captain and the colonel will say if they find oot we've been stealing wine. What will my aunts say? I'm a Stinson from Virginia and we don't steal."

"Goddammit, I'm an Osborne from Georgia and we don't steal either. Screw that cap on and hand me another jerry can."

"If this isn't stealing, I'd like to know what you call it."

Sherman Roger Jewel spat to one side. "It's liberating, by God. That's what it is. It's liberating. That's what we been doing ever since we hit France, ain't it? We're liberating."

"We're taking something that doesn't belong to us. My aunts would say that's stealing."

Jewel rose to his full height. "Fuck your aunts," he intoned. "If you don't shut up and get to toting, I'm going to stick my foot right up your ass and leave the boot up there."

500

Stinky Stinson's face flamed bright red. Then he giggled and gained Porter's approval. "Thanks for explaining things to me," he said. "I'll be right back with some more empties." He shrugged. "This may turn out to be fun."

It was impossible not to share their fun. When fellow GI's, strolling in boredom along the railway shoulder, inquired about the jerry can brigade, occupants of other cars became enthused. Some of them withheld some meager water reserve, but the two cars on each side of Porter's abandoned prudence and stockpiled the wine.

Lucetti alone in their group was adamant. "I do not drink wine. I have never tasted alcohol. I never intend to taste it. This is my personal jerry can of water and if anyone so much as touches it I'll sue. I will go straight to the first sergeant and will not stop until I reach the adjutant general. *Caveat emptor*!"

Sherman Jewel raised a canteen cup, brimming crimson, in salute. "I love to hear that fucking lawyer talk. Here's to you, Lucetti. How'd that pome go, Osborne? 'I don't care where your water goes if it doesn't get into my wine.' We ain't got but one night on the road after this one, and I don't aim to draw a sober breath till we get to Metz."

Their evening meal was hilarious. Mack and Jack were three cars up ahead and were perfectly willing to trade some hoarded C-rations for a jerry can of wine. In Porter's car they ate cold beans with weiners and washed them down with fresh French wine. They had D-bars for dessert and plenty of wine.

"It tastes a little bit like brand-new buttermilk," confided Stinky Stinson, "and it sure warms your stomach."

"'Drink it, it's good for you, Sonny,'" quoted Porter. "'It'll make you grow tall as a telephone pole.'"

"Hey, Osborne," called Jewel, "since this is our next to the last night on this luxury train of the fucking French Empire, how about reciting some more of that pome?"

Porter was flattered to be invited rather than repressed. "I don't know all of it, but the first stanza goes,

> 'Old Noah he had an ostrich farm and fowls
>   on the largest scale,
> He ate his eggs with a ladle in an egg cup big
>   as a pail,
> And the soup he took was elephant soup and
>   the fish he took was whale.

But all were small to the cellar he took when
    he set out to sail.
And Noah he often said to his wife when he sat
    down to dine,
"I don't care where the water goes if it doesn't
    get into the wine."'"

"Good old Osborne," chortled Jewel. "A fucking Georgia boy will come through in a pinch every time."

"I'll say this aboot him," said Stinson, "he's purely a caution."

"He remembers the strangest things," said Kostas.

"I know," said Lucetti. "If he'd put his mind on higher things, there's no limit to the good he might do."

Porter hiccupped and looked at Lucetti. "Fuck your aunts," he said.

"I don't have any aunts; both my parents are only children," advised Lucetti.

"Makes no difference. The message is the same," said Porter Osborne, Jr. He drained his cup and wormed into his sleeping bag.

Awakening had always been instantaneous for Porter, usually joyous, always exciting, a moment of eagerness and anticipation of a new day lying ahead to be explored and savored. Consciousness the next morning was slow to return, however. The first thing he noted was that someone was groaning, and it took long seconds to realize that the groans were on his lips and that they emanated in tortuous progress from the depths of his chest. They were triggered by the heavy pounding within his head, which seemed to be expanded to twice its usual size and was filled with lightning bolts and rolling thunder. The taste within his mouth was reminiscent of the only time he had ever tried to eat chitterlings and was heavily seasoned with rotted tobacco. His lips and even his teeth were parched. He thrust his head out of the sleeping bag to escape the fetid stench of his own breath, and when he smacked his lips they felt as dry and thick as clapping hands.

"Good morning!" said Lucetti.

"Help me, Jesus," croaked Porter.

"He will, He will," assured Lucetti, "but you have to keep asking Him. He stands at the door and knocks; all you have to do is invite Him in."

"Oh, brother. Is that Him knocking now or the wheels bumping? Is this train moving or is it just me? I think I'm dying."

"That's the way you look. Wash your face and brush your teeth and you'll feel better. We've been under way for over an hour."

Porter moved to obey before he remembered that in their car only Lucetti had water. "I can't wash in wine," he said. "Lucetti, how 'bout lending me . . . ?"

"Not a chance," the attorney from West Palm said briskly. "You yourself instigated this felony in France. You have been your own attorney, judge, and jury. You not only passed your own sentence, you embraced and executed it. Now you have to serve it. I am only an uninvolved bystander and you'll not cast me in the role of being on the Board of Pardons and Paroles."

"You're being a lawyer now. What about the Bible you're so big on? Are you going to be like the avenging Jesus? 'Woe unto you also, ye lawyers, hypocrites, for ye lade men with burdens too grievous to be borne and then lift not one finger to help them.' Or are you going to be like the Even-so Jesus? 'I was an hungered and ye gave me meat, I was thirsty and ye gave me drink, I was naked and ye clothed me . . . I was in prison and ye came unto me.' Lord God, my head hurts and I'm dry as a chip. You could give me one little cup of water."

"You know," observed Lucetti, "you really are remarkable. Your quotations are not one hundred percent accurate but, as you said last night, I get the message. I would also remind you that He said even the devil could quote Scripture to his purpose. Also, He promised us living water. Think about that awhile and get back to me later. Right now I'm busy reading about the wedding feast at Cana and trying to puzzle through it after what I've witnessed last night and this morning."

"Hey, Lucetti," said Porter, "fuck your aunts."

"Right," said Madison Lucetti and began reading.

"Water," groaned Stinson. "I need some water."

"There ain't any," said Porter. "If you want some sympathy, follow me and I'll show it to you in the dictionary. By now I know where to find it."

Jewel was the only participant who did not have a monstrous hangover. He sat propped in the half-open door, facing forward and looking up the tracks, sipping from a half-filled canteen cup. Porter flung himself prone beside him, hung his head over the side of the moving car, and uncontrollably emptied his stomach. Jewel calmly twisted a hand in the back of his collar lest his paroxysms of retching propel him headfirst from the train and, when Porter rolled over and sat up, wiping his eyes and gasping for breath, proffered the canteen cup.

"Here. Good for what ails you. Hair of the dog."

Porter's gorge rose. "No way. I'm dying."

"You ain't dying. Two quick big swallows will make you feel like a new man and also make the sun shine and the birds sing. Then you can just sip along. Trust me."

With trembling hands Porter obeyed. It worked.

"Where'd you learn that, Sherman?"

"At home. I'm from a big drinking family. One uncle cures a hangover with thin grits, one with two raw eggs. The trick is, he says, to swallow them whole without busting the yolks—they absorb the liquor and the liquor cooks the eggs and it's like you hadn't never took a drink. Another one swears by buttermilk, and I got an uncle on my mother's side puts his money on tomato juice with a touch of pepper sauce. My old man, though, always said the hair of the dog that bit you is best. Always drink some of whatever you was drinking the night before and you'll come up without no hangover." He cut his eyes at Porter. "Always said it was better if you could do it before you commence to vomick."

"Well, I sure feel like I'm going to live again," said Porter. "We better tell the others and dose them. I tell you, Sherman, I don't believe that was one of the finer wines of France that we liberated."

"Pretty raw," agreed Jewel. "Needs to set a spell yet and maybe work off a while longer. Let's tend to Stinky. We may have to hold him down and drench him like a cow, but he sure needs help. He's green as a gourd."

They were trapped in the moving forty-and-eight and had no recourse but to drink the wine. By midafternoon when their progress to Metz was once again aborted by a shunt to a siding, they were all once more drunk. They stayed that way. For five more days and nights they hurried up and waited. They would lurch a few miles and then pull onto a siding while supply trains passed them.

"Lemon said that Bosi said that Crowder told him that Capt. Sparky said we captured a bridge at a place called Remagen before the Krauts could blow it, and that the Americans are across the Rhine and have occupied Cologne."

"Big deal. Story of my life. The war'll be over before we get off this Toonerville trolley, and we'll be permanently pickled or at least marinated. I wet my hair with wine this morning to comb it, which was a mistake; it stinks and is stiff as a board. You know, even Lucetti doesn't have but a canteen of water left. We may have him asking for some wine before we get there."

"He's sure made a believer out of me. I'll never drink a drop of it again. I don't mind so much aboot being nasty and not shaving for the duration, but I'm worn oot with brushing my teeth with wine. My aunts would die."

"Don't ask Lucetti what he's reading," Porter advised. "Yesterday he was into Paul and told me, 'Drink ye then no longer water but take a little wine for thy stomach's sake and for thine own infirmities.' He's going to be the world's authority on the Christology of alcohol when this is over; God knows he's had a wealth of case studies."

"Lucetti," growled Jewel. "I've a good notion to whip his ass and fling him off the train. Christ-bitten cocksucker."

"Quit trying to talk like a Yankee," said Porter. "Besides, you couldn't do it. Lucetti's strong as a bull and quick as a cat. On top of which he's a lawyer and would have you busting rocks in Leavenworth. Leave Lucetti alone. He's at least got some convictions."

"So do you," said Kostas, "and they don't hold up. You say with one breath that I'm a Yankee and with another that Jewel talks like one. You can't have it both ways; I've never talked like that in my life."

Porter put his face close. "Touche. *Merde. C'est la guerre.* Fuck your aunts."

Kostas smiled. "Whatever you say, Georgia boy. 'Christ-bitten' is a word I've not heard before. You Southerners have picturesque speech patterns youselves. That term could well apply to Lucetti, you know."

"I keep telling you, lay off Lucetti. He and Jesus have a thing going. I may want to discuss it with him."

"I'm available," Lucetti said quietly over Porter's shoulder.

"Not now," Porter answered. "Not now. Not while I'm drunk and not while there's a war on. And not while I've got some sinning I intend to do every chance I get. I know ahead of time you're going to tell me Jesus opposes pussy, aren't you?"

"Terms are negotiable, Osborne."

"That's lawyer talk again. I may look you up later but for the time being, 'Get thee behind me, Jesus.' Way behind."

"I don't think my aunts would approve of my buddying aboot with the likes of you," said Stinky Stinson.

Sherman Jewel opened his mouth to squelch the boy, but Porter spoke first. "Pass the wine, Sherman. And fuck your uncles. Every one of them."

"Amen," said Madison Lucetti. "I'll say amen to that."

"You know, Lucetti," said Porter, "try as I will I can't help liking you."

Lucetti shrugged. "Why don't you tell that to someone who cares?"

"Southerners really are odd," said Kostas. "Interesting, but definitely odd."

"Bigot," retorted Porter and took a swallow of wine. "You really are a bigot, Kostas."

"No, I'm not. An intellectual snob, perhaps, but definitely not a bigot."

"Thank God Carter Otten can't see me now," said Porter. "Thank God he's not on this train. I wonder if he's got his stripes yet. I wonder if he's got himself laid yet."

"He's got about as much chance of either as finding Daniel D. Farbecker," said Jewel.

"The mills of the gods grind fine," said Kostas, "and they grind exceeding small."

Porter sighed and looked deep into his canteen cup. His wine glowed red. "Life used to be so simple."

He hiccupped and drained his cup.

*"The walls are hung with velvet that is black
and soft as sin,
And little dwarfs creep out of them and little
dwarfs creep in."*

38   **a**s trucks moved them through Metz from the
railroad to their billet, Porter heard comments that the cathedral was
huge, the towers of the German Gate worthy of future exploration, the
Moselle River wide and beautiful. He was too intent, however, on
holding the halves of his head together to notice or make remark. He
had drunk his fill of water for the first time in ten days upon arrival at
the train station and still could hear his belly sloshing. New dizziness
threatened his equilibrium, familiar nausea constricted his throat, and
Porter was fervently vowing to be henceforth temperate in all things,
assuming, prayerfully, that his biochemistry recovered from the present insult he had inflicted upon it. For the first twenty-four hours of
his arrival in Metz, he cared not one whit about anything beyond
personal endurance and survival.

To his joy he discovered that for the 816th General Hospital,
tents were a thing of the past. They were not even quartered in them.
Living quarters for the enlisted men stood on a hill about two miles
from the hospital, housed in a three-story masonry building equipped
with iron cots complete with springs and mattresses, electricity, flush
toilets, and even a huge communal shower. Porter had never anticipated such personal luxury in a war-torn country and marveled at his
good fortune.

The hospital was impressive. The officers and nurses were quartered near it in elegant homes set in well-tended gardens and protected
from the public eye by cloistering walls. The hospital itself was a
compound situated in solid authority behind grilled iron gates and
high walls. Its buildings were arranged in a U around lawns with turf
that puffed luxuriantly above interlacing walkways in mute testimony
to generations of meticulous care. Even the most callous GI followed
the paved walks, instinctively respecting the sanctity of those lawns.

The driveway was lined with tall cherry trees, the flower beds accentuated by groupings of smaller mirabelle trees, the atmosphere unmistakably one of assurance and security. It was said to have been built by the Germans after they appropriated Alsace-Lorraine in 1870 and had been continuously utilized as a hospital ever since, through French and the returning German administration. It had not been damaged by the Germans in their most recent occupation, the buildings and permanent fixtures still intact, only the instruments and movable equipment packed off by the retreating invaders.

Lt. Ruth Nielson was ecstatic as she equipped and organized the operating suite.

"No more dark and dingy tents or huts! Look at these tiled floors and plaster walls! These ceilings must be fifteen feet high! I can't get over the spaciousness, the big windows! The lights over the operating table even work! Sgt. Crowder, I want every floor scrubbed till it sparkles and all those walls washed down. My girls will get the sterile supplies stocked and instruments ready, so you won't have to worry about those if you'll get this place free of any speck of dust or dirt. We've got to be ready to receive our first patient in ten days. Can you and your men do it?"

"Yessum," Oliver Crowder replied, eyebrows bunched together to project his usual air of studious melancholy. "We'n do it. Hit'll take overtime and double time, but we'n do it." He sighed and looked lugubriously like a bloodhound. "Now when we could really use some them PW's, there ain't nere one to be found. What become of all of them?"

"I don't know," snapped Lt. Nielson, "but thank God we've seen the last of them. I was forever stumbling over them when I was in a hurry, and it was easier to do something yourself than explain to them what you wanted. Besides, there was something about that arrangement that smacked of slave labor. Good riddance to bad rubbish, I say. We'll run this operating room from now on with good old American sweat and elbow grease."

So they did. The pristine condition of their new quarters was indeed attained by the expenditure of American sweat and elbow grease, and to such an extent that Porter was tempted to point out the similarity of the American enlisted man's present degree of servitude to slave labor. Lt. Nielson, however, was a brisk and businesslike lady who was somewhat older than the nurses she commanded and in addition kept the distinction of rank and the authority of Chief Nurse in the Operating Room as a barrier of respect. She was born and reared in Wisconsin but had been moved to Chicago in her teens and had attended nursing school there. She spoke Norwegian fluently and the cadence of it colored her tongue just enough to give exotic lilt to her rapid-fire speech. Her eyes were ice-blue, her smile infrequent, her patience short, her opinions firm. Even Capt. Ballas trod a wide path around her and deferred to her wishes. Everyone in the hospital knew who really ran the Operating Room; it was First Lieutenant Ruth Nielson, and woe betide the hapless male who made an error in judgment about that.

Upon consideration, Porter abandoned any temptation to discuss slavery with this bustling Scandinavian Amazon. She wouldn't understand the concept of Old Missy, he thought, and she was not cut out to be one, anyhow; she worked harder than any of the slaves she directed. Besides, a lady wasn't supposed to sweat until it showed through the back of her blouse or plastered her hair in ringlets on her forehead. He followed Oliver Crowder's example and said "Yes'um" every time she spoke.

Porter had such respect for her that it approached reverence, and he willingly dropped to his knees before Queen Ruth and wielded soap and brush on the huge octagonal tiles with their mosaic borders until she snapped, "That's enough, Osborne. Any more and you'll scrub out the grout."

That operating suite became the center of Porter's existence, his anchor in reality, while he lived for the first time in a foreign city and explored its wonders. He walked to and from work daily, improved his French by visiting with *les bonnes femmes* in their tiny flower-bordered front yards along the way, chatted with merchants, broadened his horizons, but always he remembered his duties in the Operating Room as the reason for his being in Metz.

On April 12, 1945, President Franklin Delano Roosevelt died in Warm Springs, Georgia, of a cerebral hemorrhage. The news stunned the 816th General Hospital. Flags flew at half-mast. Porter accepted the tragedy as information, tucked it into the compartment with Boston Harbor Jones, Will Barton and Fritz, and went about his duties.

He avoided the concern expressed by Kostas, made no effort to commiserate with him.

"This is a terrible day for America, in fact for the whole world. It's the worst possible time for Roosevelt to die just when we're finally winning the war."

"That's what a vice-president is for. We can't do anything about it. Why worry?"

"The fate of our country is now in the hands of a shirt salesman from the Midwest. Mediocrity has been enthroned, Osborne. Why shouldn't we worry?"

"What if Roosevelt had died last term? Henry Wallace would be our president, and my daddy would be having a stroke the same as Roosevelt. Speaking of which, I'd better get back to the OR or Lt. Nielson will have one."

"Osborne, you amaze me. Global events thunder all about you and you concentrate only on your own personal world."

Porter shrugged. "'In the dew of little things the heart finds its morning and is refreshed.' *C'est la guerre*. I'm dissociating, Kostas."

Col. Draughan had black arm bands issued to his command, to be worn, Sgt. Lagerpiel explained, on the left arm above the elbow. Porter obediently wore his for a day or two and then forgot it. Mussolini and his mistress were lynched, Adolf Hitler committed suicide in his bunker, Berlin fell to the Russians. Porter noted all of these events and still felt detached, removed. The cherry trees were blooming, Lt. Nielson wanted the surgical amphitheater across the hall from their present area refurbished, and he had two Hercule Poirot mysteries he had not read before. He was occupied and reasonably content.

VE Day swept the people of France and the soldiers from America into giddy celebration, as wild and as temporary as loosened leaves dancing with abandon on unseen currents, flung beyond their control to heights beyond the grasp of gravity, tumbling pell-mell in rare sweet sunlight, heedless of the morrow.

Porter watched but did not dance. For one thing he could not yet face again the idea of imbibing alcohol and it seemed to him that all the revelers were waving bottles. Also, underlying the joy everyone felt at the final official defeat of the Boche was Porter's conviction that this did not mean homecoming for him. He felt more than ever like a cipher—no one in authority cared about his personal destiny. He was convinced in his heart that victory in Europe meant that now nothing prevented his being sent to the Pacific. Okinawa fell to the Americans shortly after VE Day, but there were still hundreds of islands before they reached Tokyo. Porter had left med school for action in the war, had been relieved when forces beyond his control shifted him into safe backwaters, and now faced with dread the near certainty that he would be sent to Japan before he saw Georgia again. He had a gut feeling that he would die on a Pacific atoll, victim of a bandy-legged, slant-eyed sniper, identifiable only as 14143150. Porter Osborne, Jr., did not dance on VE day.

He concentrated on his near surroundings and paid little attention to the rolling swell of world history on the tide of which he floated, a tiny fleck of spume, insignificant and most probably unnecessary. Through the maze of compartments he now maintained, he wound his daily path, presenting to unperceptive comrades a multifaceted face of gaity, irreverence and daring.

In the brief period after VE Day, when strangers still greeted and spoke to strangers and every American uniform clothed a nobleman who merited at least a smile, Porter wandered into a crowded market near the hospital and literally bumped into a French civilian named Lucien. He backed away from the man, smiled, bowed, apologized, and became involved in the senseless repetitive two-man sidestep that often accompanies such encounters, effectively blocking passage for each. Laughter and introductions followed, and then Lucien presented his wife, Bettie, and their infant son, Jean-George, who watched them owl-eyed from the security of a canvas stroller but seemed more interested in his newly discovered hands than in the adults towering over him.

Porter produced a Hershey bar he had procured from the Red Cross and presented it to the infant, but Bettie appropriated it, explaining in creditable English that he was too small but that his mother thanked him very much and that Porter was *très, très gentil*. With this encouragement, Porter, who long since had learned not to leave the hospital empty-handed, a convert to Lt. Fitzgerald's assertion that a nurse was entitled to her salary and all she could tote, reached into his capacious pockets and proffered a bar of soap and a packet of coffee. Bettie went into spasms of gratitude and Porter bowed before the accolades of *oo-la-la, mon Dieu, très, très gentil*. A totally incomprehensible conference between Bettie and Lucien resulted in Lucien's inviting Porter home with them.

He was flattered. He had looked wistfully at the houses in Metz, the occasional chateau, the more frequent cottage, and yearned to see inside any of them. He had not been in a French home since the old lady who wore wooden shoes and shared her thatch-roofed parlor with a cow had fed him rabbit in the countryside of Normandy; he was curious about the lifestyle of these more sophisticated city folk. He envisioned for Lucien and Bettie and little Jean-George a bungalow with flower garden in front and vegetable plot out back and followed them eagerly, explaining that his time was limited because he was working night shift in the hospital.

They led him to a building that fronted abruptly on the sidewalk with no strip of earth to succor even one blade of grass. A pass-through for trucks bisected the first floor, the scum from their exhaust griming the brick-work and greasing the windows. Their home was an apartment on the ground floor with entrance from the darkened drive-through through a heavy door with double locks. The domicile consisted of only two rooms, and Bettie had expended efforts to make them bright and cheerful. Certainly they were spotless. Crisp curtains shone as pure as communion dresses before the heavy draperies that provided privacy from passers-by. In one corner of the first room there was a tiny sofa covered in bright fabric, a coffee table adorned with formally arranged mementos, and a small green plant between it and one overstuffed chair.

The remainder of the room was given over to kitchen and dining furnishings, a sink, a small gas stove, an enamel table with two chrome-framed chairs, and multiple cupboards. There was a midget refrigerator beneath the sink that contained, Porter later discovered, Jean-George's milk and one tray of ice cubes. Bettie made coffee from her newly acquired treasures, apologizing for lack of sugar. Lucien pulled the table from in front of the window, appropriated a wooden chair from the living room and they sat down to visit. Jean-George rolled on a pallet, studying his fist with wonder and contributing an occasional gurgle to the conversation. The floor was immaculate.

Lucien told Porter that he worked on the railroad. Their expertise with language did not extend to exact details of what he did on the railroad, but daily he traveled from Metz to Nancy, sometimes to Strasbourg or Rheims, and back again. Today was his day off and what *bonne chance* that they had met each other in the marketplace. Porter must consider their home as his, must feel free to drop by at any time; Bettie would welcome him if Lucien happened not to be at home. The war was over. Soon wages would improve. Life would be better. Americans were wonderful. Porter must come often.

When he returned to the hosiptal he found the *Stars and Stripes* filled with stories of liberated captives from Dachau. There was a photograph of a trench at some place called Buchenwald, filled with a jumble of emaciated corpses, two burly Germans knee deep in the midst of them. Porter's revulsion and attention were brief. "So that's what they're doing with PW's now," he thought as he glanced at the faces of the Germans and wondered fleetingly what had happened to

512

Shorty, to Hans and his dreams of marching on Moscow. Dachau and Buchenwald were horrors of such magnitude they defied comprehension, and Porter Osborne, Jr., could do nothing about them. Why let them into his consciousness and worry about them? His thoughts were filled with the little family he had just met. He snitched a ten-pound sack of sugar and a can of coffee from the stores Sgt. Oliver Crowder maintained in the Operating Room, smuggled them to his living quarters, rose early from his cot the next afternoon and carried them to Lucien and Bettie and little Jean-George. They were within his sphere of influence and he could, by God, do something to help them.

The sugar and coffee merited a double *oo-la-la*, plus *mon Dieu, sacre couer, très, très gentil* delivered with such clarity and enthusiasm that Porter thought he might well learn to understand French if its speakers confined themselves to expletives. There was no doubt that Bettie was pleased. Lucien was not at home; he worked too long on the railroad, but it was necessary to pay the rent. Porter must come in. Lucien *aussi* thought Porter *très gentil* and *bon ami*. Come in. Come in for coffee. Lucien rides his bicycle back and forth to the *chemin de fer* every day. If the bicycle is at the door, Lucien is at home. If not, he was at work. Come back. Come back any time. Bettie was always at home except when she took Jean-George to walk in the morning and to the market in late afternoon. Porter considered the paucity of goods in the post-war shops of Metz, the housewives he had seen on the streets with their string shopping bags, containing but not concealing a single loaf of bread, sometimes only two eggs, hardly ever any meat, never bulging with plenty. He assured Bettie he would be right back and hurried the four short blocks to the hospital. He descended the back stairs to the mess hall, waited until Mack had his back turned, and made a covert swoop through the supply room. The mess sergeants would never miss the cans of Spam, of corned beef, of dried beef, of ham that he secreted beneath his baggy fatigues, and no one saw him depart.

When he returned, Bettie was in a bathrobe as nondescript and fuzzy from wear as his grandmother's, commodious and chaste. When Porter stacked his new gifts on the table, first her English failed her, then her French. Porter did his best to identify the olive green cans.

"Ham." He pointed. "*Jambon*. Pig. Oink-oink. *Compris?*"

"*Ah, oui. Oo-la-la!*"

"Corned beef. *Vache*."

"*Oui, oui, oui. Je compris. Très gentil.*"

"Dried beef." He hesitated and then improvised. "*Plus de vache. Compris?*"

"*Ah, oui. Certainement.*" She giggled. "*Moo.*"

"Right. You got it." He held up the last can. "Spam. You *compris* Spam?"

"Spam? *Qu'est-ce que* Spam?"

"Well, it's . . ." he groped for a French word. "It's just Spam, that's all. God knows what it is, but we sure eat a lot of it."

"*Je ne compris le* Spam."

Porter relaxed into normal speech. "I don't either. In fact, Bettie, I don't know a single soldier who does *compris* Spam. I don't even *compris* what holds it together and don't think I want to. I do know it can fend off starvation and that it is, in the last analysis, most likely better than nothing." He laughed. "Sort of kin to possum, I should think."

"You speak too fast. *Je ne compris.*"

"Tit for tat. I know the feeling."

He was feeling magnanimous, jovial, but his laugh choked and died; his eyes bulged.

The top of Bettie's bathrobe had come loose and was gaping all the way to the tie at her waist. She was a tiny, small-boned woman with dainty hands. Her deep-set brown eyes beneath overshot brow, together with her small snub nose and broad mouth, gave her a simian appearance, and Porter had decided she was what people in Georgia would call "cute." He had assumed, because of her face and her proportionately elongated extremities, that she was also skinny. It was obvious that he was wrong. Bettie had on not one stitch beneath the bathrobe. Bettie was not skinny. Bettie was lithe as a monkey to suit her face, perhaps, but her skin looked smooth as silk and no monkey ever had breasts like that. They slid and shifted across her chest wall, danced back again, and Porter Osborne, Jr., was mesmerized.

"*Oo-la-la,*" he breathed.

Bettie giggled, reached out, pulled his head down. "You like?" she said, and Porter was lost, temporarily devoid of any volition save one.

Later he looked around him. One corner of the bedroom was sequestered by a wall hanging, parted enough to reveal a commode and lavatory, but no tub or shower stall. Along one wall were two chests of drawers. At the foot of the bed against the wall was a baby bed, festooned now with Bettie's robe and Porter's various garments. Through and beyond these, Porter could see infant arms and legs exploring the air, could hear contented gurgles as hand grasped foot and pulled it toward mouth.

"Bettie," he whispered. "I forgot about Jean-George. My God."

"*Oui.* Good babee. You good babee, too. Now Bettie have two babee. One French. One Yankee."

"I am not a Yankee," Porter started to remonstrate but abandoned small points for larger ones. "Get him out of here so I can get my clothes on."

"He only a babee. He see nothing. He think nothing."

"Well, I can see him, and I'm not a baby. And I think I need to get dressed."

She shrugged into her robe, shook her hair into place, and carried Jean-George into the kitchen.

Porter, fully clothed, attempted stumbling rectification. "Bettie, I'm sorry. I got carried away. I didn't know what I was doing."

She put a finger across his lips. "No be sorry. You know. For be so young, you know *beaucoup* what you do. Bettie teach you more. You come back every day, *non? Oui?*"

"But Lucien. I have betrayed Lucien."

"*No compris* betray. *Qu'est-ce que?* Lucien like you."

Porter swallowed. "That's great. If I'm going to get my throat cut, it's comforting to know it'll be by someone who likes me. If Lucien is my friend, I cannot make love to his wife. *Pas zig-zig la femme de mon ami. Pas gentil,*" he essayed as explanation.

Bettie scowled in concentration. The finger came across his lips again. "*Lucien est français. Je suis française. Vous êtes américain.* All is OK. Not to worry. We no tell Lucien and he as happy next week like this week. *Compris?* No, how you say, big deal?"

Porter pulled her to him for a lingering kiss. He was lost. "Tomorrow. I'll be back tomorrow, Bettie. *Je reviens.*"

"Good. I be here. *Au 'voir.*"

"*Au revoir.*"

"One thing, Porter. No say *zig-zig. Zig-zig* not nice word."

"OK. I'll never say it again, Bettie. And in return you must promise to cover the baby bed with a sheet. You may be *française* but I am sure *américain.*"

He settled into an incredible routine. He worked all night in the hospital, grabbed a shower and a nap in his barracks through the morning hours, then hastened to a daily tryst with Bettie through the afternoons. He never went empty-handed and he was never apprehended as he raided the well-stocked pantry of the 816th, not even when he liberated a gallon of canned turkey breast that was tapped for consumption in the officers' mess.

Bosi noted that Okinawa had fallen. "We're moving but they're still killing us like flies. We're a long way yet from Tokyo."

Porter shivered a little and deferred thinking of the Pacific Theater. He was consumed with Bettie. The *Stars and tripes* made big to-do about fifty nations signing the World Security Charter in San Francisco, thus establishing the United Nations. Kostas was skeptical. "It's nothing but the same tired ploy Woodrow Wilson tried with the League of Nations. They haven't even changed the name so far as I can tell, and this one won't work either. You want to go downtown with a bunch of us this afternoon, Osborne?"

Porter declined and sped to warmer joys. He was obsessed with his monkey-faced paramour who did indeed teach him much. His concentration on sex became so consuming that he extended his visits to include a morning call also, ever careful that Lucien's bicycle was absent. Bettie's attitude became complaisant, then indulgent, and then tolerant. Porter hardly noticed; her bed and body were goals that he attained with ever increasing skill. Nothing else mattered, not even resurgence of his Baptist beliefs.

"I know I'm sinning. Up till now I've never been guilty of anything but fornication, and now I'm committing adultery. I know the Bible is a lot rougher on adultery than it is on single men just screwing around, but I'll repent later. This is the first time I've ever understood why men were willing to go to hell for a piece of pussy. I wish I had somebody to talk to."

He thought of a comment by James Callaway back in Brewton County, a family man who compensated for lack of erudition by frequent sardonic remarks that were intellectually challenging. "Don't try to tell me it's blood what makes that thing get hard. It's brains. All of a fellow's damn brains drain down into it and you better know it, for when it stands up a man ain't got a damn lick of sense left."

James, however, was not available, and Porter was imbued with the old adage that a gentleman kisses but never tells. He bore his guilt alone. Bettie accepted his gifts now as a matter of course, had even begun delineating items she desired.

"No *jambon* for two weeks. *Américain jambon tout fini?* You bring, yes? Also, we need coffee. Lucien drink *beaucoup* coffee. Lucien say you *bon ami.* Porter, the shoes. *Est-ce possible* you bring me the shoes like *Américain* nurses wear on street? In France no shoes since war began."

Porter dutifully begged a brand-new pair of shoes from Lt. Fitzgerald, who disdained the general issue oxfords and had feet he judged of a comparable size to Bettie's.

"Of course, I'm glad for you to have them, Ozzy. I think it's wonderful that you are concerned about a little old French grandmother. Most soldiers are only looking out for what they can get for themselves. You tell her I hope these help her arthritis. Isn't it wonderful about MacArthur's announcement that the Philippines are liberated?"

"Yes'm, it sure is. Thanks for the shoes. It will sure make the little old lady happy. She doesn't see too well, so the color won't bother her."

That was the day he noted that Bettie no longer said, *Oo-la-la*. Also that was the day they had their first and only argument, which, despite vocabulary differences, Porter won.

"Bettie, I don't care what you say about Jean-George not understanding. You've got to put him in the dining room when we go to bed. We can make a pen out of chairs, *comme-ça*, see? And a pallet on the floor. See? It's wicked enough for me to be seducing a friend's wife, but I draw the line at somebody's mother when he's looking straight at you. That kid has learned to pull up and he hangs on the crib with both hands and his nose hung over the railing till I feel like Kilroy is watching me. It's worse than a mirror in the ceiling. *Compris? OK?*"

"OK. OK, *mon chou*. Tomorrow, *peut-être*, you bring more soap, *oui*? I have a friend, *une bonne amie*, who like very much to have some soap like Bettie. *Est-ce possible*, yes?"

He picked her up and carried her to the bed. "No problem, *ma cherie*; soap's no problem at all. Now, where were we?"

Sgt. Crowder was talkative when Porter came on duty. "That there MacArthur's somepin else," he proclaimed and wagged his head. "Done wandered back into the Philippines; he said he was gonna come back. 'I shall return,' is what I recollect he said. I reckon we're showing them Japs now, ain't we, Osborne? Just like we done the Germans."

Porter was furtively checking Crowder's larder with an eye toward liberating more sugar and perhaps some condensed milk. "I reckon we are, Sergeant," he replied absently. "My daddy says MacArthur never should have let the Japs catch our planes on the ground and lost the Philippines in the first place, but I'm not a military strategist and I think he's something else, too. How far is Luzon from Tokyo, I wonder?"

Crowder sighed. "A fur piece. I've heerd it, but I disremember. Be sure you clean the ampitheater crost the hall good tonight. Lt. Nielson let Maj. Bloom do a case in there today, and she's worse about

517

that room than an old maid. I know you're getting wore out with night duty by now, but I can't change your shift yet."

"No problem, Sergeant. No problem at all. I'm glad to cooperate any way I can."

"Your attitude's improved, Osborne, ever since Otten transferred out. I been laying off to tell you. I 'preciate it and I'll move you to days just as soon as I can."

"No problem, Sergeant. I promise you night duty's no problem at all. I sleep good in the daytime."

A few nights later he discovered huge rolls of cloth stacked in the long room Lt. Nielson had appropriated for storage and as a sewing room to accomodate civilian seamstresses who had been hired to make new gowns, glove covers, and surgical booties. The room was adjacent to her hallowed showcase, the surgical suite, and Lt. Nielson discouraged any trespassing.

"What's all that cloth for?" he asked her as he prepared to go off duty and as she was busily directing the early morning cases.

"It's no concern of yours," she snapped. "What are you doing over there anyway?"

"Cleaning up. I dust and mop over there every night, Lt. Nielson. You said you wanted this place to shine and I try to keep it that way."

"Indeed you do," she relented. "That cloth is for drapes for the officers' club."

"Ma'am?"

"Drapes, Osborne. You know. Decorative hangings at the sides of windows."

"Yes'm. We call them draperies in Georgia. It sure is a lot of cloth." Porter looked at her in wide-eyed expectation.

"It should be adequate," she continued. "Col. Draughan is pleased. The windows in the club are terribly tall and these drapes will be elegant."

"Golly, they sure will, Lt. Nielson. I notice there're two colors of cloth, and it sure looks like fine wool to me, but then I'm no expert on cloth. What color are you going to use for the draperies?"

"I haven't decided yet. Maybe blue for one room and gray for another. Or maybe one color throughout the club. I've got to think about it."

"I can't get over your finding it. That took some doing, Lieutenant."

Her face turned unmistakably pink. "Porter, you might as well know. I've been dating a light colonel in the Quartermaster Corps and he has warehouses full of goods repossessed from the Germans. That blue cloth is the material used for Navy officers and the gray was for the *Wehrmacht*. My friend heard some of us girls talking about needing drapes and had this delivered to me. I don't have any place to store it except in that room we never use. As soon as those two French women get through with the gowns and lap sheets, I'm going to start them on that cloth."

"Yes'm. My, that sure is a fine example of what I keep hearing about being the native ingenuity of the American soldier, Miss Nielson. I bet Col. Draughan really is proud of you."

Her face pinked brighter. "Of course, he is, although he hasn't the faintest idea how I managed it. Says he really admires improvisation. Well, I have work to do or this schedule will never get off the ground, and I'm sure you want to get to your quarters and sleep." She half-raised a hand in mild deprecation. "No need to tell anybody else about that material; I don't know what got into me. It's nobody's business."

"No'm. I won't breathe it to a soul. Some time I'd like for you to tell me about the colonel in the Quartermaster Corps."

Her fading pink returned. "Speaking of nobody's business and Nosey Parkers. On your way, young man."

"Yes'm. I just want to know if he's a nice man and if he's nice to you. All of them aren't, you know."

"My word! What an archaic attitude. I'm perfectly able to take care of myself. The answer to both questions is an unqualified 'yes.' He's very lonely and quite nice."

"Yes'm. He better be or I'll get Sgt. Crowder and the OR team and we'll rock his Jeep some night and break his legs. We're your boys and we stand behind you."

"My God, what a fantasy life! Out of here, Porter Osborne! I can't spend the day visiting with you."

His assumption that Lt. Nielson would not comprehend nor accept the role of Ole Miss remained firm, but he thought she looked pleased as she hurried off. He watched till the hallway was empty, then let himself into the forbidden room. Quickly, and as deftly as if he had practiced, he took off his fatigue jacket, lowered his pants, and wrapped himself three times around with a bulky strip of the gray wool. He scissored it expertly from the roll, pulled his clothes on over it, and was gone. "I could steal the shortening from a cake and never break the crust," he thought in inadvertent recall of his grandfather's appraisal of one of the hands on their farm.

As he sauntered through the front gate and nodded with nonchalance to the guards, he remembered Lt. Fitzgerald's comforting words and added, "I'm not really a nurse and this is not nearly all I can tote, but I'm beginning to understand the program."

He went straight to Bettie's apartment. At that hour, the bicycle was still locked to the post, and it was Lucien who opened the door.

"Ah, Porter. *Bonjour. C'est un longtemps. Comment ça-va? Entrez, entrez.*"

Porter shook hands with the good-looking Frenchman he was cuckolding, concealed any revealing sign of guilt or remorse, and answered in kind. Adultery was still adultery, was assuredly one of the Big Ten, and he would be called to final account later. For the present, however, there was no need to rock the boat and he sought at least superficial expiation.

"I have a gift for you, Lucien," he said. He looked with modesty at Bettie and asked that she retire into the bedroom before he undressed and presented the gray *Wehrmacht* wool. Its reception exceeded his expectations. The room rang with *oo-la-las*. Bettie fingered the material and spontaneously kissed him on both cheeks; Lucien embraced him tightly and would have also followed through with kisses had Porter not self-consciously moved away. Little Jean-George, swept up in the contagion of joy, gave little shrieks of glee. Everyone laughed.

A new suit for Lucien! The first one since the war began! The cloth was of the finest! Nothing like it for sale in all of Alsace! How had Porter acquired it? It was two meters wide instead of one! Ah! *Oo-la-la*! There was more than enough for Lucien! Porter was *très, très, très gentil*.

No, Porter could not stay for *petit déjeuner*. He was tired. He needed to sleep. He would walk to the sidewalk with Lucien, who was going to be late for work. Bettie squeezed his hand in farewell and whispered, "*Après-midi.*" Jean-George waved but without direction. At the curb Lucien grasped his hand in both of his, assured him that he could never thank him enough, that the United States was the greatest country in the world besides France, that Porter was always welcome in his home, and that he must come more often. Porter watched him swoop away on his bicycle, his wash of guilt tinged with pity. Despite his looks, Lucien must not be much in bed or Bettie could not be so enamored of Porter. As he walked to his barracks, Porter's conscience, however, was subservient to his loins.

"*C'est la vie*," he muttered, without the least intention of missing his afternoon assignation.

He performed magnificently, he thought, listened afterwards to Bettie's prattle about the wool, rejecting indulgently her suggestion that he procure more of it for her to sell, not on the black market, of course, *oh, certainment pas*, but discreetly to neighbors or to certain wealthy acquaintances. He cajoled her into prolonged repetition and fell into the deep sleep of satiety. He awoke to whispered voices. Bettie was not in the bed. Jean-George was not in his. Porter peeked through a crack in the door. Bettie, in her bathrobe, Jean-George slung contentedly on one hip, was kissing Lucien in the doorway. It was not a perfunctory kiss of welcome for the return of a boring husband but sprang from adoration. Lucien's hands were on her buttocks. Porter picked out words. "*Pas maintenant. Il dorme. Reviens. Toujours, je t'adore.*"

He crept back into the bed and glimpsed Lucien remount his bicycle and ride away. When Porter feigned waking, he also feigned haste.

"Was good, Porter?" inquired Bettie. "You sad?"

"Ah, *non*, Bettie, I'm not sad. It's always good. You have realized your Potential."

"Pardon? Potential? *Je ne compris pas* Potential."

"Maybe it's like Spam, Bettie—no one can truly *compris* it." He gave Bettie a quick peck, Jean-George a kiss on each cheek, dissociated consummately and departed.

All night he suffered, peeling back layer after layer of events, analyzing their meaning, their intent, delineating deception. He looked hard at the people involved, their motivations, actions, and reactions. If Lucien was a pimp, what did that make Bettie? What did it make Porter? If he had been duped, used, had he not himself also actively duped and used? If he was wounded because Bettie had not truly loved him, could he honestly say that he had been in love with her or just in rut? The sin of adultery. The big A. He had always vowed he would never commit that one, the supreme and sneaky violation of trust. Yet when the temptation occurred, he had slipped into it as easily as though he had never considered it. Were only he and Bettie guilty? Or was Lucien also stained by complicity? Those were their problems, he finally decided. Porter could answer only for himself. Of three things he was certain. First, his ego was bruised in its most tender area when he contemplated that his sexual prowess had been of less consideration to his partner than the groceries he provided. "I have *zig-zigged* for soap, grease, cigarettes and chocolate," he admitted.

Second, he was not ready to face the Lord and pray about it. And third, he was bursting to talk to someone who might have experience.

"Are you feeling well, Osborne? You look green around the gills."

"I've felt better in my life, Lt. Nielson, much better. I've got things on my mind."

"Yes?"

Porter looked at this authoritative, older woman and yearned for comfort. On the one hand he could not possibly confess to a lady that he had with licentious abandon been "screwing his eyeballs out" for more than a month, but on the other hand he might wrest from her some crumb of consolation for his moral dilemma. He dressed his story, therefore, in Sunday linen and told only part of it.

"Lieutenant, I met this French family. A man, his wife, and their little boy. They are poor people and I took them some leftover food and stuff—cigarettes, some extra soap I had and things like that. They were real grateful and invited me into their apartment and all like that, you know. His wife is older than I but a real cute woman. You know how vivacious these French women are. The man works on the railroad and is gone from home a lot. Well, this woman let me know that she would, you know, go to bed with me. I was real flattered for a while but then I discovered that it's really because she's afraid if she doesn't I'll quit bringing them food and other things the civilians don't have. I'm real upset."

"About what?"

"Well, golly, wouldn't that be a form of prostitution? Plus, after all, it would be adultery. What kind of person would I be if I got involved in a situation like that?"

Her voice was sharp but her eyes were crinkled with kindness. "You're already a thief."

"Ma'am? Me?"

"Oh, come on, Osborne. Wipe that innocent look off your face. Crowder has been missing coffee, cream and sugar from his cupboard for the last month. He's been blaming the civilian maids and watching them like a hawk. It's been you, hasn't it?"

"Well, a little bit here and there, maybe. But we've got plenty, Miss Nielson." He became defensive. "That's not what I'd call stealing."

"If you take something that does not belong to you, it's stealing. I don't have time to argue about the degree of an offense. Don't worry, I'm not going to tell Sgt. Crowder. It's good for those French maids to be under surveillance. They're a shiftless lot. Sometimes I think I'd rather go back to having German PW's."

"Who did that cloth belong to that the colonel brought you, Miss Nielson?"

Her blue eyes narrowed. "Good point. Don't you touch it."

"Oh, I wouldn't think of it, Lieutenant. Me snitch cloth that's reserved for draperies for the officers' club? What kind of boy do you think I am?"

"We shan't take time to go into that."

"Yes'm." He pushed a finger along a tabletop and examined it absent-mindedly for dust. "Your friend, the colonel in the Quartermaster Corps. Is he married?"

Her blush was minimal, her syllables crackled like new lettuce. "I don't know. I have not bothered to inquire. We are both in Alsace-Lorraine and have both found out it will be months before we return to the States. I have work to do. Why don't you take a pill, go to sleep, and forget your worries?"

"Yes'm. Thanks for talking to me. I get all mixed up about things sometimes. Like I'm convinced adultery is worse than stealing."

Her spine stiffened, her neck lengthened, and Lt. Nielson looked regally into Porter's eyes. "Believe me, it's better. Remember you heard it here first."

Porter's jaw was still slack when she turned at the door and spoke again. "Osborne."

"Ma'am?"

"The next time you get propositioned by one of those French women, you take her up on it. It will be good for you and I've no doubt it will improve your whole attitude. It's time you settled into the realities of life and quit skipping around like Peter Pan."

"Wow," thought Porter, but all he uttered aloud was a meek, "Yes, ma'am."

When he awoke that afternoon, he wandered without purpose through the barracks, resisting the urge to visit Bettie and continue the game of licentious pretense. He met Kostas in the hallway and bowed formally. "Good afternoon, Stevens Peter. How is Steven?"

"I've heard that one before, Osborne, but I'm glad to see you not rushing off by yourself today and actually taking time to inquire about old friends. Want to go to town and drink some wine?"

Porter grimaced. "As they say down South, Kostas, 'Not never, nohow, no more.' The French can keep their wine; I still have scars from that dog biting me."

"Walk to town with me, anyhow. Some of us were in the old quarter down there last night and stumbled on a little woodworking shop. There's something in the window I want to see in better light and, if the shop's open, see if I can afford to buy it."

They walked along in the springtime, Kostas pointing out medieval landmarks and other sites of interest. "I can't believe you've made no effort to explore Metz; it's an absolutely marvelous city. The flying buttresses on the cathedral are world famous."

"I've been busy," Porter said and noted that this was the first time in four weeks he had spent this time of day without an erection. "I've had other things on my mind."

"Like what?"

'Well," Porter evaded, "I'm sure to get sent to the South Pacific now, and that's not a social event I'm anticipating. In fact, Steve, I have this dead certain feeling in my gut that I'm going to get killed and never see home again "

"Are you serious?"

Porter dodged into flippancy. "No, that's my brother. I'm Earnest. What is it you're so dedicated to buying on this little street? It's not wide enough for a car and I don't think the sun has ever shone in here."

"This guy has his window filled with dozens of plaques he's done in wood. *Bas-relief* things with female nudes, nearly all of them, interestingly enough, from the back. There's even one which has utilized a knot in the wood on the inner thigh and looks for all the world like a chancre."

"You want to buy that?"

"Heavens, no. What I want to examine is a woodcarving of Mephistopheles in the back of the window. He's playing a lute and it doesn't look at all like this guy's other work. He's sinister but beautiful, and as distorted and elongated as an El Greco."

"Mephistopheles was the devil in an opera, wasn't he? The one that bought men's souls? I knew a boy in med school who told me about him."

"To reduce both Goethe and Wagner to a nutshell, Osborne, the answer is 'yes'."

"And you think the devil is beautiful?"

"Always. At least until it's too late. This one certainly is. Wait until you see it. We're almost there."

"Who is El Greco?"

"Didn't you take art appreciation in college? Didn't you go to the Louvre when you went to Paris? My God, Osborne, El Greco was a world-famous artist from Spain. He was born in Greece and his real name was Domenicos Theotocopoulous but the Spanish couldn't remember that; so he was called 'The Greek.' Don't you know anything?"

"I know plenty," Porter replied, "and I'm dedicated to knowing more, which is the only reason I keep asking questions of a New Englander who is also a Mediterranean bigot. And for your information, I did not get to the Louvre when I went to Paris. I was on a mission, remember?"

"That's right, you were. I wonder if Otten has found Daniel D. Farbecker yet."

"Not a chance. I wonder if he's made sergeant. I wonder how he's doing with Ole Massa."

"Ole Massa? What are you talking about?"

"My God, Kostas, don't you know anything? Didn't you go to the Cyclorama when you were in Atlanta?"

"You're the one who's a bigot, Osborne. A real honest to God, genuine bigot."

"Takes one to know one," said Porter. His heart lifted. Camaraderie was a much less demanding relationship than adultery, he decided, and he would think no more of Bettie. Today.

Emil Rosen was in his shop. Emil Rosen spoke English. He made his living carving bas-relief profiles of customers, but his mission in life was carving bas-relief nudes. They did not sell as well as the profiles, but he was an artist and not responsible for the tastes of the public. If a person preferred a likeness of himself in wood for three hundred and fifty francs rather than a true work of art, such as this gorgeous woman seen from the rear *au bain*, Emil Rosen could not help it. He was a practical man as well as an artist, and three hundred fifty francs was much better than nothing. After all, he could carve out a ten-by-twelve likeness of an American soldier in less than an hour, whereas it took weeks to produce the detail and perspective manifest in *La nude au bain*, for which he would take not one *sou* less than fifty thousand francs, not if she hung in his shop until he was forced to burn her for kindling wood in his old age. "Notice the curve of the back just here, how naturally it flows a little to the left above the bowl. Observe the flexed thigh on that side, the outstretched leg on the right, with the foot extended, each toenail carved individually. Such perspective. Such perfection." Emil Rosen was already recognized in the art world as a master of detail; some day the public would awaken and he would no longer carve profiles to pay the rent and buy a little food. Would the young American soldiers like a work by Rosen while his prices were still so low? A souvenir of Metz by an artist who was destined one day to be world-famous? If the two of them decided to have them done this afternoon, while it happened he was not so busy, he, Emil Rosen, would even take fifty francs off the price. Did either soldier perhaps have a cigarette he could spare?

Porter pointed to the elongated Mephistopheles in the window. "How much is that statue?"

"Ah, the figure in wood *la bas*! Is not for sale, no. It does not belong to Rosen. Is property of very high woman in Metz, *une grande dame*. Here, Rosen let you hold it. See just there the crack in the leg? The lady have bring it to Rosen to repair. She trust only me."

"Would she sell it, do you think?"

"Sell it?" Rosen's eyebrows rose almost to the widow's peak from which his brown hair began a greasy, lanky course across his scalp. "*Ah, m'sieu*, you not understand. This woman is *très riche grande dame*. She never sells. She buys. Someday Emil Rosen will have a work in her salon. You wait and see. This work here, this Mefisto, is an Italian Renaissance piece. Have been in her family for generations. Is not for sale. No. Would be, how you say, insult to ask."

"It's lovely. How much do you think it's worth? If it were for sale. How many francs?"

'Ah, *m'sieu*, is hard to say. Is museum quality." The man's shoulders rose to his ear lobes, his mouth pursed. "*Peut-être* five to seven hundred thousand francs? *Je ne sais pas*. Is not for sale."

"Let me hold it," said Porter. "I'll be very careful." He stroked the figure's rounded shoulders hunched in almost voluptuous caress over the lute it cradled, traced the sword, the exaggerated slender legs, noted the detail in the face, the sly smile penetrating the van Dyke beard, the glint of mocking wisdom in the eyes, and was entranced. Emil Rosen was right about one thing, he thought — this truly was a work of art.

"Could you copy this?" he asked.

"*Pardon?*"

"Could you copy this figure? You know, make one like it if you used this one for a model?"

"*M'sieu*. Emil Rosen is an artist. Emil Rosen creates, he never copies."

526

"I understand that. All of your works here are proof of that, especially that one of the lady douching herself. It proves the subtlety of your genius because an unimaginative artist would have portrayed her from the front and that would have been, how shall I say, just too damn much. I know you are an artist, *M'sieu* Rosen, and I admire your work very much. I was just asking *could* you copy it?"

Rosen blew twin streams of smoke from his nose, squinted his eyes, and coughed for emphasis.

"*Mais certainment.* Rosen could copy this so exactly it take an expert to tell the difference. To copy is only matter of hand and eye, no need for soul or brain or heart. Of course, I could copy. But of course, also, I will not."

"I understand, *monsieur.* Have another cigarette? Keep the package, I have plenty at the barracks. I think I'm going to get you to do one of those plaques of my head, but I'm out of time right now. I have to work at night. Will you be here tomorrow?"

"*Oui, m'sieu.* But I may be busy. Perhaps tomorrow you have to wait. Most days Rosen have many American soldiers wanting their portraits in wood."

"That's OK. I'll be back tomorrow."

"One thing, *m'sieu.*"

"Yes?"

"The price tomorrow go back to three hundred fifty francs. Rosen have only time and self to sell and already I spend much time with you. *Compris?*"

"That's OK. No problem. See you tomorrow."

On the way back to the hospital, Kostas was skeptical. "Are you really going back there? The only thing in that shop worth having is that carving of Mephistopheles. I'm glad I got to see it up close, to hold it."

"Me, too. It's compelling. I identified with it the minute I touched it. I'm going to have it."

"You're dreaming. The lady won't sell and that egocentric Rosen won't copy."

"Wanta bet? There's more than one way to skin a cat. Tell me, Kostas, when he was pointing out the fine points of that carving he's trying to sell for fifty thousand francs, did it make you think of Browning's 'My Last Duchess'?"

Kostas missed a step. "Not for even one fleeting moment, Osborne. Did I ever tell you . . ."

"That Southerners are interesting? Often. Did I ever tell you I'm flattered? Other people have phrased it differently. I'm calling on Rosen again tomorrow. You want to come?"

"Why not? I want to keep you in circulation."

"You stick with me and I'll show you radishes as big as diamonds. You don't have to go to an Ivy League school to get what you want in this world."

Kostas watched as Porter posed sideways for Rosen the next day. The artist took a square of walnut and drew his profile with a heavy pencil; then began work with chisels, gouges, and scoops. Chips and shavings flew. Porter took a break.

"You truly are an artist, *Monsieur* Rosen. Even I can tell that looks like me already."

"Is nothing. In a little while you have to pose again while Rosen gets detail about eye and lines of face, yes? Right now this goes fast, is just the rough work."

"It doesn't look rough to me. It really makes me appreciate your nude over there. I wish I had fifty thousand francs and I wish that plaque wasn't three by four feet so I could get it home with me. The more you look at it, the more you see. The anatomy is perfect. I brought you three packs of Camels."

"Ah. Camels are good. American cigarettes are best in world. Except for the one called Raleigh. Not so good. Camels, Lucky Strikes, Chesterfields, all good. Thank you for the present. *Merci beaucoup*."

"*C'est mon plaisir*," Porter said smoothly and thought fleetingly of La Petite. His accent was improving. "Mr. Rosen, I recognize you are a true artist and I understand that you create and never copy, but if by chance you did consent just to think about making a replica of that figure of Mephistopheles, how much would you charge for doing it?"

"Ah, you could not afford. *Trop cher*."

"I know. But how much? Really."

"Not one *sou* less than one hundred thousand francs. *Cent mille francs*."

"Golly, that's five thousand dollars. You're right. I could never afford it. But it sure would be worth it. If I had the money, I would love to spend it that way. I really admire your work."

"Money is only symbol, my young friend. Price mean nothing. Value is relative. You understand, for Rosen know you are not like most American soldiers. You sensitive. You have heart."

"Oh, yes, sir. I understand. I'm glad you said that about value and price." Porter reached into his pocket and held out a swatch of cloth. "What do you think of this?"

Rosen laid down his chisel and felt the fine woolen weave. "Ah, very nice. Not for six, seven year have Rosen seen cloth like this. Long ago I have suit made by tailor but not so nice, *comme-ci*. Where you find?"

"I have a hidden supply available only to me. Tell me, *monsieur*, how would you like enough of this cloth to make you a suit? Immediately?"

"A suit? For Emil Rosen? From wool like this? *Ah, vraiment*, for such elegance Rosen would sell his soul."

Porter's gaze was steady. "How about a carving of Mephistopheles?"

Rosen's eyebrows rose to the accompaniment of a great sucking draft on his cigarette. Porter thought the man could accumulate a longer intact ash than anyone he had ever known, including the Bacteriology professor at Emory, but remained silent.

"How soon?"

"How soon what?"

"How soon you get cloth and bring here to Rosen?"

"How soon can you finish the carving?"

"No less than three day. No more than one week. OK?"

"Sure. OK. I can have the cloth tomorrow; that's no problem. When can you start?"

"Rosen happen to have, *bonne chance*, no customer this afternoon. I start now. Soon as I rub wax on your portrait."

"Forget that profile of me for the present, Mr. Rosen, and start on Mephistopheles. We have a deal. Can I watch?"

Rosen selected a four by four from a jumble in one corner, sawed off a two-foot segment, and began rapidly sketching on its four sides from the model. Osborne and Kostas watched in rapt silence as the figure, under the skilled hands and flashing tools, began its birth from the plain chunk of wood.

When they left, Porter was exuberant. "Can you believe the wizardry of that man, Steve? You can already tell what it's going to look like. I'm going back every day to watch."

"So am I. It really is impressive. But speaking of wizardry, just where in the hell are you going to procure enough of that material to make Rosen a suit? I learned long ago not to queer a deal, so I didn't ask in front of him."

"Don't ask now. Just trust me. The old blind hog has done stumbled up on another acorn."

The next afternoon he insisted on a detour by the hospital, sneaked undetected in and out of the sewing room, swaddled himself in *Wehrmacht* material, and adjusted the concealing fatigues to his satisfaction.

"Don't walk so fast," he requested Kostas.

"What's the matter with you? You're twisting when you walk like you'd sprained a hip or something."

Rosen had made unbelievable progress, looked up only perfunctorily, and kept busy with fine little instruments worthy of a neurosurgeon. He was working the face.

"*Bonjour*, young friends. You like? Rosen cannot sleep last night. He think about his new suit. When he *fini* Madame's statue and return it to her chateau, he will not look like *paysan*. Emil Rosen will be dress like *boulevardier*. Madame will notice, will know that Rosen prosper, that he artist but also, how you say, gentleman. She will then *peut-être* buy one of Rosen's works herself. One of your countrymen say nothing succeed like success, right? Only for this have Rosen agreed to copy; for his future. Every man have to think of his future, will do anything for his future. *N'est-ce-pas*? Right?"

"Right," agreed Porter. "As one of your countrywomen told me, 'Fair play for everybody.' Right? Mr. Rosen, it is lovely. It is magnificent. I cannot believe you have done all this in just one day. You are not only an artist; you are a genius. Can you take time out for a cigarette?"

"Ah, *oui*. Rosen also cannot himself believe he work so fast. Tomorrow I finish. Tomorrow you bring the cloth, yes?"

Porter began unbuttoning his fatigues. "The cloth is here, Mr. Rosen. *Nous sommes ici*. You like, yes? Here, Steve, help unwind me." He caught his friend's eye. "Remember that value is relative."

The Frenchman erupted into a temporary frenzy of sounds of which Porter comprehended only an occasional *mon Dieu* and a meaningless *alors*. He practically danced. "This is more than enough for a suit. Is *peut-être* enough for two suits. But what touch Rosen is you bring so soon, not wait and pay until you sure I *fini*. Like I say, you have heart. You, how you say, trust Emil Rosen, right?"

"Right. *Mais certainment, monsieur*. For Pete's sake, you have to trust somebody." He tapped Kostas with a back hand. "Ain't that right, Sport? What? What?"

"I think you're crazy, Osborne. But I agree with you about trusting someone. Even an old blind hog. I can't believe you've pulled this off. I'm envious."

"Envious?"

"Yes. I found Mephistopheles. I am the one who wanted him. You have him."

"No problem." He turned back to Emil Rosen. "*Monsieur. S'il vous plaît.* This is a gray cloth. For a blue suit would you also, *peut-être*, as a genius and an artist, make another copy for my friend here?"

Rosen smoothed his hair. "Ah. Blue, you say? *Comme-ci*, but blue?" He shrugged. "Rosen have for a long time his eye on a new model, you understand? She very fine body, a back you not believe unless you see. Rosen not have money for her, but a blue suit? *Alors,* one thing. You speak of trust. You must never let anyone in Metz or all of France see your statues. You must send them *tout de suite* to America. Yes? Madame, *la grande dame,* she trust Rosen. She die if she know he turn out copies of her treasure like a factory. Emil Rosen, himself, die of shame if it told of him." His eyes narrowed. "On the other hand, *enfin,* Rosen is a practical man; he look always to his future. This cloth *très cher, très* rare." He threw up his hands. "*Ah, oui.* Rosen do. We have, how you say, a deal, yes? My new model do anything and everything for the cloth like this."

Porter Osborne bowed to Stevens Kostas. "Value is relative. Be my guest." To Rosen he said, "Fair play for everybody. Have you signed my statue?"

"Ah, no, my young friend. One does not sign copies."

"I want mine signed."

"*Pourquoi?* Why?"

"So that years from now after the renowned and world-famous Emil Rosen has died and all his works have become collector's items, my statue in Brewtonton, Georgia, because of the relativity of values, will be worth much more than this cloth is today." He widened his eyes. "A man, as you say, must think of his future."

Rosen only looked at him.

Porter added, "Besides, think what a souvenir! When my little children, my grandchildren, sit on my knee, I will tell them that after we American soldiers, at great but unheeding peril to ourselves, had liberated Europe from the vicious German tyrant and restored Alsace-Lorraine once more to freedom and democracy, a very good French friend of mine who later became an artist as famous as Rodin or Degas insisted on rendering for me a likeness of the devil himself, lest any of us though scattered to the far reaches of the globe ever forget that war, in all its manifestations, is hell and that Mephistopheles in one guise or another is the ruler of that domain."

He took a deep breath to continue, but Rosen shook his head. "Enough. Enough. No more. Rosen not interested in politics, even less in religion. Rosen sign. See? Right here behind the foot. Bring on the cloth."

Later he remonstrated to Kostas, "You keep on and you're going to mess up my compartments, short circuit my dissociation processes. What difference does it make where I got the cloth?"

"You stole it."

"I did not. I liberated it. In fact, you would not believe how many times that wool cloth has been liberated." He thought of U-Boat commanders, SS generals, Col. Draughan, and added, "Trust me that it's more than appropriate for it to wind up where it is."

Kostas laughed. "You plainly nagged and nattered that poor man until he signed your statue in desperation just to shut you up. I guess mine will be unsigned, for I could never do that to anyone."

"In the South, it's an art form. Used mostly, I will admit, by women, Negroes, and enterprising children, but nevertheless an art form. I'll tend to getting a signature for you."

"Every time I'm around you I marvel anew at what a skilled manipulator you are."

Porter shrugged. "Words. Semantics. Rosen explained it all. Porter Osborne, Jr., has become a practical man."

"In a pig's ass," asserted Kostas.

Porter planned carefully for the rigors of the mail. A wooden box, a cradle of absorbent cotton, a sheath of stockinette, and Mephistopheles would travel safely to Georgia. He was caressing the smooth wood and studying the sardonic but enticing smile for one last time before shipping him off. Lucetti walked over to his bunk.

"What in the world is that?"

"Oh, nothing much. Just a souvenir of Metz I picked up to make me remember all the things that have happened since I got here."

"You knew Churchill just lost his election, didn't you? It's in the paper."

"I'll remember that, too, but it's way down on my list. I've lost some things myself lately."

"Like what?"

"Oh, I don't know. Trust. Virtue. Maybe even the last vestige of innocence. Nothing of any real value, I suppose. I like this statue because it makes me think. And remember."

"It's a statue of the devil, isn't it?"

"In one of his forms, yes."

"It looks expensive. How much did it cost?"

Porter took a very short breath. "Not one red dime."

"Osborne, have you sold your soul to the devil? After all the praying I've been doing for you?"

"Not a chance, Lucetti. Maybe a priest would say I've sold my soul *for* the devil, but never *to* him."

"It is a handsome thing. In an evil sort of way."

"Oh, Lucetti! The devil is historically handsome, or at least appealing, when he tempts men. Look what Jesus turned down from him in the wilderness."

"Osborne, you constantly puzzle me."

Porter continued. "I'll bet that when Satan slipped up on Eve in the Garden of Eden, she even thought his serpent's disguise was beautiful."

"All women hate snakes."

"Not until after the Fall, Lucetti." His mind was flooded with a sudden recollection of Bettie, her little monkey face, her lithe body, her bathrobe gaping open. The memory of her breasts was intensely erotic. "I'll tell you something else, Lucetti. I'll bet you that when Eve in turn tempted Adam, it was with two apples, not one."

"Where in the world would you get any such inference as that?"

"It has been revealed to me, Lucetti. Believe me, it has been revealed to me. You keep on praying. I've got to get this in the mail."

As Lucetti strolled off, Porter called after him, "It's also been revealed to me that what may be one man's god may be another man's devil."

Lucetti answered with dryness, "I'll keep on praying, Osborne. I promise you that."

"Trumpet that sayeth ha!
Domino Gloria!"

39 Sgt. Crowder put out a new duty roster which rotated Bosi to a month of night duty and Porter Osborne to days. Their caseload in the OR had dwindled now to such numbers that Capt. Ballas and Lt. Toomay were comfortably handling all of the anesthesia duties. Porter found himself bored when his morning tasks were done and searched out new chores to resolve his restlessness. Since his presence was mandatory, he preferred to be busy rather than to sit in idleness and listen to Sgt. Crowder sigh over frequent cups of coffee. The man drank this with long sucking noises, bemoaning meanwhile the slowness with which the Army was moving to return him to the States and his family in Arkansas.

He sighed and sniffed and slurped and also wagged his head in disapproval of the enlisted men serving under him. They were a frivolous lot, in his opinion, and he frequently reprimanded them for joking with the nurses or each other. They were no longer working in the crowded tents of Normandy where laxity of some rules had been expediently condoned. The traditional suite in which they now operated demanded return to formal conduct, to structured behavior and above all to serious attitude, to sincere professionalism, and, by God, Oliver Crowder was just the man to tend to it. "Effen it means the death of me," he said. He decreased his physical activity and became so increasingly mired in indolence that he was content to sit at the table in the workroom, watch the enlisted men like a brooding hawk, and issue mournful directions. He also belched a lot. Porter regarded him as an increasingly expanding blob of noncommissioned inertia and nimbly shunned his presence and attention.

In contrast, the bustling Lt. Ruth Nielson moved rapidly through her Operating Rooms, checking on the surgeons, supervising her competent, cheerful nurses, constantly busy, professionally impersonal, a little aloof. A kinship developed between her and Porter Osborne, based on their mutual preference for industriousness over sloth but widely divergent in other respects, a relationship that was unusual and memorable. He learned that he could gaze at her steadily and, if careful to look soulful and lugubrious, tell her the most outlandish truths imaginable and she would accept them as absolute lies.

"Osborne, run these packs over to Central Supply to the autoclave, if you're caught up."

"Yes, ma'am. I'll grab them in a minute."

"The seamstress said some of my cloth was missing. There was plenty for the drapes and now we're thinking about slipcovers for a sofa, too, but she reported that someone had definitely helped themselves to several yards from a couple of bolts. You wouldn't happen to know who did it, would you?"

"Oh, yes, ma'am, Lt. Nielson. I stole it."

"What? You brazen whippersnapper, don't you know that's a court-martial offense? How and why?"

"I stripped off buck naked and wound the cloth around me and then put my clothes back on over it and went to town and traded it off for the devil. I put him in a box and mailed him off to Georgia. He's going to be flabbergasted at where he winds up."

Ruth Nielson gave a short laugh. "If you're going to make up a tale, Osborne, you could do better than that. Do you take me for an idiot?"

"Oh, no, ma'am. I was just doing the best I could on the spur of the moment."

"Well, if someone really stole it instead of that seamstress just appropriating some of it for herself, it was more than likely that civilian maid who washes instruments and is always giggling and jabbering in that foreign tongue at you enlisted men. I tell you, you can't trust these French; they're a scurvy lot. I'll keep a closer eye on them."

"Yes'm. You want all these packs to go?"

Michelle was the French maid that Lt. Nielson had hired in the workroom for chores that did not require especial training or any knowledge of sterile technique. There were several jobs assigned her, but as far as the enlisted men were concerned Michelle, when she washed instruments, was fulfilling a destiny reserved specifically for her. Against one wall of the tiled, high-ceilinged workroom, directly across from the double doors that led to Operating Room A, the instrument sink was mounted. It was six feet long, of enameled cast iron, and had a drain board at each end with two shallow tubs

535

between. It was supported by four tapered wooden legs across the front, stood waist high and had no cabinets or storage space beneath it. It was obviously designed for its specific function in this specific space, and it was Michelle's work station. Porter Osborne had never seen either a sink or a woman built as they were.

Michelle's legs were muscular columns, disproportionately long, and she wore the same black skirt to work every day. It had obviously been acquired when she was much slimmer, for her buttocks were packed into it until the seams were strained and its length was revealingly less in back than in the front, hiked above her knees so that bulging pads of popliteal fat were displayed to common view, unsheathed by stockings, laced with venules surrendering in purple sprangle to pressure from above and within. She inevitably wore also a white blouse, ruffled in front, its buttons under mammary strain to rival the seams of her skirt. She was a tall woman but the high-heeled pumps upon which she teetered made her seem even taller.

The unusual height of the sink forced Michelle to hold her elbows akimbo. When she plied her scrub brush over the grooves of hemostats, the teeth of Oschner clamps, she did it with such vigor that unbelievable activity resulted. Her behind, balanced above the distant tottering heels, came alive, seemed to gyrate, gambol, and revolve incommensurately to the triggering stimulus from the scrub brush in her hands. That behind quivered, skipped along, leaped, took off in one direction, reversed itself in rapid rotation, shimmied slower for a moment, only to convulse with more rapid abandon when Michelle tackled another instrument. It had a life of its own. It was the wonder and delight of every male who beheld it.

"I never seen no ass like that in Chicago," said Bosi.

"There ain't one like it in Georgia," said Sherman Roger Jewel. "It's like it's smiling at you."

"It's so happy you almost expect it to sing," said Lemon.

"Keep your hands off'n it. Don't you dare tetch it," growled Sgt. Crowder.

"Avoid the very appearance of evil," advised Lucetti.

"What in the world are all you men doing in the corner with your heads together?" demanded Ruth Nielson. "There is work to be done."

"I know you work on the Medical wards," Porter told Kostas, "but you should make it a point to drop by the OR some morning and watch our French maid's back-end perform when she's washing instruments."

"I'm not about to stick my head in the OR; everybody says your chief nurse is an old dragon. Show me the maid and I'll watch her some time when she's walking down the hall."

"It's not the same. Nothing makes her twat truly twitch except scrubbing those hemostats. It's a work of art. Even Capt. Ballas gapes and rubs against it."

"Come on, Osborne. If you've seen one fanny, you've seen them all."

"You ever see one frolic and dance at eye level and almost hypnotize you into petting it?"

Michelle spoke no English and her efforts to learn it were primitive, limited to nouns and the present tense of a few basic verbs. She was a self-effacing, almost apologetic young giantess, unfailingly affable, tendering frequent smiles and nods as substitute for comprehension. Since she herself had no idea whatsoever of the compelling activity generated in her posterior by her work, she simply assumed that she was blocking traffic when some tech succumbed to temptation and walked close enough to her for tactile confirmation of visual stimulation. She would shift away, bob her head, and coo, "*Pardon, m'sieu.*"

"Don't you tetch it." fell often in stern caution from Sgt. Crowder's lips.

The sergeant's unsmiling face seemed to become ever more dour and he devoted ever more of his attention to rebuking any manifestation of frivolity in the techs working under him.

"All y'all barely old enough to shave and you act like a bunch of grammar school kids at recess just cause you think the war's over. You got to quit all this cutting up and carrying on and recollect that this is still the Army and we're yet at war in the Pacific. I aim for you to straighten up and fly right. You hear me? Quit tetching it."

"He's got terminal dingleberries," said Porter.

"What are dingleberries?" asked Lucetti.

"Look it up. I think you'll find a reference to them in Leviticus. Or maybe it's Exodus. Or even Deuteronomy. Samuel probably had them and I'm sure Elisha did."

"Osborne, you know I only have a New Testament with me. You're being sacrilegious again, aren't you?"

"I am not; I haven't even mentioned Paul or John the Baptist. And I'll bet if somebody did a little research, he'd discover that the Isle of Patmos was covered with dingleberries. All those men had to have something in common with Sgt. Crowder."

"Even in the presence of a forgiving God, Osborne, you should remember that there is a hell."

"Right. And I'd never thought of it before, Lucetti, but I'll bet the worst sinners of all living down in hell are also afflicted with dingleberries. Little bitty, mean, tight, and twisting ones."

"Osborne, I'd better pray for you some more, hadn't I?"

"Without ceasing," Porter said. "Especially when Michelle is busy."

Above one corner of the long work table a frayed cord snaked down from the cavernous ceiling and supported a naked light bulb which was screwed into a heavy white porcelain socket. The cord and the socket were worthy of being included in a collection of early electrical fixtures. About the time that Harry Truman met at Potsdam with Joseph Stalin and Clement Attlee to hammer out peace terms for Germany, Porter Osborne was called on to change a blown light bulb in the old fixture, inadvertently discovering thereby an unsuspected short circuit. If he grasped the socket while the switch was on, he incurred only the very faintest tingle of electrical current; but if he simultaneously touched a comrade, it induced in the second person a jolting shock and uncontrollable galvanic response. For several days he and the other GI's in the OR capered like children with a new toy until they all became gun-shy. The ever watchful Oliver Crowder glumly admonished, with new meaning, "Don't tetch it. Ain't y'all never gonna grow up? Don't grab that there light socket, you hear me now?"

At the tail end of a morning, coming up on high noon, the surgical schedule had been completed except for one case. Capt. Bloom's double herniorrhaphy had been delayed because of complications in the preceding case under the hands of Maj. Emmons but was now under way. Lt. Hormley was Bloom's assistant. Capt. Ballas was the anesthetist. Lt. Hisel was scrub nurse. Lemon was circulating, and Lt. Nielson was supervising all of it. She had sent all the other nurses on to lunch.

"You girls know there's nothing complicated about a hernia. We can handle it. Shoo along to lunch with you. Shoo, shoo."

Sgt. Crowder in turn had dismissed all his techs save Porter Osborne, who was at the distant end of the long table compiling laparotomy packs to be carried to Central Supply for sterilizing. Sgt. Crowder lounged in a chair at the near end, coffee cup before him, swallowing audibly, sighing, shifting, emitting an occasional morose burp. Michelle was attacking on teetering heels the huge pile of instruments stacked on the enameled sink. Porter, counting flats and lap pads, watched her merry buttocks over Sgt. Crowder's shoulder and remarked to himself that washing Orthopedic instruments, rongeurs and saws produced a friskier, more frolicsome exhibition than ordinary, run-of-the-mill General Surgery instruments. He noted that Michelle was balanced in a puddle of water on the cold tile floor and had best be careful not to slip.

Then it happened. Sgt. Oliver Crowder rose from his chair in exaggerated slow motion. He stepped behind the unsuspecting Michelle and stretched his arms overhead as though satisfying a deep yawn. With one hand he took a firm grip on the antique light socket and then with meaningful purpose reached out the other hand and, before Porter's incredulous gaze, grasped the enticing rump that was gyrating before him.

One shriek in that reverberating room would have paralyzed anyone within range, but Michelle emitted such a series of them that there were echoes of the echoes. At the same time, from a standing start, she instinctively leaped straight up into the sink full of instruments. The wooden legs, under her weight, immediately gave way. The heavy sink, the steel instruments, the screaming French maid all crashed to the tile floor in cacophonous bedlam. Sgt. Crowder stood frozen. Porter's hands were suspended above a lap pack.

The double doors to the Operating Room burst open and Lt. Nielson flew into the workroom. She stood for one amazed instant surveying the wreckage and then her lips began moving, obviously yelling questions. Michelle's screams were so loud Porter could hear no other sound. Lt. Nielson moved briskly forward and shook the French girl vigorously, producing staccato punctuation in the shrieks but no diminution in volume. The nurse drew back her hand and delivered such a slap that Michelle's head snapped to the side. The screams stopped abruptly and the gibbering began. Michelle pointed to the instruments scattered across the floor, the sink torn from the wall, the pool of soapy water, threw both hands up and began an outburst of high-pitched French that was rapid as a telegraph key.

"Sgt. Crowder, do something! What happened? For pity's sake, do something immediately to help stop this silly girl's hysterics!"

The sergeant, dazed and disbelieving, automatically obedient, took a tentative step toward Michelle, whereupon she backed away, pointed a trembling finger at him, and began jabbering louder and faster.

Lt. Nielson interposed herself, drew back her hand again in threat to quiet the woman. "Osborne!"

"Yes, ma'am?"

"What in the world happened? Speak the truth!"

Porter caught a glimpse of the sheepish roll of Sgt. Oliver Crowder's eyes, the accepting hang-dog shrug of his shoulders, and looked wide-eyed at Lt. Ruth Nielson.

"Well, now, ma'am, I just happened to grab that light socket up there over your head and then I goosed Michelle and she jumped straight up in the air and landed in the sink and the legs broke and everything fell to the floor."

"Osborne! I have told you about making up lies!"

"It was the best I could do on . . ."

"Don't say 'short notice' to me, young man. We all know you have an active imagination. What happened?"

"I don't think it would have been such a severe shock to her, Miss Nielson, if she hadn't been standing in a puddle of water."

"Osborne!"

Porter deliberately sighed. "Well, to tell the truth, Miss Nielson, it was just a plain ordinary commonplace little old field mouse that ran over Michelle's foot and scared her half to death."

"Field mouse!" yelled Lt. Nielson. She started to climb into a chair, collected herself, and snapped. "Oh, my God! Don't tell me there's a mouse in my operating suite!"

"There sure isn't now. He came skittering out of the room you were in, hugging up against the wall in little bursts and pauses like they do, you know, but when Michelle started screaming and that sink and all those instruments hit the floor, it went flying out in the hall with its tail straight up in the air. His whiskers were laid back and its little old beady eyes out on stems, and none of us will ever see that mouse again."

He turned to Oliver Crowder. "Sergeant, I didn't think it was quite as gray as our American mice, did you? Seemed like it had more of a russet tint to it. And I'm sure it wasn't quite as big as ours. It was a tiny little old thing, wasn't it, Sergeant?"

Oliver Crowder shifted to another foot and took a deep breath but was prevented from having to answer.

"Hush!" commanded Lt. Nielson. She shuddered. "A mouse is a mouse and I want to hear no more repulsive descriptions." She gave Michelle a soothing pat. "There, there. It's over. Quit jumping up and down and moaning. The sergeant and the privates will help you clean up this mess. There, there. You couldn't help it, poor thing."

Bosi called from Room A. "Lt. Nielson, we need you in here. Capt. Bloom was closing the first layer, and when all that racket came down he jumped so hard he lost a needle somewhere down in the patient. He needs help."

"Oh, my goodness!" responded Ruth Nielson. "Osborne, send that girl home for dry clothes and the two of you work on that mess." She hurried back into the OR and closed the doors.

Crowder squatted by Porter. "I'm much obliged to you, Osborne. You saved my ass. I hope to God that there French girl don't never learn no English. I don't know what in the world come over me."

Porter gave an exaggerated sigh. "I don't either, Sergeant. I been atelling you and telling you not to tetch neither one of them things, and then all of a sudden you up and tetch both of them at the same time. You should oughta knowed better'n to do no sech thing as that." He wagged his head. "Some days I think you just ain't never gonna grow up."

"Git serious, Osborne. I know I ain't done the best I could by you in the past, but I aim to make it up to you from now on."

"Relax, Sergeant. That's one of the most marvelous capers anybody ever pulled. I didn't know you had it in you. You know it sort of reminds me of a poem Robert Service wrote about a woman named 'Touch-the-button Nell.' Some day when I can remember all of it, I'll say it for you."

"That's all right, Osborne, ain't no call for that. You ain't got to put yourself out none for me. But I'm going to get you promoted effen it's the last thing I do."

Within a week Porter Osborne, Jr., became a corporal. He wheedled Lt. Dalrymple into sewing the double stripes on his sleeves and while she worked he mused, "Army life is ironic. You bust your butt working and trying to do a good job and get no recognition at all, and then you up and get promoted for lying. Nobody had better try to tell me virtue is its own reward."

Sgt. Crowder was faithful to his word. He took Porter under his wing and looked after him. He also stopped drinking so much coffee and became more active, but Porter always thought that was because Michelle absolutely refused to turn her back on him again and the sergeant prudently ignored her and avoided her presence. He assigned Porter to two weeks of surgical prep.

"That way ever afternoon when you git done shaving the cases for the next day you can check out and have an extry hour or so of free time."

He went further. "Here, Osborne, let me show you a trick. Take the blade out'n the razor and shave your operative area with jest the naked blade. Hit'll save you a heap of time in the long run and hit ain't near so messy getting shed of the shaved hair."

"Sergeant, isn't there a greater danger of cutting the patient?"

"Not effen you hold your wrist stiff. Like this. And keep the blade plumb straight. Like this. Effen you forget and let it slip sideways you'n git a pretty bad slice, but oncet you git use to it you won't never do it no other way."

"I never would have thought of that, Sergeant. You're ingenious."

"Naw, I ain't. I'm just a everday sort of fellow what tries to use his head for something besides a hat rack. You ain't got to be able to read arthurs and stuff like that there to study up new ways of doing things." He sighed and looked mournful. "I didn't git to be sergeant asetting around on my butt, Osborne."

Stimulated by Sgt. Crowder's goal of studying up new ways of doing things, Porter fancied that he himself might become a splendid example not only of efficiency but of the much-touted native ingenuity of the modern American soldier. The war was over and the Operating Room staff was busied now, not with the horrors of trench foot and shrapnel wounds, but, except for occasional Jeep wrecks or fights, with elective cases such as hernias and hemorrhoids. Porter's current assignment was to visit the wards and shave all body hair away from the operative sites. The task consumed most of the afternoon.

"How come you don't fetch the soldiers off'n the wards down here to git shaved, Osborne, instead of lugging that heavy old prep box around all over the hospital? I believe that'd speed things up fer ye."

"That's a good idea, Sarge. I could use the parlor, couldn't I?"

"What you calling the parlor, Osborne? I don't rightly follow you."

"The surgical amphitheater across the hall. We've never used it for a single case since we've been in Metz, except for that one time Lt. Nielson scheduled Capt. Bloom in there. She makes me keep it cleaned and everything arranged just so. That's why I call it the parlor. It's like the room back home that we never use except for funerals or for Sunday company that's extra special and not kinfolks who come all the time anyhow."

"I getcha. Sure. Use it. Hit's a waste not to. Hit's so grand I don't never myself hardly go in there nohow."

As Porter overlooked the grammar of this erstwhile adversary who had so recently become an ally, Sgt. Crowder sighed and spoke again, his voice carefully casual.

"They was five of us growing up and we never seen no parlor. Sometimes when we moved I kin recollect having a shed room or a extry room, but most of the time we never had nothing but a stove room and a front room. One the best things about me joining up in the regular Army was getting on-post housing for my ole lady and the chappies with running water and a inside toilet. We got a setting room now with the kitchen and dining room in one end of it, but I ain't never even dreamed of no parlor."

Porter said nothing.

"Hail, yeah," affirmed Sgt. Crowder in decision. "Effen anybody complains I'll cover your ass. Use the fucking parlor."

It was thus a rather unlikely confluence of events that led Porter to gather five GI patients from their respective wards one afternoon and lead them in a group through the corridors of the hospital. They were all scheduled for hemorrhoidectomies. As they walked along in the hospital uniform of blue cotton pajamas and maroon bathrobes, one or two attempted jocularity, but for the most part they were subdued young men, insouciant survivors of reckless battlefield experiences, intimidated now by the strangeness of hospital environment and soberly reconsidering the wisdom of surrendering voluntarily to surgery of the type they anticipated on the morrow.

Porter was a model of brisk efficiency. His new stripes enhanced his air of authority. When he led them into the surgical amphitheater and instructed them all to remove their pants and bathrobes, there was momentary hesitation but no remonstrance. He then proceeded to have them mount an unused operating table and lined them up in position to suit him; hands gripping the side of the table, heads down, bared buttocks at eye level, testicles swinging, anuses competently exposed.

He surveyed the result. "There's no question all of you have hemorrhoids and need surgery," he assured them. "We're going to do this on an assembly line basis now. First I lather you up with green soap. That's going to burn a little but don't worry about it; I'll wash it off before you go back to your wards. Then I have to shave you and you must be very still. This is a complicated area with lots of wrinkles and bumps, and the Major will give me hell if I leave even one little hair; so

I have to concentrate on what I'm doing and don't have time for anybody to wiggle. Also I'll be using a naked razor blade and it's to your advantage, believe me, not to move."

"You ain't got to worry about me," volunteered one.

"Do you get a new blade between patients?" asked another.

"Not unless it gets dull," said Porter.

"I never met any youse guys before," came the muffled voice of another, "but is this what they mean by asshole buddies?"

"Don't laugh," cautioned Porter. "I never noticed before, but it makes you wink and I might nick you."

"So who's laughing?" rejoined another. "I got no desire to be in no winking asshole platoon. What I wanta know is how you get out this chicken outfit?"

"Be real quiet and real still now," Porter continued. "I'm fixing to start. Our chief nurse has been in a tizzy all morning because she's getting inspected by the head nurse of the whole ETO, who's a chicken colonel and is supposed to arrive at four o'clock. It's nearly three; so I need to get you guys polished up and out of here."

It was no fault of Porter's that the Chief Nurse of the ETO, accompanied by her female retinue, arrived in Metz an hour early. He had no inkling that Lt. Nielson, as apprehensive before the chief nurse as Col. Draughn had been in the presence of Gen. Lee, would elect to display first on her tour the cold and empty surgical amphitheater. Certainly it was not intentional that his patients were aligned so that their heads were not their presenting parts.

He was not only startled but completely surprised when Lt. Nielson dramatically swung open the double doors leading into the main hall and displayed to the gaze of the women officers clustered around her Cpl. Porter Osborne's contribution to efficiency and organization. Her head bobbed, her voice rose an octave with each exclamation as she automatically counted off in acknowledgment of the vision before her.

"Oh! Oh!" she began. "Oh! Oh! Oh!"

"Ten shut!" bellowed Porter Osborne, Jr., in reflexive response to the unannounced presence of so much military brass.

"Like hell!" came a voice from the line of bowed heads. "Ain't a living soul in all the world can recognize me in this position. Stay put, fellows."

The doors slammed shut as Lt. Nielson frantically changed the itinerary of her inspection group. The doors did not close, however, before Porter got a look at the Chief Nurse of the European Theater of

544

Operations. The snappy overseas cap with the sparkling silver eagle on it rested rakishly on red hair and accented the green eyes. During the split instant before Lt. Ruth Nielson closed the doors, Col. Katie Albert from Nevada unmistakably winked at Cpl. Porter Osborne, Jr., from Georgia.

"Hey, Mack" said patient number one. "They gone?"

"Who the hell was it?" demanded patient number two. "I peeked 'tween my legs and it looked like that door was filled with dames."

"My ole lady ain't gonna believe I been on stage like this," contributed patient number three. "Showing my butt and balls to a whole bunch of broads."

"You got any pride you won't tell her," remarked number four. "I didn't hear no applause for your performance. It was right humiliating. Of course, my pecker was drawed up so tight in my belly I'm gonna have to hunt a week to find it."

"Corporal," moaned number five, "you be careful with that fucking razor blade. I been through the whole campaign with George Patton and didn't get a scratch on me. I sure don't want to qualify for no purple heart at your hands."

"All y'all hush and hold still and let's get through with this," said Porter. "I've got to find that chief nurse before she leaves and find out if she ever caught up with her husband."

Halfway through his task he said, "Like they say, it sure is a small world, fellows. I wonder how the Red Cross is doing these days."

"Can the crap," said the patient, "and hold your hand steady. I ain't winking and I don't want you blinking. Quit talking and shave."

All that Porter Osborne saw again of Katie Albert, however, was the back of her head as she sat erectly in the Jeep leading her caravan through the hospital gates. He returned to the Operating Room to face the wrath of Ruth Nielson. He was resigned to having his new corporal's stripes torn from his arm but was reluctant to endure the tongue lashing he anticipated. The lieutenant was indeed flushed bright pink and her hair was disarranged in agitation, but he was totally unprepared for the reception she tendered.

"You marvelous boy, where have you been? Col. Albert wanted to speak to you but is on a tight schedule and has to be in Rheims before dark."

"Ma'am?"

"Col. Albert said tell you 'Hello.' Aren't you listening to me? When I apologized about that debacle in the amphitheater—and I must talk to you about that later, Porter—she said I was lucky you didn't have time to coach all those patients with lines to say. Whatever was she talking about? At any rate, she was so impressed with the Operating Room that she gave me a rating of Excellent."

"That's great, Miss Nielson."

"Plus, and listen to this, she's recommended me for immediate promotion to Captain!"

"Congratulations, Miss Nielson. You sure deserve it."

"The reason, she said, is because I've been putting up with you. Furthermore, she said my being promoted to captain was contingent on my seeing that you got promoted to sergeant."

"Sergeant? Me?"

"Yes." The lieutenant paused. "I'd been warned about her brusqueness. Every nurse in the ETO is scared to death of her. I'd also been told she had a rough vocabulary, but I will confess I was almost as stunned by what she said before she left as I was by what I saw when I opened that door."

"Yes, ma'am?"

"She said, 'Nielson, I'm going to raise you to captain but it's predicated on your promise to get that goddam little scrawny-assed Porter Osborne promoted to sergeant. Stat.' Of course I said I would."

Porter waited.

"She said I had more on my hands than I could possibly realize with you in my outfit, and then when she left she said, 'No telling when he'll show up again, and I can't wait, but give that goddam incorrigible mushmouthed little son-of-a-bitch Georgia boy a great big juicy kiss. I always meant to but didn't get around to it.' What sort of hold do you have on that dragon lady of the ETO, Porter?"

Porter opened his mouth, but his reply was aborted by Capt. Ruth Nielson, who exuberantly fulfilled her mission.

"Now, get on with your business, Sgt. Osborne, but remember I'm keeping an eye on you. I've already told Crowder you're to do no more surgical preps."

Plowing his way absent-mindedly through the hordes of French children lying in wait at the gate and clamoring, "You give me gum, Yank?" Porter looked one of them in the eye and said, "Do you reckon Carter Otten has made sergeant yet?"

"You no got gum? You give gum, Yank? Please?"

Porter extracted an unopened packet of Juicy Fruit and handed it over.

"If he has," he continued, "I'll bet it was not so miraculously."

"Hey, Yank, you got candy? You give me candy, yes?"

"I wonder if Miz Albert still keeps her bandage scissors handy. I got no candy today, *enfants*. Scat!"

*"And dead is all the innocence of anger and
surprise."*

40 **f**or several weeks Porter was loath to sew on his
sergeant's stripes. He had no new duties as a result of the promotion,
had been assigned no new responsibilities, felt no nearer being a leader
of men. He did not feel unworthy of his advancement, but he was a
little embarrassed to be so capriciously singled out for advancement
while his friends who were as deserving as he still wallowed in the
quagmire of Army bureaucracy, faithfully laboring as good soldiers
should, bitching of course when their efforts were unrecognized, but
resigned to oversight, at home with futility.

"How come you ain't got your stripes on your uniform yit?"
asked Oliver Crowder.

"Maybe I feel like the people on the pavement in 'Richard Cory,'
Sergeant.

> 'So on we worked, and waited for the light,
> And went without the meat and cursed the bread.'"

Oliver Crowder sighed. "I never ast you how you feel. Reckon I
done got more sense than that by now. I ast you how come you ain't yet
sewed on your sergeant's stripes."

"To be truthful, Sergeant, I don't want my buddies to think I'm
stuck up or that I've changed. It looks to me like people resent leaders
from their own group and I don't want to be lonely." He paused a
moment. "At least no lonelier than I am."

"That's a crock of crap, Osborne. How'n hell can you be lonesome in this crazy outfit? Fretted half to death, maybe, but lonesome?"
He wagged his head. "No way. Another stripe don't change a man.
You're the same ole hawg, you jest got an extry curl in your tail. Git
your stripes sewed on."

"That poem ends,

> 'And Richard Cory one calm summer night
> Went home and put a bullet through his head.'

He was lonely, Sgt. Crowder."

The sergeant's answering sigh escaped his chest in audible moan. "And you're what we called 'tetched' back where I come from, Osborne. You was tetched when you was a private and making sergeant ain't changed you a bit. You git them stripes sewed on. Who'n hell you think you are, anyhow?"

"I am still Porter Osborne, Jr., by God." He ruminated a brief moment. "But you know something, Sergeant? I've reached the point where I don't give a shit. About anything."

Sherman Roger Jewel was walking by. "I heard that. Welcome to the club, Osborne. Want to go with me to Luxembourg tomorrow? I got transportation."

They moved away in step. "Where is Luxembourg?"

"A couple of hours up the road."

"What kind of transportation?"

"My motorcycle."

"Where in the world did you get a motorcycle?"

"Ask me no questions, I'll tell you no lies. I liberated the fucker. Been tuning and working on it for a week and it runs like a top."

"I never rode a motorcycle in my life." Porter's tone was dubious. "What if a sergeant got caught riding behind a buck private on a stolen motorcycle?"

"I thought you told old grump-and-growl Crowder you didn't give a shit."

Porter laughed. "You're on, Jewel. I'm proud to be a member of the club."

It was the first time Porter had been out of the city of Metz, and his ride through the Alsatian countryside was memorable. The trees lining the roadside were straight and tall, unsplintered by war like the ones he recalled in Normandy. Across the hayfields red poppies grew, their blazing color somehow muted to shyness by the tall grass wherein they blossomed. The sun shone. Summer sang.

"Those poppies look like the paper ones the American Legion sells back home on Armistice Day," he yelled as he bounced violently on the back edge of the seat, clinging to Jewel's back like a baby possum.

Jewel was bent over the handlebars, his shirt billowing and cracking like a towel drying on a windy clothesline. "What?" he flung into the sunlight shrieking past their ears as they popped and roared across Alsace. "What'd you say?"

"Nothing," said Porter. "I didn't say anything." His own voice sounded thin and far, far away. "Pour the juice to this baby and let's go!"

He knew this to be the wildest ride of his life, but it also ranked among the most beautiful. He thought of Brewton County, but they were going too fast for homesickness. Only the fragrance of honeysuckle was missing. With increasing confidence, he sat erect, squinting straight ahead, splitting the wind with his face, the force of the cloven air flinging water from his eyes. He was speeding into the unknown but he well knew what was behind him. For the first time in several years and for this brief hiatus on the road to the Grand Duchy of Luxembourg, Porter Osborne was content and serene. Emory University was far away, World War II in Europe was over. Japan still stood ominously between him and safe return home, but on this glorious morning Porter could not seriously believe that he would die there. He felt he just might not ever die. His heart sang with the wind. In the sun.

> "'The lark's on the wing,
> The snail's on the thorn.
> Morning's at seven,
> The hillside's dew-pearled,'" he said.

"What'd you say?" bellowed Jewel.
"Nothing. I didn't say anything."

Luxembourg was thriving, seemed busier, cleaner, brighter, and more alive than Metz. For a few minutes after he dismounted the motorcycle, Porter felt that the earth was vibrating.

"My back hurts," he said.

"Yeah," responded Jewel. He looked critically at his passenger. "You may piss blood for awhile. Skinny as you are, your kidneys take a hell of a jolting on one of these things. Don't worry."

"Not till the blood comes. Right?"

Jewel shrugged, one leg stiffly extended to support his machine. "You see that cafe right over yonder on the other side of the square? Right next to that shop says Antiques? Meet me there," he looked at his watch, "at six o'clock this evening."

"What?" expostulated Porter. "You intend to leave me all alone in this strange city?"

"You ain't alone. There's thousands of people here."

"You know what I mean. Where are you going?"

"I got to see a man about a dog."

"For what?" demanded Porter.

"His bitch had a new litter and he promised me a puppy."

"A likely story, Sherman Roger Jewel. I wasn't born yesterday. What are you up to?"

"Ask me no questions, I'll tell you no lies. You know, even for a brand-new member of the 'don't-give-a-shit' club, you're mighty tight-assed. Relax. See you at six. If I'm late, wait. I'll be back to get you." He gunned his motor, balanced expertly and was gone.

Illinois was imprinted on Porter's consciousness as a harsh land of black soil and ice, Normandy as a devastated war-scape of tents and shelled villages, Metz as a maze of cobblestones and gray buildings. His one day in Luxembourg stamped itself in his memory as a midsummer medley of flowing water, bright flowers, and gingerbread architecture; a city filled with light, beckoning to strangers with welcome and warmth. He fingered the horde of French francs he had saved from all his paychecks since Farbecker disappeared and resolved to do some serious shopping. Just as soon as he explored this delightful town, visited the palace of the Grand Duchess, dropped by the USO, sat outside at one of the sidewalk tables to eat some of the tiny mysterious pastries he had never seen before.

He was on his own, free of directional pull from any companion, moving wherever he wished at the whim of no one but himself. Toward noon, the streets became thronged with GI's pouring in by truck loads on one-day passes, roaming in groups like school children on a field trip, inquisitive about new surroundings but insulated by the compulsion to flock with familiar companions and prate of things they knew. Porter wove his aimless way through and around them, deciding that he was the only solitary visitor in all of Luxembourg. He was alone, unknown, unheeded. It was his day and he floated through it.

He did his shopping in one of the antique shops, walked out with barely the price of a meal in his pocket, carrying only two purchases, both of which fit quite neatly in one small bag.

He had begun his shopping with purpose. His mother, with VE Day safely and triumphantly behind her, casting around for material to fill her letters other than running accounts of her prayer life that from basic training at Camp Grant up until the present had focused on

Porter's safe return, had made a request. She wrote that she wanted from France a fan, a fancy fan, one that opened and closed with a snap, one preferably with a little lace on it; if he happened to run across one somewhere in a shop; if it was not too much trouble, keeping in mind, of course, that it was really of no importance whatever compared to his own safe return to the arms of his loved ones. The color of the fan did not really matter, but black would go with anything. He really should not go to too much trouble. Porter had considered the infrequency of his mother's demands for material return from him in contrast to her petitions for moral and spiritual decorum, had assessed how deficient he would appear if called upon for an accounting of the latter, and had scoured every shop he could find in Metz for a folding French fan. He had vowed that he would get one if it harelipped hell and half of Georgia. He had even enlisted Rosen's help but had found nothing.

In Luxembourg, he discovered an entire display in the window of an antique shop. There were at least a dozen lovely fans there, opened wide like resting moths. In the middle of them was exactly the one his mother wanted. The saleslady handed it to him for inspection. It had some weight to it and hefted comfortably in his hand when closed. The lady outlined its virtues. The wood, he must realize, was ebony. The design stenciled on it was real gold, the material was heavy black silk, the two-inch edging of black lace was handmade, the red roses embroidered in garland across the black silk were also done by hand. Ah, such elegance. Such, how you say, art. *M'sieu* was obviously a young man of taste; he must already know that one did not find embroidery or lace like that any more. *M'sieu* should note the fineness of the stitching, the detailed patterns of the lace. Women of today had not the patience or the eyesight to produce such fine work; indeed it was reputed that many of the old ones had gone, how you say, blind in their devotion to perfection. Ah, yes, it was true. She herself had known in her childhood such an old lace maker, the grandmother of her friend, and she could distinguish only light and had to be led everywhere by hand. Did *M'sieu* desire to purchase this lovely fan?

M'sieu definitely did. He did not even bother to dicker, to request *le dernier prix*. Porter Osborne, Jr., thought that fan the loveliest, most feminine object he had ever beheld; it became a lamb of atonement that beggared comparison. He was delighted to buy it on the spot and quelled the impulse to explain to the saleslady that eye strain did not produce cataracts.

He did, however, during the friendly cooing that resulted from his purchase spy another object in the lady's shop.

"Could I please, *s'il vous plaît, madame*, see that piece of ivory? *Comment vous dites, ivoire?*"

"Ah, *m'sieu*, like I say, you haf ze good taste. You walk first time into my shop and, *alors*, you select, *tout de suite*, two of ze best pieces. Is not so old as ze fan, but look at ze work, ze detail."

"*Ah, oui, madame*. Did the old booger who carved this go stone blind, too?"

"*Pardon, m'sieu?*"

"*Rein, madame*. It is lovely. But I am sure it is *trop cher* for a soldier's pocketbook. *Merci beaucoup*."

He made a gesture of return.

"*Un moment, m'sieu*. On zis piece ze price is not *fixe*. Let us talk."

Back and forth they went. Porter's palms grew clammy. Finally he gave a shrug, calculated that madame had announced her bottom limit, and made the purchase. While she prattled about what a good deal he had made, what a generous soul she was to release it for such a pittance, her misgivings that her good business judgment had been overbalanced by the charm of the young American soldier, but, *enfin*, how much all of Europe owed to *les Etats Unis* and in the long run money did not matter, Porter gazed raptly at his new treasure. It was an oval block of ivory with the head of a gorgeous woman carved in full relief, every feature — the eyes, the nose, the lips, each strand of hair — detailed in minute perfection. It was fashioned as a brooch with a pin on the back but had no setting or rim of gold to deflect attention from the simple beauty of the carving itself. He delivered it with reluctance to madame for wrapping in tissue and they made their farewells with much bowing and smiling and mutually flattering sentence fragments.

In late afternoon, his pulse recovered from the excitement engendered by unanticipated acquisition, feeling now a smidgen of guilt over the heedless and profligate depletion of his cash, he was strolling the crowded sidewalks of the grand square when he identified three familiar figures. They were nurses from his Operating Room, smartly attired in their dress uniforms, a real credit to the United States Army, he thought. He stepped deliberately in their path and saluted with pride. From their surprised welcome, one would have thought it had been weeks since they had seen him instead of the day before.

"Why, hello, Osborne. What are you doing here?" said Lt. Johanna Bordillon.

"Osborne! I didn't think we'd see a soul we knew in Luxembourg. What a coincidence. What a small world. What are you doing? What's going on in your life?" Lt. Fitzgerald chattered like a girl on Peachtree Street.

"My God, if it isn't Ozzy," exclaimed Lt. Dalrymple. Porter winced but forbore comment.

"What have you got in your sack?" inquired Lt. Dalrymple.

"All my worldly goods, ladies. In one afternoon I've spent every dime I'd saved in seven months."

"Oh, show us what you bought."

Porter was not unwilling to display his purchases to these Americans, anticipating with hope their approval.

"What a lovely fan! Look at the embroidery; look at that lace! It's absolutely stunning."

"I like the frame, too. That looks like twenty-four carat gold leaf. You made a nice selection, Osborne. It is for your mother? I'm sure she will love it."

Porter's chest expanded.

"It is very pretty," contributed Lt. Dalrymple, "but it looks expensive. How much did you pay for it?" Porter had hoped for that crucial but delicate question, the final indication of his purchasing skills.

"A thousand francs, Miss Dalrymple. It's an antique."

"One thousand francs? That is twenty dollars." She thrust the fan back into his hands. "My God, Ozzy, for that you could have bought an electric one!"

Porter directed a startled glance at Johanna Bordillon, who winked, grinned, and said their word. The four of them laughed on the sidewalk of Luxembourg City.

"I am curious, Osborne. The fan is for your mother. Who is this exquisite ivory brooch for?"

Porter gave a deep breath, "For me."

"For you?"

"Yes, ma'am. I have a souvenir from Normandy, that figurine named Mignonne. Remember? Then I have Mephistopheles from Metz. Y'all didn't see him, but he is the very devil. Now, in Luxembourg, I have bought this beautiful ivory woman and she will be my souvenir from all of Europe. When I go marching home."

"And what will you do with her?"

"I'll give her to the girl I marry. To wear at her bosom." He paused. "For me."

The phrase triggered a train of thought. "Have any of you ever heard Browning's 'My Last Duchess'? I'd be happy to recite it for you if you have time. And if you'd pay for the pastries. I'm broke."

"We're in a big hurry, Osborne. Some other time," said Fitzgerald.

"That is right. We have some e-shopping to do ourselves and must not miss our ride back to Metz. That would be a disaster," added Dalrymple.

Porter looked at Bordillon. "*Merde?*" he inquired.

She raised one eyebrow. "No, not *merde*, Porter Osborne. Just *au 'voir*. It will be a lucky girl who wears that brooch."

Porter had not gone twenty yards away from the nurses before he heard an unfamiliar voice call to him by a very familiar name, an evocative name that was riveting.

"Hey, Sambo! Sambo! Porter Osborne! Wait a minute."

It took him only a few seconds to identify the tall soldier hailing him. A certain willowy cant of the long limbs, a little priss in the walk, a hint of posturing, was as much recall as the swarthy pock-marked face and told Porter that this was Lawson Littleton. He remembered him as a Willingham University student a year behind him in college. He was the only child of a lumber baron in a small south Georgia town and had been an enthusiastic member of the Phi Delta Theta fraternity. He had been impressed with clothes, money, and social status and his conversational skills had been honed on gossip. Porter was a KA, had a circle of friends that did not include many Phi Delta Thetas, and had been only peripherally aware of Lawson Littleton, remembering him now as something of a dilettante, practiced and enviably graceful on the dance floor but boringly egotistical when talking. Lawson had always acquired a date for social functions but rarely the same one twice.

He was the not unusual end-product of certain small town influences that made him stand out from the rumpled, untidy, frequently unwashed herd of small boys and doomed him to be banished to girl-games throughout grammar school. By the time such a person attained adolescence, he either turned "wild," wrecking cars, flunking classes, and drinking liquor, or he continued sedately with his music lessons and was acknowledged in the community to have "tendencies," a condition that caused bluntly-spoken older men gathered on Saturdays over chewing tobacco, checkers, and memories, men who had known his ancestors for generations, to proclaim with gruff kindness, "Nothing wrong with that boy one piece of pussy wouldn't cure."

Porter had assumed at Willingham that Lawson Littleton had tendencies, was probably even seeking the universal cure, but had dismissed him as a bore. He had not been called Sambo for months and months, however, and the sound of that childhood and college nickname ringing across the square in Luxembourg produced a rush of nostalgia.

"Littleton! Lawson Littleton! Boy, am I glad to see you!"

"I've run into a lot of Willingham guys since I've been in the service and you're the first one to say that. In fact, a few didn't even remember who I was. As small as Willingham is, can you imagine forgetting any person who went there the same time you did?"

"Maybe it's the fact that you're a staff sergeant. Those stripes nearly threw me off for a minute. I'd have figured you'd be a commissioned officer. What are you doing in Luxembourg?"

"I've been in Patton's Army, but I've got in so much combat time that I'm headed home."

"You've been in combat? With Patton?"

"Bet your sweet ass. Italy. Southern France. Bastogne. All the way to Germany."

"Gosh, Lawson, you've no idea how I admire you for that. I've whiled away my days in the ETO tucked safely away in the Operating Room of a general hospital."

"Aw, shit, Sambo, get the stars out of your eyes. I went where I was told and so did you. I haven't been any damn fool hero or won any Purple Heart or anything dumb like that. I've got too much sense. First thing I learned when they put me in Quartermaster was to look after little old me. Course, I learned PDQ that sometimes that means looking after certain strategic officers if you want to get rank and position. Hell, I see you're a sergeant. You know what I mean."

"Maybe." Porter changed the subject. "Congratulations on going home. We're on alert to go to the Pacific. At least I think so. You know how rumors are."

"Have you run into any more Willingham fellows? Do you hear from any of them?"

"Not a one. You remember E. V. Derrick? He's finishing up med school at Emory. I guess. He doesn't write. And Deacon Chauncy. He's a German POW. Or at least he was. You know that sonbitch conned me into writing letters to him regularly while he was in Stalag XIV and now that he's stateside and I need the letters, do you think I hear from him? Not a word. I'm going to kick his ass if I ever see him again."

Littleton shrugged. "Be easy on all vets. 'Post war readjustment' is the magic catch word now. Don't you read the *Stars and Stripes*?"

"That's a bunch of bullshit. Nobody better try post-war read-justment on me. Assuming, of course, that I ever get back to Georgia. I'll readjust myself so quick it'll make your head swim."

"Wake up and smell the coffee, Sambo. I'm going to ride post-war readjustment for everything it's worth. They owe it to me."

"Who?"

"All those fuckers who stayed in the States, by God. I'm going to fake a complete nervous breakdown as soon as I get back on American soil, and I'm not going to recover until I get complete and total disability for the rest of my life."

"Lawson Littleton! Be ashamed. That's crooked."

"You don't for a moment imagine that I'm going back to Camilla, Georgia, and work for a living, do you?"

"But, Lawson, that's not right. You're shitting me."

"You know what the Eleventh Commandment is, don't you, Sambo? 'Thou shalt not get caught.' I've broken all the others, but I've never broken number Eleven, and I shit you not. What's in that bag you're clutching?"

"A couple of souvenirs I picked up in an antique shop, that's all. A fan for my mother. An ivory pin."

"Antiques! I just adore antiques. I've gotten to be a connoisseur. I've sent home some simply fabulous pieces. Do you mind if I see?"

Porter reluctantly complied.

"Now this fan isn't bad at all; you landed on your feet there. For your mother, you say? She'll love it." He unrolled the ivory lady from the tissue and balanced it on his palm. "Now this is truly a marvelous little find here. I've sent home a few ivories that were lying around waiting to be liberated, and none of them is more finely carved than this. I'll take this off your hands for what you paid for it and I haven't even asked the price."

"No, thanks, Lawson. She's not for sale."

"Pity. Oh, well, I can't have everything I see that I want. Who's it for?"

Porter fidgeted a little. "Me."

Lawson leveled a glance at him. "You know, Sambo, I'm decid-ing there are depths to you I never realized in college. These two pieces are really quite good. You should have had my opportunities."

"Really?"

"Yes. Part of my duties whenever we occupied a town was securing quarters for the officers, and that gave me the perfect entree into the finest homes in France and Germany. Particularly Germany. It was easy as falling off a log to requisition things ostensibly for use by the CO and hand over a fake receipt. I've sent home six complete sets of sterling flatware that are so old and heavy they make you drool, and two silver services."

Porter was too aghast to comment.

"Of course, I had to slip a few things to the captain in charge of censorship and mail inspection, but he didn't have the background to really appreciate anything." He looked at his watch. "I've got to toddle along and catch my driver. Have to be in Strasbourg by dark. Good to run into you. Wish I had more time; I think I wouldn't mind doing you. Bye, now, Sambo. I'm off for post-war readjustment."

Porter turned up the hill with his package. "'Doing me'? What in the hell did he mean by that?" He shrugged. "That snobbish sonbitch is sorry as hell and a piss poor representative for the United States." He shivered. "That's not going to be a fake nervous breakdown Lawson Littleton has; he'll be lucky if he ever works his way off the locked ward."

He was prompt for his rendezvous with Sherman Jewel, spent the last of his money on chocolate and flaky little tarts, considered that Lawson Littleton would be a perfect choice to play Dorian Gray if anyone ever made the movie, and then dismissed him from his mind. He began to fret when an hour had passed. How would he manage to get back to Metz without Jewel? What would he do for money in a strange town? What would Crowder do to him if he was AWOL?

By the time Jewel appeared, Porter's exasperation was replaced by relief.

"Where in the hell have you been? I was about to decide you'd fallen off that motorcycle and broken your damn neck."

"Not a chance. I'm here, ain't I?"

"One hour and a half after you told me to meet you. What happened?"

"Those damn puppies didn't have their eyes open yet. Let's go inside and eat. I'm starved."

"I'm broke."

"I'm not. I'll loan you the price of a meal. I know they ain't got no steak, but let's go see what they can put out in the way of chicken."

The waiter assured them that he did indeed have *le bouef-tik* and they fell upon it ravenously.

"Jewel, this is the best steak I ever put in my mouth, and what a slab of it he brought us."

"It's damn good, all right. Real tender. But it sure is dark."

"That's the sauce he's cooked it in. You know how the French are, and Luxenbourg seems mostly French."

Sherman Jewel's jaws were poked out and packed. "Good potatoes, too. Liquor ain't bad. Called mirabelle—made from them yellow plums. How come you ain't drinking?"

"I just haven't been able to get back around to it since we got off that forty-and-eight, Sherman. You're the expert on dogs, but I don't want any more hair of the one that bit me."

"Get us a dessert."

"I'm full. Aren't you?"

"Yep, but I don't want to leave this town till right at dusk dark when the MP's are patrolling the honkey-tonks. Order a dessert. I'm going to the crapper."

Talking to the waiter about desserts, Porter essayed to compliment him on the meal and to try out his French.

"*Le boeuf-steak, c'est très bon.*"

"*Merci, m'sieu.*"

"*C'etait si grand il etait une vache très grande, n'est-ce-pas?*"

"*Pas vache, m'sieu.*"

"*Pardon?*"

"*Pas vache. Cheval.*"

"*Cheval?*"

"*Oui, bickity, bickity, bickity, bick.*"

"*Mon dieu.*"

Sherman Jewel resumed his seat. "What'd he say?"

"Nothing."

"Nothing? I heard him talking and you jabbering at him in French."

"He was just saying the dessert would be a few minutes."

"Oh. I'll never get used to these johns over here, Osborne. This one ain't nothing but a trough with water running through it and two concrete footprints to hunker on. They 'sposed to be so civilized in Europe and their crappers ain't as good as a plain old Georgia privy. And what happens if you get too old to squat? Or if you miss the trough?"

"Shut up till we finish eating, will you, and thank God they have water running through the trough. Why are we dodging the MP's?"

"Cause I'm not sure I can outrun 'em on this new motorcycle. It's got a skip and I haven't really opened it up yet."

"Dammit, Jewel, you're mixed up in something crooked. What is it?"

"I ain't no crook. We got more motorcycles and Jeeps across Europe than we'll ever need and nobody misses one now and then. I got a few friends who liberate them and then I work on them, even repaint them, and we sell 'em to the French. I'm making a heap of money, but I ain't no crook."

"Sherman, you remember Z and what happened to her. You'll get caught and they'll put you under the jail."

"Naw, I won't get caught. I'm wise to 'em monitoring money every GI sends home. I go to the APO in Nancy or Luxembourg or Strasbourg or Rheims when I've got a wad saved up and send it back from a different place every time."

"So? They'll still watch you. They'll check those APO records sooner or later and you'll be in Leavenworth."

"Let 'em check. I'm sending money orders home from Daniel D. Farbecker. I'm signing with my left hand like Kostas, and ain't no lazy clerk yet asked to see my dog tags. No way they can catch me; they haven't even caught Farbecker yet."

"But, Jewel, you dumbass, they'll trace it to your home town and your family."

"Not mine. Farbecker's maybe, but not Sherman Roger Jewel. Those money orders go to Mrs. Dannie Mae Farbecker, General Delivery, Jasper, Georgia. That's fifty miles from my home town and we don't know a soul there."

"Who's cashing the money orders?"

"Ask me no questions and I'll tell you no lies. But when this Johnny goes marching home, he's going to have a gollywhopper of a nest egg to start a business with."

"I guess it's better than having tendencies and stealing silver from German women, but I still think it's crooked."

"Goddammit, Osborne, shut your self-righteous mouth. I keep telling you I ain't no crook. For somebody who doesn't give a shit, your ass is so tight it could crochet bob-wire."

"Barbed," Porter corrected. "Not bob."

"Oh shit. At any rate, haul it up and let's get moving."

"Crochet?" said Porter, but he spoke to himself.

The moon was full and the countryside radiant on their ride back to Metz. The landscape was all dark black and bright silver. Porter could not distinguish the red of the poppies but he smelled the fragrance of the curing hay. It again was one of the wildest rides of his life, remained one of the most beautiful.

When he finally reached his cot and fell asleep, he had a vivid dream. His wood carving of Mephistopheles, goat-eyed and smiling, crouched protectively over its lute which had mysteriously turned to sterling silver. It spoke softly, soothingly, "I ain't no crook, Porter Osborne. Go back to sleep." Across the pedestal, beneath the name of Rosen, was carved the number eleven.

*"And he finds his God forgotten, and he seeks
no more a sign . . ."*

41   On August 6, the Bomb dropped. Later there
would be details of the human minds and hands involved in that
project. On August 6, however, it was a manifestation of the super-
natural: so awesome, so unexpected, so magnificent, so terrible that it
challenged credulity.

"I don't believe it."

"It's on the radio."

"Just one bomb? Did all that? They're shitting us."

"Where is Hiroshima?"

"They told us at Willingham in physics class that if anybody ever
learned to split the atom it would trigger a chain reaction that would
destroy the universe. I think they're exaggerating."

"I would imagine that in Hiroshima, to all intents and purposes,
the universe is destroyed."

"Maybe now we'll get to go home."

"I still don't believe it."

"Y'all are over my head. I ain't myself never yet understood
none of that shit about atoms nohow. I still got my money on
MacArthur."

"Goddammit, where is Hiroshima?"

"It's in Japan, you dumb fucker. That's east of Pearl Harbor, and
four years ago nobody knew where that was. Now it's pay-back time."

Porter waited. He worked and listened and struggled to comprehend, but these activities seemed accomplished in slow motion,
passive and acquiescent. Waiting became an active process, demanding
fierce energy and the passion of all his hours. On August 8 the
Russians declared war on Japan.

"BFD. Who needs them?"

"Nobody. It's a political move so they'll have an excuse to grab a chunk of China or even some Japanese islands when this is over."

"You're right. Those Communists are a greedy, self-serving lot. The Russians are looking to feather their own nests when this is over."

"It ain't over, I keep telling y'all. You ain't heerd nothing out'n the Japs, have ya? I still say keep your eye on MacArthur and don't count none of them other eggs twell they hatch."

Porter Osborne, Jr., waited. Aloof. Suspended.

On August 9, it happened again. This time it was not magic. The bomb did not, after all, fall unpredictably from heaven to stun and dazzle mankind with the display of some natural cataclysm; everyone realized it was emitted with purpose from the belly of a B-29 airplane flying on course high between heaven and earth. It was the end product of mind-staggering and intermeshing human endeavor that encompassed the theory of physicists, the manufacture of plutonium, navigational use of azimuths and grids, the discipline instilled at all levels into American servicemen, the grave and soul-searching decision of political leaders. Nagasaki did not become the household word that Hiroshima did, but it was no less devastated.

"Hot damn! Harry did it again!"

"We're on a roll! Why don't they hit Tokyo?"

"How many of them bombs have we got?"

"Anybody heard anything out of the Japs?"

"Anybody heerd anything out'n MacArthur? Where's he at?"

Porter brushed away the fleeting temptation to tell Crowder that MacArthur might well be behind the 'at'. He waited.

On August 14 the news flew across the radio waves of the world that Japan had surrendered and had done so unconditionally. Porter Osborne received the news from others but always felt that he had known it first. The knowledge seeped from his bones, where it had lain for a week in dormant certainty, into his racing, exultant blood and he rejoiced. He would never go to the South Pacific; he would not be required to die on a Japanese beach; he had all of his life before him still; he would see Brewton County, Georgia, once more and he would never leave it again.

"By God, it's over."

"I can't believe it."

"When do you reckon they'll let us out of this fucking Army?"

"When our turn comes. They're giving everbody points. They calculate them on how long you've been in and how long in the ETO."

"There's a sonnet by Millay that goes,

     'Thou famished grave, I will not fill thee yet,
     Roar though thou dost, I am too happy here;
     Gnaw thine own sides, fast on; I have no fear
     Of thy dark project, but my heart is set
     On living—I have heroes to beget
     Before I die; I will not come anear
     Thy dismal jaws for many a splendid year.'"

"Oh, hush, Osborne. This is no time for personalized and romantic introspection."

"Kiss my ass, Kostas. You're the bigot who didn't trust Harry Truman."

"I bet y'all one thing. I bet they put MacArthur in charge of everthing now. Cream will rise, you know."

Porter jerked his head around. "My grandmother used to say that, Sgt. Crowder."

"So did mine, Sgt. Osborne, so did mine. Effen anybody wants to go to town and git a beer, I'll set everbody up. But I'm putting you on notice, I ain't buying nothing else. I got the points and God knows I've put in the time. I'll probly be the first one in this whole outfit gits orders cut for home and I feel like celebrating. Y'all by and large been a pretty good crew to work with and I want to set you up, but I ain't paying for no sissified, candy-assed, limber-dicking wine." Oliver Crowder gave a great sniff and a sad smile.

"I keep telling you about Southerners."

"Watch it, asshole."

"Arkansas is still in the South, isn't it?"

Even Lucetti went along on Crowder's celebration. He and Porter sat at one of the tables but did not order drinks.

"You know, Lucetti, it's going to be good to get home and settle back in for the while we have left on this earth, to a place that hasn't changed. Yet."

"Yet? What do you mean?"

"Nothing in America will ever be the same again. Probably not anywhere in the whole world. Change may come gradually in some places, but it's coming."

"Why?"

"Because of Pearl Harbor. That was the turning point. It sure changed my life."

"Yes." said Kostas. "Everybody you talk to can tell you exactly where he was and what he was doing when he heard of Pearl Harbor.

It shook the world. You're right. When all the fallout settles and is identified, Pearl Harbor will be as signal an historical event as the battles of Agincourt and Lepanto."

"I can't get all those dead people in Hiroshima and Nagasaki off my mind," mused Lucetti. "Was it right? Was it worth it?"

Porter's voice was tart. "What are you talking about? They were fighting, weren't they? They started it, didn't they? The people on the Arizona couldn't help it that they hadn't bunched up a bigger crowd of helpless sailors for them to slaughter and drown, could they? How many lives have been saved by Harry Truman deciding to cut the head off the snake instead of getting a piece at a time of the tail by all that island hopping? Including my life and your life, Lucetti. Wake up and smell the coffee. Of course it's right. Of course it's worth it. It saved both our lives."

"They were civilians. It was terrible. 'He who would save his life must lose it.' I think the world will remember Hiroshima, and I think the world will be changed because of it."

"Get that Christ-bitten fucker to drink a beer, Osborne. It'll do him whole bunches of good."

"Shut up, Jewel, and don't call him that."

"How come you defending him, Osborne? You don't buy into that shit any more'n I do. You don't believe all that crap."

"Maybe not, but I believe he believes it and he's entitled to. I've watched him all over the ETO, and he lives it. Don't call him 'Christ-bitten'."

"You ain't been the same since you made sergeant, Tight-ass. Don't tell me what to do. I'll call him what I please."

"Forget it," said Lucetti. "'Blessed are you when men revile you and persecute you for My name's sake.'"

"Aw, come on now, Lucetti," groaned Porter. "Now you're hiding behind Scripture. We were talking about nuclear fission, and to tell you the truth, I'm more comfortable with mushroom-shaped clouds than I am those damn Beatitudes. They're totally incomprehensible and illogical."

"Maybe that's why so many Southerners are Baptist," said Stevens Kostas. "Tell me, Lucetti: not nearly so many people were killed by the atomic bomb as by the gas ovens of the Nazis. They're calling that the Holocaust, you know. Do you think that has changed the world?"

"I'll answer that," said Porter. "It will. As soon as the dust settles and we have time to think about it, I'll guarantee you it will change the world. I think you can tell when something is that important because it's so big and so unimaginable that your mind can't take it in at first. Just think—we've lived, as young as we are, through three historical events that have changed forever the world as we knew it: Pearl Harbor, Hiroshima, and the Holocaust."

"Make that four," said Lucetti.

"Four?"

"Yes. Include the Resurrection. It's so big and unimaginable your mind can't take it in at first."

"Oh, come on, Lucetti. I'm talking about events that have happened in our lifetime."

"So am I. In every generation. Over and over."

"Goddammit, shut up, for Christ's sake!" said Sherman Jewel. "We're here because Crowder's going home and we aren't going to be far behind. Bomb the Japs. Fuck the Jews. Let 'em all die and drink some beer!"

"Did you know I'm Jewish?" asked Levek.

"No. But I can't help it. And neither, by God, can you. Why don't you tell somebody who gives a good goddam what church you go to and drink another beer?"

"You talk like your old man might have belonged to the Klan," ventured Porter.

"You're fucking aye. You want to get pious about that?" Jewel's freckles were light tan spots standing out against the flaming scarlet of his face. "You know something else? My mama's in the Klan, too, and all her brothers. Don't you talk like it's something to be ashamed of. Soon's I get home we're going to tend to the Catholics and niggers just like we did the Germans and Japs."

"I hope the Klan never gets the atomic bomb," said Stevens Kostas lightly.

"I want all of you fellows from up north and out west to notice that I'm leaving," said Lucetti. "Right now. Believing in Jesus Christ is not something to be ashamed of either, Jewel, and sooner or later we all have to make a stand. Osborne, are you coming with me?"

"No," said Porter. "Not so long as Levek stays. I'll stick by him, thanks. We 'also serve who only stand and wait,' and I want Levek to realize that nobody in Georgia takes the damn Klan seriously any more, that it doesn't amount to a fart in a whirlwind. Most of us hate the Klan."

"We never come out here to get serious," interposed Oliver Crowder. "Jewel is right. We come to drink beer cause I'm going home.

Nobody hates nobody no more. Nowhere. Everbody have another beer and get your hackles down. Thanks for coming, Lucetti. We'll see you around. And don't you worry none; ain't nothing wrong with being a Catholic."

"He's not a Catholic," Porter corrected as Lucetti left. "He's Methodist."

Oliver Crowder emitted a long lugubrious sigh and bunched his eyebrows. "Makes no difference. We might not all have come from the same place, Osborne, but way I look at it, we all go to the same place on down the line, and there's more'n one road to git you there. Right now all I can think of is Arkansas. Have a beer."

Jewel leaned down the table. "From what I've seen since I been in this man's Army, Osborne, Christianity ain't going to wind up being more'n a fart in a whirlwind either, smart ass."

Porter only half heard him. He turned to Kostas and mouthed, "Resurrection? I can't believe Lucetti said that."

"He said it. I heard him."

"In our lifetime? Fascinating premise."

"What's fascinating is what you people from the South can talk yourselves into believing."

"What do you mean?"

"Nothing is ever going to change."

"Why?"

"Because people are not going to change. That's why. Look at Jewel."

Porter thought a long moment before he replied. "Oh, yes, we are, Stevens Peter Kostas. We may not want to change, but sure as gun's iron we're going to. Just you wait and see."

"We're going to be sorry we dropped that bomb."

"Never! It freed me. Oppression is dead. The bomb has freed the world."

"I just hope it has not enslaved the world."

"I'm like Crowder and Jewel now, Kostas. Quit being so serious and drink some beer. I think I'll break down and have one myself. Hurrah for Harry Truman! I'm going home, too. Sooner now than later."

On the way back to the hospital, Porter and Kostas encountered Michelle out for a stroll. She was on the arm of a young Frenchman probably a few years her senior and possibly half her size. Porter hailed her as naturally and enthusiastically as he had the nurses in Luxembourg. Apparently she did not hear him.

"Hey, Kostas, that's Michelle going yonder, the one I told you about who works in the OR. She's a great gal. We're big buddies. Come meet her."

He raced to overtake the couple, planted himself squarely in their path, and with an ebullient grin presented himself.

"*Bonjour, Michelle. Bonne chance, oui?* Is this your husband? *Votre mari?*"

He held out his hand to the man. "I'm Porter Osborne, a friend of Michelle's where she works. Glad to meet you."

Michelle shrank against her companion. Her face flushed. Her tone was formal, rejecting. "*M'sieu,*" she said frigidly.

Porter's mouth gaped, his extended hand remained unclasped. The Frenchman gazed with obvious anger at Michelle and then turned his gaze on Porter.

"*Va t'en,*" he hissed. The pair stepped around him and moved away. Porter watched them disappear into the crowd. One time only Michelle looked back but her glance betrayed neither recognition nor welcome.

"I'll just be goddammed," said Porter. "What's come over her? What's the matter with him? Have I violated some taboo of French culture I don't know about? What's going on to make them treat me like that? I've been nice as everything to that girl, and there's no reason for her husband to insult me."

Kostas shrugged. "Maybe you insulted him. Who knows? Maybe they don't know you have the atomic bomb. I told you people never change. Don't worry about it. They're the ones with the problem."

"Well, I'm going to find out. Tomorrow. First thing when she shows up for work."

Porter never found out. Michelle did not return to work.

He was scrubbing instruments vigorously a few days later when he mused, "I'm going to miss Metz. A lot has happened since I came here. Roosevelt died. VE Day. Churchill got beat. Hitler committed suicide. We rescued what Jews he had missed. Truman dropped the bomb and we had V-J Day. It has to be soon I'll be going home."

He rinsed a handful of hemostats.

"I've learned a lot. I've sure learned my grandmother is right about Osborne men drinking. I've been promoted twice since we've been here, which is more than anybody in the outfit but Capt. Nielson has done. And I was the cause of that indirectly."

He thought of Katie Albert. He thought of Bettie. Of Michelle.

"One thing's for sure and certain. I have certainly joined the ranks of those who don't understand women."

He shivered. "I also don't understand religion. I've broken the Seventh Commandment over and over since I've been in this town. I've lied, stolen, and worshipped other gods. I've violated every one of the Big Ten, if you get right down to it. But yet I don't feel like a sinner. Somehow or other I still feel like I'm special in God's sight." He spread a tray of Allis clamps on a towel and began drying them. "Maybe it's because I've got my compartments sealed off from each other or maybe it's because I've managed not to break number Eleven. Yet."

He watched Capt. Nielson move industriously through the room. "I'd really like to tell her that she's right, that adultery is a damn sight better than stealing. But, Porter Osborne, you'd better keep your mouth shut. Your life is complicated enough already. Besides, maybe adultery is just another form of stealing. No need to confuse a captain. I don't want to listen to what she'd have to say."

Sgt. Crowder ambled by. Porter called out to him, "Going home next week, Sergeant? Hurrah for Harry Truman! He's going to get all of us there!"

"And many a one grows witless in his quiet room in Hell . . ."

42 nstead of being disassembled and shipped home, the 816th General Hospital was moved from Metz all the way back across France to Rouen, departing a relatively intact Alsatian city with strong Teutonic influences for one that was still mutilated by war and was Norman through and through. Rouen huddled in a curve of the Seine River as it wound to its eventual union with the Atlantic at LeHavre, the river so choked with commerce here that it lacked the romantic intimacy it displayed with the city of Paris nearer its source. Joan of Arc had been martyred in Rouen. A bronze plaque designated a small square of gold tiles set into the pavement as the true and accurate site of her pyre.

The great cathedral that Claude Monet had painted repetitively was a skeleton, impressive and majestic from a distance but unsafe to enter. Its floors were littered with shards of medieval glass, scattered by the indifferent percussion of indiscriminate bombs to glow and wink like abandoned jewels in the twilight of the vaulted nave. Jesus and the Apostles lay in tiny fragments in every color of the rainbow, an eye here, a hand or robe in red or blue there, an impossible jumble protected from vandalism by roped cordons and signs proclaiming *Entrée interdite*. The limestone rims from which the windows had been blasted gaped like eye sockets in an ancient skull. There were winding streets in the old town so narrow that one could almost touch both walls with outstretched fingertips when walking through. The village home of Baudelaire was only a short hike from Rouen.

The men of Normandy had returned from the war and the city was coming slowly alive with the energy of repair. Ruined buildings were being razed, their sites cleared, their bricks and blocks stacked in neat piles against the day of reconstruction; a feeling of hope and cheer was almost palpable. In Normandy in the fall of 1945, Americans were

570

still welcome but men and women of the United States Army were departing, not arriving, and there was a feeling of hope and cheer in the American breast also.

Porter and his mates were frustrated and grumbled frequently. They were chronically annoyed because days and then weeks dragged by without their receiving orders to return home. Their work load at the hospital was too light to keep them occupied; they noted that the majority of the patients coming through for elective surgery on their way back to the States had been in Europe less time than they; Mack and Jack were still their cooks and Spam was still as prevalent on the menu as powdered eggs and dehydrated potatoes; Col. Draughan had apparently abandoned his drive for promotion and now paid little attention to his command. Morale among the enlisted men was low; they were left to their own devices for recreation, they chafed and griped.

Kostas, in Olympian detachment, observed, "We can't go home yet, although we're entitled to, and all the colonel does is sulk in his tent like Achilles. What a war!"

"Well, he's certainly not in that tent alone," Porter contested. "Like Achilles, he's playing with the girls. You Greeks anticipated everything, didn't you?"

"What do you mean, Osborne?"

"Apparently he's trying to screw his way through the entire roster of nurses before the outfit gets sent home."

"Achilles was queer."

"You're shitting me."

"I am not. It's perfectly obvious."

"Well, that's not a condition with which our colonel is burdened. He's trying to get in all the nurses' panties."

"How do you know?"

"The nurses talk to me. It's because I'm a Southern gentleman and was raised with three sisters; I understand woman talk. Also, to be realistic, it may be because I look wormy and completely harmless and they feel safe with me. Anyhow, they tell me things. Col. Draughan hasn't cut much ice in the OR with his campaign. Capt. Nielson is mean as nine-day-old cat shit when somebody messes with her girls. She has connections with the Chief Nurse of the whole ETO, who outranks Col. Draughan, and Capt. Nielson told her nurses they didn't have to put up with any stuff out of him just because he's their CO, but to be discreet for the good of the outfit."

"'Wormy' is strictly a Southern term. You look more like someone who survived Buchenwald. That's why the nurses talk to you." Kostas's tone was too judicious to offend.

"Anyhow, they do. He got the hots for Lt. Fitzgerald back in Metz and she told me she was scared to death of him, that he had ordered her to go with him to a party at his house and help him host it. Seems that was one of his strategies — get some nurse over there as his hostess and then overpower her when everybody else clears out. I tried to tell Lt. Fitzgerald that she had the upper hand, that if it got down to a desperate situation, his old thing would be full of blood and all she'd have to do would be rake it good with those long hard fingernails of hers she's always filing and then run like hell, screaming like a banshee."

"That was poor advice. Seems like that would only make him mad and he really would overpower her."

"That was not poor advice if she'd only had the nerve to follow it. What colonel is going to be able to do anything with his pants down and his tallywhacker gushing blood? And he wouldn't dare report it because everybody would make fun of him if he did. It was good advice." Porter sighed. "But Lt. Fitzgerald wouldn't follow it. I had to rescue her."

"You? Don't make me laugh."

"You remember when the cherries got ripe in Metz? All the guys had picked the trees around the hospital clean as a November cotton stalk and Capt. Smith was issuing orders that we had to quit climbing them, that the cherries belonged to the officers. You remember that. It was about the time he decided we had gotten too uppity after V-E Day and reinstituted saluting on post if we met an officer outdoors."

"I remember that all right. That's when you got the Wafflebacks to line up ten feet apart when we saw him coming and keep him saluting like a robot all the way to lunch every day. Maj. Buster Pierce laughed at him so hard that the saluting order came off the bulletin board after three days. I remember that, but what's it have to do with St. George rescuing a damsel from the dragon? You can wander through a story worse than anybody I ever saw."

"That's because I'm Southern. The cherries were ripe. OK? There were some old, old trees in the backyard of the colonel's house loaded down with those great big pink cherries that were so sweet. Of course, they were off limits, but, Kostas, those cherries were too good for officers. A branch of one of the trees grew out over the colonel's eight-foot garden wall all the way across to the porch outside Ward

Eight. The night of his party, the OR was real quiet. I was on my way back from midnight chow and sneaked out on that porch. I took off my boots and it was easy to coon my way across into the colonel's garden. I was so busy stuffing cherries into my fatigues that I didn't hear anybody coming until it was too late to get back to the hospital porch. All I could do was grab the trunk of the tree and hide."

"Osborne, do you expect me to believe this? Next thing I know you'll tell me it was the colonel and the nurse."

"How'd you know? I haven't told a living soul before. There was a garden seat right at the very foot of the tree, not twenty feet below me, and there they sat and he started putting the moves on her. You never heard such a corny line in your life. A sophomore in Brewton County High School could do better than Col. Draughan. But then he got physical and Fitz started saying, 'Don't do that, sir. Please quit, sir. I'm engaged to be married, sir,' and Col. Draughan was saying, 'For God's sake call me Otto and drop that "sir" business. I've been wanting you for months.'"

"Osborne, I'd have fallen out of that tree."

"Believe me, you wouldn't either."

"What happened?"

"Dammit, I'm coming to that. They actually started a wrestling match. The old sonbitch is strong as a bull, you know. I heard Fitz start crying and that's when I threw a handful of cherries on them."

"You didn't."

"I did. He sat up and said, 'What's that?' but he didn't turn Fitz loose. She said, 'I believe it's cherries,' and he said, 'I know that. But where'd they come from?' and Fitz said 'The tree?' It was a real intelligent exchange down there, I tell you, Steve. I figured I might as well be hung for a sheep as a goat; so I dropped a couple more. I should have been a bombardier, because one of them hit him square on the head. He yelled, 'Somebody's up in this tree!' and turned Fitz loose. Of course, she ran like ninety, and he was hollering for somebody to bring a flashlight and call the guard. The colonel started circling like a dog that's treed a squirrel, and I kept sliding around the trunk so he couldn't see me. Finally he hollered, 'I see you, I see you! Who are you? Give me your name and that's an order!' I was quiet as the grave, and he kept on, 'You can't get down past me. What's your name?' Something came over me and I put on this real deep ghostly voice and said, 'Daniel D. Farbecker, Colonel. Button your fly.' He yelped like a snakebitten fice and ran off about ten feet hollering, 'Guard, Guard! On the double! Bring a light!' It gave me enough time to get back across the wall on my limb and back in the OR without anybody seeing me. I still had a mess of cherries, too."

"My God."

"Next afternoon I saw Lt. Fitzgerald giggling with Lt. Bordillon and asked her if she'd enjoyed the colonel's party and did she get enough cherries to eat. She said, 'Somehow I knew that was you,' and gave me a big smack on the cheek. And that's how I know the colonel's trying to screw his way through the nursing roster. Bordillon and Fitz are keeping a list of the ones he makes it with. They call them 'the Garden Girls,' but he hasn't messed with Fitz anymore."

"Osborne, there's only one reason I believe this unlikely story."

"What's that?"

"It's the only thing I've heard that explains why the colonel had that magnificent cherry tree cut down. Lt. Susan Messenholden is my ward nurse and has become a good friend of mine. You're not the only one with whom the nurses visit. She told me about it."

"She ought to know. She's a charter member of the Garden Girls."

"Osborne, you're awful. I do not understand how you ever got promoted from buck private, let alone how you made it to sergeant."

"It's a simple stairstep process, Yankee boy. I was born into this army as a PFC, I made corporal by lying, and I got to be a sergeant by shaving assholes. I've discovered that in life according to Uncle Sam it's not what you know, it's who you know, and that Eleventh Commandment is very important." He sobered. "Even if it was formulated by someone for whom the First Commandment is 'Look after Number One.' Also, don't forget the Waffleback motto: 'You dick me now, I'll get you with the big one later.'"

"You know, Osborne, as eager as I am to get back home, I'm going to miss the Army."

"You've got dingleberries of the brain. What are you going to miss?"

"This. The interchange that is not only available but unavoidable between guys from all over the country who have different ways of looking at things and most certainly different ways of expressing themselves. I'm going back to Brown to get my degree, and I know before I get there that I won't have any boys from Georgia to talk to."

"Be brave. If you graduate with honors, maybe we can find something for you to do and you can move to Georgia and live. Can you plow a mule or milk a cow?"

"No. Neither can I light a cross. My roots are as deep in Massachusetts as yours are in Georgia."

"I was only teasing, Steve. What are you going to do after you finish college?"

"I don't have the faintest idea yet, but they've got this GI Bill of Rights now and any veteran can go to school free. I figure it'll be a gravy train of a transition period and something will turn up that I want to do."

"You are not by any chance worried about that Hydra called Post-war Readjustment, are you, old buddy?"

"Quit being diversionary. Everyone doesn't have his life laid out in blocks and squares like you do, Osborne. You're going back to finish medical school and settle down in that Brewton County you're forever babbling about, live on the ancestral acres about which you also babble, and raise a dozen little Osbornes."

Porter abandoned any frivolous affect. "I don't know, Steve. I've written to my daddy about this; I'm not at all sure I still want to be a doctor. Ever since I have any recall about wanting to be anything at all when I grew up, I've always wanted to be a doctor; but as the time gets closer for me to go back to Emory, I'm having cold feet and very serious misgivings. I still want to live on the ancestral acres, as you call it, but I'm not at all sure I want to be a doctor anymore."

"For heaven's sake, what changed your mind?"

"The 816th General Hospital and the ETO, that's what. My granddaddy always said familiarity breeds contempt, and I've spent the last eighteen months living day in and day out with this bunch of officers and watching them, and there's nothing about them that makes me want to be a doctor. Look at Draughan, at Smith, at all their underlings. I sure as hell don't want to turn out to be like any of them. I'd always looked up to doctors, but I've been too closely associated with them and seen too many clay feet."

"What about Pierce? Everybody respects him."

"Right. And also Maj. Jim Emmons. But they're what my granddaddy would call the exception that proves the rule. I guess I'm just disillusioned."

"I can't believe you're abandoning a lifetime dream because of a handful of commissioned pricks and fuckups. If you really want to do something well, a negative role model is as valuable as a positive one."

"Now what is that supposed to mean?"

"It means you learn by the mistakes of others as well as by your own mistakes. It means you look at Draughan and Smith and all the others and vow that you're going to be different from them. I can't imagine your not being a doctor, Osborne. What does your father say?"

"He wrote me that I'm a grown man and must make my own decisions, and then immediately wiped out that illusion by saying that a vacancy is coming in the State Legislature next year and I could run for that and then go to law school."

"Law and politics? You?"

"I know it. On top of that, what grown man has his daddy mapping out his life for him? You know, Steve I don't feel like a man inside. I'm twenty-two years old but damned if I feel grown. When does it come?"

"Hey, old buddy, you're not by any chance having your Post-war Readjustment before you even get discharged, are you?"

"I've told you I'm not going to need any Post-war Readjustment. All I need is out; so you kiss my ass, Kostas."

"You see why I'm going to miss the Army? Where else do discussions wind up on such a lofty intellectual plane?"

The hospital they occupied in Rouen was owned by the church and staffed by nuns. It had been operated by the Germans during their occupation of Normandy, but the nuns had been banned from the building then and it had been locked and boarded up since the German evacuation in 1944. The Sisters were delighted to have it reopened and their presence re-established. They were also possessive and territorial, however, and bustled everywhere, making lists of instruments appropriated by the Boche and damage done to the building. They were not involved in patient care, since the patients were all GI's except for a rare civilian emergency, and if the hospital had been busy they would have been officiously underfoot and in the way. As it was, they added atmosphere to the old stone building with its lofty ceilings and reverberating halls, were always politely pleasant in the creaking old elevator, and kept a wary administrative eye on the way in which their brash American benefactors comported themselves. Porter remembered Flossie and her subjugating encounter with Church politics in Massachusetts and was on his best behavior when a nun was anywhere to be seen.

He noted that the hospital personnel who were Catholic tended to regard the Sisters as individual persons, more or less as indifferent to them as they would have been to minor public servants who were sustained by tax dollars. Porter, with his Protestant heritage, had difficulty regarding as mere human beings a group of women who had renounced both sex and money for all eternity and professed themselves to be the Brides of Christ. To him they were as mystifying as Vestal virgins or Druid priestesses, their theology hopelessly skewed and distorted, but their dedication to be revered as a remnant of some archaic culture.

Rouen was imprinted on his memory as a medieval city subservient still to a medieval religion, as manifested by the ruined Cathedral near the river, the hospital filled with flocks of white leghorn nuns on the other side of town, and the spot where the Maid of Orleans had burned delineated in gold halfway between the two. The Americans were interlopers and there was no doubt in his mind that as soon as they left for home, Rouen would revert to its own affairs as though they had never been there.

"I think I'm still learning a lot," he wrote to his father, "but nothing important enough to compartmentalize about. I don't see how they can possibly keep us from coming home more than another week or two at most. I have the points. Be sure I'll let you know."

He was correct about continuing to learn. Kostas and Kragel found a bar they liked near the bombed-out cathedral and pressed him to join them.

"You don't have to drink, Osborne. Come along for the fun of watching the people and really talking to them. Levek and Kelly are going. There aren't any soldiers there. It's a tiny little bar stuck up in an alley at the end of the Street of the Jews."

"The Street of the Jews? What does that mean?"

"Just what it says. It's the street where all the Jews in Rouen live. Or used to live. It's a shambles now."

"I don't believe it. This is France. They didn't have Jewish people herded off to themselves."

"Come see for yourself. The street sign on the corner says *La Rue des Juifs*. What does that mean in Georgia?"

Porter went only once, but the visit marked him. Halfway through the evening a Frenchman who had been nursing a bottle of *vin rouge* in a solitary corner approached their table bearing his bottle and a glass. His suit was neat but shabby, his black tie frayed from frequent knotting, his face furrowed and gray, his eyes a darker gray, devoid of light. His syntax was faultless, his accent piquant.

"Do you young gentlemen mind if an old man joins you? You seem so happy, so friendly with each other, and I have not had opportunity to converse with many Americans in a relaxed way. I should like to share my wine with you. May I intrude? *Garçon, une autre bouteille, s'il vous plaît."*

They made room for him politely and talked of many things. His name was Jacques Bonet, he worked for twenty years in what Americans call City Hall, he lived alone, his job meant everything to him. The conversation rose and fell like the ebb and flow of backwater, drifting without passion or purpose. Mr. Bonet may have had scant opportunity to visit with Americans, but in turn Porter Osborne had not previously met a Frenchman who had the vocabulary and the will to discuss politics or abstractions. He was charmed.

They spoke of Roosevelt, his gifts, his contributions, his death. They contrasted him to Churchill and clucked over the ingratitude of the British electorate who had thrust Clement Atlee on the world as a substitute. When deGaulle's name came up, Porter was discreetly and politely silent. Mr. Bonet touched eloquently for a while on the bravery of the British and American soldiers on V-E Day, then began a cautionary analysis of Josef Stalin and Russia.

"America must contain him," he said, "for he is as perfidious as Hitler. Roosevelt has elevated him to the level of a world leader over the protestations of Churchill, and Truman must now control him. Communism is deadening to civilization and Stalin is an able manipulator of such a system."

Kelly, Kragel, and Levek excused themselves and moved to the bar. Kostas and Osborne remained with Mr. Bonet. Osborne was spellbound in the presence of such intellect—a man of professorial detachment who could discuss world politics in as casual a voice as one might use in a civics class, and yet stimulate him to think.

"Gosh, Mr. Bonet," he said, "you are truly a remarkable man. I haven't heard anyone since my father use words the way you do. *Perfidious* is not one known by many Americans."

This led to a discussion of the importance of words, their usage, the subtleties of their meaning, even their derivation. The Americans managed to hold their own, but the Frenchman led the pack. Somehow they came to the adoption and adaptation of proper names to everyday usage. Porter contributed Mrs. Malaprop, Kostas added Don Quixote, and Mr. Bonet spoke of Rabelais and of a *Monsieur* Chauvin who had been such a fanatical admirer of Napoleon.

"Gosh, Mr. Bonet, I never before heard of anyone being called chauvinistic. You're teaching me a lot. What about *quisling*? That's a word we've seen coined right before our eyes that will probably be a permanent part of the language."

The Frenchman abstractedly took another cigarette from the package of Camels Porter had tossed on the table, tapped it on his thumbnail, and lit it. He had a faraway look in his eyes as he answered.

"Ah, yes. The Quislings. From all over Europe they appear like rats from the woodwork, at least one for every country, and for some countries more. We revel in denouncing and punishing them. But there is no name yet for the sly and secret traitor, the collaborator who sent his neighbors in Rouen to death and has not yet been discovered. I hope to live long enough to contribute such a name to the languages of the world."

He emitted white smoke in a thick cloud from his lower lip, sucked it in twin columns back up his nostrils, and then exhaled it in a blue fog that made his eyes squint. His attitude bespoke the tension and drama of recall, compelled attention. Kostas and Osborne sat in silence waiting, anticipating.

"All my married life I lived in an apartment fourteen blocks up *La Rue des Juifs* from the Cathedral. I was a model husband, then a model father. The people in my neighborhood said I doted too much on my daughters, but they and my wife were everything to me. After the Germans came I was most careful to observe all the new rules. The Germans needed a native who spoke fluent German and was familiar with the local government, the water lines, the tax records, the little details; so I was safe. I was even winkingly excused from wearing the star on my coat, a venerated symbol to my people that was during the occupation reduced to an emblem of shame, a target for unspeakable degradation you two cannot imagine. My wife was required to wear it and I forbade her the streets as much as possible. I did all the grocery shopping; my little girls went nowhere.

"For years we lived daily with caution as our guide; my family in a sense were prisoners in their own home, but at least we lived and we stayed together. After June 6, 1944, there was a great change. The Germans with whom I had worked became tense, hostile. An *ober-sergeant* followed me home one day; I looked down the stairwell as I was unlocking my apartment and saw him staring at the number above the door. They gave me next day the yellow star and commanded that I wear it.

"We received news in the Underground from the radio. We knew that the hour we longed for was approaching; the American and British troops were liberating Normandy. From my position I observed the preparation of the Germans to leave, to evacuate Rouen, to withdraw without fighting. I passed this on to my contact in the Underground and it was relayed to England. From fear for their lives, I took my wife and daughters from our apartment and hid them in the attic of the next building where we had sequestered rations and bedding behind a chimney. Three days later I overheard the Obersergeant, who never comprehended that a native of Rouen understood very well another man's mother tongue, swearing to one of his fellows that the 'damned Jew's bitch and spawn' had fled.

"To use an idiom of yours, I knew my number was up, and I slipped out of the office and disappeared. I joined my wife and daughters in that cramped crawl space and there we lived for three more days and nights. I would slip out after midnight to empty the waste bucket and meet one of my fellows from the Underground."

Mr. Bonet drained his wine glass and Porter refilled it. Silently. Waiting.

"Finally the day came — the tanks, the automobiles, the trucks. All day and half the night the city was loud with the noise of the Germans leaving. To be quite honest, they did it properly, without senseless destruction and vandalism. They are a very disciplined people. There was no doubt. They were gone.

"My friend notified headquarters in England. I moved my wife and little Rachel and Sara back to our apartment. I carried them for a stroll in the afternoon sunlight, boldly, openly on the street. That evening we dined and later sang at table. One of the songs was 'God Bless America.' When the girls were in bed, I told my wife that now a normal life was again possible.

"I told her that since I could now walk down the street like a free man again and not worry about their safety, I was going to the corner for a package of cigarettes and I would return in thirty minutes. I came to this very bar, and, young people, I strolled here! I was in no hurry. I smelled the flowers in the night; I did not look over my shoulder in fear; my heart was content.

"The bar was crowded; it seemed that every man in the neighborhood had simultaneous need for a pack of cigarettes. We laughed, we joked, we asked after absent friends. We sipped a little wine.

"Suddenly the air raid sirens sounded and all the lights went out. Everywhere. I knew that my Judith and the girls would be afraid; so I ran outside to go to them. Then the planes came, low and fast, wave after wave. Have you ever witnessed precision bombing? The entire world erupted. One moment everything was pitch black and then, poof, there were explosions and fires and colors everywhere. It was magnificent! In a terrible way, my God, it was beautiful! You should have seen the Cathedral, back-lit and glowing, the monument to hundreds of years of human aspirations, explode before your eyes in an awful, heavy instant. I saw the bombers fly straight down the Street of the Jews, dropping their fearsome loads, and I saw block after block of buildings demolished in regimented precision.

"I began running, climbing over debris, falling into craters, walls tumbling about me. That is where I got this scar you see on my forehead. I remember that all my languages left me except Hebrew. Over and over I shouted. My ears were so blocked by percussion I could not hear my own voice, but I shouted to the heavens."

Mr. Bonet shrugged. He looked at Porter but the eyes did not focus on him.

"You know that is when the emptiness began. I was never able to identify my apartment building. I think it was three weeks before we finally were sure of the block on which it had stood. There was never any question of finding Judith or Rachel or Sarah. They survive forever, floating in my emptiness."

"My God," breathed Kostas.

"What a terrible thing for the Germans to do," said Porter. "What did they hope to gain?"

"It was not the Germans. We learned that someone had broadcast in German code that their army had entrenched itself on *La Rue des Juifs*, that their evacuation had been a deceptive ploy, that they had fortified Rouen and awaited the advance of the Allies. The planes that blasted the *Rue des Juifs* were American bombers."

"I can't believe that," protested Porter.

Mr. Bonet shrugged. "Believe it or not, as you will. It is incongruous, I admit. But me? I know. In the light from the fires I saw the planes. They were American."

He looked at Porter and this time saw him.

"Do not have such a distressed look on your face. It was war. The Americans are not to be blamed. I have forgiven them. I blame myself for leaving my women, for not dying with them."

"My God, Mr. Bonet," said Porter, "how did you stand watching that? How in the world have you managed to survive?"

The man sat erect, looked deeply into Porter's eyes, and shrugged. "There are times," he said, "when you have to pretend that you are a man."

Porter stopped breathing; his head whirled, his ears rang.

"You shouldn't blame yourself," said Kostas.

"Oh, it is not only myself I blame. I live for one thing and one thing only. I will discover the traitor who sent the broadcast, the fiend who posed as friend but hates Jews enough to do such a thing. I will deal with him personally. If his name does not form a new word in the language for double-dealing, betrayal, and murder, then perhaps mine will, and it will be defined as ruthless torture in dealing with such people."

"I hope you catch him."

"I am very close. Soon, I think."

"Is that why you come to this bar where you were when the street was bombed? Does he come here, too?"

"Oh, no. I come here because it is painful and I need pain. Pain keeps me alert, alive. What night of the week is this?"

"Why, Mr. Bonet, it's Friday."

"Precisely. After the Germans left we were allowed to have a rabbi. We have a synagogue of sorts again. The good Jews go there every Friday at sundown. Me? I dress in my best clothes and I come to this bar. I force myself to buy a packet of cigarettes and I drink a bottle of wine. I remember and I hurt and I renew my vows. It is my *Shabbat*. It gets me through the next week."

When they left the bar, Porter turned to Kostas. "There's a poem about a naked man alone in the desert holding his own heart in his hands and eating it. When someone asks him if it is good he says, 'It is bitter. But I like it because it is bitter and because it is my heart.' Mr. Bonet reminds me of that man."

"You and your poetry, Osborne!"

"He also made me think about Jesus."

"Jesus? Excuse me? I'll have to get deep in left field to catch that one."

"Yes. He rattled my brain when he said there are times in life when you can only hang on and pretend that you are a man. All of a sudden I wondered if that's the way Jesus felt through all the crucifixion business."

"My word! We can go back next Friday and you ask our new friend what he thinks."

"No, we can't. I never want to see Jacques Bonet again."

"Why? I think he's fascinating."

"Because he has enriched my life and I want to leave it that way without running the risk of any disillusion. I will pretend that I am a man and I have said farewell to Jacques Bonet tonight."

"Osborne, you really are weird. You know that, don't you?"

"That, like Beauty, is in the eye of the beholder, you prick." He lofted a pebble in perfect arc with the toe of his right combat boot. "I may want to discuss it some day with Lucetti. Some day."

43

"**D**ear Dad,

What a dirty deal! For days we had been hearing that our hospital was headed home. Yesterday we learned that this is only on paper. Col. Draughan, his officers, and all the nurses are being sent back to the States right away, but the enlisted men are being transferred to other units which are scattered all over Europe. Our hospital is being broken up and it pure and simply will not exist any more. Except on paper, they say. That's what they think! Nobody who has been in this unit will ever forget it, and the 816th General Hospital will live as long as any of us live.

I have found out where they are sending me. I am being transferred to Camp Phillip Morris at LeHavre. At least it lies downriver on the Seine from Rouen and is that much closer to Brewton County. I will be in charge of a dispensary there, working under a lieutenant and a captain who will direct three dispensaries in the area. I will have eight enlisted men under me. We will treat only outpatients and will also process guys who are headed home. What really galls me is that most of them have been over here a shorter time than I have. The upshot of this is that I don't really know now when I'll get home. You told me I am a grown man, and I have decided to take your word for it, but I am still compartmentalizing all over the place. I have also taken up dissociating over the last several months, and here of late I have even begun pretending. Of the three, pretending is the most

584

realistic. I will talk to you about that when I see you, but that is going to be longer that I had hoped. Give Mother my love and tell her not to quit praying for me yet.

I know I have been bad about writing and I apologize. One of the reasons is that I went to the UK. Sgt. Lagerpiel arranged it. He was assigned six ten-day slots for our outfit for R and R in Great Britain, and he gave me one of them. He said the purpose of R and R was to improve morale and that he thought morale in the hospital would improve if I was gone. He really likes me, it's just that he has developed this great sense of humor since the war is over. Also he has orders to go back to Texas next week, so he is a happy man and kids all the fellows.

I found that I am no fonder of the English than you were. We went to London and saw Buckingham Palace, the Tower, St. Paul's, and the Abbey. I took a one-day excursion to Oxford and was disappointed. In the first place, I don't think it's a bit better than Willingham University, and in the second place there was a fly in the fish and chips I got for lunch at a stand-up booth in the town. 'Chips' is just another word for french-fried potatoes, and the fly was fried right along with them. Somehow that did not jibe with my preconception of Oxford, and the man was quite rude when I complained. In fact, most of the English were rude. They do not like us and they want us to go home. We get paid more than their soldiers do and they make snotty cracks about us, such as that we get decorated for going to a movie. They are jealous because their girls like us. My friend, Sherman Jewel, says that is because the men in England are cold-codded, but I don't know about that; there are still an awful lot of them crammed on that little island. (Don't let Mother and the girls read this letter.)

I liked Scotland. The Scots feel toward the English like we do the Yankees, and they have some humor about them. I was asking directions in Edinburgh and one of the natives told me to go to the statue of an old fat woman on a horse and turn left. The statue turned out to be Queen Victoria, and I knew I had been talking to an unreconstructed Scotsman.

Don't think I did not enjoy London. I did. I went to a play at the Haymarket Theater and I talked (only talked) to some girls at Picadilly Circus. They have the largest second-hand book store in the world in London. It covers two blocks and survived the air raid. It is called Foyle's. I spent a whole day there and came back with twenty books. I will try to get all of them home with me, but I had forgotten how heavy an armload of books can be. Poor Levek bought a sword in an antique shop the first day we were there and had to lug it all over the UK for ten days. It was pretty bad on crowded streets and subways but he hung onto it. He met a lot of people because of it and under a variety of situations; the English don't like Levek at all.

Well, this has rambled on and I must close. Do not worry about me. I will be a good soldier and get home without a court martial. I promise. As soon as I decide about med school, I will let you know. I really appreciate your interest and concern. You are the best dad a guy could have and I love you with all my heart.

Sambo"

Although rumor is as fast as firestorm through treetops, fruition can be as ponderous as a sloth. The 816th General Hospital closed its doors to patient care, with the exception of the Psychiatric ward, but it did not go anywhere, nor for several weeks was it disbanded. Porter's trip to Foyle's was fortuitous, for he had plenty of reading material. They were required to be on duty, but there was nothing to do. The remaining nurses, who were still eager beavers, set out to clean the hospital in order to leave it gleaming against the day they left it to the nuns. They badgered and cajoled the enlisted men into helping, but there was no spark in the effort, no purpose, no dedication. Lethargy prevailed.

Porter fell to reminiscing, decided that his outfit had performed as well as any other throughout the war, and became nostalgic. He felt the same mixture of relief, excitement, and sadness he had experienced during the latter days of high school and college when finals were over, grades recorded, and the students awaited only the formal ceremony of graduation. He longed for some unit ritual of farewell now and, in the noticeable absence of such, shined his combat boots, donned his dress uniform, and sought an audience with Col. Draughan.

Standing at proper attention, he struck a smart salute. "Sgt. Porter Osborne requests permission to speak to the Colonel, sir."

The colonel's shirt was rumpled and there was a smudge of pink beneath one ear lobe evocative of a lipstick smear, or at least the stimulated skin where one might recently have been scrubbed away. He removed his cigar and returned the salute lackadaisically. He could have been brushing a gnat from his eyebrow.

Porter noted the roll of flesh above the shirt collar and thought the colonel had put on some weight since last he had been this close to him.

"For God's sake, Osborne, relax. Relax. We've been through a war together, most of a war; mostly together. It's over now; over. We're headed home; we can certainly dispense with a little protocol and a lot of formality. What's on your mind? I can tell you ahead of time I can't get any orders cut to send you home sooner, if that's what's eating you."

"Oh, no sir, Colonel. I'm not requesting any special favors or preferential treatment." He quelled any defensiveness and spoke flatly. "I never have. I'm a good soldier. I just dropped in to say good-bye and to thank you."

Col. Draughan busied himself relighting the stump of his cigar. "Thank me? For what?"

"For several things, Col. Draughan. First of all, for granting my request to join this outfit in the first place and giving me the opportunity to serve overseas. Remember?"

"Remember? Of course I remember. That's not one of the things I can ever forget."

"Most importantly, I want to thank you for your leadership. This hospital has had some rough times, but you've always looked after us and brought us through. I'm proud of this and I'm grateful for your looking after us. I've learned that when all is said and done, more is usually said than done, Col. Draughan, but I think you've done a great job and I want to thank you personally. I hear you're headed for the States tomorrow. I just wanted to say good-bye, good luck, and thank you."

The colonel rose from his desk. His swagger was absent.

"I'll just be goddammed," he said. "You know, Osborne, there have been times when I wondered how wise I had been about bringing you into this unit. A CO expects a certain amount of turmoil occasionally in his outfit, but somehow it seemed that it was always your name that came up when something went wrong. Nothing we could ever put a finger on or prove, but no matter what happened your name would somehow or other be mentioned. It got to be such a pattern that I would always ask, 'Where was Porter Osborne?' That foot in the garbage can; the colonel who died with gas gangrene; two of my senior officers nearly breaking their necks one night; our records lost at Omaha; that carload of drunk soldiers stumbling off the train when we got to Metz; wrecking the sink in the OR at Metz. You were even in Luxembourg, I'm told, the day before the CID uncovered a motorcycle and Jeep theft ring."

"Theft ring? Luxembourg, sir?"

"Can the innocent crap, Osborne. Capt. Smith and I were talking just the other day. He's been after your butt ever since we hit the beaches but never could quite make a case for court-martial. Smith has mellowed a bit, and he said it had been difficult having to discipline guys like you and Otten who would be his social equals in civilian life. I've certainly had mixed feelings about you myself."

The colonel looked out the window a moment and spoke gruffly over his shoulder. "I'll tell you this, though. You're the first and only man in this outfit to approach me on a personal basis and express any semblance of gratitude or interest in me as an individual. I appreciate it. Are you going back to medical school when you get back to America?"

"I'm undecided at the moment, sir. My father has suggested law school and politics as an alternative."

"Politics? God help the whole state of Georgia. And extend my best wishes to your father. Thanks for coming by, Osborne, and lots of luck no matter what you do. So long."

"So long, Colonel."

"Osborne."

"Sir?"

"The war's over. I'm headed home tomorrow. You're shipping out to LeHavre. We'll never see each other again. Level with me about something."

"Yes, sir?"

"Who in the name of heaven and also in hell is Daniel D. Farbecker, and whatever happened to him?"

Porter forced a calm voice. "You know, Colonel, that's a great mystery to me, too. I barely knew the boy and, to tell you the truth, I've even forgotten what his face looked like. All GI's in raincoats look alike, you know. As to what happened to him, I haven't a clue. I assume he's not dead or somebody would have heard. Perhaps he'll turn up later."

"OK, be that way, Osborne. In addition to everything else you don't, by any chance, steal cherries, do you?"

Porter carefully seasoned his voice with a little indignation. "I beg your pardon, sir?"

"Nothing. Forget it. I'm a fool to bring it up. Capt. Smith was right."

"About discipline, sir?"

"Yes."

"Colonel."

"Yes, Osborne?"

"Have you ever read *Aeneas Africanus*? A story about an ex-slave trying to find his way home after the War and the stories he told about the plantation he came from?"

"No, I haven't."

"Would you give Capt. Smith a message for me?"

"Certainly."

"Tell him there's no way he could be my social equal in civilian life."

"Out of here, Osborne!"

"I'm gone, Colonel! You've been great."

Porter had assumed that the break-up of the 816th would be traumatic, that farewells would be emotional, that it would be gut-wrenching to see their officers, nurses, and most of the noncoms marching off and leaving them behind. He was mistaken. No one marched. They straggled. A few at a time, a day at a time. There were promises to write, to keep up with each other in civilian life, but farewells were accompanied by furtive glances at wrist watches, anticipation of the immediate future so keen that separation from old comrades was often desultory, assurances of fealty delivered abstractedly.

"Good God, Kostas," Porter said, "we've known all these people and worked side by side with them and shared their lives, and they all of a sudden become strangers and disappear. I feel like I'm living in a T. S. Eliot poem, and I never could abide T. S. Eliot."

"I wouldn't suppose you could; the concept of your measuring out your life in coffeespoons is incomprehensible."

"Thanks. I think. After all that Jewel and I have shared, he shoulders his duffel, sticks out that jaw, and says, 'I'm off like a big-assed bird. Keep your nose clean and don't take no wooden nickels, Osborne.' Not so much as a handshake!"

"What was your response?"

"Hell, I'm as tough as he is. I said, 'Up yours, Jewel,' and turned a page in the book I was reading."

"Maybe Southerners are like everybody else after all."

"At any rate, you and I are different, Steve. I've sure learned a lot in this war. You've contributed immensely and I'm grateful."

"Me?"

"Sure. You've shown me entirely different viewpoints from mine without preaching. You've bridged a gap between Georgia and Massachusetts that's at least a hundred years old. You've taught me that all Yankees don't look down long noses and act superior. You've taught me acceptance and tolerance. I've never had a brother in my life and always wanted one. I can't wait to tell my grandmother that I love a Yankee like a brother."

"Me?"

"Sure."

"You're off in an unrealistic dream world again, Osborne."

"You don't love me like a brother?"

"I have two brothers. It's not the same."

"What's the difference?"

"Well, in the first place, goddammit, we don't talk about it."

"Oh." Porter was silent for a long moment. "I understand. In that case, I'm going to LeHavre and later Georgia and you're leaving for Brussels and later Massachusetts, and that's my truck coming in now. I'm off like a big-assed bird. Keep your nose clean and don't take no wooden nickels, Kostas."

"Up yours, Osborne," came the quick response.

Their eyes locked and simultaneously they said, "Pretend you are a man."

Their handshake was strong and their laughter so loud that bored GI's turned and looked at them. Briefly.

*"And Christian dreadeth Christ that hath a
newer face of doom . . ."*

44 **C**amp Phillip Morris lay on a plateau above
LeHavre and was almost identical to the staging area Porter had
endured at Camp Grant. Squad tents were everywhere, occupied by
transients so briefly that it never became necessary for him to identify
the tents by numbers or street. These were troops headed out, back to
the United States, their ecstasy tempered by the sobering awareness
that although home may not have changed, the returning warriors
assuredly had. Nowhere was there any doubt expressed about whether
it had been worth it. Everyone had had a part in the liberation of
Europe, and everyone was proud of it.

To replace them there were also troops coming in from America, mostly so brash and cocky that the age difference between them
and the ones going home seemed exaggerated. Contact between the
two groups was rare and when it occurred was reminiscent of old dogs
commingling with puppies in the same backyard. The veterans were
war-seasoned, aloof, tolerant of a certain amount of youthful ebullience, but so jealous of personal space that too close an intrusion
evoked growls and snarls and, occasionally, blood-letting fights. These
encounters, however, always occurred down in the town among the
bars that cluttered the streets and alleys radiating from the waterfront.
LeHavre lay at the foot of a winding road so precipitous that it made
one's ears pop if descent from the plateau in Jeep or truck was too
rapid, far away from Porter Osborne's dispensary.

It was, indeed, Porter's dispensary. He was assigned to direct it,
to be the noncom in charge, but he had no forewarning of the extent to
which he would be in charge. His was one of three such units in the
staging area that were under the direction of two officers, 1st Lt. Milton
Goldberg of the Medical Administrative Corps and Capt. Walter
Ewing, a bona fide member of the Medical Corps. Theoretically each

dispensary had a medical officer on premises each day for sick call, a supervising physician who oversaw the treatment administered by the technicians, a real doctor who would give on-hands care to a sick soldier when such was indicated. In addition, an administrative officer supposedly toured each unit daily, inspecting the physical facility and overseeing the performance and needs of the personnel who labored there.

In no situation have theory and performance been more widely divergent. The two officers came, introduced themselves, made inquiries about Porter's background and experience, issued orders which were a puzzling mixture of explicit and general, and then showed up erratically for whirlwind appearances. It was obvious that the interests of each lay elsewhere and that neither wanted to be bothered.

Lt. Goldberg's abdication of responsibility gave Porter no problem.

"You've had experience in a general hospital working with supplies, records, and other GI's. I'll expect you to run this dispensary with no difficulty whatsoever. Fill out your requisitions and drop them by my office for signature; no need for me to come way over here in person. If I'm not there, leave them and pick them up next day."

"What about the work schedule for the men, sir? That's under your command."

"Hell, Osborne, you're sergeant-in-charge. You arrange all that. Keep them happy and if they grumble, punch their TS card and get them an appointment with the chaplain. You know the ropes. Don't clutter my mind or waste my time with inconsequential details."

"Yes, sir."

"The main thing is your paper work. Keep those records straight. Be sure your inventory is accurate. I learned a long time ago that when a SNAFU occurs, it's what's on paper that investigators trust. You got that? And be careful what you put on any GI's chart. Two weeks from any given date, if it's not written down it didn't happen. You got that?"

"Yes, sir."

Thereafter he saw Lt. Goldberg on the average of once a week.

"Any problems, Osborne?"

"No, sir."

"Good work. Carry on."

And you, appraised Porter, are a self-centered, self-serving turd who thinks of nobody but Number One, and if anything ever goes wrong it'll be my ass in a sling, and fuck you, Jack. "Thank you, sir," he said aloud. "I'm really keeping up with the paper work."

Capt. Ewing was cut from a different bolt of cloth in Porter's eyes, and that was as it should be; after all, he was a doctor. A bored doctor perhaps, even one a little on the lazy side, but not a disdainful, order-snapping surgeon nor yet a bumbling, confused mismatch. He was apparently not impressed with the military emphasis on personal appearance, for he was careless enough about his dress to have posed for Mauldin, his shirt always wrinkled, his khaki tie and cap so crumpled one fancied that he stuffed them in his shoes every night for storage. He was willing to discuss medical treatment with his supervising sergeant, however, and at least he visited the dispensary two or three times a week.

"Check their temperatures, Osborne. If a GI on sick call doesn't have a fever, chances are he's just malingering."

"Yes, sir."

"Be sure and look in their throats and ears. And use the stethoscope. Thump their chests and then listen to the heart and lungs with the almighty stethoscope. You may not have the faintest idea what you're hearing, but they won't know that. Always, always use the stethoscope. If they're really sick, it raises their comfort level, and if they're not, it makes them feel guilty because they know that you know they're goldbricking."

"Yes, sir. TPR goes on the record of every patient encounter. What about blood pressure, sir?"

"Good point, Osborne. In fact, an excellent point. By all means, take the blood pressure. In this age group it's an absolutely worthless gesture, but it does convince a patient irrefutably that he's being examined. Other than a rectal, there's nothing as reinforcing of the medical mystique as a blood pressure cuff. People were so mesmerized back in southern Illinois by that little column of mercury running up and sliding back down when they came to see me that you could damn near hypnotize them. Made me realize how you could persuade people in ancient Rome that you knew what was going to happen to them by looking at chicken entrails; it's something you can do that they can't and it impresses them. By all means, take the blood pressure."

Porter learned a lot from Capt. Ewing.

"You've left some standing orders, sir. Abrasions and minor lacerations get scrubbed with green soap, painted with iodine, sulfa crystals sprinkled on them, and sterile bandages applied. What about sutures?"

"You can quit calling me over for the minor ones. I've watched you. Remember to keep the skin edges kissing; sew up what you know I would sew up and transport the big cases to the hospital in town. Whatever you do, don't send one to the hospital without calling me first for authorization. There's a by-the-book butt-chewing colonel over there who watches like a hawk for unnecessary admissions, and I have to be sure my ass is covered. Whatever you do, don't send a wound to the hospital without giving a tetanus booster and charting it."

"Yes, sir."

"You're doing quite well on routine sick call, Osborne. I'm going to make a doctor out of you yet. There's no need for me to come over here every day. Load them up with APC's and GI gin and don't hesitate to give them a round of sulfa drug if they've got a little fever."

"Yes, sir. You want them to have plain terpin hydrate or ETH with codeine?"

"Doesn't really matter; they're not going to be around long enough to get addicted. If you get a repeater, switch him to plain. Just don't start taking the stuff yourself."

"Capt. Ewing, I wouldn't think of it."

"Another thing. You don't have to call me on that telephone every time we get a case of gonorrhea through here. They've relaxed the rule about court-martial for clap; they had to. You've seen enough of it to recognize it as good as I can. Treat it and chart it."

"With penicillin? Me?"

"Hell, yes, with penicillin. Sulfa doesn't touch it. You can let your men give the shots every six hours, but you mix up the penicillin yourself and be sure you keep it locked up. It's a hot item on the black market, and they're keeping as tight a count on it as they are on narcotics."

"Penicillin is truly a miracle drug, isn't it, Captain?"

"You can say that again. You ought to see what it's doing for pneumonia. The professors who've been working on typing the pneumococcus and producing serum are going to be out of a job. Pneumonia is licked."

Within a month Capt. Ewing was coming to the dispensary no more often than Lt. Goldberg. He was also not overly cordial on the telephone.

"Hell, Osborne, use your own judgment. You don't have to interrupt me every whipstitch for orders. You know I trust you and will back you up. Keep your ass off the telephone."

"Yes, sir."

Porter became so immersed in the day to day operation of his dispensary, in directing and supervising the men who worked under him, that he pushed everything else to the back of his mind. It could not possibly be more than a few more weeks at most before orders were cut to send him home. In the meantime, he was in a position of greater responsibility than he had ever experienced and he busied himself in response to the challenge. The dispensary was housed in the front half of a Quonset hut; Porter and his eight men had living quarters in the other half. Recalling the sergeants from his past, Porter resolved at the outset to improve upon their performances. He consequently directed his men by placation, by suggestion, by cajolery; some of these guys were older than he. He got work out of them by setting the example of working harder than anyone else, for he had observed the effectiveness of this in his beginnings on the farm. They responded, and the outfit became an insular group, individuality respected, eccentricities indulged, bonded by the resolve to get along with each other through this period of waiting. They all foresaw imminent discharge, and confidences were restricted by reluctance; no one wanted to bother finding a buddy this late in the game. The degree of grumbling and griping in the dispensary never exceeded anticipated or acceptable levels, and Porter only occasionally had to give a direct order. He rarely issued a threat, and he never, ever resorted to calling anyone a dickhead.

"Dad," he wrote, "you may be right—I may be growing up. It took a while, didn't it? Thanks for your patience and your example.

"I know I have slacked off in my letters home, but believe it or not I'm busier than I have ever been. The officers in charge of this operation have pretty well turned it over to me, and I am doing my best to rise to the challenge. I am learning a lot.

"I am still glad I did not go to OCS; being a good sergeant and looking after the few men who are under me is about all I can handle. I have learned that nobody is perfect and that nobody is all bad. I have a captain who teaches me some medicine when I can catch him. I'm about to decide that I want to go back to med school when I get home, but I've not seen anything yet to make me want to be a first lieutenant.

"Give Mother and Jimps and the little girls my love and tell them to keep those letters coming. Even if I don't answer them, I sure appreciate getting them.

"I have to run. As we say in the service, 'Keep your nose clean and don't take no wooden nickels.' Sambo"

Except for daily trips for supplies or records, utilizing either the dispensary ambulance or Jeep, Porter came to confine himself to his Quonset hut or its immediate vicinity. In the vacant office marked "Medical Officer of the Day" there was a shelf of discarded professional tomes, and he whiled away his spare time thumbing through them and reading anything that caught his fancy. The first time he looked in calculating inventory at this shelf, he discovered Boyd's *Textbook of Pathology*.

"My God," he expostulated, "there's an old friend I practically memorized two and a half years ago. What use can it possibly have in a dispensary in France that is overrun with common colds and clap?"

A later perusal revealed a two-volume set of Watson-Jones, the ultimate authority in orthopedics. "Well," he said, "Lt. Hormley was not the only doctor in the ETO to need those books. He needn't have paid for them himself after all."

He idly opened one and discovered on the flyleaf "Personal property of Lt. William Hormley, lst Lt., USMC."

"I wondered what had become of him," mused Porter. "He must have come through here on his way to the States and been overjoyed to dump these books. If he goes back to Nebraska to practice Dermatology, I hope he keeps good records, for he sure as hell gets mixed up on names."

Occasionally he would get so tired of GI food that he would accompany a group of his men to some restaurant or tavern they had discovered, but usually he stayed put. A good leader. Unlikely as it seemed, a father figure. The glaring electric bulb over the dispensary door was a substitute for the lights of home. It was up to him to keep it burning for the boys in his command.

"You guys go ahead. Sign your own passes. Somebody has to sleep out front to man the pro station and I don't mind doing it. Just leave me one guy in the back in the unlikely event I have an emergency."

Christmas Eve was no exception. He insisted on giving all his men the evening off and remained alone in the dispensary. He was making a concerted effort to compartmentalize, to dissociate, to pretend, to prove himself both a responsible and a benevolent leader.

"After all, fellows, this is my third Christmas away from home; it's no big deal for me. Y'all take off like big-assed birds and have a good time. I'll stay here and keep the store."

"But, Sarge," protested Malcolm Meadows, who was two years Porter's junior, had been transferred to his command from a defunct

Battalion Aid Station, and had the discomforting response to Porter of a starved hound that looks with abject adoration at the savior who finally gives it food and a kind word. "Come on and go with us. Nobody is going to get sick on Christmas Eve, and we haven't had a real emergency through that door since I've been here. Come on; it won't be the same without you."

"Somebody has to be here. I'd catch unshirted hell if this place got reported for being empty."

After the others had gone, he stepped outside and discovered a miraculous night over Normandy; so still and quiet that he could hear distant cock-crow, the faint and faraway bark of a lonely dog. The clear air stung his nostrils, filled his chest in sharp expansion. Starshine was so richly luminescent that the beacon above the dispensary door appeared whey-thin.

Porter found himself homesick and morose despite all efforts to the contrary. This was indeed his third Christmas in a row away from home, and he had never in his life thought he would miss even the first one. This was his second Christmas in Normandy, so far from his family in Brewton County that he had difficulty comprehending time zones, let alone the distance in miles. Although he knew guys who had missed four, or even five, Christmases with their families while in military service, contemplating the misery of others did nothing to dispel his own. He returned to his office and tried to read, but as the hours dragged by he succumbed to feeling sorry for himself. Childish, choking, consuming self-pity engulfed him; his throat swelled, his eyes stung.

His narcissism was interrupted by a loud banging on the dispensary door. He rose in answer, muttering that the damn door wasn't locked and whoever needed a pro station on Christmas Eve could just come on in. When he opened it, a buck private was standing there swaddled in his overcoat, swaying slightly from side to side, arms akimbo, all his gear complete with duffel bag lying at his feet. A corporal was loping down the walkway toward the Jeep which sat with its motor running.

"Hey!" called Porter. "What gives? You're not supposed to dump somebody here. This is not an overnight facility."

"Up yours," sang the corporal. "He just got off a Liberty ship tonight and the sergeant told me to get him to a doctor. Said this kid ain't but eighteen and is bad off. Got sick in the middle of the ocean and been getting worse every day. 'Get him to hell outa here,' the sergeant said. I've gotta go. It's Christmas Eve." He jumped in the Jeep and was gone. The soldier leaned against Porter.

"Help me," he croaked.

Porter led the stumbling figure into the brighter light of the treatment room and removed his helmet.

"What in the world is wrong with you?"

The soldier pointed to his mouth, his speech unintelligible.

"My God, your whole neck is swollen like a dog that's been snakebit; it's puffed out from your ears to your clavicle. How long have you been sick?"

The boy held up five fingers. "Can't swallow."

"You sound like you're talking around boiled eggs in your throat. Let me take a look. It's really red and swollen, but it's hard to see anything for all that old dirty white stuff stuck to it. Let me see if I can scrape some of it off. You're drooling all over the place. Didn't they have a doctor on the boat?"

The boy shook his head.

"Well, don't worry. We'll get you one. With that red swollen throat, you ought to be burning up with fever even if your skin does feel clammy. Let me get your temperature. That's the first thing the Captain will ask."

He stretched the boy on the examining table, covered him with a blanket, made his telephone call.

"Capt. Ewing, sorry to call you away from your party, but I've got a real sick one on my hands. I think you'd better come on over here as fast as you can. I don't know what to do for him. He's had a sore throat for five days and his neck is tremendously swollen on the outside."

"Osborne, I can't believe you're interrupting my evening for a damn sore throat. What's the matter with you? How many sore throats have you treated?"

"Captain, how many times have I asked you to come over here at night? This is no ordinary sore throat. Blood pressure is ninety over sixty, pulse is one hundred and twenty, and he's clammy. Temp is only ninety-nine, but he can't hold the thermometer in his mouth because he can't breathe. He's only a kid, Captain, and he's as far away from home as you and I, and it's Christmas Eve for him, too. I think you'd better come on over here."

"Osborne, I am not leaving this party! You treat that throat the best way you can!"

"The son of a bitch hung up on me," said Porter Osborne indignantly. He went back into the treatment room. The soldier was lying with eyes closed and jaws agape, struggling to pull breath through his thickened pharynx, saliva streaming from a corner of his mouth.

"I'm going to give you a shot of penicillin in your butt," Porter told him. "It's a real miracle medicine and should make you feel better pretty quick. At least I know it won't do any harm. You want a drink of water?"

The boy shook his head wearily. The look in his eyes was pleading."I'm going to call the doctor again. Don't you worry."

"Osborne, I can't believe you're back on the phone! You're prattling sentimental drivel and losing your objectivity."

"Capt. Ewing, I'm the one who's all alone with this boy and I say he's critically ill. You haven't seen him, sir. If you're not coming over here, I could bring him to you."

"Goddammit, Osborne, you're not hearing what I'm saying. Don't bother me another time with this case."

"The son of a bitch did it again," said Porter. There was now a note of panic in his voice. He took a hurried look at his patient, gave a reassuring pat to his shoulder, and went to the shelf of books in the MOD office. "This is no ordinary sore throat," he repeated.

The only book with which he had any familiarity was the Boyd's *Pathology*. He flipped through it to the section on Infections and very soon found a brief description that satisfied his quest for diagnosis. Back to the phone he raced and rang through to the irate commanding officer.

"I can't help it, Captain. I know you're at a party, but I've got to talk to you again. This man I'm worried about has diphtheria! . . . Yes, he has, too. There's the grayish membrane in his throat that bleeds if you try to remove it and occludes breathing, and he has a classic example of what Boyd calls 'bull neck' . . . .No, sir, I know. I'd never heard of bull neck before either, Captain. Boyd says it is a sign found only in the terminal stages . . . No, sir, I do not think I'm smarter than a doctor . . . But, Capt. Ewing, I'm calling to request admission of this guy to the hospital . . . What do you mean, 'Request denied', sir? This man may . . . I'm a son of a bitch if the son of a bitch didn't do it again!"

Porter went back to check the boy. The mouth was gaping, the lips parched and shriveled with dried mucus, the chest straining. He bathed the lips and said, "We're going to the hospital, fellow. I think you've got diphtheria. Haven't you ever had any shots?"

The boy opened his eyes and shrugged.

"Where are you from? What's your name? I've got to fill out an admission sheet, and I don't even know your name."

The boy pointed to his dog-tags, fumbled to produce his wallet, but his speech was unintelligible.

"Ah, here it is. Keith McLean. West Virginia. I don't think I've met anybody from West Virginia before." He was prattling and realized it, but the sound of his own voice directed attention from the terrible stertor of the boy's breathing. "Don't you worry. You're going to be all right, Keith. I had diphtheria when I was a little kid and I can remember Dr. Wallis and Dr. Lester coming out to my house and giving me antitoxin. I'm going to get you to the hospital where you can get some antitoxin, and you're going to do great and get well, Keith. Just hang in there, fellow, and let me type up this form."

He filled out all the blanks on the form for emergency hospital admission with surprisingly few mistakes in his typing. Under diagnosis he boldly specified "Diphtheria, acute, severe." Under clinical findings he delineated "occluding membrane, bull neck."

Under admitting officer he without pause typed "Walter D. Ewing, M.D., Capt." and scrawled an illegible signature above it.

"One last phone call and we're on our way, fellow. You're going to be all right, Keith. Just keep hanging in there for me, you hear?"

This time, although he requested Capt. Ewing, he got Lt. Goldberg.

"Osborne, the captain won't come to the phone for you anymore. He sent me instead. He said to tell you that if you call him one more time tonight he's going to tie your ass up in Europe so long you'll be gray-haired before you ever see Georgia again."

"Lt. Goldberg, I don't have time to argue. I'm heading to the hospital with Pvt. Keith McLean right now. I don't really give a damn whether you tell the captain or not, but this admission is over his signature."

He slammed the receiver down in Lt. Goldberg's ear and enjoyed the sensation. "Two can play that game."

He draped McLean's arm over his shoulders and managed to get him into the Jeep. He tucked blankets hurriedly around him and held a protective hand across his chest as he careened the vehicle down the precipitous road to the hospital.

"Help me!" he yelled to the tech when he arrived at the Emergency Room. "I need a stretcher!"

"Help me," attempted Keith McLean in echo but could not get his lips together to mouth the words satisfactorily.

Porter was quickly relieved of his burden by medics who wore whites instead of work fatigues and moved with speed and efficiency through the bright lights of the coldly clean emergency suite, barking orders back and forth to each other. Nurses rushed in, doctors followed. Porter eddied into a corner with feelings of inadequacy as he admired the professional competence now surrounding him.

"You can go on back to your outfit, Sergeant," an enlisted man said. "We'll take it from here. He's sick as hell."

"I know," said Porter. "I thought I'd hang around a while."

"Then grab a seat in that waiting area around the corner where you'll be out of our way, and I'll keep you posted. They're doing an emergency tracheotomy on him right now. I heard the colonel bragging on that Capt. Ewing of yours and saying he is sure a smart doctor. Who'd ever have thought of diphtheria in a young, healthy GI?"

"Yeah," said Porter. "He's smart all right. Y'all giving McLean antitoxin?"

"Are you kidding? We got tetanus, but nobody ever even thought of stocking diphtheria antitoxin. The colonel's got everybody scouring local French hospitals now, hunting some. You sit down. I'll let you know."

Porter was looking carefully at the toes of the boots on his outstretched feet when someone else walked up. He did not rise for Lt. Goldberg.

"Hi, Osborne."

Porter only looked at him, dully expectant.

"You did a good job getting McLean down here."

"I disobeyed orders."

"I know, and thank God you did. In addition to looking after McLean, you also covered Ewing's ass, even when he was hell bent on showing it. You should hear the medics and docs back there bragging on the good captain for making that diagnosis and moving on it so fast."

Porter did not flinch. "What are you doing here, Lieutenant?"

"I figured some officer somewhere tonight had best exhibit a little responsibility. You had a desperate tone in your voice and I came down to back you up. I've never known you to screw up before, and I was betting that you weren't this time."

"And did I, Lieutenant?" Porter carefully cleansed his voice of sarcasm. "Was my paper work in order?"

"Your paper work is brilliant. Everything is written down and so everything happened the way you said it did. I'm damn glad to be your superior officer and I'm damn glad I came down to bail you out in case you needed me. You're an exceptional person, Osborne, and I admire you for what you've done tonight. Don't worry about breaking rules and disobeying orders."

"I wasn't. I'm worried about McLean."

"I know. All the guys in the back are, too. Mind if I sit down?"

The silence between them grew but did not become tense. Rather it became a vibrant, mystic, almost pulsating source of comfort. Porter felt a closeness to Milton Goldberg unlike any he had experienced before. The man's entire attention, he felt, was directed toward him; the silence was supporting him as surely as the arms of a father. For some reason he thought briefly of Dick Faulkner. He drew a deep breath and released an audible sigh.

"You're going to be a good doctor, Osborne." Goldberg's voice was soft, almost detached.

"I am?" Porter replied. "Maybe." He shrugged. "Maybe not." He looked at Lt. Goldberg. "I've not been exposed to anybody lately who made me want to emulate them."

"Good." said Melvin Goldberg. "Now you're free to strike out on your own and be the sort of doctor you want to be. You can be Dr. Porter Osborne and not have to force yourself into any kind of mold."

"Yeah," said Porter. "And while I'm at it I could grow up and be a man, too, couldn't I, Lieutenant? I have a buddy named Kostas who talked to me about negative role models. If I decide to go back to med school, I've sure found another one of those tonight."

"Good boy! Everybody has a different reason for doing things."

Porter was silent for a long while. "I had a friend who died before he could finish med school. He didn't flunk out; he really was kicked out. He told me that there are people in this world who give and people who take. He wanted to be a doctor because he said he was born to give." He rose slowly from his chair. "I think I'll line up with Will Barton, Lieutenant," he replied. "Hell, yes, I'm going to be a doctor!"

"Good boy, Osborne! If nobody else ever says it, I'm proud of you."

"Thanks." Porter scowled. "I don't know, of course, when I'll make it. The captain may follow through with his threat to tie me down over here."

"Leave the captain to me, Osborne. He's still playing poker at the top of the hill and doesn't have the faintest idea what's on that admission sheet. When I get through with him, his ass will be so tight you couldn't drive a pin in it with a ball-peen hammer."

"You're beginning to talk like a Southerner, Lieutenant."

"I've got leanings, Osborne, I've got leanings. Don't fret about leaving the ETO. I'll have you on a boat headed home in less than a week, I promise you, and those orders will be signed by no less than Capt. Ewing himself, because I'll see to it that he knows you've got him by the balls and hold his future in your fist. I'll work this so that his feeling will be one of immeasurable relief when you ship out."

"Speaking of feelings and remembering Will Barton, Lieutenant, if you get a chance, ask the captain how he'd feel if I jerked his head off and shit in his neck."

"I wouldn't think of it, Osborne. My word, you're making me lose my Southern leanings. You go on back to quarters and go to bed. I'm back up the hill to break up a poker game."

"I'm going to stick around, Lieutenant. I couldn't sleep anyway."

"OK, it's your call. Thank God for your guts; McLean's alive because of you. See you around."

Porter watched the retreating figure, the narrow shoulders, the pigeon-toed drag of the right foot and decided that you just never could tell about folks.

He dashed to the door and called across the parking lot, "Hey, Lieutenant!"

Goldberg turned his head. "Yes?"

"Merry Christmas!"

There was a short hesitation. "Yeah." The shoulders squared. "Up yours, too, Osborne. You need some sleep!"

At 4:30 A.M. Porter's vigil was interrupted by a weary medic in rumpled whites. "You can haul it home, Sergeant. He checked out on us."

"McLean's dead?"

"Deader'n hell. Or, to get precise and proper with our fucking terminology, the patient expired at precisely o-four-o-six hours. Nice try, Sergeant, but no save."

"But the trach, the IV's, the oxygen. I thought . . ."

"Too late, too little. We even got some antitoxin from a French hospital and flooded him with that. The colonel says the diphtheria toxin had already hit his heart and he never had a chance."

"What if you'd gotten him two hours earlier?"

"No difference, according to the colonel. Full court press, good last shot, Sergeant, but no basket. That's the way the ball bounces. We all fouled out. Whistle blew. Game's over. Tough." He spread his hands. "Sorry."

"Yeah. Me, too. So long."

He dragged to his Jeep, grasped the steering wheel, turned the key. Lifting his head to the stars, he gazed through the windshield and spoke aloud. "OK, Will Barton. Fuck us all if we can't take a joke. Right?"

He turned the ignition off, laid his head forward and wept. Gut-wrenching sobs swept him until his eyes were dry and hiccups shook his frame. Still he did not raise his head.

He felt a hand on his shoulder. "My word, it's Porter Osborne! What's the trouble, fellow? Can I help?"

"Hi, Lucetti," he responded without wonder. "Where'd you come from? I thought you shipped home before we left Rouen."

"I wish. I'm stuck in the OR here and was coming on duty early to let some of the other guys off for Christmas. What's bugging you? Bad news from home? Can I help?"

"Bad news right here. A kid who doesn't even shave yet just died on Christmas Day in the morning a million miles from West Virginia and his folks. It got to me."

"I'm sorry. Have you prayed?"

Porter looked at him and hiccupped. "You might call it that." He blew his nose. "And to answer your question, hell, no, you can't help. You're all hung up on Jesus and I'm not in the mood to hear about Him any more than I want to discuss Santa Claus. Not on Christmas day in the morning in LeHavre, France. When you're dead, Lucetti, you're dead, dead, dead. No matter whether you're named Barton, Fritz, or McLean, and don't hand me any of that 'in-my-Father's-house-are-many-mansions' crap and 'I go to prepare a place for you.' I've listened my entire life to those fairy stories and I've had a belly full. Where is God when you really need Him? Hell, He even let Jesus die, and I've never really understood that."

"You're not supposed to understand, Osborne. You don't have to intellectualize about an experience that is basically an emotional one. All you have to do is believe."

"I don't know what I believe any more. Next thing I know you'll be prattling about faith."

"Why not? You know what faith is, don't you?"

"You're mighty right I know what faith is; it's believing something you know goddam well ain't so. You think when you're dead that's not the end of you, Lucetti, but it is. I've seen too many corpses to believe anything else. What about Aushwitz? Buchenwald?"

Lucetti's voice was patient. "Faith is believing something in the face of doubt, Porter Osborne. If you don't ever doubt, you can't have faith. There's a big difference between knowledge and faith. I've come to welcome my doubts; they strengthen my faith."

"You? Running around all the time with that Bible? You have doubts? Look out, Lucetti, God's gonna get you. He'll zap you for sure."

When there was no reply, Porter asked, "What do you really believe, Lucetti?"

"I've got to get on duty, Porter, but let me try to put it in as much of a nutshell as I can. What do I really believe? I'm a good Methodist; I believe in God the Father Almighty, creator of Heaven and Earth, and in His only Son, our Lord, who was conceived by the Holy Spirit, born of the Virgin Mary, suffered under Pontius Pilate, was crucified, dead and buried. On the third day He rose from the dead. He ascended into Heaven where He sitteth on the right hand of God the Father Almighty."

Porter rolled his eyes and sighed. Lucetti paused.

"But me? Personally? Madison Lucetti? What do I believe? I believe that through the ages God got tired of the people He had chosen for His own developing so many misconceptions and false ideas about Him that their worship became top-heavy with rules that were really of their own making. And so, to show us what God is really like and to set us free from those silly rules, He came and lived among us as a plain ordinary carpenter's son. He showed us every day the beauty in a human heart when it is full of love, compassion, and grace. Into the mouth of Jehovah, man had put promises of lands. And herds. And victory over enemies. And even great wealth if we kept His commandments and obeyed all those rules. That was about like promising a kid when he loses a tooth that if he doesn't put his tongue in the hole, a gold one will grow back in.

"Jesus promised us one thing and one thing only. Peace. 'My peace I leave with you, my peace I give unto you. Not as the world gives give I unto you, but the peace that passeth understanding. And the gates of hell shall not prevail against you.' It really does pass understanding, Porter. I've been given the Peace and nothing can take it from me."

"Nothing?"

"Nothing."

"As that guy told Stephen, 'Almost thou persuadest me.' But not quite, Lucetti. In fact, not by a long damn shot. There's a fury in my soul and a fire in my belly, and peace is not even an option right now. I don't want peace; I want to fight. I want to run. I want to suck every day into my soul until I am choked with the surfeit of its grandeur. I want to experience everything. I want to savor every minute as though it might be my last."

"Go ahead, do that. 'Rejoice, oh young man, in thy youth and let thy heart cheer thee in the days of thy youth, while the evil days come not when thou shalt say I have no pleasure in them.'"

Porter stared at him. Lucetti continued. "'But know thou that for all these things God will bring thee into judgment.'"

"That's Old Testament, Lucetti. What about those rules?"

"I know it. Frightening, isn't it? Makes you appreciate the love of someone who would die for the sins we commit, doesn't it? We can't be excused from the responsibility for our actions or the consequences of them, but at least we know we are forgiven. When you accept that, you will forgive yourself, and then you, too, will find the peace. It will come to you some day. I know it as sure as I'm standing here."

"Fuck peace."

"I'm sorry your friend died tonight."

"He wasn't my friend; I never saw him before in my life."

"Oh. In that case it looks like you're really getting where we've been talking about. Look, I've got to run. There's got be great faith beneath that great doubt of yours. I'll pray for you, Porter Osborne."

"You'll do no such a damn thing. Don't you dare pray for me! This is a personal matter between me and God, and He and I will tend to it. You keep your mouth out of it."

"Merry Christmas, Osborne."

"Up yours, too, Lucetti."

"Cervantes on his galley sets the sword back in the sheath.
(Don John of Austria rides homeward with a wreath.)
And he sees across a weary land a straggling road in Spain,
Up which a lean and foolish knight forever rides in vain,
And he smiles, but not as Sultans smile, and settles back the
blade . . .
(But Don John of Austria rides home from the Crusade.)"

45   "That's correct, operator. Number one-six in Brewtonton, Georgia. Collect. This is Porter Osborne, Jr. . . . . Sure, I'll speak to whoever answers. This time of day there can only be one person there."

Porter could hear the hum of distance being surmounted and pressed the receiver against his ear until it hurt. He was a little dizzy.

"Hell, yes, I'll accept the call, operator. Thanks for putting it through. Sambo! Where are you, son?"

"Fort Bragg. Fayetteville, North Carolina, Dad. Got here yesterday on the bus but this is the first time I could grab a phone. I'd have called from New York the minute I got off that Victory ship that bucked us across the Atlantic, but it was before you got to the office. Is everybody all right?"

"All right? Everybody's fine and they're going to be even better when they find out you're safely back on American soil. God, you have no idea how glad we are you're coming home!"

"I'm twice as glad as any of y'all are. I thought for a while I was going to be stuck in Europe another year, but somebody greased the chute for me and here I am in Fort Bragg, and it's only the first day of February. I'll never have to be away from home again on Christmas the longest day I live. It doesn't even seem cold."

"When will you be coming in?"

"They're processing us as fast as they can, sort of like cattle in a slaughter pen, so it'll only be a couple of days. I would have been through late this afternoon and on my way, but I had a run-in with a master sergeant and he called a captain in on me, and I'm being held up an extra day. Probably Wednesday. I hope no later than Thursday. I'll call you this same time tomorrow."

"Sambo, what are you having a disagreement about?"

"Aw, they're running us through this discharge mill in groups of fifty, as many as they can pack into a room at the time. 'Sign this, sign that, get the lead out and move on to Corridor E, Room 222.' Don't give us time to read anything, and all the guys are so eager to get out of the Army they just put their names on anything pushed at them. This sergeant was wanting us all to sign up for the ERC and that's where I balked."

"What's the ERC?"

"Enlisted Reserve Corps. He acted like it was routine until I asked what was the purpose of it. They want a pool of soldiers in the Reserves, he said, especially the noncoms, in case there's another war or a national emergency and they need to mobilize in a hurry. I refused to sign it and he made an issue out of it."

"Why not sign it? Sounds routine to me, also."

"I told him there wasn't supposed to be another war, that we had all been told this was the war to end all wars and I was tired of the Army double-talking us. He said it was just in case they needed us, nobody was expecting anything to happen, but if it did they wanted to know where to find us. One word led to another and forty-seven out of the fifty guys joined me and refused to sign either." He fell silent.

"I'm waiting. This had better turn out all right."

"That got the sergeant befuddled and he called in a captain who went through exactly the same song and dance and then actually threatened us by saying if we didn't sign, it could hold up our discharge for days or even weeks. I knew that was a lie because they want us out of here every bit as much as we want to get out. You wouldn't believe how many troops are piling in here every hour. Then he wheedled us and went through that business about love of country and the possibility of needing us again in a hurry, and I stood up and told him that I had volunteered before and I would do it again if it becomes necessary, but that I reserve the right to judge that necessity as an individual of free will; that is what I thought the war had been about and that is what I thought made America great. The captain had a Yankee accent and he said, 'You see that flag, Sergeant? Don't you love it?' And I said, 'I love it with all my heart, Captain, but I'm from Georgia and have the advantage of loving two flags. All my life. I was raised to fight for what those flags represent, and if you need me again, I'll be there without your having to send for me.' That's when the guys around me all cheered and clapped and we didn't sign."

"Are you sure you're getting discharged this week?"

"Yes, sir! They tried to single me out of the herd and say they'd lost my immunization records and I'd have to take all my shots over, but when that bluff didn't work I heard the captain say an ugly word and tell the sergeant to forget it. I'll be home no later than Wednesday."

"Good. Don't pick any more fights till you get home. You've got to be at Emory by Monday."

"Sir? Monday?"

"That's right. Otten is already back in the class."

"What?"

"That's right. He got discharged a month ago."

"I can't believe it. What rank did he make before discharge?"

"He's still a PFC, I'm told."

"God. I dread seeing him. How'd you find out?"

"When I got that letter you wrote the day after Christmas saying you had definitely decided to go back to med school, I took my letter from Astenheimer and made a little trip out to Emory on your behalf. He's not dean any more and they acted like they weren't going to honor his commitment to reinstate you; so I looked Dr. Thebault up. That building where his office is stinks to high heaven, I don't know how he stands it, but my visit paid off. He went to bat for us and you've got a slot in this class if you can get there by Monday. Otherwise you'll have to wait until September and he's not sure about a place then."

"Golly, Dad, that's coming up quick and calling things close."

"I thought you said you'd made up your mind to be a doctor."

"I have, but what's the rush? Next Monday is right on top of me. I had thought I'd have a few days, or even weeks, to see the family and buy some clothes. Get out of this uniform." He took a deep breath. "You know, get a little Post-war Readjustment under my belt."

"That's a bunch of baloney."

"What?"

"Post-war Readjustment. You'll be involved in that the rest of your life and you'll never get done with it. Take it from me. I know. Hello, are you still there?"

"Yes, sir. I was just thinking."

"Well, don't do it over long distance. You're going to have plenty of time for that when you get home. Just don't find any more rebel causes till you get those discharge papers in your hand and get on the bus. You don't know how hungry I am to see you."

"I think I do. Me, too. I'll let you go, Dad. See you Wednesday. Maybe Thursday. Certainly by Friday."

"Sambo."

"Sir?"

"Before you hang up. One thing. You've kept writing me all through this war that you were learning a lot. The last time we had a talk, I told you how I felt about IFMS. Remember?"

"I do, now that you mention it."

"I told you I wanted those letters that stood for I Flunked Med School to mean I Found My Self. Remember?"

"I remember."

"Well?"

"Well, what?"

"Can you say, 'I found myself'?"

Porter was silent so long that the lines could be heard humming again. There was reflection and honest doubt in his answer. "I don't know, Dad. I truly do not know."

His father waited.

"I can't stand here in this phone booth in North Carolina and honestly tell you I've found myself, not with all that statement implies." Porter's voice strengthened; a hint of thunder invaded it. "But I can tell you one thing I do know. Beyond the shadow of a doubt."

"What's that?"

"I have sure as hell discovered America!"